新制多益 聽力高分金榜演練

關鍵10回滿分模擬1000題

作者 YBM TOEIC R&D　譯者 黃詩韻／蔡裴驊／劉嘉珮

目錄

多益測驗簡介

TOEIC 為 Test of English for International Communication 的縮寫，針對母語非英語的人士所設計，測驗其在日常生活或國際業務上所具備的英語應用能力。該測驗的評量重點在於「與他人溝通的能力」（communication ability），著重「英語的運用與其功能」層面，而非單純針對「英語知識」出題。

1979 年美國 ETS（Educational Testing Service）研發出 TOEIC，而後在全世界 160 個國家中獲得超過 14,000 個機構採用，作為升遷、外派、人才招募的依據，全球每年超過 700 萬人次報考。

›› 多益測驗題型

<table>
<tr><th></th><th>Part</th><th colspan="2">測驗題型</th><th>題數</th><th>時間</th><th>分數</th></tr>
<tr><td rowspan="4">聽力
Listening Comprehension</td><td>1</td><td colspan="2">照片描述</td><td>6</td><td rowspan="4">45 分鐘</td><td rowspan="4">495 分</td></tr>
<tr><td>2</td><td colspan="2">應答問題</td><td>25</td></tr>
<tr><td>3</td><td colspan="2">簡短對話</td><td>39</td></tr>
<tr><td>4</td><td colspan="2">簡短獨白</td><td>30</td></tr>
<tr><td rowspan="4">閱讀
Reading Comprehension</td><td>5</td><td colspan="2">句子填空</td><td>30</td><td rowspan="4">75 分鐘</td><td rowspan="4">495 分</td></tr>
<tr><td>6</td><td colspan="2">段落填空</td><td>16</td></tr>
<tr><td rowspan="2">7</td><td rowspan="2">閱測</td><td>單篇閱讀</td><td>29</td></tr>
<tr><td>多篇閱讀</td><td>25</td></tr>
<tr><td>總計</td><td></td><td colspan="2"></td><td>200</td><td>約 150 分鐘 ✷</td><td>990 分</td></tr>
</table>

✷ 含基本資料及問卷填寫

›› 報名方式

請上官網 www.toeic.com.tw 確認測驗日期、報名時間等相關細節。報名時，請先查看定期場次和新增場次的時間，再選擇欲報考的測驗日期。完成報名後，請務必再次確認報考測驗日期與應試地點。

›› 應試攜帶物品

- **指定身分證件**：國民身分證、有效期限內之護照等，詳細資訊請以多益官網公告為準（如未攜帶者，不得入場考試）。
- **考試用具**：2B 鉛筆和橡皮擦（不可使用原子筆或簽字筆）。
- **手錶**：指針式手錶（不可使用電子手錶）。

›› 成績查詢

通常於測驗後的二至三週內開放網路查詢。成績單將於測驗結束後 12 個工作日（不含假日）寄發，一般郵局大宗郵件平信寄送作業約需 3–5 個工作天（不含假日）。申請成績單補發 / 證書的期限為自測驗日起的兩年內。

›› 多益測驗如何計分？

多益分數分為聽力與閱讀部分的分數，每部分的分數以 5 分為單位，範圍在 5 分至 495 分，總分則會落在 10 分至 990 分。多益測驗成績會針對題本內容，設定不同量尺轉換方法，最後分數是以「答對」的題數，經過量尺轉換而來。

多益聽力測驗出題趨勢分析

共 6 道題

PART 1 照片描述 Photographs

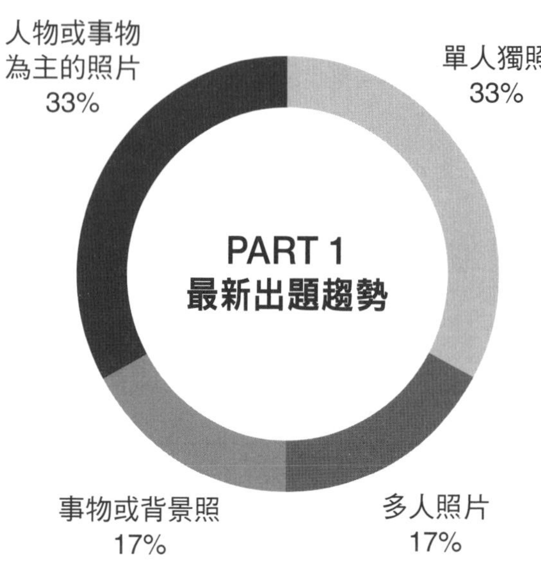

>> 單人獨照

主詞為 He/She、A man/woman 等，主要出現在該大題的**前半段**。

>> 多人照片

主詞為 They、Some men/women/people、One of the men/women 等，主要出現在該大題的**中段**。

>> 事物或背景照

主詞為 A car、some chairs 等，主要出現在該大題的**後半段**。

>> 以人物或事物為主的照片

主詞為部分的人物或事物，主要出現在該大題的**後半段**。

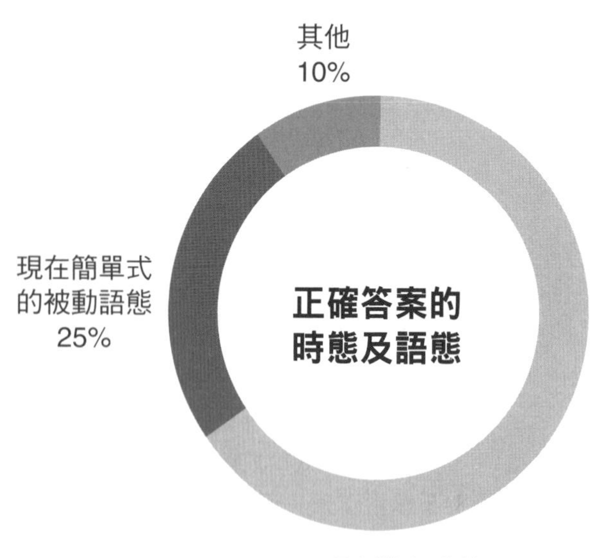

>> 現在進行式的主動語態

以「is/are ＋現在分詞」的形態呈現，主詞以**人物**為主。

>> 現在簡單式的被動語態

以「is/are ＋過去分詞」形態呈現，主詞以**事物**為主。

>> 其他

包含：

- 以「is/are ＋ being ＋過去分詞」形態呈現的**現在進行式被動**語態
- 以「has/have ＋ been ＋過去分詞」形態呈現的**現在完成式被動**語態
- 以「及物動詞＋受詞」形態呈現的**現在簡單式主動**語態
- 「There is/are」型態的**現在簡單式**。

共 25 道題

PART 2 應答問題 Question-Response

>> 直述句

非問句，陳述客觀**事實**或說話者**意見**的句子。

>> 祈使句

以**原形動詞**或 **Please** 等詞開頭的句子。

>> 疑問詞開頭的問句

各類疑問詞會出現**一至兩個**。疑問詞會單獨出現，也會與**名詞**或**形容詞**結合，像是「What time . . . ?」、「How long . . . ?」、「Which room . . . ?」等。

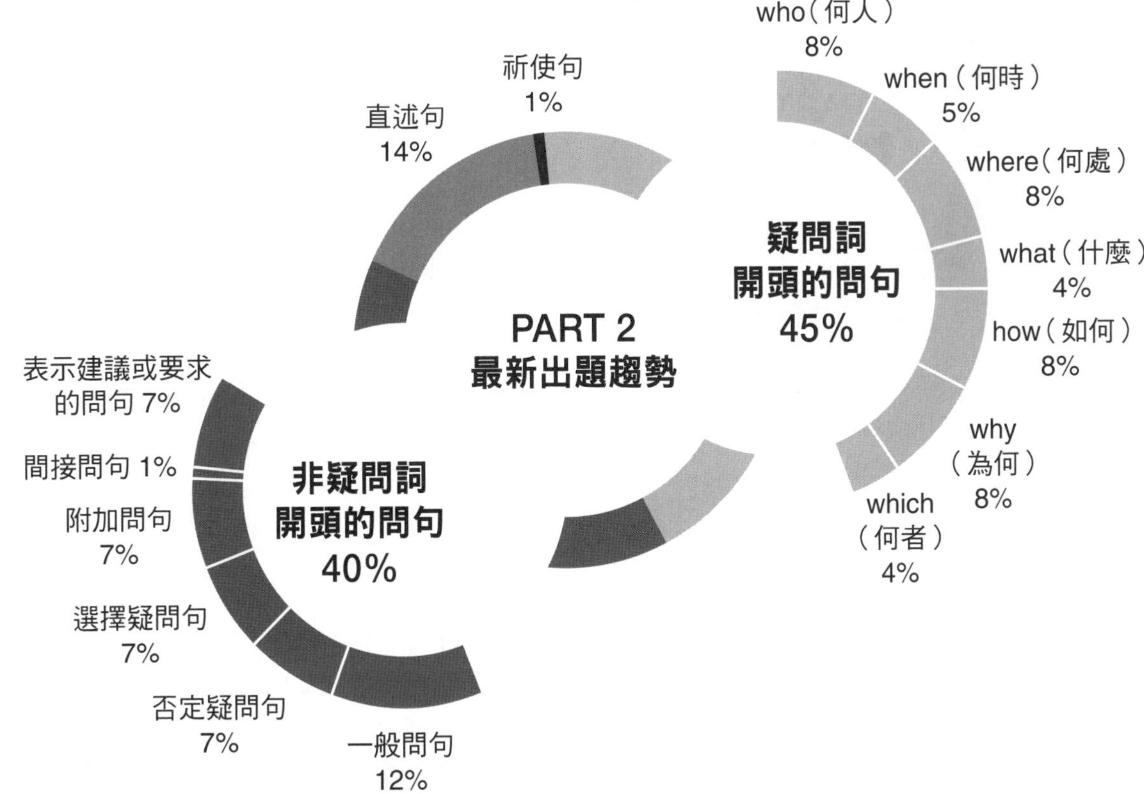

>> 非疑問詞開頭的問句

一般 Yes/No 問句	少則出現**一至兩題**，多則出現**三至四題**。
否定疑問句	以「Don't you . . . ?」、「Isn't he . . . ?」等開頭的句子，較一般肯定疑問句少出現。
選擇疑問句	以 A or B 的形態呈現，A 和 B 的可能為單字、片語或子句。若為片語或子句，**句子長度較長時，難度也較高**。
附加問句	以「. . . , don't you?」、「. . . , isn't he?」等結尾的問句，出題頻率與一般否定疑問句差不多。
間接問句	疑問詞不會置於句首，而是置於句子的**中間**。
表示建議或要求的問句	目的並非取得資訊，而是用於**尋求對方的幫助或同意**

共 13 組對話，39 題（每組考 3 題）

PART 3 簡短對話 Conversations

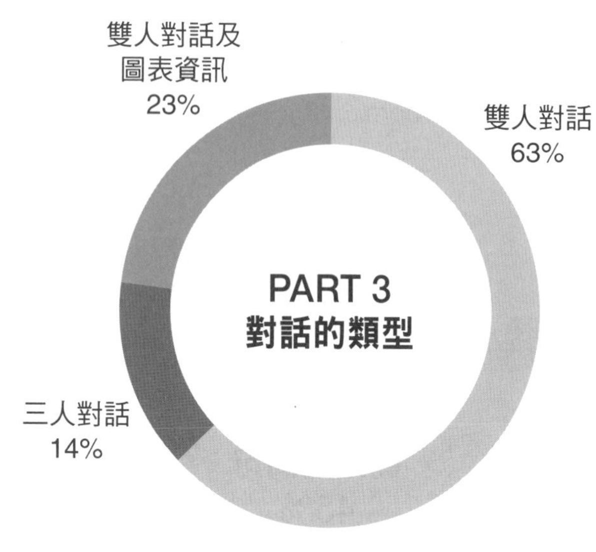

- 若為三人對話，可能會出現兩名男性和一名女性、或是一名男性和兩名女性，因此有別於雙人對話，題目中不太會使用 the man 或 the woman，而是使用 **the men** 或 **the women**，或**直接提及特定的姓名**。

- **對話 + 圖表資訊整合題**通常會出現在該大題的**後半部**。

- 圖表資訊包含：
chart（圖表）、map（地圖）、floor plan（平面圖）、schedule（時程表）、table（表格）、weather forecast（天氣預報）、directory（指引）、list（清單）、invoice（帳單）、receipt（收據）、sign（標示）、packing slip（裝箱單）等多種類型資料。

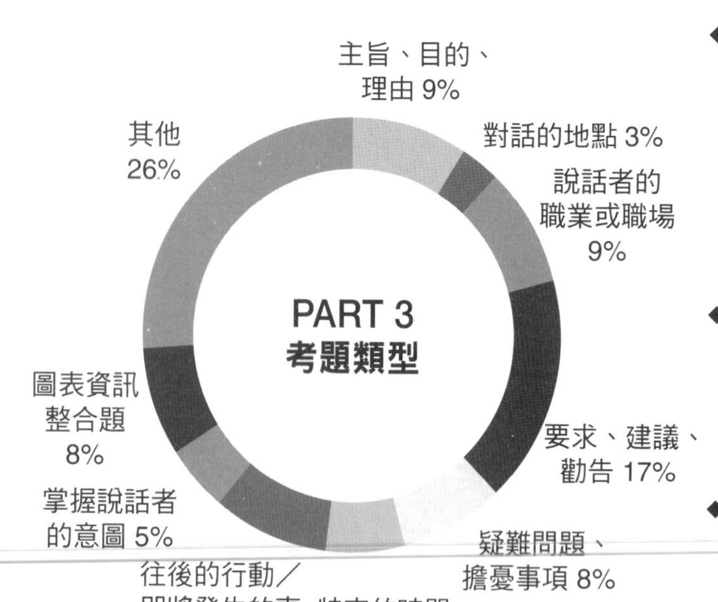

- 詢問**主旨**、**目的**、**理由**、**對話地點**、**說話者的職業**或**職場**等相關考題，主要會出現在**對話題組中的第 1 題**；詢問**往後的行動**、或**即將發生的事**等相關考題，則通常出現在對話題組中的**第 3 題**。

- 詢問說話者**意圖**的考題，通常會出現在雙人對話題組，偶爾也會出現在三人對話題組中，但是通常並**不會出現在圖表資訊整合的題組**中。

- 在 PART 3 中，詢問**說話者意圖**的考題通常會出現 **2 題**；**圖表資訊整合**題則會考 **3 題**。

共 10 段獨白，30 題（每段考 3 題）

PART 4 簡短獨白 Talks

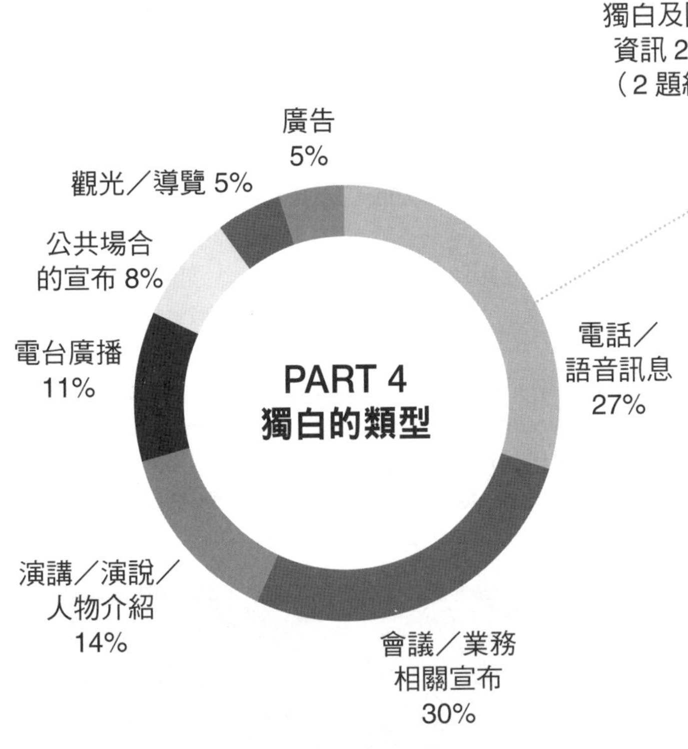

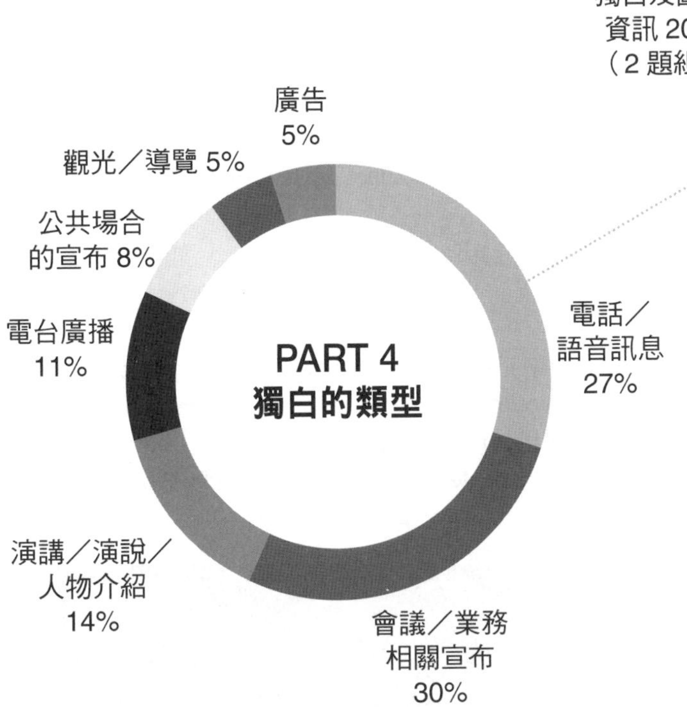

◆ 電話留言（telephone message）和會議摘錄（excerpt from a meeting）基本上是**一定會出現**的題型，有時甚至會占整個大題的 **50%** 至 **60%**。

◆ **獨白 + 圖表資訊整合題**通常會出現在該大題的**後半部**。

◆ 圖表資訊包含：chart（圖表）、map（地圖）、floor plan（平面圖）、schedule（時程表）、table（表格）、weather forecast（天氣預報）、graph（圖解）、survey（調查）、order form（訂單）、expense report（開銷報告）、advertisement（廣告）、coupon（優惠券）、brochure（手冊）等多種類型資料。

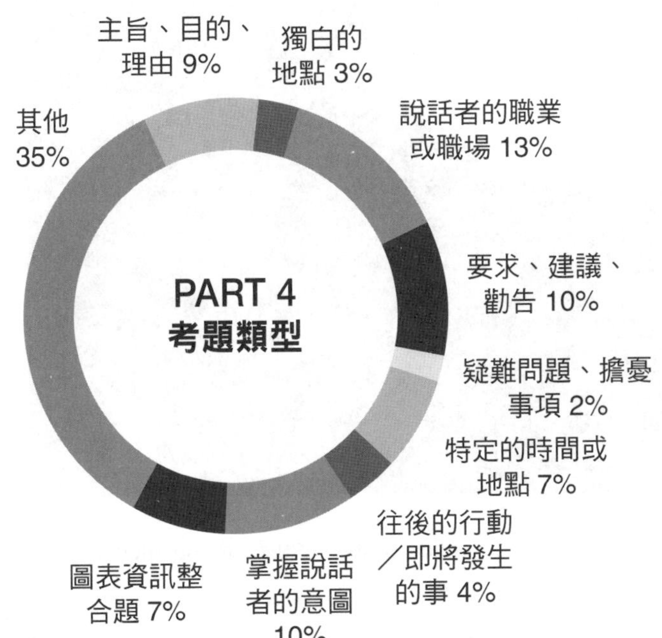

◆ 考題類型基本上與 Part 3 幾乎相同。

◆ 詢問**主旨**、**目的**、**理由**、**獨白地點**、說話者的**職業**或**職場**等相關考題，主要會出現在獨白題組中的**第 1 題**；詢問往後的**行動**、或**即將發生的事**等相關考題，則通常出現在獨白題組中的**第 3 題**。

◆ 在 Part 4 中，詢問**說話者意圖**的考題通常會出現 **3 題**；**圖表資訊整合題**則會出現 **2 題**。

ACTUAL TEST 1

LISTENING TEST 01

In the Listening test, you will be asked to demonstrate how well you understand spoken English. The entire Listening test will last approximately 45 minutes. There are four parts, and directions are given for each part. You must mark your answers on the separate answer sheet. Do not write your answers in your test book.

PART 1

Directions: For each question in this part, you will hear four statements about a picture in your test book. When you hear the statements, you must select the one statement that best describes what you see in the picture. Then find the number of the question on your answer sheet and mark your answer. The statements will not be printed in your test book and will be spoken only one time.

Statement (C), "They're sitting at a table," is the best description of the picture, so you should select answer (C) and mark it on your answer sheet.

1.

2.

GO ON TO THE NEXT PAGE

3.

4.

5.

6.

GO ON TO THE NEXT PAGE

PART 2 (02)

Directions: You will hear a question or statement and three responses spoken in English. They will not be printed in your test book and will be spoken only one time. Select the best response to the question or statement and mark the letter (A), (B), or (C) on your answer sheet.

7. Mark your answer on your answer sheet.

8. Mark your answer on your answer sheet.

9. Mark your answer on your answer sheet.

10. Mark your answer on your answer sheet.

11. Mark your answer on your answer sheet.

12. Mark your answer on your answer sheet.

13. Mark your answer on your answer sheet.

14. Mark your answer on your answer sheet.

15. Mark your answer on your answer sheet.

16. Mark your answer on your answer sheet.

17. Mark your answer on your answer sheet.

18. Mark your answer on your answer sheet.

19. Mark your answer on your answer sheet.

20. Mark your answer on your answer sheet.

21. Mark your answer on your answer sheet.

22. Mark your answer on your answer sheet.

23. Mark your answer on your answer sheet.

24. Mark your answer on your answer sheet.

25. Mark your answer on your answer sheet.

26. Mark your answer on your answer sheet.

27. Mark your answer on your answer sheet.

28. Mark your answer on your answer sheet.

29. Mark your answer on your answer sheet.

30. Mark your answer on your answer sheet.

31. Mark your answer on your answer sheet.

PART 3 03

Directions: You will hear some conversations between two or more people. You will be asked to answer three questions about what the speakers say in each conversation. Select the best response to each question and mark the letter (A), (B), (C), or (D) on your answer sheet. The conversations will not be printed in your test book and will be spoken only one time.

32. Where most likely does the man work?
(A) At an interior design firm
(B) At an apartment management office
(C) At a moving company
(D) At a hotel

33. What problem does the woman describe?
(A) An appliance is not working.
(B) A wall has been damaged.
(C) Some loud noises can be heard.
(D) Some furniture is uncomfortable.

34. What does the man ask the woman to do?
(A) Take some measurements
(B) Wait for a company representative
(C) Send him some pictures
(D) Read a set of instructions

---

35. Where most likely are the speakers?
(A) At a train terminal
(B) On an airplane
(C) At a restaurant
(D) At a park

36. What does the woman say has caused a problem?
(A) Some meals were not cooked properly.
(B) Some boxes have not been unpacked.
(C) A tour has too many participants.
(D) A form was filled out incorrectly.

37. What does the man ask for?
(A) A partial refund
(B) Some extra food
(C) Directions to a store
(D) A different seat assignment

---

38. What kind of service does the men's company provide?
(A) Advertising
(B) Catering
(C) Accounting
(D) Web design

39. Why has the woman hired the men's company?
(A) To grow her business
(B) To save money
(C) To follow a regulation
(D) To give herself more free time

40. What does the woman say about a suggestion?
(A) It has been tried before.
(B) It may not be effective.
(C) It would be expensive.
(D) It is complicated.

---

41. Which department does the woman most likely work in?
(A) Public Relations
(B) Human Resources
(C) Information Technology
(D) Sales and Marketing

42. What problem are the speakers discussing?
(A) A slow response time
(B) A scheduling conflict
(C) A customer complaint
(D) A missing detail

43. What does the woman recommend the man do first?
(A) Speak with his manager
(B) Check some software settings
(C) Post a correction notice
(D) Restart a machine

GO ON TO THE NEXT PAGE

44. What is the man about to do?

(A) Clean some clothing
(B) Use a sewing machine
(C) Arrange a window display
(D) Test some product samples

45. What does the woman point out about a fabric?

(A) Its color is due to special chemicals.
(B) It has been decorated with beads.
(C) Its cost has recently risen.
(D) It is lightweight.

46. What does the woman agree to do?

(A) Increase some lighting
(B) Hold a hand tool
(C) Postpone a photo session
(D) Provide some training

---

47. Why does the man say he comes to the bakery frequently?

(A) It is near his home.
(B) It has a pleasant atmosphere.
(C) It sells a special type of baked goods.
(D) It has convenient operating hours.

48. Why does the woman say, "these chocolate cupcakes have marshmallow frosting"?

(A) To point out a mistake on a label
(B) To propose an alternative purchase
(C) To express surprise at a suggestion
(D) To explain a pricing decision

49. What does the woman offer the man?

(A) A onetime discount
(B) A list of the ingredients in a recipe
(C) A chance to attend a tasting session
(D) A takeout container

---

50. Where do the speakers most likely work?

(A) At a construction company
(B) At a warehouse
(C) At a farm
(D) At a car repair shop

51. What has caused a problem?

(A) Some packages have been misplaced.
(B) Some roads are closed.
(C) A staff member is out sick.
(D) A vehicle has broken down.

52. What does the woman say she will do?

(A) Work overtime today
(B) Put up a warning sign
(C) Conduct a safety inspection
(D) Contact another company

---

53. Who most likely is Ms. Lee?

(A) A journalist
(B) A city official
(C) A travel agent
(D) A researcher

54. What does the man say about the construction of a train line?

(A) It caused him to be late.
(B) It will take many years to complete.
(C) It will relieve crowding on another line.
(D) It has shortened his commute.

55. What does Ms. Lee ask the man to do next?

(A) Show her a ticket
(B) Watch a video clip
(C) Sit down at a table
(D) Sign a document

---

56. What most likely is the mission of the speakers' organization?
(A) To educate children
(B) To take care of animals
(C) To protect the environment
(D) To support the arts

57. What does the man say he will do soon?
(A) Earn a degree
(B) Move away
(C) Take a vacation
(D) Donate some supplies

58. What does the woman mean when she says, "You've been an excellent volunteer"?
(A) She is happy to fulfill the man's request.
(B) She is sorry that the man is quitting.
(C) She is surprised by the man's mistake.
(D) She is pleased that the man will become more involved.

---

59. What are the speakers discussing?
(A) A promotion
(B) A career fair
(C) An interview
(D) A transfer

60. What does the woman say she has been doing?
(A) Collecting some records
(B) Processing some applications
(C) Communicating with some recruiters
(D) Replacing some equipment

61. What does the man give the woman?
(A) A job advertisement
(B) An applicant's résumé
(C) An employment agreement
(D) An orientation schedule

Bus Departures

Destination	Boarding Area	Time
Grammett	D	DEPARTED
Cookville	E	7:20 a.m.
Owenton	B	7:53 a.m.
Grammett	D	8:04 a.m.
Cookville	E	8:10 a.m.

62. What are the speakers going to do?
(A) Visit a factory
(B) Oversee a building project
(C) Participate in a conference
(D) Attend an awards ceremony

63. What did the woman initially forget to bring?
(A) A set of gifts
(B) A travel document
(C) Some special clothing
(D) Some presentation materials

64. Look at the graphic. When does the man suggest departing?
(A) At 7:20 a.m.
(B) At 7:53 a.m.
(C) At 8:04 a.m.
(D) At 8:10 a.m.

GO ON TO THE NEXT PAGE

Brooks Gym

Buy a class package and save!

	Total	Savings per class
5 classes	$90	$2
10 classes	$160	$4
15 classes	$210	$6
20 classes	$240	$8

65. Where most likely did the man get the coupon?

(A) At a gym class
(B) On the street
(C) In the mail
(D) On a Web site

66. Look at the graphic. How much will the man save per class?

(A) $2
(B) $4
(C) $6
(D) $8

67. What does the woman say about the class packages?

(A) They were recently introduced.
(B) They are valid for a limited time.
(C) They are not eligible for refunds.
(D) They allow entry to any type of class.

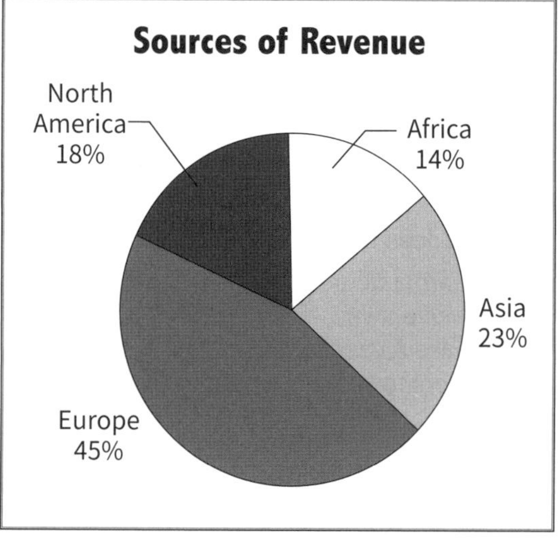

68. Look at the graphic. Which figure does the woman say is larger than before?

(A) 14%
(B) 18%
(C) 23%
(D) 45%

69. According to the man, what does the company plan to do?

(A) Enter an additional industry
(B) Replace its chief executive
(C) Relocate its headquarters
(D) Expand into a new region

70. What does the man recommend reading?

(A) A section of a report
(B) An article on a Web page
(C) A summary of some laws
(D) An invitation to a celebration

PART 4 

Directions: You will hear some talks given by a single speaker. You will be asked to answer three questions about what the speaker says in each talk. Select the best response to each question and mark the letter (A), (B), (C), or (D) on your answer sheet. The talks will not be printed in your test book and will be spoken only one time.

71. What is the message mainly about?
(A) A prescription medication
(B) An appointment time
(C) A doctor's specialty
(D) A hospital bill

72. What does the speaker say he has received?
(A) An electronic payment
(B) An insurance authorization
(C) Some promotional brochures
(D) Some past medical records

73. What does the speaker say will happen tomorrow?
(A) He will update a database.
(B) He will call the listener again.
(C) A business will be closed.
(D) A delivery will arrive.

---

74. What have some employees complained about?
(A) The quality of a workplace amenity
(B) The temperature of their office
(C) The distribution of a workload
(D) The behavior of their coworkers

75. What does the speaker say about Human Resources?
(A) It is currently understaffed.
(B) It follows specific procedures.
(C) It handles only significant matters.
(D) It has made an announcement.

76. What does the speaker ask the listeners to do?
(A) Review part of the employee handbook
(B) Participate in a team-building activity
(C) Brainstorm some possible solutions
(D) View an online training film

---

77. What field does Ms. Datta most likely work in?
(A) Politics
(B) Medicine
(C) Engineering
(D) Publishing

78. What will Ms. Datta talk about?
(A) A book about her experiences
(B) A documentary about a journey
(C) An organization she founded
(D) A prize she received

79. What does the speaker imply when she says, "there are a hundred other people here"?
(A) Some of the listeners do not usually attend lectures.
(B) It will be easy to reach a fund-raising goal.
(C) There are not enough seats for the whole audience.
(D) The listeners should not take too long with their questions.

---

80. Where most likely is the announcement being made?
(A) At a public library
(B) At a shopping mall
(C) At an amusement park
(D) At a conference center

81. What does the speaker say about Mr. Adams?
(A) He is searching for an acquaintance.
(B) One of his possessions has been found.
(C) He is about to act as the host of an event.
(D) Information about him has been put on display.

82. What does the speaker say is newly available?
(A) A dining facility
(B) A mobile app
(C) A job opportunity
(D) A transportation service

GO ON TO THE NEXT PAGE

83. Who most likely are the listeners?
(A) Bank tellers
(B) Store clerks
(C) Factory workers
(D) Real estate agents

84. What does the speaker list?
(A) Pieces of equipment
(B) Marketing strategies
(C) Employee rest areas
(D) Customer complaints

85. Why does the speaker say, "There are some pencils on that table"?
(A) To show disappointment that a facility is messy
(B) To suggest that the listeners have lost some belongings
(C) To recommend using the pencils to take notes
(D) To offer the pencils to the listeners as gifts to take home

---

86. What type of service does the speaker's company provide?
(A) Security
(B) Shipping
(C) Landscaping
(D) Telecommunications

87. What is the speaker calling about?
(A) A review posted on a Web site
(B) An account password
(C) A reward for certain customers
(D) A malfunctioning electronic device

88. Why should the listener return the phone call?
(A) To schedule a home visit
(B) To learn more about a discount
(C) To receive installation instructions
(D) To find out where to send an item

---

89. Where is the tour taking place?
(A) On a mountain
(B) In a forest
(C) By a lake
(D) In a desert

90. What does the speaker imply when he says, "the van will be close behind us"?
(A) Listeners do not have to worry about getting lost.
(B) Listeners can ride in the van during the tour.
(C) Listeners should be careful around a vehicle.
(D) Listeners can access their baggage at any time.

91. What are the listeners asked to do next?
(A) Look at a route map
(B) Fill out some paperwork
(C) Put on some safety gear
(D) Throw away some trash

---

92. What does the speaker thank the listeners for?
(A) Taking part in the meeting
(B) Reporting some problems
(C) Working additional hours
(D) Going to an exposition

93. According to the speaker, what will happen in June?
(A) A competition will be held.
(B) An executive will retire.
(C) A new branch will open.
(D) A holiday will be celebrated.

94. What does the speaker clarify?
(A) The names included on a guest list
(B) The availability of some hotel rooms
(C) The requirements for a submission
(D) The responsibilities of a position

Project Schedule

Planning	July 1–19
Data collection	July 22–August 30
Data analysis	September 2–6
Report preparation	September 9–20
Presentation of results	September 23

95. Look at the graphic. On which date is the speaker calling?
(A) July 1
(B) July 22
(C) September 2
(D) September 9

96. What has the speaker just finished doing?
(A) Calculating an expense
(B) Arranging some interviews
(C) Running some software
(D) Meeting with team members

97. What does the speaker want to discuss with the listener?
(A) The size of the research team
(B) The due date of the report
(C) The format of the questionnaire
(D) The strategy for attracting participants

Festival Floor Plan

98. What kind of organization is holding the festival?
(A) An art school
(B) A museum
(C) A student-run association
(D) A city government department

99. When did the festival begin?
(A) Three weeks ago
(B) Last week
(C) Yesterday
(D) This morning

100. Look at the graphic. In which hall will a special event take place?
(A) The North Hall
(B) The West Hall
(C) The East Hall
(D) The South Hall

This is the end of the Listening test.

ACTUAL TEST 2

LISTENING TEST 05

In the Listening test, you will be asked to demonstrate how well you understand spoken English. The entire Listening test will last approximately 45 minutes. There are four parts, and directions are given for each part. You must mark your answers on the separate answer sheet. Do not write your answers in your test book.

PART 1

Directions: For each question in this part, you will hear four statements about a picture in your test book. When you hear the statements, you must select the one statement that best describes what you see in the picture. Then find the number of the question on your answer sheet and mark your answer. The statements will not be printed in your test book and will be spoken only one time.

Statement (C), "They're sitting at a table," is the best description of the picture, so you should select answer (C) and mark it on your answer sheet.

1.

2.

3.

4.

5.

6.

PART 2 06

Directions: You will hear a question or statement and three responses spoken in English. They will not be printed in your test book and will be spoken only one time. Select the best response to the question or statement and mark the letter (A), (B), or (C) on your answer sheet.

7. Mark your answer on your answer sheet.

8. Mark your answer on your answer sheet.

9. Mark your answer on your answer sheet.

10. Mark your answer on your answer sheet.

11. Mark your answer on your answer sheet.

12. Mark your answer on your answer sheet.

13. Mark your answer on your answer sheet.

14. Mark your answer on your answer sheet.

15. Mark your answer on your answer sheet.

16. Mark your answer on your answer sheet.

17. Mark your answer on your answer sheet.

18. Mark your answer on your answer sheet.

19. Mark your answer on your answer sheet.

20. Mark your answer on your answer sheet.

21. Mark your answer on your answer sheet.

22. Mark your answer on your answer sheet.

23. Mark your answer on your answer sheet.

24. Mark your answer on your answer sheet.

25. Mark your answer on your answer sheet.

26. Mark your answer on your answer sheet.

27. Mark your answer on your answer sheet.

28. Mark your answer on your answer sheet.

29. Mark your answer on your answer sheet.

30. Mark your answer on your answer sheet.

31. Mark your answer on your answer sheet.

PART 3 (07)

Directions: You will hear some conversations between two or more people. You will be asked to answer three questions about what the speakers say in each conversation. Select the best response to each question and mark the letter (A), (B), (C), or (D) on your answer sheet. The conversations will not be printed in your test book and will be spoken only one time.

32. Where most likely are the speakers?
(A) At an airport
(B) At a hotel
(C) On a bus
(D) In a taxi

33. What is the purpose of the man's trip?
(A) To evaluate a facility
(B) To attend a social event
(C) To receive some training
(D) To promote a business

34. What does the woman recommend doing?
(A) Trying a local dish
(B) Visiting a tourist attraction
(C) Storing some baggage temporarily
(D) Taking a certain route to a destination

35. What has the man agreed to do?
(A) Proofread some writing
(B) Participate in an interview
(C) Analyze an industry
(D) Produce some graphics

36. Why is the woman calling?
(A) To determine a fee
(B) To check some statistics
(C) To introduce a journalist
(D) To change a schedule

37. What will the man receive today?
(A) An electronic payment
(B) A draft of an article
(C) Some guidelines
(D) Some contact information

38. What are the speakers mainly discussing?
(A) A power outage
(B) Some poor weather
(C) An employee absence
(D) Some roadwork

39. What does the woman suggest doing?
(A) Closing down for the day
(B) Notifying a neighboring business
(C) Teaching a skill to some workers
(D) Buying a special machine

40. What does the woman mean when she says, "Shaun is posting on social media right now"?
(A) Shaun is neglecting his duties.
(B) Shaun is making an announcement.
(C) Shaun is seeking more detailed information.
(D) Shaun is more familiar with a marketing method.

41. What problem does the man mention?
(A) He has not received his paycheck.
(B) His paycheck is not itemized clearly.
(C) His pay amount is different from before.
(D) His pay was issued using an inconvenient method.

42. According to the woman, what caused the problem?
(A) An address is incorrect.
(B) A tax law has been revised.
(C) A software program is not working properly.
(D) A form was misplaced.

43. What does the man say he is currently doing?
(A) Setting aside some money
(B) Taking overtime shifts
(C) Applying for a departmental transfer
(D) Renting an apartment

GO ON TO THE NEXT PAGE

44. What does Edith want to do?

(A) Take on more responsibility
(B) Relieve some physical discomfort
(C) Improve a workplace relationship
(D) Increase her efficiency

45. What does the man recommend asking Jackie for?

(A) An opinion
(B) An apology
(C) Some paperwork
(D) Some equipment

46. What does Jackie offer to do?

(A) Help with an installation procedure
(B) Look in the company handbook
(C) Show Edith a computer accessory
(D) Connect Edith with another coworker

---

47. What does the woman say she just did?

(A) Spoken with a patron
(B) Read a publication
(C) Attended a lecture
(D) Posted a notice

48. What does the woman suggest offering?

(A) Private meeting facilities
(B) Classes on library resources
(C) A mobile library service
(D) A longer borrowing period

49. What does the woman agree to do?

(A) Clean out a space
(B) Create a document
(C) Gather some colleagues
(D) Review a budget

---

50. What is the main topic of the conversation?

(A) A shipping service
(B) A building process
(C) A rental contract
(D) A vehicle repair

51. Why is Mr. Swanson surprised?

(A) A request has been denied.
(B) A cost estimate has risen.
(C) A task has not been completed.
(D) A project manager has been replaced.

52. What does Pete explain?

(A) The reason for a change
(B) The steps of a procedure
(C) The features of some software
(D) The options of a choice

---

53. What has the man become interested in?

(A) Fishing
(B) Cooking
(C) Playing an instrument
(D) Learning a new language

54. What is the man planning to do this weekend?

(A) Purchase some supplies
(B) Join a hobby club
(C) Go on a group trip
(D) Stream some videos

55. What kind of event does the woman mention?

(A) A dinner party
(B) A television show shoot
(C) A skills demonstration
(D) A competition

---

56. What kind of business does the woman work for?
(A) An information technology consulting firm
(B) An employment agency
(C) A research laboratory
(D) An educational institute

57. What does the man ask about?
(A) A number of people
(B) A source of funding
(C) A required qualification
(D) A usual start time

58. Why does the woman say, "information security would be a difficult area"?
(A) To indicate that she is impressed
(B) To recommend an additional service
(C) To justify a heavy workload
(D) To give the man a warning

---

59. How did the man learn about the woman's business?
(A) From an industry magazine
(B) From an outdoor advertisement
(C) From a local newspaper
(D) From a Web site

60. What does the man say about his store?
(A) Some of its merchandise is out of stock.
(B) It does not have many customers.
(C) Part of it is being remodeled.
(D) A parking area is being added.

61. What does the woman propose doing first?
(A) Inspecting a manufacturing plant
(B) Discussing the terms of an agreement
(C) Distributing some product samples
(D) Reviewing some sales figures

Directory

Floor	Products
1	Cosmetics & Jewelry
2	Women's Clothing
3	Men's Clothing
4	Home Goods

62. Look at the graphic. Which floor are the speakers on?
(A) The first floor
(B) The second floor
(C) The third floor
(D) The fourth floor

63. Why is the woman uncertain about buying an item?
(A) It may be the wrong size.
(B) It would be easy to damage.
(C) It has an unusual design.
(D) It is expensive.

64. What does the man suggest doing?
(A) Trying on an item
(B) Paying in installments
(C) Going to online stores
(D) Looking for a salesperson

GO ON TO THE NEXT PAGE

References

Timothy Ward *(Manager at Slangal)*	555-0145
Maureen Jacobs *(Supervisor at Zubina Consultants)*	555-0182
Anita Bajwa *(Director at Soares Engineering)*	555-0176
Frank Oliver *(Manager at Soares Engineering)*	555-0109

65. Who most likely is the woman?

(A) A job applicant
(B) A hiring manager
(C) A department head
(D) A corporate recruiter

66. Look at the graphic. Which phone number is the man having trouble with?

(A) 555-0145
(B) 555-0182
(C) 555-0176
(D) 555-0109

67. What does the woman say caused a problem?

(A) A technological issue
(B) A typing error
(C) A company policy
(D) A personnel change

Crabtree Deli

Order Form

Item	Quantity
Ham sandwich	3
Tuna sandwich	4
Potato salad (container)	1
House salad	2

68. What is taking place at the woman's company?

(A) A board meeting
(B) A client visit
(C) A sales workshop
(D) An orientation session

69. Look at the graphic. What is the woman missing?

(A) A ham sandwich
(B) A tuna sandwich
(C) A container of potato salad
(D) A house salad

70. What does the man say he will do next?

(A) Send a scanned copy of a form
(B) Refund the cost of the order
(C) Contact a delivery person
(D) Make some more food

PART 4 08

Directions: You will hear some talks given by a single speaker. You will be asked to answer three questions about what the speaker says in each talk. Select the best response to each question and mark the letter (A), (B), (C), or (D) on your answer sheet. The talks will not be printed in your test book and will be spoken only one time.

71. What is the purpose of the meeting?
(A) To describe a tourism campaign
(B) To announce an office relocation
(C) To report on a construction process
(D) To recommend a company outing

72. What does the speaker say about Valtside?
(A) It hosts an annual festival.
(B) It is beautiful in spring.
(C) It is the oldest part of the city.
(D) It is accessible by public transportation.

73. What does the speaker show the listeners?
(A) A neighborhood map
(B) A train schedule
(C) A floor plan
(D) An organization chart

---

74. What type of product is being advertised?
(A) Furniture
(B) Electronics
(C) Luggage
(D) Footwear

75. According to the speaker, what has the company done?
(A) Invented a production technique
(B) Conducted market research
(C) Begun exporting to other countries
(D) Collaborated with a famous designer

76. What will happen on December 4 ?
(A) A new store branch will open.
(B) A sales promotion will begin.
(C) New products will be launched.
(D) The winner of a contest will be chosen.

77. What will the listener hold a party to celebrate?
(A) A marriage anniversary
(B) A retirement
(C) A promotion
(D) A birthday

78. What does the speaker confirm a change to?
(A) The menu for a celebration
(B) The theme of some decorations
(C) The time of a reservation
(D) The size of a group

79. What does the speaker imply when she says, "we just booked a band for that night"?
(A) A preference has been accommodated.
(B) An additional charge will be imposed.
(C) A seating arrangement must be modified.
(D) Some noise at a venue is inevitable.

---

80. What will the survey results be used for?
(A) Making an expansion decision
(B) Developing new programs
(C) Attracting advertisers
(D) Planning in-person events

81. What does the speaker say about the survey?
(A) It is targeted toward listeners of a certain age.
(B) It only has multiple choice questions.
(C) There are two ways to access it.
(D) The station has conducted it before.

82. What will survey participants have the chance to win?
(A) A cash prize
(B) Concert tickets
(C) Branded merchandise
(D) A station tour

GO ON TO THE NEXT PAGE

83. Where most likely is the workshop taking place?

(A) At a bank
(B) At a law firm
(C) At a government office
(D) At an accounting company

84. What does the speaker mean when she says, "you'd be surprised"?

(A) Some problems happen frequently.
(B) Some conflicts have already been resolved.
(C) Some mistakes have serious consequences.
(D) Some errors are easy to prevent.

85. What does the speaker say she will do next?

(A) Tell a true story
(B) Give a short quiz
(C) Pass out an agenda
(D) Begin a slide show

---

86. What is the purpose of the message?

(A) To offer a referral
(B) To ask for approval
(C) To apologize for a delay
(D) To answer a question

87. What does the speaker say about a landscaping project?

(A) It will lead to other work opportunities.
(B) It involves special materials.
(C) It has been postponed.
(D) It requires several permits.

88. What does the speaker say will happen if the listener does not act quickly?

(A) Seasonal weather will become a problem.
(B) Discounted prices will no longer be available.
(C) A potential customer will hire a competitor.
(D) A property may fail an inspection.

---

89. What industry will be featured at the trade show?

(A) Pharmaceuticals
(B) Construction
(C) Energy
(D) Agriculture

90. What does the speaker imply when she says, "Hall C in particular gets a lot of foot traffic"?

(A) Hall C exhibitors paid the highest registration fee.
(B) Hall C staff should take extra care not to block the aisles.
(C) Hall C would be a good place to hand out a resource.
(D) Hall C must be cleaned more often than other halls.

91. Why should listeners speak to Mr. Hayashi?

(A) To have their working hours recorded
(B) To obtain a communication device
(C) To report problems on the trade show floor
(D) To be reimbursed for a travel expense

---

92. What do the listeners most likely have in common?

(A) They studied at the same university.
(B) They hold the same type of job.
(C) They work for the same employer.
(D) They support the same sports team.

93. What does the speaker encourage listeners to do?

(A) Stop by a photo booth
(B) Make a financial donation
(C) Join a regional association
(D) Cast a vote

94. What will take place next?

(A) A keynote speech
(B) An award ceremony
(C) A dance performance
(D) A buffet meal

	Width x Length
Table 1	4 ft. x 6 ft.
Table 2	4 ft. x 7 ft.
Table 3	6 ft. x 6 ft.
Table 4	7 ft. x 7 ft.

95. Where will a new table be placed?
(A) In a patio
(B) In a lobby
(C) In a dining room
(D) In a conference room

96. Look at the graphic. Which table does the speaker prefer?
(A) Table 1
(B) Table 2
(C) Table 3
(D) Table 4

97. What does the speaker ask the listener to do?
(A) Place a purchase order
(B) Read a reply e-mail
(C) Arrange a furniture removal
(D) Verify the space's measurements

Yowek, Inc.

LONG-TERM PARKING PASS

#011923

Issued: January 1
Valid until: December 31

98. Who most likely are the listeners?
(A) Delivery drivers
(B) Graphic designers
(C) Parking attendants
(D) Senior executives

99. Look at the graphic. Which piece of information looked different before?
(A) The company name
(B) The pass type
(C) The pass number
(D) The expiration date

100. What does the speaker mention about an earlier design?
(A) It featured an image.
(B) It was a darker color.
(C) It included additional text.
(D) It made use of a heavier material.

This is the end of the Listening test.

ACTUAL TEST 3

LISTENING TEST 09

In the Listening test, you will be asked to demonstrate how well you understand spoken English. The entire Listening test will last approximately 45 minutes. There are four parts, and directions are given for each part. You must mark your answers on the separate answer sheet. Do not write your answers in your test book.

PART 1

Directions: For each question in this part, you will hear four statements about a picture in your test book. When you hear the statements, you must select the one statement that best describes what you see in the picture. Then find the number of the question on your answer sheet and mark your answer. The statements will not be printed in your test book and will be spoken only one time.

Statement (C), "They're sitting at a table," is the best description of the picture, so you should select answer (C) and mark it on your answer sheet.

1.

ACTUAL TEST 03 PART 1

2.

GO ON TO THE NEXT PAGE

3.

4.

5.

6.

GO ON TO THE NEXT PAGE

PART 2 10

Directions: You will hear a question or statement and three responses spoken in English. They will not be printed in your test book and will be spoken only one time. Select the best response to the question or statement and mark the letter (A), (B), or (C) on your answer sheet.

7. Mark your answer on your answer sheet.

8. Mark your answer on your answer sheet.

9. Mark your answer on your answer sheet.

10. Mark your answer on your answer sheet.

11. Mark your answer on your answer sheet.

12. Mark your answer on your answer sheet.

13. Mark your answer on your answer sheet.

14. Mark your answer on your answer sheet.

15. Mark your answer on your answer sheet.

16. Mark your answer on your answer sheet.

17. Mark your answer on your answer sheet.

18. Mark your answer on your answer sheet.

19. Mark your answer on your answer sheet.

20. Mark your answer on your answer sheet.

21. Mark your answer on your answer sheet.

22. Mark your answer on your answer sheet.

23. Mark your answer on your answer sheet.

24. Mark your answer on your answer sheet.

25. Mark your answer on your answer sheet.

26. Mark your answer on your answer sheet.

27. Mark your answer on your answer sheet.

28. Mark your answer on your answer sheet.

29. Mark your answer on your answer sheet.

30. Mark your answer on your answer sheet.

31. Mark your answer on your answer sheet.

PART 3 (11)

Directions: You will hear some conversations between two or more people. You will be asked to answer three questions about what the speakers say in each conversation. Select the best response to each question and mark the letter (A), (B), (C), or (D) on your answer sheet. The conversations will not be printed in your test book and will be spoken only one time.

32. Where do the speakers work?
(A) At a factory
(B) At an airport
(C) At a restaurant
(D) At a movie theater

33. What does the man suggest?
(A) Putting up a sign
(B) Hiring more staff
(C) Widening an entrance
(D) Automating a process

34. What does the woman say the man's suggested action might cause?
(A) Service delays
(B) A shortage of space
(C) An unpleasant atmosphere
(D) A budget problem

35. What does the man plan to do?
(A) Move to a different residence
(B) Purchase a new appliance
(C) Put his belongings in storage
(D) Renovate an apartment

36. Why does the man say he is concerned?
(A) A job must be completed quickly.
(B) An activity will be noisy.
(C) An item may be damaged.
(D) A room may be too small.

37. What does the woman offer to give the man?
(A) Referrals to other companies
(B) An informal cost estimate
(C) A legal document
(D) Packaging supplies

38. What is the topic of the conversation?
(A) Keeping a current client account
(B) Attracting internship applicants
(C) Meeting shareholders' expectations
(D) Maintaining employee satisfaction

39. What does the man propose?
(A) Making use of a local resource
(B) Reducing time spent commuting
(C) Starting a volunteer program
(D) Expanding an orientation session

40. What do the speakers agree to do?
(A) Develop the man's suggestion
(B) Seek alternative options
(C) Announce a decision
(D) Ask for workers' opinions

41. Who most likely is the man?
(A) A trade show exhibitor
(B) A tour guide
(C) A workshop leader
(D) An airline representative

42. What does the man tell the group about?
(A) A building entrance
(B) A form of transportation
(C) An instruction manual
(D) A storage facility

43. What does the man say is causing a problem?
(A) He is not used to dealing with large groups.
(B) His audio equipment is malfunctioning.
(C) Some demonstration machinery is very loud.
(D) The usual venue for a talk is unavailable.

44. Where are the speakers?

(A) At a law firm
(B) At a hair salon
(C) At a doctor's office
(D) At an auto repair shop

45. Why did the woman schedule her appointment for today?

(A) She completed some preparations yesterday.
(B) She does not have to work this afternoon.
(C) She will attend a banquet this evening.
(D) She will leave for a trip tomorrow.

46. What does the man suggest doing?

(A) Updating some records
(B) Postponing a service
(C) Talking to a manager
(D) Saving a copy of a form

---

47. What has the speakers' organization received?

(A) A grant from a government agency
(B) A prize from a national contest
(C) Additional funds from its headquarters
(D) A donation from a businessperson

48. What does the woman suggest doing with the money?

(A) Producing some brochures
(B) Giving bonuses to employees
(C) Holding a speaker series
(D) Offering a school scholarship

49. What does Jonas decide to do?

(A) Plan a gathering
(B) Issue a questionnaire
(C) Call a consultant
(D) Draft an article

---

50. Why is the man calling the woman?

(A) To get some feedback
(B) To notify her of a problem
(C) To confirm some instructions
(D) To volunteer for an assignment

51. What does the woman imply when she says, "our main priority is our visitors' comfort"?

(A) She is not concerned about cost.
(B) She does not mind extending a deadline.
(C) A room should have more open space.
(D) Some seating looks uncomfortable.

52. What does the woman agree to do?

(A) Pay a deposit
(B) Visit a store
(C) Approve a design
(D) Wait for a shipment

---

53. Who most likely is the woman?

(A) A bookstore clerk
(B) A repair technician
(C) A pharmacist
(D) A librarian

54. What does the woman offer to do?

(A) Provide a refund
(B) Assist with a search
(C) Restart a computer system
(D) Recommend an alternative

55. What does the man say will happen next month?

(A) A registration period will begin.
(B) A product will be removed from the market.
(C) A certification exam will be held.
(D) A return policy will become invalid.

---

56. What did the woman post on social media?

(A) Some images
(B) Some statistics
(C) Some questions
(D) Some advice

57. Why does the man say, "this got a lot of people talking"?

(A) To reject the woman's request
(B) To point out an unintended benefit of an action
(C) To express concern about some criticism
(D) To admit that he was wrong about a strategy

58. What does the man ask the woman to do?

(A) Edit a sentence
(B) Write another post
(C) Monitor a discussion
(D) Respond to some comments

---

59. What type of event is about to take place?

(A) An arts festival
(B) A career fair
(C) A store opening
(D) An advertising seminar

60. Why is the woman pleased?

(A) Some marketing materials are attractive.
(B) A piece of furniture is larger than expected.
(C) The man has agreed to her proposal.
(D) A space is in a busy area.

61. What did the man forget to do?

(A) Clean some decorations
(B) Seal a box tightly
(C) Bring some refreshments
(D) Put fuel in a vehicle

	Wednesday	Thursday
Morning shift	Christina	Christina
Afternoon shift	Neil	Ruby
Night shift	Alton	Hakeem

62. What is causing a scheduling conflict for the man?

(A) A family gathering
(B) Some planned travel
(C) A medical appointment
(D) A university course

63. Look at the graphic. Who will the man next ask to take his shift?

(A) Christina
(B) Alton
(C) Ruby
(D) Hakeem

64. What does the woman suggest doing when a manager arrives?

(A) Making a reminder note
(B) Getting some contact details
(C) Referring a friend for employment
(D) Reporting the status of a task

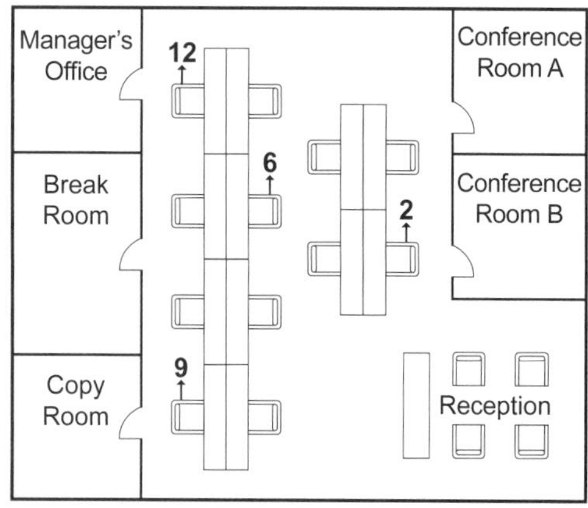

65. What does the woman ask about?
(A) Computer sizes
(B) Privacy measures
(C) Meeting frequencies
(D) Temperature conditions

66. Look at the graphic. Which desk does the woman choose?
(A) 2
(B) 6
(C) 9
(D) 12

67. What will the speakers do next?
(A) Fill out paperwork
(B) Greet a department head
(C) Shop online for supplies
(D) Go to a workstation

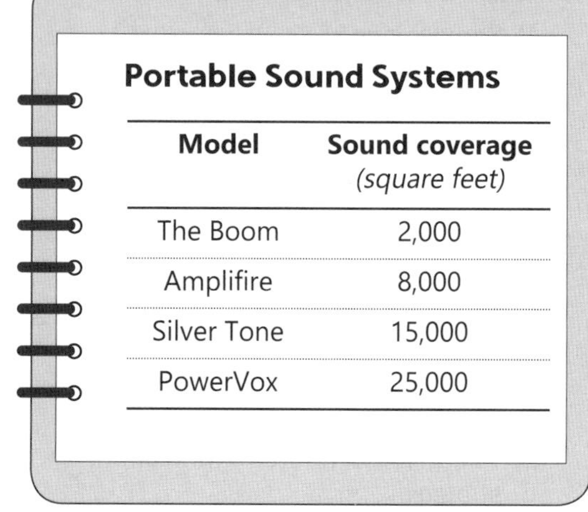

Portable Sound Systems

Model	**Sound coverage** *(square feet)*
The Boom	2,000
Amplifire	8,000
Silver Tone	15,000
PowerVox	25,000

68. What does the woman plan to do?
(A) Perform some music
(B) Organize some lectures
(C) Host a sports event
(D) Hold a party

69. Look at the graphic. Which model does the man recommend?
(A) The Boom
(B) Amplifire
(C) Silver Tone
(D) PowerVox

70. What does the man say about the store's portable sound systems?
(A) They are kept behind the counter.
(B) They can be paid for in installments.
(C) A new model will be released this month.
(D) Some of them may be rented.

PART 4 (12)

Directions: You will hear some talks given by a single speaker. You will be asked to answer three questions about what the speaker says in each talk. Select the best response to each question and mark the letter (A), (B), (C), or (D) on your answer sheet. The talks will not be printed in your test book and will be spoken only one time.

71. What does the speaker say EMC Furniture received recognition for?
(A) Their excellent customer service
(B) Their innovative loyalty program
(C) Their large inventory
(D) Their reasonable prices

72. According to the speaker, what can shoppers do in the store?
(A) Access the Internet
(B) Watch a repair process
(C) Sit down to take a break
(D) Receive personalized advice

73. What is currently on sale?
(A) A disposal method
(B) A club membership
(C) Furniture customization
(D) A product guarantee

---

74. What is the main purpose of the talk?
(A) To promote some cleaning products
(B) To outline the schedule of a tour
(C) To give assignments to a work crew
(D) To introduce some safety videos

75. What does the speaker say about Ranvex Spray?
(A) It smells good.
(B) It is powerful.
(C) It is a window cleaner.
(D) It comes in a small bottle.

76. According to the speaker, what has each listener received?
(A) A communication device
(B) Some protective clothing
(C) Some brochures
(D) A floor plan

---

77. What news from the city does the speaker mention?
(A) An inspector will visit local businesses.
(B) An area's power will be turned off.
(C) A construction project will begin.
(D) A major road will be closed.

78. What does the speaker mean when he says, "That'll be the only change"?
(A) Employees should use the same login information.
(B) Employees should not submit extra reports.
(C) Employees should work their usual hours.
(D) Employees should not prepare for an evaluation.

79. What type of project are the listeners working on?
(A) Doing market research
(B) Designing an automobile
(C) Remodeling an office
(D) Building a Web site

---

80. What is the speaker most likely talking about?
(A) Rearranging a work space
(B) Preparing for a workshop
(C) Setting up some interviews
(D) Handling some vacation requests

81. What problem does the speaker mention?
(A) Some equipment cannot be located.
(B) Some furniture is very heavy.
(C) A conference room is unavailable.
(D) A software program is slow.

82. What does the speaker mean when she says, "Ms. Kwak's flight arrives at 4 p.m., right"?
(A) She is offering assistance to the listener.
(B) She recommends postponing a decision.
(C) She thinks a message contains incorrect information.
(D) She is grateful for the listener's support.

GO ON TO THE NEXT PAGE 

83. What does Patton Enterprises sell?

(A) Power tools
(B) Floor coverings
(C) Home appliances
(D) Safety gear

84. What does the speaker mention about the business's merchandise?

(A) It is energy-efficient.
(B) It is made from recycled materials.
(C) Its ratings are consistently positive.
(D) Its availability changes regularly.

85. What does the speaker offer to do for the listener?

(A) Send a catalog
(B) Deliver items for free
(C) Give a demonstration
(D) Provide a consultation

---

86. What kind of event is taking place?

(A) A sports competition
(B) A groundbreaking ceremony
(C) An outdoor fund-raiser
(D) A street parade

87. Why does the speaker say, "I got here at 6 a.m."?

(A) To make a recommendation about future events
(B) To emphasize how popular the event is
(C) To explain how she got an advantage
(D) To indicate frustration with a delay

88. What is available on a Web site?

(A) A route map
(B) Game highlights
(C) Athlete biographies
(D) A public discussion

---

89. Where most likely is the announcement being made?

(A) At a television studio
(B) At a shopping mall
(C) At a sports stadium
(D) At a manufacturing plant

90. What does the speaker say about a television show episode?

(A) It will include an action scene.
(B) It will be broadcast next week.
(C) It will feature a guest star.
(D) It will be one hour long.

91. What are the listeners asked to do?

(A) Distribute costumes to employees
(B) Conduct an inspection of a facility
(C) Avoid certain parts of a workplace
(D) Review the contents of a document

---

92. What does the speaker say she recently did?

(A) She went to an industry conference.
(B) She contacted a start-up company.
(C) She spoke with an acquaintance.
(D) She read a retail trade magazine.

93. How does the speaker propose increasing sales?

(A) By making a deal to buy some goods in bulk
(B) By expanding into new areas of the country
(C) By selling discount vouchers through an online platform
(D) By raising the commission paid to salespeople

94. What does the speaker ask the listeners to discuss?

(A) Their departments' achievements
(B) The creation of a project team
(C) A possible launch date
(D) Disadvantages of her idea

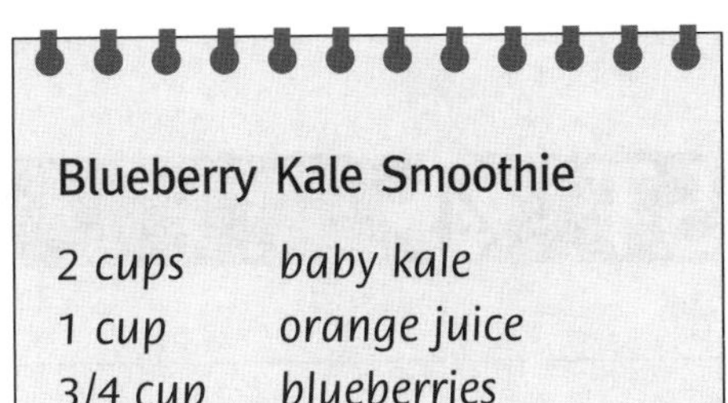

95. Who most likely are the listeners?
(A) Viewers of an online video
(B) Visitors to a supermarket
(C) Students at a cooking school
(D) The audience of a radio show

96. Look at the graphic. Which amount does the speaker say can be adjusted?
(A) 2 cups
(B) 1 cup
(C) 3/4 cup
(D) 1/8 cup

97. What does the speaker recommend doing?
(A) Consuming the smoothie immediately
(B) Refrigerating the ingredients beforehand
(C) Serving small amounts as appetizers
(D) Using a special setting on the blender

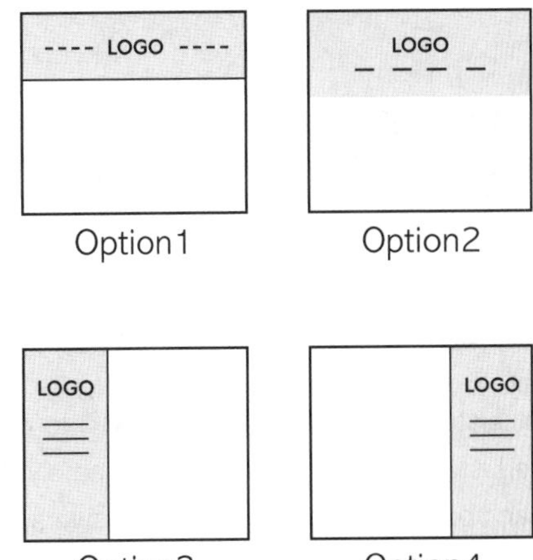

98. Look at the graphic. Which option does the speaker prefer?
(A) Option 1
(B) Option 2
(C) Option 3
(D) Option 4

99. Where most likely does the speaker work?
(A) At a real estate firm
(B) At a photography studio
(C) At a hotel chain
(D) A tour agency

100. What does the speaker suggest doing over the phone?
(A) Discussing layout styles
(B) Apologizing to a client
(C) Carrying out an interview
(D) Giving some driving directions

This is the end of the Listening test.

ACTUAL TEST 4

LISTENING TEST 13

In the Listening test, you will be asked to demonstrate how well you understand spoken English. The entire Listening test will last approximately 45 minutes. There are four parts, and directions are given for each part. You must mark your answers on the separate answer sheet. Do not write your answers in your test book.

PART 1

Directions: For each question in this part, you will hear four statements about a picture in your test book. When you hear the statements, you must select the one statement that best describes what you see in the picture. Then find the number of the question on your answer sheet and mark your answer. The statements will not be printed in your test book and will be spoken only one time.

Statement (C), "They're sitting at a table," is the best description of the picture, so you should select answer (C) and mark it on your answer sheet.

1.

2.

ACTUAL TEST 04

PART 1

3.

4.

5.

6.

PART 2 14

Directions: You will hear a question or statement and three responses spoken in English. They will not be printed in your test book and will be spoken only one time. Select the best response to the question or statement and mark the letter (A), (B), or (C) on your answer sheet.

7. Mark your answer on your answer sheet.

8. Mark your answer on your answer sheet.

9. Mark your answer on your answer sheet.

10. Mark your answer on your answer sheet.

11. Mark your answer on your answer sheet.

12. Mark your answer on your answer sheet.

13. Mark your answer on your answer sheet.

14. Mark your answer on your answer sheet.

15. Mark your answer on your answer sheet.

16. Mark your answer on your answer sheet.

17. Mark your answer on your answer sheet.

18. Mark your answer on your answer sheet.

19. Mark your answer on your answer sheet.

20. Mark your answer on your answer sheet.

21. Mark your answer on your answer sheet.

22. Mark your answer on your answer sheet.

23. Mark your answer on your answer sheet.

24. Mark your answer on your answer sheet.

25. Mark your answer on your answer sheet.

26. Mark your answer on your answer sheet.

27. Mark your answer on your answer sheet.

28. Mark your answer on your answer sheet.

29. Mark your answer on your answer sheet.

30. Mark your answer on your answer sheet.

31. Mark your answer on your answer sheet.

PART 3 15

Directions: You will hear some conversations between two or more people. You will be asked to answer three questions about what the speakers say in each conversation. Select the best response to each question and mark the letter (A), (B), (C), or (D) on your answer sheet. The conversations will not be printed in your test book and will be spoken only one time.

32. What are the speakers most likely doing?
(A) Delivering some groceries
(B) Giving a cooking demonstration
(C) Catering a celebration
(D) Holding a bake sale

33. According to the woman, what is causing a problem?
(A) An inefficient process
(B) A large number of people
(C) Damage to an appliance
(D) Bad weather

34. Where will the woman most likely go next?
(A) To an automobile
(B) To a front entrance
(C) To a storage area
(D) To a kitchen

---

35. What are the women doing?
(A) Touring an office space
(B) Shopping for electronics
(C) Checking in at a conference
(D) Learning to use a software program

36. Why is Theresa concerned?
(A) A retail price is high.
(B) A piece of equipment is large.
(C) An opportunity might be missed.
(D) A conflict might occur.

37. What does the man emphasize the availability of?
(A) A special transportation service
(B) A form of commercial insurance
(C) A short-term commitment option
(D) A free training resource

---

38. Why has the woman come to the gallery?
(A) To see a new piece of artwork
(B) To inquire about exhibiting
(C) To finalize a purchase
(D) To listen to a talk

39. What does the man ask the woman to provide?
(A) Proof of a membership
(B) The name of her friend
(C) The title of a painting
(D) A credit card

40. Why will the woman be unable to enter Garrett Hall?
(A) Its contents have been loaned out.
(B) It is being renovated.
(C) Business hours are over.
(D) A pass has some restrictions.

---

41. What service does the woman plan to receive?
(A) Pet care
(B) Vehicle washing
(C) Interior decorating
(D) Plumbing repair

42. What mistake did the woman make?
(A) She gave the wrong address.
(B) She failed to provide an important detail.
(C) She chose an inconvenient appointment time.
(D) She did not realize that a deal had ended.

43. What does the man say about his business?
(A) It uses advanced technology.
(B) It charges a fee to fulfill certain requests.
(C) It encourages staff to receive certifications.
(D) It tries to accommodate customers.

---

44. Why is the man calling the woman?

(A) To arrange an interview with her
(B) To ask for a document
(C) To offer her a job
(D) To assess her professional qualifications

45. What does the woman say is attractive about a position?

(A) The salary for it is high.
(B) The work involved seems enjoyable.
(C) It is with a famous company.
(D) Its hours are flexible.

46. What does the woman agree to do?

(A) Send some paperwork
(B) Visit a workplace
(C) Make a phone call
(D) Prepare a presentation

---

47. Who most likely is the woman?

(A) An auto mechanic
(B) A fitness instructor
(C) A medical clinic receptionist
(D) A real estate agent

48. What do the men want to know about?

(A) A customized service
(B) A routine inspection
(C) Some test results
(D) Some safety rules

49. Why does the woman ask the men to wait?

(A) A supervisor must approve a request.
(B) A budget has not been finalized yet.
(C) She must rearrange some furniture.
(D) She needs to check a schedule.

---

50. Why is the man in the conference room?

(A) To have a quick snack
(B) To prepare for a seminar
(C) To lead a videoconference
(D) To work in a quiet place

51. What does the woman say she recently did?

(A) She calculated some costs.
(B) She complained to a manager.
(C) She made plans to travel abroad.
(D) She went to another floor of the building.

52. What might the speakers' company buy for employees?

(A) Some audio equipment
(B) Some special seating
(C) A cooling appliance
(D) A beverage machine

---

53. What are the speakers mainly discussing?

(A) An activity group
(B) A business trip
(C) A promotional event
(D) An employee newsletter

54. What does the man say about a book?

(A) He has not started reading it.
(B) He owns several copies.
(C) It is very popular.
(D) It gives investment tips.

55. What does the woman imply when she says, "that's a really big book"?

(A) The book will not fit in a display.
(B) It will take a long time to read the book.
(C) The book probably contains certain information.
(D) It will be uncomfortable to carry the book.

---

56. What is the purpose of the call?
(A) To order some office supplies
(B) To complain about the quality of some goods
(C) To ask about a charge on an invoice
(D) To check the status of a shipment

57. Why does the man mention his coworkers?
(A) To describe how a mistake was noticed
(B) To explain the need for some items
(C) To clarify whom the woman should contact
(D) To highlight an advantage of a proposal

58. What does the woman offer the man?
(A) A discount coupon
(B) A tracking number
(C) A branded gift
(D) A return authorization

---

59. Where is the conversation taking place?
(A) At a flower shop
(B) At a clothing retailer
(C) At an art supply store
(D) At a supermarket

60. What does the man say about some merchandise?
(A) It should be added to a display.
(B) It is in the stockroom.
(C) It has sold out.
(D) It needs to be organized.

61. What does the man imply when he says, "It's lucky that Chae-Young was here"?
(A) A task required two people.
(B) He was very busy today.
(C) Chae-Young has a special skill.
(D) Chae-Young provided useful information.

Framing Assignments

Area	Crew Leader
Stairs	Whitney
Roof	Grant
Walls	Santos
Windows	Jim

62. What most likely is being built?
(A) An apartment complex
(B) A store
(C) A hotel
(D) A school building

63. What does the woman suggest doing?
(A) Hiring some subcontractors
(B) Postponing an opening day
(C) Installing a protective covering
(D) Contacting other suppliers

64. Look at the graphic. Whom are the speakers going to see?
(A) Whitney
(B) Grant
(C) Santos
(D) Jim

GO ON TO THE NEXT PAGE

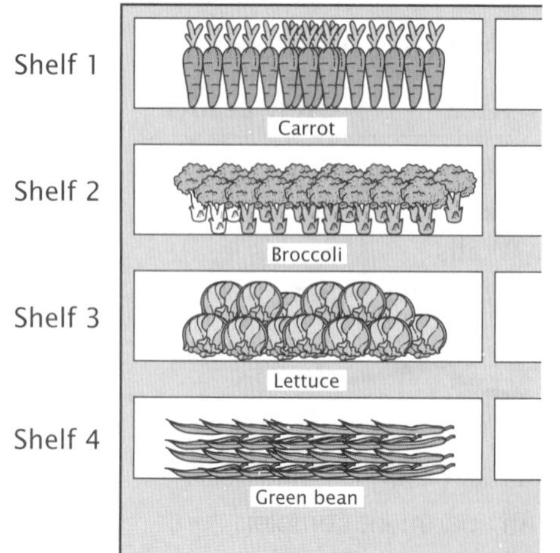

65. Look at the graphic. Which shelf's vegetables is the woman concerned about?

(A) Shelf 1
(B) Shelf 2
(C) Shelf 3
(D) Shelf 4

66. What does the woman say she will make a list of?

(A) Types of produce
(B) Staff members
(C) Cleaning tasks
(D) Purchase dates

67. What will the man most likely do next to some vegetables?

(A) Carry them to another area
(B) Spray water on them
(C) Examine them for defects
(D) Rearrange them into piles

Beginners' Classes

Class	Current Registrants/Capacity
Rumba	7 / 22
Salsa	16 / 16 (FULL)
Swing	11 / 18
Waltz	19 / 20

68. What does the woman ask about?

(A) How long each session lasts
(B) Whether she can attend alone
(C) How much experience an instructor has
(D) What kind of dance the man recommends

69. Look at the graphic. Which class does the woman want to sign up for?

(A) Rumba
(B) Salsa
(C) Swing
(D) Waltz

70. What does the woman agree to do online?

(A) Order some merchandise
(B) Get driving directions
(C) Register for a class
(D) Read some advice

PART 4 (16)

Directions: You will hear some talks given by a single speaker. You will be asked to answer three questions about what the speaker says in each talk. Select the best response to each question and mark the letter (A), (B), (C), or (D) on your answer sheet. The talks will not be printed in your test book and will be spoken only one time.

71. Where do the listeners work?
(A) At a moving company
(B) At a manufacturing plant
(C) At a storage facility
(D) At a construction firm

72. What does the speaker remind the listeners to do first?
(A) Put on some safety gear
(B) Refer to a floor plan
(C) Study a warning label
(D) Inspect the parts of a machine

73. According to the speaker, where can listeners find additional information?
(A) On a handout
(B) In a user manual
(C) On a Web site
(D) In a break room

---

74. Whom did the speaker meet with today?
(A) Potential investors
(B) Current clients
(C) Business consultants
(D) Government regulators

75. What does the speaker mean when she says, "my flight just started boarding"?
(A) Her trip is behind schedule.
(B) She has to end the call.
(C) It is too late to make a change.
(D) She will be unable to get a message.

76. What does the speaker ask the listener to do?
(A) Reply to an e-mail
(B) Pick her up from the airport
(C) Set up a morning meeting
(D) Eat a meal with her

---

77. Where is the tour taking place?
(A) A city street
(B) A nature reserve
(C) An aircraft factory
(D) A movie studio

78. What are the listeners asked to do?
(A) Remain seated in a vehicle
(B) Save questions until the end
(C) Watch an introductory video
(D) Turn off personal electronics

79. What will the speaker talk about next?
(A) A company's expansion plans
(B) The course of the tour
(C) The history of a site
(D) An upcoming celebration

---

80. According to the broadcast, what type of event will occur on Saturday?
(A) An athletic competition
(B) A career fair
(C) An exhibition opening
(D) A trade show

81. Why does the speaker say attendees should arrive to the event early?
(A) To ensure entrance
(B) To meet a local celebrity
(C) To gain discounted admission
(D) To find parking nearby

82. What will listeners most likely hear next?
(A) An interview
(B) A weather report
(C) A sports update
(D) An advertisement

GO ON TO THE NEXT PAGE

83. What does the speaker congratulate the listeners on?
(A) Finishing a team-building program
(B) Launching a new product
(C) Breaking a sales record
(D) Receiving promotions

84. Who is the speaker?
(A) A previous customer
(B) A business researcher
(C) A current supervisor
(D) A city official

85. Why does the speaker say, "Now, I know we need to do this again"?
(A) An activity was effective.
(B) Some results were unexpected.
(C) Participants performed poorly.
(D) Other people should observe an activity.

---

86. What is the topic of the talk?
(A) Carpet cleaning
(B) House painting
(C) Light fixture repair
(D) Window installation

87. What does the speaker say about a product?
(A) It is durable.
(B) It comes with instructions.
(C) It is sold in a variety of colors.
(D) It is affordable.

88. What does the speaker say she did before the talk?
(A) Cleared out a room
(B) Mixed some chemicals
(C) Covered some surfaces
(D) Measured an object

---

89. What is the announcement mainly about?
(A) A project for a client
(B) A corporate merger
(C) An office relocation
(D) An annual budget

90. Why does the speaker say, "Have you seen the amenities they offer"?
(A) To inquire about some facilities
(B) To suggest a policy change
(C) To criticize a venue's management
(D) To emphasize some benefits

91. What does the speaker ask listeners to do?
(A) Download some computer software
(B) Pack up their personal items
(C) Register for a meeting time
(D) Look at an employee handbook

---

92. What is taking place?
(A) A charity dinner
(B) A music festival
(C) A groundbreaking ceremony
(D) An industry conference

93. What does the speaker say the listeners can do?
(A) Purchase event merchandise
(B) Meet a company executive
(C) Network with others
(D) Sample some refreshments

94. What does the speaker say has changed?
(A) The focus of an organization
(B) The location of an event
(C) The date of a launch
(D) The cost of a ticket

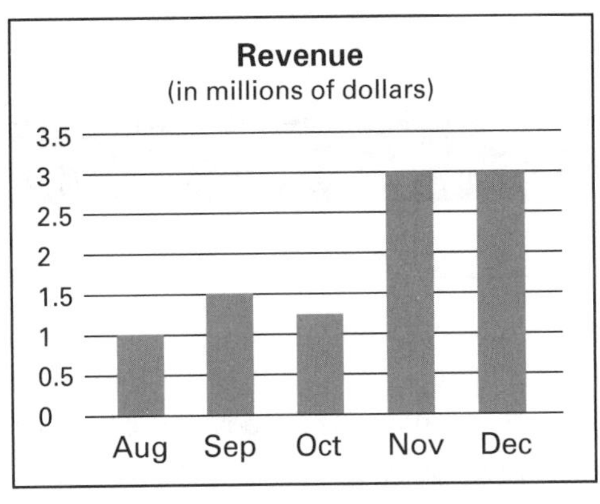

95. Who most likely are the listeners?
(A) Snack food developers
(B) Financial analysts
(C) Grocery store managers
(D) Advertising professionals

96. Look at the graphic. In which month was a product line released?
(A) September
(B) October
(C) November
(D) December

97. What will Takuya most likely do?
(A) Assign some responsibilities to the listeners
(B) Address the listeners' concerns about a policy
(C) Teach the listeners some promotional techniques
(D) Present an award to one of the listeners

Rewards for Fund-raiser Participants

Level	Minimum amount raised	Prize(s)
1	$10	Certificate
2	$50	Certificate + bag
3	$100	Certificate + bag + T-shirt
4	$200	Certificate + bag + T-shirt + movie tickets

98. What did some fund-raiser participants do?
(A) They completed a sports challenge.
(B) They gave a musical performance.
(C) They donated some homemade food.
(D) They decorated an outdoor space.

99. Look at the graphic. Which level did the participating listeners most likely reach?
(A) Level 1
(B) Level 2
(C) Level 3
(D) Level 4

100. What will the funds be used for?
(A) Medical research
(B) Improvements to a park
(C) The renovation of a community center
(D) An educational program

This is the end of the Listening test.

ACTUAL TEST 5

LISTENING TEST 

In the Listening test, you will be asked to demonstrate how well you understand spoken English. The entire Listening test will last approximately 45 minutes. There are four parts, and directions are given for each part. You must mark your answers on the separate answer sheet. Do not write your answers in your test book.

PART 1

Directions: For each question in this part, you will hear four statements about a picture in your test book. When you hear the statements, you must select the one statement that best describes what you see in the picture. Then find the number of the question on your answer sheet and mark your answer. The statements will not be printed in your test book and will be spoken only one time.

Statement (C), "They're sitting at a table," is the best description of the picture, so you should select answer (C) and mark it on your answer sheet.

1.

2.

GO ON TO THE NEXT PAGE

3.

4.

5.

6.

GO ON TO THE NEXT PAGE

PART 2 18

Directions: You will hear a question or statement and three responses spoken in English. They will not be printed in your test book and will be spoken only one time. Select the best response to the question or statement and mark the letter (A), (B), or (C) on your answer sheet.

7. Mark your answer on your answer sheet.

8. Mark your answer on your answer sheet.

9. Mark your answer on your answer sheet.

10. Mark your answer on your answer sheet.

11. Mark your answer on your answer sheet.

12. Mark your answer on your answer sheet.

13. Mark your answer on your answer sheet.

14. Mark your answer on your answer sheet.

15. Mark your answer on your answer sheet.

16. Mark your answer on your answer sheet.

17. Mark your answer on your answer sheet.

18. Mark your answer on your answer sheet.

19. Mark your answer on your answer sheet.

20. Mark your answer on your answer sheet.

21. Mark your answer on your answer sheet.

22. Mark your answer on your answer sheet.

23. Mark your answer on your answer sheet.

24. Mark your answer on your answer sheet.

25. Mark your answer on your answer sheet.

26. Mark your answer on your answer sheet.

27. Mark your answer on your answer sheet.

28. Mark your answer on your answer sheet.

29. Mark your answer on your answer sheet.

30. Mark your answer on your answer sheet.

31. Mark your answer on your answer sheet.

PART 3 (19)

Directions: You will hear some conversations between two or more people. You will be asked to answer three questions about what the speakers say in each conversation. Select the best response to each question and mark the letter (A), (B), (C), or (D) on your answer sheet. The conversations will not be printed in your test book and will be spoken only one time.

32. What kind of business do the speakers most likely work for?
(A) A hardware store
(B) A construction firm
(C) A building equipment manufacturer
(D) A landscaping company

33. What has the woman recently done?
(A) Rearranged a storage area
(B) Met with potential investors
(C) Attended a live demonstration
(D) Replaced one of her belongings

34. What does the woman say has changed about the Wenton X Series?
(A) It now has additional features.
(B) It is now made of a different metal.
(C) It has become less expensive.
(D) It has become safer to use.

35. What are the speakers mainly discussing?
(A) A video shoot
(B) A department supervisor
(C) A training program
(D) An upcoming presentation

36. Why does the woman say, "I don't think anyone thought that"?
(A) To decline an offer
(B) To justify a decision
(C) To agree with the man
(D) To correct a misunderstanding

37. What does the man say he will do tomorrow?
(A) Arrive to work late
(B) Wear attractive clothes
(C) Watch a television broadcast
(D) Bring in his camera

38. What does the woman ask about?
(A) A size limit
(B) A bulk price
(C) A minimum quantity
(D) A likely completion date

39. What does Demetri recommend that the woman do?
(A) Inquire at other print shops
(B) Wait until new stock is delivered
(C) Look at some samples online
(D) Choose a different material

40. What does the woman say about Demetri's recommendation?
(A) She will consider it.
(B) She will implement it.
(C) She wants to hear more about it.
(D) She does not believe it is suitable.

41. Where most likely does the conversation take place?
(A) At a real estate agency
(B) At a medical clinic
(C) At a post office
(D) At a law firm

42. What problem does the woman describe?
(A) She did not receive a piece of mail.
(B) She did not understand some instructions.
(C) She misplaced a document.
(D) She is uncertain about a proposal.

43. What does the man ask the woman to choose?
(A) When an appointment will be rescheduled for
(B) Whether she will authorize a transaction
(C) How she will fill out some forms
(D) Where a shipment will be sent

GO ON TO THE NEXT PAGE

44. What is the main topic of the conversation?
(A) An employee's performance evaluation
(B) A technical difficulty with some software
(C) A system for issuing scheduling reminders
(D) A convenience facility in a building

45. What does the woman want to do?
(A) Administer a companywide survey
(B) Lower some maintenance spending
(C) Learn about upgrade options
(D) Clarify some guidelines

46. What does the woman ask the man to do?
(A) Set up a meeting
(B) Draft a notice
(C) Clean out a room
(D) Search a database

---

47. Why is the man at the store?
(A) To have some footwear repaired
(B) To buy a gift for a family member
(C) To return some unwanted goods
(D) To place an advance order

48. What does the woman request that the man do?
(A) Estimate a person's shoe size
(B) Complete some paperwork
(C) Provide proof of a purchase
(D) Show her the problem with an item

49. What does the woman apologize for?
(A) A long shipping duration
(B) An unfavorable store policy
(C) The small selection of merchandise
(D) A malfunctioning payment system

---

50. What do the women hope to do?
(A) Reserve an earlier train
(B) Use a self-service machine
(C) Take advantage of a promotion
(D) Change their seating assignments

51. What problem does the man describe?
(A) Some tickets have sold out.
(B) Some departures will be delayed.
(C) A computer server is down.
(D) A voucher has expired.

52. What will the women most likely do next?
(A) Notify a coworker
(B) Reevaluate a budget
(C) Divide up some work tasks
(D) Consider other travel methods

---

53. What most likely is the man's job?
(A) A journalist
(B) A graphic designer
(C) A newspaper editor
(D) A receptionist

54. According to the woman, what is the problem with an article?
(A) Some details are missing.
(B) There are some errors.
(C) The meaning of its title is unclear.
(D) It was placed in the wrong section.

55. What does the man ask the woman to do?
(A) Verify her professional qualifications
(B) Check the online version of the article
(C) Wait for him to locate a colleague
(D) File her complaint electronically

---

56. What is the man calling about?
(A) A sales event
(B) A repair service
(C) A new business
(D) A product order

57. What does the woman mean when she says, "I'm at work right now"?
(A) She does not have access to an item.
(B) She forgot about an appointment.
(C) She does not have time to talk.
(D) She is unaware of an issue that has arisen.

58. What will the woman most likely do next?
(A) Write down some contact information
(B) Stand near the entrance to a building
(C) Make a drawing of a space
(D) Take a bus to her house

---

59. What does the man thank the woman for?
(A) Lending him a resource
(B) Introducing him to an acquaintance
(C) Allowing him to use a workstation
(D) Looking over his writing

60. What does the man say happened last week?
(A) A publishing decision was announced.
(B) A research interview took place.
(C) A university institution was closed.
(D) A submission was made.

61. What does the man ask the woman about?
(A) Her experience with a process
(B) Her favorite coffee drink
(C) Her opinions on a book
(D) Her availability in the near future

Order Form

Item	No.
File organizers	3
Paper clips boxes	5
Pen sets	2
Staplers	1
Sticky notes pads	4

62. Who most likely is Mr. Han?
(A) A government inspector
(B) A board member
(C) A new hire
(D) A vendor

63. What does the man say he is currently doing?
(A) Organizing some files
(B) Making a schedule
(C) Reviewing an agreement
(D) Collecting some supplies

64. Look at the graphic. Which number does the woman recommend changing?
(A) 3
(B) 5
(C) 2
(D) 4

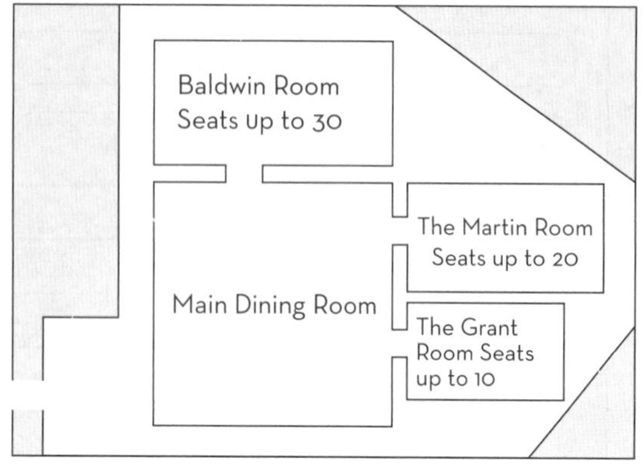

65. What is the woman organizing?
   (A) A fund-raiser
   (B) An office dinner
   (C) An awards ceremony
   (D) A retirement party

66. Look at the graphic. What room will the woman's group use?
   (A) The Main Dining Room
   (B) The Baldwin Room
   (C) The Martin Room
   (D) The Grant Room

67. What does the man say the woman will have to do?
   (A) Make a partial payment beforehand
   (B) Approve a fixed menu of dishes
   (C) Vacate the room by a certain time
   (D) Read some guidelines for patrons

68. What problem does the man mention?
   (A) A news report criticized the company.
   (B) It is difficult to attract new staff.
   (C) A client did not renew a contract.
   (D) Several employees have quit their jobs.

69. Look at the graphic. Which category does the woman want to know more about?
   (A) Career Opportunities
   (B) Management
   (C) Pay and Benefits
   (D) Work-Life Balance

70. What will the man do today?
   (A) Share a Web link with the woman
   (B) Alert other supervisors about a discovery
   (C) Create a summary of some content
   (D) Post a review on the Web site

PART 4 (20)

Directions: You will hear some talks given by a single speaker. You will be asked to answer three questions about what the speaker says in each talk. Select the best response to each question and mark the letter (A), (B), (C), or (D) on your answer sheet. The talks will not be printed in your test book and will be spoken only one time.

71. What is the purpose of the hotline?
(A) To give updates
(B) To provide advice
(C) To accept donations
(D) To take reports on community problems

72. What does the speaker mention about potential call recipients?
(A) They follow strict rules.
(B) They are currently busy.
(C) They are given regular training.
(D) They are not paid workers.

73. What does the speaker ask listeners to do during their call?
(A) Be brief
(B) Take notes
(C) Speak clearly
(D) Remain polite

---

74. What is Edge Thinking?
(A) A company that promotes healthy workplaces
(B) A government campaign targeting an industry
(C) An annual human resources conference
(D) A Web site operated by a research organization

75. What did the speaker arrange?
(A) A tour of a factory
(B) A team-building outing
(C) An assessment of an office
(D) A seminar on well-being

76. What does the speaker show the listeners?
(A) Some revisions to a floor plan
(B) Images of furniture
(C) A list of job benefits
(D) A potential itinerary

---

77. What kind of event is the speaker most likely attending?
(A) A cosmetics convention
(B) An arts and crafts festival
(C) A food and beverage exposition
(D) A pharmaceutical trade show

78. What does the speaker imply when she says, "I have about twenty sample bottles left"?
(A) More giveaway stock is urgently needed.
(B) Her return journey will not be difficult.
(C) A prediction about a product was correct.
(D) A display should be removed from a booth.

79. What does the speaker say she will do?
(A) Have lunch with a possible distributor
(B) Check the details of a contract
(C) Take an overnight flight
(D) Send the listener an e-mail

---

80. What does the speaker emphasize about the Cessna Institute?
(A) Its long history
(B) Its convenient location
(C) Its high admission requirements
(D) Its variable entrance costs

81. What does the speaker say about Mr. Duncan?
(A) He opened a new restaurant.
(B) His classroom is well-equipped.
(C) He studied at the Cessna Institute.
(D) His business received an award.

82. Why are the listeners encouraged to register soon?
(A) Classes are filling up quickly.
(B) A special offer is about to end.
(C) The deadline is approaching.
(D) A new policy will be adopted shortly.

GO ON TO THE NEXT PAGE

83. Who is the announcement most likely for?
(A) Theater patrons
(B) Shoppers
(C) Gym users
(D) Travelers

84. What does the speaker announce?
(A) A correction to an advertisement
(B) An issue with some plumbing
(C) A shortage of inventory
(D) A change in venue

85. What does the speaker say some staff members will do?
(A) Arrange a form of compensation
(B) Oversee the sharing of a resource
(C) Make further announcements
(D) Help listeners leave the area

---

86. Where does the speaker work?
(A) At a research facility
(B) At a manufacturing plant
(C) At a city government agency
(D) At a shipping center

87. What does the speaker mean when he says, "there's a reason we put that sign up"?
(A) An activity can be dangerous.
(B) Storage spaces must be kept secure.
(C) Visitors need special assistance.
(D) Some old equipment is fragile.

88. What does the speaker apologize for?
(A) Not noticing a mistake earlier
(B) Not explaining a procedure
(C) Addressing all of the listeners
(D) Limiting access to an amenity

---

89. What event are the listeners attending?
(A) A guest lecture
(B) A welcome reception
(C) An exhibition opening
(D) A tour of an artist's workshop

90. Who most likely is Ms. Carlson?
(A) An art scholar
(B) A painter
(C) A gallery owner
(D) A museum donor

91. According to the speaker, what will happen after Ms. Carlson speaks?
(A) Some refreshments will be served.
(B) Some photographs will be taken.
(C) The listeners will ask questions.
(D) The listeners will walk around.

---

92. What is the main topic of the broadcast?
(A) A special status for a residence
(B) The activities of a citizens' organization
(C) The possible purchase of a structure
(D) A publication on a city's history

93. Why does the speaker say, "the building is in bad condition"?
(A) To express disapproval of a proposal
(B) To report the result of an official inspection
(C) To suggest that a project will be harder than expected
(D) To explain an assumption she has made

94. What does the speaker encourage some listeners to do?
(A) Apply for membership in a group
(B) Provide financial support for a cause
(C) Make a public comment on a matter
(D) See a property in person

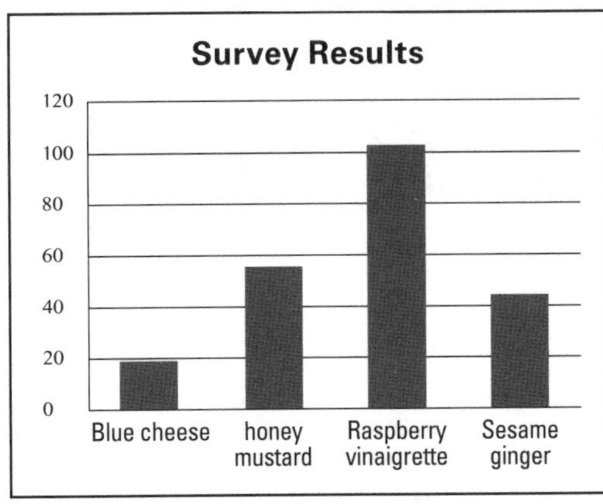

95. Who most likely are the listeners?

(A) Restaurant staff
(B) Lunch customers
(C) Product developers
(D) Marketing specialists

96. Look at the graphic. Which type of salad dressing does the speaker point out?

(A) Blue cheese
(B) Honey mustard
(C) Raspberry vinaigrette
(D) Sesame ginger

97. What has the speaker decided to do?

(A) Contact an outside consultant
(B) Offer a promotional discount
(C) Discontinue two types of dressing
(D) Increase a regular supply order

Boheim Horse Show

Ticket pricing (per person)	
1–3 people	£30
4–10 people	£27
11+ people	£24

98. Who will the speaker attend the show with?

(A) Work colleagues
(B) Relatives
(C) Potential clients
(D) Fellow members of a club

99. Look at the graphic. How much would the speaker like to pay per person?

(A) £33
(B) £30
(C) £27
(D) £24

100. What is the speaker concerned about?

(A) Rules may prohibit bringing certain items.
(B) The tickets may not be refundable.
(C) Part of the show may be canceled.
(D) A sale period may have ended.

This is the end of the Listening test.

ACTUAL TEST 6

LISTENING TEST 21

In the Listening test, you will be asked to demonstrate how well you understand spoken English. The entire Listening test will last approximately 45 minutes. There are four parts, and directions are given for each part. You must mark your answers on the separate answer sheet. Do not write your answers in your test book.

PART 1

Directions: For each question in this part, you will hear four statements about a picture in your test book. When you hear the statements, you must select the one statement that best describes what you see in the picture. Then find the number of the question on your answer sheet and mark your answer. The statements will not be printed in your test book and will be spoken only one time.

Statement (C), "They're sitting at a table," is the best description of the picture, so you should select answer (C) and mark it on your answer sheet.

1.

2.

3.

4.

5.

6.

PART 2 22

Directions: You will hear a question or statement and three responses spoken in English. They will not be printed in your test book and will be spoken only one time. Select the best response to the question or statement and mark the letter (A), (B), or (C) on your answer sheet.

7. Mark your answer on your answer sheet.

8. Mark your answer on your answer sheet.

9. Mark your answer on your answer sheet.

10. Mark your answer on your answer sheet.

11. Mark your answer on your answer sheet.

12. Mark your answer on your answer sheet.

13. Mark your answer on your answer sheet.

14. Mark your answer on your answer sheet.

15. Mark your answer on your answer sheet.

16. Mark your answer on your answer sheet.

17. Mark your answer on your answer sheet.

18. Mark your answer on your answer sheet.

19. Mark your answer on your answer sheet.

20. Mark your answer on your answer sheet.

21. Mark your answer on your answer sheet.

22. Mark your answer on your answer sheet.

23. Mark your answer on your answer sheet.

24. Mark your answer on your answer sheet.

25. Mark your answer on your answer sheet.

26. Mark your answer on your answer sheet.

27. Mark your answer on your answer sheet.

28. Mark your answer on your answer sheet.

29. Mark your answer on your answer sheet.

30. Mark your answer on your answer sheet.

31. Mark your answer on your answer sheet.

PART 3 (23)

Directions: You will hear some conversations between two or more people. You will be asked to answer three questions about what the speakers say in each conversation. Select the best response to each question and mark the letter (A), (B), (C), or (D) on your answer sheet. The conversations will not be printed in your test book and will be spoken only one time.

32. Where are the speakers?
(A) At a restaurant
(B) At a vacation resort
(C) At a conference center
(D) At a car rental agency

33. What problem does the woman mention?
(A) She has misplaced a set of keys.
(B) She does not know how long a trip will take.
(C) She did not receive an e-mail.
(D) She is unsure about operating a device.

34. What does the woman say she will do?
(A) Check some instructions
(B) Use a storage compartment
(C) Make an initial payment
(D) Watch a video

---

35. What does the man mean when he says, "the delivery was this morning"?
(A) He needs to put away some stock.
(B) He is available to have a discussion.
(C) He does not require the woman's help.
(D) He is confused about a work schedule.

36. According to the woman, what does the CEO want to do?
(A) Open a new branch
(B) Hire more servers
(C) Expand a menu
(D) Offer a discount

37. What does the woman decide to do?
(A) Share an idea with an executive
(B) Visit a competitor
(C) Conduct online research
(D) Make an official announcement

---

38. Who most likely is the woman?
(A) An office receptionist
(B) A human resources manager
(C) An information technology technician
(D) A maintenance supervisor

39. What problem does the man have?
(A) He forgot a password.
(B) He missed an orientation.
(C) He cannot get into his office.
(D) His computer is malfunctioning.

40. What will the woman probably do next?
(A) Go to pick up a machine
(B) Search for a publication
(C) Assign a task to a worker
(D) Approve a spending request

---

41. What most likely is the man's job?
(A) Vehicle mechanic
(B) Parking attendant
(C) Car salesperson
(D) Delivery driver

42. What does the man say he dislikes about his job?
(A) The lack of promotion opportunities
(B) The competitive colleagues
(C) The irregular finish time
(D) The long commute

43. What does the woman suggest that the man do?
(A) Submit an application form
(B) Accompany her to an event
(C) Speak to their mutual friend
(D) Read a job advertisement

GO ON TO THE NEXT PAGE

44. Who most likely are the men?
(A) City officials
(B) Real estate agents
(C) Interior decorators
(D) Event planners

45. What does the woman mention about the property?
(A) It is currently unfurnished.
(B) It will also be used for business.
(C) It is located downtown.
(D) It is in need of repairs.

46. What will the men probably do next?
(A) Show the woman some paperwork
(B) Unload some equipment
(C) Interview the woman
(D) Tour the residence

---

47. Why does the woman say she is unable to accept an assignment?
(A) Her workload is too heavy.
(B) She does not have a necessary skill.
(C) It would violate a company policy.
(D) She is going out of town soon.

48. What does the woman suggest asking Angelina to do?
(A) Provide some training
(B) Contact new clients
(C) Update a database
(D) Postpone a vacation

49. What does the man say he will check?
(A) A building directory
(B) A work calendar
(C) A staff handbook
(D) A survey report

---

50. What is the man concerned about?
(A) The price of a service
(B) The quality of an image
(C) The color of a logo
(D) The size of an order

51. What does the woman say her assistant will do this afternoon?
(A) Prepare a revised invoice
(B) Print additional copies
(C) Send a design electronically
(D) Pack up some posters

52. Why does the man want to change an appointment time?
(A) He has to attend a business gathering.
(B) His coworker is using a company car.
(C) He needs to pick up some clients.
(D) His office is scheduled to close early.

---

53. What type of business do the speakers most likely work for?
(A) A movie theater
(B) A hotel
(C) A museum
(D) A travel agency

54. What does the woman mention about the surrounding neighborhood?
(A) It has a new leisure facility.
(B) It has an interesting history.
(C) It has a confusing layout.
(D) It lacks parking.

55. What does the woman imply when she says, "Michael knows the area pretty well"?
(A) It is surprising that Michael made a mistake.
(B) Michael might be able to answer a question.
(C) The man should not be concerned about a delay.
(D) She thinks Michael is suitable for a role.

---

56. What types of products does Harumi want to review?
(A) Security systems
(B) Digital cameras
(C) Game consoles
(D) Audio equipment

57. What does the man ask Harumi about?
(A) Determining some standards
(B) Encouraging readers to leave comments
(C) Clearing out a space for shipments
(D) Negotiating a deal with manufacturers

58. What does the man request that Janelle do?
(A) Monitor an online discussion
(B) Locate a project file
(C) Meet with a coworker
(D) Edit some articles

---

59. What does the man ask for the woman's advice on?
(A) Evaluating suppliers
(B) Recruiting volunteers
(C) Participating in conferences
(D) Attracting customers

60. What does the woman recommend?
(A) Relaxing some communication rules
(B) Analyzing posts on a Web platform
(C) Subscribing to a news source
(D) Increasing marketing methods

61. Why is the man uncertain about the woman's suggestion?
(A) A venue may not be available.
(B) A budget may not be large enough.
(C) A timeline cannot be extended.
(D) A law may not allow a change.

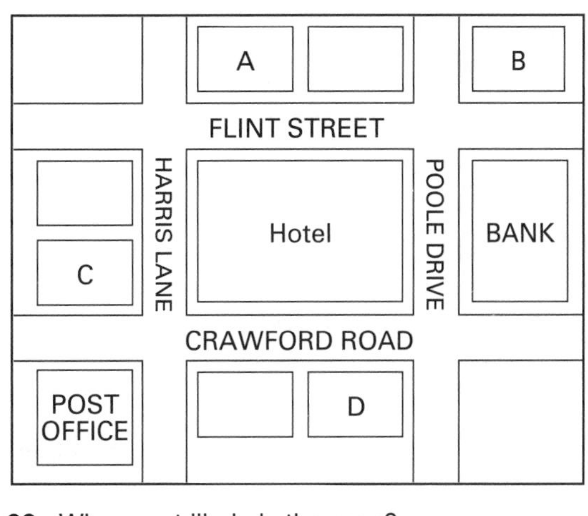

62. Who most likely is the man?
(A) A painter
(B) A gardener
(C) A caterer
(D) A repair person

63. Look at the graphic. Where does the woman live?
(A) At Location A
(B) At Location B
(C) At Location C
(D) At Location D

64. What is the problem?
(A) A service has been canceled.
(B) The man had the wrong address.
(C) A road has been closed to traffic.
(D) The woman's house has been renovated.

Northside Home Goods

Sale on Shanter brand floral dinnerware sets!

sets for
4 people:
$10 off

sets for
8+ people:
$15 off

65. What does the man want to know about the dinnerware sets?

(A) Why they are on sale
(B) How they should be washed
(C) How many pieces they include
(D) Whether they can be heated

66. Look at the graphic. How much money will the man save?

(A) $5
(B) $10
(C) $15
(D) $20

67. What does the woman say about Shanter's products?

(A) They are easy to return.
(B) They are designed to be long-lasting.
(C) They are not offered by many retailers.
(D) They are not discontinued often.

Destination	Scheduled Departure	Status
Detroit	07:35	Delayed (30 minutes)
Indianapolis	07:55	On Time
Toledo	08:15	Delayed (45 minutes)
Milwaukee	08:25	Delayed (2 hours)

68. What does the woman say she has brought?

(A) A computer accessory
(B) Some refreshments
(C) Some gifts
(D) A printout

69. Look at the graphic. What is the speakers' destination?

(A) Detroit
(B) Indianapolis
(C) Toledo
(D) Milwaukee

70. What does the woman suggest doing?

(A) Making a phone call
(B) Reviewing some plans
(C) Going to a departure platform
(D) Reserving some accommodations

PART 4 (24)

Directions: You will hear some talks given by a single speaker. You will be asked to answer three questions about what the speaker says in each talk. Select the best response to each question and mark the letter (A), (B), (C), or (D) on your answer sheet. The talks will not be printed in your test book and will be spoken only one time.

71. Who most likely is the listener?
(A) A job applicant
(B) A reference provider
(C) An external recruiter
(D) A career coach

72. What does the speaker say the listener has?
(A) Relevant experience
(B) A large number of contacts
(C) A sample legal agreement
(D) Generous funding

73. What does the speaker ask the listener to do?
(A) Submit a document
(B) Return his call
(C) Visit a Web site
(D) Confirm some data

---

74. What product does the speaker's company sell?
(A) Automobiles
(B) Electronics
(C) Furniture
(D) Luggage

75. What does the company's target market want?
(A) Better durability
(B) Increased comfort
(C) Improved safety
(D) Reduced cost

76. What does the speaker say she has done?
(A) Employed a consultant
(B) Ordered some materials
(C) Talked to a facility manager
(D) Made a list of features

---

77. What event will the listener attend on Thursday?
(A) A trade exposition
(B) A recruitment fair
(C) A training workshop
(D) A grand opening

78. What does the speaker say about a form?
(A) It is incomplete.
(B) It was submitted relatively late.
(C) It includes an unusual request.
(D) It has been misplaced.

79. Why does the speaker say, "West Coast Air flies direct to San Francisco"?
(A) To point out a mistake that he discovered
(B) To answer a question the listener about an itinerary
(C) To suggest an alternative travel option
(D) To explain why he made a decision

---

80. What type of event is the speaker advertising?
(A) An outdoor concert
(B) A movie festival
(C) A street parade
(D) A sports tournament

81. What are listeners encouraged to do?
(A) Try a special kind of food
(B) Wear warm clothing
(C) Bring their own seating
(D) Use public transportation

82. Why should listeners visit a Web site?
(A) To become a volunteer worker
(B) To download a map of a venue
(C) To see an entertainment lineup
(D) To purchase tickets in advance

GO ON TO THE NEXT PAGE

83. What is being discussed?
(A) A park restoration
(B) A building expansion
(C) An educational program
(D) An election campaign

84. What does the speaker imply when she says, "we're still waiting for Joslyn Associates"?
(A) She is worried that a deadline will not be met.
(B) She is unable to grant a request at this time.
(C) Joslyn Associates will contribute to an initiative.
(D) Joslyn Associates has a lot of influence in the city.

85. What was the speaker concerned about before?
(A) Expensive permit fees
(B) A shortage of personnel
(C) Negative public opinion
(D) Poor seasonal weather

---

86. What is the topic of the podcast?
(A) Writing advice
(B) Book reviews
(C) Famous authors
(D) Publishing trends

87. What does the speaker apologize for?
(A) Pronouncing a name incorrectly
(B) Misunderstanding a listener question
(C) Including a segment with bad sound quality
(D) Interrupting the show for an advertisement

88. What does the speaker encourage listeners to do?
(A) Report any errors she makes
(B) Recommend ideas for future episodes
(C) Support the podcast's sponsor
(D) Follow her social media account

---

89. According to the speaker, what will happen soon?
(A) A project team will be formed.
(B) A leadership position will be filled.
(C) A product will be announced.
(D) A mobile app will be released.

90. What does the speaker want the listeners to do?
(A) Provide some feedback
(B) Create a recording
(C) Gather some supplies
(D) Revise some sales figures

91. What does the speaker ask Barbara to hand out?
(A) Entrance passes
(B) A set of prototypes
(C) A draft of a script
(D) Notepads

---

92. Where most likely is the talk taking place?
(A) At a fitness center
(B) At a construction site
(C) In a hospital
(D) In a factory

93. What does the speaker ask the listeners to do?
(A) Wear safety gear
(B) Watch a demonstration
(C) Clean some machines
(D) Pack some boxes

94. What does the speaker mean when he says "Just look around at the other workers"?
(A) A requirement applies to everyone at a workplace.
(B) The listeners can learn a task by observing others.
(C) The listeners' negative feelings are common.
(D) There is serious competition for an opportunity.

---

requested quantities of wireless keyboards

Branch	Quantity
Bristol	25
Manchester	35
Norwich	40
Liverpool	45

95. Who most likely will use the keyboards?
(A) Customer service representatives
(B) Data entry specialists
(C) Software designers
(D) Newspaper staff

96. Look at the graphic. Which branch does the speaker work for?
(A) Bristol
(B) Manchester
(C) Norwich
(D) Liverpool

97. What does the speaker ask about?
(A) When a shipment will arrive
(B) How to start a return process
(C) Whom to notify about an issue
(D) Whether an order has been finalized

Exeter Science Museum

Family fun Day Demonstrations

9:00 A.M.	Invisible Ink
11:00 A.M.	Homemade Slime
1:00 P.M.	Glitter Volcano
3:00 P.M.	Miniature Windmill
5:00 P.M.	Rocket Balloon Car

98. Look at the graphic. Which demonstration does the speaker say will take place twice?
(A) Invisible Ink
(B) Homemade Slime
(C) Glitter Volcano
(D) Rocket Balloon Car

99. What does the speaker say he will do?
(A) Post an announcement
(B) Lead visitors on a tour
(C) Set up a temporary exhibit
(D) Hand out some badges

100. Why will Mr. Dixon observe some of the listeners?
(A) To prepare to write an article
(B) To give performance evaluations
(C) To carry out scientific research
(D) To receive training for his job

This is the end of the Listening test.

ACTUAL TEST 7

LISTENING TEST 

In the Listening test, you will be asked to demonstrate how well you understand spoken English. The entire Listening test will last approximately 45 minutes. There are four parts, and directions are given for each part. You must mark your answers on the separate answer sheet. Do not write your answers in your test book.

PART 1

Directions: For each question in this part, you will hear four statements about a picture in your test book. When you hear the statements, you must select the one statement that best describes what you see in the picture. Then find the number of the question on your answer sheet and mark your answer. The statements will not be printed in your test book and will be spoken only one time.

Statement (C), "They're sitting at a table," is the best description of the picture, so you should select answer (C) and mark it on your answer sheet.

1.

2.

3.

4.

5.

6.

GO ON TO THE NEXT PAGE

PART 2 (26)

Directions: You will hear a question or statement and three responses spoken in English. They will not be printed in your test book and will be spoken only one time. Select the best response to the question or statement and mark the letter (A), (B), or (C) on your answer sheet.

7. Mark your answer on your answer sheet.

8. Mark your answer on your answer sheet.

9. Mark your answer on your answer sheet.

10. Mark your answer on your answer sheet.

11. Mark your answer on your answer sheet.

12. Mark your answer on your answer sheet.

13. Mark your answer on your answer sheet.

14. Mark your answer on your answer sheet.

15. Mark your answer on your answer sheet.

16. Mark your answer on your answer sheet.

17. Mark your answer on your answer sheet.

18. Mark your answer on your answer sheet.

19. Mark your answer on your answer sheet.

20. Mark your answer on your answer sheet.

21. Mark your answer on your answer sheet.

22. Mark your answer on your answer sheet.

23. Mark your answer on your answer sheet.

24. Mark your answer on your answer sheet.

25. Mark your answer on your answer sheet.

26. Mark your answer on your answer sheet.

27. Mark your answer on your answer sheet.

28. Mark your answer on your answer sheet.

29. Mark your answer on your answer sheet.

30. Mark your answer on your answer sheet.

31. Mark your answer on your answer sheet.

PART 3 (27)

Directions: You will hear some conversations between two or more people. You will be asked to answer three questions about what the speakers say in each conversation. Select the best response to each question and mark the letter (A), (B), (C), or (D) on your answer sheet. The conversations will not be printed in your test book and will be spoken only one time.

32. Where most likely is the woman going?
(A) To a shopping mall
(B) To a city park
(C) To a conference center
(D) To a railway terminal

33. What is mentioned about Bryson Rotary?
(A) It usually has heavy traffic.
(B) It is the site of a city festival.
(C) It has a subway stop.
(D) It is partially under construction.

34. What does the man recommend doing?
(A) Parking in a garage
(B) Walking along a pedestrian street
(C) Returning via a different bus route
(D) Postponing a trip for a few hours

---

35. Where most likely do the speakers work?
(A) At a fitness center
(B) At a home furnishings store
(C) At a coffee shop
(D) At a clothing store

36. What is scheduled to take place Saturday?
(A) A grand opening celebration
(B) A safety inspection
(C) A closure for inventory
(D) A recycling collection event

37. What does the man say he will do next?
(A) Prepare some discount vouchers
(B) Place some boxes in storage
(C) Update a planning spreadsheet
(D) Process a customer refund

---

38. Why does the man want to purchase an electric bike?
(A) To add to a city's bike-share program
(B) To replace an older sport bike
(C) To transport building materials
(D) To shorten his daily commute

39. According to the woman, what is a disadvantage of the Y10 bike?
(A) Its size
(B) Its appearance
(C) Its battery life
(D) Its cost

40. What does the woman say the store is offering that week?
(A) Trial use of a charging station
(B) Extended warranties on bikes
(C) Reduced prices for repair services
(D) Free installation of accessories

---

41. Who most likely is the man?
(A) A customer service manager
(B) A software designer
(C) A shipping clerk
(D) An event planner

42. Why most likely does the woman say, "I've done that before"?
(A) To argue that a task must be possible
(B) To acknowledge a mistake she made
(C) To explain why she is working alone
(D) To show understanding of a problem

43. What does the woman suggest doing?
(A) Asking a team leader for additional help
(B) Referring to an instruction book during a process
(C) Sending a product back to its manufacturer
(D) Keeping a record of some actions

---

44. What did Mr. Taylor just finish doing?
(A) Cleaning a power tool
(B) Unloading a truck
(C) Landscaping a yard
(D) Repairing a sink

45. What does the woman say she will do?
(A) Organize a neighborhood event
(B) Refer others to Mr. Taylor's business
(C) Pay for services with a credit card
(D) Move a parked vehicle

46. What does Tom ask Mr. Taylor for?
(A) A cost estimate
(B) A regular client discount
(C) A printed receipt
(D) A copy of a contract

---

47. What does the man say he is looking for?
(A) A souvenir T-shirt
(B) A camera carrying bag
(C) An illustrated guidebook
(D) A set of drawing tools

48. According to the woman, why is the museum special?
(A) It has free admission.
(B) It is the city's oldest museum.
(C) It has exhibits on sporting history.
(D) It allows visitors to take photographs.

49. What will the woman ask a manager for?
(A) A product code
(B) A key to a cabinet
(C) Some gift wrapping
(D) Some business cards

---

50. What does the speakers' company most likely manufacture?
(A) Soft drinks
(B) Skin care products
(C) Eating utensils
(D) Food seasonings

51. What will the woman help the man do?
(A) Place products into shipping boxes
(B) Adjust a machine's operating speed
(C) Change the design of a logo
(D) Order additional equipment

52. What will the man most likely do next?
(A) Phone a company technician
(B) Search for an instruction manual
(C) Inform a team of a work interruption
(D) Choose an alternative type of packaging

---

53. According to the man, what needs improvement?
(A) A promotional flyer
(B) Some guidance signs
(C) Some outdoor gardens
(D) A restaurant in a food court

54. Who most likely will participate in next week's focus group?
(A) Maintenance workers
(B) Mall shoppers
(C) Store owners
(D) Real estate developers

55. What does Susan offer to do?
(A) Contact a consultant
(B) Post notices in a building
(C) Lead a training session
(D) Redesign a questionnaire

56. What are the speakers mainly discussing?
(A) A new work-from-home policy
(B) The layout of a workplace
(C) An upcoming video shoot
(D) New procedures for collecting data

57. What problem does the woman report?
(A) Some documents are hard to access.
(B) Some employees have long commutes to work.
(C) Some storage areas have no more space.
(D) Some hallways are often noisy.

58. What will the woman ask Mr. Kim to do?
(A) Move to a smaller office
(B) Purchase a piece of furniture
(C) Revise a research report
(D) Extend a submission deadline

---

59. What did the speakers' business do recently?
(A) Expanded its range of products
(B) Held an anniversary celebration
(C) Joined an industry association
(D) Renovated a shopping area

60. Why most likely does the man say, "other organic grocery stores have hands-on cooking classes"?
(A) To show surprise at a local trend
(B) To suggest offering in-store activities
(C) To highlight the health benefits of organic foods
(D) To express doubt about the effectiveness of a promotion

61. What will the man probably do next?
(A) Water some plants
(B) Visit a nearby farm
(C) Clear off a display shelf
(D) Request a catalog

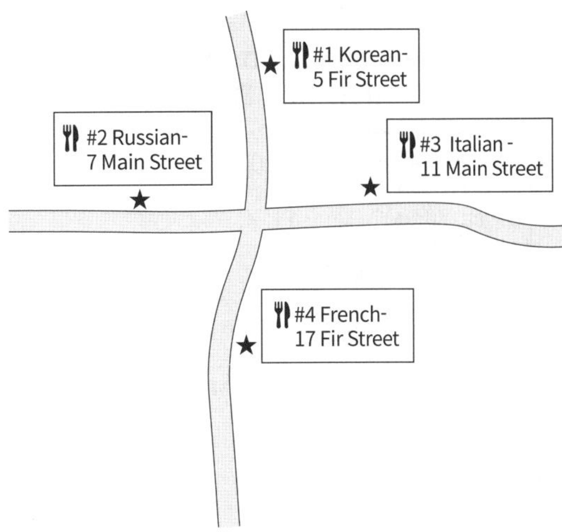

62. What does the man say he put on the business's Web site?
(A) A link
(B) An apology
(C) Some praise
(D) Some prices

63. What does the woman say she will do next week?
(A) Arrange a staff appreciation party
(B) Speak with a local business owner
(C) Purchase a navigation device
(D) View some vacant apartments

64. Look at the graphic. Which location number is no longer accurate?
(A) #1
(B) #2
(C) #3
(D) #4

Interview Schedule
Conference Room

David Meyer	10:00 A.M.
Erica Yang	11:00 A.M.
LUNCH BREAK	12:00 P.M.-1:00 P.M.
Lance Dedham	1:30 P.M.
Joy Nelson	3:00 P.M.

65. What does the woman say the magazine will start doing next month?

(A) Reducing rates for advertisements
(B) Publishing letters from subscribers
(C) Giving tours of its headquarters complex
(D) Releasing special issues regularly

66. What does the man plan to do?

(A) Take photos for a Web site
(B) Proofread some writing
(C) Set up audiovisual equipment
(D) Send out text messages

67. Look at the graphic. Which candidate will be interviewed in a different room?

(A) David Meyer
(B) Erica Yang
(C) Lance Dedham
(D) Joy Nelson

General Goods Section

Aisle 1	Garden supplies
Aisle 2	Carpet and flooring
Aisle 3	Sports equipment
Aisle 4	Office stationery

68. What problem do the speakers mention?

(A) A missing form
(B) A delayed delivery
(C) A shortage of employees
(D) An out-of-date training manual

69. Look at the graphic. Which aisle will the speakers work in that afternoon?

(A) Aisle 1
(B) Aisle 2
(C) Aisle 3
(D) Aisle 4

70. According to the woman, what happened last week?

(A) A staff recruiting event
(B) A district managers' meeting
(C) A building renovation
(D) A seasonal sale

PART 4 (28)

Directions: You will hear some talks given by a single speaker. You will be asked to answer three questions about what the speaker says in each talk. Select the best response to each question and mark the letter (A), (B), (C), or (D) on your answer sheet. The talks will not be printed in your test book and will be spoken only one time.

71. Where is the announcement being given?
(A) On a high-speed train
(B) On an airport shuttle bus
(C) In a baggage claim area
(D) At an airport departure lounge

72. What does the speaker mention about Delray Airport?
(A) It is one of two airports in the city.
(B) It mainly handles cargo planes.
(C) It offers international flights.
(D) It was recently expanded.

73. What does the speaker encourage listeners to do?
(A) Observe airport operations
(B) Make use of luggage racks
(C) Request additional station stops
(D) Register for a notification service

---

74. What is the main purpose of the meeting?
(A) To address listeners' feedback on a plan
(B) To brainstorm names for a product
(C) To familiarize attendees with a software program
(D) To review a consultant's report

75. According to the speaker, what is the problem with a mobile phone app?
(A) High user fees
(B) Slow loading speed
(C) Unclear illustrations
(D) Complex navigation

76. What will the speaker probably do next?
(A) Evaluate design proposals
(B) Welcome a guest speaker
(C) Pass out sample items
(D) Discuss a presentation slide

---

77. What does the speaker mention about Lorna's Market?
(A) It was recently remodeled.
(B) It has a seafood department.
(C) It has a loyalty card program.
(D) Its management has changed.

78. What is the main purpose of the announcement?
(A) To remind shoppers about extended hours
(B) To publicize current job openings
(C) To encourage use of self-checkout machines
(D) To share the results of a survey

79. According to the announcement, what will start on June 1 ?
(A) A series of cooking demonstrations
(B) The construction of a new location
(C) A home delivery service
(D) A prize giveaway contest

---

80. Where most likely does the speaker work?
(A) At a transportation service
(B) At an architecture firm
(C) At an educational institution
(D) At a dining establishment

81. What does the speaker mean when she says, "remember that people do live here"?
(A) Listeners should be respectful toward residents.
(B) Older homes are more attractive to buyers.
(C) Residents depend on tourism revenue.
(D) It is unusual for a historic district to be occupied.

82. What does the speaker say the listeners will see next?
(A) A live performance
(B) Some architectural drawings
(C) Some classic vehicles
(D) A body of water

---

83. What is the main topic of the news report?

(A) A profile of a local politician
(B) An upcoming community activity
(C) Driving conditions on area roadways
(D) Problems with an environmental project

84. What are listeners invited to do?

(A) Participate in an opinion poll
(B) Attend an outdoor event
(C) Join a volunteer organization
(D) View an online catalog

85. What most likely will be heard next?

(A) A list of business closures
(B) A paid advertisement
(C) A call from a radio listener
(D) An explanation of a competition

---

86. Who most likely is the speaker?

(A) An interior designer
(B) A convention organizer
(C) A hotel manager
(D) A real estate agent

87. Why most likely does the speaker say, "the wallpaper and lamps are quite old"?

(A) To indicate that she is impressed by some materials' durability
(B) To justify the decision to change a venue
(C) To emphasize the need to make updates
(D) To compliment a structure's vintage decorations

88. What does the speaker say she will do later that day?

(A) Recruit additional workers
(B) Introduce the listener to a colleague
(C) Provide a written proposal
(D) Issue a partial refund

---

89. Where most likely is the introduction taking place?

(A) At a university student center
(B) At an art museum
(C) At a formal garden
(D) At a photo studio

90. What will the speaker give the listeners?

(A) An audio device
(B) A gift shop coupon
(C) A guide map to a facility
(D) A link to a mobile phone app

91. What does the speaker suggest doing?

(A) Watching an introductory film
(B) Ordering a meal in advance
(C) Starting a tour in a less crowded area
(D) Filling out a feedback survey

---

92. Why most likely does the speaker congratulate the listener?

(A) He gave a successful presentation.
(B) He recently purchased a new house.
(C) His transfer request was granted.
(D) His sales team won an award.

93. What does the speaker imply when she says, "there are a lot of moving companies in this area"?

(A) She needs more details about a project.
(B) The region has many new residents.
(C) It will not be difficult to hire a mover.
(D) A new company might struggle at first.

94. What does the speaker say will be helpful for the listener?

(A) Browsing a Web site
(B) Modifying a travel itinerary
(C) Completing an electronic form
(D) Holding a special staff meeting

Name of Trainer	Room number
Gregor	305
Jim	307
Becky	309
Yuko	311

95. What kind of business does the speaker most likely work for?
(A) At a merchandise display distributor
(B) At a software development firm
(C) At a footwear manufacturer
(D) At a package shipping company

96. According to the speaker, what will interns be required to do?
(A) Oversee an online messaging board
(B) Create posts for a social media account
(C) Test a feature of a computer program
(D) Compile statistics about clients

97. Look at the graphic. Which room will most likely NOT be used for training?
(A) 305
(B) 307
(C) 309
(D) 311

Sign

1	Delivery Drivers Must Sign in at Office
2	Visitors Must Wear ID Badges
3	Area Monitored by Security Camera
4	Parking for Delivery Vehicles Only

98. What does the speaker first announce a change to?
(A) A work schedule
(B) The staff dress code
(C) A stocking system
(D) A floor plan

99. According to the speaker, what will happen in the summer?
(A) A new product will be launched.
(B) A busy period will begin.
(C) A facility will close temporarily.
(D) A sales contest will take place.

100. Look at the graphic. Which sign did the speaker install yesterday?
(A) Sign #1
(B) Sign #2
(C) Sign #3
(D) Sign #4

This is the end of the Listening test.

ACTUAL TEST 8

LISTENING TEST 29

In the Listening test, you will be asked to demonstrate how well you understand spoken English. The entire Listening test will last approximately 45 minutes. There are four parts, and directions are given for each part. You must mark your answers on the separate answer sheet. Do not write your answers in your test book.

PART 1

Directions: For each question in this part, you will hear four statements about a picture in your test book. When you hear the statements, you must select the one statement that best describes what you see in the picture. Then find the number of the question on your answer sheet and mark your answer. The statements will not be printed in your test book and will be spoken only one time.

Statement (C), "They're sitting at a table," is the best description of the picture, so you should select answer (C) and mark it on your answer sheet.

1.

2.

3.

4.

5.

6.

PART 2 (30)

Directions: You will hear a question or statement and three responses spoken in English. They will not be printed in your test book and will be spoken only one time. Select the best response to the question or statement and mark the letter (A), (B), or (C) on your answer sheet.

7. Mark your answer on your answer sheet.

8. Mark your answer on your answer sheet.

9. Mark your answer on your answer sheet.

10. Mark your answer on your answer sheet.

11. Mark your answer on your answer sheet.

12. Mark your answer on your answer sheet.

13. Mark your answer on your answer sheet.

14. Mark your answer on your answer sheet.

15. Mark your answer on your answer sheet.

16. Mark your answer on your answer sheet.

17. Mark your answer on your answer sheet.

18. Mark your answer on your answer sheet.

19. Mark your answer on your answer sheet.

20. Mark your answer on your answer sheet.

21. Mark your answer on your answer sheet.

22. Mark your answer on your answer sheet.

23. Mark your answer on your answer sheet.

24. Mark your answer on your answer sheet.

25. Mark your answer on your answer sheet.

26. Mark your answer on your answer sheet.

27. Mark your answer on your answer sheet.

28. Mark your answer on your answer sheet.

29. Mark your answer on your answer sheet.

30. Mark your answer on your answer sheet.

31. Mark your answer on your answer sheet.

PART 3 (31)

Directions: You will hear some conversations between two or more people. You will be asked to answer three questions about what the speakers say in each conversation. Select the best response to each question and mark the letter (A), (B), (C), or (D) on your answer sheet. The conversations will not be printed in your test book and will be spoken only one time.

32. What does the woman say she is pleased with?
(A) A larger work area
(B) An extended vacation
(C) Some budget decisions
(D) Some recent sales results

33. What kind of business most likely is B & R Services?
(A) An event planning firm
(B) A temporary staffing agency
(C) An interior decorating provider
(D) A carpet cleaning company

34. What will the speakers probably do next?
(A) Review information on a Web site
(B) Prepare a presentation
(C) Rearrange some devices
(D) Ask for approval from a manager

---

35. According to the woman, what has changed about a trip itinerary?
(A) The operator of a flight
(B) The departure point
(C) The duration
(D) The number of connecting flights

36. What does the man say happened on Friday?
(A) He received a notification message.
(B) He canceled a previous booking.
(C) He changed the date of a trip.
(D) He was given a ticket discount.

37. What does the man want to know about?
(A) Choosing a seating option
(B) Checking in large baggage
(C) Requesting special meals
(D) Using an airport lounge

---

38. What was the man previously instructed to do?
(A) Bring his old dental records
(B) Enter through a side door
(C) Arrive early for an appointment
(D) Refer acquaintances to a clinic

39. What does the woman say about some paperwork?
(A) It had already been filled out electronically.
(B) It has marked sections for completion.
(C) It contains some printing errors.
(D) It was recently revised.

40. What does the woman give the man?
(A) Some tooth care tools
(B) Some customized stationery
(C) Some coupons for future visits
(D) Some bottled water

---

41. Who most likely is Nancy Batra?
(A) A visiting professor
(B) An in-house translator
(C) A departmental intern
(D) A newspaper journalist

42. Why does the man say, "many students are learning from home"?
(A) To decline an assignment
(B) To suggest delaying a product release
(C) To express agreement with the woman
(D) To admit that he is concerned about market competition

43. What will the woman probably do next?
(A) Contact a consultant
(B) Make a delivery
(C) Proofread a report
(D) Set up some equipment

GO ON TO THE NEXT PAGE

44. What has caused a problem?
(A) An outdated software program
(B) A malfunctioning monitor
(C) A loose cable connection
(D) A faulty electrical outlet

45. What does Stan mention about himself?
(A) He supervises an intern.
(B) He has a project due soon.
(C) He previously tried to fix a computer.
(D) He referred Ms. Jacobs to a service.

46. What is the woman asked to do?
(A) Distribute his business card
(B) Provide online feedback
(C) Present a warranty document
(D) Review an installation procedure

---

47. According to the woman, what did the man do recently?
(A) Took a knowledge test
(B) Opened a souvenir shop
(C) Published a guidebook
(D) Trained a tour leader

48. Why does the woman say the city's history museum is important?
(A) It is the city's oldest tourist attraction.
(B) It is larger than other museums.
(C) It has new interactive exhibits.
(D) It is the starting point for walking tours.

49. What does the man ask the woman about?
(A) Taking special transportation to a venue
(B) Introducing himself to a group of people
(C) Earning a professional qualification
(D) Keeping a record of a conversation

---

50. Where most likely is the conversation taking place?
(A) At a city park
(B) At a garden supply shop
(C) At an organic farm
(D) At a natural history museum

51. What does the man suggest doing for a project?
(A) Placing some plants in an indoor area
(B) Checking a local weather forecast daily
(C) Choosing plants that normally grow in a region
(D) Starting it during a warmer season

52. What does the man show the woman?
(A) A directional sign
(B) An informational Web site
(C) An artificial body of water
(D) A price list for services

---

53. What kind of products does the man's company sell?
(A) Adjustable desks
(B) Instructional books
(C) Business software
(D) Motivational posters

54. What do the women say they like about the man's company?
(A) It provides a fast delivery service.
(B) It uses environmentally-friendly materials.
(C) It participates in community fundraisers.
(D) It has a wide selection of products.

55. What does Sandra say about her department?
(A) It will sponsor a running race.
(B) It will be given a different name.
(C) It will have team-building day.
(D) It will merge with another department.

---

56. What kind of event is the woman planning?

(A) An awards banquet
(B) A birthday party
(C) An anniversary celebration
(D) A cooking contest

57. What does the man say to reassure the woman about a catering service?

(A) It has won recognition from publications.
(B) It is used by the area's biggest companies.
(C) It can be provided in a range of venues.
(D) It is available outside of regular business hours.

58. What does the man suggest doing?

(A) Requesting a discount for a large group
(B) Reserving a particular banquet room
(C) Phoning a business proprietor directly
(D) Ordering meals from an online menu

---

59. What does the woman say she did?

(A) Uploaded some images to the Internet
(B) Repaired some harvesting equipment
(C) Packed a box of produce for pick-up
(D) Submitted an order form to a manufacturer

60. Why most likely does the man say, "I grew up on a farm"?

(A) To support an opinion
(B) To explain a misunderstanding
(C) To offer assistance
(D) To show curiosity

61. What does the woman suggest the man do?

(A) Feed some farm animals
(B) Park closer to an entrance
(C) Read over a promotional flyer
(D) Look at some flower arrangements

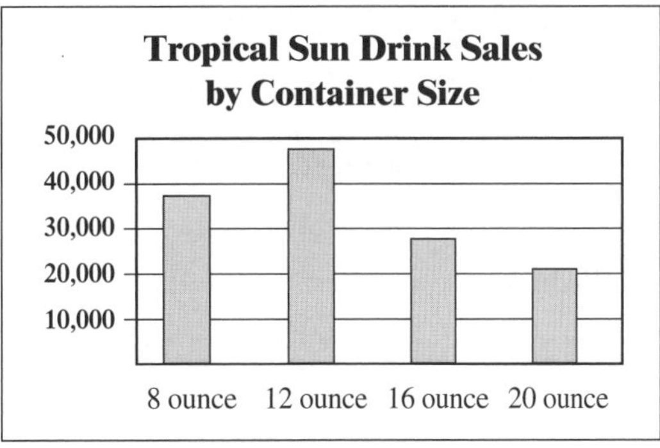

62. According to the speakers, what has the company done?

(A) Relocated its head office
(B) Expanded its sales territory
(C) Created a new corporate logo
(D) Replaced a celebrity spokesperson

63. What is mentioned about the Tropical Sun drink?

(A) It is stocked mostly in restaurants.
(B) It has a combination of flavors.
(C) It will soon be sold at discounts.
(D) It comes in glass bottles.

64. Look at the graphic. Which size of drink's sales data will the speakers focus on?

(A) 8 ounce
(B) 12 ounce
(C) 16 ounce
(D) 20 ounce

Enzio's Cafe—Daily Specials

Monday	Chicken curry $13
Tuesday	Vegetable pasta $10
Wednesday	Cheese pizza $12
Thursday	Grilled salmon $14

65. What does the man say about some employees?

(A) They have been telecommuting.
(B) They will transfer to overseas offices.
(C) Their workloads have been reduced.
(D) They are attending a product launch.

66. According to the woman, what has Enzio's Café recently done?

(A) Raised its food prices
(B) Renovated its dining room
(C) Opened an additional location
(D) Simplified an ordering process

67. Look at the graphic. What special will the speakers probably order for delivery?

(A) Chicken curry
(B) Vegetable pasta
(C) Cheese pizza
(D) Grilled salmon

Return code	Reason for return
01	Damaged in shipping
02	Defective—does not work properly
03	Wrong item shipped
04	Changed mind—do not want

68. What does the man mention about the woman?

(A) She is working overtime.
(B) She is a new employee.
(C) She will soon go on vacation.
(D) She is handling a colleague's responsibilities.

69. Look at the graphic. Which return code will most likely be entered?

(A) Code 01
(B) Code 02
(C) Code 03
(D) Code 04

70. What will the man probably do next?

(A) Go to a different part of a building
(B) Use a loudspeaker to ask for assistance
(C) Write down some questions
(D) Restart a handheld device

PART 4 (32)

Directions: You will hear some talks given by a single speaker. You will be asked to answer three questions about what the speaker says in each talk. Select the best response to each question and mark the letter (A), (B), (C), or (D) on your answer sheet. The talks will not be printed in your test book and will be spoken only one time.

71. What kind of business most likely is Caldarr Center?
(A) A home furnishings retailer
(B) An electronics store
(C) A telecommunications service
(D) A maker of office supplies

72. According to the advertisement, what has Caldarr Center done recently?
(A) Added a new way to shop
(B) Launched a loyalty program
(C) Expanded its range of products
(D) Hired new staff members

73. What does the speaker encourage listeners to do?
(A) Browse a customer feedback page
(B) Upgrade some warranty coverage
(C) Purchase special gift cards
(D) Vote on a potential improvement

---

74. What is mentioned about the Northern Express Train?
(A) It costs more than ordinary trains.
(B) It operates several times each day.
(C) It makes no stops en route to its destination.
(D) It is divided into two seating classes.

75. What are passengers in Car Four of the train asked to do?
(A) Present photo identification
(B) Store luggage between cars
(C) Avoid mobile phone conversations
(D) Move forward to the next car

76. According to the announcement, what will happen shortly?
(A) Tickets will be inspected.
(B) A video will be shown.
(C) Boarding will be completed.
(D) Refreshments will be available.

---

77. What kind of business recorded the message?
(A) A real estate firm
(B) A travel agency
(C) A medical clinic
(D) A mobile app developer

78. What does the speaker apologize for?
(A) A recent price increase
(B) An upcoming holiday closure
(C) Extended holding times
(D) Possible audio problems

79. What is the listener encouraged to do?
(A) Meet a representative in person
(B) Prepare some documentation
(C) Use a business's other locations
(D) Try calling on another day

---

80. Who most likely is the listener?
(A) A neighbor
(B) A plumber
(C) A house painter
(D) A delivery person

81. What most likely does the speaker mean when she says, "there are a lot of white houses in the area"?
(A) A maintenance service could become popular.
(B) A neighborhood has few nearby businesses.
(C) Some renovations will make a home stand out.
(D) Some instructions may have been unclear.

82. What does the speaker say she will do next?
(A) Add her signature to an agreement
(B) Make a space available for parking
(C) Take some letters to a post office
(D) Put up some signs outside a structure

GO ON TO THE NEXT PAGE

83. According to the report, what delayed the mall's completion?

(A) Changes to its floor plan
(B) Difficulty receiving some permits
(C) A shortage of construction workers
(D) The hiring of a new contractor

84. What does the speaker say is a feature of the mall?

(A) A performance space
(B) An indoor garden
(C) A large entrance hall
(D) A public transportation stop

85. What are listeners invited to do?

(A) Stream footage of an opening-day event
(B) Submit feedback surveys to mall management
(C) Register for an e-mail update program
(D) Participate in a phone-in talk show

---

86. What kind of business most likely is Revdecc Plus?

(A) A publishing company
(B) A real estate developer
(C) A fitness center
(D) An advertising agency

87. Why most likely does the speaker say, "we've had design challenges before"?

(A) To suggest buying new design software
(B) To emphasize the need to recruit more staff
(C) To reassure the listeners about a task
(D) To praise the listeners for an accomplishment

88. What does the speaker recommend doing in the afternoon?

(A) Distributing some brochures
(B) Holding a team meeting
(C) Working past the end of a shift
(D) Visiting a client together

---

89. What most likely is being taught in the workshop?

(A) Hiking for fitness
(B) Growing plants
(C) Writing journals
(D) Painting pictures

90. According to the speaker, what is special about the workshop?

(A) It has a high enrollment.
(B) It is being held outdoors.
(C) It is taught by two instructors.
(D) It takes place over multiple days.

91. What are listeners advised to do?

(A) Obtain parking permits
(B) Carry minimal belongings
(C) Avoid picking flowers
(D) Walk carefully

---

92. What will the speaker's company do soon?

(A) Relocate to a different office
(B) Host a visit from potential clients
(C) Rearrange its current workspace
(D) Undergo a safety inspection

93. What does the speaker imply when he says, "it's Thursday afternoon"?

(A) An executive is probably busy.
(B) A deadline is approaching.
(C) A previously stated date is incorrect.
(D) A meeting will be postponed.

94. What does the speaker say he will do next?

(A) Clean a workstation
(B) Wait next to an external door
(C) Organize a supply closet
(D) Set up a waste container

Imported Items

95. According to the speaker, what is being sold at reduced prices?
(A) Health foods
(B) Cooking tools
(C) Products sold in bulk
(D) Discontinued merchandise

96. Look at the graphic. Which shelf did the speaker remove items from?
(A) The top shelf
(B) The third shelf
(C) The second shelf
(D) The bottom shelf

97. What are listeners asked to emphasize about a sale?
(A) It applies mostly to high priced items.
(B) It involves a mobile app.
(C) It will last for only one day.
(D) It does not require coupons.

Day 2 training
1:00 P.M. to 5:00 P.M.

Module 1	Company policies
Module 2	Making presentations
Module 3	Software training
Module 4	Customer relations

98. Where most likely is the introduction taking place?
(A) At a luggage manufacturer
(B) At a graphic design firm
(C) At a jewelry seller
(D) At a software developer

99. Look at the graphic. Which module most likely will be shortened?
(A) Module 1
(B) Module 2
(C) Module 3
(D) Module 4

100. What does the speaker tell the listeners to do?
(A) Look at some product samples
(B) Share materials with a partner
(C) Ensure that a booklet is complete
(D) Turn off any personal electronics

This is the end of the Listening test.

ACTUAL TEST 9

LISTENING TEST 33

In the Listening test, you will be asked to demonstrate how well you understand spoken English. The entire Listening test will last approximately 45 minutes. There are four parts, and directions are given for each part. You must mark your answers on the separate answer sheet. Do not write your answers in your test book.

PART 1

Directions: For each question in this part, you will hear four statements about a picture in your test book. When you hear the statements, you must select the one statement that best describes what you see in the picture. Then find the number of the question on your answer sheet and mark your answer. The statements will not be printed in your test book and will be spoken only one time.

Statement (C), "They're sitting at a table," is the best description of the picture, so you should select answer (C) and mark it on your answer sheet.

1.

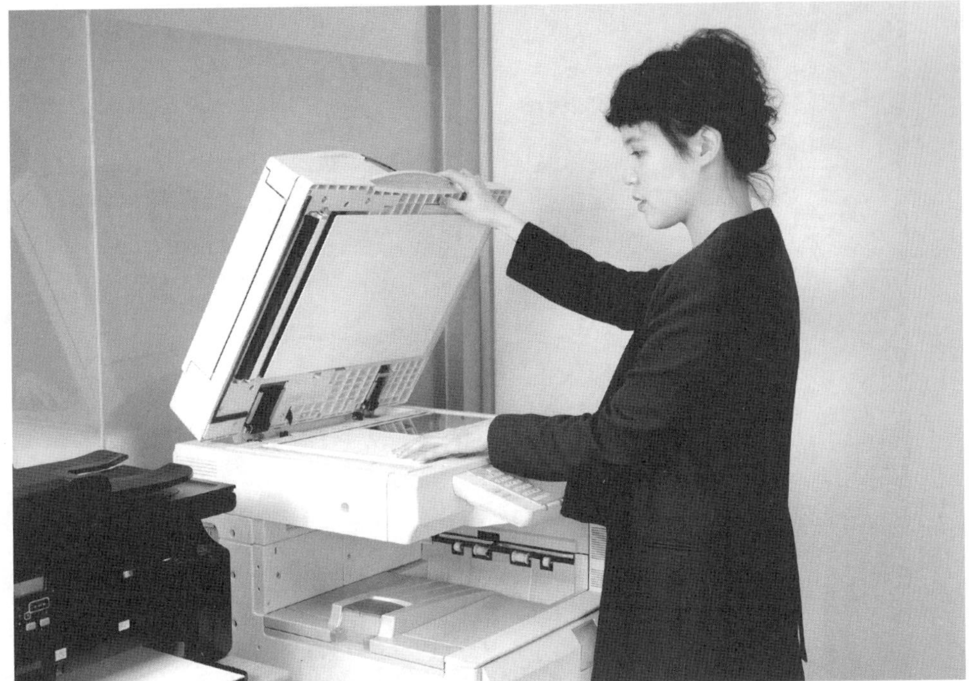

2.

GO ON TO THE NEXT PAGE

3.

4.

5.

6.

PART 2 (34)

Directions: You will hear a question or statement and three responses spoken in English. They will not be printed in your test book and will be spoken only one time. Select the best response to the question or statement and mark the letter (A), (B), or (C) on your answer sheet.

7. Mark your answer on your answer sheet.

8. Mark your answer on your answer sheet.

9. Mark your answer on your answer sheet.

10. Mark your answer on your answer sheet.

11. Mark your answer on your answer sheet.

12. Mark your answer on your answer sheet.

13. Mark your answer on your answer sheet.

14. Mark your answer on your answer sheet.

15. Mark your answer on your answer sheet.

16. Mark your answer on your answer sheet.

17. Mark your answer on your answer sheet.

18. Mark your answer on your answer sheet.

19. Mark your answer on your answer sheet.

20. Mark your answer on your answer sheet.

21. Mark your answer on your answer sheet.

22. Mark your answer on your answer sheet.

23. Mark your answer on your answer sheet.

24. Mark your answer on your answer sheet.

25. Mark your answer on your answer sheet.

26. Mark your answer on your answer sheet.

27. Mark your answer on your answer sheet.

28. Mark your answer on your answer sheet.

29. Mark your answer on your answer sheet.

30. Mark your answer on your answer sheet.

31. Mark your answer on your answer sheet.

PART 3 35

Directions: You will hear some conversations between two or more people. You will be asked to answer three questions about what the speakers say in each conversation. Select the best response to each question and mark the letter (A), (B), (C), or (D) on your answer sheet. The conversations will not be printed in your test book and will be spoken only one time.

32. What does the man say will happen next month?
(A) A conference will take place.
(B) A new law will go into effect.
(C) A tour will be given.
(D) A staff member will retire.

33. What does the woman say she did?
(A) Picked up some materials
(B) Made some reservations
(C) Had lunch with a client
(D) Posted a job listing

34. What does the man ask the woman to do immediately?
(A) Listen to a telephone message
(B) Make copies of a file
(C) Correct a mistake
(D) Send a notification

---

35. What does the woman ask for?
(A) A take-away cup
(B) A sales receipt
(C) A gift certificate
(D) An ingredient replacement

36. What does Bill correct Carl about?
(A) The name of a drink
(B) The operating hours of a café
(C) The availability of an item
(D) The cost of a change

37. How does the woman want to pay for her order?
(A) With cash
(B) With a voucher
(C) With a credit card
(D) With a mobile app

---

38. What are the speakers most likely choosing cast members for?
(A) A television program
(B) A feature film
(C) A stage show
(D) An online advertisement

39. What does the man say about Mr. Witherspoon?
(A) He does not have a necessary skill.
(B) He should play another character.
(C) He will have to audition again.
(D) He has a scheduling conflict.

40. What does the man decide to do?
(A) Speak with an investor
(B) Rewatch a performance
(C) Postpone a discussion
(D) Move a location

---

41. Where most likely is the conversation taking place?
(A) In a parking garage
(B) In a banquet hall
(C) In a seminar room
(D) In a hotel lobby

42. What does the woman imply when she says, "I arrived yesterday morning"?
(A) She was not present for a talk.
(B) There is an error on an invoice.
(C) She did not have time for a social activity.
(D) There was strong competition for an opportunity.

43. What will the woman most likely do next?
(A) Look over a timetable
(B) Make a call to a colleague
(C) Search through her handbag
(D) E-mail the man from a device

GO ON TO THE NEXT PAGE

44. Who most likely is the woman?

(A) An assembly line manager
(B) A truck driver
(C) A warehouse worker
(D) A sales clerk

45. What is the man concerned about?

(A) The status of a shipment
(B) The woman's health
(C) The opinion of an executive
(D) The woman's job satisfaction

46. What does the man offer the woman?

(A) Help from another staff member
(B) Use of a special piece of equipment
(C) A career development opportunity
(D) A referral to a service provider

---

47. What does the man hope to do?

(A) Release some music
(B) Rent some machinery
(C) Sell a piece of property
(D) Relocate a retail store

48. What problem does the woman mention?

(A) A contract's terms are unfavorable.
(B) A space has some security issues.
(C) A local regulation is complicated.
(D) A certification has expired.

49. What does the woman ask the man about?

(A) His familiarity with a process
(B) His willingness to negotiate
(C) His ability to prove a claim
(D) His access to a resource

---

50. What does the man mention about the meeting?

(A) It was not originally scheduled for today.
(B) It includes a remote participant.
(C) It is being recorded.
(D) It might last past closing time.

51. What kind of project are the speakers working on?

(A) Recruiting for staff openings
(B) Developing a questionnaire
(C) Organizing a training program
(D) Rewriting a set of policies

52. What will the speakers do next?

(A) Give individual progress updates
(B) Read the minutes of a previous meeting
(C) Choose their preferred assignments
(D) Wait for an additional attendee

---

53. What does the man say about his trip?

(A) He plans to visit a friend.
(B) It will be one week long.
(C) It has been enjoyable.
(D) He is traveling for work.

54. How does the woman assist the man?

(A) By giving him an extra cushion
(B) By agreeing to talk to another passenger
(C) By accepting a container for disposal
(D) By lending him a writing tool

55. According to the woman, what can the man do?

(A) Lean his seat back
(B) Access a storage area
(C) Leave part of a form blank
(D) Turn off an overhead light

---

56. Where do the speakers most likely work?
(A) At a public relations agency
(B) At an architectural firm
(C) At a recording studio
(D) At an art museum

57. What does the man say will happen soon?
(A) A computer program will be upgraded.
(B) A building will be remodeled.
(C) Some interns will be selected.
(D) Business hours will change temporarily.

58. What does the woman agree to do?
(A) Calculate a budgetary requirement
(B) Telecommute for a short period
(C) Deliver a speech to a group
(D) Conduct some phone interviews

---

59. What does the man say he is currently doing?
(A) Repairing some electronics
(B) Assembling some furniture
(C) Packing a moving crate
(D) Installing an appliance

60. What is the problem with a nearby building?
(A) It is blocking some light.
(B) It is increasing noise levels.
(C) It is reflecting some heat.
(D) It is causing higher winds.

61. What does the man mean when he says, "I left my blue screwdriver on my desk"?
(A) He is willing to lend his belongings to the woman.
(B) He will not be able to complete his task right away.
(C) He does not mind returning to his work station.
(D) He would like the woman to bring a tool to him.

18°C / 24°C	15°C / 21°C	16°C / 21°C	17°C / 26°C
Tuesday	Wednesday	Thursday	Friday

62. What industry do the speakers most likely work in?
(A) Energy utilities
(B) Rail transportation
(C) Road construction
(D) Groundskeeping

63. Look at the graphic. Which day does the woman suggest scheduling extra workers for?
(A) Tuesday
(B) Wednesday
(C) Thursday
(D) Friday

64. What does the man recommend doing first?
(A) Asking a supervisor for approval
(B) Giving workers a chance to volunteer
(C) Determining some crews' responsibilities
(D) Checking some different forecasts

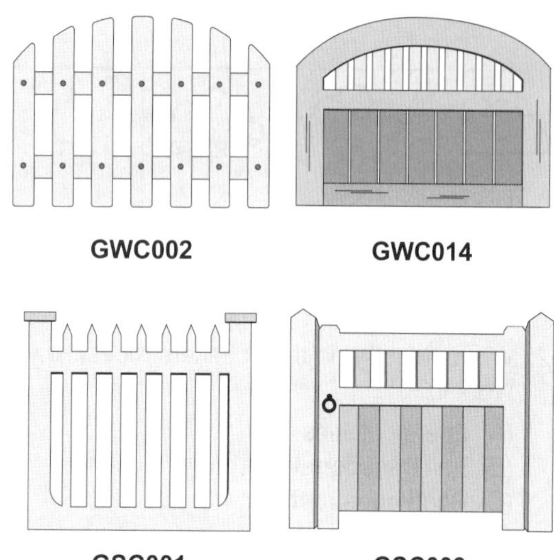

65. Look at the graphic. Which gate does the man choose?

(A) GWC002
(B) GWC014
(C) GSC001
(D) GSC009

66. What does the man say about his yard?

(A) He will keep a pet there.
(B) He will grow produce there.
(C) He plans to have parties there.
(D) He will put in a swimming pool there.

67. Who will the woman most likely call next?

(A) A supplier
(B) An employee
(C) Another client
(D) An inspector

Showing: Newest first ▼

"Amita Mittal" June 23	40 minutes
"Mateo Lozano" June 16	39 minutes
"Josh Dennis" June 9	42 minutes
"Verna Armstrong" June 2	44 minutes

68. What most likely has the man just finished doing?

(A) Buying food at a roadside store
(B) Putting fuel in a vehicle
(C) Arranging some baggage
(D) Receiving advice about a route

69. What is mentioned about the people featured on the podcast?

(A) They founded their own businesses.
(B) They have spoken at a famous event.
(C) They are in the same industry.
(D) They conducted interesting research.

70. Look at the graphic. Which episode will the man play first?

(A) "Amita Mittal"
(B) "Mateo Lozano"
(C) "Josh Dennis"
(D) "Verna Armstrong"

PART 4 (36)

Directions: You will hear some talks given by a single speaker. You will be asked to answer three questions about what the speaker says in each talk. Select the best response to each question and mark the letter (A), (B), (C), or (D) on your answer sheet. The talks will not be printed in your test book and will be spoken only one time.

71. What kind of business is the speaker calling?
(A) A fitness center
(B) A hardware store
(C) An employment agency
(D) A shipping company

72. What is the purpose of the call?
(A) To confirm an address
(B) To make an appointment
(C) To ask about parking options
(D) To learn about a pricing system

73. What is the speaker concerned about?
(A) An additional fee
(B) A limited amount of time
(C) An identification requirement
(D) A large number of customers

74. What has caused traffic problems?
(A) Bad weather
(B) A street closure
(C) Holiday travel
(D) A major event

75. According to the speaker, what has a government department done?
(A) Issued a mass text message
(B) Sent personnel to an area
(C) Posted a statement online
(D) Suspended a transportation service

76. What are the listeners asked to do?
(A) Visit a city Web site
(B) Avoid a neighborhood
(C) Drive more slowly than usual
(D) Await a second radio announcement

77. What does the speaker thank Jeremy for?
(A) Creating some visual aids
(B) Leading a discussion group
(C) Organizing the current meeting
(D) Preparing some lotion samples

78. Why does the speaker say, "the 'scent' category received the highest approval rating, at 74%"?
(A) To show disappointment with all of the results
(B) To indicate a new direction for a marketing campaign
(C) To congratulate some of the listeners on an achievement
(D) To request that the listeners ignore some design flaws

79. What does the speaker ask for the listeners' opinions on?
(A) Performing more market research
(B) Contacting a manufacturer
(C) Forming a special team
(D) Extending a deadline

80. What type of service is being advertised?
(A) Sign printing
(B) Clothes cleaning
(C) Automobile repair
(D) Air conditioner maintenance

81. What does the speaker say is available for free?
(A) A care product
(B) Delivery service
(C) An initial inspection
(D) An extended warranty

82. How can listeners receive the offer?
(A) By installing a mobile app
(B) By mentioning the advertisement to a clerk
(C) By spending a certain amount of money
(D) By joining a mailing list

83. What did the speaker interview Mr. Young about?

(A) An award he won
(B) A structure he built
(C) His personal Web site
(D) His new book

84. What does the speaker encourage listeners to do?

(A) Attend a celebration
(B) Phone the radio station
(C) Make an online purchase
(D) Write down some information

85. What does the speaker imply when she says, "he's a full-time parent to three kids"?

(A) Mr. Young does not have much time to talk.
(B) Mr. Young's productivity is impressive.
(C) Mr. Young is an expert on a topic.
(D) Mr. Young often engages in an activity.

---

86. What does Londa help users do?

(A) Learn a foreign language
(B) Improve their physical fitness
(C) Manage their finances
(D) Follow current affairs

87. Why does the speaker say, "Londa is designed to be simple"?

(A) To provide reassurance about user-friendliness
(B) To justify a lack of sophisticated features
(C) To explain why an optional service is not necessary
(D) To express confusion about some advertising claims

88. According to the speaker, what is an advantage of Londa?

(A) It can be downloaded for free.
(B) It offers excellent customer support.
(C) It can retrieve data from many sources.
(D) It does not require much storage space.

---

89. Why is the speaker interested in buying a car?

(A) She often has to move large items.
(B) She wants to go on unplanned trips out of town.
(C) She lives in an area with unreliable public transportation.
(D) She likes to have privacy when going on journeys.

90. What feature does the speaker ask about?

(A) Electronic door locks
(B) Power seats
(C) Darkened windows
(D) Temperature control systems

91. What does the speaker say she will do in the evening?

(A) Go for a test drive
(B) Attend a job interview
(C) Have dinner with friends
(D) Suggest a sale price

---

92. What does the speaker mention about his appointment to CEO?

(A) It has not been officially announced.
(B) It has caused controversy.
(C) It will be temporary.
(D) It was unexpected.

93. What does the speaker say he will try to do?

(A) Expand a training initiative
(B) Improve internal communication
(C) Upgrade the safety of a facility
(D) Increase employee benefits

94. What most likely will take place next?

(A) A question-and-answer session
(B) A welcome reception
(C) A slide presentation
(D) A photo shoot

Vallond Video Hosting Packages

Package	Features	Monthly Cost
Package A	20 videos	Free
Package B	100 videos	$25
Package C	500 videos + viewing statistics	$100
Package D	Unlimited videos + viewing statistics	$300

95. Where most likely do the listeners work?
(A) At a commercial farm
(B) At a plant shop
(C) At a public park
(D) At a landscaping firm

96. What does the speaker say all packages allow customers to do?
(A) Customize the video player's appearance
(B) Place regional restrictions on videos
(C) Enable viewers to share videos
(D) Display a Web link in a video

97. Look at the graphic. Which package does the speaker recommend?
(A) Package A
(B) Package B
(C) Package C
(D) Package D

Appointment Confirmation
Line 2 — Steele Salon
Line 3 — Stylist Greg Byrd
Line 4 — Saturday, October 17
Line 5 — 1:30 p.m.
Text "Yes" to confirm or call 555-0148 to change.

98. What does the speaker say he was doing when the text message arrived?
(A) Playing a sport
(B) Making a call
(C) Seeing a movie
(D) Boarding a flight

99. Look at the graphic. Which line includes information that the speaker would like to change?
(A) Line 2
(B) Line 3
(C) Line 4
(D) Line 5

100. What does the speaker want to know about the salon?
(A) Whether its shampoos contain certain chemicals
(B) Whether it offers a product for purchase
(C) How much it charges for a hair treatment
(D) How long the effects of one of its services will last

This is the end of the Listening test.

ACTUAL TEST 10

LISTENING TEST 37

In the Listening test, you will be asked to demonstrate how well you understand spoken English. The entire Listening test will last approximately 45 minutes. There are four parts, and directions are given for each part. You must mark your answers on the separate answer sheet. Do not write your answers in your test book.

PART 1

Directions: For each question in this part, you will hear four statements about a picture in your test book. When you hear the statements, you must select the one statement that best describes what you see in the picture. Then find the number of the question on your answer sheet and mark your answer. The statements will not be printed in your test book and will be spoken only one time.

Statement (C), "They're sitting at a table," is the best description of the picture, so you should select answer (C) and mark it on your answer sheet.

1.

2.

GO ON TO THE NEXT PAGE

3.

4.

5.

6.

ACTUAL TEST 10

PART

PART 2 38

Directions: You will hear a question or statement and three responses spoken in English. They will not be printed in your test book and will be spoken only one time. Select the best response to the question or statement and mark the letter (A), (B), or (C) on your answer sheet.

7. Mark your answer on your answer sheet.

8. Mark your answer on your answer sheet.

9. Mark your answer on your answer sheet.

10. Mark your answer on your answer sheet.

11. Mark your answer on your answer sheet.

12. Mark your answer on your answer sheet.

13. Mark your answer on your answer sheet.

14. Mark your answer on your answer sheet.

15. Mark your answer on your answer sheet.

16. Mark your answer on your answer sheet.

17. Mark your answer on your answer sheet.

18. Mark your answer on your answer sheet.

19. Mark your answer on your answer sheet.

20. Mark your answer on your answer sheet.

21. Mark your answer on your answer sheet.

22. Mark your answer on your answer sheet.

23. Mark your answer on your answer sheet.

24. Mark your answer on your answer sheet.

25. Mark your answer on your answer sheet.

26. Mark your answer on your answer sheet.

27. Mark your answer on your answer sheet.

28. Mark your answer on your answer sheet.

29. Mark your answer on your answer sheet.

30. Mark your answer on your answer sheet.

31. Mark your answer on your answer sheet.

PART 3 (39)

Directions: You will hear some conversations between two or more people. You will be asked to answer three questions about what the speakers say in each conversation. Select the best response to each question and mark the letter (A), (B), (C), or (D) on your answer sheet. The conversations will not be printed in your test book and will be spoken only one time.

32. What is the purpose of the man's visit?
(A) To inquire about a bill
(B) To pick up an order
(C) To renew a prescription
(D) To request a fit adjustment

33. What does the woman say is available?
(A) Some publications
(B) Some beverages
(C) Internet access
(D) Charging stations

34. What problem does the man mention?
(A) He did not bring a required item.
(B) He is unable to use an amenity.
(C) He can only wait a short duration.
(D) His contact information has changed.

---

35. Where does the woman work?
(A) At a city department
(B) At a financial institution
(C) At a news outlet
(D) At a law office

36. What does the man plan to do?
(A) Donate money to a charity
(B) Bid for a government contract
(C) Organize a community activity
(D) Launch a retail business

37. Why does the woman ask the man to visit her office?
(A) To discuss an idea
(B) To submit a payment
(C) To review some paperwork
(D) To meet a manager

---

38. According to the man, what took place in the morning?
(A) A training workshop
(B) A laboratory meeting
(C) A university class
(D) An inventory check

39. Why does the man say, "I took detailed notes"?
(A) To explain why he could not be contacted
(B) To emphasize the value of some information
(C) To show willingness to share a resource with the woman
(D) To decline the woman's offer of assistance

40. What is the woman nervous about?
(A) Leading a research project
(B) Interviewing for a job opening
(C) Learning the result of an application
(D) Giving a conference presentation

---

41. What has the woman's crew come to do?
(A) Connect power wiring
(B) Modify an outdoor space
(C) Install some interior surfaces
(D) Set up temperature control systems

42. What problem does Eric report?
(A) A budget limit has been reached.
(B) Some design plans have been revised.
(C) Some construction materials have flaws.
(D) The weather has been unfavorable.

43. What does Eric say to reassure the woman?
(A) Her company's expertise will still be necessary.
(B) Her company can probably complete a job swiftly.
(C) Her company will not be blamed for an issue.
(D) Her company will receive a cancelation fee.

GO ON TO THE NEXT PAGE

44. What has the woman decided to do?

(A) Ask for a pay raise
(B) Suspend a subscription
(C) Obtain an academic degree
(D) Resign from her position

45. What problem does the woman mention?

(A) Her compensation is unusually small.
(B) The market for a service is shrinking.
(C) A required task is unpleasant.
(D) Her workload has increased.

46. What does the man promise to do?

(A) Consider a request
(B) Supervise a transition
(C) Deliver some feedback
(D) Make an introduction

---

47. Who is the man?

(A) An author
(B) A musician
(C) An entrepreneur
(D) A politician

48. What does Tracy ask the man about?

(A) Challenges he faced
(B) His advice for youth
(C) His hopes for the future
(D) People who influenced him

49. What does the man recommend doing?

(A) Seeking a mentor relationship
(B) Reading a certain book
(C) Traveling to other countries
(D) Choosing a small university

---

50. What does the woman tell the man about?

(A) A negative review
(B) A broken Web link
(C) A scheduling error
(D) A security risk

51. Why will the man speak to Ashley?

(A) To ask for her help
(B) To give her some news
(C) To express his gratitude
(D) To provide some guidance

52. According to the woman, what must the speakers' company do?

(A) Issue a partial refund
(B) Save copies of some images
(C) Replace a software program
(D) Make an official announcement

---

53. What does the man's store mainly sell?

(A) Cosmetics
(B) Health food
(C) Housewares
(D) Stationery

54. What do we know about the journal the woman buys?

(A) It was recently released.
(B) It is imported from abroad.
(C) It is not often sold at a discount.
(D) It has been discontinued.

55. What does the woman most likely mean when she says, "I'll be back soon"?

(A) She expects to use up a purchase quickly.
(B) She hopes that the man will do a favor for her.
(C) She parked close to the store's entrance.
(D) She intends to become a regular customer.

---

56. What does the woman say about a company executive?
(A) He does not speak a local language.
(B) He will bring a lot of luggage.
(C) He has a minor injury.
(D) He will not have much time.

57. According to the woman, what will not be necessary?
(A) Arranging ground transportation
(B) Giving a special greeting
(C) Reserving a private rest space
(D) Sending electronic flight updates

58. What will the woman most likely do after the conversation?
(A) Forward a confirmation e-mail
(B) Make another phone call
(C) Begin a car journey
(D) Visit a travel Web site

---

59. What service does the man say he has scheduled?
(A) Plant care
(B) Appliance repair
(C) Window cleaning
(D) Furniture removal

60. According to the man, what is special about the service?
(A) It is done outside of business hours.
(B) It does not involve hazardous chemicals.
(C) It is not available in all seasons.
(D) It is performed by machines.

61. What does the woman say she will do?
(A) Watch a demonstration
(B) Inform some colleagues
(C) Permit an inconvenience
(D) Take the rest of the day off

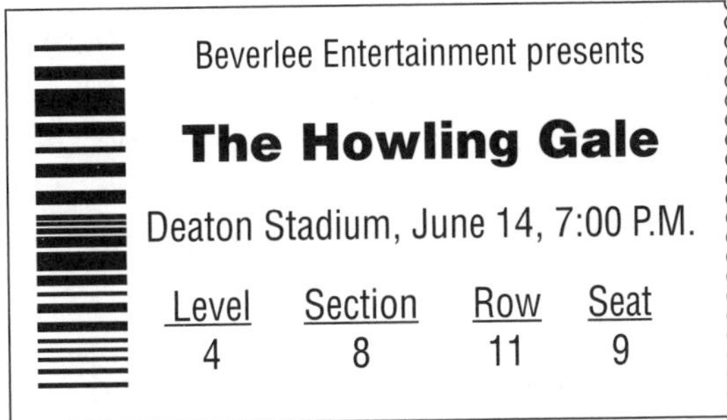

62. Why is the woman late?
(A) It took her a long time to find parking.
(B) She was unaware of an admission policy.
(C) She misunderstood a spoken invitation.
(D) There was traffic around the stadium.

63. Look at the graphic. What section did the woman go to by mistake?
(A) 4
(B) 8
(C) 11
(D) 9

64. What does the man ask the woman to do?
(A) Bring him some refreshments
(B) Send him a photograph
(C) Look for concert staff
(D) Wait by a landmark

GO ON TO THE NEXT PAGE

2nd Annual Jasper
Environmental Awards Winners

Conservation
Jamie Wright

Waste Management
Taylor Bowers

Technology
Hyun-Jin Wi

Communications
Cameron Kennedy

65. Who most likely is the woman?

(A) A city official
(B) A reporter
(C) A nonprofit executive
(D) A marketing consultant

66. What does the woman say about the awards program?

(A) It deserves more publicity.
(B) It selects surprising winners.
(C) It added a new category this year.
(D) Its ceremony can be viewed online.

67. Look at the graphic. Whom will the woman most likely contact?

(A) Jamie Wright
(B) Taylor Bowers
(C) Hyun-Jin Wi
(D) Cameron Kennedy

Operating Expenses

520	Business Supplies
530	Utilities
540	Telecommunications
550	Repair and Maintenance

68. Look at the graphic. Which code will the expense most likely be entered under?

(A) 520
(B) 530
(C) 540
(D) 550

69. Why is the man concerned about the invoice?

(A) Its due date has already passed.
(B) It does not include some details.
(C) It is from an unfamiliar company.
(D) It requests an unusual amount of money.

70. What did the woman most likely do recently?

(A) Watched a television news show
(B) Cleared out a storage area
(C) Attended an industry event
(D) Delegated a task to an employee

PART 4 40

Directions: You will hear some talks given by a single speaker. You will be asked to answer three questions about what the speaker says in each talk. Select the best response to each question and mark the letter (A), (B), (C), or (D) on your answer sheet. The talks will not be printed in your test book and will be spoken only one time.

71. What did the company recently adopt a policy on?
(A) How meeting notifications are sent out
(B) How many people must attend a meeting
(C) How meeting spaces can be used
(D) How long meetings can last

72. What does the speaker ask the listeners to do first?
(A) Put away some snacks
(B) Examine an agenda
(C) Prepare to take notes
(D) Write their names on a form

73. What is the purpose of the meeting?
(A) To discuss a safety issue
(B) To choose a new employee
(C) To evaluate a training program
(D) To plan an annual gathering

---

74. What did the speaker do in the morning?
(A) Finalized a digital drawing
(B) Browsed a furniture catalog
(C) Checked a sample item
(D) Received a sales proposal

75. What does the speaker imply when she says, "I guess it's not native to your area"?
(A) She knows why a cost might be high.
(B) She understands how a mistake happened.
(C) She is suggesting entering a new market.
(D) She is doubtful about a product's authenticity.

76. What does the speaker ask the listener to do?
(A) Give his opinion
(B) Expedite an order
(C) Update some machinery
(D) Search for an alternative

---

77. Where most likely are the listeners?
(A) On a bus
(B) On a boat
(C) On a footpath
(D) On an aircraft

78. What does the speaker point out to the listeners?
(A) Some wild animals
(B) Some rare plants
(C) A famous building
(D) A large body of water

79. What does the speaker encourage listeners to do later?
(A) Return some rental gear
(B) Purchase a video souvenir
(C) Post their photographs online
(D) Recommend the tour to others

---

80. What is the speaker announcing?
(A) The revision of a document
(B) The relocation of a workplace
(C) The reorganization of a company
(D) The retirement of an executive

81. What does the speaker imply when he says, "this will be a major change"?
(A) The listeners might be feeling concerned.
(B) A process will take place over a long period.
(C) He is optimistic about an outcome.
(D) A previous project had a limited impact.

82. What are the listeners asked to do?
(A) Schedule regular planning sessions
(B) Conserve some office supplies
(C) Monitor the results of a transition
(D) Avoid disclosing some information

---

83. Where does the speaker work?

(A) At a hotel
(B) At a travel agency
(C) At an architectural firm
(D) At a cleaning company

84. What does the speaker indicate about the listener?

(A) He has recently been hired.
(B) He has won a competition.
(C) He is a member of a rewards club.
(D) He is a professional public speaker.

85. What does the speaker say the listener can do?

(A) Try out a new offering
(B) Submit a form electronically
(C) Enjoy upgraded accommodations
(D) Participate in a celebration remotely

---

86. Who most likely are the listeners?

(A) Company shareholders
(B) Potential clients
(C) Volunteer workers
(D) Safety inspectors

87. What does the speaker mention about the convention center?

(A) It is the largest venue in the region.
(B) It will be renovated soon.
(C) It is affordable to rent.
(D) It uses modern technology.

88. What type of company is A Perfect Night?

(A) A prepared-meal delivery provider
(B) A chauffeur service
(C) An event organizer
(D) An employment agency

---

89. What does the speaker show on a screen?

(A) A list of actions
(B) A customer profile
(C) A set of statistics
(D) A Web page

90. Why does the speaker say, "Would you like to hear that"?

(A) To confirm that she should set up some audio equipment
(B) To express surprise at the listeners' interest in a story
(C) To make the listeners consider another person's perspective
(D) To indicate that a certain part of the workshop is unpopular

91. What will the listeners most likely do next?

(A) Take a short break
(B) Vote on a suggestion
(C) Open some packages
(D) Engage in role plays

---

92. What is the news report mainly about?

(A) A forthcoming mode of transportation
(B) The banning of automobiles from a street
(C) Some work to improve the quality of a road
(D) The creation of additional parking facilities

93. What does the speaker indicate about a project?

(A) It is intended to reduce environmental damage.
(B) It is opposed by a merchants' association.
(C) Its scope might expand in the future.
(D) It was carried out successfully in other cities.

94. What did the city government do for citizens in the past month?

(A) Notified them of an upcoming change
(B) Surveyed them about a proposal
(C) Relaxed a local regulation
(D) Held a special public event

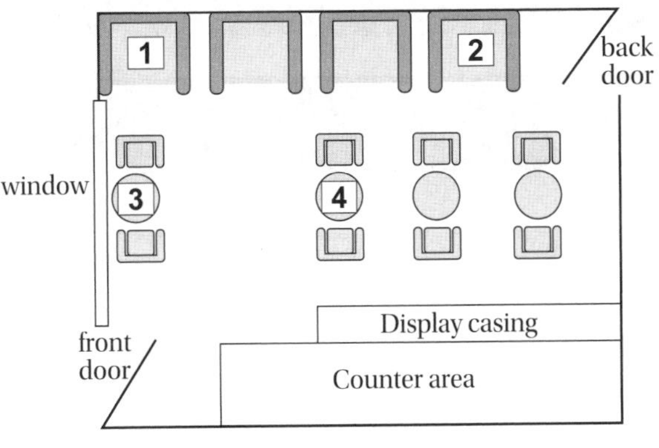

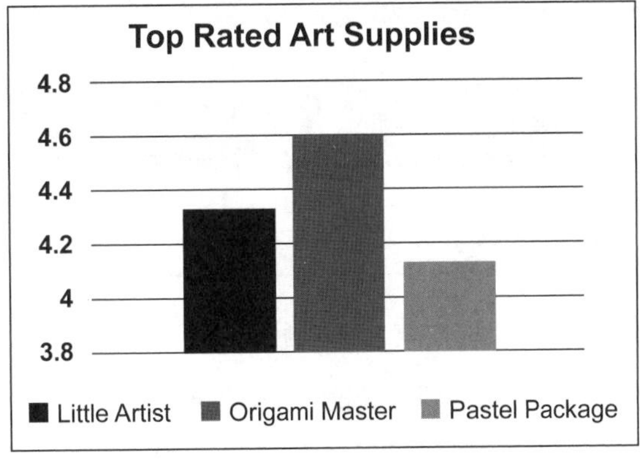

95. What was the speaker mainly doing at the café?
(A) Engaging in a leisure activity
(B) Completing some freelance work
(C) Speaking with a business associate
(D) Studying for a professional exam

96. Look at the graphic. At which location was the speaker sitting?
(A) 1
(B) 2
(C) 3
(D) 4

97. What does the speaker say about the umbrella?
(A) It was expensive.
(B) It was a gift.
(C) Its design is unique.
(D) It belongs to a relative.

98. Look at the graphic. What Web site is the chart for?
(A) Hall's Market
(B) Success Arts
(C) Delta Mall Online
(D) Creative Ideas

99. What does the speaker propose doing?
(A) Hiring a consulting firm
(B) Expanding a product line
(C) Renegotiating a contract
(D) Increasing a promotional effort

100. What does the speaker ask Jenny about?
(A) Some financial resources
(B) Some employees' availability
(C) A manufacturing process
(D) A competitor's practices

This is the end of the Listening test.

ACTUAL TEST 1

PART 1 P. 8–11

01

1. 單人獨照——描寫人物的動作 加

(A) She's drinking coffee in a café.
(B) She's arranging books on a windowsill.
(C) She's plugging in a notebook computer.
(D) She's talking on a mobile phone.

(A) 她在咖啡廳裡喝咖啡。
(B) 她在整理窗台上的書籍。
(C) 她在給筆記型電腦接上電源。
(D) 她在用手機通話。

- arrange (v.) 整理；擺放 windowsill (n.) 窗台 plug in 插上……的插頭以接電源

2. 單人獨照——描寫人物的動作 英

(A) He's pulling a string to close some blinds.
(B) He's painting the outside of a house.
(C) He's cleaning a window with a cloth.
(D) He's using a tool to repair a roof.

(A) 他在拉繩關百葉窗。
(B) 他在粉刷房子的外牆。
(C) 他在用布擦窗戶。
(D) 他在用工具修理屋頂。

- string (n.) 繩子 blind (n.) 百葉窗；窗簾 cloth (n.) 布 repair (v.) 修理

3. 綜合照片——描寫人物或事物 澳

(A) Some passengers are seated in an airplane.
(B) Some food has been placed on a tray.
(C) Some suitcases are standing in an aisle.
(D) Some storage compartments have been left open.

(A) 一些乘客在飛機上坐著。
(B) 一些食物被放在餐盤上。
(C) 幾個手提箱立在走道上。
(D) 有些行李置物櫃敞開著。

- passenger (n.) 乘客 tray (n.) 托盤；餐盤 suitcase (n.) 手提箱 aisle (n.)（座席、貨架間的）走道 storage compartment 置物櫃

4. 事物與背景照——描寫戶外事物的狀態 美 難

(A) Railings are being installed on a platform.
(B) There is a row of signs inside a warehouse.
(C) A set of stairs leads to a doorway.
(D) A truck is parked near an intersection.

(A) 平台上正在裝設欄杆。
(B) 倉庫內有一排標示牌。
(C) 樓梯通向門口。
(D) 卡車停在十字路口附近。

- railing (n.) 欄杆 install (v.) 安裝 platform (n.) 平台 row (n.) 排 sign (n.) 告示；標誌 warehouse (n.) 倉庫 lead to 通向 doorway (n.) 門口 intersection (n.) 交叉路口；十字路口

5. 綜合照片——描寫人物或事物 加

(A) Some charts are being projected onto a screen.
(B) A group of people are looking at some papers.
(C) A woman is writing on a whiteboard.
(D) Some cups are being stacked on a table.

(A) 幾張圖表被投射到螢幕上。
(B) 一群人正在查看幾份文件。
(C) 一名女子在白板上寫字。
(D) 幾個杯子堆在桌子上。

- project (v.) 投射；放映 stack (v.) 堆放；把……疊成堆

6. 事物與背景照——描寫戶外事物的狀態 英 難

(A) Some bushes are being planted.
(B) There are chairs next to a swimming pool.
(C) A fence has been built around a grassy area.
(D) A small lawn is being mowed.

(A) 有人在種植一些灌木。
(B) 游泳池邊有數張椅子。
(C) 草地周圍建有圍欄。
(D) 有人在小草坪上除草。

- **bush (n.)** 灌木 **plant (v.)** 種植；栽種 **fence (n.)** 柵欄；籬笆 **grassy (adj.)** 長滿草的 **lawn (n.)** 草地；草坪 **mow (v.)** 割（草）；修剪

PART 2 P. 12 02

7. 以 Where 開頭的問句，詢問購物中心的位置 加⇄英

Where's the shopping mall you're going to?
(A) Let's use the company credit card.
(B) Mostly clothing and electronics stores.
(C) Over on the north side of town.

你要去的購物中心在哪裡？
(A) 我們用公司的信用卡吧。
(B) 主要是服飾店跟電子用品店。
(C) 在城鎮的北邊。

- **mostly (adv.)** 大部分地；主要地 **electronics (n.)** 電子產品

8. 以 When 開頭的問句，詢問伯納德加入讀書會的時間點 美⇄加

When did Bernard join this study group?
(A) For conversation practice.
(B) Last semester.
(C) Twice a week.

伯納德是什麼時候加入這個讀書會的？
(A) 為了會話練習。
(B) 上學期。
(C) 每週兩次。

- **semester (n.)** 學期

9. 以 Why 開頭的問句，詢問希爾小姐為何提前離開 澳⇄美

Why is Ms. Hill leaving the conference early?
(A) On the express train.
(B) To attend an important meeting.
(C) Yes, the session on marketing.

希爾小姐為什麼提前離開會議？
(A) 在直達車上。
(B) 為了參加重要會面。
(C) 是的，是行銷方面的講習。

- **conference (n.)** 會議；討論會 **express train (n.)** 直達車 **session (n.)** 會議；講習

10. 以 Who 開頭的問句，詢問是誰想到要貼標籤 英⇄澳 

Who had the idea of labeling these drawers?
(A) Only the locked ones.
(B) Use green labels for current clients.
(C) It has certainly helped, hasn't it?

給這些抽屜貼標籤，是誰的點子？
(A) 只有鎖著的抽屜。
(B) 給現有客戶用綠色標籤。
(C) 確實很有用，不是嗎？

- **label (v.)** 貼標籤於 **drawer (n.)** 抽屜 **locked (adj.)** 鎖著的 **current (adj.)** 當前的；現在的

11. 以 **How often** 開頭的問句，詢問換電池的頻率 英⇄加 難

How often should we change the batteries?	我們應多久換一次電池？
(A) This light will flash when they start to run out.	**(A)** 電池快沒電的時候，這個燈就會閃爍。
(B) You don't like the way it looks now?	(B) 你不喜歡現在的樣子嗎？
(C) It's our latest energy bill.	(C) 這是我們最新的電費／瓦斯費單。

- run out 用完；耗盡　latest (adj.) 最新的　bill (n.) 帳單

12. 表示請託或要求的問句 美⇄加

Can I borrow your pen to fill out this questionnaire?	我可以跟你借筆寫這份問卷嗎？
(A) Just answer as honestly as possible.	(A) 儘量誠實作答即可。
(B) Sure, as soon as I'm finished with it.	**(B)** 當然可以，等我寫完就借你。
(C) Sorry, it's already full.	(C) 抱歉，已經滿了。

- fill out 填寫　questionnaire (n.) 問卷；調查表

13. 以助動詞 **Has** 開頭的問句，確認印表機是否已經修好 美⇄澳 難

Has the printer been repaired yet?	印表機已經修好了嗎？
(A) Yes, a faster model.	(A) 是的，速度更快的機型。
(B) They charge ten cents per page.	(B) 每頁要價 10 美分（1 美分即 0.01 美元）。
(C) I haven't tried using it.	**(C)** 我還沒去試用過。

- repair (v.) 維修　charge (v.) 收費；要價　per (prep.) 每……

14. 以 **What** 開頭的問句詢問醫師的建議 加⇄澳 難

What did the doctor recommend?	醫師有什麼建議？
(A) My appointment was cancelled.	**(A)** 我的約診被取消了。
(B) Just a minor cold.	(B) 只是個小感冒。
(C) I like the clinic on Morton Street.	(C) 我喜歡莫頓街的那家診所。

- recommend (v.) 建議；推薦　appointment (n.) 預約；約定會面　cancel (v.) 取消
  minor (adj.) 輕微的；不嚴重的

15. 以否定疑問句詢問克雷格是否曾在找這本書 加⇄英

Wasn't Craig looking for this book?	克雷格之前不是在找這本書嗎？
(A) Yes—we should take it to him.	**(A)** 是的，我們該把書拿去給他。
(B) Try page eighty-two.	(B) 試試第 82 頁吧。
(C) No, it was already booked.	(C) 不，已經預訂好了。

16. 表示建議或提案的問句 美⇄澳 難

Why don't you ask Nick Reynolds to interview for the position?	你何不叫尼克・雷諾茲來面試這個職位呢？
(A) I don't have the required experience.	(A) 我沒有所需的經驗。
(B) Well, he seems happy with his current job.	**(B)** 唔，他似乎對目前的工作很滿意。
(C) In an e-mail to all of the candidates.	(C) 在發給所有應徵者的電子郵件中。

- position (n.) 職位　required (adj.) 要求的　candidate (n.) 應徵者

17. 以 **How** 開頭的問句，詢問前往工廠的方法 加⇄美

How are we getting to the factory for the inspection?	我們要怎麼前往工廠視察？
(A) The household appliances it makes.	(A) 工廠生產的家電。
(B) Sure, that would be fine.	(B) 沒問題，那樣可以。
(C) Don't worry, I brought my car today.	**(C) 別擔心，我今天開車。**

- **inspection (n.)** 檢查；視察 **household appliances** 家用電器

18. 以選擇疑問句，詢問要在哪一家餐廳訂餐 澳⇄英

Do you want to order lunch from Haley's Diner again, or try somewhere new?	午餐你是想再跟哈雷餐廳訂餐，還是想換別家嘗鮮？
(A) Haley's sounds good.	**(A) 哈雷餐廳還不錯。**
(B) Yes, I cooked it myself.	(B) 對，我自己煮的。
(C) In front of the restaurant.	(C) 在餐廳前面。

- **order (v.)** 訂購；點餐 **diner (n.)** 小餐館 **somewhere (n.)** 某個地方

19. 以否定疑問句確認新家具到貨的時間點 加⇄美 難

Isn't the new office furniture arriving this afternoon?	新的辦公家具不是今天下午要送來嗎？
(A) The address is written here.	(A) 地址寫在這裡。
(B) I've found it very comfortable.	(B) 我覺得這很舒適。
(C) There's been a shipping delay.	**(C) 送貨延遲了。**

- **furniture (n.)** 家具 **address (n.)** 地址 **comfortable (adj.)** 舒服的 **shipping (n.)** 運輸 **delay (n.)** 延誤

20. 以直述句傳達資訊 英⇄美 難

It looks like there are two open seats in that row.	那一排看起來有兩個空位。
(A) The five p.m. showing.	(A) 下午 5 點的那場。
(B) But isn't Sung-Won coming, too?	**(B) 可是，成元不是也要來嗎？**
(C) They're supposed to be that low.	(C) 本來就應該那麼低的。

- **row (n.)** 排 **showing (n.)** 表演；播映 **be supposed to** 應該

21. 以 **When** 開頭的問句，詢問實習生的到職時間 澳⇄英 難

When will the accounting interns start work?	會計部的實習生什麼時候開始上班？
(A) The London branch.	(A) 倫敦分公司。
(B) They're not hiring any this year.	**(B) 他們今年不打算招募（實習生）。**
(C) We'll count them again.	(C) 我們會再算一遍。

- **accounting (n.)** 會計 **intern (n.)** 實習生 **branch (n.)** 分支機構 **count (v.)** 計算；數

22. 以助動詞 **Did** 開頭的問句，確認對方是否弄懂相機操作方法 美⇄澳

Did you figure out how to operate the camera?	你弄懂怎麼操作這台相機了嗎？
(A) This silver one here, please.	(A) 請給我這邊這台銀色的。
(B) The figures have been updated.	(B) 數據已更新。
(C) I'm reading the manual right now.	**(C) 我正在看使用說明書。**

- **figure out** 弄懂；想明白 **operate (v.)** 操作 **figure (n.)** 數字 **manual (n.)** 使用手冊

23. 以助動詞 **Have** 確認對方是否看了預估成本 英⇄加 難

Have you seen the expected cost of that project?
(A) That's why we're considering other options.
(B) It was put in storage after the inspection.
(C) I'm not sure what he looks like.

你看到那件專案的預估成本了嗎？
(A) 這就是我們正考慮其他選項的原因。
(B) 檢查後就入庫了。
(C) 我不確定他的長相。

- cost (n.) 成本　option (n.) 可選擇的事物　storage (n.) 儲藏；倉庫　inspection (n.) 檢查

24. 以 **Where** 開頭的問句，詢問薪資部的位置 美⇄加

Where's the office of the payroll department?
(A) No, it's always free for employees.
(B) Ayuka would probably know that.
(C) The first business day of every month.

薪資部的辦公室在哪裡？
(A) 不，員工向來都是免費的。
(B) 步佳大概知道吧。
(C) 每個月的第一個營業日。

- payroll department 薪資部

25. 以否定疑問句確認是否有要更換櫥窗的展示內容 澳⇄美

Weren't you going to change the window display?
(A) Would you like to try them on?
(B) I'll do it after we close tonight.
(C) I don't know how to play.

你不是打算更換櫥窗展示內容嗎？
(A) 您要不要試穿？
(B) 我等今晚打烊後再換。
(C) 我不知道怎麼玩。

- display (n.) 布置；陳列；展示　try on 試穿

26. 以直述句傳達資訊 英⇄澳

I'm here to deliver a package to Catrina Ortiz.
(A) Her desk is over there.
(B) A box and a roll of tape.
(C) Yes, she has some baggage.

我來送交包裹給卡翠娜．歐提茲。
(A) 她的辦公桌在那邊。
(B) 一個箱子跟一卷膠帶。
(C) 是的，她有幾件行李。

- package (n.) 包裹　baggage (n.) 行李

27. 以附加問句確認對方是否去了馬修的生日派對 加⇄英

You went to Matthew's birthday party, didn't you?
(A) I had an urgent deadline at work.
(B) Twenty-nine years old.
(C) Birthday cards are in Aisle Four.

你去了馬修的生日派對，對嗎？
(A) 我當時在趕工作的緊急截止日。
(B) 29 歲。
(C) 生日賀卡放在第 4 排走道。

- urgent (adj.) 緊急的　aisle (n.)（貨架間的）走道

28. 以 **Where** 開頭的問句，詢問取得安全裝備的地點 美⇄加

Where can we get those vests and helmets?
(A) To keep you safe during your visit.
(B) Here's a list of our investment activities.
(C) They're provided at the construction site.

哪裡可以取得那種背心跟安全帽？
(A) 為維護您參訪期間的安全。
(B) 這是我們投資活動的清單。
(C) 施工現場會提供。

- vest (n.) 背心　investment (n.) 投資　construction site（建築）工地

29. 以選擇疑問句，詢問傳單的處理方式 美⇄澳

Are we hanging these flyers up or handing them out?	這些傳單是要掛起來，還是發送出去？
(A) Because we're having a sale.	(A) 因為我們在做促銷。
(B) The plan is to do both.	**(B) 計畫是兩者都進行。**
(C) I think Peter agreed to.	(C) 我想彼得有同意。

- flyer (n.)（廣告）傳單　hand out 分發

30. 以直述句傳達資訊 英⇄澳　難

The lights in the gallery were left on again last night.	昨晚畫廊裡的燈又開著沒關。
(A) Some of the paintings are quite heavy.	(A) 有幾幅畫很重。
(B) You'd better remind Sylvia to be careful.	**(B) 你最好提醒席薇亞要留意點。**
(C) Thanks–the interior designer chose them.	(C) 謝謝，是室內設計師選的。

- gallery (n.) 畫廊；美術館　remind (v.) 提醒

31. 表示建議或提案的問句 加⇄英　難

Should we send out a paper memo about the new policy?	關於新政策，我們是否該寄出紙本的備忘錄？
(A) Staff don't often check their inboxes.	**(A) 員工不常查看他們的收件匣。**
(B) The expense reimbursement process.	(B) 費用核銷的步驟。
(C) I'll show you how to use the shredder.	(C) 我會教你怎麼使用碎紙機。

- policy (n.) 政策　inbox (n.) 郵箱；收件匣　expense (n.) 費用　reimbursement (n.) 退款；償還　process (n.) 步驟；過程　shredder (n.) 碎紙機

PART 3 P. 13–16

03

32-34 Conversation / 32-34 對話 美⇄澳

W: Hi, this is Kim Solomon. **(32) Your firm renovated my apartment last month.**	女：你好，我是琪恩．索羅門。**(32) 貴公司上個月有來整修我的公寓。**
M: Hello, Ms. Solomon. What can we do for you today?	男：您好，索羅門女士，目前有什麼我們能為您服務的嗎？
W: **(33) Well, I was just moving around some furniture while vacuuming my living room, and I noticed large scratches on the wall behind the sofa.** I'm sure I didn't cause them, so . . .	女：**(33) 嗯，我在客廳吸地板的時候，搬動了幾件家具，然後就注意到沙發後面的牆上有幾道大刮痕**，我很確定那不是我造成的，所以⋯⋯
M: Oh, I'm sorry to hear that. We'll take care of it. **(34) Could you take a few clear photographs of the problem and e-mail them to me?** We need to know how serious it is.	男：噢，您反映的事項，我們很抱歉。我們會妥善處理，**(34) 能否請您拍下幾張問題所在的清楚照片，然後用電子郵件寄給我？** 我們需要了解嚴重程度。

- firm (n.) 公司　renovate (v.) 翻修；整修　vacuum (v.) 用吸塵器清掃　scratch (n.) 刮痕　take a photograph 拍照

32. 全文相關——男子的工作地點

Where most likely does the man work?
(A) At an interior design firm
(B) At an apartment management office
(C) At a moving company
(D) At a hotel

男子最有可能在哪裡工作？
(A) 在室內設計公司
(B) 在公寓管理處
(C) 在搬家公司
(D) 在旅館

33. 相關細節——女子提出的問題

What problem does the woman describe?
(A) An appliance is not working.
(B) A wall has been damaged.
(C) Some loud noises can be heard.
(D) Some furniture is uncomfortable.

女子描述的是什麼問題？
(A) 電器故障。
(B) 牆面毀損。
(C) 能聽到很大的噪音。
(D) 有些家具不甚舒適。

- appliance (n.) 電器 damage (v.) 損壞

34. 相關細節——男子對女子的要求

What does the man ask the woman to do?
(A) Take some measurements
(B) Wait for a company representative
(C) Send him some pictures
(D) Read a set of instructions

男子要求女子做什麼事？
(A) 測量尺寸
(B) 等待公司專員前去
(C) 寄幾張照片給他
(D) 閱讀一套說明書

- measurement (n.) 測量；尺寸 representative (n.) 代表；代理人 instruction (n.) 用法說明

換句話說 photographs（照片）→ pictures（照片／圖片）

35-37 Conversation

W: All right, everyone. (35) **Now that we've handed out your packed lunches, you'll have half an hour to eat before we continue our tour of Fannon Park.**

M: Ms. Sasaki, can I talk to you? The sandwich in my meal has ham in it, but I'm a vegetarian.

W: I'm sorry, Mr. Johnson, but I looked over the tour registration forms very carefully. (36) **You must have forgotten to check the "vegetarian" box in the meal preference section.** We do have some extra lunches, but they're all non-vegetarian.

M: (37) **Well, could I have some of the fruit and snacks from those meals?** I'm really hungry from all this walking.

35-37 對話

美⇄加

女：好了，各位，(35) **現在午餐盒都已經發給大家了，在我們繼續參觀法儂公園之前，各位有半小時的時間可以用餐。**

男：佐佐木小姐，我可以跟妳談談嗎？我午餐的三明治裡有火腿，可是我吃素。

女：不好意思，強生先生，但我很仔細確認過旅遊報名表。(36) **飲食偏好這部分，您一定忘記勾選「素食」選項了。**我們是有多餘的午餐盒，但沒有素食的。

男：(37) **好吧，那我可以從那些午餐盒裡拿一些水果和點心嗎？**走了這麼久的路，我真的餓壞了。

- hand out 分發 continue (v.) 繼續 vegetarian (n./adj.) 素食者／素食的 registration form 報名表 meal preference 飲食偏好 section (n.) 部分

35. 全文相關——對話的地點

Where most likely are the speakers?
(A) At a train terminal
(B) On an airplane
(C) At a restaurant
(D) At a park

說話者們最有可能在哪裡？
(A) 在火車總站
(B) 在飛機上
(C) 在餐廳
(D) 在公園

36. 相關細節——女子提及引起問題的原因

What does the woman say has caused a problem?
(A) Some meals were not cooked properly.
(B) Some boxes have not been unpacked.
(C) A tour has too many participants.
(D) A form was filled out incorrectly.

據女子所說，何事造成問題發生？
(A) 有些餐點未妥善烹煮。
(B) 有些餐盒還沒有打開。
(C) 參加旅行團的人太多了。
(D) 並未正確填寫表格。

- properly (adv.) 正確地；妥當地　unpack (v.) 打開　fill out 填寫　incorrectly (adv.) 不正確地

37. 相關細節——男子提出的要求

What does the man ask for?
(A) A partial refund
(B) Some extra food
(C) Directions to a store
(D) A different seat assignment

男子有何要求？
(A) 退還部分款項
(B) 一些額外食物
(C) 去商店的路線指引
(D) 換到別的座位

- partial (adj.) 部分的　refund (n.) 退款　directions (n.)（恆用複數）路線指引　assignment (n.) 分配

換句話說 some of the fruit and snacks（一些水果和點心）→ some extra food（一些額外食物）

38-40 Conversation with three speakers

M1: (38) **Ms. Ortega, thank you again for choosing us to create your Web site.** Now, tell us more about your wedding planning business.

W: I started the company a year ago, and it's been going well. (39) **I'm hoping that the Web site can attract even more clients.**

M2: Sure. What sets you apart from your competitors?

W: We focus on what clients want, not on following trends. It means we've planned some really unusual ceremonies!

M1: That's interesting! Would you like to feature photos of them on the Web site?

W: Actually . . . I'm not sure. (40) **That might make some potential clients less likely to choose us.**

M2: OK. We'll put that idea aside for now.

38-40 三人對話

加⇄英⇄澳

男 1： (38) **奧爾特加女士，再次感謝您選擇本公司為您建立網站。**現在麻煩您跟我們更進一步說明您的婚禮規劃公司。

女： 我一年前成立了這家公司，生意一直都很上軌道，(39) **我希望網站能吸引到更多的客戶。**

男 2： 沒問題。請問貴公司何以能從同業競爭者中脫穎而出？

女： 我們會專注於客戶想要什麼，而不是一味跟風，這意味著我們曾辦過幾場獨樹一幟的婚禮！

男 1： 那挺有趣的！您會想在公司的網站上，展示當時現場的照片嗎？

女： 老實說……我不確定。(40) **有些潛在客戶看了，可能會因而不選擇我們公司。**

男 2： 好吧，我們暫且把這個想法放一邊。

- set apart 區別；使……與眾不同　competitor (n.) 競爭對手　ceremony (n.) 典禮；儀式
feature (v.) 以……為特色　potential (adj.) 潛在的　for now 此時；暫時

38. 全文相關——男子們的公司提供的服務類型

What kind of service does the men's company provide?
(A) Advertising
(B) Catering
(C) Accounting
(D) Web design

男子們的公司提供何種服務？
(A) 廣告
(B) 餐飲
(C) 會計
(D) 網站設計

---

39. 相關細節——女子選擇男子公司的理由

Why has the woman hired the men's company?
(A) To grow her business
(B) To save money
(C) To follow a regulation
(D) To give herself more free time

女子為何僱用男子們的公司？
(A) 為了使業務成長
(B) 為了省錢
(C) 為了遵守規定
(D) 為了讓自己有更多自由時間

- regulation (n.) 規定；條例

換句話說 attract even more clients（吸引到更多的客戶）→ grow her business（使業務成長）

---

40. 相關細節——女子對於建議的看法 難

What does the woman say about a suggestion?
(A) It has been tried before.
(B) It may not be effective.
(C) It would be expensive.
(D) It is complicated.

女子覺得建議怎麼樣？
(A) 以前已經試過了。
(B) 可能沒有效果。
(C) 會很昂貴。
(D) 很複雜。

- effective (adj.) 有效的　complicated (adj.) 複雜的

41-43 Conversation

M: Hi, Monica? This is Paul in Sales. (41) **I need some technical help with the new vacation scheduling system.** (42) **I'm not seeing the submission date on my team members' electronic request forms.**

W: Are you looking at the bottom right-hand side of the forms?

M: Yes—there's no information there. I think there must be a problem with the software.

W: Maybe. (43) **But let's start by making sure your display settings are correct.** You can find that information in the "Options" menu. I'll wait.

41-43 對話 澳⇄英

男：嗨，莫妮卡嗎？我是業務部的保羅。**(41) 有關新的排休系統，我需要一點技術支援。(42) 我在我們部門人員的電子假單上，無法檢視提交日期。**

女：你看的地方是請假單的右下角嗎？

男：對的，那裡沒有資訊，想必是軟體出了問題。

女：有這個可能，**(43) 不過我們還是先來確認一下你的顯示設定是否正確。**你可以從選單上的「選項」欄位找到該項資訊。等你確認喔。

- vacation (n.) 假期　scheduling (n.) 安排；調度　submission (n.) 提交；呈遞
electronic (adj.) 電子的　request form 申請表　right-hand side 右側；右手邊　option (n.) 選項

41. 全文相關——女子工作的部門

Which department does the woman most likely work in?
(A) Public Relations
(B) Human Resources
(C) Information Technology
(D) Sales and Marketing

女子最有可能在哪個部門任職？
(A) 公共關係部
(B) 人力資源部
(C) 資訊技術部
(D) 業務行銷部

42. 相關細節——說話者討論的問題 難

What problem are the speakers discussing?
(A) A slow response time
(B) A scheduling conflict
(C) A customer complaint
(D) A missing detail

說話者在討論什麼問題？
(A) 反應時間緩慢
(B) 排程上的衝突
(C) 顧客的投訴
(D) 缺漏的細節

- **response (n.)** 反應 **conflict (n.)** 衝突 **complaint (n.)** 抱怨；投訴 **missing (adj.)** 缺失的

43. 相關細節——女子建議男子先做的事

What does the woman recommend the man do first?
(A) Speak with his manager
(B) Check some software settings
(C) Post a correction notice
(D) Restart a machine

女子建議男子先做什麼？
(A) 與經理談話
(B) 檢查軟體設定
(C) 發布更正啟示
(D) 重啟裝置

- **post (v.)** 發布；張貼 **notice (n.)** 公告；通知

44-46 Conversation

M: Shanice, could I ask you about this dress that a customer just brought in?
W: Sure, Brandon.
M: **(44) The label says that only certain chemicals can be used on it, and I want to know why before I put it into the dry-cleaning machine.**
W: **(45) Oh, it's because of all of these plastic beads that have been sewn onto the fabric. Some dry-cleaning chemicals can damage them.**
M: Got it. You know, I'd like to learn more of this kind of background information. **(46) Could we hold informal training sessions every now and then?**
W: I'd be happy to do that. How about starting next Monday before work?

44-46 對話 加⇄美

男：萱妮絲，有關客人剛送來的這件洋裝，我可以跟妳請教一下嗎？
女：當然可以，布蘭登。
男：**(44) 標籤上面說，洋裝只能使用特定化學藥劑，而我想先了解原因，再將衣服放進乾洗機。**
女：**(45) 噢，這是因為洋裝上縫了很多這些塑膠珠子，有些乾洗用的化學藥劑會使塑膠珠毀損。**
男：了解。妳也知道，我想多了解這方面的背景知識，**(46) 我們能不能偶爾舉辦非正式的培訓課程？**
女：樂意之至。下週一的上班前就開始培訓，怎麼樣？

- **label (n.)** 標籤 **chemical (n.)** 化學藥品 **bead (n.)** 珠子 **sew (v.)** 縫 **background (n./adj.)** 背景（的）
informal (adj.) 非正式的 **every now and then** 偶爾；有時

44. 相關細節——男子打算要做的事

What is the man about to do?
(A) Clean some clothing
(B) Use a sewing machine
(C) Arrange a window display
(D) Test some product samples

男子正要做什麼？
(A) 清洗衣物
(B) 使用縫紉機
(C) 布置櫥窗展示
(D) 測試樣品

- be about to 即將；正要 sewing machine 縫紉機

45. 相關細節——女子針對衣料提及的內容

What does the woman point out about a fabric?
(A) Its color is due to special chemicals.
(B) It has been decorated with beads.
(C) Its cost has recently risen.
(D) It is lightweight.

女子指出衣料的什麼事項？
(A) 顏色來自特殊的化學藥劑。
(B) 使用珠子裝飾。
(C) 最近價格上漲了。
(D) 質地輕薄。

- decorate (v.) 裝飾 lightweight (adj.) 重量輕的

46. 相關細節——女子同意做的事

What does the woman agree to do?
(A) Increase some lighting
(B) Hold a hand tool
(C) Postpone a photo session
(D) Provide some training

女子同意做什麼？
(A) 增加一些照明
(B) 拿著手持器具
(C) 延後拍照時間
(D) 提供一些培訓

- lighting (n.) 燈光；照明 hand tool 手持工具 postpone (v.) 延後

47-49 Conversation

M: Excuse me. This is the third time that I've come in to find that you don't have any strawberry cupcakes with marshmallow frosting. May I speak to a manager about that?
W: Absolutely, sir. I'm the manager today.
M: Oh. (47) **Well, I come to this bakery every week just to get those cupcakes, even though I don't live nearby. You know, they're not sold anywhere else. What's going on?**
W: (48) **I'm sorry, but those cupcakes have actually been discontinued.** But these chocolate cupcakes have marshmallow frosting.
M: Hmm . . . I don't know. They're more expensive.
W: (49) **Well, I could lower the price just this once.** Consider it our apology for getting rid of the strawberry flavor option.

47-49 對話 加⇄美

男：打擾一下，我已經來了貴店三次，每次都找不到澆有棉花糖霜的草莓杯子蛋糕，我可以跟你們經理談談這件事嗎？
女：當然可以，先生，我就是今天的值班經理。
男：噢。(47) **是這樣的，我並不住在這附近，但每週都特地跑來這家麵包店，就是為了買那款杯子蛋糕，妳也知道，別家店都沒在賣。不知道發生了什麼事？**
女：(48) **我很抱歉，但是那款杯子蛋糕其實已經停售了。**不過，這款巧克力杯子蛋糕上面有澆棉花糖霜。
男：呃⋯⋯我不知道，那款蛋糕比較貴。
女：(49) **那這樣吧，這一次我可以降價賣給您，**就當是本店對於停賣草莓口味蛋糕的道歉吧。

- frosting (n.) 糖霜 nearby (adv.) 在附近 anywhere else 其他地方 discontinue (v.) 停止 lower (v.) 降低 apology (n.) 道歉；歉意 get rid of 擺脫；去除 flavor (n.) 味道；口味 option (n.) 選擇；選項

47. 相關細節——男子經常光顧麵包店的理由 難

Why does the man say he comes to the bakery frequently?
(A) It is near his home.
(B) It has a pleasant atmosphere.
(C) It sells a special type of baked goods.
(D) It has convenient operating hours.

男子說他為什麼經常來這家麵包店？
(A) 就在他家附近。
(B) 店裡氣氛愉快。
(C) 店裡有賣特別的烘焙食品。
(D) 該店的營業時間很便利。

- **frequently (adv.)** 時常；經常 **pleasant (adj.)** 令人愉快的 **atmosphere (n.)** 氣氛 **goods (n.)** 商品；產品 **convenient (adj.)** 方便的；便利的 **operating hours** 營業時間

48. 掌握說話者意圖——提及「這款巧克力杯子蛋糕上面有澆棉花糖霜」的意圖 難

Why does the woman say, "these chocolate cupcakes have marshmallow frosting"?
(A) To point out a mistake on a label
(B) To propose an alternative purchase
(C) To express surprise at a suggestion
(D) To explain a pricing decision

女子為什麼說：「這款巧克力杯子蛋糕上面有澆棉花糖霜」？
(A) 指出標籤上的錯誤
(B) 提議購買替代產品
(C) 對建議表示驚訝
(D) 解釋定價決策

- **label (n.)** 標籤 **propose (v.)** 提議；提出 **alternative (adj.)** 替代的 **express (v.)** 表達 **pricing decision** 定價決策

49. 相關細節——女子提供給男子的東西

What does the woman offer the man?
(A) A onetime discount
(B) A list of the ingredients in a recipe
(C) A chance to attend a tasting session
(D) A takeout container

女子提供了什麼給男子？
(A) 僅限一次的折扣
(B) 食譜裡的成分列表
(C) 參加試吃會的機會
(D) 外帶餐盒

- **ingredient (n.)** 食材；材料 **recipe (n.)** 食譜 **tasting session** 試吃會；品鑑會 **takeout (n./adj.)** 外賣（的） **container (n.)** 容器

換句話說 lower the price just this once（這一次可以降價）→ onetime discount（僅限一次的折扣）

50-52 Conversation

W: (50) **Adam, why haven't those boxes been moved to their storage shelves?** I thought they were unloaded from the trucks an hour ago.

M: (51) **Oh, one of the regular forklift operators wasn't feeling well enough to come in today.** The backup driver isn't as skilled, so we're a little behind.

W: Hmm. Will the shipment to Prentell Industries go out by two p.m. as scheduled?

M: That might be a little difficult. It'll more likely be ready at around two-thirty or three.

50-52 對話 英⇄澳

女：(50) **亞當，那些箱子怎麼還沒搬到儲貨架上？**我想那些箱子一個小時前，就從卡車上卸下來了吧。

男：(51) **噢，一名值班的堆高機操作員今天身體不舒服，沒來上班，**支援的駕駛員沒那麼熟練，所以我們進度有點落後。

女：唔，那在下午兩點前，會如期出貨給普倫特工業嗎？

男：可能有點困難，比較有可能在兩點半或三點左右準備好。

W: Well, that doesn't sound too bad. (52) **But just to be safe, I'm going to call Prentell.** They like to be warned about potential problems.

女： 好吧，聽起來不算太嚴重，(52) **但為了保險起見，我會打電話通知普倫特**。若有潛在問題，他們會希望事先知會。

- storage (n.) 儲藏室；倉庫　shelf (n.) 架子　unload (v.) 卸（貨）　forklift (n.) 堆高機　operator (n.) 司機；操作員　backup (adj.) 備用的　skilled (adj.) 熟練的　shipment (n.) 貨物　potential (adj.) 潛在的；可能的

50. 全文相關——說話者們的工作地點

Where do the speakers most likely work?

(A) At a construction company

(B) At a warehouse

(C) At a farm

(D) At a car repair shop

說話者最有可能是在哪裡工作？

(A) 在建設公司

(B) 在倉庫

(C) 在農場

(D) 在汽車維修廠

51. 相關細節——引發問題的原因

What has caused a problem?

(A) Some packages have been misplaced.

(B) Some roads are closed.

(C) A staff member is out sick.

(D) A vehicle has broken down.

問題的起因為何？

(A) 有些包裹找不到。

(B) 有些道路封閉。

(C) 有名員工請病假。

(D) 有輛車壞了。

- misplace (v.) 誤置　vehicle (n.) 車輛　break down 故障；拋錨

換句話說 **wasn't feeling well enough to come in**（身體不舒服，沒來上班）→ **is out sick**（請病假）

52. 相關細節——女子將要做的事

What does the woman say she will do?

(A) Work overtime today

(B) Put up a warning sign

(C) Conduct a safety inspection

(D) Contact another company

女子說她會做什麼？

(A) 今天會加班

(B) 豎起警示牌

(C) 進行安全檢查

(D) 聯絡另一家公司

- conduct (v.) 實施　inspection (n.) 檢查

53-55 Conversation with three speakers

W1: Excuse me, sir. (53) **My name is Min-Sun Lee, and I'm a reporter with Channel Six News.** Would you be willing to be interviewed on camera about the new metro train line the city plans to construct?

M: Sure. Uh, right now?

W1: Yes, just stand right there. So, what do you think about the new line?

53-55 三人對話

美⇄澳⇄英

女 1： 先生您好，(53) **我叫李敏生，是第六頻道新聞台的記者**。您願意針對本市計劃興建的新地鐵路線，在鏡頭前接受我們的採訪嗎？

男： 當然願意。呃，現在嗎？

女 1： 是的，站在原地即可。那麼，您對這條新路線有什麼看法？

M: It's a good idea. (54) **I've been commuting on the Norman line for years, and it's become packed with people. The new line will help with that.**	男： 這是很好的構想。(54) **我搭諾曼線通勤好多年了，該路線現在已經人滿為患，新的路線會有助解決這個問題。**
W1: Great. That was perfect.(55) **Now I just need your signature on the consent form my producer is holding.**	女 1： 好的，訪談圓滿結束。(55) **現在，我的製作人手上拿著同意書，請您在上頭簽名即可。**
W2: It gives us permission to broadcast the clip we just made. Here's a pen, too.	女 2： 簽名代表允許我們播出剛才拍攝的片段。這支筆也給您。

- metro train 地鐵 commute (v.) 通勤 be packed with 擠滿；塞滿 signature (n.) 簽名 consent form 同意書 permission (n.) 許可 broadcast (v.) 播放 clip (n.)（電視節目等的）片段

53. 相關細節——李小姐的職業

Who most likely is Ms. Lee?

(A) A journalist
(B) A city official
(C) A travel agent
(D) A researcher

李小姐最有可能的身分為何？

(A) 新聞記者
(B) 市府官員
(C) 旅行社職員
(D) 研究人員

54. 相關細節——男子針對地鐵路線工程提及的內容 難

What does the man say about the construction of a train line?

(A) It caused him to be late.
(B) It will take many years to complete.
(C) It will relieve crowding on another line.
(D) It has shortened his commute.

男子對地鐵線的興建有何說法？

(A) 讓他因此而遲到了。
(B) 需耗時多年才能完工。
(C) 會緩解另一條路線的人潮。
(D) 已縮短了他的通勤時間。

- relieve (v.) 緩解 crowding (n.) 人潮 shorten (v.) 縮短

換句話說 packed with people（人滿為患）→ crowding（人潮）
help with（有助）→ relieve（緩解）

55. 相關細節——李小姐要求男子做的事

What does Ms. Lee ask the man to do next?

(A) Show her a ticket
(B) Watch a video clip
(C) Sit down at a table
(D) Sign a document

李小姐要求男子接下來做什麼？

(A) 出示車票
(B) 看一段影片
(C) 在桌旁坐下
(D) 簽署文件

56-58 Conversation

56-58 對話 美⇄加

W: Oh, hi Martin. (56) **Did you finish walking the dogs and cleaning their cages?**	女： 噢，嗨，馬丁。(56) **你遛完狗兒們、也清理過狗籠了嗎？**
M: Hi, Ms. Cruz. Yes, I did. Uh, do you have a minute? I wanted to talk to you about something.	男： 嗨，克魯茲小姐。是的，我都完成了。呃，您現在有空嗎？我想跟您說件事。

W: Sure. Have a seat.	女：當然有空，請坐。
M: Thanks. (57) **As you know, I'm about to graduate from university, so I'm starting to look for jobs.** I already listed my work with this organization on my résumé. (58) **Could I give your name as a reference as well?**	男：謝謝。(57) **您也知道，我馬上就要大學畢業，所以正在開始找工作**，我已經把這家機構的工作經歷列在履歷表上，(58) **不知能否將您的名字也列上去，作為推薦人？**
W: (58) **Absolutely.** You've been an excellent volunteer. Do you already know my official job title and contact details?	女：(58) **當然可以**，你擔任志工期間，一直都很優秀，你知道我的正式職稱和聯絡方式嗎？
M: I do. Thank you so much!	男：我知道的，非常感謝您！

- cage (n.) 籠子　graduate (v.) 畢業　organization (n.) 機構；組織　résumé (n.) 履歷表　reference (n.) 推薦人（信）　volunteer (n.) 志工　official (adj.) 正式的；官方的　contact (n.) 聯絡；聯繫

56. 相關細節——說話者所屬機構的工作內容 難

What most likely is the mission of the speakers' organization?

(A) To educate children

(B) To take care of animals

(C) To protect the environment

(D) To support the arts

說話者任職的機構，最有可能從事何種任務？

(A) 教育孩童

(B) 照顧動物

(C) 保護環境

(D) 支持藝術

- mission (n.) 使命；任務　educate (v.) 教育　environment (n.) 環境　support (v.) 支持

57. 相關細節——男子即將要做的事

What does the man say he will do soon?

(A) Earn a degree

(B) Move away

(C) Take a vacation

(D) Donate some supplies

男子說他很快就會做什麼？

(A) 取得學位

(B) 搬家

(C) 休假

(D) 捐贈物資

換句話說 graduate from university（大學畢業）→ earn a degree（取得學位）

58. 掌握說話者的意圖——提及「你擔任志工期間，一直都很優秀」的意圖 難

What does the woman mean when she says, "You've been an excellent volunteer"?

(A) She is happy to fulfill the man's request.

(B) She is sorry that the man is quitting.

(C) She is surprised by the man's mistake.

(D) She is pleased that the man will become more involved.

女子說：「你擔任志工期間，一直都很優秀」，其意思為何？

(A) 她很樂意答應男子的要求。

(B) 她很遺憾男子要離職。

(C) 她對男子的失誤感到驚訝。

(D) 她樂見男子更加投入。

- fulfill (v.) 實現；滿足　request (n.) 要求　quit (v.) 辭職；離開　involved (adj.) 參與的；涉及的

59-61 Conversation

59-61 對話

加⇄英

M: Sandy, thanks for coming in. (59) **I have some news—the move you requested came through.** You'll be able to start working at the Lambert office on August first.

W: Wow, that's soon! (60) **It's a good thing that I've already started gathering documentation on my work processes to give to my replacement.**

M: Oh, have you? That's excellent. (61) **Now, here's a draft of your new job contract.** It's very similar to your current one, but there are a few differences. Take a look at it and let me know if you have any questions.

男：姍蒂，謝謝妳過來。(59) **我有個消息：妳轉調的申請已經批下來了，** 8 月 1 日開始，妳就要去蘭伯特辦公室上班了。

女：哇，這麼快啊！(60) **還好我已經開始彙整我這邊業務進度的文件，好交接給要接替我的同仁。**

男：噢，有在進行嗎？那太好了。(61) **那麼，這份是妳的新工作合約草稿，** 跟妳現在的合約大同小異，但有幾個地方不一樣。請妳查看一下，如果有什麼問題再跟我說。

- **come through** 通過；批准 **documentation (n.)** 文件 **process (n.)** 流程；程序 **replacement (n.)**（工作）接替者 **draft (n.)** 草稿

59. 全文相關——對話主題

What are the speakers discussing?
(A) A promotion
(B) A career fair
(C) An interview
(D) A transfer

說話者正在討論什麼事？
(A) 升遷
(B) 就業博覽會
(C) 面試
(D) 轉調

---

60. 相關細節——女子持續在做的事 難

What does the woman say she has been doing?
(A) Collecting some records
(B) Processing some applications
(C) Communicating with some recruiters
(D) Replacing some equipment

女子說她持續在做什麼事？
(A) 收集一些紀錄
(B) 處理一些應徵表
(C) 與一些招聘人員溝通
(D) 更換一些設備

- **process (v.)** 處理 **application (n.)** 申請書 **recruiter (n.)** 招聘人員 **replace (v.)** 更換 **equipment (n.)** 設備

---

61. 相關細節——男子給女子的東西

What does the man give the woman?
(A) A job advertisement
(B) An applicant's résumé
(C) An employment agreement
(D) An orientation schedule

男子給女子什麼東西？
(A) 求職廣告
(B) 求職者的履歷
(C) 聘用契約
(D) 新人培訓時程表

- **applicant (n.)** 求職者 **employment (n.)** 聘僱；工作 **orientation (n.)** 職前訓練；始業訓練

換句話說 job contract（工作合約）→ **employment agreement**（聘用契約）

62-64 Conversation + Departure board

M: Vera, where are you? Our bus is leaving in five minutes. (62) **It's going to make a bad impression on the other industry attendees if we miss the beginning of the conference.**

W: I'm so sorry, Nathan. (63) **I was halfway to the bus terminal this morning before I realized that I'd left two of my structural models at home.** I wouldn't be able to lead my session without them. Anyway, I won't arrive at the departure area for another twenty minutes, so you should go ahead without me.

M: No, that's all right. (64) **I think you'll be able to make the bus to Cookville that leaves after eight.** I'll try to get us tickets for that one.

Bus Departures

Destination	Boarding Area	Time
Grammett	D	DEPARTED
Cookville	E	7:20 a.m.
Owenton	B	7:53 a.m
Grammett	D	8:04 a.m
(64) **Cookville**	**E**	**8:10** a.m

62-64 對話＋公車時刻表 澳⇄英

男：薇拉，妳人在哪？我們的客運五分鐘後就要發車了。(62) **要是我們錯過了會議的開場，會給業界的其他與會者留下不好的印象。**

女：抱歉，內森。(63) **我今天早上去客運總站的半路上，發覺我把兩個結構模型忘在家裡了**，沒有模型，我就沒辦法主持我負責的講座。總之，我還要再 20 分鐘才會到乘車處，所以你不用等我，先出發吧。

男：不用，沒關係的，(64) **我想妳趕得上八點後開往庫克維爾的那班車**，我會想辦法買票供我們搭那班車。

客運發車時間

終點站	乘車處	時間
格雷姆特	D	已離站
庫克維爾	E	上午 7：20
歐文頓	B	上午 7：53
格雷姆特	D	上午 8：04
(64) **庫克維爾**	**E**	**上午 8：10**

- impression (n.) 印象　industry (n.) 產業；工業　attendee (n.) 與會者　conference (n.) 會議；研討會　halfway (adj./adv.) 半路的／地　realize (v.) 意識到　structural (adj.) 結構的　ahead (adv.) 在前

62. 相關細節——說話者們要做的事

What are the speakers going to do?

(A) Visit a factory

(B) Oversee a building project

(C) Participate in a conference

(D) Attend an awards ceremony

說話者將要做什麼？

(A) 參觀工廠

(B) 監督建案

(C) 參加會議

(D) 出席頒獎典禮

- oversee (v.) 監督　participate in 參加

63. 相關細節——女子忘記帶的東西 難

What did the woman forget to bring?

(A) A set of gifts

(B) A travel document

(C) Some special clothing

(D) Some presentation materials

女子忘記帶什麼了？

(A) 一組禮物

(B) 旅行證件

(C) 特殊服裝

(D) 發表用的素材

- document (n.) 文件；證件　material (n.) 材料；資料

64. 圖表整合題——男子建議的出發時間

Look at the graphic. When does the man suggest departing?

(A) At 7:20 a.m.

(B) At 7:53 a.m.

(C) At 8:04 a.m.

(D) At 8:10 a.m.

請看圖表作答。男子建議何時出發？

(A) 上午 7：20

(B) 上午 7：53

(C) 上午 8：04

(D) 上午 8：10

65-67 Conversation + Coupon

W: Welcome to Brooks Gym. How can I help you today?

M: **(65) I was just handed this coupon as I was passing by outside, so I wanted to come in and see what kind of classes you offer.**

W: Sure. Here's a list.

M: Oh, kickboxing! I'd like to try that.

W: Great. Which class package would you like?

M: Let's see . . . **(66) I don't want to make a big commitment before I know if I like it, so I'll go with the ten-class package.**

W: Great choice. **(67) And you should know—these packages don't have any limits on the kind of class.** If you decide that kickboxing isn't for you, you can try another activity.

Brooks Gym

Buy a class package and save!

	Total	Savings per class
5 classes	$90	$2
(66) **10 classes**	**$160**	**$4**
15 classes	$210	$6
20 classes	$240	$8

65-67 對話＋優惠券 美⇄澳

女： 歡迎光臨布魯克健身房，目前有什麼能為您服務的嗎？

男： **(65) 我經過外面的時候，有人發給我這張優惠券，所以我想進來看看你們有提供哪些課程。**

女： 沒問題，請參考這張表。

男： 哦，有踢拳道！我想試試這個。

女： 當然好，您想選擇哪種課程方案呢？

男： 我看看⋯⋯ **(66) 我不知道會不會喜歡上踢拳道，還不想做長遠安排，所以就選 10 堂課的方案吧。**

女： 很好的選擇。**(67) 這邊跟您說明一下：這些方案可不限課程種類使用。**如果您覺得踢拳道不適合您，就可以嘗試別項活動。

布魯克健身房

選購課程方案，多買多省！

	總價	每堂課省下
5堂課	90 美元	2 美元
(66) 10堂課	160 美元	4 美元
15堂課	210 美元	6 美元
20堂課	240 美元	8 美元

- **hand (v.)** 傳遞；給 **pass by** 經過；走過 **commitment (n.)** 承諾；投入（金錢、時間、人力）
  limit (n.) 限制

65. 相關細節——男子拿到優惠券的地方 難

Where most likely did the man get the coupon?

(A) At a gym class

(B) On the street

(C) In the mail

(D) On a Web site

男子最有可能從哪裡拿到優惠券？

(A) 在健身課上

(B) 在街上

(C) 在郵件裡

(D) 在網站上

66. 圖表整合題——男子可省下的課程費用

Look at the graphic. How much will the man save per class?

(A) $2　**(B) $4**

(C) $6　(D) $8

請看圖表作答。男子每堂課可以省下多少錢？

(A) 2 美元　**(B) 4 美元**

(C) 6 美元　(D) 8 美元

67. 相關細節——女子針對課程方案提到的內容 難

What does the woman say about the class packages?

(A) They were recently introduced.

(B) They are valid for a limited time.

(C) They are not eligible for refunds.

(D) They allow entry to any type of class.

關於課程方案，女子說了什麼？

(A) 最近才推出的。

(B) 限時有效。

(C) 無法退費。

(D) 適用各種類課程。

- introduce (v.) 採用；引進　valid (adj.) 有效的　limited (adj.) 限定的　eligible (adj.) 符合條件的；有資格的　entry (n.) 參加；進入

換句話說 don't have any limits on the kind of class（不限課程種類）
→ allow entry to any type of class（適用各種類課程）

68-70 Conversation + Pie chart

M: Sabrina, have you read the company's annual report yet?

W: I'm doing that right now, actually. This "Sources of Revenue" chart is surprising. (68) **You know, it's been less than five years since we started doing business in Africa, and look how much it's grown as a source of revenue.**

M: It's impressive, isn't it? (69) **I think that's why the company is planning to enter the South American market.** The CEO is predicting similar success there.

W: Oh really?

M: (70) **Yes, the last few pages are about that. You'll definitely want to read that part.**

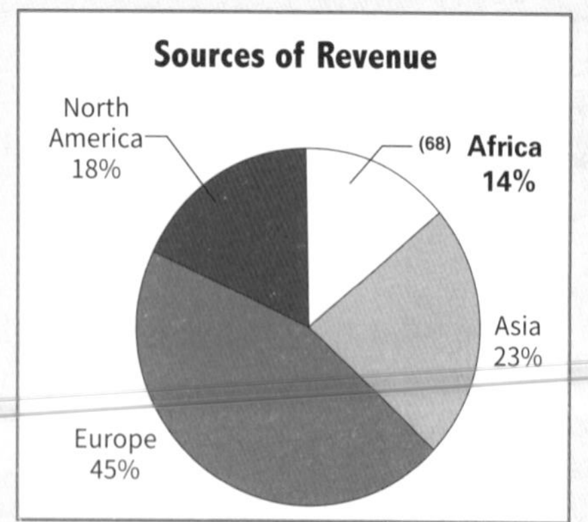

68-70 對話＋圓餅圖 加⇄英

男： 莎賓娜，妳看過公司的年報了嗎？

女： 其實我現在正在看。這張「收益來源」的圖表還真令人驚訝。(68) **你也知道，我們從開始在非洲做生意至今，還不到五年的時間，現在一看，這個地區的收益來源，成長竟是如此可觀。**

男： 令人刮目相看，不是嗎？(69) **我想這就是公司正計劃進軍南美市場的原因，**執行長預期將在南美同樣大獲成功。

女： 噢，真的嗎？

男： (70) **真的，最後幾頁有寫到相關內容，妳一定會想一睹為快。**

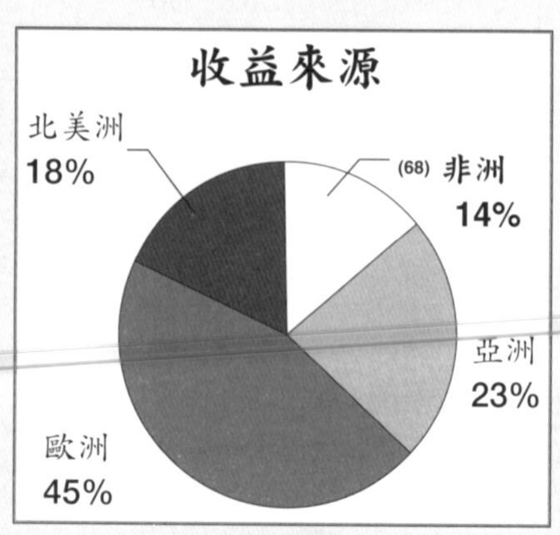

- annual (adj.) 年度的　source (n.) 來源　revenue (n.) 收益；收入　impressive (adj.) 令人印象深刻的　predict (v.) 預測　definitely (adv.) 絕對地

68. 圖表整合題——女子提及數值增長的情形

Look at the graphic. Which figure does the woman say is larger than before?
(A) 14% (B) 18%
(C) 23% (D) 45%

請看圖表作答。女子說何項數字超越以往？
(A) 14% (B) 18%
(C) 23% (D) 45%

- figure (n.) 數字

69. 相關細節——男子提及的公司計畫

According to the man, what does the company plan to do?
(A) Enter an additional industry
(B) Replace its chief executive
(C) Relocate its headquarters
(D) Expand into a new region

根據男子說法，該公司有何計畫？
(A) 涉足其他產業
(B) 更換執行長
(C) 遷移總部
(D) 擴展到新地區

- industry (n.) 行業 chief executive 執行長；總裁 relocate (v.) 搬遷 headquarters (n.) 總部 expand (v.) 擴展；擴大 region (n.) 區域

換句話說 enter the South American market（進軍南美市場）
→ expand into a new region（擴展到新地區）

70. 相關細節——男子建議閱讀的東西

What does the man recommend reading?
(A) A section of a report
(B) An article on a Web page
(C) A summary of some laws
(D) An invitation to a celebration

男子建議閱讀什麼？
(A) 報告的一部分
(B) 網頁的文章
(C) 法律的摘要
(D) 慶祝會的邀請函

- section (n.) 部分 summary (n.) 摘要 celebration (n.) 慶祝（會）

PART 4 P. 17–19

04

71-73 Telephone message

Hi, Ms. Gibson. This is Kwang-Ho at Pelston Pharmacy. (71) **The medicine that Doctor Walsh prescribed for your eye condition is ready.** I apologize for the delay. (72) **It took some time to get your insurance provider's approval. But we finally did, so you won't have to pay anything out-of-pocket for the medicine.** You can come by and pick it up during our business hours, which are from eight to six. (73) **Oh, but we have to close down tomorrow for maintenance reasons, so don't come then.** Call us if you have any questions. Thanks.

71–73 電話留言 澳

吉布森女士您好，我是佩爾斯頓藥局的光浩。(71) **沃爾許醫師開給您治療眼睛的藥物已經備妥**，很抱歉耽擱了。(72) **為了得到您保險公司的批准，我們花了一些時間，但我們最終還是成功了，所以您不用自付任何藥費。**您可以在我們的營業時間，也就是八點到六點間來取藥。(73) **噢，但我們因為維修，明日沒有營業，請您不要白跑一趟。**如果有任何問題，敬請來電，謝謝。

- pharmacy (n.) 藥局 prescribe (v.) 開藥 insurance (n.) 保險 approval (n.) 批准；許可 out-of-pocket (adj.)（費用）實付的 maintenance (n.) 維修

71. 全文相關——留言的主旨

What is the message mainly about?
(A) A prescription medication
(B) An appointment time
(C) A doctor's specialty
(D) A hospital bill

這段留言的主題為何？
(A) 處方藥物
(B) 約診時間
(C) 醫師專長
(D) 就醫帳單

- prescription (n.) 處方　medication (n.) 藥　specialty (n.) 專業；特長

---

72. 相關細節——說話者提及他取得的東西

What does the speaker say he has received?
(A) An electronic payment
(B) An insurance authorization
(C) Some promotional brochures
(D) Some past medical records

說話者說他取得了什麼？
(A) 電子付款
(B) 保險授權
(C) 宣傳手冊
(D) 過去病歷

- electronic (adj.) 電子的　authorization (n.) 授權　promotional (adj.) 宣傳的；促銷的　brochure (n.) 小冊子

換句話說 insurance provider's approval（保險公司的批准）→ insurance authorization（保險授權）

---

73. 相關細節——說話者提及明天將發生的事

What does the speaker say will happen tomorrow?
(A) He will update a database.
(B) He will call the listener again.
(C) A business will be closed.
(D) A delivery will arrive.

說話者說明天將發生什麼事？
(A) 他會更新資料庫。
(B) 他會再打電話給聽者。
(C) 店家將不營業。
(D) 貨物將送達。

74-76 Excerpt from a meeting

Before we finish up this office-wide meeting, I'd like to address a problem that's come to my attention. (74) **It seems that several of you have complained to Human Resources about your coworkers taking calls from family and friends at their workstations.** I know that it can be difficult to concentrate when you can hear others' personal conversations, but this is not the kind of matter that should be brought to HR. (75) **Human Resources deals with major workplace issues.** (76) **Its functions are clearly laid out in the staff handbook, which you should all have a copy of. When you return to your desks today, please take a minute to look over that section.** Thank you.

74-76 會議摘錄 (加)

這次的全公司會議結束前，我想談談最近注意到的問題。(74) **似乎有數名同仁跟人資部投訴說，有同事在座位上接聽家人和朋友的來電。**我知道聽見別人的私人對話，會讓人會很難專心工作，但這類情事不應該是向人資部反映。(75) **人資部是負責處理公司內的重大問題，**(76) **該部門的職能在員工手冊上有清楚說明，手冊應該人人都有一本。請大家等下回到座位後，抽空查閱那個部分的內容，**謝謝各位。

- office-wide (adj.) 全公司的　Human Resources 人資部　concentrate (v.) 專注；專心　deal with 處理　lay something out（以書寫方式）清楚說明　staff handbook 員工手冊　section (n.) 部分

74. 相關細節——部分員工投訴的事情

What have some employees complained about?
(A) The quality of a workplace amenity
(B) The temperature of their office
(C) The distribution of a workload
(D) The behavior of their coworkers

有些員工投訴什麼問題？
(A) 公司休閒設施的品質
(B) 辦公室的溫度
(C) 工作量的分配
(D) 同事的行為

- amenity (n.) 休閒設施　temperature (n.) 溫度　distribution (n.) 分配　workload (n.) 工作量
  behavior (n.) 行為

75. 相關細節——說話者針對人資部的敘述

What does the speaker say about Human Resources?
(A) It is currently understaffed.
(B) It follows specific procedures.
(C) It handles only significant matters.
(D) It has made an announcement.

說話者對人資部有什麼說法？
(A) 目前人手不足。
(B) 遵循特定程序。
(C) 只處理重要事項。
(D) 已發表聲明。

- understaffed (adj.) 人員短缺的　specific (adj.) 特定的；具體的　procedure (n.) 程序
  handle (v.) 處理　significant (adj.) 重大的；重要的　announcement (n.) 宣布；通知

換句話說 deals with major workplace issues（處理公司內的重大問題）
→ handles significant matters（處理重要事項）

76. 相關細節——說話者要求聽者做的事情

What does the speaker ask the listeners to do?
(A) Review part of the employee handbook
(B) Participate in a team-building activity
(C) Brainstorm some possible solutions
(D) View an online training film

說話者要求聽者做什麼？
(A) 重讀部分員工手冊內容
(B) 參加團隊建立活動
(C) 發想可能的解決辦法
(D) 觀看線上培訓影片

- review (v.) 查看　brainstorm (v.) 腦力激盪；集思廣益

換句話說 look over that section（查閱那個部分）→ review part of（重讀部分）

77-79 Introduction

Welcome to this evening's lecture. I'm pleased to introduce our speaker, Gurleen Datta. (77) **Over her thirty-year career, Ms. Datta has been involved in the design and construction of dams all over the country, including one on the enormous Cataldo River.** (78) **To share some of the wisdom she has acquired, she has written an autobiography detailing her successes and failures, and she's going to tell us all about it today.** Ms. Datta will speak for one hour and then take questions from the audience. (79) **One note about the Q and A—the time will be limited, so if you decide to participate,** please remember that there are a hundred other people here. All right. Please welcome Gurleen Datta!

77-79 介紹 (美)

歡迎蒞臨今晚的講座，在此我非常開心地向大家介紹主講人：古爾倫·達塔。(77) **達塔女士 30 年的從業生涯中，參與過全國各地水壩的設計與興建，包括坐落於卡達多大河的水壩。**(78) **為了分享一路上獲得的智慧結晶，她寫了一本自傳，娓娓道出她成功與失敗的經驗，而今晚她就要跟我們聊聊這一切。**達塔女士將在一小時的演講後，接受觀眾提問，(79) **但有關問答環節，要請各位注意：問答時間有限，所以如果各位有心提問，**請記住現場還有一百個人。那麼，歡迎古爾倫·達塔上台！

- lecture (n.) 演講　be involved in 參與　enormous (adj.) 巨大的　wisdom (n.) 知識；學問　acquire (v.) 獲得　autobiography (n.) 自傳　detail (v.) 詳細描述　audience (n.) 觀眾　limited (adj.) 有限的　participate (v.) 參加

77. 相關細節——達塔女士從事的行業　難

What field does Ms. Datta most likely work in?
(A) Politics
(B) Medicine
(C) Engineering
(D) Publishing

達塔女士最有可能從事何種行業？
(A) 政治
(B) 醫療
(C) 工程
(D) 出版

78. 相關細節——達塔女士的演講主題　難

What will Ms. Datta talk about?
(A) A book about her experiences
(B) A documentary about a journey
(C) An organization she founded
(D) A prize she received

達塔女士將會談到什麼？
(A) 有關人生經歷的書
(B) 旅遊的紀錄片
(C) 她成立的組織
(D) 她獲得的獎項

- documentary (n.) 紀錄片　organization (n.) 組織　found (v.) 成立

換句話說 autobiography detailing her successes and failures（娓娓道出她成功與失敗經驗的自傳）
→ book about her experiences（有關人生經歷的書）

79. 掌握說話者的意圖——提及「現場還有一百個人」的意圖　難

What does the speaker imply when she says, "there are a hundred other people here"?
(A) Some of the listeners do not usually attend lectures.
(B) It will be easy to reach a fund-raising goal.
(C) There are not enough seats for the whole audience.
(D) The listeners should not take too long with their questions.

說話者說：「現場還有一百個人」，言下之意為何？
(A) 有些聽眾不常聽演講。
(B) 募款目標很容易達成。
(C) 座位不足，無法容納所有聽眾。
(D) 聽眾提問時間不宜過長。

- fund-raising (n.) 募款

80-82 Announcement

(80) Good afternoon, Prensfield Plaza shoppers. We have some brief announcements to make. **(81) First, the youth talent show, presided over by local news anchor Dean Adams, is starting in ten minutes.** Join Mr. Adams in the central atrium for a wonderful display of singing, dancing, and more. **(82) Also, we encourage our shoppers to download Prensfield Plus, our new application for smartphones and other mobile devices.** It features detailed information on our shops and restaurants, alerts about sales and entertainment events, and exclusive coupons. That's Prensfield Plus, available through all major app stores. Thank you, and enjoy your visit to Prensfield Plaza.

80-82 宣布　英

(80) 潘斯菲德購物廣場的貴賓們，大家午安，在此有些簡短的消息要通知大家。**(81) 首先，由本地新聞主播迪安．亞當斯主持的青年才藝表演，將在 10 分鐘後開始，**敬請移步中央大廳，和亞當斯先生一起欣賞精彩的勁歌熱舞等多項表演。**(82) 此外，也鼓勵所有貴賓下載本公司專為智慧型手機、以及其他行動裝置開發的新款應用程式「潘斯菲德 Plus」，**上面主打本商場商店、餐廳方面的詳細資訊，並會通知用戶促銷、娛樂活動，並提供專屬優惠。請指名「潘斯菲德 Plus」，在各大 APP 商店皆可下載，謝謝您，祝您在潘斯菲德購物廣場購物愉快。

- brief (adj.) 簡短的　preside over 主持　atrium (n.) 中庭；中央大廳　device (n.) 裝置
  feature (v.) 以……為特色　detailed (adj.) 詳細的　alert (n.) 提醒　exclusive (adj.) 專屬的
  available (adj.) 可取得

80. 全文相關——宣布出現的地點

Where most likely is the announcement being made?
(A) At a public library
(B) At a shopping mall
(C) At an amusement park
(D) At a conference center

這段宣布最有可能在哪裡播出？
(A) 在公共圖書館
(B) 在購物中心
(C) 在遊樂園
(D) 在會議中心

---

81. 相關細節——說話者針對亞當斯先生的敘述

What does the speaker say about Mr. Adams?
(A) He is searching for an acquaintance.
(B) One of his possessions has been found.
(C) He is about to act as the host of an event.
(D) Information about him has been put on display.

說話者提到了何項亞當斯先生的相關資訊？
(A) 他在找一名熟人。
(B) 他的物品已尋獲。
(C) 他即將擔任活動主持人。
(D) 他的相關資訊已公開展示。

- search for 尋找　acquaintance (n.) 熟人；認識的人　possession (n.) 所有物；財物
  be about to 即將　host (n.) 主持人

---

82. 相關細節——說話者提及新推出的事物

What does the speaker say is newly available?
(A) A dining facility
(B) A mobile app
(C) A job opportunity
(D) A transportation service

說話者說有新推出何物？
(A) 餐飲設施
(B) 行動裝置應用程式
(C) 工作機會
(D) 交通運輸服務

- dining (n.) 用餐　facility (n.) 場所；設施　transportation (n.) 運輸；交通工具

83-85 Instructions

Thank you all for coming in to learn about our new point-of-sale system. (83) **Once you've all been fully trained on it, you'll find that you can check out customers twice as fast as you did with the old cash registers.** (84) **Now, the system includes a touch screen, a barcode scanner, a credit card reader, a receipt printer, and a cash drawer—and today you'll find out how to use all of them.** To help, I've made these copies of the directions provided by the manufacturer. (85) **Still, as I demonstrate how to use the system, you'll want to write down some extra details or clarifications.** There are some pencils on that table. All right? Ready.

83-85 解說 澳

謝謝大家前來了解我們的新款銷售點管理系統。(83) **等大家完整受訓之後，就會發現幫顧客結帳的速度，會是你使用舊款收銀機的時兩倍，**(84) **本系統備有包括觸控螢幕、條碼掃描器、信用卡讀卡機、收據列印機、存放現金的抽屜，而你們今天將會學會如何操作以上設備。**為了幫大家學習，我已經印好製造廠商提供的說明指引，(85) **不過在我示範操作本系統的時候，各位不妨記下一些額外細節或說明，**那張桌上些有鉛筆。了解了嗎？我們準備開始。

- point-of-sale system 銷售點管理系統　cash register 收銀機　cash drawer 存放現金的抽屜
  directions (n.) 說明指引　manufacturer (n.) 製造商　demonstrate (v.) 示範　detail (n.) 細節；詳情
  clarification (n.) 說明；澄清

83. 全文相關——聽者的職業

Who most likely are the listeners?
(A) Bank tellers
(B) Store clerks
(C) Factory workers
(D) Real estate agents

聽者最有可能的身分為何？
(A) 銀行櫃員
(B) 商店店員
(C) 工廠員工
(D) 房地產仲介

84. 相關細節——說話者列出的項目

What does the speaker list?
(A) Pieces of equipment
(B) Marketing strategies
(C) Employee rest areas
(D) Customer complaints

說話者列舉了什麼？
(A) 設備項目
(B) 行銷策略
(C) 員工休息場所
(D) 顧客投訴

85. 掌握說話者的意圖——提及「那張桌上有些鉛筆」的意圖 難

Why does the speaker say, "There are some pencils on that table"?
(A) To show disappointment that a facility is messy
(B) To suggest that the listeners have lost some belongings
(C) To recommend using the pencils to take notes
(D) To offer the pencils to the listeners as gifts to take home

為何說話者要說：「那張桌上有些鉛筆」？
(A) 表示場地凌亂，令人失望
(B) 暗示聽者有人遺失了隨身物品
(C) 建議用鉛筆來做筆記
(D) 請聽者將鉛筆當贈品帶回家

- messy (adj.) 凌亂的 belongings (n.) 隨身物品；所有物

換句話說 write down some extra details（記下一些額外細節）→ take notes（做筆記）

86-88 Telephone message

Hello, Mr. Odiatu. This is Alyssa at Nealon Global. (86) **We've just reviewed your account and noticed that you've been using our Internet, phone, and cable services for five years.** (87) **It's Nealon Global's policy to show our appreciation to loyal customers like you, so we'd like to give you a digital home assistant made by our partner company—for free.** This voice-activated device, which retails for one hundred dollars, can play music, search the Internet, issue reminders, and much more. (88) **If you're interested, call me back at 1-800-555-0156, extension 85, and let me know when to send a technician to your house to install the device.** And again, thank you for being a Nealon Global customer.

86-88 電話留言 美

奧迪亞圖先生您好，我是尼隆環球公司的艾莉莎。(86) **我們剛查看了您的帳戶，發現您已持續五年使用本公司的網路、電話、有線電視服務。**(87) **向您這樣的忠實客戶表達感謝，是本公司一貫政策，因此想贈送給您由我們合作廠商製造的數位居家助理——完全免費喔。**這款裝置可語音聲控，市價 100 美元，具備播放音樂、上網搜尋、發送提醒通知等多項功能。(88) **若您有興趣，請撥打 1-800-555-0156，85 號分機回電給我，並告知什麼時候方便派技術員到府上安裝設備。**再次感謝您使用尼隆環球公司的服務。

- review (v.) 查看 account (n.) 帳戶 notice (v.) 注意到；發現 policy (n.) 政策 loyal (adj.) 忠實的 voice-activated (adj.) 聲控的 retail (v.) 零售 reminder (n.) 提醒 extension (n.) 分機 technician (n.) 技術員 install (v.) 安裝

86. 相關細節——說話者公司提供的服務

What type of service does the speaker's company provide?
(A) Security
(B) Shipping
(C) Landscaping
(D) Telecommunications

說話者的公司提供何種類型的服務？
(A) 保全
(B) 物流
(C) 造景
(D) 電信

87. 全文相關——電話留言的主旨

What is the speaker calling about?
(A) A review posted on a Web site
(B) An account password
(C) A reward for certain customers
(D) A malfunctioning electronic device

說話者的來電與何事有關？
(A) 網站上發布的評論
(B) 帳戶密碼
(C) 給特定客戶的回饋
(D) 故障的電子設備

- **post (v.)** 發布；張貼 **malfunctioning (adj.)** 故障的 **electronic (adj.)** 電子的

換句話說 show our appreciation to loyal customers（向忠實客戶表達感謝）
→ reward for certain customers（給特定客戶的回饋）

88. 相關細節——聽者需要回電的理由

Why should the listener return the phone call?
(A) To schedule a home visit
(B) To learn more about a discount
(C) To receive installation instructions
(D) To find out where to send an item

聽者為何應該回電？
(A) 為了安排到府服務時間
(B) 為了進一步了解折扣
(C) 為了取得安裝說明書
(D) 為了得知產品寄送地點

89-91 Tour information

Wow, isn't that a beautiful sky? OK, now that the sun has risen fully, it's time to begin the second part of our tour. (89) **Luke has gotten our bikes out of the tour van so that we can cycle back down the mountain.** As you know, this is expected to take four hours. (90) **We will stop twice for breaks, but if you still start to feel too tired to keep riding,** the van will be close behind us. You can see the same beautiful views from the van, so don't hesitate to speak to me if you need it. (91) **OK, please get your bike helmets on.** They're in this box here.

89-91 旅遊資訊 加

哇，多美麗的藍天啊？好的，既然已經太陽已經完全升起，我們該進入第二部分的旅遊行程了。(89) **盧克幫我們把自行車從旅遊小巴上搬下來了，我們可以騎車返回山下。**各位都知道，回程預計要四個小時，(90) **中間會停下來休息兩次，不過要是途中還是開始覺得累到騎不動了，**小巴就在後方緊緊跟著，在車上同樣可以欣賞到美麗的山色風光，所以如果有需要，請不吝隨時告知。(91) **好了，請大家戴上自行車安全帽，**安全帽在這個箱子。

- **van (n.)** 廂型車；麵包車 **cycle (v.)** 騎腳踏車 **break (n.)** 休息 **hesitate (v.)** 猶豫

89. 全文相關——該趟行程的地點

Where is the tour taking place?
(A) On a mountain
(B) In a forest
(C) By a lake
(D) In a desert

這趟旅遊行程在哪裡進行？
(A) 在山上
(B) 在森林裡
(C) 在湖邊
(D) 在沙漠裡

90. 掌握說話者的意圖——提及「小巴就在後方緊緊跟著」的意圖 難

What does the speaker imply when he says, "the van will be close behind us"?
(A) Listeners do not have to worry about getting lost.
(B) Listeners can ride in the van during the tour.
(C) Listeners should be careful around a vehicle.
(D) Listeners can access their baggage at any time.

說話者說：「小巴就在後方緊緊跟著」，言下之意為何？
(A) 聽者不必擔心迷路。
(B) 聽者在旅遊途中可以坐車。
(C) 聽者在車輛周圍時要小心。
(D) 聽者能隨時取用行李。

- get lost 迷路　vehicle (n.) 車輛　access (v.) 接近；使用　baggage (n.) 行李

91. 相關細節——聽者接下來要做的事情

What are the listeners asked to do next?
(A) Look at a route map
(B) Fill out some paperwork
(C) Put on some safety gear
(D) Throw away some trash

聽者被指示接著做什麼？
(A) 查看路線圖
(B) 填寫文件
(C) 戴上安全裝備
(D) 扔掉垃圾

- route map 路線圖　fill out 填寫　safety gear 安全裝備　trash (n.) 垃圾

換句話說 get your bike helmets on（大家戴上自行車安全帽）
→ put on some safety gear（戴上安全裝備）

92-94 Excerpt from a meeting

Let's get started. (92) **First, I want to express my gratitude to all of you for taking on extra shifts while the business exposition was in town.** Our hotel handled the increase in guests without any major problems. (93) **That said, we have another busy week coming up in June during the annual Waltsville Marathon.** So in today's meeting, we'll discuss the issues we did have and how to avoid them in the future. For example, we sometimes had long check-in lines because front desk staff were answering tourism-related questions. (94) **But I want to make it clear that that's not actually part of their job.** Instead, guests with such inquiries should be directed to use the concierge desk.

92-94 會議摘錄 英

我們開始開會吧。(92) **首先我要感謝全體員工，在本市舉辦商業博覽會期間加班輪值。**我們飯店面對客人增加，接待上沒有出現重大問題。(93) **儘管如此，沃茨維爾年度馬拉松賽即將在六月舉行，屆時我們又會迎接忙碌的一週，**因此在今天的會議上，我們要討論先前確實遇過的問題，以及今後如何防範於未然，例如，等待辦理入住的客人有時會大排長龍，因為前檯人員忙著回答旅遊相關問題。(94) **但我想說清楚：這其實不是前檯人員的工作範疇，**應該引導需要這類諮詢的客人前往禮賓服務檯才對。

- gratitude (n.) 感謝　shift (n.) 輪班工作時間　exposition (n.) 博覽會；展覽會　handle (v.) 處理　major (adj.) 主要的；重大的　that said 儘管如此　annual (adj.) 年度的　avoid (v.) 避免　related (adj.) 相關的　inquiry (n.) 詢問；諮詢　direct (v.) 給……指路　concierge (n.)（旅館的）禮賓部；禮賓接待員

92. 相關細節——說話者感謝聽者的事情

What does the speaker thank the listeners for?
(A) Taking part in the meeting
(B) Reporting some problems
(C) Working additional hours
(D) Going to an exposition

說話者為何事感謝聽者？
(A) 參加會議
(B) 回報問題
(C) 加班工作
(D) 參加博覽會

- take part in 出席；參加

93. 相關細節——說話者表示將於六月發生的事情

According to the speaker, what will happen in June?
(A) A competition will be held.
(B) An executive will retire.
(C) A new branch will open.
(D) A holiday will be celebrated.

根據說話者所言，六月將會發生什麼事？
(A) 將舉行比賽。
(B) 主管將退休。
(C) 新分店將開幕。
(D) 將慶祝節日。

- competition (n.) 比賽　executive (n.) 主管　branch (n.) 分支機構　celebrate (v.) 慶祝

換句話說 marathon（馬拉松）→ competition（競賽）

94. 相關細節——說話者澄清的事情 難

What does the speaker clarify?
(A) The names included on a guest list
(B) The availability of some hotel rooms
(C) The requirements for a submission
(D) The responsibilities of a position

說話者澄清了什麼事？
(A) 房客名單上的名字
(B) 飯店部分客房的供應情況
(C) 提交的條件
(D) 職位的職責

- clarify (v.) 澄清；說清楚　availability (n.) 可利用性　requirement (n.) 要求；條件
  submission (n.) 提交　responsibility (n.) 責任

95-97 Telephone message + Schedule

Hi, Kioshi. I hope this message catches you before you leave work. (95) **As you know, today was the first day of data collection for the Gilfoy Airport employee satisfaction survey.** We administered the surveys to fifteen people, which is within our target range. (96) **But I just gathered the team to discuss how the project is going so far, and it seems there's a problem.** Just as we tried to warn airport management, the questionnaire is too long. Employees seem to be getting tired and not giving thoughtful answers by the end. (97) **I think we should shorten or at least rearrange it to address this issue.** Can we talk about this tomorrow morning? Let me know.

95-97 電話留言＋時程表 澳

嗨，紀志。希望你下班前有聽到這則留言。(95) **你知道，今天是我們為吉爾佛機場員工滿意度調查收集資料的第一天，**我們對 15 人進行了問卷調查，這落在目標範圍內，(96) **但是我剛召集組員討論專案目前的進展，結果好像有個問題，**就跟我們之前想提醒機場管理部門留意的一樣，這份問卷太長了，員工好像越填來越疲乏，到後來就沒有太用心回答。(97) **要解決這個問題，我認為我們應該縮短問卷長度，或者至少重新編排。**我們明天早上能談談這個問題嗎？再請告知。

Project Schedule	
Planning	July 1–19
(95) **Data collection**	**July 22–August 30**
Data analysis	September 2–6
Report preparation	September 9–20
Presentation of results	September 23

專案時程表	
規劃	7月1日至19日
(95) **資料收集**	**7月22日至8月30日**
資料分析	9月2日至6日
準備報告	9月9日至20日
報告結果	9月23日

- collection (n.) 蒐集　satisfaction (n.) 滿意（度）　survey (n.) 調查　administer (v.) 給予；施行　range (n.) 範圍　gather (v.) 召集；聚集　questionnaire (n.) 問卷；調查表　thoughtful (adj.) 用心的　shorten (v.) 縮短　rearrange (v.) 重新整理　address (v.) 處理；對付

95. 圖表整合題——說話者來電的日期

Look at the graphic. On which date is the speaker calling?

(A) July 1

(B) July 22

(C) September 2

(D) September 9

請看圖表作答。說話者是在哪一天打電話的？

(A) 7 月 1 日

(B) 7 月 22 日

(C) 9 月 2 日

(D) 9 月 9 日

96. 相關細節——說話者剛完成的事情

What has the speaker just finished doing?

(A) Calculating an expense

(B) Arranging some interviews

(C) Running some software

(D) Meeting with team members

說話者剛做完了什麼？

(A) 計算費用

(B) 安排面試

(C) 操作軟體

(D) 和組員開會

- calculate (v.) 計算　expense (n.) 費用　arrange (v.) 安排；準備

97. 相關細節——說話者想與聽者討論的事情

What does the speaker want to discuss with the listener?

(A) The size of the research team

(B) The due date of the report

(C) The format of the questionnaire

(D) The strategy for attracting participants

說話者想要跟聽者討論什麼事？

(A) 研究團隊的規模

(B) 報告的截止日期

(C) 問卷調查表的編排

(D) 吸引參與者的策略

- research (n.) 研究　due date 截止日期　format (n.) 形式；編排　strategy (n.) 策略　participant (n.) 參與者

98-100 Broadcast + Floor plan

98-100 電台廣播＋平面圖 美

(98) In local news, the Raffden Student Arts Festival organized by the city's Office of Arts and Culture has proven popular among residents and tourists. An average of two thousand visitors per day have come to Raffden Convention Center to see works and performances by university students. **(99) Today, the festival kicks off its second week with a special event.** Devon Keller, the young handicraft enthusiast who has become an Internet sensation, will teach thirty lucky visitors how to make one of her clay jewelry pieces. **(100) This free class will be held in the festival's "Activities Corner" at three p.m., but festival organizers recommend arriving earlier in order to reserve a seat.** Now, the weather forecast.

(98) 本地新聞方面，本市藝文局主辦的拉夫登學生藝術節，已受到當地居民與遊客的熱烈響應，每天平均有兩千名遊客來到拉夫登會議中心，觀賞大學生的作品與演出。**(99) 藝術節在今天邁入第二週，並會以特別活動拉開序幕。**戴玟．凱勒是一名年輕的手工藝品愛好者，已在網路爆紅，她將在現場教導 30 名幸運觀眾，如何用黏土製作她創作的飾品。**(100) 這個免費課程將於下午三點在藝術節會場的「活動專區」舉行，但活動主辦單位建議提早到場劃位，以免向隅。**接下來是天氣預報。

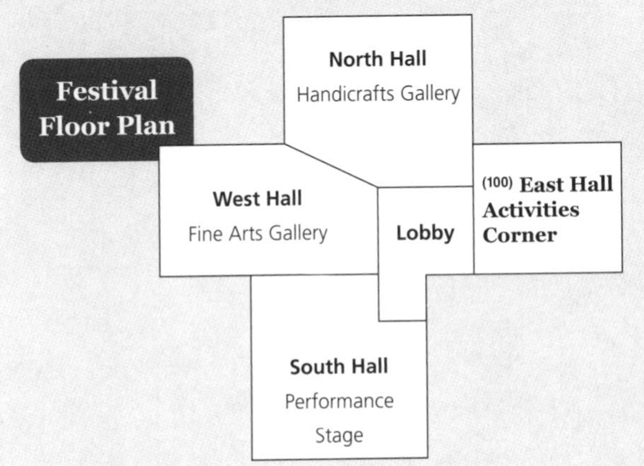

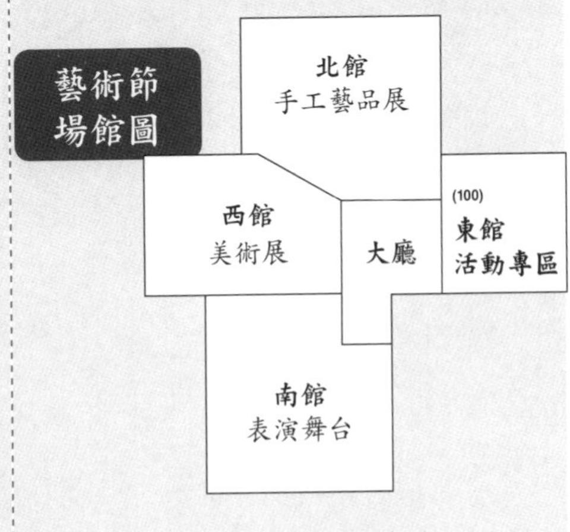

- organize (v.) 組織；籌辦　prove (v.) 證明；顯示　resident (n.) 居民　average (n.) 平均值　per (prep.) 每（一）　performance (n.) 表演；演出　kick off 開始　handicraft (n.) 手工藝（品）　enthusiast (n.) 愛好者　sensation (n.) 引起轟動的人（或事）　clay (n.) 黏土　jewelry (n.) 飾品；珠寶　organizer (n.) 主辦單位　reserve (v.) 預訂；保留

98. 相關細節——活動的主辦單位 

What kind of organization is holding the festival?
(A) An art school
(B) A museum
(C) A student-run association
(D) A city government department

藝術節由何種單位舉辦？
(A) 藝術學校
(B) 博物館
(C) 學生自治團體
(D) 市府部門

- association (n.) 協會　government (n.) 政府

99. 相關細節——藝術節開始的時間 難

When did the festival begin?
(A) Three weeks ago
(B) Last week
(C) Yesterday
(D) This morning

藝術節何時開始？
(A) 三週前
(B) 上週
(C) 昨天
(D) 今天早上

100. 圖表整合題——特別活動的舉行地點

Look at the graphic. In which hall will a special event take place?

(A) The North Hall

(B) The West Hall

(C) The East Hall

(D) The South Hall

請看圖表作答。特別活動將在哪個館場舉行？

(A) 北館

(B) 西館

(C) 東館

(D) 南館

ACTUAL TEST 2

PART 1 P. 20–23

05

1. 單人獨照——描寫人物的動作 加

(A) He's eating a cookie.
(B) He's opening a kitchen drawer.
(C) He's cooking on a stove.
(D) He's holding a baking tray.

(A) 他在吃餅乾。
(B) 他在打開廚房抽屜。
(C) 他在爐子上煮飯。
(D) 他端著烤盤。

- drawer (n.) 抽屜 stove (n.)（烹飪用的）爐子 baking tray 烤盤

2. 雙人照片——描寫人物的動作 澳

(A) The man is writing on a document.
(B) The man is looking in a cabinet.
(C) The woman is using a microscope.
(D) The woman is pouring some liquid.

(A) 男子在文件上寫字。
(B) 男子在櫃子裡找東西。
(C) 女子在使用顯微鏡。
(D) 女子在倒入一些液體。

- microscope (n.) 顯微鏡 pour (v.) 傾倒；灌注 liquid (n.) 液體

3. 綜合照片——描寫人物或事物 英

(A) A stone barrier runs along a bridge.
(B) Some people are climbing a set of steps.
(C) A woman is working out outdoors.
(D) A path is being cleared off.

(A) 一道石牆順著橋延伸。
(B) 有些人在爬樓梯。
(C) 女子在戶外運動。
(D) 道路正在淨空中。

- barrier (n.) 隔欄；屏障 step (n.) 階梯；臺階 work out 鍛鍊身體 outdoors (adv.) 在戶外 path (n.) 小徑；路

4. 綜合照片——描寫人物或事物 美

(A) Computers have been arranged in two rows.
(B) A group of people is watching a presentation.
(C) A pair of headphones has been left on a keyboard.
(D) One of the men is distributing some papers.

(A) 電腦排成兩列。
(B) 一群人在看簡報。
(C) 一副耳機擱在鍵盤上。
(D) 有個男子在分發文件。

- arrange (v.) 排列 row (n.) 排 presentation (n.) 簡報；演講 distribute (v.) 分發

5. 綜合照片——描寫人物或事物 英 

(A) A shelving unit is being assembled.
(B) Goods are being moved around a warehouse.
(C) A technician is using tools to repair a machine.
(D) Workers are carrying a package together.

(A) 貨架正在組裝中。
(B) 倉庫內貨物正在搬移當中。
(C) 技術員正在用工具修理機器。
(D) 工人一起搬運一包貨物。

- shelving unit 貨架；置物架 assemble (v.) 組裝 goods (n.) 貨物 warehouse (n.) 倉庫 technician (n.) 技術員；技師 tool (n.) 工具

6. 事物與背景照——描寫室內事物的狀態 加

(A) There is a large rug on the floor.	**(A) 地板上鋪著一塊大地毯。**
(B) Curtains have been closed over windows.	(B) 窗戶的窗簾已經關上了。
(C) A wooden deck is filled with furniture.	(C) 木製露台上擺滿了家具。
(D) A home fireplace is being cleaned.	(D) 家裡的壁爐正在清潔中。

- rug (n.) 地毯　deck (n.) 露天平台　be filled with 充滿；填滿　fireplace (n.) 壁爐

PART 2 P. 24

06

7. 以 **Who** 開頭的問句，詢問會議參加者 加⇄美

Who's coming to this afternoon's meeting?	誰會來參加今天下午的會議？
(A) It was moved to four p.m.	(A) 改到下午四點。
(B) I'll reserve the conference room.	(B) 我會去預約會議室。
(C) Just Ms. Fisher's team.	**(C) 只有費雪女士的團隊。**

- reserve (v.) 預約；預訂

8. 以 **Be** 動詞開頭的問句，詢問是否為對方的傘 澳⇄英

Excuse me—is this your umbrella?	請問這是你的雨傘嗎？
(A) No, I haven't.	(A) 不是，我還沒有。
(B) Oh, thank you!	**(B) 噢，謝謝你！**
(C) Check the weather forecast.	(C) 請查看天氣預報。

9. 以 **Where** 開頭的問句，詢問鄰近超市的位置 美⇄加

Where's the closest supermarket?	最鄰近的超市在哪？
(A) Over on Third Avenue.	**(A) 在第三大道。**
(B) No, it's still open.	(B) 不，仍在營業中。
(C) Excellent customer service.	(C) 優質的客戶服務。

- avenue (n.) 大道　excellent (adj.) 優良的

10. 以 **When** 開頭的問句，詢問休假何時結束 英⇄澳

When did you get back from vacation?	你什麼時候休假回來的？
(A) Yes, and I got one for you too.	(A) 是的，我也幫你買了一個。
(B) To help with an urgent project.	(B) 為了協助一項緊急專案。
(C) Today's my first day back.	**(C) 今天是我回來的第一天。**

- vacation (n.) 度假；休假　urgent (adj.) 緊急的

11. 以 **What** 開頭的問句，詢問製作圖表的工具 美⇄加

What did you use to make this graphic?	你是用什麼繪製這張圖的？
(A) The program is called "Shin Image Pro."	**(A) 叫做「欣影像 Pro」的程式。**
(B) That's right—until last year.	(B) 沒錯——到去年為止。
(C) The blue line shows our sales.	(C) 藍色線顯示公司的銷售額。

- graphic (n.) 圖表

12. 以否定疑問句，確認是否有徵得新的辦公室經理 澳⇄美

Haven't you found a new office manager yet?
(A) I didn't know it had been lost.
(B) We're still holding interviews.
(C) At his welcome party.

你們還沒找到新的辦公室經理嗎？
(A) 我不知道它遺失了。
(B) 我們還在進行面試。
(C) 在他的迎新會上。

- welcome party 迎新會；歡迎會

13. 以 **Why** 開頭的問句，詢問表演取消的原因 英⇄加 難

Why was the second performance on Sunday canceled?
(A) I hadn't heard that—how disappointing!
(B) Performance reviews will be done annually.
(C) Early Saturday evening.

週日的第二場演出為什麼取消了？
(A) 我還沒聽說呢——真失望！
(B) 績效評估每年都會進行一次。
(C) 週六晚間稍早。

- performance (n.) 表演；（工作）表現　review (n.) 審查；檢討

14. 以選擇疑問句，詢問折扣適用的對象 英⇄澳 難

Is the discount just for employees, or can our families use it too?
(A) It's a great benefit, isn't it?
(B) Your close family members can.
(C) For a more reliable way of counting.

只有員工才能享有折扣嗎，還是我的家屬也可以？
(A) 福利很棒，對不對？
(B) 與您親近的家人可以。
(C) 為了更可靠的計算方法。

- benefit (n.) 福利；待遇　reliable (adj.) 可靠的　count (v.) 計算

15. 以 **How quickly** 開頭的問句，詢問對方翻譯文件的速度 加⇄美

How quickly could you translate this document?
(A) Some spelling mistakes.
(B) With translation software.
(C) Let me look over the contents.

你可以多快翻譯好這份文件？
(A) 有些拼字錯誤。
(B) 用翻譯軟體。
(C) 我要瀏覽一下內容。

- translate (v.) 翻譯　look over （快速）查看

16. 以附加問句，確認義大利麵裡是否有含肉 加⇄英 難

The cream pasta has meat in it, doesn't it?
(A) We could make it vegetarian for you.
(B) By putting it in the microwave.
(C) It's one of our lunch specials on Fridays.

這道奶油義大利麵裡面有肉，對嗎？
(A) 我們可以幫您做成素食的。
(B) 藉由把它放到微波爐裡。
(C) 這是週五午餐的特餐。

- vegetarian (adj.) 素食的　microwave (n.) 微波爐

17. 以直述句傳達資訊 澳⇄英 難

That potted plant is in bad condition.
(A) Sarah works at a pottery plant.
(B) It's supposed to keep the air fresh.
(C) I haven't been able to water it regularly.

那個盆栽裡的植物狀況很差。
(A) 莎拉在一家陶瓷廠工作。
(B) 它應該會使空氣保持清新。
(C) 我一直沒能定期澆水。

- potted plant 盆栽植物　pottery (n.) 陶器　plant (n.) 植物／工廠　be supposed to 應該　water (v.) 澆水　regularly (adv.) 定期；經常

18. 以 **Be** 動詞開頭的問句，詢問對方是否有興趣參加研討會 美⇄加 難

Are you interested in attending the technology workshop?	你有興趣參加技術研習會嗎？
(A) Isn't the registration fee really expensive?	**(A)** 報名費不是很貴嗎？
(B) The updated list of attendees.	(B) 更新的與會者名單。
(C) Oh, I took attendance a few minutes ago.	(C) 噢，我幾分鐘前點過名了

- attend (v.) 參與；出席　technology (n.) 技術；科技　registration fee 報名費　attendee (n.) 與會者；參加者　take attendance 點名

19. 以附加問句確認對方是否會去機場接人 英⇄美 難

You're picking the guest speaker up from the airport, aren't you?	你會去機場接特邀講者，對嗎？
(A) About his life as a photographer.	(A) 關於他的攝影生涯。
(B) I'm planning to leave at three-thirty.	**(B) 我打算三點半出發。**
(C) The director always picks the speaker.	(C) 演講者總是由主管挑選。

- guest speaker 特邀演講者　photographer (n.) 攝影師　director (n.) 主管；董事

20. 表示建議或提案的問句 澳⇄英 難

Why don't we try advertising on social media?	我們何不試著在社群媒體上打廣告呢？
(A) Since the site was launched.	(A) 自從網站成立以來。
(B) That was Lloyd's advice, too.	**(B) 羅伊德也是這麼建議的。**
(C) I believe so.	(C) 我相信是的。

- advertise (v.) 打廣告；做宣傳　social media 社群媒體　launch (v.) 發起；啟動　advice (n.) 建議

21. 以 **Where** 開頭的問句，詢問產品測試結果在哪裡 美⇄澳 難

Where are the results of the product test?	產品測試的結果在哪裡？
(A) We're pleased with most of them.	(A) 我們對大部分（的結果）都感到滿意。
(B) The quality of some sample items.	(B) 部分樣品的品質。
(C) Are you sure it's been completed?	**(C) 你確定測試完成了嗎？**

- result (n.) 結果　quality (n.) 品質　complete (v.) 完成

22. 以 **What** 開頭的問句，詢問建議租賃的車種 美⇄加 難

What type of car do you recommend renting?	你建議租什麼類型的車？
(A) During your business trip out of state.	(A) 在你到別的州出差期間。
(B) I have some suggestions, but it's really up to you.	**(B) 我有幾個建議，但這真的取決於你。**
(C) The keys are in the top drawer of my desk.	(C) 鑰匙在我辦公桌最上面的抽屜裡。

- rent (v.) 出租；租用　state (n.) 州　suggestion (n.) 建議；提議　drawer (n.) 抽屜

23. 以選擇疑問句，詢問對方偏好的聯絡方式 英⇄澳

Would you like to be contacted by text message or by e-mail?	你想以簡訊還是電子郵件聯繫？
(A) Here's our staff directory.	(A) 這是我們的職員通訊錄。
(B) Only if there's a problem with my order.	(B) 只在我的訂單出問題時。
(C) I'd prefer to receive a phone call, actually.	**(C) 我其實比較想以電話聯繫。**

- contact (v.) 聯繫；聯絡　staff directory 員工通訊錄　order (n.) 訂單　receive (v.) 接到

24. 以助動詞 Do 開頭的問句，詢問對方是否常用咖啡機 加⇄澳 難

Do you use the coffee machine much? **(A) I mostly drink tea.** (B) For color copies. (C) Kenji has the invoice.	你很常使用咖啡機嗎？ **(A) 我大都是喝茶。** (B) 用於彩色影印。 (C) 帳單在賢治那裡。

- mostly (adv.) 通常；主要；一般　invoice (n.) 發貨單；帳單

25. 以直述句傳達資訊 加⇄英

I enjoyed your article in the company newsletter. **(A) That's kind of you to say.** (B) On page two, I think. (C) Oh, are you taking letters to the mailroom?	我很喜歡你在公司刊物上發表的文章。 **(A) 謝謝你的誇獎。** (B) 我想是在第二頁。 (C) 噢，你要把信送去郵件收發室嗎？

- article (n.) 文章　newsletter (n.) 通訊刊物；電子報　mailroom (n.) 郵件收發室

26. 以 How 開頭的問句，詢問飯店健身設施如何 美⇄澳

How are the fitness facilities in this hotel? (A) Whenever you're ready. **(B) I've never stayed here before.** (C) In the west wing of the ground floor.	這家飯店的健身設施怎麼樣？ (A) 只要你準備好了（，隨時都可以）。 **(B) 我沒住過這家飯店。** (C) 在一樓西側。

- facility (n.) 設施　wing (n.) 建築翼部；側廳　ground floor 一樓

27. 以 Why 開頭的問句，詢問公車停下來的原因 加⇄美

Why is the driver stopping the bus here? (A) By a field on the side of the road. **(B) Go and ask the tour guide.** (C) OK, I'll tell them to stop if possible.	公車司機為什麼要在這裡停車？ (A) 在路邊的田地旁。 **(B) 去問導遊看看。** (C) 好的，可以的話，我會叫他們停下。

28. 表示請託或要求的問句 澳⇄英

Would you mind taking this survey about our store? (A) It's printed on the sign near the entrance. **(B) I'm running late to work right now.** (C) Hmm—let's revise Question Five.	您是否方便做一下本店的意見調查？ (A) 門口旁的告示上寫著。 **(B) 我現在上班快要遲到了。** (C) 嗯⋯⋯我們修改一下第五題吧。

- survey (n.) 意見調查　entrance (n.) 入口；門口　revise (v.) 修改

29. 以助動詞 Do 開頭的問句，確認公寓是否設有洗衣機 澳⇄美 難

Does this washing machine come with the apartment? (A) About seven kilograms of clothing. (B) A local cleaning service does it. **(C) It belongs to the current tenant—sorry.**	這台洗衣機是本棟公寓提供的嗎？ (A) 大約七公斤的衣物。 (B) 本地清潔業者會做。 **(C) 抱歉，洗衣機是現任房客的。**

- washing machine 洗衣機　come with 與⋯⋯一起供給　tenant (n.) 承租人；房客

30. 以否定疑問句確認合約是否於十月到期 加⇄美 難

Didn't our contract with that supplier end in October?
(A) This payment will settle our account.
(B) They sell manufacturing materials.
(C) Yes, it looks like I'm free then.

我們與那家供應商的合約不是十月到期了嗎？
(A) 這筆款項後我們就結清了。
(B) 他們販售製造原料。
(C) 是的，看起來我到時有空。

- contract (n.) 合約 supplier (n.) 供應商 settle (v.) 結清 manufacturing (n.) 製造業 material (n.) 材料；原料

31. 以直述句傳達資訊 英⇄加

The shirt part of my uniform doesn't fit very well.
(A) Does she need to be taken to a hospital?
(B) The large white logo on the back.
(C) We have a few other women's sizes available.

我制服的襯衫部分不是很合身。
(A) 需要送她去醫院嗎？
(B) 背面那個大的白色標誌。
(C) 我們還有幾件別的女性尺碼。

- fit (v.) 合身 available (adj.) 可用的；在手邊的

PART 3 P. 25–28

07

32-34 Conversation

W: Good morning. (32) **Where can I take you today?**

M: Holligan Square, please. And would you mind turning on the air conditioning?

W: No problem. So, I can guess from your suitcase that you're probably a visitor here. What brings you to Mavner City?

M: (33) **I'm giving a presentation on my company's products to a potential client.** It's Romari Industries. Have you heard of them?

W: Yes—their offices are by Elmbrook Bridge, right? (34) **If you get a chance, you should take a walk across there. It has some of the most famous views in the city.**

32-34 對話 英⇄澳

女：早安。(32) **請問您今天要去哪裡？**

男：霍利根廣場，謝謝。還有，能麻煩妳開一下空調嗎？

女：沒問題。那麼，從您的行李箱來看，我猜您是外地人吧，您為何來到馬夫納市呢？

男：(33) **我是來向潛在客戶發表簡報，介紹我們公司的產品**，對方公司名叫「羅馬力工業」，不知道妳有沒有聽說過？

女：有的，他們公司的辦公室在艾姆布魯克橋旁，對嗎？(34) **您要是有機會，不妨到那座橋附近走走，那裡有好幾處本市相當著名的景觀。**

- square (n.) 廣場 suitcase (n.) 手提行李箱 potential (adj.) 潛在的 client (n.) 客戶 across (prep.) 遍及；穿過 view (n.) 景色

32. 全文相關——對話地點

Where most likely are the speakers?
(A) At an airport
(B) At a hotel
(C) On a bus
(D) In a taxi

說話者最有可能身在何處？
(A) 在機場
(B) 在飯店
(C) 在公車上
(D) 在計程車裡

33. 相關細節——男子的行程目的

What is the purpose of the man's trip?
(A) To evaluate a facility
(B) To attend a social event
(C) To receive some training
(D) To promote a business

男子此行的目的為何？
(A) 評估設施
(B) 參加社交活動
(C) 受訓
(D) 推廣業務

- **evaluate (v.)** 評估　**facility (n.)** 設施；場地　**promote (v.)** 宣傳；推廣

34. 相關細節——女子提出的建議

難

What does the woman recommend doing?
(A) Trying a local dish
(B) Visiting a tourist attraction
(C) Storing some baggage temporarily
(D) Taking a certain route to a destination

女子建議做什麼？
(A) 品嚐當地美食
(B) 參觀旅遊景點
(C) 暫時存放行李
(D) 走特定路線到目的地

- **dish (n.)** 菜餚；料理　**tourist attraction** 旅遊景點　**store (v.)** 存放；儲存　**temporarily (adv.)** 暫時地　**route (n.)** 路線　**destination (n.)** 目的地

35-37 Conversation

英⇄加

W: Alex, it's Chinami. I'm calling about my article for the industry journal. (35) **Thanks again for agreeing to check it for errors.**

M: I'm happy to do it. You're sending it over today, right?

W: Well, actually, I wanted to let you know that I wasn't able to finish it on time. (36) **Could I send it to you on Friday instead, and get it back by Wednesday?**

M: Let me check my planner . . . Yeah, that should be OK.

W: Great. I appreciate your flexibility. (37) **Oh, but I'll send you the journal's style manual right now.** It'll give you an idea of their standards.

M: That's a good idea. I'll familiarize myself with it before Friday.

35-37 對話

女： 艾力克斯，我是千奈美。我這次來電是有關我為產業期刊寫的那篇文章。(35) **再次感謝你同意幫忙檢查錯誤。**

男： 我很樂意幫忙。妳今天會把文章寄來，對嗎？

女： 呃，其實我想跟你說，我無法準時完稿，(36) **我可以改成週五寄給你，然後在下週三前收到回覆嗎？**

男： 我看一下我的行事曆……可以，應該沒問題。

女： 太好了，謝謝你給予彈性。(37) **噢，不過我現在就會把期刊的格式手冊寄給你，**讓你了解一下他們的規範標準。

男： 這是個好主意，我會在週五前熟悉一下。

- **journal (n.)** 期刊；雜誌　**appreciate (v.)** 感謝　**flexibility (n.)** 彈性；靈活度　**manual (n.)** 使用手冊；操作指南　**standard (n.)** 標準　**familiarize (v.)** 使熟悉

35. 相關細節——男子同意做的事

難

What has the man agreed to do?
(A) Proofread some writing
(B) Participate in an interview
(C) Analyze an industry
(D) Produce some graphics

男子同意做什麼？
(A) 校對文章
(B) 參加面試
(C) 分析產業
(D) 製作圖表

- **proofread (v.)** 校對　**analyze (v.)** 分析

換句話說 check . . . for errors（檢查錯誤）→ proofread（校對）

36. 全文相關——女子來電的目的

Why is the woman calling?
(A) To determine a fee
(B) To check some statistics
(C) To introduce a journalist
(D) To change a schedule

女子致電的原因為何？
(A) 確定費用
(B) 檢查統計數字
(C) 介紹記者
(D) 變更時程

• determine (v.) 確定　fee (n.) 費用　statistics (n.) 統計資料；統計數字　journalist (n.) 記者

37. 相關細節——男子將於今日收到的東西

What will the man receive today?
(A) An electronic payment
(B) A draft of an article
(C) Some guidelines
(D) Some contact information

男子今天會收到什麼？
(A) 電子支付的款項
(B) 文章的草稿
(C) 一些規範
(D) 聯繫方式

• electronic (adj.) 電子的　draft (n.) 草稿　guideline (n.) 準則

換句話說 manual（手冊）→ guidelines（規範）

38-40 Conversation

M: Uchenna, I just got back from lunch. What's going on? (38) **Why doesn't the print shop have any electricity?**
W: The wind caused a big tree to fall on a transformer on Carlton Street. The power is out across the whole neighborhood.
M: Really? The restaurant I was at didn't seem to have any problems.
W: (39) **They must have a power generator. We should consider getting one too.** They're saying that we might not get electricity until tomorrow afternoon.
M: That's going to put us behind on all of our printing jobs. (40) **We'd better let our customers know.**
W: Shaun is posting on social media right now. We're lucky that he could log into our company account.

38-40 對話　澳⇄英

男： 烏琴娜，我剛吃完午餐回來。(38) **發生了什麼事？影印店怎麼停電了？**
女： 卡爾頓街有棵大樹被風吹倒，砸到變電器了。整個街區都停電了。
男： 真的嗎？我剛去用餐的餐廳好像沒有任何問題。
女： (39) **他們一定設有發電機。我們也應該考慮購置一台。**聽說要到明天下午才會恢復供電。
男： 這會讓店裡所有的影印工作落後，(40) **我們最好要向客戶告知。**
女： 肖恩正在社群媒體上發文。他還能登入公司的帳號，真是不幸中的大幸。

• electricity (n.) 電力　transformer (n.) 變電器；變壓器　power (n.) 電力　power generator 發電機　post (v.) 發布；張貼

38. 全文相關——對話主題

What are the speakers mainly discussing?
(A) A power outage
(B) Some poor weather
(C) An employee absence
(D) Some roadwork

說話者主要討論的是什麼問題？
(A) 停電
(B) 天候不佳
(C) 員工缺勤
(D) 道路工程

• absence (n.) 缺席；缺勤

換句話說 doesn't . . . have any electricity（停電）→ power outage（停電）

39. 相關細節——女子提出的建議

What does the woman suggest doing?
(A) Closing down for the day
(B) Notifying a neighboring business
(C) Teaching a skill to some workers
(D) Buying a special machine

女子建議做什麼？
(A) 今天關店
(B) 通知附近商家
(C) 教導工人技能
(D) 購買特殊機器

- **close down** 關閉商店　**notify (v.)** 通知

40. 掌握說話者的意圖——提及「肖恩正在社群媒體上發文」的意圖 難

What does the woman mean when she says, "Shaun is posting on social media right now"?
(A) Shaun is neglecting his duties.
(B) Shaun is making an announcement.
(C) Shaun is seeking more detailed information.
(D) Shaun is more familiar with a marketing method.

女子說：「肖恩正在社群媒體上發文」，其意思為何？
(A) 肖恩怠乎職守。
(B) 肖恩在製作公告。
(C) 肖恩在找更詳細的資料。
(D) 肖恩更熟悉行銷手法。

- **neglect (v.)** 忽略　**duty (n.)** 職責　**announcement (n.)** 宣布；公告　**detailed (adj.)** 詳細的　**familiar (adj.)** 熟悉的　**method (n.)** 方法

換句話說 let . . . know（向……告知）→ make an announcement（製作公告）

41-43 Conversation

M: Hi, Dora. You handle payroll, right? Well, I was looking at my electronic paycheck this week, and . . . I think I've been overpaid. (41) **It's about a hundred dollars higher than usual.**

W: Ah, you're not the first person who's come by to ask about that! (42) **It's because of a change to the income tax code.** It just came into effect this month. So don't worry— that money belongs to you.

M: That's great news! (43) **I'm saving up for an apartment these days, so that will really help.** Thanks, Dora.

41-43 對話 澳⇄美

男： 嗨，朵拉，妳負責薪資單，對嗎？嗯，我正在看我這週的電子薪資單，然後……我覺得我多領了，**(41) 比平常多出 100 美元左右。**

女： 噢，除了你，很多人都有過來問我！**(42) 原因是因為所得稅法有異動**，從這個月開始生效，所以別擔心——那筆錢是你的。

男： 真是個好消息！**(43) 我這陣子在存錢買公寓，所以真是不無小補。**謝啦，朵拉。

- **payroll (n.)** 工資表　**electronic (adj.)** 電子的　**paycheck (n.)** 薪水；付薪水的支票　**overpay (v.)** 多付(金額)　**income (n.)** 所得；收入　**tax code** 稅法　**come into effect** 開始生效；開始實施　**belong to** 屬於

41. 相關細節——男子提出的問題

What problem does the man mention?
(A) He has not received his paycheck.
(B) His paycheck is not itemized clearly.
(C) His pay amount is different from before.
(D) His pay was issued using an inconvenient method.

男子提到什麼問題？
(A) 他還沒有領到薪水。
(B) 他的薪水沒有條列清楚。
(C) 他的薪水金額與以前不同。
(D) 他的薪水支付方式不便利。

- **itemize (v.)** 詳細列舉　**clearly (adv.)** 清楚地；明確地　**issue (v.)** 核發　**inconvenient (adj.)** 不便利的　**method (n.)** 方法

42. 相關細節——女子提及引發問題的原因 難

According to the woman, what caused the problem?
(A) An address is incorrect.
(B) A tax law has been revised.
(C) A software program is not working properly.
(D) A form was misplaced.

根據女子所言，導致問題的原因為何？
(A) 地址不正確。
(B) 稅法已修正。
(C) 軟體程式運作不正常。
(D) 表格遺失。

- revise (v.) 修改 properly (adv.) 正確地 misplace (v.) 亂放而一時找不到

---

43. 相關細節——男子表示近期在做的事情

What does the man say he is currently doing?
(A) Setting aside some money
(B) Taking overtime shifts
(C) Applying for a departmental transfer
(D) Renting an apartment

男子說他目前在做什麼？
(A) 存錢
(B) 加班
(C) 部門請調
(D) 租公寓

- set aside 撥出 shift (n.) 輪班 apply for 申請 departmental (adj.) 部門的 transfer (n.) 調動 rent (v.) 承租

44-46 Conversation with three speakers

M: OK, Edith. What did you want to speak to me about?

W1: My wrist has been sore, and I think it's from using my computer all day. (44) **I'd like to find a way to make it stop hurting.**

M: Well, you can request ergonomic equipment, but it's a lot of paperwork. Actually, Jackie just did it. (45) **You should ask her if she thinks the process was worth it.**

W1: OK. Oh, there she is now. Jackie!

W2: Hi, Edith. What's up?

W1: I heard you got some ergonomic equipment. I'm considering doing the same thing.

W2: That's a great idea. (46) **I got a special computer mouse, and it has helped a lot. I'd be happy to show it to you, if you'd like.**

44-46 三人對話 加⇄美⇄英

男： 嗨，伊迪絲，妳之前要跟我說什麼事？

女1： 我的手腕一直感到痠痛，我想是因為整天用電腦的關係，(44) **我想找個消除痠痛的辦法。**

男： 嗯，妳可以請領符合人體工學的設備，但這要走很多書面程序。其實潔姬剛跑完這項流程，(45) **妳該問問她覺得這個過程值不值得。**

女1： 好的。噢，她人就在那！潔姬！

女2： 嗨，伊迪絲，有什麼事呢？

女1： 我聽說妳請領了符合人體工學的設備，我也正在考慮申請。

女2： 那是個好主意。(46) **我拿到了特製的電腦滑鼠，對我很有幫助，如果妳有興趣，我很樂意拿給妳看看。**

- wrist (n.) 手腕 sore (adj.) 疼痛發炎的 ergonomic (adj.) 符合人體工學的 equipment (n.) 設備 process (n.) 過程；程序 worth (adj.) 值得做的

44. 相關細節——伊迪絲想做的事情 

What does Edith want to do?
(A) Take on more responsibility
(B) Relieve some physical discomfort
(C) Improve a workplace relationship
(D) Increase her efficiency

伊迪絲想要做什麼？
(A) 承擔更多責任
(B) 緩解身體不適
(C) 改善職場人際關係
(D) 提高效率

- take on 承擔 relieve (v.) 緩解 physical (adj.) 身體的 discomfort (n.) 不適；不舒服 efficiency (n.) 效率

換句話說 make . . . stop hurting（消除痠痛）→ relieve some physical discomfort（緩解身體不適）

45. 相關細節——男子建議詢問潔姬的事情

What does the man recommend asking Jackie for?

(A) An opinion

(B) An apology

(C) Some paperwork

(D) Some equipment

男子建議可向潔姬尋求什麼？

(A) 意見

(B) 道歉

(C) 文書作業

(D) 設備

46. 相關細節——潔姬提出的建議

What does Jackie offer to do?

(A) Help with an installation procedure

(B) Look in the company handbook

(C) Show Edith a computer accessory

(D) Connect Edith with another coworker

潔姬提議做什麼？

(A) 協助完成安裝程序

(B) 查閱公司員工手冊

(C) 給伊迪絲看電腦配件

(D) 幫伊迪絲與其他同事接洽

- installation (n.) 安裝　procedure (n.) 程序　handbook (n.) 員工手冊　accessory (n.) 配件　coworker (n.) 同事

換句話說 a computer mouse（電腦滑鼠）→ a computer accessory（電腦配件）

47-49 Conversation

W: (47) **Leroy, I was talking with Ms. Brissette as she checked out a book just now.** Did you know she works at an assisted living facility for elderly people?

M: No, I didn't. But—why do you bring that up?

W: Well, she was saying the residents there sometimes ask her to borrow library books for them. (48) **I was thinking—what if we brought some of our books directly to the facility for the residents' use?**

M: Oh, that's a great idea! And I think we already have the funds for it. (49) **You should write up an official proposal for the director.**

W: (49) **OK, I will.** Thanks for the encouragement.

47-49 對話　美⇄加

女：(47) **里羅伊，布里塞特小姐剛才借書的時候，我和她聊了一下，**你知道她在一家老人安養中心工作嗎？

男：不，我不知道。不過—妳怎麼會提到這件事？

女：是這樣的，她說養老院的住戶有時候會請她幫忙來圖書館借書，(48) **我在思考—不如我們乾脆直接把部分書籍，送到安養中心給居民借閱？**

男：哦，好主意！而且我想我們已經有經費了，(49) **妳應該寫份正式的提案給主管。**

女：(49) **好，我會的，**謝謝你的鼓勵。

- check out 借（書）　assisted living facility 養護機構　elderly people 年長者　bring up 提起；談到　resident (n.) 居民；住戶　directly (adv.) 直接地　official (adj.) 正式的　proposal (n.) 提案　director (n.) 主管；主任　encouragement (n.) 鼓勵

47. 相關細節——女子提及她剛做的事情　難

What does the woman say she just did?

(A) Spoken with a patron

(B) Read a publication

(C) Attended a lecture

(D) Posted a notice

女子說她剛做了什麼？

(A) 跟讀者說話

(B) 閱讀刊物

(C) 參加講座

(D) 張貼公告

- patron (n.) 主顧；常客　publication (n.) 出版物；刊物　lecture (n.) 演講　post (v.) 張貼；發布　notice (n.) 公告；通知

48. 相關細節——女子建議提供的事物 難

What does the woman suggest offering?
(A) Private meeting facilities
(B) Classes on library resources
(C) A mobile library service
(D) A longer borrowing period

女子建議主動提供什麼？
(A) 私人聚會設施
(B) 圖書館資源課程
(C) 行動圖書館服務
(D) 借閱期延長

- **period (n.)** 期間 **private (adj.)** 私人的；不公開的 **resource (n.)** 資源 **mobile (adj.)** 行動的

49. 相關細節——女子同意做的事情

What does the woman agree to do?
(A) Clean out a space
(B) Create a document
(C) Gather some colleagues
(D) Review a budget

女子同意做什麼？
(A) 打掃某地
(B) 撰寫文件
(C) 召集同事
(D) 審查預算

- **gather (v.)** 召集 **colleague (n.)** 同事 **budget (n.)** 預算

換句話說 write up an proposal（寫份提案）→ create a document（撰寫文件）

50-52 Conversation with three speakers

M1: Hi, this is Dan Swanson. (50) **You called about my car?**

W: Ah, Mr. Swanson. Uh, unfortunately, (50) **it seems the estimate we gave you for the repair work was incorrect** . . . It's going to be more like fifteen hundred dollars.

M1: (51) **Wow, that's a lot more than you quoted me at first . . .**

W: Yes, sorry about that. Would you like to speak with Pete, the mechanic handling your vehicle? He's right here.

M1: That would be nice.

M2: Hi Mr. Swanson. (52) **We thought the problem was your fuel filter, but it turns out it's the catalytic converter.** That's a much more expensive part to replace, but it has to be done.

M1: I see. Well, OK then.

50-52 三人對話 加⇄美⇄澳

男 1： 嗨，我是丹・史瓦森。(50) **妳之前來電是想討論我車輛的事宜嗎？**

女： 噢，史瓦森先生。呃，很抱歉，(50) **我們之前給您估算的維修費好像並不正確**……似乎會是約莫一千五百美元才對。

男 1： (51) **哇，這比你們一開始開給我的報價高出很多……**

女： 是的，真的很抱歉。您想跟皮特談談嗎？他是負責維修您車子的技師，現在人就在這裡。

男 1： 好的。

男 2： 史瓦森先生您好，(52) **我們剛開始以為問題出在燃油濾清器上，但結果發現是觸媒轉化器的問題**，更換這個零件的價格貴出很多，可是不得不更換。

男 1： 知道了，那麼沒有問題。

- **unfortunately (adv.)** 不幸地；遺憾地 **estimate (n.)** 估價（單） **incorrect (adj.)** 不正確 **quote (v.)** 報價 **mechanic (n.)** 技師 **vehicle (n.)** 車輛 **fuel (n.)** 燃油 **turn out** 結果發現；證明為 **catalytic converter** 觸媒轉化器（防空污的裝置）

50. 全文相關——對話主題

What is the main topic of the conversation?
(A) A shipping service
(B) A building process
(C) A rental contract
(D) A vehicle repair

這段對話所討論的主題為何？
(A) 運輸服務
(B) 建設過程
(C) 租賃契約
(D) 車輛維修

- shipping (n.) 運輸　process (n.) 過程　rental (adj.) 租賃的　contract (n.) 合約　vehicle (n.) 車輛

51. 相關細節——史瓦森先生感到驚訝的理由

Why is Mr. Swanson surprised?
(A) A request has been denied.
(B) A cost estimate has risen.
(C) A task has not been completed.
(D) A project manager has been replaced.

史瓦森先生為什麼感到驚訝？
(A) 要求遭到駁回。
(B) 估價費用增加。
(C) 工作尚未完成。
(D) 專案經理遭撤換。

- deny (v.) 拒絕；否定　task (n.) 工作

52. 相關細節——皮特解釋的內容

難

What does Pete explain?
(A) The reason for a change
(B) The steps of a procedure
(C) The features of some software
(D) The options of a choice

皮特說明了什麼？
(A) 變動的理由
(B) 流程的步驟
(C) 軟體的特色
(D) 可選擇的項目

- step (n.) 步驟　procedure (n.) 過程　feature (n.) 特色　option (n.) 選擇

53-55 Conversation

美⇄加

W: Fabian, I just saw the picture you posted of the amazing French fish dish you made. It looked delicious!

M: Oh thanks, Sherry. (53) **Now that I have more free time, I've gotten interested in making my own meals.**

W: That's great.

M: Yes, I'm enjoying it. (54) **This weekend, I'm actually going to the Garrisville Farmers Market to pick up some ingredients for a special dish.**

W: How fun! (55) **Speaking of Garrisville, did you hear that Taylor Kirby is coming there to put on a live cooking exhibition?** He's going to show how to make some of his famous recipes.

M: The chef who won that TV competition? Wow! I'd love to go to that.

53-55 對話

女： 法比安，我剛看到你發布的照片了，你做了美味的法式魚料理，看起來好好吃！

男： 噢，謝謝，雪莉，(53) **因為我現在比較有空，所以就有興致自己做飯。**

女： 那很不錯呢。

男： 是啊，我樂在其中。(54) **其實，我這個週末要到加里斯維爾農民市場去購買食材，製作一道特殊料理。**

女： 真是有趣！(55) **說到加里斯維爾，你有聽說泰勒．柯比要去那裡舉辦現場廚藝秀嗎？**他會示範做幾道他聞名遐邇的招牌料理。

男： 就是電視烹飪大賽中奪冠的那位主廚？哇！我很想去看看。

- post (v.) 發布；張貼　delicious (adj.) 美味的　ingredient (n.) 食材　speaking of 說到
  live (adj.) 現場的　exhibition (n.) 展示　recipe (n.) 食譜；烹飪法

53. 相關細節——男子感興趣的事情

What has the man become interested in?
(A) Fishing
(B) Cooking
(C) Playing an instrument
(D) Learning a new language

男子對什麼產生興趣？
(A) 釣魚
(B) 烹飪
(C) 演奏樂器
(D) 學習新的語言

換句話說 **making my own meals**（自己做飯）→ **cooking**（烹飪）

---

54. 相關細節——男子週末的計畫

What is the man planning to do this weekend?
(A) Purchase some supplies
(B) Join a hobby club
(C) Go on a group trip
(D) Stream some videos

男子這個週末打算做什麼？
(A) 購買用品
(B) 參加同好會
(C) 跟團旅行
(D) 串流播放影片

- **purchase (v.)** 購買 **supplies (n.)**（複數）用品 **hobby (n.)** 嗜好 **stream (v.)** 在網路上收聽／看

換句話說 **pick up some ingredients**（購買食材）→ **purchase some supplies**（購買用品）

---

55. 相關細節——女子提及的活動

What kind of event does the woman mention?
(A) A dinner party
(B) A television show shoot
(C) A skills demonstration
(D) A competition

女子提到什麼樣的活動？
(A) 晚宴
(B) 電視節目拍攝
(C) 技藝展示
(D) 競賽

- **shoot (n.)** 拍攝 **demonstration (n.)** 示範 **competition (n.)** 競賽

56-58 Conversation

W: (56) **Hawkins Technical Academy, Kelsie speaking.**
M: Hello. I'm looking to get into the computer science field, and I thought I'd start by taking classes at your school.
W: Sure, our academy has helped many people become qualified for jobs in computing.
M: Right. Uh, I just have a question about some information that's not on your Web site. (57) **How many students are there in your weekend classes, usually?**
W: The limit is thirty, but there are typically around twenty.
M: Great. (58) **Then I'd like to sign up for the information security class starting next month.**
W: Hmm. (58) **Given your likely knowledge level,** information security would be a difficult area. (58) **May I suggest some alternatives?**

56-58 對話 英⇄澳

女： (56) **您好，這裡是霍金斯技術學堂，我叫凱爾西。**
男： 您好，我希望踏入電腦科學領域，認為可在貴學校修課，作為入門磚。
女： 沒有問題，本校已經幫助許多人取得電腦方面的工作資格。
男： 好的。呃，我有個問題，在你們網站上找不到資訊，想在此請教：(57) **請問你們週末的課堂通常有多少位學生？**
女： 人數限制是 30 人，但是通常是 20 人左右。
男： 那太好了。(58) **那麼，我想要報名下個月開課的資訊安全課程。**
女： 唔，(58) **考量到您目前可能的知識程度，**資訊安全領域會很吃力，(58) **能否容我向您推薦其他課程呢？**

- field (n.) 領域 academy (n.) 專科學院 qualified (adj.) 有資格的 computing (n.) 電腦學 limit (n.) 限制 typically (adv.) 通常；一般地 sign up for 報名；註冊 security (n.) 安全 given (prep.) 考慮到 alternative (n.) 替代方案

56. 全文相關——女子工作的地點

What kind of business does the woman work for?
(A) An information technology consulting firm
(B) An employment agency
(C) A research laboratory
(D) An educational institute

女子在何種業者工作？
(A) 資訊科技顧問公司
(B) 人力仲介
(C) 研究實驗室
(D) 教育機構

- employment (n.) 就業；工作 research (n.) 研究 laboratory (n.) 實驗室 educational (adj.) 教育的 institute (n.) 機構

換句話說 academy（學堂）→ educational institute（教育機構）

57. 相關細節——男子詢問的事項

What does the man ask about?
(A) A number of people
(B) A source of funding
(C) A required qualification
(D) A usual start time

男子詢問什麼方面的問題？
(A) 人數
(B) 資金來源
(C) 必備資格條件
(D) 通常的開始時間

- source (n.) 來源 funding (n.) 資金 required (adj.) 必備的；所需的 qualification (n.) 資格；條件

58. 掌握說話者的意圖——提及「資訊安全領域會很吃力」的意圖 難

Why does the woman say, "information security would be a difficult area"?
(A) To indicate that she is impressed
(B) To recommend an additional service
(C) To justify a heavy workload
(D) To give the man a warning

女子為何要說：「資訊安全領域會很吃力」？
(A) 以表示她印象很深刻
(B) 以推薦額外的服務
(C) 以為繁重的工作量找理由
(D) 以提醒男子

- indicate (v.) 表示 impressed (adj.) 印象深刻的 additional (adj.) 額外的 justify (v.) 證明……正當（有理） workload (n.) 工作量

59-61 Conversation

M: Ms. Kang, welcome to our store. Have a seat.

W: Thank you, Mr. Redford. (59) **So, you said that you became interested in distributing my company's products after you saw our advertisement in the latest issue of *Hardware Retailers Monthly*.**

M: That's right. I don't know if you noticed, (60) **but we're renovating and expanding the southwest corner of the store.** I thought that stocking your home safe boxes could be a great use of some of that new space.

59-61 對話 加⇄英

男： 康小姐，歡迎蒞臨本店，請坐。

女： 謝謝您，瑞德福先生。(59) **聽您說，您在最新一期的《五金零售商月刊》上看到我們刊登的廣告後，便有興趣經銷本公司的產品。**

男： 是的，不知道您是否有注意到，(60) **但我們正在整修及擴建賣場的西南角，**我認為在那裡擺放向貴公司進貨的家用保險箱，能善用那個新空間的一部分。

W: Excellent. I think our products would sell very well here. (61) **What are your expectations for the distribution contract? It's helpful to make sure we have similar ideas about the major points before going forward.**	**女：** 好極了，我想本公司的產品會在貴店大賣，(61) **不知您對經銷合約有什麼期望？若我們能對重點有所共識，會很有助我們接著做後續的討論。**
M: OK. Where would you like to start?	**男：** 好的，您希望從什麼事項開始談？

- **distribute (v.)** 經銷（產品） **advertisement (n.)** 廣告 **latest (adj.)** 最新的 **notice (v.)** 注意到 **renovate (v.)** 整修；翻修 **expand (v.)** 擴增；擴大 **stock (v.)** 進貨 **expectation (n.)** 期望 **go forward** 繼續；進展

59. 相關細節——男子得知女子公司的途徑

How did the man learn about the woman's business?

(A) From an industry magazine

(B) From an outdoor advertisement

(C) From a local newspaper

(D) From a Web site

男子如何得知女子公司？

(A) 從產業雜誌上

(B) 從戶外廣告上

(C) 從當地報紙上

(D) 從網站上

- **industry (n.)** 產業 **outdoor (adj.)** 戶外的

60. 相關細節——男子針對商店提及的內容

What does the man say about his store?

(A) Some of its merchandise is out of stock.

(B) It does not have many customers.

(C) Part of it is being remodeled.

(D) A parking area is being added.

對於他的商店，男子提到了什麼事？

(A) 有些商品缺貨。

(B) 顧客不多。

(C) 局部區域正在整修。

(D) 正在新增停車區。

- **merchandise (n.)** 商品 **out of stock** 缺貨 **remodel (v.)** 改造；整修

換句話說 **renovating and expanding the southwest corner of the store**（在西南角進行整修及擴建）
→ **part of it is being remodeled**（局部區域正在整修）

61. 相關細節——女子建議優先做的事 難

What does the woman propose doing first?

(A) Inspecting a manufacturing plant

(B) Discussing the terms of an agreement

(C) Distributing some product samples

(D) Reviewing some sales figures

女子提議先做什麼事？

(A) 視察製造工廠

(B) 討論合約條款

(C) 分銷產品樣品

(D) 審查銷售數據

- **inspect (v.)** 視察 **manufacturing plant** 製造廠 **terms (n.)**（合約）條款 **figure (n.)** 數字

62-64 Conversation + Directory

62-64 對話＋樓層指南 美⇄加

W: Oh, look at those stylish watches. That reminds me—I need to get a graduation gift for one of my relatives. (62) **Would you mind if we looked at the bracelets for a moment?**	**女：** 噢，你看，那些手錶真是時尚有型。這倒提醒了我——我需要買送給一個親戚的畢業禮物，(62) **我們可以來看一下手鐲嗎？**
M: Oh, no problem. How about this gold one with green stones?	**男：** 哦，沒問題。這只鑲綠寶石的金手鐲怎麼樣？

W: Wow, it's beautiful. (63) **But look at the price! I don't want to get something so valuable that my relative never wears it because she's afraid of damaging it.**

M: Good point. (64) **Well, why don't you try looking for a cheaper price for it on the Internet?** I'm sure there are sites that have discounts.

W: You're probably right. But I'd like to walk around here a little more first.

Directory

Floor	Products
(62) **1**	**Cosmetics & Jewelry**
2	Women's Clothing
3	Men's Clothing
4	Home Goods

女： 哇，好漂亮。(63) **可是，看看這個價格！我可不想買個太貴重的東西，結果我親戚因為怕弄壞而不敢戴。**

男： 有道理。(64) **那妳要不要上網，看看這只手鐲有沒有人提供較便宜的價格？**肯定會有網站給予折扣。

女： 你說的可能沒錯，但是我還想先在這裡多逛一下。

樓層指南

樓層	產品
(62) **1**	**化妝品與珠寶**
2	女性服飾
3	男性服飾
4	家居用品

- graduation (n.) 畢業　relative (n.) 親戚　bracelet (n.) 手鐲　valuable (adj.) 寶貴的　damage (v.) 損毀

62. 圖表整合題——說話者所在的樓層

Look at the graphic. Which floor are the speakers on?

(A) The first floor

(B) The second floor

(C) The third floor

(D) The fourth floor

請看圖表作答。說話者在哪一層樓？

(A) 1 樓

(B) 2 樓

(C) 3 樓

(D) 4 樓

63. 相關細節——女子不確定是否要購買該項商品的原因 難

Why is the woman uncertain about buying an item?

(A) It may be the wrong size.

(B) It would be easy to damage.

(C) It has an unusual design.

(D) It is expensive.

女子為什麼不確定是否要購買商品？

(A) 尺寸可能不合。

(B) 容易損壞。

(C) 設計獨特。

(D) 價格昂貴。

- unusual (adj.) 獨特的；不同尋常的

64. 相關細節——男子提出的建議

What does the man suggest doing?

(A) Trying on an item

(B) Paying in installments

(C) Going to online stores

(D) Looking for a salesperson

男子建議做什麼？

(A) 試戴產品

(B) 分期付款

(C) 前往網路商店

(D) 找銷售員

- try on 試戴（穿）　in installments 分期付款　salesperson (n.) 銷售員

換句話說 try looking for . . . on the Internet（上網看看……）→ going to online stores（前往網路商店）

65-67 Conversation + Reference list

M: Hello, Ms. Bajwa. This is Craig Anderson from Rylon Group. We spoke earlier about Fiona Morris's candidacy for a job at my company.

W: Oh, hello again. (65) **Do you need more information about Fiona's performance when she worked in my department?**

M: No, but it's a related issue. (66) **Ms. Morris has also suggested we speak to Frank Oliver, a manager at your company. But I can't get through to the number she gave us.** Do you know why that might be?

W: (67) **Oh, it's because Frank left the company a few weeks ago.** Fiona must not have heard. Let me see if I have his new contact information.

References

Timothy Ward *(Manager at Siangal)*	555-0145
Maureen Jacobs *(Supervisor at Zubina Consultants)*	555-0182
Anita Bajwa *(Director at Soares Engineering)*	555-0176
(66) **Frank Oliver** *(Manager at Soares Engineering)*	555-0109

65-67 對話＋推薦人名單 澳⇄美

男： 巴札爾小姐您好，我是萊隆集團的克雷格・安德森。我們稍早有通過電話，談過菲歐娜・莫里斯應徵我們公司職缺的事。

女： 噢我記得，您好。(65) **您需要進一步了解菲歐娜在我部門的工作表現嗎？**

男： 不是的，不過也有關聯。(66) **莫里斯小姐也曾建議我們，來跟貴公司的經理法蘭克・奧利佛聯繫，她給了我們他的電話號碼，可是電話卻打不通**，您知道可能是什麼原因嗎？

女： (67) **噢，那是因為法蘭克數週前離職了**，菲歐娜肯定是不知道這項消息。我看看有沒有他新的聯繫方式。

推薦人

提摩西・沃德 （斯朗格爾公司經理）	555-0145
茉琳・雅各布斯 （朱比納顧問公司主管）	555-0182
安妮塔・巴札爾 （蘇亞雷斯工程公司總監）	555-0176
(66) **法蘭克・奧利佛** （蘇亞雷斯工程公司經理）	555-0109

- **candidacy (n.)** 候選人資格（或身分） **performance (n.)** 績效；表現 **related (adj.)** 相關的 **get through to** 打通電話；接通

65. 全文相關——女子的職業

Who most likely is the woman?

(A) A job applicant

(B) A hiring manager

(C) A department head

(D) A corporate recruiter

女子最有可能是什麼人？

(A) 求職者

(B) 招募經理

(C) 部門主管

(D) 公司的招聘人員

- **applicant (n.)** 求職者 **head (n.)** 領導人；負責人 **corporate (adj.)** 公司的；企業的 **recruiter (n.)** 招聘人員

66. 圖表整合題——有問題的電話號碼

Look at the graphic. Which phone number is the man having trouble with?

(A) 555-0145

(B) 555-0182

(C) 555-0176

(D) 555-0109

請看圖表作答。下列何者是男子打不通的電話號碼？

(A) 555-0145

(B) 555-0182

(C) 555-0176

(D) 555-0109

67. 相關細節——女子提及造成問題的理由

What does the woman say caused a problem?
(A) A technological issue
(B) A typing error
(C) A company policy
(D) A personnel change

女子提到問題的成因為何？
(A) 技術問題
(B) 打字錯誤
(C) 公司政策
(D) 人事變動

• technological (adj.) 技術的　type (v.) 打字　error (n.) 錯誤　personnel (n.) 人員；員工

68-70 Conversation + Order form

W: Hi. This is Kate at Coomer Software. **(68) We ordered lunch from your deli this morning for a sales client who dropped by unexpectedly.** It just arrived, right on time, but now that we've opened up the bags, it seems there's a problem.

M: OK, I've found your order form in our records. What's the problem?

W: **(69) We only got three of each type of sandwich.** As you can tell, that means we're missing one.

M: Yes, I see. Well, I'm pretty sure that we made all seven sandwiches. **(70) Let me call the employee who dropped off your order, and see what he says.**

Crabtree Deli
Order Form

Item	Quantity
Ham sandwich	3
(69) Tuna sandwich	4
Potato salad (container)	1
House salad	2

68-70 對話＋訂單

英⇄澳

女： 你好，我是庫莫軟體公司的凱特。**(68) 今天早上我們向你們熟食店訂了午餐，給突然來訪的業務客戶**，餐點剛才準時送到，可是現在我們把袋子打開了，發現似乎有個問題。

男： 好的，我在紀錄中找到了您的訂單，請問有什麼問題？

女： **(69) 我們每種三明治只拿到了三個**，如你所知，這表示還少了一個。

男： 好的，我明白了。嗯，我很確定我們七份三明治都有做，**(70) 我打電話問一下給您送餐的同仁，看看他怎麼說。**

蟹樹熟食店
訂單

品名	數量
火腿三明治	3
(69) 鮪魚三明治	**4**
馬鈴薯沙拉（盒裝）	1
招牌沙拉	2

68. 相關細節——女子公司發生的事

What is taking place at the woman's company?
(A) A board meeting
(B) A client visit
(C) A sales workshop
(D) An orientation session

女子的公司裡正發生什麼事？
(A) 董事會會議
(B) 客戶造訪
(C) 銷售研習會
(D) 新人培訓會

• board (n.) 董事會　orientation (n.) 員工新訓　session (n.)（某項活動的）一段時間

換句話說 drop by（來訪）→ visit（造訪）

69. 圖表整合題——女子未收到的餐點

Look at the graphic. What is the woman missing?
(A) A ham sandwich
(B) A tuna sandwich
(C) A container of potato salad
(D) A house salad

請看圖表作答。女子少拿到什麼？
(A) 一個火腿三明治
(B) 一個鮪魚三明治
(C) 一盒馬鈴薯沙拉
(D) 一份招牌沙拉

70. 相關細節——男子表示他接下來要做的事

What does the man say he will do next?
(A) Send a scanned copy of a form
(B) Refund the cost of the order
(C) Contact a delivery person
(D) Make some more food

男子說他接下來會做什麼？
(A) 傳送掃描後的表格
(B) 退還訂單金額
(C) 聯繫外送員
(D) 多做一些餐點

- form (n.) 表格　refund (v.) 退款

換句話說 call the employee who dropped off your order（打電話問一下給您送餐的同仁）
→ contact a delivery person（聯繫外送員）

PART 4 P. 29–31

08

71-73 Excerpt from a meeting

All right, everyone, I have some big news. (71) **We just signed the lease agreement for a new place of business—a whole floor of the Ashbrook Building in the Valtside neighborhood—and we'll be moving in in spring.** Now, I know that might feel like a big change, but Valtside is still within the city. (72) **And several bus and subway lines run through it, so it's actually easier to reach than our current area.** But best of all, we'll have more space in the Ashbrook Building than we do here. (73) **Let me put the layout up on the screen.** See? Our organization will finally get a real break room.

71-73 會議摘錄

英

好了，各位，我有個大消息。(71) **我們剛簽下新營業處的租約，就在沃特塞德街區的梣樹溪辦公大樓，有一整層樓的空間，而且明年春天就會搬進去。**現在，我知道這感覺變化很大，但是沃特塞德還是在市區裡，(72) **且還有好幾條公車跟地鐵路線經過，所以那個地方其實比我們現在的位置交通更便利。**不過最大的優點是，梣樹溪辦公大樓那邊的空間，比我們目前的地點還要大。(73) **我把空間配置圖放到螢幕上給大家看。**看到了嗎？我們機構終於會有真正的員工休息室了。

- lease (n.) 租約　agreement (n.) 協議；契約　neighborhood (n.) 街區；鄰近　layout (n.) 布局　organization (n.) 組織；機構　break room 休息室

71. 全文相關——會議的目的

What is the purpose of the meeting?
(A) To describe a tourism campaign
(B) To announce an office relocation
(C) To report on a construction process
(D) To recommend a company outing

這場會議的目的為何？
(A) 說明旅遊活動
(B) 宣布辦公室搬遷
(C) 報告施工過程
(D) 推薦公司出遊

- describe (v.) 描述　relocation (n.) 搬遷　report (v.) 報告　process (n.) 過程　recommend (v.) 推薦　outing (n.)（集體）出遊

72. 相關細節——說話者針對沃特塞德提及的內容 難

What does the speaker say about Valtside?
(A) It hosts an annual festival.
(B) It is beautiful in spring.
(C) It is the oldest part of the city.
(D) It is accessible by public transportation.

有關沃特塞德，說話者說了什麼？
(A) 每年都會舉辦慶典。
(B) 春天時景色優美。
(C) 是本市最老舊的一區。
(D) 可搭乘公共運輸到達。

- host (v.) 舉辦　annual (adj.) 年度的　accessible (adj.) 可到達的　public (adj.) 公共的；公眾的　transportation (n.) 運輸；交通工具

換句話說 several bus and subway lines run through it（好幾條公車跟地鐵路線經過）
→ it is accessible by public transportation（可搭乘公共運輸到達）

73. 相關細節——說話者給聽者看的東西

What does the speaker show the listeners?
(A) A neighborhood map
(B) A train schedule
(C) A floor plan
(D) An organization chart

說話者向聽者展示了什麼？
(A) 社區地圖
(B) 火車時刻表
(C) 樓層平面圖
(D) 組織結構圖

換句話說 layout（空間配置圖）→ floor plan（樓層平面圖）

74-76 Advertisement

Do you find that all you can do after a long day on your feet is sit on the sofa? (74) **Then Carnahan shoes were made for you.** They're specially designed to be both stylish and comfortable. (75) **Our researchers developed a new manufacturing method to create durable soles that provide amazing cushioning and support.** With Carnahan shoes, you'll be able to walk all day and still enjoy your evening. (76) **And on December fourth and fifth, we'll be celebrating the one-year anniversary of the launch of Carnahan Shoes with a special sales event.** Visit one of our stores for huge discounts on select products. Carnahan Shoes—live comfortably.

74-76 廣告 加

您是否感覺在站了一整天後，只能癱坐在沙發上呢？(74) **那麼，卡納漢鞋就是專為您量身訂做的。**卡納漢鞋經過特殊設計，既時尚又舒適，(75) **我們的研究員開發出新製程，生產出耐用的鞋底，可提供神奇的避震效果和支撐感。**有了卡納漢鞋，就算走了一整天，晚上依然輕鬆舒適，(76) **而且在 12 月 4 日、5 日這兩天，我們將舉辦特賣活動，歡慶卡納漢鞋上市一週年。**蒞臨門市即可享有精選鞋款的高額折扣。卡納漢鞋——就是要你活得舒適。

- on one's feet 站立著　researcher (n.) 研究員　manufacture (v.) 製造　durable (adj.) 經久耐用的　sole (n.) 鞋底　cushioning (n.) 緩衝　support (n.) 支撐　anniversary (n.) 週年　launch (n.) 上市；推出　select (adj.) 精選的

74. 全文相關——廣告的產品

What type of product is being advertised?
(A) Furniture
(B) Electronics
(C) Luggage
(D) Footwear

廣告推銷的是何種產品？
(A) 家具
(B) 電子產品
(C) 行李箱
(D) 鞋類

換句話說 shoes（鞋）→ footwear（鞋類）

75. 相關細節——說話者提及公司完成的事情

難

According to the speaker, what has the company done?

(A) Invented a production technique

(B) Conducted market research

(C) Begun exporting to other countries

(D) Collaborated with a famous designer

根據說話者所言，該公司完成了何事？

(A) 開創生產技術

(B) 進行市場調查

(C) 開始出口到海外

(D) 與著名設計師合作

- **invent (v.)** 發明 **technique (n.)** 技術；技法 **conduct (v.)** 實施；執行 **research (n.)** 研究；調查 **export (v.)** 出口 **collaborate (v.)** 合作

換句話說 **developed a new manufacturing method**（開發出新製程）
→ **invented a production technique**（開創生產技術）

---

76. 相關細節——將於 12 月 4 日發生的事情

What will happen on December 4 ?

(A) A new store branch will open.

(B) A sales promotion will begin.

(C) New products will be launched.

(D) The winner of a contest will be chosen.

12 月 4 日這天會發生什麼事？

(A) 新分店將開張。

(B) 促銷活動將開始。

(C) 新產品將上市。

(D) 將選出比賽優勝者。

- **branch (n.)** 分店 **promotion (n.)** 促銷活動

77-79 Telephone message

Hi Mr. Cha. (77) **This is Jody at Melting Moon Grill calling about your upcoming party for your colleague's promotion.** (78) **Our host said you left a message to ask if it would be all right to change your reservation from ten to fifteen people. That will be just fine.** We'll still be able to provide our special chocolate cake for everyone. (79) **Oh, and when we spoke before, you mentioned that your colleague likes live music, right?** Well, we just booked a band for that night. You can see information about them on our Web site. OK, call me back if you have any other questions or concerns.

77-79 電話留言

美

查先生您好，(77) **我是熔月燒烤店的裘蒂，來電是想討論您即將為升遷同事舉辦派對的事宜。**(78) **本店領檯人員說您有留言，問能不能將預約人數從 10 人更改為 15 人，這部分沒問題，**我們還是能為每位貴賓提供特製巧克力蛋糕。(79) **啊，我們之前洽談的時候，您提到您的同事喜歡現場音樂演奏，對嗎？**這部分，我們剛才為當晚預訂了樂隊，您可到我們的網站上查看樂隊資訊。好的，如果您有任何其他問題或疑慮，再請回電。

- **upcoming (adj.)** 即將到來的 **colleague (n.)** 同事 **promotion (n.)** 升遷 **host (n.)**（負責帶位的）領檯人員 **reservation (n.)** 預約

77. 相關細節——聽者舉辦派對慶祝的事情

What will the listener hold a party to celebrate?

(A) A marriage anniversary

(B) A retirement

(C) A promotion

(D) A birthday

聽者將舉辦派對，是為了慶祝何事？

(A) 結婚週年紀念

(B) 退休

(C) 升遷

(D) 生日

78. 相關細節——說話者確認的變更事項

What does the speaker confirm a change to?
(A) The menu for a celebration
(B) The theme of some decorations
(C) The time of a reservation
(D) The size of a group

說話者確認何項異動？
(A) 慶祝活動的菜單
(B) 裝飾的主題
(C) 預約的時間
(D) 團體的人數

- celebration (n.) 慶祝活動　theme (n.) 主題　decoration (n.)（室內）裝飾

79. 掌握說話者的意圖——提及「我們剛才為當晚預訂了樂隊」的意圖　難

What does the speaker imply when she says, "we just booked a band for that night"?
(A) A preference has been accommodated.
(B) An additional charge will be imposed.
(C) A seating arrangement must be modified.
(D) Some noise at a venue is inevitable.

說話者說：「我們剛才為當晚預訂了樂隊」，其言下之意為何？
(A) 一項偏好獲得配合。
(B) 將會加收費用。
(C) 必須修改座位安排。
(D) 場地噪音無法避免。

- preference (n.) 偏好　accommodate (v.) 考慮到；照顧到　impose (v.) 強行施加　modify (v.) 修改　venue (n.) 場地　inevitable (adj.) 不可避免的

80-82 Broadcast

UFM Radio fans, we need your help! This month, we are carrying out a survey of our regular listeners to find out who you are and what you're interested in. (80) **The information you provide will enable us to draw in the brand-name advertisers we need to continue broadcasting all of your favorite UFM shows.** (81) **To participate, either go to www.ufmradio.com/survey, or text "Survey" to 555-0182 to receive a text-message version.** That's www.ufmradio.com/survey or texting "Survey" to 555-0182. (82) **Everyone who fills out the entire survey will be entered into a drawing for a chance to visit our station and meet our DJs.** You might even see a famous musician while you're here! Do the survey today to secure your chance to win.

80-82 廣播　澳

UFM 廣播電台的粉絲們，我們需要大家幫忙！這個月，我們將對經常收聽本電台的聽眾進行問卷調查，來了解各位是什麼人、以及對什麼感興趣。(80) **您提供的資訊，將能讓我們招攬本台所需的各大品牌廣告商，以便能夠繼續播放各項您最喜愛的 UFM 節目。**(81) **若有意參與調查，請至官網 www.ufmradio.com/survey，或者以簡訊輸入「調查」兩字並發送到 555-0182 以獲取簡訊版問卷。** 請記好，網址為 www.ufmradio.com/survey，或輸入「調查」傳簡訊到 555-0182。(82) **完整填寫者將可參加抽獎，中籤者可獲得參觀本電台並與本台 DJ 見面的機會。** 您甚至有可能在參觀時，見到某位知名的音樂家哦！現在就來做調查，獲得中獎機會吧。

- carry out 實施；執行　survey (n.) 問卷調查　enable (v.) 使能夠；使成為可能　draw (v.) 吸引　advertiser (n.) 廣告客戶　fill out 填寫　entire (adj.) 整個的　drawing (n.) 抽籤　secure (v.) 獲得

80. 相關細節——問卷調查結果的用途

What will the survey results be used for?
(A) Making an expansion decision
(B) Developing new programs
(C) Attracting advertisers
(D) Planning in-person events

問卷調查的結果將用於何處？
(A) 制定擴張決定
(B) 開發新節目
(C) 吸引廣告客戶
(D) 規劃現場活動

- expansion (n.) 擴張　decision (n.) 決定　in-person (adj.) 親臨的；親身的

換句話說 draw in . . . advertisers（招攬……廣告商）→ attract advertisers（吸引廣告商）

81. 相關細節——說話者針對問卷調查提及的內容 難

What does the speaker say about the survey?
(A) It is targeted toward listeners of a certain age.
(B) It only has multiple choice questions.
(C) There are two ways to access it.
(D) The station has conducted it before.

關於問卷調查，說話者說了什麼？
(A) 以特定年齡層的聽眾為目標對象。
(B) 只有選擇題。
(C) 有兩種方式可參與調查。
(D) 該電台以前曾做過。

- **target (v.)** 以……為目標 **certain (adj.)** 特定的 **multiple (adj.)** 多個的；多種的 **access (v.)** 使用 **conduct (v.)** 實施

82. 相關細節——問卷調查參與者有機會贏得的東西

What will survey participants have the chance to win?
(A) A cash prize
(B) Concert tickets
(C) Branded merchandise
(D) A station tour

參與問卷調查的人，將有機會贏得什麼？
(A) 現金獎金
(B) 音樂會門票
(C) 名牌商品
(D) 廣播電台參訪

- **cash prize** 現金獎勵 **branded (adj.)** 名牌的 **merchandise (n.)** 商品

83-85 Excerpt from a workshop

Welcome to today's workshop. (83) **As you know, I've been invited to your offices to discuss ethical issues that you might encounter in your role as city employees.** We'll talk about types of issues, relevant laws and regulations, and possible resolutions. (84) **Now, some of you might be thinking, "I'm just an entry-level employee—am I really likely to face an ethical issue?"** Well, you'd be surprised. So I hope that you'll all take this workshop seriously and participate wholeheartedly. (85) **OK, I'd like to start by sharing with you a real experience that happened to a participant in a workshop I gave last year.**

83-85 研習會節錄 英

歡迎蒞臨今天的研習。(83) **如各位所知，我經常受到貴機關邀請，來討論身為市府官員的大家，可能面臨的道德問題。**我們將要談到問題的類型、相關法律與規章，以及可能的解決辦法。(84) **現在，在座有些人可能會想：「我只是基層職員，真的有可能面臨到道德問題嗎？」**嗯，你們會大吃一驚的。所以，我希望你們都能認真看待這次的研習，用心參與。(85) **好，那我首先就跟大家分享一個真實案例，這是我去年主持的研習中，有一個學員遭遇的真實案例。**

- **ethical (adj.)** 道德的；倫理的 **encounter (v.)** 遇到 **relevant (adj.)** 相關的 **regulation (n.)** 規範 **resolution (n.)** 解決 **entry-level (adj.)**（組織）最底層的 **face (v.)** 面臨 **seriously (adv.)** 認真地；嚴肅地 **participate (v.)** 參與 **wholeheartedly (adv.)** 全神貫注地 **participant (n.)** 參與者

83. 相關細節——研討會的舉辦地點

Where most likely is the workshop taking place?
(A) At a bank
(B) At a law firm
(C) At a government office
(D) At an accounting company

這場研習最有可能是在哪裡舉行的？
(A) 在銀行
(B) 在法律事務所
(C) 在政府機關
(D) 在會計師事務所

84. 掌握說話者的意圖——提及「你們會大吃一驚的」的意圖 難

What does the speaker mean when she says, "you'd be surprised"?

(A) Some problems happen frequently.
(B) Some conflicts have already been resolved.
(C) Some mistakes have serious consequences.
(D) Some errors are easy to prevent.

說話者說：「你們會大吃一驚的」，其意思為何？

(A) 有些問題經常發生。
(B) 有些衝突已經解決。
(C) 有些失誤會導致嚴重的後果。
(D) 有些錯誤易於防範。

- **frequently (adv.)** 經常 **conflict (n.)** 衝突；矛盾 **resolve (v.)** 解決 **consequence (n.)** 後果 **prevent (v.)** 預防

85. 相關細節——說話者表示接下來要做的事情 難

What does the speaker say she will do next?

(A) Tell a true story
(B) Give a short quiz
(C) Pass out an agenda
(D) Begin a slide show

說話者說她接下來要做什麼？

(A) 講述真實故事
(B) 進行簡短的測驗
(C) 分發議程表
(D) 開始播放投影片

- **pass out** 分發 **agenda (n.)** 議程表

換句話說 **share with you a real experience**（跟大家分享一個真實案例）
→ **tell a true story**（講述真實故事）

86-88 Telephone message

Anna, it's Jessie. Mr. Stout just called about our bid for the landscaping project at his office. He says that Crinton Landscaping offered to do it for twelve thousand dollars. That's six hundred dollars less than what we proposed. But Mr. Stout would like to hire us if we can match that price. (86) **Will you authorize me to revise our bid?** I think it's a good idea. (87) **The project does require using some unusual plants and stones, but not much labor.** We could still make a profit from it. (88) **Call me back as soon as you decide, because Mr. Stout wants to get started and will go with Crinton Landscaping if we take too long to respond.** Thanks.

86-88 電話留言 加

安娜，我是傑西。史托特先生剛才來電，要討論我方針對他公司的景觀工程案的報價，他說克林頓園藝工程公司願意以 12,000 元承包，比我們提出的還要少 600 元，不過史托特先生說，如果我們能比照這個價格，他就想僱用我們。(86) **請問妳是否准許我修改報價？**我覺得這是明智之舉，(87) **雖然這個案子的確要用到特殊的植物與石材，但人力需求並不大**，我們依然有獲利空間。(88) **妳決定後，就馬上打電話給我，因為史托特先生想要動工了，要是我們拖太久才回覆，他就會選擇克林頓園藝工程公司**，謝謝。

- **bid (n.)** 出價；投標 **landscaping (n.)** 園林造景；景觀美化 **propose (v.)** 提出 **match (v.)** 比得上 **authorize (v.)** 授權給；允許；批准 **revise (v.)** 修改 **unusual (adj.)** 不尋常的 **labor (n.)** 勞動；工作 **profit (n.)** 盈利；利潤

86. 全文相關——留言的目的

What is the purpose of the message?

(A) To offer a referral
(B) To ask for approval
(C) To apologize for a delay
(D) To answer a question

這則留言的目的為何？

(A) 提供推薦
(B) 請求許可
(C) 為延誤致歉
(D) 回答問題

- **referral (n.)** 推薦 **approval (n.)** 許可；同意 **delay (n.)** 延誤

換句話說 authorize me to . . .（准許我）→ approval（許可）

87. 相關細節——說話者針對景觀工程提及的內容

What does the speaker say about a landscaping project?
(A) It will lead to other work opportunities.
(B) It involves special materials.
(C) It has been postponed.
(D) It requires several permits.

說話者對於景觀工程案有何看法？
(A) 將帶來其他工作機會。
(B) 會用到特殊用材。
(C) 已經延期。
(D) 需要數張許可證。

- lead to 導致；引起　opportunity (n.) 機會　involve (v.) 包含　material (n.) 材料　permit (n.) 許可（證）

換句話說 require using unusual plants and stones（要用到特殊的植物與石材）
→ involves special materials（用到特殊用材）

88. 相關細節——說話者提及若聽者不盡快行動，可能會發生的事情 難

What does the speaker say will happen if the listener does not act quickly?
(A) Seasonal weather will become a problem.
(B) Discounted prices will no longer be available.
(C) A potential customer will hire a competitor.
(D) A property may fail an inspection.

說話者說，如果聽者不快點行動，將會發生什麼事？
(A) 季節性氣候將造成問題。
(B) 將不再享有優惠價。
(C) 潛在客戶將聘僱同業。
(D) 建物可能無法通過檢查。

- seasonal (adj.) 季節（性）的　available (adj.) 可用的；可得到的　potential (adj.) 潛在的　competitor (n.) 競爭對手　property (n.) 建築物；房地產　inspection (n.) 檢查；視察

89-91 Talk

(89) Thank you all again for joining the Stoneville Farm Show as temporary event staff this week. Starting today, you'll help us showcase the latest innovations in growing crops and raising livestock. I hope that by now, you're all clear on your duties—answering visitor questions, assisting exhibitors, reporting problems through your two-way radio **(90) Please be accessible to attendees but also stay out of the way, so that they can circulate easily.** Uh, Hall C in particular gets a lot of foot traffic. So staff there will need to be aware of that. **(91) Finally, don't forget to see Mr. Hayashi each day to clock in and out.** He'll be in the convention center office.

89-91 談話 美

(89) 再次感謝大家加入，擔任本週石谷農貿展的臨時工作人員。各位從今天開始，將協助我們展示農作物種植、家畜飼養的創新方法，希望現在大家都已經清楚自己的職責——也就是回答來賓的問題、協助參展人員，以及用對講機回報問題。**(90) 請隨時協助與會者，但不要妨礙到動線，以方便來賓走動參觀。**哦，特別是 C 展區，客流人潮很多，所以同仁要注意那個區域。**(91) 最後，別忘了每天都要找林先生記錄上下班時間，**他都在大會中心辦公室裡。

- temporary (adj.) 臨時的　showcase (v.) 展示　innovation (n.) 創新；新方法　crop (n.) 農作物　livestock (n.) 家畜　duty (n.) 責任；職責　assist (v.) 協助　exhibitor (n.) 參展者　two-way (adj.) 雙向的（收發兩用的）　radio (n.) 無線電設備　accessible (adj.) 可接近的　circulate (v.) 走動　in particular 特別；尤其　foot traffic 顧客流量　be aware of 注意　clock in and out 上下班打卡

89. 相關細節——預計參展的產業類別

What industry will be featured at the trade show?

(A) Pharmaceuticals

(B) Construction

(C) Energy

(D) Agriculture

貿易展的主題是何項產業？

(A) 製藥

(B) 建築

(C) 能源

(D) 農業

90. 掌握說話者的意圖——提及「特別是 C 展區，客流人潮很多」的意圖 難

What does the speaker imply when she says, "Hall C in particular gets a lot of foot traffic"?

(A) Hall C exhibitors paid the highest registration fee.

(B) Hall C staff should take extra care not to block the aisles.

(C) Hall C would be a good place to hand out a resource.

(D) Hall C must be cleaned more often than other halls.

說話者說：「特別是 C 展區，客流人潮很多」，言下之意為何？

(A) C 展區參展商支付的報名費最高。

(B) C 展區的工作人員應格外小心，不要擋住通道。

(C) C 展區是適合發放資料的地方。

(D) C 展區比別的展區更須經常打掃。

- **registration fee** 報名費；註冊費 **block (v.)** 擋住 **aisle (n.)** 走道 **hand out** 發放 **resource (n.)** 資料；資源

換句話說 **stay out of the way**（不要妨礙到動線）→ **not to block the aisles**（不要擋住通道）

91. 相關細節——聽者需要找林先生的理由 難

Why should listeners speak to Mr. Hayashi?

(A) To have their working hours recorded

(B) To obtain a communication device

(C) To report problems on the trade show floor

(D) To be reimbursed for a travel expense

聽者為什麼要找林先生交談？

(A) 為了記錄工時

(B) 為了取得通訊器材

(C) 為了回報展場上的問題

(D) 為了報銷差旅費

- **record (v.)** 記錄 **obtain (v.)** 取得 **communication device** 通訊器材 **reimburse (v.)** 報銷；償付 **expense (n.)** 費用

換句話說 **clock in and out**（記錄上下班時間）→ **have working hours recorded**（記錄工時）

92-94 Talk

Good evening. (92) **As the alumni relations manager for Welksfield University, it's my honor to welcome our graduates back to campus for tonight's dinner.** This is a chance for you to share memories of your time here and make some new ones. However, that's not the only purpose of tonight's dinner. It's also for funding scholarships awarded to current and future Welksfield students. (93) **Please visit the booth in the back to contribute money to this worthy cause.** All right, alumni association president Gustavo Costa will give the keynote address later this evening, (94) **but first, you may help yourselves to the delicious spread that the caterers are setting out on the side tables now.** Thank you.

92-94 談話 英

晚安。(92) **身為維克斯菲爾德大學校友公關經理，我很榮幸歡迎各位本校畢業生返校參加今晚的晚宴。**各位可藉此機會與大家分享就學時期的美好時光，同時創造新的回憶。不過，這並非今晚晚宴的唯一目的，晚宴也希望募取資金，提供給本校在學生以及未來學生的獎學金之用，(93) **請至後面的攤位，捐款響應這項有意義的計畫。**好的，校友會會長古斯塔夫．柯斯塔將在今晚稍晚發表主題演講，(94) **但在此之前，大家可自行取用美味佳餚，外燴業者正在把餐點擺放到邊桌上。**謝謝。

- alumni (n.) 校友 relation (n.) 關係 graduate (n.) 畢業生 purpose (n.) 目的 scholarship (n.) 獎學金 award (v.) 授予 contribute (v.) 捐獻 worthy (adj.) 值得支持的 cause (n.) 理由；目標 association (n.) 協會 keynote address 專題演講 spread (n.) 盛宴 caterer (n.) 酒席承辦業者

92. 相關細節——聽者們的共通點

What do the listeners most likely have in common?
(A) They studied at the same university.
(B) They hold the same type of job.
(C) They work for the same employer.
(D) They support the same sports team.

聽者最有可能有什麼共通點？
(A) 他們曾就讀同一所大學。
(B) 他們從事同類型工作。
(C) 他們為同一雇主工作。
(D) 他們支持相同體育隊伍。

- employer (n.) 雇主 support (v.) 支持

93. 相關細節——說話者向聽者提出的建議

What does the speaker encourage listeners to do?
(A) Stop by a photo booth
(B) Make a financial donation
(C) Join a regional association
(D) Cast a vote

說話者鼓勵聽者做什麼？
(A) 前往拍照亭
(B) 捐款
(C) 加入地方協會
(D) 投票

- financial (adj.) 財政的；金融的 donation (n.) 捐款 cast a vote 投票

換句話說 contribute money（捐款）→ make a financial donation（捐款）

94. 相關細節——接下來將發生的事情

What will take place next?
(A) A keynote speech
(B) An award ceremony
(C) A dance performance
(D) A buffet meal

下一個排程為何？
(A) 專題演講
(B) 頒獎典禮
(C) 舞蹈演出
(D) 自助餐點

- ceremony (n.) 典禮 buffet (n.) 自助餐 submission (n.) 提交 responsibility (n.) 責任

95-97 Telephone message + Table size options

Hi, Carl. (95) **Thanks for putting together the list of options for replacing the meeting room table.** I'm looking over your e-mail now, and (96) **I think we should avoid the two widest ones.** I know that it was my idea to look into them, but I've changed my mind. We don't want clients to feel crowded. I think it would be better to buy a smaller table and just put chairs in the corners if needed. Uh, and the seven-foot-long table isn't very attractive, in my opinion. (96) **So I like the six-foot-long option the best.** (97) **Please go ahead and order it when you get into work tomorrow.** Then we can talk about removing the old one.

95-97 電話留言＋桌子尺寸清單 澳

嗨，卡爾，(95) **謝謝你為更換會議室的會議桌，整理出可供選擇的各款尺寸桌子，**我正在看你寄來的電子郵件，(96) **我覺得應該不要選用最寬的那兩款，**我知道是我提議要找那種會議桌，可是我改變主意了，我不希望客戶覺得會議室很擠，我覺得買小一點的會議桌會比較好，如果有需要的話可在角落放置椅子。噢，而我個人認為，七呎長的桌子不怎麼好看，(95) **所以我最喜歡六呎長的桌子。**(97) **請你明天上班就時，下訂那張會議桌吧，**然後我們再來討論怎麼移走舊桌子。

	Width x Length
(96) Table 1	4 ft. x 6 ft.
Table 2	4 ft. x 7 ft.
Table 3	6 ft. x 6 ft.
Table 4	7 ft. x 7 ft.

	寬 X 長
(96) 桌子 1	4呎 x 6呎
桌子 2	4呎 x 7呎
桌子 3	6呎 x 6呎
桌子 4	7呎 x 7呎

- put together 整理出　option (n.) 選擇；選項　replace (v.) 更換　avoid (v.) 避免　crowded (adj.) 擁擠的　attractive (adj.) 吸引人的　opinion (n.) 意見；評價　go ahead 進行；發生　order (v.) 訂購　remove (v.) 搬開；除去

95. 相關細節——放置新桌子的地點

Where will a new table be placed?

(A) In a patio

(B) In a lobby

(C) In a dining room

(D) In a conference room

新桌子會放到哪裡使用？

(A) 在露臺裡

(B) 在大廳裡

(C) 在餐廳裡

(D) 在會議室裡

換句話說 meeting room（會議室）→ conference room（會議室）

96. 圖表整合題——說話者偏好的桌子

Look at the graphic. Which table does the speaker prefer?

(A) Table 1

(B) Table 2

(C) Table 3

(D) Table 4

請看圖表作答。說話者偏好哪張桌子？

(A) 桌子 1

(B) 桌子 2

(C) 桌子 3

(D) 桌子 4

97. 相關細節——說話者要求聽著做的事情

What does the speaker ask the listener to do?

(A) Place a purchase order

(B) Read a reply e-mail

(C) Arrange a furniture removal

(D) Verify the space's measurements

說話者要求聽者做什麼？

(A) 下單採購

(B) 閱讀電子郵件的回信

(C) 安排家具搬運離開

(D) 確認空間大小

- purchase (n.) 訂購　arrange (v.) 安排；處理　removal (n.) 移開　verify (v.) 查清；核對　measurement (n.) 尺寸；大小

換句話說 order（訂購）→ place a purchase order（下單採購）

98-100 Excerpt from a meeting + Sample parking pass

98-100 會議摘錄＋停車證樣本 加

Good morning, everyone. The reason I've asked you all to come in a little early is to see the final design of our new parking pass. (98) **I'm happy to say that the graphic designer listened to your input on how she could make it easier for you to check whether vehicles in the parking area belong there.** Here's the sample pass that she made. (99) **As you can see, the information on the third line is larger than it was before.** I think it's much better now. (100) **The background is also a lighter shade of silver than the previous design so that all of the text is more visible.** It looks good, doesn't it?

大家早安。我讓你們早點來的原因，就是為了讓大家看看新停車證的最終版設計，(98) **很高興的要跟大家說，平面設計師聽取了各位的建議，設計的方式可讓你們更方便檢查停車場的車輛是否屬於本停車場。**這裡有張她設計的停車證樣本，(99) **大家可以看到，第三行資訊的文字比以前更為放大，**我覺得現在好多了，(100) **底色的銀色也比之前設計調得更淺，讓所有文字更清晰可見，**看起來很不錯吧，對吧？

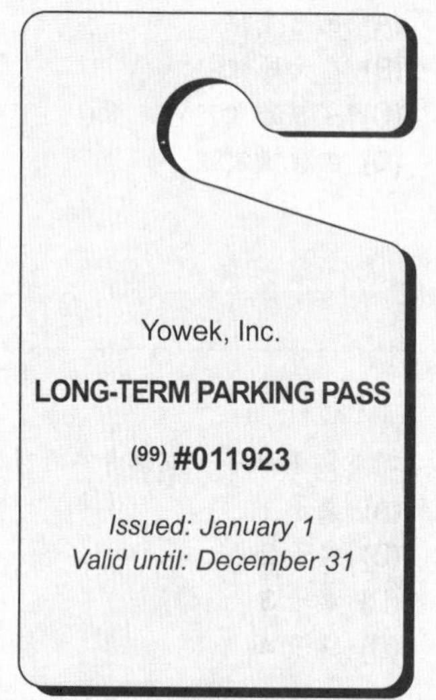

- **reason (n.)** 理由；原因 **parking pass** 停車證 **input (n.)** 建議 **vehicle (n.)** 車輛 **background (n.)** 背景 **shade (n.)** 濃淡；色度 **previous (adj.)** 先前的 **visible (adj.)** 明顯的；顯眼的

98. 全文相關——聽者們的職業

Who most likely are the listeners?

(A) Delivery drivers

(B) Graphic designers

(C) Parking attendants

(D) Senior executives

聽者最有可能是什麼人？

(A) 貨運司機

(B) 平面設計師

(C) 停車場服務員

(D) 高層主管

99. 圖表整合題——與先前的差異

Look at the graphic. Which piece of information looked different before?

(A) The company name

(B) The pass type

(C) The pass number

(D) The expiration date

請看圖表作答。哪項資訊看起來跟先前不同？

(A) 公司名稱

(B) 停車證種類

(C) 停車證號碼

(D) 到期日

- **expiration (n.)** 到期；截止

100. 相關細節——說話者針對先前設計提及的內容 難

What does the speaker mention about an earlier design?

(A) It featured an image.

(B) It was a darker color.

(C) It included additional text.

(D) It made use of a heavier material.

關於先前的設計，說話者提到了什麼？

(A) 其中有圖像。

(B) 顏色較深。

(C) 包括額外文字。

(D) 用了較重的材質。

- **feature (v.)** 以……為特色；以……為主要組成　**include (v.)** 包括　**additional (adj.)** 額外的；附加的　**material (n.)** 材料

ACTUAL TEST 3

PART 1 P. 32-35

09

1. 單人獨照——描寫人物的動作 加

(A) The woman is searching in a backpack.
(B) The woman is cleaning a bottle.
(C) The woman is exploring an exhibition.
(D) The woman is standing in front of a ticket window.

(A) 女子正在翻背包找東西。
(B) 女子正在清洗瓶子。
(C) 女子正在參觀展覽。
(D) 女子正站在售票窗口前。

- backpack (n.) 背包 explore (v.) 探索；探究 exhibition (n.) 展覽

2. 雙人照片——描寫人物的動作 美

(A) They're placing dishes in a sink.
(B) They're bending over an oven.
(C) They're looking at a piece of paper.
(D) They're stacking some clipboards.

(A) 他們正把盤子放進水槽裡。
(B) 他們正俯身在烤箱上方。
(C) 他們正在看一張紙。
(D) 他們堆疊文件夾板。

- place (v.) 放置 sink (n.) 水槽 bend (v.) 彎；俯 stack (v.) 堆疊；堆放

3. 綜合照片——描寫人物或事物 澳

(A) There is a line of customers in a store.
(B) Produce has fallen onto the floor.
(C) A cashier is handing a bag to a man.
(D) A woman is reaching out to touch a screen.

(A) 店裡有一排客人。
(B) 農產品掉到地上。
(C) 收銀員正把袋子遞給男子。
(D) 女子正伸手去觸摸螢幕。

- produce (n.) 農產品 hand (v.) 傳遞；給 reach out 伸手

4. 綜合照片——描寫人物或事物 英

(A) A farmer is operating some machinery.
(B) A gardener is watering some plants.
(C) Some tree branches are being trimmed.
(D) A rake is being used in a field.

(A) 農夫正在操作機械。
(B) 園丁正在給植物澆水。
(C) 有人正在修剪樹枝。
(D) 有人正在田裡使用耙子。

- operate (v.) 操作 machinery (n.) 機械；機器 gardener (n.) 園丁 plant (n.) 植物 branch (n.) 樹枝 trim (v.) 修剪 rake (n.)（長柄的）耙；草耙

5. 綜合照片——描寫人物或事物 加

(A) Some people are sitting in an auditorium.
(B) Some chairs have been arranged around a table.
(C) One of the women is pointing at a bookcase.
(D) The curtains in a conference room have been closed.

(A) 有些人正坐在禮堂裡。
(B) 桌子周圍擺放了一些椅子。
(C) 其中一名女子手指著書櫃。
(D) 會議室裡的窗簾已被拉上了。

- auditorium (n.) 禮堂 arrange (v.) 安排；排列 point at 指向 bookcase (n.) 書架；書櫃 conference room 會議室

6. 事物與背景照——描寫室內事物的狀態 (美)

(A) There is a large sign next to a doorway.	(A) 門口旁有個大型告示。
(B) A sofa is being moved into a café.	(B) 沙發正被搬進咖啡廳。
(C) A lamp is hanging from the ceiling.	**(C) 天花板上懸掛著一盞燈。**
(D) A jar has been left on a display counter.	(D) 罐子被放在展示櫃上。

- sign doorway 門口；出入口 ceiling (n.) 天花板 jar (n.) 罐子 display counter 陳列櫃；展示架

PART 2 P. 36

10

7. 表示請託或要求的問句 (加)⇄(英)

Could you put these books back on the shelves?	你可以把這些書放回書架上嗎？
(A) Sure, I'll do that right now.	**(A) 沒問題，我現在就去放。**
(B) Here's my library card.	(B) 這是我的借書證。
(C) Sorry—I meant the front of the shelves.	(C) 抱歉——我是說書架的正面。

- shelf (n.) 架子（複數為 shelves）

8. 以 **How long** 開頭的問句，詢問準備開胃菜的所需時間 (美)⇄(澳)

How long will it take to prepare the appetizers?	準備開胃菜需要多久的時間？
(A) I'd love some garlic bread.	(A) 我想吃點大蒜麵包。
(B) About four inches each.	(B) 每個大約四英吋。
(C) We'll work as fast as we can.	**(C) 我們會盡快完成。**

- prepare (v.) 準備 appetizer (n.) 開胃菜

9. 以 **Where** 開頭的問句，詢問員工電梯的位置 (英)⇄(加)

Where's the service elevator?	員工電梯在哪裡？
(A) Around that corner and to the left.	**(A) 繞過那個轉角，就在左邊。**
(B) The tenth floor, please.	(B) 請按 10 樓。
(C) To improve customer satisfaction.	(C) 為了提高顧客滿意度。

- service elevator 員工或送貨員使用的電梯 satisfaction (n.) 滿意

10. 以助動詞 **Did** 開頭的問句，確認對方是否有參加遠足 (澳)⇄(美)

Did you go on the walking tour that Ivan organized?	你有參加伊凡辦的遠足嗎？
(A) Yes—it was quite interesting.	**(A) 有啊——辦得相當有趣。**
(B) Those files are organized by type.	(B) 那些文件有分門別類整理。
(C) Some tourists from out of town.	(C) 幾個外地來的觀光客。

- organize (v.) 組織；規劃 quite (adv.) 相當；很

11. 以 **What** 開頭的問句，詢問對方正在設計的建築種類 (澳)⇄(英)

What kind of building are you designing?	你在設計什麼樣的建築？
(A) In the Clancy neighborhood.	(A) 在克蘭西街區。
(B) A freelance architect.	(B) 自由接案的建築師。
(C) It's a distribution center for retail goods.	**(C) 零售商品的配送中心。**

- architect (n.) 建築師 distribution (n.) 分配；分銷 retail (n.) 零售 goods (n.)（複數）商品

12. 以 When 開頭的問句，詢問上次更新軟體的時間 美⇄加

When did we last update this software program?
(A) No—let's find another date.
(B) Near the end of January.
(C) So that it would run faster.

我們上次更新這個軟體是什麼時候？
(A) 不是——我們找別的日期吧。
(B) 接近一月底。
(C) 這樣會運行得更快。

13. 以否定疑問句，確認對方是否完成受訓 澳⇄美 難

Didn't you complete that training course already?
(A) I've heard the instructor is great.
(B) Well, that was a long time ago.
(C) Changes to safety procedures.

你不是已經完成那個培訓課程了嗎？
(A) 我聽說那位講師很棒。
(B) 嗯，那是很久以前的事了。
(C) 安全程序的異動。

- complete (v.) 完成　instructor (n.) 教師；指導者　safety (n.) 安全　procedure (n.) 程序

14. 以 Where 開頭的問句，詢問影印紙的箱子放在哪裡 英⇄加

Where did you set that big box of printer paper?
(A) From Rimson Stationery.
(B) Oh, do you need some?
(C) I used company funds.

你把那一大箱的影印紙放哪裡了？
(A) 從林森文具店。
(B) 噢，你需要一些嗎？
(C) 我用了公司的資金。

- stationery (n.) 文具　fund (n.) 資金

15. 以間接問句詢問如何去倉庫 美⇄加 難

Do you know how to get to the warehouse from here?
(A) I'll just use the mapping app on my smartphone.
(B) She lives in an apartment, not a house.
(C) My brother grew up here, but moved away.

你知道怎麼從這裡去倉庫嗎？
(A) 我會用智慧型手機裡的地圖應用程式。
(B) 她住在公寓裡，而不是房子裡。
(C) 我弟弟在這裡長大，但後來搬走了。

- warehouse (n.) 倉庫

16. 表示建議或提案的問句 加⇄英

Why don't you call a taxi to take you to the airport?
(A) The flight to Hong Kong.
(B) Hmm, I suppose I'd better.
(C) He's not a tax specialist.

你何不打電話叫計程車載你去機場？
(A) 飛往香港的班機。
(B) 嗯，我想我最好這麼做。
(C) 他不是稅務專員。

- flight (n.) 班機；航班　suppose (v.) 猜想　tax specialist 稅務專家

17. 以選擇疑問句，詢問對方想做哪一項工作 澳⇄美

Do you want to sweep the aisles or set up the sale display?
(A) The display will be set up between aisles.
(B) As soon as the last shopper leaves.
(C) I don't mind either job.

你想要打掃走道，還是要擺設展示商品？
(A) 商品展示區將設置在走道之間。
(B) 等最後一位顧客離開就開始。
(C) 任一項工作我都能做。

- sweep (v.) 掃地　aisle (n.) 走道　display (n.) 展示；陳列

18. 以 Why 開頭的問句，詢問赫南德茲請客的理由 英⇄加 難

Why is Mr. Hernandez treating everyone to lunch?
(A) I think it's launching soon.
(B) Barnette Restaurant, on Fifth Street.
(C) It's just the administrators, actually.

為什麼赫南德茲先生要請大家吃午餐？
(A) 我想很快就會推出了。
(B) 巴內特餐廳，在第五街。
(C) 其實只有宴請管理人員。

- treat (v.) 請客　launch (v.) 推出；上市　administrator (n.) 管理者

19. 以 Who 開頭的問句，詢問撰寫報導的人 澳⇄美

Who's writing the articles on the food festival?
(A) The cooking competition and the concert.
(B) They should be under five hundred words.
(C) Check the assignment spreadsheet.

誰正在寫美食節的報導文章？
(A) 烹飪比賽跟音樂會。
(B) 應該在 500 字以內。
(C) 查看一下工作分配表。

- competition (n.) 比賽　assignment (n.) 工作；任務　spreadsheet (n.) 電子試算表

20. 以附加問句，確認佳茵是否在處理調查結果 英⇄澳 難

Ga-Young is processing the results of the intern survey, isn't she?
(A) She's going to present them next week.
(B) The university's summer vacation.
(C) Thanks—I'll let her know you told me.

佳茵在處理實習生意見調查的結果，對不對？
(A) 她下星期會發表結果。
(B) 大學的暑假。
(C) 謝謝——我會跟她說妳告訴我了。

- process (v.) 處理　intern (n.) 實習生　present (v.) 展示；發表　vacation (n.) 假期

21. 以 When 開頭的問句，詢問完成裝修的時間 加⇄美 難

When will they finish renovating the café in the lobby?
(A) The menu is a lot longer now.
(B) That would be great, if you're free.
(C) Is the noise making it hard for you to focus?

他們何時能完成大廳裡咖啡廳的整修工程？
(A) 現在的菜單長很多。
(B) 如果你有空的話，那就太好啦。
(C) 這噪音是不是讓你難以專心？

- renovate (v.) 翻新；改造　focus (v.) 集中；專心

22. 以否定疑問句，確認對方是否會在家工作 加⇄澳 難

Weren't you scheduled to work from home today?
(A) A new person in the scheduling department.
(B) Some clients asked to meet this afternoon.
(C) I'm hoping to buy a home in the suburbs.

你不是安排好今天在家工作嗎？
(A) 規劃部的新人。
(B) 幾位客戶要求今天下午會面。
(C) 我想在郊區買間房子。

- scheduling (n.) 排程；調度　suburb (n.) 郊區

23. 以 Who 開頭的問句，詢問委員會的成員 美⇄澳 

Who's on the selection committee for the research prize?
(A) Its members are appointed by the board.
(B) Oh, I've already chosen my topic.
(C) Julia Herrera won first place, I read.

研究獎的甄審委員會裡有哪些人？
(A) 委員是由董事會任命的。
(B) 哦，我已經選好我的主題了。
(C) 我看到茱莉亞・赫瑞拉拿下第一。

- selection (n.) 選擇；選拔　committee (n.) 委員會　research (n.) 研究　appoint (v.) 任命　board (n.) 董事會

24. 表示請託或要求的直述句 加⇄英 難

We need proof of your income to complete your loan application.	我們需要您的收入證明，才能完成您的貸款申請。
(A) Would a copy of my paycheck be all right?	**(A) 可以用我的薪資單複本嗎？**
(B) She's about to make a deposit at the bank.	(B) 她正要去銀行存錢。
(C) The money to start my own business.	(C) 我要自行創業的資金

- proof (n.) 證明；證據　income (n.) 收入　loan application 貸款申請　paycheck (n.) 工資　make a deposit 存錢

25. 以 Why 開頭的問句，詢問未清洗地毯的原因 澳⇄英 難

Why aren't we having the carpets deep-cleaned this year?	我們今年何不請人把地毯徹底清潔一下？
(A) When everyone's at the company retreat.	(A) 在大家都去員工旅遊的時候。
(B) No, we're buying a new copy machine.	(B) 不，我們要買新的影印機。
(C) Facilities maintenance is Corey's area.	**(C) 設施維護是柯瑞負責的。**

- retreat (n.) 靜修　facility (n.) 設施　maintenance (n.) 維護；保養

26. 以 Be 動詞開頭的問句，詢問是否可保留旅遊回饋點數 美⇄加 難

Am I allowed to keep travel rewards points I earn during business trips?	我可以保留出差期間累積的旅遊回饋點數嗎？
(A) Samford Bank's rewards program participants.	(A) 桑福德銀行的獎勵方案參與者。
(B) That's not necessary—just check your e-mail often.	(B) 不必——只要你常查看電子郵件就行了。
(C) I'm not aware of any policies against it.	**(C) 就我所知，沒有規定禁止。**

- allow (v.) 允許　reward (n.) 獎勵（金）　business trip 出差　participant (n.) 參與者　aware (adj.) 知道的　policy (n.) 政策；方針

27. 以助動詞 Do 開頭的問句，詢問最後一班工作人員是否有特別職責 澳⇄美 難

Do workers on the closing shift have any special responsibilities?	打烊時間的輪班員工有什麼特別的職責嗎？
(A) Yes, the store closed down last June.	(A) 是的，該商店去年六月就結束營業了。
(B) Nothing that you wouldn't expect.	**(B) 都是你可以料想到的。**
(C) When does it start and end?	(C) 起迄時間為何？

- shift (n.) 輪班（時間）　responsibility (n.) 職責；責任

28. 以附加問句詢問是否發布新聞稿 英⇄澳 難

We're issuing a press release about the expansion, aren't we?	我們要就擴大營業發布新聞稿，對嗎？
(A) The new president is from Philadelphia.	(A) 新任董事長來自費城。
(B) Not until all of the plans are finalized.	**(B) 等所有計畫都落定後才會發布。**
(C) Try pressing the "release" button on the side.	(C) 按一下旁邊那個「釋出」鍵看看。

- issue (v.) 發布；發行　press release 新聞稿　expansion (n.) 擴張；發展　finalize (v.) 敲定；定案　press (v.) 按　release (v./n.) 釋放

29. 以 Which 開頭的問句，詢問該修改的部分 美⇄加 難

Which part of the manual did you say we should revise? **(A) Most sections need at least some revisions.** (B) Because some of the instructions aren't clear. (C) Each employee is given a manual at orientation.	你說我們應該修改說明書的哪個部分？ **(A) 大部分章節都起碼需要一些修改。** (B) 因為有些說明不太清楚。 (C) 每位員工在入職訓練時都會拿到說明書。

- **manual (n.)** 使用手冊；說明書 **revise (v.)** 修改；修訂 **section (n.)** 部分 **at least** 至少 **revision (n.)** 修改 **instruction (n.)** 說明；指示 **orientation (n.)** 新人培訓

30. 以直述句傳達資訊 英⇄美 難

The sales projections for this quarter are higher than I expected. (A) There were several very good applicants. **(B) Management believes demand is going to grow.** (C) We could mount the projector on the ceiling.	本季的銷售預測比我先前預期還要高。 (A) 有幾位很優秀的應徵者。 **(B) 管理高層認為需求量將會增加。** (C) 我們可以把投影機安裝在天花板上。

- **projection (n.)** 預測 **quarter (n.)** 季度 **applicant (n.)** 應徵者；求職者 **management (n.)** 管理層 **demand (n.)** 需求 **projector (n.)** 投影機 **mount (v.)** 架設；安裝 **ceiling (n.)** 天花板

31. 以 How many 開頭的問句，詢問派去協商的人數 加⇄英 難

How many representatives are we sending to the negotiations? **(A) That's not as important as what our strategy is.** (B) I sent a couple out by express mail. (C) Ellen suggested offering a five percent price cut.	我們要派多少名代表去參加談判？ **(A) 這一點（人數）沒有我們的策略重要。** (B) 我用快捷郵件寄了一些。 (C) 艾倫建議提供 5% 降價。

- **representative (n.)** 代表 **negotiation (n.)** 談判；協商 **strategy (n.)** 策略；戰略 **express mail** 快捷郵件

PART 3 P. 37–40

11

32-34 Conversation / 32-34 對話 英⇄澳

W: [32] **Ray, have you noticed that some customers are staying at their tables for a long time without ordering more food or drinks?**	女：[32] **雷伊，你有沒有注意到，有些客人會在位子上待很久，卻沒有再加點餐點或飲料？**
M: Oh yeah, it does seem like that's becoming a problem. [33] **What if we posted a notice near the entrance that told people they had to leave promptly after they finish eating?**	男：噢，有的，似乎確實越來越讓人困擾，[33] **不如我們在門口邊張貼公告，告訴客人用餐完後就得儘快離開，怎麼樣？**
W: I don't know . . . [34] **That seems like it would make a lot of customers feel pressured and uncomfortable.** I was thinking about a more targeted approach, like just bringing the bill to slow tables before they ask.	女：我不知道耶⋯⋯[34] **感覺這麼做會讓很多客人感到有壓力、不自在，** 我正在思考能更精準對症下藥的辦法，比如針對坐得太久的客人，就不等他們開口，直接先送上帳單。
M: Ah, I see. Yes, that sounds like a better plan.	男：噢，我懂了。是啊，這個辦法聽起來比較好。

- **notice (v.)** 注意；留意 **post (v.)** 張貼；公布 **entrance (n.)** 門口；入口 **promptly (adv.)** 立即 **feel pressured** 感到有壓力 **targeted (adj.)** 針對（目標）的 **approach (n.)** 方法 **bill (n.)** 帳單

32. 全文相關——說話者工作的地點

Where do the speakers work?
(A) At a factory
(B) At an airport
(C) At a restaurant
(D) At a movie theater

說話者在哪裡工作？
(A) 在工廠
(B) 在機場
(C) 在餐廳
(D) 在電影院

33. 相關細節——男子提出的建議

What does the man suggest?
(A) Putting up a sign
(B) Hiring more staff
(C) Widening an entrance
(D) Automating a process

男子有什麼建議？
(A) 張貼告示
(B) 招聘更多員工
(C) 拓寬門口
(D) 將流程自動化

- **widen (v.)** 加寬 **automate (v.)** 使自動化 **process (n.)** 過程

換句話說 posted a notice（張貼公告）→ putting up a sign（貼張告示）

34. 相關細節——女子表示男子的建議可能會引發的狀況 難

What does the woman say the man's suggested action might cause?
(A) Service delays
(B) A shortage of space
(C) An unpleasant atmosphere
(D) A budget problem

女子說男子建議的做法可能導致什麼結果？
(A) 服務延遲
(B) 空間不足
(C) 氣氛尷尬
(D) 預算問題

- **delay (n.)** 延遲 **shortage (n.)** 缺少；不足 **unpleasant (adj.)** 使人不愉快的 **atmosphere (n.)** 氣氛；氛圍 **budget (n.)** 預算

35-37 Conversation

M: Hi, Ms. Griffin. Thank you for coming.

W: It's nice to meet you in person, Mr. Marsh. (35) **Now, as I said on the phone, I'd like you to show me everything that you'll need my company to pack up and transport to your new apartment.**

M: Sure. Let's start with the most difficult part—the living room. (36) **As you can see, I have a piano. I'm afraid that it won't survive the trip in good condition.**

W: Well, we've moved pianos before with no problems. (37) **And all of our work will be insured under a formal agreement drafted by lawyers. Would you like a sample copy of it?** I have one here.

35-37 對話

加⇄英

男： 妳好，葛林芬小姐，謝謝妳前來。

女： 很高興能和您現場碰面，馬許先生。(35) **現在，正如我在電話中說的，我希望給我看一下所有您需要我們公司打包、運送到新公寓的物品。**

男： 沒問題。我們從最困難的部分開始吧，也就是客廳。(36) **如妳所見，我有一台鋼琴。我擔心鋼琴在運送過程中，無法保持完好的狀態。**

女： 嗯，我們過去搬運過鋼琴，完全沒有發生問題，(37) **而且我們所有的作業，都有律師擬定的正式合約提供保險保障。您要看一下合約樣本嗎？**我這裡有一份。

- **pack (v.)** 包裝；裝（箱） **transport (v.)** 運輸 **survive (v.)** 經歷……而倖存 **condition (n.)** 狀態 **insure (v.)** 為……投保 **agreement (n.)** 契約；協議 **draft (v.)** 制定；起草 **lawyer (n.)** 律師

35. 相關細節——男子計劃要做的事情

難

What does the man plan to do?
(A) Move to a different residence
(B) Purchase a new appliance
(C) Put his belongings in storage
(D) Renovate an apartment

男子打算做什麼？
(A) 搬到別的住所
(B) 購買新的家電產品
(C) 儲放他的物品
(D) 翻修公寓

- **residence (n.)** 住所；住宅 **appliance (n.)** 家用電器 **belongings (n.)** 隨身物品 **storage (n.)** 倉庫；儲藏室 **renovate (v.)** 翻新；改造

換句話說 **your new apartment**（您的新公寓）→ **a different residence**（別的住所）

36. 相關細節——引發男子擔憂的理由

Why does the man say he is concerned?
(A) A job must be completed quickly.
(B) An activity will be noisy.
(C) An item may be damaged.
(D) A room may be too small.

男子說他為何擔心？
(A) 工作必須迅速完成。
(B) 活動會很吵雜。
(C) 物品可能會損壞。
(D) 房間可能太小。

- **complete (v.)** 完成 **activity (n.)** 活動 **damage (v.)** 損壞；損傷

37. 相關細節——女子向男子提出的建議

What does the woman offer to give the man?
(A) Referrals to other companies
(B) An informal cost estimate
(C) A legal document
(D) Packaging supplies

女子提議給男子什麼？
(A) 到其他公司的轉介
(B) 非正式的估價
(C) 法律文件
(D) 包裝用料

- **referral (n.)** 轉介；推薦 **informal (adj.)** 非正式的 **estimate (n.)** 估價 **legal (adj.)** 和法律相關的 **supplies (n.)** 物資；日用品

換句話說 **a formal agreement drafted by lawyers**（律師擬定的正式合約）
→ **a legal document**（法律文件）

38-40 Conversation

W: (38) **Ernest, since pay raises will be a little low this year, I think we need to find other ways to keep the staff happy.** Do you have any suggestions?

M: Let me think . . . (39) **How about creating a company community service program?**

W: Wait, why would that help?

38-40 對話

美⇄澳

女：(38) **恩斯特，由於今年的加薪幅度會有點低，我想我們得找別的辦法來讓員工保持開心。**你有什麼建議嗎？

男：我想想看喔⋯⋯ (39) **成立公司的社區服務計畫怎麼樣？**

女：等一下，這麼做有什麼用？

M: Well, people feel good when they help others, and spending time together outside the office would build stronger relationships between staff members.	**男：** 這個嘛，助人為快樂之本，而且讓同仁們能在辦公室以外的地方相處互動，也會加強員工之間的連結。
W: Those are good points, but . . . I don't know. Some employees might see it as a burden. **(40) Let's try to think of some other ideas before we move forward with that one.**	**女：** 這些想法是不錯啦，可是……我不知道，有些員工可能會把這個看成是負擔。**(40) 在我們繼續討論這個方案之前，再想想別的辦法吧。**
M: Sure, Lula. I'll see what I can come up with.	**男：** 沒問題，露拉。我再看看還能想出什麼辦法來。

- **raise (n.)** 加薪（額） **suggestion (n.)** 建議 **community service** 社會服務；地方服務活動 **relationship (n.)** 關係 **burden (n.)** 負擔

38. 全文相關——對話主題

難

What is the topic of the conversation?
(A) Keeping a current client account
(B) Attracting internship applicants
(C) Meeting shareholders' expectations
(D) Maintaining employee satisfaction

這段對話的主題為何？
(A) 留住現有的客戶帳戶
(B) 吸引實習應徵者
(C) 滿足股東期望
(D) 維持員工滿意度

- **account (n.)** 帳戶 **applicant (n.)** 求職者；申請人 **shareholder (n.)** 股東 **expectation (n.)** 期望 **satisfaction (n.)** 滿意

換句話說 **keep the staff happy**（讓員工保持開心）
→ **maintaining employee satisfaction**（維持員工滿意度）

39. 相關細節——男子提出的建議

What does the man propose?
(A) Making use of a local resource
(B) Reducing time spent commuting
(C) Starting a volunteer program
(D) Expanding an orientation session

男子有什麼提議？
(A) 利用當地資源
(B) 減少通勤所需時間
(C) 啟動志工計畫
(D) 擴大員工新訓的環節

- **resource (n.)** 資源 **reduce (v.)** 減少 **commute (v.)** 通勤 **expand (v.)** 擴展 **orientation (n.)** 入職培訓；迎新會 **session (n.)**（活動的）一段時間

40. 相關細節——說話者同意做的事情

What do the speakers agree to do?
(A) Develop the man's suggestion
(B) Seek alternative options
(C) Announce a decision
(D) Ask for workers' opinions

說話者同意做什麼？
(A) 延伸男子的建議
(B) 尋找替代方案
(C) 宣布一項決定
(D) 徵求員工的意見

- **alternative (adj.)** 替代的 **option (n.)** 選項 **announce (v.)** 宣布 **opinion (n.)** 意見

41-43 Conversation with three speakers

41-43 三人對話

加⇄美⇄英

M: Hi, everyone. (41) **My name is Tae-Min, and I'll be taking you around the museum today.** Are there any questions before we get started?

W1: I have one—is there somewhere I could leave this bag? It's quite heavy.

M: (42) **Yes, we have lockers near the entrance.** If you head over there now, you should be able to meet us in Gilmore Hall in a few minutes.

W1: Thanks. I'll do that.

W2: Um, I'm having trouble hearing you. Would you mind speaking up?

M: Oh, sorry about that. (43) **This is a bigger crowd than I usually handle. Yes, I'll try to speak more loudly.**

男：大家好。(41) **我叫做泰民，今天將由我來帶領各位參觀博物館。**在我們開始之前，大家有什麼問題嗎？

女1：我有個問題——有哪裡可以讓我寄放這個包包嗎？包包很重。

男：(42) **有的，我們入口附近有置物櫃**，如果您現在前往的話，幾分鐘後應當可以和我們在吉爾摩廳會合。

女1：謝謝，就這麼辦吧。

女2：呃，我聽不太清楚你的聲音，能麻煩說話再大聲一點嗎？

男：噢，抱歉，(43) **今天團員的人數比我平常負責的人數還多。好的，我說話會盡量大聲一點。**

41. 全文相關——男子的職業

Who most likely is the man?

(A) A trade show exhibitor

(B) A tour guide

(C) A workshop leader

(D) An airline representative

男子最有可能是什麼人？

(A) 商展參展商

(B) 導覽人員

(C) 研習會主持人

(D) 航空公司代表

42. 相關細節——男子向團體告知的事項

What does the man tell the group about?

(A) A building entrance

(B) A form of transportation

(C) An instruction manual

(D) A storage facility

男子向團員們說明了什麼？

(A) 建築物入口

(B) 交通運輸方式

(C) 說明手冊

(D) 置物設施

換句話說 lockers（置物櫃）→ a storage facility（置物設施）

43. 相關細節——男子表示造成問題的原因

What does the man say is causing a problem?

(A) He is not used to dealing with large groups.

(B) His audio equipment is malfunctioning.

(C) Some demonstration machinery is very loud.

(D) The usual venue for a talk is unavailable.

男子說何事造成了問題？

(A) 他不習慣應對大型團體。

(B) 他的音訊設備故障中。

(C) 有些展示機具聲音很大聲。

(D) 常用的演講場地無法使用。

- deal with 處理；應付 equipment (n.) 設備 malfunction (v.) 故障 demonstration (n.) 示範 venue (n.) 場地 unavailable (adj.) 無法使用的

換句話說 handle（負責〔處理〕）→ dealing with（應對）

44-46 Conversation

44-46 對話 英⇄澳

W: **(44) Hi, I have an appointment for a tune-up on my sedan.** My name is Yolanda Garcia.

M: I'm sorry, Ms. Garcia, but we're pretty busy today. We might not be able to get to your car until the early evening. **(45) Would you like me to check our schedule for openings tomorrow morning instead?**

W: **(45) Oh, I'm going out of town then. Driving, actually. That's why I scheduled my appointment for this afternoon.** Is there anything you can do to speed up the process, at least?

M: Let me see . . . Our records say you don't really need an oil change yet. **(46) Why don't we save that job for later?**

W: That sounds good. Here are my keys.

女：**(44) 你好，我有預約要為我的轎車要進行檢修**，我的名字是尤蘭達・賈西亞。

男：抱歉，賈西亞小姐，我們今天業務繁忙，可能要到傍晚才能幫您的車進行檢修，要不要我幫您查一下時間表，幫您改約明天早上的空檔？

女：**(45) 噢，到時我就要出發去外地了，其實就是要開車去，這就是為何我預約在今天下午檢修**，你有沒有辦法至少加快一下檢修過程？

男：我看一下……我們的紀錄顯示，您的車還不太需要更換機油，**(46) 我們何不把這項工作留到以後呢？**

女：聽起來可行。這邊是我的鑰匙。

- appointment (n.) 預約　tune-up (n.) 把（引擎）調試到最佳運轉狀態　sedan (n.) 轎車　opening (n.) 空缺　instead (adv.) 作為替代　process (n.) 過程　at least 無論如何；至少　save (v.) 保留

44. 全文相關——對話地點

Where are the speakers?
(A) At a law firm
(B) At a hair salon
(C) At a doctor's office
(D) At an auto repair shop

說話者人在何處？
(A) 在律師事務所
(B) 在美髮沙龍
(C) 在醫師診間
(D) 在汽車維修廠

45. 相關細節——女子預約在今天的理由

Why did the woman schedule her appointment for today?
(A) She completed some preparations yesterday.
(B) She does not have to work this afternoon.
(C) She will attend a banquet this evening.
(D) She will leave for a trip tomorrow.

女子為何把預約安排在今天？
(A) 她昨天做好了準備。
(B) 她今天下午不用工作。
(C) 她今天晚上要參加宴會。
(D) 她明天要外出遠行。

- preparation (n.) 準備　banquet (n.) 宴會

換句話說 going out of town（到外地）→ leave for a trip（外出遠行）

46. 相關細節——男子提出的建議

What does the man suggest doing?
(A) Updating some records
(B) Postponing a service
(C) Talking to a manager
(D) Saving a copy of a form

男子建議怎麼做？
(A) 更新紀錄
(B) 延後一項服務
(C) 與經理談話
(D) 保存表格副本

- postpone (v.) 延遲　form (n.) 表格

換句話說 save that job for later（把這項工作留到以後）→ postponing a service（延後一項服務）

47-49 Conversation with three speakers

M1: Hi, Jonas. What did you want to talk to us about?

M2: (47) **Some good news—the owner of Jessup Supermarkets has given our organization a fifty-thousand-dollar gift.**

W: Wow! What will it be used for?

M2: She only specified that we put it towards community outreach.

W: (48) **OK. Well, I heard about an environmental nonprofit in Florida that has been inviting famous climate scientists to give lectures . . . How about we plan something similar?**

M2: That could certainly bring us some publicity.

M1: True, but educational events that are fun for schoolchildren too might engage more local citizens.

M2: Hmm, you both make good points. (49) **I'd like to get our employees' input too. Let's set up an organization-wide meeting this week to discuss ideas.**

47-49 三人對話 加⇄澳⇄美

男 1： 嗨，喬納斯，你要跟我們說什麼事？

男 2： (47) **有個好消息：傑瑟普超市的老闆捐了五萬元給我們組織。**

女： 哇！這筆錢要如何運用？

男 2： 她只指定要我們將款項用於社區外展服務。

女： (48) **好的。那麼，我聽說佛羅里達州有個非營利環保組織，會邀請知名氣候科學家進行演講⋯⋯我們要不要也規劃類似活動？**

男 2： 這肯定會讓我們獲得大眾關注。

男 1： 確實，但是如果舉辦學童們也能樂在其中的教育活動，可望能吸引更多當地民眾參與。

男 2： 嗯，兩位都提出了很好的意見。(49) **我也想聽聽我們員工們的建議，本週我們來就開場全體會議、腦力激盪一下吧。**

- organization (n.) 組織；機構　specify (v.) 明確指出　outreach (n.) 外展服務；推廣服務　nonprofit (n.) 非營利組織　climate (n.) 氣候　publicity (n.) 宣傳；關注　engage (v.) 吸引　input (n.) 意見

47. 相關細節——說話者收到的東西 難

What has the speakers' organization received?

(A) A grant from a government agency

(B) A prize from a national contest

(C) Additional funds from its headquarters

(D) A donation from a businessperson

說話者的組織收到了什麼？

(A) 政府單位的補助金

(B) 全國比賽的獎金

(C) 總公司追加的資金

(D) 商人的捐款

- grant (n.)（政府）撥款；補助金　headquarters (n.) 總部；總公司　donation (n.) 捐贈；捐款

換句話說 the owner of . . . a fifty-thousand-dollar gift（⋯⋯的老闆捐了五萬元）
→ a donation from a businessperson（商人的捐款）

48. 相關細節——女子對使用這筆錢的建議 難

What does the woman suggest doing with the money?

(A) Producing some brochures

(B) Giving bonuses to employees

(C) Holding a speaker series

(D) Offering a school scholarship

女子建議如何運用這筆錢？

(A) 製作宣傳手冊

(B) 給員工發獎金

(C) 舉辦系列講座

(D) 提供學校獎學金

- brochure (n.) 小冊子　scholarship (n.) 獎學金

49. 相關細節——喬納斯決定做的事情

What does Jonas decide to do?
(A) Plan a gathering
(B) Issue a questionnaire
(C) Call a consultant
(D) Draft an article

喬納斯決定做什麼？
(A) 計劃開會
(B) 發放調查問卷
(C) 打電話給顧問
(D) 草擬文章

- **gathering (n.)** 聚會；集會 **issue (v.)** 發給 **draft (v.)** 起草；制定

50-52 Conversation

M: Hi, Melinda? It's Chikashi. (50) **I'm calling about the interior design drawings I sent you earlier this week. I'd love to hear what you think of them.**

W: Hi, Chikashi. Well, for the most part, I'm very pleased. (51) **But . . . the chairs that you chose for the waiting room are very stylish, while** our main priority is our visitors' comfort. Do you have some other options you could show me?

M: I do, but I want you to know that I did choose those chairs with comfort in mind. (52) **Would you consider trying them out at the wholesale shop before you decide against them?** It's not far from your office.

W: (52) **OK, I guess I can do that.**

50-52 對話

加⇄美

男： 嗨，是梅琳達嗎？我是誓志。(50) **我打電話來，是想問一下我本週稍早寄給妳的室內設計圖，我想聽聽妳的看法。**

女： 嗨，誓志。嗯，我大致上很滿意，(51) **不過……你幫等候室挑選的椅子相當時髦，然而**我們的首要考量是訪客的舒適度，你還有其他幾款椅子可以讓我參考嗎？

男： 確實有的，可是我想讓妳了解一下，我當初選這款椅子時，就有將舒適度考慮在內，(52) **妳否決這款椅子之前，能否考慮到家具批發店試坐看看呢？**那家店離妳的公司不遠。

女： (52) **好的，我想可以的。**

- **waiting room** 等候室；候診室 **priority (n.)** 優先考慮的事 **comfort (n.)** 舒適 **option (n.)** 選擇；選項 **wholesale (adj.)** 批發的

50. 全文相關——男子來電的目的

Why is the man calling the woman?
(A) To get some feedback
(B) To notify her of a problem
(C) To confirm some instructions
(D) To volunteer for an assignment

男子為什麼會打電話給女子？
(A) 為了取得意見回饋
(B) 為了告知她問題
(C) 為了確認幾項指示
(D) 為了自願接下任務

- **notify (v.)** 通知 **confirm (v.)** 確認 **instruction (n.)** 指示；說明 **assignment (n.)** 工作；任務

換句話說 hear what you think of them（聽聽妳的看法）→ get some feedback（取得意見回饋）

51. 掌握說話者的意圖——提及「我們的首要考量是訪客的舒適度」的意圖 難

What does the woman imply when she says, "our main priority is our visitors' comfort"?
(A) She is not concerned about cost.
(B) She does not mind extending a deadline.
(C) A room should have more open space.
(D) Some seating looks uncomfortable.

女子說：「我們的首要考量是訪客的舒適度」，言下之意為何？
(A) 她不擔心費用。
(B) 她不介意延長期限。
(C) 室內應該有更多的開放空間。
(D) 座椅看起來不舒適。

- **concerned (adj.)** 擔心的；關心的 **extend (v.)** 延長 **seating (n.)** 座位 **uncomfortable (adj.)** 不舒適的；令人不舒服的

52. 相關細節——女子同意做的事情

What does the woman agree to do?
(A) Pay a deposit
(B) Visit a store
(C) Approve a design
(D) Wait for a shipment

女子同意做什麼？
(A) 支付訂金
(B) 造訪商店
(C) 批准設計
(D) 等待送貨

- **deposit (n.)** 訂金 **approve (v.)** 批准 **shipment (n.)** 運輸的貨物

換句話說 trying them out the wholesale shop（到家具批發店試坐看看）→ visit a store（造訪商店）

53-55 Conversation

M: (53) **Excuse me—I'm looking for the book Guide to Brockler.** You know, for the programming language "Brockler"? Your computer system says it's in stock, but (53) **I can't find it on the shelf. Does that mean that another customer has bought the last copy?**

W: It might, but it could also mean that someone has just put it back in the wrong location. If that's the case, it's probably in the same general area. (54) **Would you like me to help you look?**

M: That would be great, thanks. (55) **I've registered to take a Brockler certification test next month, and apparently Guide to Brockler is the best prep book on the market.** I'm really hoping to pick it up today and start studying.

53-55 對話

澳⇄英

男： (53) **請問一下，我在找《柏克勒指南》這本書。**你知道的，就是針對程式語言「柏克勒」的書？你們的電腦系統顯示有庫存，可是 (53) **我在架上找不到。這代表有別的客人買走了最後一本嗎？**

女： 有可能，不過也可能只是有人把書歸位時放錯位置了。如果是這樣，書可能同樣還在綜合書區。(54) **需要我幫您找找看嗎？**

男： 那就太好了，謝謝。(55) **我已經報名參加下個月的柏克勒檢定考，而顯然《柏克勒指南》是市面上最好的備考書，**我真的希望今天能買到書，然後開始研讀。

- **shelf (n.)** 架子；書架 **general (adj.)** 綜合的；一般的 **register (v.)** 報名；註冊
  certification (n.) 檢定；證明 **apparently (adv.)** 顯然地

53. 全文相關——女子的職業

Who most likely is the woman?
(A) A bookstore clerk
(B) A repair technician
(C) A pharmacist
(D) A librarian

女子最有可能的職業為何？
(A) 書店店員
(B) 維修技術員
(C) 藥師
(D) 圖書館員

---

54. 相關細節——女子提議做的事情

What does the woman offer to do?
(A) Provide a refund
(B) Assist with a search
(C) Restart a computer system
(D) Recommend an alternative

女子提議做什麼？
(A) 提供退款
(B) 協助尋找
(C) 重新啟動電腦系統
(D) 推薦替代選項

- **refund (n.)** 退款 **search (n.)** 搜尋 **alternative (n.)** 替代品

換句話說 help you look（幫您找找看）→ assist with a search（協助尋找）

55. 相關細節——男子提及下個月將發生的事情

What does the man say will happen next month?
(A) A registration period will begin.
(B) A product will be removed from the market.
(C) A certification exam will be held.
(D) A return policy will become invalid.

男子說下個月會發生什麼事？
(A) 報名期間將開始。
(B) 某產品將撤出市場。
(C) 將舉行檢定考。
(D) 退貨政策將失效。

- period (n.) 期間 remove (v.) 去掉；移開 exam (n.) 考試 invalid (adj.) 無效的

56-58 Conversation

W: Oliver, I need your advice. (56) **Do you remember how I posted a quiz about the association's history on our social media account?** It's getting hundreds of comments, and not all of them are positive.

M: Hold on. Let me open up my browser . . . Oh, I see.

W: Yeah. (57) **I didn't realize that the answer to number five is controversial.** What should I do?

M: (57) **Well, the point of our social media presence is to increase member engagement,** and this got a lot of people talking.

W: That's true.

M: (58) **We don't want to discourage debate, so for now, just keep an eye on these comments.** You can take action later if needed.

56-58 對話 英⇄加

女： 奧利佛，我需要你的建議，(56) **你還記得我曾在我們的社群媒體帳戶上，發布了有關協會歷史的小測驗嗎？**那則貼文獲得好幾百則留言，而並不全部都是正面回饋。

男： 稍等，我開一下瀏覽器……哦，我明白了。

女： 是啊，(57) **沒想到第五題的答案居然有爭議，**我該怎麼辦？

男： (57) **這個嘛，我們在社群媒體上活動的用意，就是增加會員的參與度，**而這一題引起很多人的討論。

女： 確實如此。

男： (58) **我們並不希望制止人們討論，所以目前就先留意留言狀況吧，**如有必要，後續再採取措施就行了。

- association (n.) 協會；社團 account (n.) 帳戶 comment (n.) 評論；留言 positive (adj.) 正面的 realize (v.) 意識到 controversial (adj.) 有爭議的 presence (n.) 存在 engagement (n.) 參與 discourage (v.) 阻擋；阻撓 debate (n.) 辯論

56. 相關細節——女子發在社群媒體上的貼文

What did the woman post on social media?
(A) Some images
(B) Some statistics
(C) Some questions
(D) Some advice

女子在社群媒體上發布了何種內容？
(A) 一些圖片
(B) 一些統計數字
(C) 一些問題
(D) 一些建議

換句話說 a quiz（小測驗）→ some questions（一些問題）

57. 掌握說話者的意圖——提及「這一題引起很多人的討論」的意圖 難

Why does the man say, "this got a lot of people talking"?
(A) To reject the woman's request
(B) To point out an unintended benefit of an action
(C) To express concern about some criticism
(D) To admit that he was wrong about a strategy

為何男子要說：「這一題引起很多人的討論」？
(A) 以拒絕女子的要求
(B) 以指出一項行動的意外好處
(C) 以表達對批評的擔憂
(D) 以承認他在策略上的錯誤

- reject (v.) 拒絕 unintended (adj.) 無意的 benefit (n.) 益處 concern (n.) 擔心；關切 criticism (n.) 批評 strategy (n.) 策略；戰略

58. 相關細節——男子向女子提出的要求

What does the man ask the woman to do?
(A) Edit a sentence
(B) Write another post
(C) Monitor a discussion
(D) Respond to some comments

男子要求女子做什麼？
(A) 修訂句子
(B) 寫另一則貼文
(C) 監看討論
(D) 回應留言

- edit (v.) 編輯；修訂 post (n.)（網路）貼文 monitor (v.) 監控

換句話說 keep an eye on these comments（留意留言狀況）→ monitor a discussion（監看討論）

59-61 Conversation

M: OK, this is our booth space—number sixteen. [59] **Let's set up quickly so we have some time to review our recruiting strategy before the jobseekers arrive.**

W: Good idea. I'll start opening the boxes. [60] **Wow, the new "About Howlert Corporation" pamphlets look great!** I think they're really going to get people interested in working for us.

M: Yes, they did turn out well, didn't they? But where's the table cover with our logo on it? We should put that down first.

W: It's right here. But, Giuseppe . . . [61] **where are the soft drinks and energy bars?** I don't see them anywhere.

M: [61] **Ah, I forgot to put that box in the car!** Do you think there's a supermarket nearby?

59-61 對話 加⇄美

男： 好的，這就是我們的展覽攤位——第16號，(59) **我們趕緊做好布置吧，以便在求職者過來以前，有時間再複習一下我們的招聘方針。**

女： 好主意。我先來把箱子打開。(60) **哇，這份「豪樂特公司簡介」宣傳冊看起來真棒！**我想這肯定會激起很多人的興趣，想要到我們公司工作。

男： 對啊，製作得很精美，對不對？不過，上面印有我們公司標誌的桌布在哪裡？我們應該要先把桌布鋪上。

女： 就在這裡。不過，朱塞佩……(61) **飲料跟能量棒放在哪裡呢？**我到處都找不到。

男： (61) **噢，我忘記把那一箱搬上車了！**妳覺得這附近會有超市嗎？

- booth (n.) 攤位；展位 review (v.) 再檢查 recruit (v.) 招聘；僱用 strategy (n.) 策略 jobseeker (n.) 求職者 pamphlet (n.) 小冊子 cover (n.) 遮蓋物

59. 相關細節——即將舉辦的活動類型

What type of event is about to take place?
(A) An arts festival
(B) A career fair
(C) A store opening
(D) An advertising seminar

何種活動即將舉辦？
(A) 藝術節
(B) 就業博覽會
(C) 商店開幕會
(D) 廣告討論會

60. 相關細節——女子感到滿意的理由

Why is the woman pleased?
(A) Some marketing materials are attractive.
(B) A piece of furniture is larger than expected.
(C) The man has agreed to her proposal.
(D) A space is in a busy area.

女子為什麼很滿意？
(A) 行銷資料很吸引人。
(B) 家具大小超乎預期。
(C) 男子同意她的提議。
(D) 場地所在區域人潮眾多。

- material (n.) 資料；素材 attractive (adj.) 吸引人的 proposal (n.) 提案

61. 相關細節——男子忘記做的事情

What did the man forget to do?
(A) Clean some decorations
(B) Seal a box tightly
(C) Bring some refreshments
(D) Put fuel in a vehicle

男子忘記做什麼？
(A) 清洗裝飾品
(B) 把箱子封緊
(C) 攜帶點心飲料
(D) 給車輛加油

- decoration (n.) 裝飾（品） seal (v.) 封；密封 tightly (adv.) 緊緊地；牢固地 refreshment (n.) 茶點；點心 fuel (n.) 燃料 vehicle (n.) 車輛

換句話說 soft drinks and energy bars（飲料跟能量棒）→ refreshments（點心飲料）

62-64 Conversation + Shift schedule

M: Oh no, (62) **I've been scheduled to work on Wednesday afternoon! That's when my university's Japanese class meets.** I'll have to switch shifts with somebody. You're working in the morning—could you switch with me?

W: (63) **Sorry, Neil, but I'm also busy on Wednesday afternoon. Try asking whoever's working the night shift that day.**

M: (63) **OK, I will.** But this is frustrating. I definitely told Mr. Romero that I wasn't free on Wednesday afternoons.

W: Well, as a manager, he has a lot of information to keep track of. (64) **You should write down your availability for him when he comes in today. Then he'll have something to refer to when he makes the next shift schedule.**

	Wednesday	Thursday
Morning shift	Christina	Christina
Afternoon shift	Neil	Ruby
(63) Night shift	**Alton**	Hakeem

62-64 對話＋排班日程表 澳⇄美

男： 噢，不好了，(62) **我星期三下午有被排到班！那個時段是我大學日文課的上課時間，** 我得跟別人換班。妳那天上早班吧，可以跟我換班嗎？

女： (63) **對不起，尼爾，星期三下午我也很忙，問看看那天上晚班的人吧。**

男： (63) **好吧，我會去問，** 但這就是讓人氣惱，我確實有跟羅梅羅先生說過，我星期三下午並沒有空檔。

女： 嗯，他是經理，要留意的事情千頭萬緒，(64) **你應該把你的空檔時段寫下來，等他今天來上班時交給他，這樣他下次他排班表的時候，就有資料可以參照。**

	星期三	星期四
早班	克莉絲汀娜	克莉絲汀娜
午班	尼爾	露比
(63) 晚班	**奧爾頓**	哈基姆

- switch (v.) 調換；交換 shift (n.) 輪班 frustrating (adj.) 令人懊惱的 keep track of 記錄 availability (n.) 可得性；能參加 refer to 參考；查閱

62. 相關細節——男子排班上有衝突的原因

What is causing a scheduling conflict for the man?
(A) A family gathering
(B) Some planned travel
(C) A medical appointment
(D) A university course

何事造成男子的排班時間衝突？
(A) 家庭聚會
(B) 旅行規畫
(C) 預約就診
(D) 大學課程

- **conflict (n.)** 衝突 **gathering (n.)** 聚會 **appointment (n.)** 預約

63. 圖表整合題——男子將要求換班的對象

Look at the graphic. Who will the man next ask to take his shift?
(A) Christina
(B) Alton
(C) Ruby
(D) Hakeem

請看圖表作答。男子接下來會請誰接手他的輪班？
(A) 克莉絲汀娜
(B) 奧爾頓
(C) 露比
(D) 哈基姆

64. 相關細節——女子建議在經理抵達時做的事情

What does the woman suggest doing when a manager arrives?
(A) Making a reminder note
(B) Getting some contact details
(C) Referring a friend for employment
(D) Reporting the status of a task

經理到達後，女子建議做什麼？
(A) 製作提醒便條
(B) 取得聯繫方式
(C) 推薦朋友就業
(D) 回報工作狀態

- **reminder (n.)** 提醒用的事物 **detail (n.)** 詳細資訊；細節 **refer (v.)** 介紹；推薦 **status (n.)** 狀態 **task (n.)** 任務；工作

換句話說 write down（寫下）→ make a note（製作便條）

65-67 Conversation + Floor plan

M: As one of the first new hires in our expanded office, you have a choice between a couple of open desks. Here's the floor plan. Where would you like to sit?

W: Hmm . . . (65) **Well, I'm going to be handling sensitive information on my computer. Is there a way to ensure that people passing by me can't see it?**

M: Oh yes, we can get you a privacy screen that fits over your monitor.

W: Great! (66) **Then I'd like the empty desk by the copy room.** That would be convenient.

M: All right. (67) **Let's head over there now so you can see what kind of equipment and supplies you already have.** Then we can order the screen and anything else you need.

65-67 對話＋平面圖 澳⇄英

男： 妳是我們辦公室擴建後，招募來的第一批新人，所以有不少空的辦公座位可讓妳選擇，這裡是平面圖，不知妳會想坐哪裡？

女： 唔……(65) **嗯，我之後會在電腦上處理敏感資訊，有什麼辦法來確保經過我座位的人，看不到螢幕上的內容呢？**

男： 噢，有的，我們可以提供防窺片，裝設在妳的電腦螢幕上。

女： 好極了！(66) **那麼我想坐在影印室旁邊的空桌**，那會很方便。

男： 好的。(67) **我們現在一起過去那邊，讓妳可以看看現有的設備和用品有哪些**，然後就可以下單購買螢幕防窺片和其他所需物品。

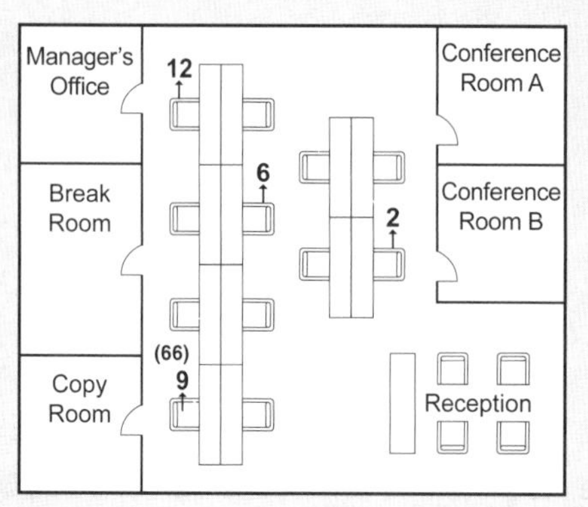

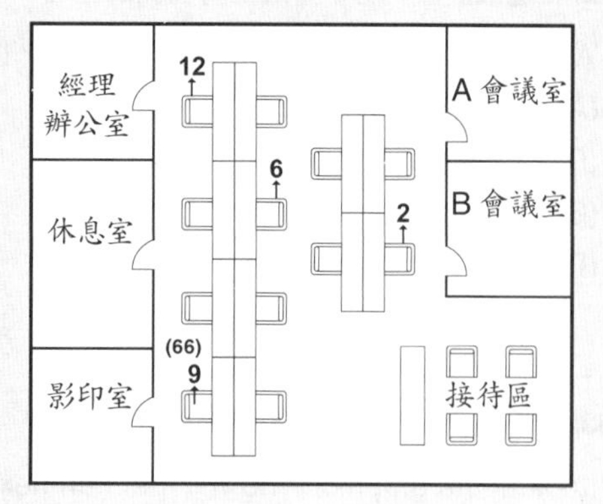

- hire (n.) 新雇員　expanded (adj.) 擴大的　floor plan 平面圖　handle (v.) 處理　sensitive (adj.) 敏感的　ensure (v.) 確保　privacy (n.) 隱私　fit (v.) 安裝；適合　empty (adj.) 空的；未佔用的　convenient (adj.) 方便的　head (v.) 前往　equipment (n.) 設備　supplies (n.) 用品

65. 相關細節——女子提出的問題

What does the woman ask about?

(A) Computer sizes

(B) Privacy measures

(C) Meeting frequencies

(D) Temperature conditions

女子詢問了什麼事？

(A) 電腦尺寸

(B) 隱私保護措施

(C) 開會頻率

(D) 溫度狀況

換句話說 **a way to ensure that people passing by me can't see it**（辦法來確保經過我座位的人，看不到螢幕上的內容）→ **privacy measures**（隱私保護措施）

66. 圖表整合題——女子選擇的辦公桌

Look at the graphic. Which desk does the woman choose?

(A) 2

(B) 6

(C) 9

(D) 12

請看圖表作答。女子選擇哪個座位？

(A) 2

(B) 6

(C) 9

(D) 12

67. 相關細節——說話者接下來要做的事情

What will the speakers do next?

(A) Fill out paperwork

(B) Greet a department head

(C) Shop online for supplies

(D) Go to a workstation

說話者下一步要做什麼？

(A) 填寫文件

(B) 跟部門主管打招呼

(C) 上網購買用品

(D) 前往工作位置

- fill out 填寫　paperwork (n.) 資料；文檔　greet (v.) 問候；打招呼　workstation (n.) 個人工作區

68-70 Conversation + List

W: Hi. Could you help me choose a portable sound system?

M: Sure. What do you need one for?

W: (68) **I'm in a band, and we need equipment for performing in public places and at parties.** Do you think "The Boom" would be powerful enough for that?

M: Two thousand square feet isn't actually a very big area. (69) **I'd recommend buying the model with eight thousand square feet of sound coverage instead and turning the volume down as needed.**

W: Let me see the price tag . . . Hmm . . . That's not cheap.

M: (70) **Well, we offer a very affordable monthly payment plan on most of our electronics, including portable sound systems.** Let me show you at the counter.

Portable Sound Systems

Model	Sound coverage (*square feet*)
The Boom	2,000
(69) **Amplifire**	**8,000**
Silver Tone	15,000
PowerVox	25,000

68-70 對話＋清單 美⇄加

女：你好，可以請你幫我挑選一台可攜式音響系統嗎？

男：當然可以，請問裝置的用途為何呢？

女：(68) **我是樂團成員，我們樂團需要可供在公共場所、派對上演出時使用的音響設備，** 你覺得這款「轟鳴」的聲音強度夠嗎？

男：2,000平方英尺的覆蓋範圍，其實並不算大，(69) **我推薦您改選用聲音覆蓋範圍8,000平方英尺的那款，然後根據需求調低音量。**

女：我看看價格標籤……唔……不便宜呢。

男：(70) **啊，本店大部分的電子產品，都提供有非常划算的月付方案，可攜式音響系統也在包含在內。** 請移步櫃檯，讓我向您介紹。

可攜式音響

機型	聲音覆蓋範圍（平方英尺）
轟鳴	2,000
(69) **爆音**	**8,000**
銀音	15,000
力聲	25,000

- portable (adj.) 便攜的；手提的　equipment (n.) 設備　perform (v.) 表演；演出　square feet 平方英尺　coverage (n.) 覆蓋範圍　instead (adv.) 作為替代　price tag 價格標籤　affordable (adj.) 價格實惠的　plan (n.) 計畫；方案　electronics (n.) 電子用品

68. 相關細節——女子的計畫

What does the woman plan to do?

(A) Perform some music

(B) Organize some lectures

(C) Host a sports event

(D) Hold a party

女子計畫從事什麼？

(A) 演奏音樂

(B) 籌辦講座

(C) 主持體育賽事

(D) 舉辦派對

- organize (v.) 組織；安排　lecture (n.) 演講　host (v.) 主持

69. 圖表整合題——男子推薦的機型

Look at the graphic. Which model does the man recommend?

(A) The Boom

(B) Amplifire

(C) Silver Tone

(D) PowerVox

請看圖表作答。男子推薦哪個機型？

(A) 轟鳴

(B) 爆音

(C) 銀音

(D) 力聲

---

70. 相關細節一男子針對店內可攜式音響提及的內容 

What does the man say about the store's portable sound systems?

(A) They are kept behind the counter.

(B) They can be paid for in installments.

(C) A new model will be released this month.

(D) Some of them may be rented.

對於店裡的可攜式音響系統，男子有何說明？

(A) 都放在櫃檯後方。

(B) 可以分期付款。

(C) 本月會推出新款。

(D) 部分機台可供租用。

- in installments 分期地　release (v.) 推出；上市　rent (v.) 出租；租用

換句話說 offer a monthly payment plan（提供有月付方案）
→ can be paid for in installments（可以分期付款）

PART 4 P. 41–43 12

71-73 Announcement

71-73 宣布 美

Good evening, shoppers. (71) **Did you know that EMC Furniture was voted the best value for the money by Detroit shoppers?** (72) **While you browse our merchandise, we invite you to compare prices by going online at any of our Internet kiosks located conveniently throughout the store.** If you can find another store offering one of our products for less, we'll beat their price. And for a limited time you can receive a fantastic deal on an extended warranty. (73) **Our two-hundred-dollar warranty is half price through the weekend.** Thanks for visiting EMC, where we're always looking for ways to save you money.

各位顧客，大家好。(71) **您知道 EMC 家具賣場，被底特律的消費者票選為性價比最高的店家嗎？** (72) **我們邀請您在查看本店商品同時，可以利用本店隨處可見的網路服務機台，上網比較商品價格。**如果針對本賣場的商品，您能找到別家商店開出更便宜的價格，我們將提供更加優惠的價格。目前本店也有限時優惠，可供您以非常優惠的價格取得商品延長保固。(73) **週末期間，本店兩百元的保固方案皆以半價提供給您。**感謝各位光臨 EMC，本店一直為您的荷包把關。

- vote (v.) 投票　value for money 物美價廉　browse (v.) 瀏覽　merchandise (n.) 商品
compare (v.) 比較　conveniently (adv.) 便利地　beat (v.) 打敗；勝過　limited (adj.) 有限的
extended (adj.) 延長的　warranty (n.) 保固

71. 相關細節——說話者提及 EMC 家具獲得認可的部分 

What does the speaker say EMC Furniture received recognition for?

(A) Their excellent customer service

(B) Their innovative loyalty program

(C) Their large inventory

(D) Their reasonable prices

說話者提到，EMC 家具賣場因何事受到肯定？

(A) 優質的顧客服務

(B) 創新的熟客回饋方案

(C) 庫存量大

(D) 價格公道

- excellent (adj.) 優秀的　innovative (adj.) 創新的　loyalty program 常客回饋方案　inventory (n.) 存貨；庫存　reasonable (adj.) 合理的

換句話說 the best value for the money（性價比最高）→ their reasonable prices（價格公道）

72. 相關細節——說話者提及購物者可以在店內做的事情

According to the speaker, what can shoppers do in the store?

(A) Access the Internet

(B) Watch a repair process

(C) Sit down to take a break

(D) Receive personalized advice

根據說話者所述，購物者能在賣場裡做什麼？

(A) 使用網路連線

(B) 觀看維修過程

(C) 坐下休息

(D) 取得客製化建議

- access (v.) 使用　process (n.) 過程　personalized (adj.) 客製化的

換句話說 going online（上網）→ access the Internet（使用網路連線）

73. 相關細節——現在正在優惠的東西

What is currently on sale?

(A) A disposal method

(B) A club membership

(C) Furniture customization

(D) A product guarantee

目前何者正在優惠中？

(A) 處理方法

(B) 會員資格

(C) 家具客製

(D) 產品保修

- disposal (n.) 處理　method (n.) 方法　customization (n.) 客製化　guarantee (n.) 保固；品質保證

換句話說 our warranty（本店的保固方案）→ a product guarantee（產品保修）

74-76 Talk

All right, gather around. (74) **Let me tell you what you'll be doing here today.** Dorothy and Krista, I'd like you to dust the desks and bookcases and wash the windows. Max, you vacuum the carpets. Travis and Deepak, you clean the break room. Uh, there's some mildew in there, so you'll need this bottle of Ranvex Spray. (75) **It's pretty strong, so use a small amount and keep the windows open.** (76) **Now, this isn't a big office, but I'd still like everyone to keep the two-way radio I gave you turned on, just in case.** OK, let's get started.

74-76 談話 英

好了，大家請集合。(74) **我要跟大家宣布今天在這裡要做的事項。**桃樂絲跟克麗斯塔，妳們負責清理桌子跟書架上的灰塵，並要清洗窗戶；麥克斯，你負責用吸塵器清潔地毯，特拉維斯和狄帕克，你們要打掃休息室。呃，休息室裡有點發霉，所以你們會需要用到這瓶「朗維克斯噴劑」。(75) **噴劑的效力強勁，所以用量只需一點，窗戶也要打開。**(76) **雖然辦公室不大，但還是希望大家把我給你們的無線電對講機打開，以備不時之需。**好的，我們開始工作吧。

- gather (v.) 集合　dust (v.) 除塵　vacuum (v.) 用吸塵器打掃　mildew (n.) 黴菌　two-way radio 無線電對講機

74. 全文相關——獨白的目的

難

What is the main purpose of the talk?
(A) To promote some cleaning products
(B) To outline the schedule of a tour
(C) To give assignments to a work crew
(D) To introduce some safety videos

本段談話的主要目的為何？
(A) 宣傳清潔產品
(B) 概述旅遊行程
(C) 分配工作給團隊成員
(D) 介紹安全影片

- promote (v.) 宣傳；推銷　outline (v.) 概述　assignment (n.) 工作；任務　work crew 工作團隊

75. 相關細節——說話者針對「朗維克斯噴劑」提及的內容

What does the speaker say about Ranvex Spray?
(A) It smells good.
(B) It is powerful.
(C) It is a window cleaner.
(D) It comes in a small bottle.

對於「朗維克斯噴劑」，說話者有何說法？
(A) 味道很好。
(B) 效力很強。
(C) 是窗戶清潔劑。
(D) 是以小瓶裝。

換句話說 strong（效力強勁）→ powerful（效力很強）

76. 相關細節——說話者提及聽者拿到的東西

According to the speaker, what has each listener received?
(A) A communication device
(B) Some protective clothing
(C) Some brochures
(D) A floor plan

根據說話者所說，每位聽者都有拿到什麼？
(A) 通訊器材
(B) 防護衣物
(C) 小冊子
(D) 樓層平面圖

換句話說 the two-way radio（無線電對講機）→ a communication device（通訊器材）

77-79 Excerpt from a meeting

[77] The last thing I'd like to discuss is, um, some news we received from the city. Apparently, they're doing some maintenance and this whole block won't have electricity for most of Tuesday. I think it will make more sense for everyone to just work from home that day. I know it's a bit unusual, but most of us can get everything we need from our computers and make all of our calls from home. That'll be the only change. **[78] I expect everyone to be available for team calls or anything else that comes up during the workday. [79] We promised we'd finish making Calliban Financial's Web site by Friday, so I don't want to lose any time.**

77-79 會議摘錄

澳

[77] 我想討論的最後一件事是，唔，我們從市政府接收到的消息。顯然，市府正在進行修護工程，而在這星期二的大半天，這整個街區都會停電。我認為在當天，讓大家在家辦公會是比較合理的做法。我知道這跟平常有所不同，但我們大多在家中都可以用電腦取得一切所需資料，也可以撥打電話，除此變動外，一切都照舊。**[78] 我希望當天上班期間，大家能隨時待命，以便處理團隊通話或者其他公務，[79] 我們已經承諾要在星期五之前，完成卡里班財務公司的網站，所以我不想浪費任何時間。**

- apparently (adv.) 顯然地　maintenance (n.) 維護；維修　electricity (n.) 電力
make sense 合理；可行　available (adj.) 聯絡得到的　promise (v.) 承諾　lose (v.) 失去；浪費

77. 相關細節—說話者提及他聽到的消息 難

What news from the city does the speaker mention?
(A) An inspector will visit local businesses.
(B) An area's power will be turned off.
(C) A construction project will begin.
(D) A major road will be closed.

說話者提到，從市政府有接收到何項消息？
(A) 稽查員將訪視當地企業。
(B) 地區的供電將切斷。
(C) 建案將開始動工。
(D) 主要道路將封閉。

- inspector (n.) 檢查員；視察員　power (n.) 電力　construction (n.) 建築　major (adj.) 主要的

換句話說 this whole block won't have electricity（整個街區都會停電）
→ an area's power will be turned off（地區的供電將切斷）

78. 掌握說話者的意圖——提及「除此變動外，一切都照舊」的意圖 難

What does the speaker mean when he says, "That'll be the only change"?
(A) Employees should use the same login information.
(B) Employees should not submit extra reports.
(C) Employees should work their usual hours.
(D) Employees should not prepare for an evaluation.

說話者說：「除此變動外，一切都照舊」，意思為何？
(A) 員工應用相同資訊登入系統。
(B) 員工不應繳交額外報告。
(C) 員工應按時照常上班。
(D) 員工不應準備評鑑。

- submit (v.) 提交　evaluation (n.) 評估；評價

79. 相關細節——聽者正在處理的工作項目

What type of project are the listeners working on?
(A) Doing market research
(B) Designing an automobile
(C) Remodeling an office
(D) Building a Web site

聽者目前正在進行何種專案？
(A) 市場調查
(B) 汽車設計
(C) 辦公室改建
(D) 網站架設

80-82 Telephone message

Hi, Anne. It's Terry. (80) **I got your message, and I brought the handouts for the Elsa Kwak workshop to your desk like you requested.** And they look great, by the way. (81) **Uh, but since you weren't at your desk, I guess that you're still trying to find the projector for the large conference room.** I have no idea why it's missing or where it would be, so I can't help you with that task. But—Ms. Kwak's flight arrives at four p.m., right? (82) **I could have her back here by six for the group dinner as planned. That would give you some extra time to set up.** Call me back and let me know what you think.

80-82 電話留言 英

嗨，安，我是特麗。(80) **我收到妳的訊息了，也已經按照妳的吩咐，把艾莎・夸克的研習會要用的講義，放到妳的桌上。**對了，講義看起來很不錯哦。(81) **呃，但既然妳不在位子上，我猜妳還在找大會議室要用的投影機。**我不知道為何投影機會不見，也不知道會在哪裡，所以幫不上忙。不過，夸克女士的班機是下午四點抵達，對吧？(82) **我可以按照計畫，在六點時接她回來這裡參加團隊晚餐。這樣妳就有一些額外時間做準備了。**請回電，讓我知道妳的想法。

- handout (n.) 講義；印出的資料　missing (adj.) 遺失的；找不到的

80. 全文相關——電話留言的主題

What is the speaker most likely talking about?
(A) Rearranging a work space
(B) Preparing for a workshop
(C) Setting up some interviews
(D) Handling some vacation requests

說話者最有可能在談論何事？
(A) 重新布置辦公空間
(B) 為研習會做準備
(C) 安排面試
(D) 處理休假申請

- rearrange (v.) 重新安排 handle (v.) 處理 vacation (n.) 休假

81. 相關細節——說話者提及的問題 難

What problem does the speaker mention?
(A) Some equipment cannot be located.
(B) Some furniture is very heavy.
(C) A conference room is unavailable.
(D) A software program is slow.

說話者提到什麼問題？
(A) 設備下落不明。
(B) 家具非常沉重。
(C) 會議室無法使用。
(D) 軟體程式運作緩慢。

- locate (v.) 找出；確定……的地點 unavailable (adj.) 不可用的；無法得到的

換句話說 still trying to find the projector（還在找投影機）
→ some equipment cannot be located（設備下落不明）

82. 掌握說話者的意圖——提及「夸克小姐的班機是下午四點抵達，對吧？」的意圖 難

What does the speaker mean when she says, "Ms. Kwak's flight arrives at 4 p.m., right"?
(A) She is offering assistance to the listener.
(B) She recommends postponing a decision.
(C) She thinks a message contains incorrect information.
(D) She is grateful for the listener's support.

說話者說：「夸克女士的班機是下午四點抵達，對吧」，意思為何？
(A) 她正在向聽者提供協助。
(B) 她建議延後某項決定。
(C) 她認為訊息裡包含錯誤資訊。
(D) 她感謝聽者的支持。

- assistance (n.) 協助 postpone (v.) 延後；延期 contain (v.) 包含 grateful (adj.) 感謝的

83-85 Telephone message

Hello, my name is Frederick Lund, and (83) **I'm calling from Patton Enterprises.** I understand that you are a contractor who specializes in residential properties, and I'd like to introduce my company to you. (83) **We are the area's leading supplier of carpet remnants—that is, pieces that are left over from fitted carpet jobs.** You can pick up these pieces at incredible prices, and (84) **the items we have in stock are different every week.** (85) **Best of all, if you purchase at least three items, I can ship them to you at no cost.** Please call me back at 555-0188 to discuss this further if you're interested. Thank you.

83-85 電話留言 加

您好，我是 (83) **派頓企業**的弗雷德里克・倫德。我知道貴公司是專營住宅房地產的承包商，而我想向您介紹一下我們公司。(83) **我們是本地零頭地毯的主要供應商，也就是販售那些鋪設大面地毯後，剩下的邊角地毯布。**您可以用超乎想像的價格，購買這些地毯布，而且 (84) **我們的供貨每週都不同。**(85) **最優惠的是，若購買三件以上商品，還可享有免運費送貨到府。**如果您有興趣，請撥打 555-0188 回電給我，以便進一步討論，謝謝您。

- contractor (n.) 承包商 specialize in 專門經營 residential (adj.) 住宅的 supplier (n.) 供應商 remnant (n.) 邊角剩料；剩餘部分 incredible (adj.) 驚人的 in stock 有庫存；有現貨

83. 相關細節—派頓企業販售的商品 難

What does Patton Enterprises sell?
(A) Power tools
(B) Floor coverings
(C) Home appliances
(D) Safety gear

派頓企業販售何物？
(A) 電動工具
(B) 鋪地板的用料
(C) 家電產品
(D) 安全裝備

換句話說 carpet remnants（零頭地毯）→ floor coverings（鋪地板的用料）

84. 相關細節——說話者針對公司產品提及的內容

What does the speaker mention about the business's merchandise?
(A) It is energy-efficient.
(B) It is made from recycled materials.
(C) Its ratings are consistently positive.
(D) Its availability changes regularly.

關於該公司的產品，說話者提到了什麼？
(A) 節省能源。
(B) 由再生材料製成。
(C) 評價一向良好。
(D) 現貨定期更換。

- **efficient (adj.)** 效率高的　**recycled (adj.)** 回收再製的　**material (n.)** 材料；原料　**rating (n.)** 評價　**consistently (adv.)** 始終如一地　**availability (n.)** 可得到的東西　**regularly (adv.)** 定期的

換句話說 items we have in stock are different every week（我們的供貨每週都不同）
→ its availability changes regularly（現貨定期更換）

85. 相關細節——說話者提供給聽者的東西

What does the speaker offer to do for the listener?
(A) Send a catalog
(B) Deliver items for free
(C) Give a demonstration
(D) Provide a consultation

說話者主動提供聽者什麼？
(A) 寄送型錄
(B) 免費配送
(C) 示範說明
(D) 提供諮詢

- **demonstration (n.)**（使用方法等的）示範說明　**consultation (n.)** 諮詢

換句話說 ship them to you at no cost（免運費送貨到府）→ deliver items for free（免費配送）

86-88 Broadcast

I'm Luisa Peters, reporting from Cavette for *Sports News Today*. As you can see, I'm here at the celebration of the Cavette Mustangs' national baseball championship. (86) **There are the team's players and coaches, cruising by in open vehicles and waving at the cheering crowd.** And what a crowd it is! (87) **Most of these people were here when I arrived,** and I got here at 6 a.m.! Clearly there is a lot of excitement about the Mustangs' historic win. (88) **If you missed the game, you can visit sportsnewstoday.com right now to see clips of its most exciting moments.** But don't forget to tune back in to our program. At the end of the route, some of the players are going to give speeches.

86-88 電視播報 美

我是路易莎·彼得斯，目前在卡維特現場為您播報《今日體育新聞》。如大家所看到，我現在位於「卡維特野馬隊」在全國棒球賽奪冠的慶祝會現場。(86) **球隊選手跟教練都坐在敞篷車上，向歡呼的群眾揮手致意。**真是人山人海！(87) **我抵達時，大部分的人潮就已經聚集在這裡，**我可是早上六點就來了！顯然，大家對野馬隊獲得歷史性的勝利，都感到熱血沸騰。(88) **如果各位錯過了那場比賽，現在可以到 sportsnewstoday.com 回顧最刺激的賽事片段，**但別忘了回來收看本節目。在遊行結束時，將有幾名球員發表演說。

- celebration (n.) 慶祝　cruise (v.) 緩慢巡行　vehicle (n.) 車輛　wave (v.) 向……揮手致意　cheer (v.) 歡呼　crowd (n.) 人群　excitement (n.) 興奮　miss (v.) 錯過　clip (n.)（剪輯的）片段　route (n.) 路線

86. 相關細節——活動類型 難

What kind of event is taking place?
(A) A sports competition
(B) A groundbreaking ceremony
(C) An outdoor fund-raiser
(D) A street parade

何種活動正在舉行當中？
(A) 體育競賽
(B) 動土典禮
(C) 戶外募款
(D) 街頭遊行

87. 掌握說話者的意圖——提及「我可是早上六點就來了」的意圖 難

Why does the speaker say, "I got here at 6 a.m."?
(A) To make a recommendation about future events
(B) To emphasize how popular the event is
(C) To explain how she got an advantage
(D) To indicate frustration with a delay

說話者為何要說：「我可是早上六點就來了」？
(A) 對未來的活動提出建議
(B) 強調活動的受歡迎程度
(C) 解釋她如何獲得優勢
(D) 對於延誤表示失望

- recommendation (n.) 建議；推薦　emphasize (v.) 強調　advantage (n.) 優勢；好處　indicate (v.) 表示　frustration (n.) 沮喪；失望　delay (n.) 延遲

88. 相關細節—網站上提供的東西

What is available on a Web site?
(A) A route map
(B) Game highlights
(C) Athlete biographies
(D) A public discussion

網站上有提供什麼內容？
(A) 路線圖
(B) 賽事亮點
(C) 運動員傳記
(D) 公開討論

- biography (n.) 傳記

換句話說 clips of its most exciting moments（最刺激的賽事片段）→ game highlights（賽事亮點）

89-91 Announcement

Good morning, managers. (89) **I need to inform you of an upcoming interruption to our factory's operations.** Management approved a request from Foster Television Network to film part of an episode of the show *Bertram* here next week. (90) **As I understand it, the show's star is going to chase another character through the facility and have a big fight with him.** Sounds exciting, doesn't it? Anyway, both the afternoon and night shifts will be affected during the two days of filming. (91) **All of the important details are in the memo that I'm handing out now. Please go over it briefly with your employees so that they know what to expect.**

89-91 宣布 澳

各位主管早安。(89) **我要通知大家，我們工廠的運作即將因故有所中斷。**公司管理高層已批准了福斯特電視網的申請，讓他們下週在我們這裡拍攝影集《伯特蘭》的部分內容。(90) **據我所知，劇中的影星會在工廠裡追逐另一個角色，並與他展開激烈打鬥**，聽起來很刺激，對不對？總之，在為期兩天的拍攝期間，午班和晚班工作都會受到影響。(91) **重要的細節資訊，全都列在現在我要發給大家的備忘錄裡。請與同仁一起簡短地查看一遍，讓他們知道會有什麼狀況。**

- inform (v.) 通知　upcoming (adj.) 即將到來的　interruption (n.) 打斷；干擾　approve (v.) 批准　film (v.) 拍攝　chase (v.) 追逐　facility (n.) 場所；設施　shift (n.) 輪班（工作時間）　affect (v.) 影響

hand out 分發　go over 查看

89. 全文相關——這則宣布出現的地點

Where most likely is the announcement being made?
(A) At a television studio
(B) At a shopping mall
(C) At a sports stadium
(D) At a manufacturing plant

這項宣布最有可能是在何處發表？
(A) 在電視攝影棚
(B) 在購物中心
(C) 在體育館
(D) 在製造工廠

換句話說 our factory（我們工廠）→ a manufacturing plant（製造工廠）

90. 相關細節——說話者針對電視節目談及的內容

What does the speaker say about a television show episode?
(A) It will include an action scene.
(B) It will be broadcast next week.
(C) It will feature a guest star.
(D) It will be one hour long.

關於該集電視節目，說話者說了什麼？
(A) 會包含動作場景。
(B) 將在下週播出。
(C) 將有客串明星登場。
(D) 時長將為一小時。

- include (v.) 包括　broadcast (v.) 播出；播放　feature (v.) 由……主演；特寫

91. 相關細節——要求聽者做的事情

What are the listeners asked to do?
(A) Distribute costumes to employees
(B) Conduct an inspection of a facility
(C) Avoid certain parts of a workplace
(D) Review the contents of a document

聽者被要求做什麼？
(A) 分發戲服給員工
(B) 執行設施檢查
(C) 避開工作場所的特定區域
(D) 審視文件內容

- distribute (v.) 分發　costume (n.) 戲服　conduct (v.) 執行；實施　inspection (n.) 檢查　avoid (v.) 避開　content (n.) 內容

換句話說 go over（查看）→ review（審視）

92-94 Excerpt from a meeting

OK, here's an idea I've been considering for improving our sales numbers. (92) **A few weeks ago, I ran into a personal contact who's also in the retail industry, and she told me about a Web site called "Zatmo".** (93) **It sells electronic coupons for discounts on other businesses' goods.** Zatmo gets a commission if a minimum number of people buy the coupons. My contact said it really raised her store's profile. (93) **I think we should try it.** (94) **But—does anybody see any possible downsides to working with Zatmo? If so, let's talk them over now.**

92-94 會議摘錄 英

好啦，我這裡一直有個想法，希望藉此提高我們的業績。(92) **數週前，我偶然碰到了一個熟人，她同樣在零售業工作，而她向我提起一個叫「扎特莫」的網站。**(93) **該網站販售的是其他店家的電子折價券。**針對售出一定數量折價券的店家，「扎特莫」就會向其收取佣金。我朋友說，這個方式確實提高了她賣場的知名度，(93) **我想我們也該試試看。**(94) **可是有沒有人思考到，和「扎特莫」合作可能會有哪些缺點？若有的話，我們現在就來討論一下。**

- run into 巧遇　contact (n.) 熟人；人脈　retail (n.) 零售　electronic (adj.) 電子的　commission (n.) 佣金；服務費　raise (v.) 提高；增加　profile (n.) 知名度；大眾的注意　downside (n.) 缺點

92. 相關細節——說話者提及她最近做的事情 難

What does the speaker say she recently did?
(A) She went to an industry conference.
(B) She contacted a start-up company.
(C) She spoke with an acquaintance.
(D) She read a retail trade magazine.

說話者說，她最近做了什麼事？
(A) 她參加了產業會議。
(B) 她聯絡上一家新創公司。
(C) 她跟一位熟人交談過。
(D) 她閱讀了零售產業雜誌。

- conference (n.) 會議　start-up company 新創公司　acquaintance (n.) 熟人　trade magazine 產業誌

換句話說 a personal contact（熟人）→ an acquaintance（熟人）

---

93. 相關細節——說話者提議增加銷售量的方式

How does the speaker propose increasing sales?
(A) By making a deal to buy some goods in bulk
(B) By expanding into new areas of the country
(C) By selling discount vouchers through an online platform
(D) By raising the commission paid to salespeople

說話者建議要如何提高業績？
(A) 達成大量商品採購的交易
(B) 擴展到國內其他地區
(C) 在網路平台販售折價券
(D) 提高支付給業務員的佣金

- deal (n.) 交易　in bulk 大量　expand (v.) 擴展　voucher (n.) 優惠券

換句話說 coupons for discounts（折價券）→ discount vouchers（折價券）

---

94. 相關細節——說話者要求聽者討論的事宜 

What does the speaker ask the listeners to discuss?
(A) Their departments' achievements
(B) The creation of a project team
(C) A possible launch date
(D) Disadvantages of her idea

說話者要求聽者討論何事？
(A) 該部門的成就
(B) 專案小組的成立
(C) 可能推出的日期
(D) 她的想法的缺點

- achievement (n.) 業績；成就　creation (n.) 創建；創造　launch (n.) 推出；上市
disadvantage (n.) 缺點

換句話說 downsides（缺點）→ disadvantages（缺點）

95-97 Talk + Recipe

Welcome to the latest episode of *Quentin's Kitchen*. (95) **A couple of the comments under last week's video asked for healthy snacks for summer.** So, today I'm going to show you how to make my favorite smoothies. Let's start with the blueberry kale smoothie. You'll need blueberries, baby kale, orange juice, and plain yogurt in the amounts you can see on the screen here. (96) **You can add more or less yogurt depending on how creamy you want the smoothie to be.** Then, just toss it all into the blender! It's ready once the kale is fully blended. (97) **I recommend drinking it right away so that the ingredients don't separate.** It becomes a little unappetizing then.

95-97 談話＋食譜 

歡迎大家收看最新一集《昆丁的廚房》。(95) **上週的影片下面，有不少留言敲碗要看適合夏天的健康點心**，所以，今天我要教教大家，如何製作我最愛的幾款奶昔。我們從藍莓羽衣甘藍奶昔開始吧，各位需要的食材有藍莓、嫩羽衣甘藍、柳橙汁跟原味優格，份量就如螢幕畫面所示，(96) **大家可以依照對奶昔綿密程度的偏好，來調整優格添加的多寡。**然後，就把所有食材放進攪拌機裡攪拌！等甘藍完全拌開之後，這道點心就完成了。(97) **完成後會建議馬上飲用，以免食材彼此散開**，這樣味道就會差了點。

Blueberry Kale Smoothie	
2 cups	baby kale
1 cup	orange juice
3/4 cup	blueberries
(96) 1/8 cup	yogurt

藍莓羽衣甘藍奶昔	
2 杯	嫩羽衣甘藍
1 杯	柳橙汁
3/4 杯	藍莓
(96) 1/8 杯	**優格**

- latest (adj.) 最新的 comment (n.) 評論；意見 kale (n.) 羽衣甘藍 depend on 取決於；根據 toss (v.) 扔；攪拌 blender (n.) 攪拌機 blend (v.) 攪拌 ingredient (n.) 食材 separate (v.) 分離 unappetizing (adj.) 令人沒有食慾的

95. 全文相關——聽者的身分 難

Who most likely are the listeners?
(A) Viewers of an online video
(B) Visitors to a supermarket
(C) Students at a cooking school
(D) The audience of a radio show

聽者最有可能是什麼人？
(A) 網路影片的觀眾
(B) 超市的顧客
(C) 烹飪學校的學生
(D) 廣播節目的聽眾

96. 圖表整合題——說話者提及可以調整的量

Look at the graphic. Which amount does the speaker say can be adjusted?
(A) 2 cups
(B) 1 cup
(C) 3/4 cup
(D) 1/8 cup

請看圖表作答。據說話者說，何項份量可以調整？
(A) 2 杯
(B) 1 杯
(C) 3/4 杯
(D) 1/8 杯

97. 相關細節——說話者提出的建議

What does the speaker recommend doing?
(A) Consuming the smoothie immediately
(B) Refrigerating the ingredients beforehand
(C) Serving small amounts as appetizers
(D) Using a special setting on the blender

說話者建議做何事？
(A) 立即享用奶昔
(B) 預先將食材冰鎮
(C) 少量食用作為開胃菜
(D) 使用攪拌機的特殊設定

- consume (v.) 食／飲用 immediately (adv.) 立刻 refrigerate (v.) 冷藏 beforehand (adv.) 事先；預先 serve (v.) 招待；上菜 appetizer (n.) 開胃菜 setting (n.) 設定

換句話說 drinking it right away（馬上飲用）→ consuming the smoothie immediately（立即享用冰沙）

98-100 Telephone message + Web page layout

Hi Wakana, it's Leo. I'm just looking over the layout options for our Web site that you sent over. (98) **If I have to choose, I prefer the one that has both our logo and the drop-down menus on the left side of the screen.** (99) **But will it allow us to feature high-quality photographs of our property listings?** That's the most important feature, anyway.

98-100 電話留言＋網頁版式 澳

嗨，若奈，我是里歐。妳有傳來幾款我們網站版面的選項，我現在正在查看，(98) **如果要選的話，我比較喜歡將公司商標和下拉選單，都放在螢幕左邊的那一款，**(99) **可是如此一來，我們有辦法再放上房地產商品的高畫質照片嗎？**畢竟，網站最重要的要素就是這個。

(100) Uh, also, I know you wanted to interview me for the site's "About Us" section, but I'm just too busy to meet in person this week. I do have a long car drive to meet a prospective buyer tomorrow morning, though. **(100) Could we talk on the phone as I drive?** Let me know.

(100) 哦還有，我知道妳想要和我做訪談，以便製作網站的「關於我們」頁面，但我本週太忙碌了，無法親自跟妳見面，不過，我明天早上要開很久的車，去和潛在買家碰面，(100) 到時我可以邊開車邊跟妳做電話對談嗎？請再告訴我。

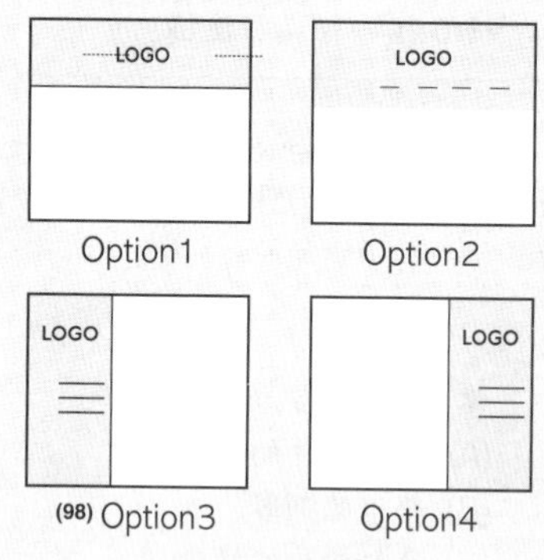

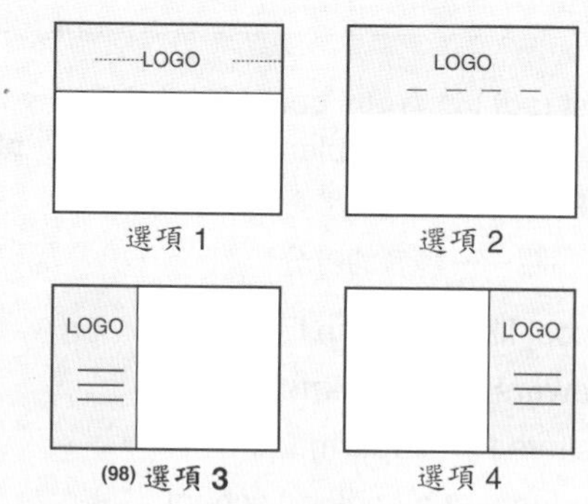

- layout (n.) 版面編排　option (n.) 選項　feature (n.) 特徵　property (n.) 房地產　listing (n.) 列表；清單　section (n.) 部分　in person 親自；面對面的　prospective (adj.) 預期的；未來的

98. 圖表整合題——說話者偏好的排版

Look at the graphic. Which option does the speaker prefer?

(A) Option 1

(B) Option 2

(C) Option 3

(D) Option 4

請看圖表作答。說話者偏好那個選項？

(A) 選項 1

(B) 選項 2

(C) 選項 3

(D) 選項 4

99. 全文相關——說話者的工作地點

Where most likely does the speaker work?

(A) At a real estate firm

(B) At a photography studio

(C) At a hotel chain

(D) A tour agency

說話者最有可能在哪裡工作？

(A) 在房地產公司

(B) 在攝影工作室

(C) 在連鎖飯店

(D) 在旅行社

100. 相關細節——說話者建議在電話上做的事情

What does the speaker suggest doing over the phone?

(A) Discussing layout styles

(B) Apologizing to a client

(C) Carrying out an interview

(D) Giving some driving directions

說話者建議透過電話做什麼事？

(A) 討論版面風格

(B) 向客戶致歉

(C) 進行採訪

(D) 提供行車路線

- apologize (v.) 道歉　carry out 實施；執行　directions (n.)〔複〕路線指引

ACTUAL TEST 4

PART 1 P. 44–47 13

1. 雙人照片——描寫人物的動作 英

A) They're lifting a box in an office.
(B) They're shaking hands with each other.
(C) One of the men is checking his watch.
(D) One of the men is touching a keyboard.

(A) 他們在辦公室裡抬起箱子。
(B) 他們彼此握手。
(C) 其中一名男子在查看手錶。
(D) 其中一名男子正觸碰著鍵盤。

- lift (v.) 抬起 shake hands 握手

2. 單人獨照——描寫人物的動作 澳

(A) A man is using a pole for a task.
(B) A man is watering some plants.
(C) A man is swimming in a pool.
(D) A man is painting a deck.

(A) 男子正在用桿子進行作業。
(B) 男子正在給植物澆水。
(C) 男子正在泳池游泳。
(D) 男子正在粉刷露台。

- pole (n.) 桿子 task (n.) 工作 deck (n.) 露台

3. 綜合照片——描寫人物或事物 加

(A) Some people are standing around a conference table.
(B) Images are being projected on a whiteboard.
(C) A woman is handing out bottles of water.
(D) A woman is addressing meeting participants.

(A) 有些人正站在會議桌周圍。
(B) 圖像正被投影到白板上。
(C) 女子正在分發瓶裝水。
(D) 女子正在對與會者說話。

- conference (n.) 會議 hand out 分發 address (v.) 向……談話 participant (n.) 與會者；參與者

4. 事物與背景照——描寫室內事物的狀態 美 

(A) One of the glass jars is empty.
(B) There are several pieces of silverware in a cup.
(C) A kitchen knife has been left on a plate.
(D) Bowls have been stacked on a counter.

(A) 其中一個玻璃罐是空的。
(B) 杯子裡有好幾件銀製餐具。
(C) 廚刀擺在盤子裡。
(D) 碗堆疊在流理台上。

- jar (n.) 瓶罐 empty (adj.) 空的 silverware (n.) 銀製餐具 plate (n.) 盤子 bowl (n.) 碗 stack (v.) 堆疊

5. 綜合照片——描寫人物或事物 英

(A) A gallery tour is taking place.
(B) A man is putting a picture in a frame.
(C) A group of people is being photographed.
(D) Lights have been turned toward some artwork.

(A) 畫廊導覽正在進行。
(B) 男子正把相片放進相框裡。
(C) 一群人正在拍照。
(D) 燈光被調整照向藝術作品。

- take place 發生；舉行 frame (n.) 框 photograph (v.) 照相 artwork (n.) 藝術作品

6. 綜合照片——描寫人物或事物 澳 難

(A) Some shirts have been hung on racks.	**(A) 掛衣架上掛著幾件襯衫。**
(B) Some hats have been placed in a shopping cart.	(B) 購物車裡放著幾頂帽子。
(C) A woman is laying a product on a shelf.	(C) 女子把產品放到貨架上。
(D) A window display is being rearranged.	(D) 有人在重新布置櫥窗展示品。

- rack (n.) 架子；掛物架 lay (v.) 放；擱 shelf (n.) 架子 rearrange (v.) 重新布置

PART 2 P. 48

14

7. 以 Why 開頭的問句，詢問員工獎提名梅蘭妮的原因 澳⇄英

Why did you nominate Melanie for an employee award?	你為什麼要提名梅蘭妮爭取員工獎？
(A) I wish I could, but I'm busy.	(A) 我希望我可以，但我很忙。
(B) Because she works really hard.	**(B) 因為她很努力工作。**
(C) The "Team Player" award.	(C) 「優秀團隊成員」的獎項。

- nominate (v.) 提名 employee (n.) 員工 award (n.) 獎

8. 表示請託或要求的問句 美⇄加

Would you mind picking up some napkins next time you go to the store?	下次你去商店時，可以順便幫我買些餐巾紙嗎？
(A) Sometime this morning.	(A) 今天早上的某個時間。
(B) I already picked up my trash.	(B) 我已經收拾了我的垃圾。
(C) We might have some in storage, though.	**(C) 但我們可能還有一些庫存。**

- pick up 買 trash (n.) 垃圾 storage (n.) 倉庫；儲藏

9. 以助動詞 Will 開頭的問句，詢問是否要預訂晚餐席位 澳⇄英 難

Will I need to reserve a table for dinner?	需要我為晚餐訂位嗎？
(A) A pasta dish with vegetables on the side.	(A) 一道義大利麵佐蔬菜。
(B) Let me see—Mr. Carter, party of four?	(B) 我看看——卡特先生，四位嗎？
(C) The restaurant isn't full in the evenings.	**(C) 那間餐廳晚上不會客滿。**

- reserve (v.) 預約 party (n.)（共同參加活動的）一行人

10. 以附加問句確認面試的結果 美⇄加

The interview with Ellen Bradley went well, didn't it?	和愛倫．布拉德利的面試進行得很順利，對吧？
(A) I think we should hire her.	**(A) 我認為我們該僱用她。**
(B) Her career history and skills.	(B) 她的工作經歷和技能。
(C) I prefer the view from Paul's workstation.	(C) 我更喜歡從保羅座位看出去的景色。

- career (n.) 職業；事業 view (n.) 景色；風光

11. 以 **Who** 開頭的問句，詢問應向誰提問 澳⇄美

Who should I talk to if I have questions about payroll? (A) I think the receptionist did. **(B) That would be Jin-Woo.** (C) Yes—how often will I be paid?	如果我有工資方面的問題，應該找誰討論？ (A) 我想是接待員做的。 **(B) 應該找秦禹。** (C) 是的，我多久能領一次薪水？

- payroll (n.) 工資表；工資單　receptionist (n.) 接待員

12. 以 **Where** 開頭的問句，詢問看新聞的管道 加⇄英

Where do you usually get your news? **(A) From the local newspaper.** (B) I haven't heard anything about it. (C) Every few hours.	你通常從哪裡看新聞？ **(A) 從地方報紙上。** (B) 我沒聽說過這件事。 (C) 每隔幾個小時。

13. 以 **How** 開頭的問句詢問，如何使用乾洗服務 美⇄澳

How do I use the hotel's dry-cleaning service? **(A) Did you ask the front desk staff?** (B) For my suit and shirts. (C) Our rooms are cleaned twice daily.	我要怎麼使用飯店的乾洗服務？ **(A) 你問過櫃檯人員了嗎？** (B) 為了我的西裝和襯衫。 (C) 本飯店客房每天打掃兩次。

- front desk 服務台；櫃檯　suit (n.) 西裝；套裝

14. 以助動詞 **Did** 開頭的問句，詢問設備是否有帶齊 英⇄澳

Did you pack up all of the equipment in the seminar room? (A) An overseas manufacturer. (B) It was quite easy to operate. **(C) There weren't enough boxes for everything.**	研討室的設備你全都打包收拾好了嗎？ (A) 一家海外製造商。 (B) 很容易操作。 **(C) 沒有夠多箱子裝下所有物品。**

- pack up 打包；收拾　equipment (n.) 設備　overseas (adj.) 海外的　manufacturer (n.) 製造商　operate (v.) 操作

15. 以 **When** 開頭的問句，詢問租約何時到期 加⇄美　難

When does the lease on our current space end? (A) We pay rent plus property taxes. **(B) Oh, we just got a notice about that.** (C) How much space are you looking for?	我們現在這地方的租約何時到期？ (A) 我們支付租金，外加上財產稅。 **(B) 噢，我們剛收到相關通知。** (C) 你們要找多大的空間？

- lease (n.) 租賃契約　current (adj.) 現在的　rent (n.) 租金　property tax 財產稅　notice (n.) 通知；公告

16. 以否定疑問句，確認對方剛是否有跟自己通電話 澳⇄美　難

Aren't you the sales clerk I spoke to on the phone? (A) Yes, a buy-one-get-one-free sale. (B) I believe it's 555-0130. **(C) My shift only started five minutes ago.**	你是和我通過話的那個店員，不是嗎？ (A) 是的，買一送一的促銷活動。 (B) 我想是 555-0130。 **(C) 我 5 分鐘前才剛開始值班。**

- sales clerk 店員　shift (n.) 輪班（工作時間）

17. 以選擇疑問句，詢問員工的用餐方式 英⇄澳

Do staff here usually bring lunch from home or go out to eat?	這裡的員工通常會自己帶午餐，還是去外面吃？
(A) Most people bring their own food.	**(A) 大部分的人會自備食物。**
(B) In the cafeteria on the ground floor.	(B) 在一樓的自助餐廳裡。
(C) Sure, that sounds good.	(C) 當然可以，聽起來不錯。

- cafeteria (n.) 自助餐廳

18. 以 How 開頭的問句，詢問對方準備演講的方法 加⇄美 難

How are you preparing for your conference speech?	你打算怎麼準備會議演說？
(A) It's going to be in the auditorium.	(A) 會是在禮堂。
(B) Well, it's still a month away.	**(B) 呃，（演說）還有一個月的時間。**
(C) Some stories about my research.	(C) 與研究相關的小故事。

- auditorium (n.) 禮堂 research (n.) 研究

19. 以直述句傳達資訊 英⇄加 難

Ms. Hardin's goodbye party has been scheduled for May second.	哈丁女士的送別會定於五月二日舉行。
(A) I didn't know she was leaving.	**(A) 我不知道她要離職了。**
(B) No, it will be the first time.	(B) 不，這會是第一次。
(C) There was a cake and some gifts.	(C) 有一塊蛋糕跟幾件禮物。

20. 以 What 開頭的問句，詢問錯誤訊息的意思 美⇄澳

What does this error message mean?	這個錯誤訊息代表什麼？
(A) Mr. Walsh stopped by while you were out.	(A) 威爾許先生在你外出時，有順道來訪。
(B) I didn't find any errors when I looked.	(B) 我看的時候，沒有發現錯誤。
(C) Isn't it listed in the product manual?	**(C) 這不是有列在產品說明書裡嗎？**

- stop by 順路造訪 list (v.) 列出 manual (n.) 說明書

21. 以否定疑問句，詢問某個人是否為某演員 加⇄英

Isn't that the actor from that television show you watch?	那不是你看的那部電視劇的演員嗎？
(A) Tuesday nights at eight.	(A) 每週二晚上八點。
(B) I think that man just looks like him.	**(B) 我覺得那個人只是長得像他。**
(C) Thanks—my brother asked for a watch for his birthday.	(C) 謝謝，我弟弟說要手錶當作生日禮物。

- look like 看起來像

22. 以 Where 開頭的問句，詢問可以學金融投資的地點 美⇄澳

Where can I learn about financial investing?	我可以到哪裡學習金融投資？
(A) Yes, very interesting.	(A) 是的，非常有趣。
(B) How about taking a course online?	**(B) 參加線上課程如何？**
(C) Into a savings account.	(C) 存入儲蓄帳戶裡。

- financial (adj.) 財金的 invest (v.) 投資 savings account 儲蓄帳戶

23. 以助動詞 **Did** 開頭的問句，詢問蔡先生是否已核准設計 英⇄加 難

Did Mr. Chae approve the designs for the lobby renovation?
(A) Unfortunately, it isn't.
(B) We have enough proof already.
(C) After a few revisions.

蔡先生是否已批准大廳整修的設計案？
(A) 很可惜，這不是。
(B) 我們已經有了足夠證據。
(C) 在經過幾次修改後。

- approve (v.) 批准　renovation (n.) 整修；改造　proof (n.) 證據　revision (n.) 修改

24. 以 **Who** 開頭的問句，詢問募到最多捐款的人 澳⇄美

Who collected the most donations for the fund-raiser?
(A) We're announcing it at tomorrow's meeting.
(B) Over six hundred dollars.
(C) I really care about this cause.

誰為募款活動籌集了最多的捐款？
(A) 我們明天開會時會公布。
(B) 超過六百美元。
(C) 我真的很關心這項慈善任務。

- donation (n.) 捐款　fund-raiser (n.) 募款活動　announce (v.) 公布　cause (n.) 目標；理想

25. 以選擇疑問句，詢問對方偏好的約診時間 英⇄加

Would you prefer Thursday afternoon or Friday morning for your next appointment?
(A) Three days' worth of medicine.
(B) I want to hear my test results in person.
(C) Let me open up my calendar app.

下次你比較想約週四下午，還是週五早上？
(A) 三天的藥量。
(B) 我想親自聽取檢驗報告。
(C) 讓我打開行事曆的應用程式。

- appointment (n.) 預約　medicine (n.) 藥　calendar (n.) 行事曆

26. 以附加問句，確認是否會重新裝修停車場 英⇄美 難

The parking area's going to be remodeled soon, isn't it?
(A) I don't drive here, so I'm not aware of it.
(B) It's past the stoplight, on your left.
(C) One of our older models, actually.

停車場很快就要改建了，對吧？
(A) 我不開車來，所以我不知道。
(B) 過了紅綠燈，就在左邊。
(C) 實際上，是我們較舊的機型。

- remodel (v.) 改建　stoplight (n.) 紅綠燈　actually (adv.) 實際上

27. 以 **Be** 動詞開頭的問句，詢問是否還接受交件 美⇄澳

Are we still accepting submissions for the new logo?
(A) The deadline is today at five.
(B) A white "M" on a blue circle.
(C) I submitted mine by e-mail.

我們還繼續新標誌設計的收件嗎？
(A) 最後期限是今天五點。
(B) 藍色圓圈上有白色的 M 字。
(C) 我用電子郵件把我的交出去了。

- accept (v.) 接受　submission (n.) 提交　deadline (n.) 截止日期；最後期限

28. 以 **When** 開頭的問句，詢問店家開始販售家居用品的時間點 加⇄美 難

When did Vaskin Apparel start selling household goods?
(A) I guess you missed the big promotional campaign.
(B) That's kind of you, but I don't need anything.
(C) No, they don't let you put items on hold.

瓦司金服飾何時開始賣起了家居用品？
(A) 看來你錯過了大型宣傳活動。
(B) 承蒙好意，可是我什麼都不需要。
(C) 不，他們不會讓你預留商品的。

- household goods 家庭日用品　miss (v.) 錯過　promotional (adj.) 促銷的　on hold 擱置

29. 以直述句傳達資訊 澳⇄英

The scanner in this self-service kiosk won't recognize my passport. (A) A major international airline. **(B) You'll have to check in at the counter, then.** (C) He's probably a new employee.	自助服務台的掃描器無法辨識我的護照。 (A) 一家大型國際航空公司。 **(B) 那麼，您得到櫃檯辦理登機手續。** (C) 他可能是新進員工。

- recognize (v.) 辨識；認出　passport (n.) 護照　international (adj.) 國際的　airline (n.) 航空公司

30. 以 Which 開頭的問句，詢問封街的區域 美⇄英　難

Which section of Harrison Street is closed? (A) OK, I'll take Stokes Avenue instead. (B) The city is repairing a water pipe. **(C) They finished up the roadwork yesterday.**	哈里遜街的哪個路段封閉了？ (A) 好吧，我會改走斯托克斯大道。 (B) 本市正在進行水管維修。 **(C) 道路工程昨天就完工了。**

- section (n.) 區域；地段　instead (adv.) 代替　repair (v.) 修理　roadwork (n.) 道路施工

31. 表示請託或要求的直述句 加⇄美　難

Please examine our utility bills for any extra charges. (A) To save money on electricity. **(B) There's never been a mistake in them before.** (C) You can pay by check or automatic withdrawal.	請檢查我們的水電費帳單，看是否有額外費用。 (A) 為了節省電費。 **(B) 之前從沒有出過差錯。** (C) 您可以用支票或自動扣款來支付。

- utility bill (n.) 水、電等費用帳單　charge (n.) 費用　electricity (n.) 電力　by check 以支票支付　withdrawal (n.) 提取

PART 3 P. 49–52　15

32-34 Conversation　32-34 對話　加⇄英

M: Ah, there you are, Alice. (32) **Do you know why the party guests are finishing the appetizers so quickly? Our servers are coming back with empty trays in just minutes.**	男：啊，愛麗絲，妳在這裡呀，(32) **宴會上的客人一下就把開胃菜一掃而空，妳知道原因嗎？才不過幾分鐘，服務生就把空托盤端回來了。**
W: I was just coming to talk to you about that. (33) **The greeter we stationed at the entrance says that she's already counted more than fifty guests.**	女：我正要來跟你說這件事，(33) **我們發派到門口的迎賓接待員說，據她計算，賓客人數已經有五十幾個人了。**
M: Really? (33) **There were only supposed to be thirty!** OK, I'll call Gene and ask him to bring some extra food from our kitchen. (34) **Could you drive to the nearest supermarket and pick up some more? The truck is parked by the back door.**	男：真的嗎？(33) **客人應該只有三十名才對啊！**好吧，我會打電話給吉恩，要他從廚房多帶些餐點過來，(34) **妳可以開車到最近的超市，購買更多食材嗎？卡車就停在後門附近。**
W: Sure. Let's see, I'll get dinner rolls and lettuce . . . Anything else?	女：沒問題。我看看，我會採買圓麵包跟生菜……還需要什麼嗎？

- server (n.) 服務生　tray (n.) 托盤　greeter (n.) 迎賓員；接待員　station (v.) 配置　entrance (n.) 出入口；門口　count (v.) 計數　be suppose to 應該　lettuce (n.) 生菜；萵苣

32. 相關細節——說話者正在做的事情

What are the speakers most likely doing?
(A) Delivering some groceries
(B) Giving a cooking demonstration
(C) Catering a celebration
(D) Holding a bake sale

說話者最有可能正在從事何事？
(A) 運送食品雜貨
(B) 進行烹飪示範
(C) 為慶祝活動供餐
(D) 舉辦烘焙食品義賣

- **grocery (n.)** 食品雜貨　**demonstration (n.)** 示範；演示　**cater (v.)** 提供餐飲服務　**celebration (n.)** 慶祝活動　**bake sale**（為募款舉辦的）烘焙食品義賣

33. 相關細節——女子提及造成問題的原因

According to the woman, what is causing a problem?
(A) An inefficient process
(B) A large number of people
(C) Damage to an appliance
(D) Bad weather

根據女子說法，問題的成因為何？
(A) 流程效率低下
(B) 來客人數眾多
(C) 電器產品損壞
(D) 天候不佳

- **inefficient (adj.)** 低效率的　**process (n.)** 過程；流程　**damage (n.)** 損壞　**appliance (n.)** 電器

34. 相關細節——女子接下來要去的地方

Where will the woman most likely go next?
(A) To an automobile
(B) To a front entrance
(C) To a storage area
(D) To a kitchen

女子接下來最有可能前往何處？
(A) 車輛
(B) 前門
(C) 庫存設施
(D) 廚房

換句話說 the truck（卡車）→ an automobile（車輛）

35-37 Conversation with three speakers

M: **(35) Finally, here are the conference rooms that you and your employees could use.** As you can see, each one has state-of-the-art presentation equipment. You can reserve them through a convenient online system.

W1: OK. I think this would fit our start-up's needs pretty well. **(36) What do you think, Theresa?**

W2: I agree, but I'm still uncertain about sharing a space with other companies. **(36) I mean, what happens if there's a disagreement between us and another tenant?**

M: Those are very rare. **(37) And remember, we offer month-to-month usage contracts.** If you choose that, you'd be free to leave relatively quickly even if a problem did arise.

35-37 三人對話　澳⇄美⇄英

男： **(35) 最後，這幾間是可供妳們和員工使用的會議室。**如妳們所見，每間會議室都配置了最先進的簡報設備，且透過便利的線上系統，就可以預約使用。

女1： 好的，我覺得這很符合我們這間新創公司的需求。**(36) 特瑞莎，妳覺得怎麼樣？**

女2： 我同意，可是對於要跟別家公司共用空間，我還是感到猶豫。**(36) 我的意思是，要是我們跟另一家承租人之間意見不合，該怎麼辦？**

男： 這種情況極少發生，**(37) 而且別忘了，我們有提供按月承租的使用合約**，若是妳們選擇了這個方案，即使真的發生問題，也能夠相當快速地解約搬離。

- **state-of-the-art (adj.)** 先進的　**reserve (v.)** 預約；預訂　**fit (v.)** 適合；符合　**start-up (n.)** 新創公司　**disagreement (n.)** 意見分歧　**tenant (n.)** 承租者　**rare (adj.)** 罕見的　**usage (n.)** 使用　**contract (n.)** 合約　**relatively (adv.)** 相當地　**arise (v.)** 出現；形成

35. 相關細節——女子們正在做的事

What are the women doing?
(A) Touring an office space
(B) Shopping for electronics
(C) Checking in at a conference
(D) Learning to use a software program

女子們正在進行何事？
(A) 參觀辦公空間
(B) 購買電子產品
(C) 簽到參加會議
(D) 學習使用軟體程式

- electronics (n.) 電子產品　check in 報到

36. 相關細節——特瑞莎擔憂的理由

Why is Theresa concerned?
(A) A retail price is high.
(B) A piece of equipment is large.
(C) An opportunity might be missed.
(D) A conflict might occur.

特瑞莎擔心什麼？
(A) 零售價格太高。
(B) 有件設備太大。
(C) 可能錯失機會。
(D) 可能發生爭執。

換句話說 a disagreement（意見不合）→ a conflict（爭執）

37. 相關細節——男子強調的事情

What does the man emphasize the availability of?
(A) A special transportation service
(B) A form of commercial insurance
(C) A short-term commitment option
(D) A free training resource

男子強調有提供何者？
(A) 特別的運輸服務
(B) 商業保險的表格
(C) 短期租約的選項
(D) 免費的培訓資源

- transportation (n.) 運輸　commercial (adj.) 商業的　insurance (n.) 保險
  commitment (n.) 承諾；投入　option (n.) 選擇；方案　resource (n.) 資源

換句話說 month-to-month usage contracts（按月承租的使用合約）
→ a short-term commitment（短期租約）

38-40 Conversation

M: Good evening, and [(38)] **welcome to Flatner Art Gallery. Are you here for Ms. Greenbaum's lecture?**

W: [(38)] **Yes—I loved her book on famous exhibitions. I couldn't miss the chance to hear her speak in person.**

M: We're glad that she agreed to come. [(39)] **Uh, may I see your "Friends of the Gallery" membership card?**

W: Here it is. Oh, and since I'm a little early, could I take a quick walk through Garrett Hall? I heard that it was just renovated.

M: [(40)] **I'm sorry, but since it's past six p.m., all parts of the gallery are closed except for the lecture area.**

38-40 對話 加⇄美

男： 晚安，[(38)] **歡迎蒞臨弗雷納美術館，請問您是來聽格林鮑姆女士的演講嗎？**

女： [(38)] **是的，她那本關於著名展覽的書，我相當喜歡，我不能錯過現場聽她演講的機會。**

男： 我們也很高興她能應邀前來。[(39)] **啊，方便讓我看一下您的「美術館之友」會員卡嗎？**

女： 在這邊。噢，因為我有點提早到，我能快速參觀一下加勒特廳嗎？我聽說加勒特廳才剛整修過。

男： [(40)] **很抱歉，由於已經過了下午六點，整間美術館除了演講會場以外，其他場館都已閉館了。**

- lecture (n.) 演講　exhibition (n.) 展覽　miss (v.) 錯過　renovate (v.) 翻新；整修　except for 除了

38. 相關細節——女子前來美術館的理由

Why has the woman come to the gallery?
(A) To see a new piece of artwork
(B) To inquire about exhibiting
(C) To finalize a purchase
(D) To listen to a talk

女子為何來到美術館？
(A) 看新展出的藝術品
(B) 詢問展覽事宜
(C) 敲定採購案
(D) 聆聽演講

- **artwork (n.)** 藝術作品 **inquire (v.)** 詢問 **finalize (v.)** 敲定；定案

39. 相關細節——男子要求女子提供的東西

What does the man ask the woman to provide?
(A) Proof of a membership
(B) The name of her friend
(C) The title of a painting
(D) A credit card

男子要求女子提供何者？
(A) 會員資格證明
(B) 她朋友的姓名
(C) 畫作的名稱
(D) 信用卡

換句話說 your membership card（您的會員卡）→ proof of a membership（會員資格證明）

40. 相關細節——女子無法進入加勒特廳的理由

Why will the woman be unable to enter Garrett Hall?
(A) Its contents have been loaned out.
(B) It is being renovated.
(C) Business hours are over.
(D) A pass has some restrictions.

女子為何無法進入加勒特廳？
(A) 廳內展品已外借。
(B) 正在進行整修。
(C) 開放時間已過。
(D) 通行證有所限制。

- **content (n.)** 內容物 **loan (v.)** 借出 **pass (n.)** 通行證 **restriction (n.)** 限制

換句話說 all parts of the gallery are closed（整間個美術館的場館已經關閉館了）
→ business hours are over（開放時間已過）

41-43 Conversation

W: Hi. (41) **My name is Glinda Stokes, and I made an appointment to have my dog washed and groomed on Saturday.**

M: Hello, Ms. Stokes. Yes, the miniature poodle at two o'clock. How can I help you today?

W: (42) **Well, uh, when I made that appointment, I forgot that a friend from out of town will be visiting that afternoon.** Do you happen to have any openings in the morning, instead? I'm sorry about the mistake.

M: Oh, no problem. (43) **We're always happy to try to satisfy customer requests as long as we have some advance notice.** Let's see . . . Would nine a.m. be too early?

W: No, that would be perfect. Thank you so much.

41-43 對話

英⇄加

女： 嗨，(41) **我的名字是葛琳達·史托克斯，我有幫我的狗狗預約星期六要做洗澡和美容服務。**

男： 哈囉，史托克斯小姐。對的，是一隻迷你貴賓狗，約在下午兩點，請問今天有什麼需要服務的嗎？

女： (42) **是這樣的，呃，我當初預約的時候，忘了那天下午會有朋友從外地來訪，**請問那天早上是否剛好還有空檔？對於這個疏失，我感到很抱歉。

男： 噢，沒有問題。(43) **只要有事先通知，我們都很樂意滿足顧客的要求。**我看看……早上九點會太早嗎？

女： 不會，那個時間很合適。非常謝謝你。

- appointment (n.) 預約　groom (v.) 使變整潔；打理……　opening (n.) 機會；空缺　instead (adv.) 作為替代　satisfy (v.) 滿足　advance notice 事先通知

41. 相關細節——女子欲接受的服務類型

What service does the woman plan to receive?
(A) Pet care
(B) Vehicle washing
(C) Interior decorating
(D) Plumbing repair

女子預計取得何項服務？
(A) 寵物打理
(B) 車輛清洗
(C) 室內裝飾
(D) 管線維修

換句話說 **have my dog washed and groomed**（幫我的狗狗做洗澡和美容服務）→ **pet care**（寵物打理）

42. 相關細節——女子犯下的失誤

What mistake did the woman make?
(A) She gave the wrong address.
(B) She failed to provide an important detail.
(C) She chose an inconvenient appointment time.
(D) She did not realize that a deal had ended.

女子有何疏失？
(A) 她給錯地址了。
(B) 她並未提供一項重要資訊。
(C) 她預約了不方便的時間。
(D) 她沒有注意到協議結束了。

- detail (n.) 細節　inconvenient (adj.) 不方便的　realize (v.) 意識到　deal (n.) 協議；交易

43. 相關細節——男子針對自己的商家提及的內容 難

What does the man say about his business?
(A) It uses advanced technology.
(B) It charges a fee to fulfill certain requests.
(C) It encourages staff to receive certifications.
(D) It tries to accommodate customers.

男子對於他的店有什麼說法？
(A) 使用了先進科技。
(B) 為滿足特定要求，會收取費用。
(C) 鼓勵員工取得證照。
(D) 努力配合顧客。

- advanced (adj.) 先進的　charge (v.) 收取（費用）　fee (n.) 費用　fulfill (v.) 達成；滿足　certification (n.) 證照　accommodate (v.) 為……提供方便

換句話說 **satisfy customer requests**（滿足顧客的要求）→ **accommodate customers**（配合顧客）

44-46 Conversation

M: Hi, Myra? This is Juan from Haslop Global calling. (44) **I'm happy to say that, based on your qualifications and yesterday's interview, we'd like to invite you to join the company as an in-house financial consultant.**

W: Oh, that's great! I was really impressed by everything I heard yesterday. (45) **I'm particularly excited about the chance to decide for myself when to start and finish work.**

M: Yes, our current staff really enjoy that perk. Now, the terms of our contract can be complex. (46) **Could you come in to the office tomorrow to look over them together?**

W: (46) **Sure.** But I hope you don't expect me to make a decision right then.

44-46 對話　澳⇄英

男： 嗨，是麥菈嗎？我是哈斯洛普環球公司的胡安。(44) **我很高興通知您，有鑑於您的資歷以及昨天面試的結果，我們想要邀請您加入本公司內部團隊，擔任財務顧問。**

女： 噢，真是好消息！昨天在貴公司的所見所聞，真的讓我非常佩服，(45) **對於有機會自行決定上下班時間，我尤其感到躍躍欲試。**

男： 沒錯，本公司目前的員工都很喜歡這項福利。接著呢，我們的合約條款可能會很複雜。(46) **能否請您明天來一趟公司，一起查看合約條款？**

女： (46) **當然可以。**可是希望您不會期望我到時要當下做出決定。

• based on 根據 qualification (n.) 資歷；條件 in-house (adj.)（機構、公司）內部的 impressed (adj.) 印象深刻的 particularly (adv.) 尤其地 perk (n.) 福利待遇 complex (adj.) 複雜的

44. 全文相關——男子致電的目的

Why is the man calling the woman?
(A) To arrange an interview with her
(B) To ask for a document
(C) To offer her a job
(D) To assess her professional qualifications

男子為何打電話給女子？
(A) 要安排與她面試
(B) 要索取文件
(C) 要提供她工作機會
(D) 要評估她的專業資格

• arrange (v.) 安排 assess (v.) 評估

換句話說 invite you to join the company as . . .（邀請您到加入本公司擔任……）
→ offer her a job（提供她工作職缺）

45. 相關細節——女子提及該職缺的吸引力

What does the woman say is attractive about a position?
(A) The salary for it is high.
(B) The work involved seems enjoyable.
(C) It is with a famous company.
(D) Its hours are flexible.

女子說這份工作吸引人的地方為何？
(A) 薪水很高。
(B) 經手的工作似乎很有趣。
(C) 是在知名公司工作。
(D) 上班時間很彈性。

• salary (n.) 薪資 involved (adj.) 有關的 enjoyable (adj.) 有樂趣的 flexible (adj.) 彈性的

換句話說 decide for myself when to start and finish work（自行決定上下班時間）
→ its hours are flexible（上班時間很彈性）

46. 相關細節——女子同意做的事情

What does the woman agree to do?
(A) Send some paperwork
(B) Visit a workplace
(C) Make a phone call
(D) Prepare a presentation

女子同意做什麼？
(A) 寄出文件資料
(B) 到工作地點
(C) 撥打電話
(D) 準備簡報

• paperwork (n.) 文件資料 workplace (n.) 工作場所 prepare (v.) 準備

換句話說 come in to the office（來一趟公司）→ visit a workplace（到工作地點）

47-49 Conversation with three speakers

W: Oh, hi, Keith and Randy. (47) **I noticed you haven't been coming to my cycling class lately. Is everything all right?**

M1: Hi, Fuyuko. My work schedule changed, so now we exercise in the evenings instead of the mornings.

M2: But we do miss your class! (48) **You don't offer personal training, do you?**

47-49 三人對話 美⇄澳⇄加

女： 嗅，季斯、藍迪，你們好。(47) **我注意到你們最近都沒有來上我的飛輪課程，一切都還好吧？**

男 1： 嗨，冬子。我的工作時間有變動，所以我們現在的運動時間不在早上，改到晚上運動了。

男 2： 不過我們真的很想念妳上的課！(48) **妳沒有提供個人化訓練課程，是嗎？**

M1: (49) **Yes, we'd love to have you lead just the two of us through a tailored cycling routine once a week or so.**	男 1：(49) **對啊，我們想請妳大概每週一次，就帶領我們兩個人，進行為我們量身打造的飛輪有氧課。**
W: I'd be happy to do that.	女：這個我很樂意喔。
M2: Great! How about on Thursdays?	男 2：好極了！每週四上課怎麼樣？
W: That could work. (49) **Could you wait a moment while I go to my desk to review my calendar?**	女：我覺得可行。(49) **你們兩位可以等我一下嗎？我回座位查看我的時間表。**
M2: Sure. We'll be lifting weights over here for a while.	男 2：沒問題，我們會在這裡做一下重訓。
M1: Yes, take your time.	男 1：對啊，妳慢慢來。

- notice (v.) 注意到　lately (adv.) 最近　lead (v.) 帶領　tailored (adj.) 量身定做的　lift (v.) 舉起　weight (n.) 重物；重量

47. 全文相關——女子的職業

Who most likely is the woman?
(A) An auto mechanic
(B) A fitness instructor
(C) A medical clinic receptionist
(D) A real estate agent

女子最有可能是什麼身分？
(A) 汽車維修工人
(B) 健身教練
(C) 醫療診所接待員
(D) 房地產仲介

48. 相關細節——男子們想知道的事情 難

What do the men want to know about?
(A) A customized service
(B) A routine inspection
(C) Some test results
(D) Some safety rules

男子們想知道什麼相關資訊？
(A) 客製化的服務
(B) 定期檢查
(C) 測試結果
(D) 安全規定

- customized (adj.) 客製化的　routine (adj.) 常規的；例行的　inspection (n.) 檢查　safety (n.) 安全

換句話說 tailored（專門設計的）→ customized（客製化的）

49. 相關細節——女子請男子們稍等的原因

Why does the woman ask the men to wait?
(A) A supervisor must approve a request.
(B) A budget has not been finalized yet.
(C) She must rearrange some furniture.
(D) She needs to check a schedule.

女子為何要求男子們等候？
(A) 主管必須批准請求。
(B) 預算尚未定案。
(C) 她必須重新擺設家具。
(D) 她需要查看時間表。

- supervisor (n.) 主管　approve (v.) 批准　budget (n.) 預算　finalize (v.) 定案　rearrange (v.) 重新安排

換句話說 review my calendar（查看我的時間表）→ check a schedule（查看時間表）

50-52 Conversation

50-52 對話

加⇄美

M: Oh, hi, Rosemary. Do you need the conference room? (50) **I just brought my laptop in here because I was having trouble concentrating. The noise from the construction site next door is so loud out in the office.**

W: I came in here for the same reason. It's frustrating, isn't it? (51) **Actually, yesterday I told my boss that I was having a hard time with it. I was hoping she'd have some ideas for solutions.**

M: What did she say?

W: (52) **She promised to ask the company to pay for noise-cancelling headphones staff can use at their seats.** I hope that they agree.

M: If they do, I might have to look into getting a pair as well.

男：哦，嗨，羅絲瑪麗，妳需要使用會議室嗎？(50) **因為我沒辦法專心工作，所以就帶著筆電來這裡，隔壁工地的噪音實在是太大，外面辦公室都聽得到。**

女：我也是為了這個，才過來這裡，真的很讓人火大，對吧？(51) **其實，我昨天就跟我主管說過我受不了，我當時希望她能想出些解決辦法。**

男：結果她怎麼說？

女：(52) **她答應會要求公司出錢購買降噪耳機，讓員工在自己的座位上可以使用，**希望公司會同意。

男：如果公司同意，我可能也得考慮取得一副了。

- concentrate (v.) 全神貫注　loud (adj.) 吵鬧的；大聲的　frustrating (adj.) 令人懊惱的

50. 相關細節——男子待在會議室的理由

Why is the man in the conference room?

(A) To have a quick snack

(B) To prepare for a seminar

(C) To lead a videoconference

(D) To work in a quiet place

男子為何會在會議室？

(A) 為了簡單吃個點心

(B) 為研討會做準備

(C) 為了主持視訊會議

(D) 為了在安靜的地方工作

- prepare (v.) 準備　videoconference (n.) 視訊會議

51. 相關細節——女子提及最近所做的事情

What does the woman say she recently did?

(A) She calculated some costs.

(B) She complained to a manager.

(C) She made plans to travel abroad.

(D) She went to another floor of the building.

女子說她不久前做了什麼事？

(A) 她把費用算出來了。

(B) 她跟主管抱怨過。

(C) 她做了出國旅遊的計畫。

(D) 她去了別的樓層。

- calculate (v.) 計算　complain (v.) 抱怨　abroad (adv.) 到國外

換句話說 told my boss that I was having a hard time with it（跟我主管說過我受不了）
→ complained to a manager（跟主管抱怨過）

52. 相關細節——說話者的公司可能會為員工購入的東西

What might the speakers' company buy for employees?

(A) Some audio equipment

(B) Some special seating

(C) A cooling appliance

(D) A beverage machine

說話者的公司有可能會買什麼給員工？

(A) 音訊設備

(B) 特殊座椅

(C) 冷卻裝置

(D) 飲料機

- equipment (n.) 設備；器材　appliance (n.) 裝置　beverage (n.) 飲料

換句話說 noise-cancelling headphones（降噪耳機）→ some audio equipment（音訊設備）

53-55 Conversation

W: (53) **Omar, Matt has been telling me that your employee book club is really fun.** How can I join?

M: I'm glad to hear that you're interested, Ursula! I'll just put you on the e-mail list. That's all there is to it.

W: Great! When's the next meeting?

M: It's this Thursday. Here's the book we're reading now. (54) **It's a bestseller that has some great tips on management techniques.** You'll need to get your own copy.

W: Oh! That sounds great but . . . that's a really big book. (55) **And the meeting is on Thursday?**

M: (55) **Ah, you don't have to finish the whole thing by then.** Just chapters three and four.

53-55 對話 英⇄澳

女：(53) **奧馬，麥特一直跟我說你開的員工讀書會樂趣十足**，我要如何才能參加呢？

男：烏蘇拉，聽妳說妳有興趣，我很開心！我會把妳加進電子郵件的收件名單，這樣就行了。

女：太好了！下次的讀書會是什麼時候？

男：這個星期四。我們現在正在讀的書是這本，(54) **是一本暢銷書，書裡提供不少管理技巧的高明訣竅**，妳得要自己去買一本。

女：哦！聽起來很不錯，可是……這本書好厚一本，(55) **而且讀書會就在週四？**

男：(55) **噢，妳不需要在那之前把整本書都讀完**，只要看第三、第四章就行了。

• interested (adj.) 感興趣的　management (n.) 管理　technique (n.) 技巧；技能

53. 全文相關——對話主題

What are the speakers mainly discussing?

(A) An activity group

(B) A business trip

(C) A promotional event

(D) An employee newsletter

說話者主要在討論什麼？

(A) 活動團體

(B) 商務旅行

(C) 促銷宣傳活動

(D) 員工電子報

54. 相關細節——男子針對書籍提及的事情

What does the man say about a book?

(A) He has not started reading it.

(B) He owns several copies.

(C) It is very popular.

(D) It gives investment tips.

有關書籍，男子提到了什麼事？

(A) 他還沒開始讀那本書。

(B) 他有好幾本書。

(C) 這本書大受歡迎。

(D) 書裡提供投資建議。

• own (v.) 擁有　investment (n.) 投資

換句話說 a bestseller（一本暢銷書）→ very popular（大受歡迎）

55. 掌握說話者的意圖——提及「這本書好厚一本」的意圖 難

What does the woman imply when she says, "that's a really big book"?

(A) The book will not fit in a display.

(B) It will take a long time to read the book.

(C) The book probably contains certain information.

(D) It will be uncomfortable to carry the book.

女子說：「這本書好厚一本」，言下之意為何？

(A) 書架放不下這本書。

(B) 讀這本書要很久的時間。

(C) 這本書可能包含特定資訊。

(D) 這本書攜帶不便。

• fit (v.) 適合　contain (v.) 含有　uncomfortable (adj.) 不舒服的　carry (v.) 攜帶

56-58 Conversation

56-58 對話 加⇄英

M: Hello. This is Wallace Dunn calling from Lensard Incorporated. (56) **I ordered some office supplies from you last week, and the invoice said they'd arrive by March third. But that was yesterday, and we haven't gotten anything. What's going on?**

W: Let me just find your account . . . OK. It appears that your shipment was delayed by a road closure. It should arrive tomorrow.

M: Well, I hope so. (57) **My colleagues are running out of the supplies required to keep our business running smoothly.**

W: I'm sorry about that. (58) **We don't usually allow this, but—would you like the shipment's ID code? If you enter it into a box on our Web site, you can follow your order's progress along its route.**

男：您好，這裡是連沙德公司的華利士·鄧恩。(56) **上週我跟你們訂了一批辦公用品，而發貨單上面寫著三月三日前會到貨，可是昨天就是三月三日，而我們未收到任何貨品。不知道發生了什麼事？**

女：請讓我查一下貴公司的帳號……找到了，看來貴公司的這批貨，因為道路封閉而延誤了，明天應該就會到貨。

男：好吧，希望如此。(57) **我們需要多項辦公用品，讓公司能順利營運，但現在同事們都快要把用品用完了。**

女：我對此感到很抱歉。(58) **我們通常不會容許這類情事，但是——您需要該批貨的識別編號嗎？如果您到我們網站，在欄位裡輸入這個編號，就可以追蹤您的訂單在路程上的進度。**

- incorporated (adj.) 組成公司的　invoice (n.) 發貨單；帳單　shipment (n.) 運輸的貨物　closure (n.) 關閉　colleague (n.) 同事　smoothly (adv.) 順暢的　progress (n.) 進展　route (n.) 路線

56. 全文相關——這通電話的目的

What is the purpose of the call?
(A) To order some office supplies
(B) To complain about the quality of some goods
(C) To ask about a charge on an invoice
(D) To check the status of a shipment

這通電話的目的為何？
(A) 訂購一些辦公用品
(B) 客訴一些商品的品質
(C) 詢問帳單上的費用
(D) 查詢貨物運送狀態

- goods (n.) 產品；商品　charge (n.) 費用　status (n.) 狀態

57. 相關細節——男子提及同事的理由 難

Why does the man mention his coworkers?
(A) To describe how a mistake was noticed
(B) To explain the need for some items
(C) To clarify whom the woman should contact
(D) To highlight an advantage of a proposal

男子為何提到他的同事？
(A) 說明錯誤是怎麼發現的
(B) 解釋對某些物品的需求
(C) 說明女子應該聯絡的對象
(D) 強調提案的好處

- describe (v.) 講述　clarify (v.) 澄清　highlight (v.) 強調　advantage (n.) 好處　proposal (n.) 提案

58. 相關細節——女子提供男子的東西

What does the woman offer the man?
(A) A discount coupon
(B) A tracking number
(C) A branded gift
(D) A return authorization

女子提供了什麼給男子？
(A) 折價券
(B) 追蹤編號
(C) 品牌禮品
(D) 退貨許可

- track (v.) 追蹤　branded (adj.) 有品牌的　return (n.) 退貨　authorization (n.) 批准；授權

換句話說 the shipment's ID code（該批貨的識別編號）→ a tracking number（追蹤編號）

59-61 Conversation

W: **(59) Aaron, those displays of blue jeans that you set up look very nice.** I think you're really starting to master this job.

M: Thanks, Ms. Soto. I'm enjoying the work. It's fun to help customers find what they need.

W: That's great. Well, I'm going to head home. Is there anything I should know before I go?

M: **(60) Oh, did you see that we're completely out of the Rothland-brand padded jackets?**

W: Aren't there some in the stockroom?

M: No, we sold those too. **(61) Though I didn't realize they were back there, actually, when the first customer asked me about them.** It's lucky that Chae-Young was here.

W: Yes, I see. Well, I'll order some more, then.

59-61 對話 美⇄澳

女： **(59) 艾隆，你把貨架上的那些藍色牛仔褲擺得有模有樣呢。**我看這份工作，你是駕輕就熟囉。

男： 謝謝，索托女士。這份工作讓我樂在其中。幫助客人找到他們所需的衣物，總是讓我樂此不疲。

女： 那好極了。對了，我準備回家了。在我離開前，有什麼事情是我需要知道的嗎？

男： **(60) 噢，妳有發現到，店裡「羅特蘭」品牌的襯墊外套，都已經完全沒貨了嗎？**

女： 倉庫裡不是還有幾件嗎？

男： 沒有了，那幾件也都賣完了。**(61) 不過其實，第一位客人問起那款外套的時候，我並不知道倉庫裡還有貨。**幸好當時彩瑛有在現場。

女： 好的，我知道了。那麼，我就再多訂一些貨吧。

- padded jacket 襯墊外套　stockroom (n.) 倉庫；商品儲藏室

59. 全文相關——對話的地點

Where is the conversation taking place?
(A) At a flower shop
(B) At a clothing retailer
(C) At an art supply store
(D) At a supermarket

這段對話是在哪裡發生的？
(A) 在花店
(B) 在服飾零售店
(C) 在美術用品店
(D) 在超級市場

60. 相關細節——男子針對商品提及的事情

What does the man say about some merchandise?
(A) It should be added to a display.
(B) It is in the stockroom.
(C) It has sold out.
(D) It needs to be organized.

對於某樣商品，男子有何說法？
(A) 應新增到展示區。
(B) 在倉庫裡。
(C) 已經完售。
(D) 需要整理。

- add (v.) 添加　sell out 售罄；賣光

61. 掌握說話者的意圖——提及「幸好當時彩瑛有在現場」的意圖 難

What does the man imply when he says, "It's lucky that Chae-Young was here"?
(A) A task required two people.
(B) He was very busy today.
(C) Chae-Young has a special skill.
(D) Chae-Young provided useful information.

男子說：「幸好當時彩瑛有在現場」，言下之意為何？
(A) 工作需要兩個人。
(B) 他今天非常忙。
(C) 彩瑛有特殊技能。
(D) 彩瑛提供了有用的資訊。

62-64 Conversation + Work assignment

62-64 對話＋工作分配表 加⇄美

M: Kara, hi. I got your latest status update on the construction and wanted to stop by. What's going on?

W: Well, the rain has put the framing work behind by several days, and I just heard that the flooring materials won't arrive until May.

M: Uh-oh. (62) **So will we be ready for guests in time for tourist season?**

W: It's going to be close. (63) **To be safe, I think we should bring in a specialist company to handle the flooring.**

M: OK, I'll think about it. For now, can you show me how the framing is going? (64) **Let's start with the walls.**

W: (64) **Sure, I'll take you to the crew leader.** Follow me.

Framing Assignments

Area	Crew Leader
Stairs	Whitney
Roof	Grant
(64) **Walls**	**Santos**
Windows	Jim

男： 嗨，卡拉，我收到妳寄來的最新施工狀況回報了，所以想要過來看看，不知道發生了什麼事？

女： 是這樣的，框架工程因為雨勢延宕了好幾天，而且我剛才聽說，地板用料要五月才會到貨。

男： 噢，真糟糕，(62) **這樣我們來得及在旅遊旺季前，準備好迎接客人嗎？**

女： 時間上會壓得很緊。(63) **保險起見，我認為我們應該延請專門的公司，來處理地板工程。**

男： 好的，我會考慮。現在可以帶我看看框架工程的進展嗎？(64) **我們從牆壁開始來看。**

女： (64) **沒問題，我帶你去找領班。**請跟我來。

框架工作分配表

區域	領班
樓梯	惠特尼
屋頂	葛蘭特
(64) **牆壁**	**桑托斯**
窗戶	吉姆

- **latest (adj.)** 最新的 **status (n.)** 情況 **construction (n.)** 工程 **framing (n.)** 框架 **flooring (n.)** 鋪地板 **material (n.)** 材料 **in time for** 及時趕上 **specialist (adj.)** 專業的；專門的 **handle (v.)** 處理 **crew (n.)** 工作人員

62. 相關細節——正在興建的建物

What most likely is being built?

(A) An apartment complex

(B) A store

(C) A hotel

(D) A school building

何者正在建造當中？

(A) 公寓大樓

(B) 商店

(C) 飯店

(D) 學校校舍

63. 相關細節——女子提出的建議 難

What does the woman suggest doing?

(A) Hiring some subcontractors

(B) Postponing an opening day

(C) Installing a protective covering

(D) Contacting other suppliers

女子建議做什麼？

(A) 僱用轉包商

(B) 延後開幕日期

(C) 安裝保護屏障

(D) 聯繫其他供應商

- **subcontractor (n.)** 轉包商 **postpone (v.)** 延後 **install (v.)** 安裝 **protective (adj.)** 保護的 **supplier (n.)** 供應商

換句話說 bring in a specialist company（延請專門的公司）
→ hiring some subcontractors（僱用轉包商）

---

64. 圖表整合題——說話者要去見的人

Look at the graphic. Whom are the speakers going to see?
(A) Whitney
(B) Grant
(C) Santos
(D) Jim

請看圖表作答。說話者將要去見何人？
(A) 惠特尼
(B) 葛蘭特
(C) 桑托斯
(D) 吉姆

65-67 Conversation + Display case

W: Howard, could you come over here for a second?
M: Sure, Ms. Quinn. What's up?
W: (65) **These carrots are looking a little dry. When was the last time you sprayed water on them?**
M: Oh, do they need to be sprayed with water? I thought it was only the broccoli in this section.
W: No, it isn't. You know, this isn't the first time there's been confusion about this. (66) **I'm going to make a list of the fruits and vegetables that need regular spraying. I'll post it in the staff room.**
M: That would be really helpful. (67) **And I'll go get a spray bottle to take care of these carrots.**

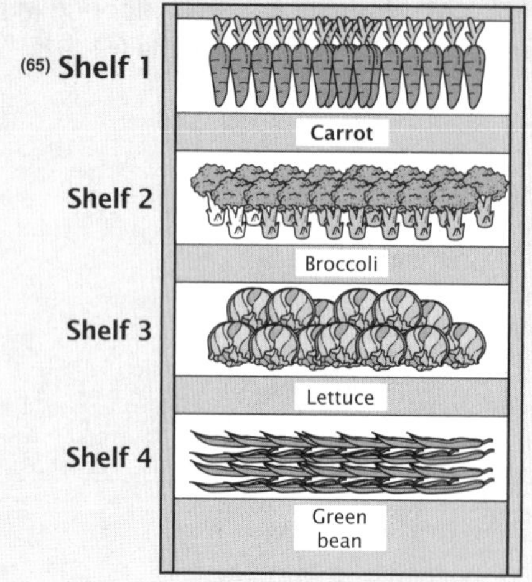

65-67 對話＋陳列架 英⇄澳

女： 霍華德，可以請你過來一下嗎？
男： 當然可以，昆尼女士。請問怎麼了嗎？
女： (65) **這些紅蘿蔔看起來有點乾癟。你上一次幫紅蘿蔔噴灑水分，是多久以前？**
男： 噢，需要幫紅蘿蔔灑水嗎？我還以為這個區域，只有青花菜需要灑水。
女： 不，不是那樣。你知道，這已經不是第一次有人搞錯了，(66) **我之後會把需要定時灑水的蔬果列成清單，貼在員工休息室。**
男： 那就幫了大忙了。(67) **那我去拿噴霧器，幫這些紅蘿蔔灑一下水。**

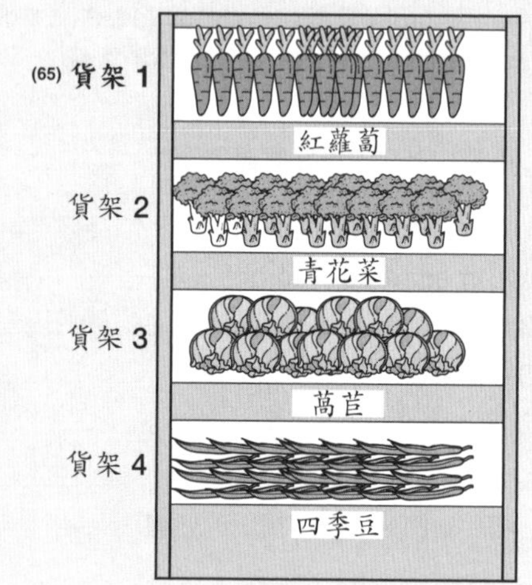

- spray (v.) 噴灑 section (n.) 區域 confusion (n.) 混淆；誤解 vegetable (n.) 蔬菜 regular (adj.) 定期的 take care of 處理；照顧

65. 圖表整合題——女子關切的蔬菜

Look at the graphic. Which shelf's vegetables is the woman concerned about?

(A) Shelf 1

(B) Shelf 2

(C) Shelf 3

(D) Shelf 4

請看圖表作答。女子關切的是哪層貨架的蔬菜？

(A) 貨架 1

(B) 貨架 2

(C) 貨架 3

(D) 貨架 4

66. 相關細節——女子欲製作的清單

What does the woman say she will make a list of?

(A) Types of produce

(B) Staff members

(C) Cleaning tasks

(D) Purchase dates

女子說她會將何物列成清單？

(A) 農產品種類

(B) 工作人員

(C) 清潔工作

(D) 購買日期

換句話說 fruits and vegetables（蔬果）→ produce（農產品）

67. 相關細節——男子接下來要對部分蔬菜做的事情

What will the man most likely do next to some vegetables?

(A) Carry them to another area

(B) Spray water on them

(C) Examine them for defects

(D) Rearrange them into piles

男子接下來最有可能替蔬菜做何事？

(A) 把它們移到另一區

(B) 在它們上面灑水

(C) 查看有無瑕疵

(D) 重新整理成堆

68-70 Conversation + Class information

M: Colland Studios. How can I help you?

W: (68) **I'm interested in taking a social dance class, but I was wondering—is it OK to go without a partner?**

M: Absolutely. Your instructor will partner you up with one of your classmates at each session.

W: That's good. But I guess I'd better choose a class with a lot of participants. (69) **Could you sign me up for whichever beginner class has the most people registered so far?**

M: (70) **Sorry, but we don't allow sign-ups over the phone. You can either stop by our studio or follow the directions on our Web site.**

W: Oh, I see. (70) **I'll go to your Web site.** Thanks.

68-70 對話＋課程資訊 　澳⇄美

男：這裡是柯藍舞蹈教室，有什麼我能協助的嗎？

女：(68) **我有興趣參加社交舞課程，但我想請教一下——若沒有跟舞伴一起，也能參加課程嗎？**

男：當然可以。每節上課時，課程的講師會幫您跟一位同學搭檔跳舞。

女：這樣很好，但我覺得最好選擇學員人數很多的班別。(69) **你可以幫我報名目前報名人數最多的初級班課程嗎？**

男：(70) **抱歉，我們沒辦法受理電話報名。您可以過來我們教室、或是按照我們官網上的指示報名。**

女：哦，我明白了，(70) **我會到你們的網站上報名**，謝謝。

Beginners' Classes	
Class	Current Registrants/Capacity
Rumba	7 / 22
Salsa	16 / 16 (FULL)
Swing	11 / 18
(69) Waltz	**19 / 20**

初級班	
課程	當前報名人數／人數上限
倫巴	7 / 22
索沙舞	16 / 16（額滿）
搖擺舞	11 / 18
(69) 華爾滋	**19 / 20**

- **instructor (n.)** 教練；教師 **partner up with** 與（某人）成為搭檔 **session (n.)** 上課期間 **sign up for** 報名 **register (v.)** 登記；註冊 **stop by** 造訪 **direction (n.)** 指示

68. 相關細節——女子提出的疑問 難

What does the woman ask about?
(A) How long each session lasts
(B) Whether she can attend alone
(C) How much experience an instructor has
(D) What kind of dance the man recommends

女子詢問什麼事？
(A) 每節課的上課時間
(B) 她是否可單獨去上課
(C) 講師有多少經驗
(D) 男子推薦的舞蹈類型

69. 圖表整合題——女子欲報名參加的課程

Look at the graphic. Which class does the woman want to sign up for?
(A) Rumba
(B) Salsa
(C) Swing
(D) Waltz

請看圖作答表。女子想要報名何項課程？
(A) 倫巴
(B) 索沙舞
(C) 搖擺舞
(D) 華爾滋

70. 相關細節——女子同意線上處理的事情

What does the woman agree to do online?
(A) Order some merchandise
(B) Get driving directions
(C) Register for a class
(D) Read some advice

女子同意在網路上做什麼？
(A) 訂購商品
(B) 取得行車指引
(C) 報名課程
(D) 查閱建議

PART 4 P. 53–55

16

71-73 Instructions

All right, everyone. (71) **Now that you've been given an overview of our operations here at the warehouse, it's time to talk about some specific tasks.** I'll start by showing you how to use the forklift to move items around. (72) **Now, safety is important, so the first thing you need to do is look carefully at each component of the forklift.** You should make

71-73 說明 英

好吧，各位。(71) **既然你們已經大致了解了倉庫這裡的運作情況，是時候講解具體的工作了。**首先我會示範給你們看，要怎麼使用堆高機來搬運物品。(72) **話說，安全很重要，所以你們要做的第一步驟，就是仔細檢查堆高機的每個部件，**你們務必要確保沒有損壞，尤其是

sure there is no damage, especially to the tires. (73) **For a full list of what you need to check, please refer to the printout I'm giving you now.**	輪胎的部分。(73) **有關需檢查項目的完整清單，請參閱我現在發給各位的列印資料。**

- overview (n.) 概述　operation (n.) 運作；操作　warehouse (n.) 倉庫　specific (adj.) 具體的；特定的　task (n.) 工作；任務　forklift (n.) 堆高機　safety (n.) 安全　component (n.) 零件；組件　damage (n.) 損壞　printout (n.) 印出的資料

71. 全文相關——聽者的工作地點

Where do the listeners work?	聽者在哪裡工作？
(A) At a moving company	(A) 在搬家公司
(B) At a manufacturing plant	(B) 在製造工廠
(C) At a storage facility	**(C) 在倉儲場所**
(D) At a construction firm	(D) 在建設公司

換句話說 the warehouse（倉庫）→ a storage facility（倉儲場所）

72. 相關細節——說話者要求聽者優先做的事情 難

What does the speaker remind the listeners to do first?	說話者提醒聽者要先做什麼？
(A) Put on some safety gear	(A) 穿戴安全裝備
(B) Refer to a floor plan	(B) 查閱平面圖
(C) Study a warning label	(C) 研究警示標籤
(D) Inspect the parts of a machine	**(D) 檢查機械的組成部件**

- gear (n.) 裝置；設備　refer to 參考；查閱　floor plan 平面圖　warning (n.) 警告　inspect (v.) 檢查　part (n.) 零件；部件

換句話說 look carefully at each component of the forklift（仔細檢查堆高機的每個部件）
→ inspect the parts of a machine（檢查機械的組成部件）

73. 相關細節——聽者可以找到更多相關資訊的地方

According to the speaker, where can listeners find additional information?	根據說話者所言，聽者可以在何處找到額外資訊？
(A) On a handout	**(A) 在講義資料**
(B) In a user manual	(B) 在使用手冊
(C) On a Web site	(C) 在網站上
(D) In a break room	(D) 在休息室裡

換句話說 the printout I'm giving you（我現在發給各位的列印資料）→ a handout（講義資料）

74-76 Telephone message

74-76 電話留言 美

Hi Don, it's me. I'm about to fly home. Sorry I didn't call you until now—it's been a busy day. **(74) But I'm happy to say that the meetings went extremely well—both Ervitt Partners and Wyant Capital said they would be interested in funding our business!** We can expect their offers within the week. Oh, my flight just started boarding. **(75) But, uh, I'd love to tell you more when I land. (76) Can we meet up for dinner?** I should be back in the city by seven. Let me know.

嗨，唐，是我，我馬上就要搭飛機回家了。對不起，現在才打電話給你，今天忙了一天，**(74) 可是我很開心要跟你說：會議進行得非常順利，艾弗特公司和懷安資本公司都說有興趣提供資金給我們公司！**本週以內，我們可望就能收到他們的投資提案。噢，我的班機剛要開始登機了。**(75) 不過，嗯，等我下機之後，我有更多事情想跟你說。(76) 我們可以見面吃頓晚餐嗎？**我應該七點前就能回到城裡。再告訴我吧。

- **be about to** 即將；正要 **extremely (adv.)** 非常；極其 **fund (v.)** 提供資金 **offer (n.)** 提案 **board (v.)** 登上（飛機、船等） **land (v.)** 抵達；著陸

74. 相關細節——說話者今天見面的對象 難

Whom did the speaker meet with today?

(A) Potential investors

(B) Current clients

(C) Business consultants

(D) Government regulators

說話者今天和誰見面？

(A) 潛在投資者

(B) 現有客戶

(C) 商業顧問

(D) 政府監管人員

- **potential (adj.)** 潛在的 **investor (n.)** 投資者 **regulator (n.)** 監管人；監管機構

---

75. 掌握說話者的意圖——提及「我的班機剛要開始登機了」的意圖

What does the speaker mean when she says, "my flight just started boarding"?

(A) Her trip is behind schedule.

(B) She has to end the call.

(C) It is too late to make a change.

(D) She will be unable to get a message.

說話者說：「我的班機剛要開始登機了」，意思為何？

(A) 她的行程延誤了。

(B) 她必須結束通話。

(C) 可做異動的時限已過。

(D) 她將無法收到訊息。

---

76. 相關細節——說話者向聽者提出的要求

What does the speaker ask the listener to do?

(A) Reply to an e-mail

(B) Pick her up from the airport

(C) Set up a morning meeting

(D) Eat a meal with her

說話者要求聽者做什麼？

(A) 回覆電子郵件

(B) 去機場接她

(C) 安排上午會議

(D) 與她吃頓飯

換句話說 **meet up for dinner**（見面吃頓晚餐）→ **eat a meal with**（與……吃頓飯）

77-79 Tour information

77-79 旅遊資訊 澳

[77] **Hello, and welcome to this tour of Frazier Pictures' back lot. I'm so excited to show you the well-preserved sets on which our most famous movies were made.** If we're lucky, you may even see one or two productions being filmed today! [78] **Now, the tour will last about forty-five minutes, and we ask that you stay seated in these electric carts the whole time.** If you have any problems or questions, you may speak to me or an assistant guide at any time. OK, we're coming up on our first stop—Soundstage 1. [79] **Let me tell you the colorful past of this building, which was one of the first constructed on our lot.**

[77] **大家好，歡迎來參觀弗雷澤電影公司的外景片場，我很高興能向各位展示這些保存完好的場景，這裡是本公司幾部知名大片的拍攝場地。**要是我們運氣好，今天甚至能看到一、兩部作品的拍攝過程！[78] **那麼現在，本次參觀行程時間大約45分鐘，請各位全程都坐在電動接駁車裡。**如果你們有任何問題或疑問，可以隨時告訴我或助理導遊。好的，我們即將來到參訪的第一站，也就是「一號攝影棚」，[79] **這是片場最早落成的第一批建築，我來跟大家說說這棟建築的輝煌歷史吧。**

- back lot 外景用的露天片場　preserve (v.) 保存　production (n.) 製作；攝製　last (v.) 持續　electric (adj.) 電動的

77. 全文相關——獨白出現的地點

Where is the tour taking place?

(A) A city street
(B) A nature reserve
(C) An aircraft factory
(D) A movie studio

參訪進行的地點為何？

(A) 城市街道
(B) 自然保護區
(C) 飛機製造廠
(D) 電影製片廠

- reserve (n.) 保護區　aircraft (n.) 飛機

換句話說 the . . . sets on which our . . . movies were made（本公司……大片的拍攝場地）
→ a movie studio（電影製片廠）

78. 相關細節——要求聽者做的事情

What are the listeners asked to do?

(A) Remain seated in a vehicle
(B) Save questions until the end
(C) Watch an introductory video
(D) Turn off personal electronics

聽者被要求做什麼？

(A) 保持坐在車裡
(B) 留待最後再提問
(C) 觀看介紹影片
(D) 關閉個人電子設備

- seated (adj.) 就坐的　introductory (adj.) 介紹的　electronics (n.) 電子產品

換句話說 stay seated in these electric carts（坐在電動接駁車裡）
→ remain seated in a vehicle（保持坐在車裡）

79. 相關細節——說話者接下來要講的內容 難

What will the speaker talk about next?

(A) A company's expansion plans
(B) The course of the tour
(C) The history of a site
(D) An upcoming celebration

說話者接下來會講述什麼？

(A) 公司擴張計畫
(B) 參觀的路線
(C) 場地的歷史
(D) 即將舉行的慶祝活動

- expansion (n.) 擴張　site (n.) 地點　upcoming (adj.) 即將到來的　celebration (n.) 慶祝活動

換句話說 the . . . past of this building（這棟建築的歷史）→ the history of a site（場地的歷史）

80-82 Broadcast

This is your hourly local news update on CWT, Winnipeg's most trusted news source. [(80)] **The Canadian Board of Better Business Practices is hosting a job fair in the Arabesque Convention Center downtown this Saturday, starting at ten a.m.** Anyone looking for a job should stop by to meet hiring directors from some of the largest Winnipeg employers. There will also be career counselors offering free consultations and career aptitude tests for anyone interested. [(81)] **The event is free to attend, but it is expected to fill up quickly, so consider arriving early to make sure you get in.** [(82)] **Now, let's hear about the incoming storm from Kyung-Ho Jang.** Hi, Kyung-Ho.

80-82 電台廣播 加

歡迎收聽溫尼伯最值得信賴的新聞來源「CWT」，以下為您播報本地最新整點新聞。[(80)] **加拿大「商業實踐改進委員會」將於本週六上午十點起，於市中心的阿拉貝斯克展覽館舉辦就業博覽會**，有求職需求的民眾應可到場，與溫尼伯各大頂尖企業的招聘主管面談。現場也會有職涯顧問，為感興趣者提供免費諮詢與職業適性測驗。[(81)] **活動免費參加，但預計很快就會人滿為患，因此請考慮提早抵達，以確保您能入場。**[(82)] **現在，讓我們一起聽聽張景胡帶來未來近期暴風雨的消息。**景胡，你好。

- hourly (adj.) 每小時的　trusted (adj.) 值得信賴的　source (n.) 來源　director (n.) 主管　counselor (n.) 諮商師；顧問　consultation (n.) 諮詢　aptitude (n.) 傾向；天賦　fill up 充滿　incoming (adj.) 正來臨的

80. 相關細節——於週六舉行的活動類型

According to the broadcast, what type of event will occur on Saturday?

(A) An athletic competition

(B) A career fair

(C) An exhibition opening

(D) A trade show

根據廣播內容，週六將會舉辦何種活動？

(A) 體育比賽

(B) 就業博覽會

(C) 展覽開幕

(D) 商展

換句話說 a job fair（就業博覽會）→ a career fair（就業博覽會）

---

81. 相關細節——建議參加者提早抵達活動現場的理由

Why does the speaker say attendees should arrive to the event early?

(A) To ensure entrance

(B) To meet a local celebrity

(C) To gain discounted admission

(D) To find parking nearby

說話者表示參加者應提早抵達現場，原因為何？

(A) 以確保入場

(B) 以和當地名人見面

(C) 以獲得門票優惠

(D) 以找附近的停車位

- ensure (v.) 確保　entrance (n.) 進入權　celebrity (n.) 名人　admission (n.) 門票價格　nearby (adv.) 在附近

換句話說 to make sure you get in（以確保您能入場）→ to ensure entrance（以確保入場）

---

82. 相關細節——聽者將於接下來聽到的內容

What will listeners most likely hear next?
(A) An interview
(B) A weather report
(C) A sports update
(D) An advertisement

聽眾接下來最有可能會聽到什麼？
(A) 訪談
(B) 天氣預報
(C) 最新體育消息
(D) 廣告

- sports (adj.) 運動的　advertisement (n.) 廣告

83-85 Speech

83-85 演說 美

(83) **Congratulations, everyone, on completing the first annual Employee Enrichment Week at Jenson and Grieves Marketing. This week, we challenged ourselves with rigorous team-building activities,** and we learned a lot about each other. I saw bonds formed between colleagues, and new talents discovered in each of you. (84) **It makes me very happy as your operations manager to see such remarkable growth in everyone.** I'm sure the work we did this week will contribute to a more productive work environment for all of us. (85) **Since this is the first time we conducted the Employee Enrichment Week, I wasn't sure if it would be worth repeating next year.** Now, I know we need to do this again. Thank you.

(83) **我們「詹森與格里夫斯行銷公司」舉辦的第一屆年度員工充實週，活動到這邊圓滿結束，在此恭喜大家。我們在本週，透過嚴格的企業內訓活動來挑自我，**也使同仁彼此更加了解。我看到同事間萌生情誼，也發現到各位全新的才能嶄露頭角，(84) **身為各位的營運經理，看到大家有突飛猛進的成長，我感到非常欣慰。**我相信我們在本週的一切努力，將為大家創造更具生產效能的職場環境。(85) **由於這是我們首次舉辦員工充實週，我本來不確定明年是否還值得舉辦。**現在，我知道我們需要再辦一次。謝謝大家。

- annual (adj.) 每年一次的　enrichment (n.) 加強；充實　challenge (v.) 挑戰　rigorous (adj.) 嚴格的　bond (n.) 關係；聯繫　form (v.) 形成　colleague (n.) 同事　talent (n.) 天賦；天分　remarkable (adj.) 顯著的　contribute to 促成；導致　productive (adj.) 生產力高的　environment (n.) 環境　conduct (v.) 實施　worth (adj.) 值得的

83. 相關細節——說話者向聽者道賀的事情

What does the speaker congratulate the listeners on?
(A) Finishing a team-building program
(B) Launching a new product
(C) Breaking a sales record
(D) Receiving promotions

說話者向聽者祝賀什麼事？
(A) 完成企業內訓
(B) 推出新產品
(C) 打破銷售紀錄
(D) 獲得升職

- launch (v.) 推出　break (v.) 打破　record (n.) 紀錄　promotion (n.) 晉升；升遷

84. 全文相關——說話者的職業

Who is the speaker?
(A) A previous customer
(B) A business researcher
(C) A current supervisor
(D) A city official

說話者的身分為何？
(A) 以前的客戶
(B) 企業研究員
(C) 現任主管
(D) 市府官員

- previous (adj.) 以前的　researcher (n.) 研究員　supervisor (n.) 主管　official (n.) 公職人員

換句話說 your operations manager（各位的營運經理）→ supervisor（主管）

85. 掌握說話者的意圖——提及「現在，我知道我們需要再辦一次」的意圖 難

Why does the speaker say, "Now, I know we need to do this again"?

(A) An activity was effective.

(B) Some results were unexpected.

(C) Participants performed poorly.

(D) Other people should observe an activity.

說話者為什麼會說：「現在，我知道我們需要再辦一次」？

(A) 活動成效良好。

(B) 結果出乎意料。

(C) 參與者表現很差。

(D) 其他人應要觀察活動。

- **effective (adj.)** 有效的 **unexpected (adj.)** 出乎意料的 **participant (n.)** 參加者 **perform (v.)** 表現 **observe (v.)** 觀察

86-88 Talk

86-88 談話 英

Hi, I'm Stella Hogan. Thanks for watching the latest in my line of home improvement how-to videos. [(86)] **In this one, I'm going to show you how to paint the inside walls of your home without damaging your windows or anything else.** All right, here are my supplies. There are details about them in the notes for this video. Uh, you may be wondering why I chose Dewitt-brand paint. [(87)] **It's because it's inexpensive and sold in most stores, so I thought that many people would be likely to use it.** [(88)] **Now, as you can see, I've already removed all of the furniture and other objects from this room.** Next, I'll lay down this plastic sheet to protect the carpet.

嗨，我是史黛拉·霍根，感謝收看我的家居裝修系列，最新一集的教學影片。[(86)] **本集影片中，我要教大家怎麼粉刷家裡內部的牆壁，而不會損壞家中的窗戶等其他物品。**好的，我需要的用品都在這裡了。這些用品的詳細資訊，請參閱影片的註解。唔，大家可能想知道我為什麼會選擇「德威特」牌的油漆，[(87)] **這是因為價格不貴，而且大部分商店都有販售，所以我想很多人可能會選用。**[(88)] **現在，如各位所見，我已經把房間裡所有的家具跟其他物品搬走了。**接下來我會鋪設塑膠墊，用來保護地毯。

- **latest (n.)** 最新的事物 **improvement (n.)** 改善 **inside (adj.)** 在屋裡的 **damage (v.)** 損壞 **supplies (n.)** 〔複〕用品 **detail (n.)** 細節 **wonder (v.)** 想知道 **inexpensive (adj.)** 便宜的 **remove (v.)** 移除 **object (n.)** 物體 **protect (v.)** 保護

86. 全文相關——獨白的主題

What is the topic of the talk?

(A) Carpet cleaning

(B) House painting

(C) Light fixture repair

(D) Window installation

談話的主題是什麼？

(A) 地毯清潔

(B) 居家油漆

(C) 燈具維修

(D) 窗戶安裝

87. 相關細節——說話者針對產品提及的內容

What does the speaker say about a product?

(A) It is durable.

(B) It comes with instructions.

(C) It is sold in a variety of colors.

(D) It is affordable.

有關一項產品，說話者說了什麼？

(A) 它經久耐用。

(B) 它有附使用說明。

(C) 它有賣各種顏色。

(D) 它的價格實惠。

- **durable (adj.)** 耐用的 **instructions (n.)** 說明書 **a variety of** 各式各樣的 **affordable (adj.)** 價格親民的

換句話說 inexpensive（價格不貴）→ affordable（價格實惠）

88. 相關細節——說話者提到先前完成的事情

What does the speaker say she did before the talk?
(A) Cleared out a room
(B) Mixed some chemicals
(C) Covered some surfaces
(D) Measured an object

說話者表示，她在說話前已經做了何事？
(A) 清空房間
(B) 混合化學物質
(C) 遮蓋地面
(D) 測量物品

- mix (v.) 混合 chemical (n.) 化學物質 surface (n.) 表面 measure (v.) 測量

換句話說 removed all of the furniture and other objects from this room（把房間裡所有的家具跟其他物品搬走了）→ cleared out a room（清空房間）

89-91 Excerpt from a meeting

(89) **OK, let's talk about the new office space we're moving into.** (90) **First—I've heard some people say they'll miss our current location, but I really think you're all going to love the new building.** Have you seen the amenities they offer? (90) **It's a big step up.** Now, we can move into our new space on October fifth, and the lease on this building ends three days later. We have to move everything in between those days. (91) **We've hired a mover to handle the bigger items, like desks and computers, but I'd like you all to move your own belongings. You should start boxing those up this week.** Does that seem doable?

89-91 會議摘錄 加

(89) **好的，我們來討論即將搬進的新辦公室。**(90) **首先，我聽到有人說，將會很想念我們現在的辦公室，但是我真的認為，你們會愛上新的辦公大樓，**你們有看到新大樓提供的便利設施嗎？(90) **水準大有提升。**目前，我們十月五日就可以搬進新的辦公室，而那之後再過三天，在這棟大樓的租約就會到期，所以我們要在那幾天內，把所有物品搬到新辦公室。(91) **我們已經請搬家公司來處理大件物品，像是辦公桌、電腦等，至於你們的私人物品，我希望大家可以自己帶過去。本週就應該開始收拾裝箱了，**大家覺得可行嗎？

- location (n.) 場所；位置 amenity (n.) 便利設施 lease (n.) 租賃契約 handle (v.) 處理 belongings (n.) 個人物品 box (v.) 把……裝箱 doable (adj.) 可行的

89. 全文相關——宣布的主題

What is the announcement mainly about?
(A) A project for a client
(B) A corporate merger
(C) An office relocation
(D) An annual budget

這段宣布的主要內容為何？
(A) 客戶的專案
(B) 公司合併
(C) 辦公室搬遷
(D) 年度預算

- merger (n.) 合併 relocation (n.) 搬遷 budget (n.) 預算

換句話說 moving into（搬進）→ relocation（搬遷）

---

90. 掌握說話者的意圖——提及「你們有看到新大樓提供的便利設施嗎？」的意圖

Why does the speaker say, "Have you seen the amenities they offer"?
(A) To inquire about some facilities
(B) To suggest a policy change
(C) To criticize a venue's management
(D) To emphasize some benefits

為什麼說話者會說：「你們有看到新大樓提供的便利設施嗎」？
(A) 以詢問設施相關事宜
(B) 以提議政策異動
(C) 以批評場地管理
(D) 以強調優點

- inquire (v.) 詢問　facility (n.) 設施　policy (n.) 政策　criticize (v.) 批評　venue (n.) 場所　emphasize (v.) 強調

91. 相關細節——說話者要求聽者做的事情

What does the speaker ask listeners to do?
(A) Download some computer software
(B) Pack up their personal items
(C) Register for a meeting time
(D) Look at an employee handbook

說話者要求聽者做什麼？
(A) 下載電腦軟體
(B) 打包私人物品
(C) 登記會面時間
(D) 查閱員工手冊

- software (n.) 軟體　pack up 收拾妥當　register (v.) 登記　handbook (n.) 手冊

換句話說 your own belongings（你們的私人物品）→ personal items（私人物品）

92-94 Talk

Hello, ladies and gentleman. My name is Wayne Beck, and I'm the president of the Western Cosmetics Association. (92) **The WCA is proud to have organized this incredible gathering of cosmetics professionals, and glad that you have all come.** (93) **Over the next two days, you'll listen to expert lecturers and meet many other members of this exciting field.** We hope that you enjoy your time. Oh, but before you head to the first workshops, I need to make an announcement. (94) **Due to some unavoidable circumstances, tonight's after-dinner networking party cannot be held in the Grand Ballroom, as it says in your program. Instead, it will be held in the Rose Ballroom.** Thank you.

92-94 談話 澳

各位先生、各位女士，大家好。我的名字叫韋恩．貝克，是「西方化妝品協會」的會長。(92) **本協會很榮幸能籌辦此次盛會，也很高興各方美妝專業人士受邀齊聚一堂。**(93) **接下來兩天裡，各位來賓將聽取專業講師的演講，並與這個迷人的業界裡的許多其他同行見面交流**，我們希望大家都能盡興而歸。噢，但在各位前往第一場研習會之前，我有件事要宣布。(94) **由於一些猝不及防的情況，今天晚宴後的交流會將無法如節目表所寫的在主宴會廳舉行，而會改到玫瑰舞廳舉辦。**謝謝大家。

- association (n.) 協會　incredible (adj.) 極好的　gathering (n.) 聚會　professional (n.) 專業人士　expert (adj.) 專家的　lecturer (n.) 講師　field (n.) 領域　head (v.) 前往　announcement (n.) 宣布　unavoidable (adj.) 不可避免的　circumstance (n.) 情況　networking (n.) 交際人脈

92. 相關細節——正在舉辦的活動 難

What is taking place?
(A) A charity dinner
(B) A music festival
(C) A groundbreaking ceremony
(D) An industry conference

正在舉辦什麼活動？
(A) 慈善晚宴
(B) 音樂節
(C) 破土儀式
(D) 產業會議

換句話說 gathering of . . . professionals（專業人士……齊聚）→ industry conference（產業會議）

93. 相關細節——聽者可以做的事情 難

What does the speaker say the listeners can do?
(A) Purchase event merchandise
(B) Meet a company executive
(C) Network with others
(D) Sample some refreshments

說話者提到，聽者能做何事？
(A) 購買活動商品
(B) 與公司主管會面
(C) 與他人交際
(D) 品嚐茶點

- merchandise (n.) 商品　executive (n.) 主管　network (v.) 建立人脈　sample (v.) 品嚐

換句話說 meet many other members（許多其他同行見面）→ network with others（與他人交際）

94. 相關細節——說話者提及有所更動的部分

What does the speaker say has changed?
(A) The focus of an organization
(B) The location of an event
(C) The date of a launch
(D) The cost of a ticket

說話者說，何者會有異動？
(A) 組織的重點
(B) 活動的場地
(C) 發布會的日期
(D) 票券費用

• organization (n.) 組織　location (n.) 地點　launch (n.) 發布會

95-97 Excerpt from a meeting + Graph

Let's get started. (95) **As you know, our firm's promotional campaign for Dorints Foods' new line of potato chips has been a huge success.** Take a look at this graph of the company's sales revenues over the last few months. (96) **The month that their new line actually came out, there was only this small, temporary increase. Then we took over the marketing for it, and the numbers skyrocketed.** Just amazing. Now other clients are asking for similar campaigns. (97) **That's why Takuya, the leader of the team responsible for the campaign, is going to speak next. He's going to present some of the innovative marketing methods they developed for it so that you can start making use of them yourselves.**

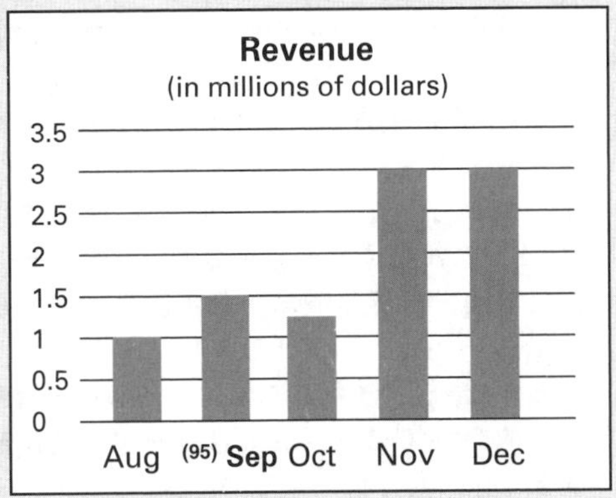

95-97 會議摘錄＋圖表 美

開始開會吧。(95) **大家都知道，本公司為「多林茲食品」新系列洋芋片所策劃的宣傳活動大獲成功。**大家看一下這張圖表，這是該公司近幾個月的銷售收入，(96) **在該公司新產品實際上市的月分，收入只有小幅、暫時的增加，但等到我們接手行銷工作後，數字就一飛衝天了，**簡直是不可思議。現在，其他客戶都在要求我們進行類似活動。(97) **這就是為何接下來，要請拓哉上台跟大家報告，他是負責該次行銷的團隊主管，他會跟大家說明這次發想出的幾種創新行銷方法，這樣各位就可以開始運用。**

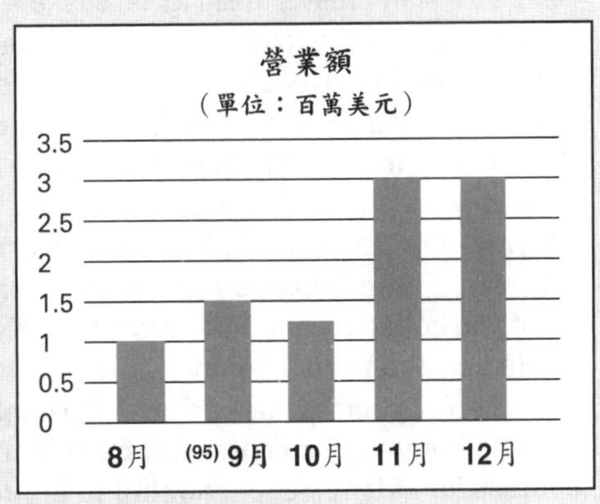

• promotional (adj.) 宣傳的；促銷的　revenue (n.) 營業收入　temporary (adj.) 臨時的　increase (n.) 增加；提高　skyrocket (v.) 飆升　present (v.) 展示　innovative (adj.) 創新的　method (n.) 方法

95. 全文相關——聽者的職業

Who most likely are the listeners?
(A) Snack food developers
(B) Financial analysts
(C) Grocery store managers
(D) Advertising professionals

聽者最有可能是什麼身分？
(A) 休閒食品開發員
(B) 金融分析師
(C) 雜貨店經理
(D) 專業廣告人員

換句話說 promotional campaign（宣傳活動）→ advertising（廣告）

96. 圖表整合題——產品推出的月分 難

Look at the graphic. In which month was a product line released?

(A) September

(B) October

(C) November

(D) December

請看圖表作答。新系列產品是在哪個月分上市的？

(A) 九月

(B) 十月

(C) 十一月

(D) 十二月

97. 相關細節——拓哉要做的事情

What will Takuya most likely do?

(A) Assign some responsibilities to the listeners

(B) Address the listeners' concerns about a policy

(C) Teach the listeners some promotional techniques

(D) Present an award to one of the listeners

拓哉最有可能將要做何事？

(A) 為聽者分配工作職責

(B) 解決聽者對政策的擔憂

(C) 教給聽者宣傳技巧

(D) 將獎項頒給其中一位聽者

- assign (v.) 分配　address (v.) 處理；解決　concern (n.) 擔憂　technique (n.) 技巧
  present (v.) 頒發　award (n.) 獎

換句話說 present some of the innovative marketing methods（說明幾種創新行銷方法）
→ teach some promotional techniques（教導宣傳技巧）

98-100 Announcement + Table

Before we start today's meeting, let's take a minute to recognize the employees who represented our company in the recent community center fund-raiser. Could you all stand up? (98) **I know that singing in a talent show was a big challenge for some of you, but you did it anyway.** Your dedication to the community is inspiring. (99) **And I'm proud to announce that all of you collected enough donations to earn a tote bag and even a T-shirt**—wow! Feel free to wear the T-shirt on casual Fridays. (100) **Thanks to citizens like you, the center will be able to offer courses for elderly people hoping to improve their computer skills.** Great job.

Rewards for Fund-raiser Participants

Level	Minimum amount raised	Prize(s)
1	$10	Certificate
2	$50	Certificate + bag
(99) 3	$100	**Certificate + bag + T-shirt**
4	$200	Certificate + bag + T-shirt + movie tickets

98-100 宣布＋表格 加

今天的會議開始前，讓我們花點時間，表揚在最近社區活動中心舉行的募款活動裡，代表公司與會的員工，可以麻煩你們幾位起立一下嗎？(98) **我知道對你們當中有些人來說，要在才藝表演中唱歌是件艱困的挑戰，但無論如何，你們做到了**，你們對社區的奉獻精神值得欽佩。(99) **在此榮幸的宣布，你們大家都募到了足夠的款項，有資格領取一個手提包，還可以領到T恤**——哇！週五便服日時，別拘束，就穿來上班吧。(100) **多虧有你們這樣的居民，活動中心將能開設課程，提供給想提升電腦技能的年長者**，你們做得很好。

募捐活動參加者回饋一覽

等級	最低募款金額	獎項
1	$10	獎狀
2	$50	獎狀＋手提袋
(99) 3	$100	**獎狀＋手提袋＋T恤**
4	$200	獎狀＋手提袋＋T恤＋電影票

- recognize (v.) 表揚　represent (v.) 代表　community (n.) 社區　fund-raiser (n.) 募款活動　talent (n.) 才藝　challenge (n.) 挑戰　dedication (n.) 奉獻　inspiring (adj.) 鼓舞人心的　donation (n.) 捐款　citizen (n.) 居民　elderly (adj.) 年長的　improve (v.) 提升

98. 相關細節——募款活動參與者完成的事情

What did some fund-raiser participants do?
(A) They completed a sports challenge.
(B) They gave a musical performance.
(C) They donated some homemade food.
(D) They decorated an outdoor space.

募款活動的參與者做了何事？
(A) 他們完成了體能挑戰。
(B) 他們出演音樂表演。
(C) 他們捐了自製的食物。
(D) 他們布置了戶外場地。

- complete (v.) 完成　performance (n.) 表演；演出　donate (v.) 捐贈　decorate (v.) 布置；裝飾　outdoor (adj.) 戶外的

換句話說 singing in a talent show（在才藝表演中唱歌）→ gave a musical performance（出演音樂表演）

99. 圖表整合題——參與的聽者達到的等級

Look at the graphic. Which level did the participating listeners most likely reach?
(A) Level 1
(B) Level 2
(C) Level 3
(D) Level 4

請看圖表作答。參與活動的聽者最有可能達到了那個等級？
(A) 等級 1
(B) 等級 2
(C) 等級 3
(D) 等級 4

100. 相關細節——款項的用途

What will the funds be used for?
(A) Medical research
(B) Improvements to a park
(C) The renovation of a community center
(D) An educational program

募得的資金將用於何處？
(A) 醫療研究
(B) 公園改善
(C) 社區中心的整修
(D) 教育課程

- improvement (n.) 改善　renovation (n.) 翻新；整修　educational (adj.) 教育的

換句話說 courses . . . to improve their computer skills（課程……提升電腦技能）
→ an educational program（教育課程）

ACTUAL TEST 5

PART 1 P. 56–59 17

1. 單人獨照──描寫人物的動作 澳

(A) He's rolling down a window.
(B) He's replacing a tire.
(C) He's putting fuel in a vehicle.
(D) He's examining an engine.

(A) 他在把車窗搖下。
(B) 他在更換輪胎。
(C) 他在給汽車加油。
(D) 他在檢查引擎。

- roll down 搖下；放下 replace (v.) 更換 fuel (n.) 燃料；燃油 vehicle (n.) 車輛 examine (v.) 檢查

2. 雙人照片──描寫人物的動作 美

(A) The woman is pointing upward.
(B) They're looking at a clipboard.
(C) They're wearing safety glasses.
(D) The man is wrapping a box in plastic.

(A) 女子正指著上方。
(B) 他們正看著文件板夾
(C) 他們正戴著護目鏡。
(D) 男子正在用塑膠包裝盒子。

- point (v.) 指；指向 upward (adv.) 向上 safety glasses 護目鏡 wrap (v.) 包；裹 plastic (n.) 塑膠

3. 單人獨照──描寫人物的動作 英

(A) She's cooking on a stove.
(B) She's standing at a buffet.
(C) She's carrying a tray of food.
(D) She's pouring soup into a bowl.

(A) 她正在爐灶上做飯。
(B) 她正站在自助餐前。
(C) 她正用拖盤端著食物。
(D) 她正把湯倒進碗裡。

- stove (n.) 爐灶 buffet (n.) 自助餐 tray (n.) 托盤；一盤的量 pour (v.) 倒（液體） bowl (n.) 碗

4. 綜合照片──描寫人物或事物 加

(A) Some people are applauding a performance.
(B) A floor is being polished.
(C) A mirror covers most of one wall.
(D) A man is dancing on a stage.

(A) 一些人正在為表演鼓掌。
(B) 有人正在給地板上光。
(C) 鏡子幾乎占據一面牆。
(D) 男子正在舞台上跳舞。

- applaud (v.) 鼓掌；喝采 performance (n.) 表演 polish (v.) 磨光；擦亮 cover (v.) 覆蓋

5. 事物與背景照──描寫戶外事物的狀態 美 難

(A) Cars are parked along a waterway.
(B) Boats are being rowed toward the shore.
(C) A bridge connects two parts of a forest.
(D) A row of tents faces the ocean.

(A) 車輛沿著水路停放。
(B) 有人正划著小船朝向岸邊。
(C) 一座橋連接森林的兩邊。
(D) 一排帳篷朝向海洋。

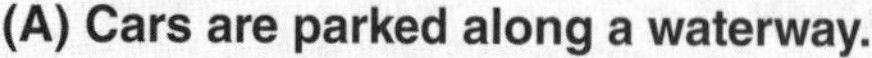

- waterway (n.) 水路；航道 row (v.)（用槳）划船 shore (n.) 岸邊 face (v.) 面向；正對

6. 綜合照片——描寫人物或事物 澳

(A) The woman is drinking from a glass. (B) One of the men is gesturing at a projector screen. **(C) A laptop computer has been opened.** (D) There are file folders on the table.	(A) 女子正在用玻璃杯喝東西。 (B) 其中一名男子正對著投影螢幕比劃。 **(C) 筆記型電腦是打開的。** (D) 桌上有資料夾。

- gesture (v.) 打手勢；用動作示意

PART 2 P. 60

18

7. 以 When 開頭的問句，詢問末班車發車時間 美⇄加

When does the last train to Montreal leave from this station? **(A) At eleven-fifteen at night.** (B) Just a few more stations. (C) No, I'm going to Toronto today.	開往蒙特婁的末班車，何時從本站發車？ **(A) 晚上十一點十五分。** (B) 還有幾站。 (C) 不是，我今天要去多倫多。

8. 以助動詞 Have 開頭的問句，詢問是否聽過威廉森家電 英⇄澳

Have you ever heard of Williamson Appliances? (A) I need a new refrigerator. **(B) That name does seem familiar.** (C) Go ahead and turn up the volume.	你聽說過「威廉森家電」嗎？ (A) 我需要新的冰箱。 **(B) 這名字的確似乎很耳熟。** (C) 請便，把音量調大聲。

- appliance (n.) 家用電器　refrigerator (n.) 冰箱

9. 表示建議或提案的直述句 加⇄英

I could reserve a conference room for the performance reviews. (A) It's down the hall to your left. (B) The top performers in each department. **(C) That would be great.**	我可以預約一間會議室來做績效評估。 (A) 順著走廊走，在左手邊。 (B) 各部門表現最好的員工。 **(C) 那就太好了。**

- reserve (v.) 預約；保留　conference (n.) 會議　performance (n.) 績效；表現

10. 以否定疑問句，詢問是否為安吉拉的辦公桌 美⇄加 難

Isn't this Angela's desk? (A) Oh, where did you find it? **(B) She said I could sit here when she's away.** (C) Yes, the latest lab test.	這不是安吉拉的桌子嗎？ (A) 噢，你在哪裡找到的？ **(B) 她說她不在時，我可以坐這裡。** (C) 是的，最新的實驗室測試。

- latest (adj.) 最新的　lab (n.) 實驗室（=laboratory）

11. 以 **Which** 開頭的問句，詢問製作表格該點選哪個按鈕 美⇄澳

Which button do I click on to create a graph?	我應該要點選哪個按鍵，來繪製圖表？
(A) The one with three colored lines.	**(A) 有三條色線的那個。**
(B) It's a good way to display figures.	(B) 這是展示數據的好方法。
(C) I didn't know you took photographs.	(C) 我不知道你拍了照片。

• display (v.) 顯示　figure (n.) 數據　photograph (n.) 照片

12. 以選擇疑問句，詢問較適合這份工作的人 英⇄加　難

Do you think Chris Cole or Jane Barr is a better candidate for the job?	你覺得誰較適合這份工作，克里斯·柯爾還是簡·巴爾？
(A) That's the hiring manager's opinion.	(A) 那是招聘經理的意見。
(B) Yes, the earliest date possible.	(B) 是的，盡可能越早的日期。
(C) Based on the interviews, I'd choose Chris.	**(C) 根據面試結果，我會選克里斯。**

• candidate (n.) 候選人；人選　based on 根據；依據

13. 以附加問句，確認今天是否為城市藝術節首日 澳⇄美

This is the first day of the city arts festival, isn't it?	今天是城市藝術節的第一天，對嗎？
(A) An exhibition of works by local artists.	(A) 本地藝術家的作品展。
(B) This painting won second prize, actually.	(B) 這幅畫其實獲得了第二名。
(C) Check the official event Web site.	**(C) 去查看活動的官方網站。**

• exhibition (n.) 展覽　work (n.) 作品　prize (n.) 獎　official (adj.) 官方的

14. 以 **Where** 開頭的問句，詢問可換錢的地方 英⇄加

Where can I exchange these dollars for British pounds?	我可以到哪裡將這些美元兌換成英鎊？
(A) There's a bank across the street.	**(A) 這條街對面有家銀行。**
(B) Sure, we have plenty of change.	(B) 當然好，我們有很多零錢。
(C) A little lower than yesterday.	(C) 比昨天低了一點。

• exchange (v.) 兌換　plenty of 大量的；很多　change (n.) 零錢

15. 以 **Why** 開頭的問句，詢問表格中為何要填寫電子信箱 澳⇄加　難

Excuse me—why does this form ask for an e-mail address?	請問一下，為何此表格要求填寫電子郵件地址？
(A) Try looking in the staff directory first.	(A) 先去查一下員工通訊錄。
(B) I e-mailed it to jsmith@rppo.com.	(B) 我用電郵寄到 jsmith@rppo.com 了。
(C) You can leave that part blank if you want.	**(C) 那部分可以空著，看你的意願。**

• form (n.) 表格　directory (n.) 電話簿；姓名地址通訊錄　blank (adj.) 空白的

16. 以否定疑問句，確認是否有庫存的冬裝 澳⇄英

Don't you have any winter clothing in stock yet?	你們還沒有任何冬裝供貨嗎？
(A) What exactly are you looking for?	**(A) 具體來說，您在要找什麼類型的衣服？**
(B) A group skiing trip in January.	(B) 一月的滑雪旅行團。
(C) We're having a heating unit installed soon.	(C) 我們很快就會安裝暖氣設備。

• in stock 有現貨　heating (n.) 暖氣　unit (n.) 裝置　install (v.) 安裝

17. 以 Who 開頭的問句，詢問誰是數位行銷部主任 加⇄美 難

Who's the director of digital marketing?	數位行銷部的主任是誰？
(A) At Creldon Associates.	(A) 在克里頓企業。
(B) I've only met the assistant director.	**(B) 我只見過助理主任。**
(C) It's a series of Web advertisements.	(C) 這是一系列的網路廣告。

- **director (n.)** 主任；總監　**associate (n.)** 關聯企業　**advertisement (n.)** 廣告

18. 以 How 開頭的問句，詢問如何維持制服的整潔 加⇄英 難

How do you keep your uniform so clean?	你的制服怎麼保持得這麼乾淨？
(A) You have to use the right laundry detergent.	**(A) 你得用對洗衣精。**
(B) Just to wipe down the counters.	(B) 只為了把櫃檯擦乾淨。
(C) I thought we had to keep it there.	(C) 我以為得把它留在這裡。

- **laundry (n.)** 洗衣　**detergent (n.)** 洗滌劑　**wipe (v.)** 擦拭

19. 表示請託或要求的直述句 美⇄英 難

Please place any metal items in this basket.	請把所有金屬物品放在這個籃子裡。
(A) A couple pounds of apples.	(A) 幾磅的蘋果。
(B) Let me get my keys out of my pocket.	**(B) 讓我從口袋裡拿出鑰匙。**
(C) So-Hee is training to replace Mark.	(C) 昭熙正在受訓，要接馬克的工作。

- **metal (adj.)** 金屬的　**basket (n.)** 籃子　**pound (n.)** 磅（重量單位）　**replace (v.)** 接替；取代

20. 以附加問句確認對方是否要去郵局 美⇄加

You're going to the post office this afternoon, aren't you?	你今天下午會去郵局，對嗎？
(A) No, it wasn't on the poster.	(A) 不，沒有在海報上。
(B) Here's a roll of first-class stamps.	(B) 這是一捆第一類郵票。
(C) After I repackage this shipment.	**(C) 等我重新包裝這批貨後。**

- **post office** 郵局　**roll (n.)** 捲；捆　**stamp (n.)** 郵票　**repackage (v.)** 重新包裝　**shipment (n.)** 運送的貨物

21. 以 Where 開頭的問句，詢問參考資料室的位置 澳⇄美

Where's this law firm's reference library?	這家律師事務所的參考資料室在哪裡？
(A) Our large collection of law books and documents.	(A) 我們對法律書籍及文件的大量收藏。
(B) I'll show you the building's floor plan.	**(B) 我給你看這棟大樓的平面圖。**
(C) Ms. Garcia certainly writes good reference letters.	(C) 賈西亞女士肯定很會寫推薦信。

- **law firm** 律師事務所　**reference library**（書籍不外借的）參考書閱覽室　**collection (n.)** 收集；收藏品　**floor plan** 平面圖　**reference letter** 推薦信

22. 表示請託或要求的問句 英⇄澳

Could I borrow your mobile phone charger?	我可以借用你的手機充電器嗎？
(A) Did you lose yours again?	**(A) 你的（充電器）又弄丟了嗎？**
(B) The charges are explained on your invoice.	(B) 這些費用在你的帳單上有說明。
(C) Almost one hundred percent.	(C) 幾乎百分之一百。

- **charger (n.)** 充電器　**lose (v.)** 遺失　**charge (n.)** 費用；收費　**invoice (n.)** 發貨單；請款帳單

23. 以 **Who** 開頭的問句，詢問該向誰請教維修要求的進度 (美)⇄(加) 

Who can I ask about the status of my maintenance request? **(A) I'd wait another day before following up.** (B) Yes, during the question-and-answer session. (C) Because this electrical outlet still isn't working.	關於維修申請的進度，我可以問誰呢？ **(A) 如果是我，我會多等一天再追蹤進度。** (B) 是的，在問答時間中。 (C) 因為這個電源插座仍無法運作。

- status (n.) 狀態；進度　maintenance (n.) 維護　follow up 追查……的情況；對……採取進一步行動　session (n.)（活動的）一段時間；一場　electrical outlet 電源插座

24. 以 **How long** 開頭的問句，詢問預估研究調查的時間 (美)⇄(澳) 難

How long do you expect the research study to take? (A) It was carefully inspected in June. **(B) There is a lot of data to gather.** (C) Through an Internet search portal.	你預估這項調查研究需要多久時間？ (A) 六月時就仔細檢查過了。 **(B) 有很多資料要收集。** (C) 透過網路搜尋入口網站。

- research (n.) 研究；調查　study (n.) 研究　inspect (v.) 檢查

25. 以 **Be** 動詞開頭的問句，詢問是否準備分發講義 (加)⇄(英)

Are the handouts ready to be distributed? (A) It's a summary of my main points. **(B) We just need to staple them.** (C) Each person in the seminar.	這些印出的資料準備好分發出去了嗎？ (A) 這是我的重點概要。 **(B) 只要再裝釘起來，就可以了。** (C) 研討會上的每個人。

- handout (n.) 講義　distribute (v.) 分發　summary (n.) 總結；摘要　staple (v.)（用釘書機）釘住

26. 以 **What** 開頭的問句，詢問瓷碗的用途 (澳)⇄(英) 難

What are these small ceramic bowls for? (A) Five thousand won for a set of three. **(B) The waiter will let us know when he comes back.** (C) Do you remember where you last saw it?	這些小瓷碗是做什麼用的？ (A) 一組三件，售價五千韓元。 **(B) 等服務生回來，就會告訴我們。** (C) 你記得你何時最後一次看到它嗎？

- ceramic (adj.) 陶瓷的

27. 表示建議或提案的問句 (加)⇄(美)

Would you like me to order a new copy machine? (A) Yokoyama Office Electronics, I believe. (B) The user's manual is in the box. **(C) The technician is still trying to fix the old one.**	你要我去訂購一台新的影印機嗎？ (A) 我想是橫山辦公電器公司。 (B) 使用說明書在箱子裡。 **(C) 技術人員仍試著修復舊的那台。**

- order (v.) 訂購　copy machine 影印機　manual (n.) 使用手冊；說明書　fix (v.) 維修

28. 以 **Be** 動詞開頭的問句，詢問是否會舉辦員工野餐 (英)⇄(澳)

Are we going to have an employee picnic again this year? (A) I'd love to go with you. (B) That's OK—the park is within walking distance. **(C) If the weather allows it.**	我們今年還要舉辦員工野餐嗎？ (A) 我很樂意跟你一起去。 (B) 沒關係，公園可以步行抵達。 **(C) 如果天候許可的話。**

- employee (n.) 員工　distance (n.) 距離　allow (v.) 允許；使成為可能

29. 以選擇疑問句詢問繳回合約書的方法 英⇄澳 難

Do I have to return this contract in person, or can I mail it back?

(A) That's your copy to keep.

(B) Once you've signed and dated it.

(C) I'm sorry, but we don't accept returns.

我必須親自把合約送回，還是可以郵寄回去？

(A) 這份是供你留存的副本。

(B) 一旦你簽了名、寫了日期後。

(C) 很抱歉，我們不接受退貨。

- return (v.) 歸還；退回　contract (n.) 合約　in person 親自　once (conj.) 一旦……就　date (v.) 在……上標明日期　accept (v.) 接受

30. 以 Why 開頭的問句，詢問門口停放搬家貨車的原因 加⇄美 難

Why is there a moving truck parked out front?

(A) It's all right as long as it's not moving quickly.

(B) We'll need permission from the building supervisor.

(C) They must have found a tenant for the office next door.

為什麼有輛搬家公司的卡車停在門口？

(A) 只要它未在快速移動就沒有問題。

(B) 我們需要得到辦公大樓管理人的許可。

(C) 一定是隔壁辦公室找到了租戶。

- permission (n.) 許可　supervisor (n.) 主管；經理　tenant (n.) 承租人；房客

31. 以直述句傳達資訊 澳⇄美 難

Fonson Bridge is closed, and I don't know another route.

(A) No, we're still pretty far from the river.

(B) Oh, I forgot that you're not from around here.

(C) Whichever is the fastest.

弗森橋關閉了，而我不知道別條路怎麼走。

(A) 不，我們離河邊還遠著呢。

(B) 噢，我忘了你不是本地人。

(C) 就選最快的路線。

- route (n.) 路線　pretty (adv.) 相當；很　whichever (pron.) 任何一個

PART 3 P. 61–64

19

32-34 Conversation

加⇄英

M: OK, Georgia, (32) **I can install the rest of the flooring myself. I'd like you to climb up onto the roof and help Rick attach the tiles.** (33) **Say, is that a new toolbox?**

W: (33) **Oh—yes, it is. You know, my old blue toolkit was falling apart and never could carry that much anyway. So I thought I'd invest in a new one.**

M: It's really nice. Wait, is it a Wenton X Series? With the adjustable handle feature? I thought those cost like a hundred dollars.

W: (34) **Well, now that it's been on the market for a few years, its price has dropped.** If you like it, you should look into getting one, too.

32-34 對話

男：好了，喬琪雅，(32) **我可以自己完成剩下的地板鋪設，我想請妳爬到屋頂上，幫忙里克貼瓦片。**(33) **唉唷，那個工具箱是新的嗎？**

女：(33) **噢，對啊，你也知道，我舊的那個藍色工具箱都快要四分五裂了，而且一直都裝不了多少東西，所以我就想花點錢買個新的。**

男：挺不錯的，等等，這個是溫頓 X 系列嗎？手把附有調整功能的那個？我以為那系列產品大概要價 100 美元。

女：(34) **嗯，畢竟該系列已經上市好幾年，價格已經調降了**，如果你喜歡，不妨考慮也去買一個。

- install (v.) 裝設；安裝　flooring (n.) 地板材料　attach (v.) 貼上　toolkit (n.) 工具箱　invest (v.) 花錢買；投資　adjustable (adj.) 可調整的　feature (n.) 功能；性能　look into 調查

32. 全文相關——說話者的工作地點

What kind of business do the speakers most likely work for?

(A) A hardware store

(B) A construction firm

(C) A building equipment manufacturer

(D) A landscaping company

說話者最有可能在哪種企業工作？

(A) 五金行

(B) 建設公司

(C) 建築設備製造商

(D) 景觀工程公司

33. 相關細節——女子最近做的事情 難

What has the woman recently done?

(A) Rearranged a storage area

(B) Met with potential investors

(C) Attended a live demonstration

(D) Replaced one of her belongings

女子最近做了什麼事？

(A) 重新整理了倉儲區。

(B) 與潛在投資者會面。

(C) 參加了現場展示會。

(D) 更換了她的個人物品。

- rearrange (v.) 重新整理　storage (n.) 儲存　potential (adj.) 潛在的　investor (n.) 投資者　demonstration (n.) 展示；示範　belonging (n.)（常用複數）個人物品

34. 相關細節——女子提到有關溫頓 X 的變化

What does the woman say has changed about the Wenton X Series?

(A) It now has additional features.

(B) It is now made of a different metal.

(C) It has become less expensive.

(D) It has become safer to use.

女子說到，溫頓 X 系列有了何種變化？

(A) 現在有了額外功能。

(B) 如今是由不同金屬製成。

(C) 變得沒那麼昂貴。

(D) 現在使用更安全了。

- additional (adj.) 額外的　metal (n.) 金屬　expensive (adj.) 昂貴的

換句話說 its price has dropped（價格已經調降了）→ it has become less expensive（變得沒那麼昂貴）

35-37 Conversation

W: **(35) Devon, did you hear about the television ad the marketing department is creating? It will feature some real employees working in our office.**

M: Really? That's interesting.

W: Yeah. So, tomorrow they're going to send a film crew here to record us working.

M: **(36) Wow! I never thought I'd be on TV for working in the accounting department.**

W: I don't think anyone thought that!

M: **(37) I guess I'll wear my best-looking suit tomorrow, then.** I want to make sure I look good on camera!

35-37 對話

美⇄澳

女： **(35) 德文，你有聽說行銷部正在製作的電視廣告嗎？據說我們辦公室有一些員工會實際入鏡。**

男： 真的嗎？挺有趣的。

女： 對啊，所以明天他們會派拍攝組到這裡，記錄我們工作的樣子。

男： **(36) 哇！我從來沒想過，我會因為在會計部工作而上電視。**

女： 我想沒有人料想得到！

男： **(37) 那我明天想穿我最好看的西裝穿來上班**，在鏡頭前一定得看起來體面上相！

- feature (v.) 由⋯⋯擔任主演　crew (n.) 工作人員　record (v.) 錄製　accounting (n.) 會計

35. 全文相關——對話主題

What are the speakers mainly discussing?

(A) A video shoot

(B) A department supervisor

(C) A training program

(D) An upcoming presentation

說話者主要在討論什麼事？

(A) 影片拍攝

(B) 部門主管

(C) 培訓課程

(D) 即將進行的簡報

- shoot (n.) 拍攝　supervisor (n.) 主管　upcoming (adj.) 即將到來的

36. 掌握說話者的意圖——提及「我想沒有人料想得到」的意圖 難

Why does the woman say, "I don't think anyone thought that"?

(A) To decline an offer

(B) To justify a decision

(C) To agree with the man

(D) To correct a misunderstanding

女子為什麼會說：「我想沒有人料想得到」？

(A) 以拒絕提議

(B) 要為決定辯解

(C) 以同意男子的觀點

(D) 以糾正誤會

- decline (v.) 拒絕　offer (n.) 提議　justify (v.) 對……做出解釋　correct (v.) 糾正　misunderstanding (n.) 誤解

37. 相關細節——明天男子將做的事情

What does the man say he will do tomorrow?

(A) Arrive to work late

(B) Wear attractive clothes

(C) Watch a television broadcast

(D) Bring in his camera

男子說他明天要做什麼？

(A) 晚點去上班

(B) 穿好看的衣服

(C) 收看電視播出

(D) 帶他的相機來

換句話說 wear my best-looking suit（穿我最好看的西裝）→ wear attractive clothes（穿好看的衣服）

38-40 Conversation with three speakers

M1: Eastlake Printing. How can I help you?

W: Hi, I'd like to have some posters printed and covered in protective plastic. (38) **How large of a document can you do that for?** Would three feet by two feet be too big?

M1: Hmm, let me check with my coworker. (39) **Demetri, can we laminate a three-foot-by-two-foot poster?**

M2: (39) **No, but we could print it on special, thicker paper instead.** That gives a similar effect.

M1: OK. Thanks, Demetri. Ma'am, did you hear that?

W: I did. (40) **But I don't think that's a good idea. Paper wouldn't be durable enough for my needs.** I'll try some other print shops.

38-40 三人對話 澳⇄美⇄加

男 1： 歡迎光臨東湖印刷公司，請問您需要什麼服務？

女： 你好，我想印製幾張海報，然後用塑膠保護膜護貝起來。(38) **你們能護貝多大尺寸的文件資料？**三呎長、兩呎寬的話會太大嗎？

男 1： 唔，讓我跟同事確認一下。(39) **德梅奇，我們能護貝大小 3 X 2 呎的海報嗎？**

男 2： (39) **沒有辦法，不過我們可以使用特製的厚紙印刷，**可以有相似的效果。

男 1： 我知道了。謝謝你，德梅奇。女士，您有聽到嗎？

女： 我聽到了，(40) **但是我不認為那是個好辦法。紙質材料的耐用度不夠，無法滿足我的需求，**我再到別家印刷店看看。

- coworker (n.) 同事　laminate (v.) 給……護貝　durable (adj.) 耐用的

38. 相關細節——女子提出的問題

What does the woman ask about?
(A) A size limit
(B) A bulk price
(C) A minimum quantity
(D) A likely completion date

女子詢問何事？
(A) 尺寸限制
(B) 大量印製的價格
(C) 最低印刷量
(D) 可能的完成日期

39. 相關細節——德梅奇建議女子做的事情

What does Demetri recommend that the woman do?
(A) Inquire at other print shops
(B) Wait until new stock is delivered
(C) Look at some samples online
(D) Choose a different material

德梅奇建議女子做什麼？
(A) 到別家影印店洽詢
(B) 等新的存貨送達
(C) 在網路上看樣品
(D) 選擇不同的材質

- inquire (v.) 詢問；查詢 stock (n.) 存貨；庫存 material (n.) 材質

40. 相關細節——女子對於德梅奇建議的想法

What does the woman say about Demetri's recommendation?
(A) She will consider it.
(B) She will implement it.
(C) She wants to hear more about it.
(D) She does not believe it is suitable.

女子對德梅奇的建議有何說法？
(A) 她會考慮。
(B) 她會付諸實行。
(C) 她想更深入了解。
(D) 她認為不適合。

- implement (v.) 實施；執行 suitable (adj.) 適合的

41-43 Conversation

W: Hi, my name is Natalie Reeves. [41] **I have a two o'clock appointment with Dr. Dhawan.**

M: Let me see . . . yes, there you are. [41] **Did you bring the patient update paperwork we sent to your address on Evans Drive?**

W: [42] **Oh, I actually moved last month, so no, I never even got those documents.** Is that going to be a problem?

M: [43] **No, it just means you'll need to complete them now, before your appointment. Would you like the paper version, or the electronic version on this tablet computer?**

41-43 對話 英⇄加

女：你好，我的名字是娜塔莉．李斯，**(41) 我跟達萬醫生約了下午兩點看診。**

男：我看看……有的，找到了。**(41) 我們之前有寄一份病患資料的更新表單，到您在艾文斯路的住址，請問您有帶過來嗎？**

女：**(42) 噢，其實我上個月搬家了，甚至連收到那份資料都沒有，所以無法帶來。**這會造成什麼問題嗎？

男：**(43) 不會，只是這表示您現在得在約診開始前，完成表格填寫。您想以紙本填寫，還是使用這邊平板電腦的電子檔？**

- appointment (n.) 預約 patient (n.) 病患 paperwork (n.) 文書；資料 address (n.) 地址 document (n.) 文件 complete (v.) 完成 electronic (adj.) 電子的

41. 全文相關——對話的地點

Where most likely does the conversation take place?
(A) At a real estate agency
(B) At a medical clinic
(C) At a post office
(D) At a law firm

這段對話最有可能是在哪裡發生的？
(A) 在房地產仲介商
(B) 在醫療診所
(C) 在郵局
(D) 在律師事務所

42. 相關細節——女子描述的問題

What problem does the woman describe?
(A) She did not receive a piece of mail.
(B) She did not understand some instructions.
(C) She misplaced a document.
(D) She is uncertain about a proposal.

女子提到了什麼問題？
(A) 她沒有收到郵件。
(B) 她未理解指示說明。
(C) 她忘記文件放置位置。
(D) 她對提議猶豫不決。

- **receive (v.)** 收到 **mail (n.)** 郵件 **instruction (n.)** 指示；說明書 **misplace (v.)** 忘記……放在哪裡 **uncertain (adj.)** 猶豫的 **proposal (n.)** 提議

43. 相關細節——男子要求女子選擇的事項

What does the man ask the woman to choose?
(A) When an appointment will be rescheduled for
(B) Whether she will authorize a transaction
(C) How she will fill out some forms
(D) Where a shipment will be sent

男子要求女子選擇何事？
(A) 約診變更的時間
(B) 是否授權一筆交易
(C) 填寫表格的方式
(D) 貨物要送往何處

- **reschedule (v.)** 改期 **authorize (v.)** 授權 **transaction (n.)** 交易 **form (n.)** 表格 **shipment (n.)** 運送的貨物

44-46 Conversation

M: Hi, Ms. Griffith. (44) **I just wanted to remind you that elevator technicians will be coming in next week to perform routine maintenance.**

W: Thanks, Lester. (45) **Actually—I've been thinking about improving or maybe even replacing our elevators to speed them up. When the technicians are here, I'd like to ask them what the possibilities are.**

M: Well, they're maintenance technicians, so I'm not sure they'd know much about important factors like pricing.

W: Good point. Hmm . . . (46) **Then please call the company and arrange for a consultant to come in and talk to me.** Sometime in the next few weeks would be great.

44-46 對話 澳⇄英

男：嗨，格里菲斯女士，(44) **我只是想提醒您：電梯技師會在下週過來，進行例行的檢修。**

女：謝謝你，萊斯特。(45) **其實對於電梯，我一直在考慮要不要進行改善或甚至更換，以便加快電梯的速度。技師到達之後，我想問問看他們有哪些可能的做法。**

男：這個嘛，他們是維修保養的技術人員，所以我不確定他們會很了解價格等重要因素。

女：說得有道理。嗯……(46) **那麼請你打電話給那家公司，安排諮詢人員到公司跟我討論，**時間理想上是接下來數週之內的時間。

- **remind (v.)** 提醒 **technician (n.)** 技術人員 **perform (v.)** 執行 **possibility (n.)** 可能的選項 **maintenance (n.)** 檢修 **factor (n.)** 因素；要素 **arrange (v.)** 安排

44. 全文相關——對話主題

難

What is the main topic of the conversation?
(A) An employee's performance evaluation
(B) A technical difficulty with some software
(C) A system for issuing scheduling reminders
(D) A convenience facility in a building

這段對話的主題為何？
(A) 一名員工的績效評估
(B) 部分軟體的技術難題
(C) 發送日程提醒通知的系統
(D) 大樓裡的便利設施

- performance (n.) 績效；考績 evaluation (n.) 評估 issue (v.) 發出 scheduling (n.) 排程 reminder (n.) 提醒物 convenience (n.) 便利 facility (n.) 設施

換句話說 elevator（電梯）→ a convenience facility（便利設施）

45. 相關細節——女子想要做的事情

What does the woman want to do?
(A) Administer a companywide survey
(B) Lower some maintenance spending
(C) Learn about upgrade options
(D) Clarify some guidelines

女子想要做什麼？
(A) 執行全公司的調查
(B) 降低一些檢修支出
(C) 了解設備更新的選項
(D) 釐清一些指導原則

- administer (v.) 施行 companywide (adj.) 全公司的 lower (v.) 降低 spending (n.) 支出；開銷 option (n.) 可選擇的方案 clarify (v.) 澄清 guideline (n.) 準則；指導原則

46. 相關細節——女子要求男子做的事情

What does the woman ask the man to do?
(A) Set up a meeting
(B) Draft a notice
(C) Clean out a room
(D) Search a database

女子要求男子做什麼？
(A) 安排會面
(B) 草擬通知
(C) 清理房間
(D) 搜尋資料庫

- draft (v.) 草擬 notice (n.) 通知；公告

換句話說 arrange for a consultant to come in and talk to me（安排諮詢人員到公司跟我討論）
→ set up a meeting（安排會面）

47-49 Conversation

W: Welcome to Nashlin Shoes.

M: Hi. I was given this pair of sneakers as a gift, but they're not really my style. (47) **I'd like to exchange them for a refund.**

W: I can help you with that. (48) **I'll need to see the receipt, though—do you happen to have it?**

M: Yes, the person who gave me the sneakers included it in the box, just in case. Here it is.

W: Great. (49) **Oh, I'm sorry, but since it's been more than thirty days since these were purchased, we can't give you a cash refund.** You'll only be able to get store credit.

47-49 對話

美⇄加

女： 歡迎光臨納什林鞋店。

男： 妳好，有人送我這雙運動鞋當作禮物，可是真的不符合我喜歡的風格，(47) **我想來退貨，換取退款。**

女： 我可以幫您處理，(48) **不過我需要查看收據，不知您有帶來嗎？**

男： 有的，送我這雙運動鞋的人，有把收據放在盒子裡，以備不時之需，就在這裡。

女： 好極了。(49) **噢，很抱歉，但因為這雙鞋自購買日起已經超過 30 天，所以我們沒辦法退現金給您，**只能提供您本店的折抵額度。

- pair (n.) 雙　exchange (v.) 交換　refund (n.) 退款　receipt (n.) 收據　purchase (v.) 購買
  store credit 購物折抵單（退貨後得到，可供下次購物折抵）

47. 相關細節——男子來店裡的理由

Why is the man at the store?
(A) To have some footwear repaired
(B) To buy a gift for a family member
(C) To return some unwanted goods
(D) To place an advance order

男子為何會到商店裡？
(A) 修理鞋子
(B) 為家人買禮物
(C) 退回不想要的商品
(D) 下單預購

- repair (v.) 修理　unwanted (adj.) 不需要的　advanced order 預購

換句話說 exchange them for a refund（退貨換取退款）
→ return some unwanted goods（退回不想要的商品）

48. 相關細節——女子要求男子做的事情

What does the woman request that the man do?
(A) Estimate a person's shoe size
(B) Complete some paperwork
(C) Provide proof of a purchase
(D) Show her the problem with an item

女子要求男子做什麼？
(A) 推估某人的鞋碼
(B) 完成文件填寫
(C) 提供購買證明
(D) 給她看產品的問題

- estimate (v.) 估計；推測　paperwork (n.) 文件資料　proof (n.) 證明；證據

換句話說 the receipt（收據）→ proof of a purchase（購買證明）

49. 相關細節——女子道歉的理由 難

What does the woman apologize for?
(A) A long shipping duration
(B) An unfavorable store policy
(C) The small selection of merchandise
(D) A malfunctioning payment system

女子為什麼道歉？
(A) 送貨時間漫長
(B) 商店政策不盡人意
(C) 商品選擇少
(D) 支付系統故障

- shipping (n.) 運輸　duration (n.) 持續期間　unfavorable (adj.) 不利的　policy (n.) 政策
  selection (n.) 選擇　merchandise (n.) 商品　malfunction (v.) 故障　payment (n.) 付款

50-52 Conversation with three speakers

W1: Hi. (50) **My colleague and I just used the kiosk to print out our reserved tickets, and we see that we've been seated in different rows.**

W2: We were planning to get some work done on the train. (50) **Could we possibly sit together? Here are our tickets.**

M: Oh, you're going down to Hingdon? (51) **I'm sorry, but all of the trains going there are completely full.** The Hingdon Music Festival is this weekend.

W1: I see. Well, that's disappointing. But thanks anyway.

50-52 三人對話 美⇄英⇄澳

女 1： 你好，(50) **我同事跟我剛剛使用服務機台，把我們預訂的車票印出來了，可是卻發現我們的座位在不同排。**

女 2： 我們打算在列車上把一些工作完成。(50) **有辦法讓我們坐在一起嗎？這是我們的車票。**

男： 噢，兩位要南下去新登？(51) **很抱歉，目前開往該地的列車全部都滿座，**這個週末有舉辦「新登音樂節」。

女 1： 我明白了。唉，可惜無法如願，不過還是謝謝你。

M: No problem.
W2: Well, what should we do, Tara? We need to get ready for our presentation.
W1: We'll have to do the preparations separately. (52) **Let's sit down and figure out who will handle what.**

男： 不客氣。
女 2： 那麼塔拉，我們該怎麼辦？我們必須準備好我們的簡報內容。
女 1： 我們只好分頭做準備工作。(52) **我們先坐下來，討論各自要負責的部分吧。**

- reserve (v.) 預訂　row (n.) 一排（列）　possibly (adv.) 可能　full (adj.) 滿的　disappointing (adj.) 令人失望的　separately (adv.) 分別地　handle (v.) 處理

50. 相關細節——女子們希望做的事情

What do the women hope to do?
(A) Reserve an earlier train
(B) Use a self-service machine
(C) Take advantage of a promotion
(D) Change their seating assignments

女子們希望做何事？
(A) 預訂更早的列車
(B) 使用自助機台
(C) 利用促銷活動
(D) 變更座位分配

- take advantage of 利用　promotion (n.) 促銷活動　assignment (n.) 分配；安排

51. 相關細節——男子描述的問題

What problem does the man describe?
(A) Some tickets have sold out.
(B) Some departures will be delayed.
(C) A computer server is down.
(D) A voucher has expired.

男子說到有何種問題？
(A) 車票已售罄。
(B) 列車將延後發車。
(C) 電腦伺服器當機。
(D) 優惠券已過期。

- departure (n.) 出發　delay (v.) 延遲　voucher (n.) 優惠券　expire (v.) 到期；失效

換句話說 all of the trains going there are completely full（開往該地的列車全部都滿座）
→ some tickets have sold out（車票已售罄）

52. 相關細節——女子們接下來要做的事情 難

What will the women most likely do next?
(A) Notify a coworker
(B) Reevaluate a budget
(C) Divide up some work tasks
(D) Consider other travel methods

女子們接下來最有可能做什麼？
(A) 通知同事
(B) 重新評估預算
(C) 分配工作任務
(D) 考慮其他交通方式

- notify (v.) 通知　coworker (n.) 同事　reevaluate (v.) 重新評估　budget (n.) 預算　divide up 劃分；分配　consider (v.) 考慮　method (n.) 方法

換句話說 figure out who will handle what（討論各自要負責的部分）
→ divide out some work tasks（分配工作任務）

53-55 Conversation

53-55 對話

加⇄英

M: [53] ***Pinterville Times* front desk, this is Matt.** How can I help you?

W: Hi, I was hoping to speak to one of your reporters—uh, Denise Webber.

M: May I ask what this is about?

W: I'd like to express my dissatisfaction about her article on Pinterville Park. [54] **There's some incorrect information in it that needs to be cleared up.**

M: [55] **Ah, in that case, please fill out the reporting form on our Web site.** You can access it from the "Contact Us" menu.

W: Oh, OK. Once I do that, how long will it take for a correction to be printed?

M: Well, we have to verify the information, so it usually takes a few days.

男：[53] **這裡是《品特威爾時報》服務台，我是麥特。**請問有什麼需要協助的地方？

女：你好，我希望和貴報社的一名記者談談——嗯，名叫丹妮絲．韋伯。

男：方便請教一下是什麼事嗎？

女：她針對品特威爾公園寫了一篇文章，我讀了不甚滿意，想跟她反映，[54] **文章裡有些不正確的資訊，需要予以澄清。**

男：[55] **哦，那樣的話，麻煩您到我們的網站填寫回報單，**表單可以在「與我們聯繫」的選單上取得。

女：噢，好的。等我填完後，需要多久的時間才會刊出更正的資訊？

男：這個嘛，由於我們必須查證資訊，所以通常需要幾天的時間。

- **front desk** 服務台 **express (v.)** 表達 **dissatisfaction (n.)** 不滿 **article (n.)** 文章 **incorrect (adj.)** 不正確的 **clear up** 澄清 **fill out** 填寫 **access (v.)**（電腦）存取 **correction (n.)** 更正 **verify (v.)** 查清；證實

53. 全文相關——男子的職業

What most likely is the man's job?

(A) A journalist

(B) A graphic designer

(C) A newspaper editor

(D) A receptionist

男子最有可能從事何種職業？

(A) 記者

(B) 平面設計師

(C) 報紙編輯

(D) 接待員

---

54. 相關細節——女子提及報導中的問題

According to the woman, what is the problem with an article?

(A) Some details are missing.

(B) There are some errors.

(C) The meaning of its title is unclear.

(D) It was placed in the wrong section.

根據女子所言，文章有什麼問題？

(A) 遺漏了某些細節。

(B) 有一些錯誤。

(C) 標題語意不清。

(D) 放錯版面。

- **detail (n.)** 細節 **missing (adj.)** 遺漏的 **error (n.)** 錯誤 **section (n.)** 部分

換句話說 some incorrect information（有些不正確的資訊）→ some errors（一些錯誤）

---

55. 相關細節——男子要求女子做的事情

What does the man ask the woman to do?

(A) Verify her professional qualifications

(B) Check the online version of the article

(C) Wait for him to locate a colleague

(D) File her complaint electronically

男子要求女子做什麼？

(A) 證明她的專業資格

(B) 查看網路版文章

(C) 等待他找到同事所在

(D) 以電子方式提出客訴

- professional (adj.) 專業的　qualification (n.) 資格；條件　locate (v.) 找出……的位置　complaint (n.) 客訴　electronically (adv.) 以電子方式

換句話說 on our Web site（到我們的網站）→ electronically（以電子方式）

56-58 Conversation

M: Ms. Bowers? This is Orlando from Ankins Electronics. [56] **I'm calling about the order for spare camera parts that you placed through our Web site.**

W: Yes, this is Emily Bowers. Is there a problem?

M: No, we just need a little more information to make sure we send you the right products. [57] **Could you look at the underside of your camera and tell me its full model number?**

W: Oh, I'm at work right now. [57] **And I don't have the number memorized or anything.**

M: All right. [58] **Can I give you the direct phone number for customer service so you can call us from home later?**

W: Sure. [58] **Let me just get a pen. OK, I'm ready.**

56-58 對話　加⇄美

男：鮑爾斯女士嗎？我是「安金斯電子」的奧蘭多，[56] **本次來電是關於您在本公司的網站上，下單購買的備用相機零件。**

女：是的，我是艾蜜莉・鮑爾斯。有什麼問題嗎？

男：沒有的，我們只是需要更多一點資訊，以確保我們寄給您正確的產品。[57] **可以請您查看一下相機底部、告訴我完整的型號嗎？**

女：噢，現在我在上班，[57] **而我也沒有把型號之類的記下來。**

男：好的。[58] **我可否給您客服部的直撥電話號碼？這樣晚點您可以從家裡打電話給我們。**

女：好啊。[58] **我拿支筆。好了，我準備好了。**

- order (n.) 訂單　spare (adj.) 備用的　part (n.) 部件；零件　underside (n.) 底部；下面　memorize (v.) 記住；背誦　direct (adj.) 直接的

56. 全文相關——來電的目的

What is the man calling about?

(A) A sales event
(B) A repair service
(C) A new business
(D) A product order

男子的來電所為何事？

(A) 促銷活動
(B) 維修服務
(C) 新開的商家
(D) 產品訂單

---

57. 掌握說話者的意圖——提及「現在我在上班」的意圖　難

What does the woman mean when she says, "I'm at work right now"?

(A) She does not have access to an item.
(B) She forgot about an appointment.
(C) She does not have time to talk.
(D) She is unaware of an issue that has arisen.

女子說：「現在我在上班」，意思為何？

(A) 她無法取用某件物品。
(B) 她忘了有預約。
(C) 她沒時間講話。
(D) 她渾然不知已出現問題。

- access (n.) 使用（某物）的機會　appointment (n.)（事務性的）約會　unaware (adj.) 未察覺到的　issue (n.) 問題　arise (v.) 出現

---

58. 相關細節——女子接下來要做的事情

What will the woman most likely do next?

(A) Write down some contact information

(B) Stand near the entrance to a building

(C) Make a drawing of a space

(D) Take a bus to her house

女子接下來最有可能做什麼？

(A) 寫下聯絡方式

(B) 站在大樓入口旁

(C) 繪製空間圖

(D) 搭公車回家

換句話說 the . . . phone number（電話號碼）→ some contact information（聯絡方式）

59-61 Conversation

59-61 對話

澳⇄美

M: Hi, Michelle. It's Leland. (59) **I wanted to call and thank you for letting me borrow that book by Theresa Riley.** I ended up referring to it a lot while writing my article.

W: Oh, it was no problem. I'm glad I could help.

M: You really did. (60) **If I'd had to wait for the university library to order the book, I'd never have been able to get the article to the journal last week before the cutoff date.**

W: Yeah, the library's system is pretty slow sometimes.

M: I've certainly learned that lesson. (61) **Anyway, do you have a free hour sometime this week?** I'd like to meet up to return the book and buy you a coffee.

男：嗨，蜜雪兒，我是利蘭。(59) **我打電話是想謝謝妳把泰瑞莎．萊利的書借給我**，我的文章寫到後來，參考了很多這本書的內容。

女：噢，這沒什麼，我很高興能幫上忙。

男：妳真的幫了大忙，(60) **如果我得等到大學圖書館訂購到這本書，那我上週絕對沒辦法趕在截止日前，把文章送交給期刊。**

女：對啊，圖書館的系統有時相當緩慢。

男：我已徹底學到教訓了。(61) **話說回來，妳這個星期能不能撥出一個小時？**我想跟妳見面還書，並請妳喝杯咖啡。

- **borrow (v.)** 借入 **end up** 到頭來；結束 **refer to** 參考 **article (n.)** 文章 **cutoff date** 截止日期 **lesson (n.)** 教訓；經驗

59. 相關細節——男子感謝女子的事情

What does the man thank the woman for?

(A) Lending him a resource

(B) Introducing him to an acquaintance

(C) Allowing him to use a workstation

(D) Looking over his writing

男子為何事感謝女子？

(A) 借他一本參考書

(B) 把他介紹給熟人

(C) 允許他使用工作區

(D) 檢查他寫的文章

- **lend (v.)** 借出 **resource (n.)** 資源 **introduce (v.)** 介紹 **acquaintance (n.)** 熟人 **workstation (n.)** 工作區

---

60. 相關細節——男子提到上週發生的事情 難

What does the man say happened last week?

(A) A publishing decision was announced.

(B) A research interview took place.

(C) A university institution was closed.

(D) A submission was made.

男子說上個星期發生了什麼事？

(A) 宣布了出版的決定。

(B) 進行了研究訪談。

(C) 大學的機構關閉了。

(D) 已經交稿了。

- **publish (v.)** 出版 **decision (n.)** 決定 **announce (v.)** 宣布；公布 **research (n.)** 研究 **take place** 發生 **institution (n.)** 機構 **submission (n.)** 提交；繳交

---

61. 相關細節——男子詢問女子的事情

What does the man ask the woman about?
(A) Her experience with a process
(B) Her favorite coffee drink
(C) Her opinions on a book
(D) Her availability in the near future

男子詢問女子何事？
(A) 她對某個過程的經驗
(B) 她最喜歡的咖啡
(C) 她對書本的看法
(D) 她最近是否有空

- process (n.) 過程 favorite (adj.) 最喜愛的 opinion (n.) 意見 availability (n.) 能出席；能參加

換句話說 a free hour sometime this week（這個星期撥出一個小時）
→ availability in the near future（最近是否有空）

62-64 Conversation + Order form

W: Hi, Dave. (62) **I wanted to check how your preparations for Byung-Hoon Han's first day are going. I'd like to get him ready to start contributing to the team right away.**

M: Sure, Claudette. (63) **I'm arranging his orientation sessions right now.** It looks like we should be able to get them all done on the first day.

W: That's great. And how about the office supplies he'll need? Have you ordered them yet?

M: Oh, I'd like your opinion on that, actually. Here's the order form I filled out. Does it look all right? Or did I forget anything?

W: Hmm . . . (64) **That seems like too many paper clips. Two boxes would probably be enough. Otherwise, it looks good.**

Order Form

Item	No.
File organizers	3
(64) **Paper clips boxes**	**5**
Pen sets	2
Staplers	1
Sticky notes pads	4

62-64 對話＋訂購單 英⇄加

女： 嗨，戴夫。(62) **我想確認韓秉動第一天上班的準備工作，你進行得怎麼樣了？我希望他可以馬上就緒，對團隊做出貢獻。**

男： 沒問題，克勞黛。(63) **我現在正在安排他的新人培訓課程**，看樣子在第一天，我們就能結束所有的課程。

女： 太好了。那麼他會需要的辦公用品呢？你都訂好了嗎？

男： 哦，其實對此我想聽聽妳的意見。這是我填好的訂購單，看起來沒問題吧？還是我漏掉了什麼東西？

女： 嗯……(64) **迴紋針好像太多了，兩盒也許就夠用了。除此之外，看起來挺好的。**

訂購單

品項	數量
文件架	3
(64) 盒裝迴紋針	**5**
筆組	2
釘書機	1
便利貼	4

- preparation (n.) 準備 contribute (v.) 貢獻 arrange (v.) 安排；準備 orientation (n.) 新人培訓 session (n.)（活動的）一段時間；一場 office supplies 辦公用品 order (n.) 訂購（單） opinion (n.) 意見 fill out 填寫 otherwise (adv.) 除此以外

62. 相關細節——韓先生的職業

Who most likely is Mr. Han?
(A) A government inspector
(B) A board member
(C) A new hire
(D) A vendor

韓先生最有可能是什麼人？
(A) 政府督察員
(B) 董事會成員
(C) 新進員工
(D) 小販

63. 相關細節——男子提到自己正在做的事情 難

What does the man say he is currently doing?
(A) Organizing some files
(B) Making a schedule
(C) Reviewing an agreement
(D) Collecting some supplies

男子說他目前正在做什麼？
(A) 整理檔案
(B) 制定時間表
(C) 審查合約
(D) 領取用品

- **organize (v.)** 整理；組織 **review (v.)** 審查；審閱 **collect (v.)** 領取 **supplies (n.)**〔複〕用品

64. 圖表整合題——女子建議更改的數量

Look at the graphic. Which number does the woman recommend changing?
(A) 3
(B) 5
(C) 2
(D) 4

請看圖表作答。女子建議變更哪個數字？
(A) 3
(B) 5
(C) 2
(D) 4

65-67 Conversation + Floor plan

W: (65) **Hi, I'm calling to make an evening reservation for my office's annual holiday party.** Can you serve twenty-five people? Preferably in one of your private rooms.

M: Certainly. (66) **We just renovated our largest dining room besides the main one, and I must say it's lovely. We'll put your party in there.** What day and time will you be coming?

W: Well, the party's this Friday and we'll be coming at six o'clock.

M: Let's see . . . Yes, we do have an opening at six. (67) **Now, we require a one-hundred-dollar deposit to hold a dining room for an event.**

W: That shouldn't be a problem.

(66) **Baldwin Room**
Seats up to 30
The Martin Room
Seats up to 20
Main Dining Room
The Grant Room Seats up to 10

65-67 對話＋平面圖 英⇄澳

女： (65) **你好，我來電是想預約晚間時段，要舉行公司的年度假期聚會，**你們能夠接待 25 人嗎？最好是能在你們的私人包廂舉辦。

男： 當然可以。(66) **我們才剛整修過除了主宴會廳以外，最大的一間包廂。不得不說，那間包廂真是美輪美奐，我們會把貴公司一行人安排到那間包廂，**請問您們打算在哪一天、幾點鐘前來？

女： 這個嘛，聚會是在本週五舉行，我們六點會到餐廳。

男： 我看看哦……有，六點正好有位子。
(67) **那麼，我們要跟您收取一百美元的訂金，以便預留活動用的包廂。**

女： 沒有問題。

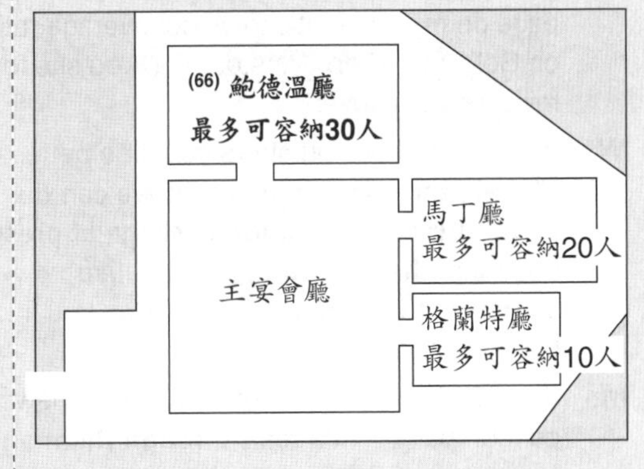

- **reservation (n.)** 預約 **annual (adj.)** 年度的 **preferably (adv.)** 更佳地
private (adj.) 不受打擾的；不對外開放的 **renovate (v.)** 翻修；改建 **besides (prep.)** 除……之外
I must say 在我看來；我認為 **party (n.)** 一行人 **deposit (n.)** 押金；訂金；保證金

65. 相關細節——女子負責籌辦的活動

What is the woman organizing?
(A) A fund-raiser
(B) An office dinner
(C) An awards ceremony
(D) A retirement party

女子正在籌辦什麼活動？
(A) 募款活動
(B) 公司晚宴
(C) 頒獎典禮
(D) 退休派對

66. 圖表整合題——女子一行人將會使用的包廂

Look at the graphic. What room will the woman's group use?
(A) The Main Dining Room
(B) The Baldwin Room
(C) The Martin Room
(D) The Grant Room

請看圖表作答。女子一行人將會使用哪間包廂？
(A) 主宴會廳
(B) 包德溫廳
(C) 馬丁廳
(D) 格蘭特廳

67. 相關細節——男子提及女子必須要做的事情

What does the man say the woman will have to do?
(A) Make a partial payment beforehand
(B) Approve a fixed menu of dishes
(C) Vacate the room by a certain time
(D) Read some guidelines for patrons

男子說女子必須做何事？
(A) 提前支付部分款項
(B) 批准固定菜單
(C) 在特定時間前離開包廂
(D) 閱讀客戶須知

- **partial (adj.)** 部分的 **payment (n.)** 付款 **beforehand (adv.)** 提前；事先 **approve (v.)** 批准；允許 **fixed (adj.)** 固定的 **vacate (v.)** 空出；騰出 **guideline (n.)** 指引；準則 **patron (n.)** 客戶

換句話說 require a . . . deposit（要收取……的訂金）
→ make a partial payment beforehand（提前支付部分款項）

68-70 Conversation + Web page

M: [68] **Ms. Tucker, I think I've discovered why we haven't been getting enough applicants for job openings lately.** Take a look at the Web page on my tablet. It shows our average ratings on Gold-Star-Employers.com, a Web site for reviewing employers.

W: Ah . . . yes, these numbers could be better. [69] **Well, there isn't much that we can do about our compensation package at present, but this other low rating seems like something we could address.** Can you find out more about it?

M: Sure. The site also has some longer reviews of our company. [70] **I'll read through them and prepare an outline of the important points for you by the end of the day.**

68-70 對話＋網頁

澳⇄美

男：[68] **塔克女士，有關我們最近的缺職吸引不到足夠應徵者，我想我已經發現原因了。**看一下我平板電腦上的網頁吧，上面顯示的是我們公司在 Gold-Star-Employers.com 上的平均分數，這是個用來評比企業主的網站。

女：哦……是啊，這些分數尚有進步空間。[69] **是說，薪酬待遇方面，我們目前無能為力，但是另一個評分低迷的項目，似乎是我們可以處理的，**你能去進一步了解嗎？

男：沒問題。針對我們公司，這個網站上還有幾篇較長的評論，[70] **我會在今天看完，然後在下班前準備好一份重點概要給妳過目。**

http://gold-employers.com	http://gold-employers.com
Average ratings for Custas Associates	**卡斯塔思事務所的平均評分**
Career Opportunities ★★★☆☆	工作前景 ★★★☆☆
Management ★★★★☆	管理 ★★★★☆
Pay and Benefits ★★☆☆☆	薪酬及福利 ★★☆☆☆
(69) **Work-Life Balance** ★★☆☆☆	(69) **工作／生活的平衡** ★★☆☆☆

- **discover (v.)** 發現；找到 **applicant (n.)** 應徵者 **job opening** 職缺 **rating (n.)** 評分；等級 **review (v./n.)** 評論 **employer (n.)** 雇主 **compensation package** 薪酬待遇 **at present** 目前 **address (v.)** 處理（問題） **outline (n.)** 大綱；概要

68. 相關細節——男子提及的問題

What problem does the man mention?
(A) A news report criticized the company.
(B) It is difficult to attract new staff.
(C) A client did not renew a contract.
(D) Several employees have quit their jobs.

男子提到了什麼問題？
(A) 新聞報導批評了公司。
(B) 難以招攬新員工。
(C) 客戶沒有續約。
(D) 數名職員已辭職。

- **criticize (v.)** 批評 **attract (v.)** 吸引 **renew (v.)** 使續簽 **contract (n.)** 合約 **quit (v.)** 辭職

69. 圖表整合題——女子想要深入了解的項目 難

Look at the graphic. Which category does the woman want to know more about?
(A) Career Opportunities
(B) Management
(C) Pay and Benefits
(D) Work-Life Balance

請看圖表作答。女子想要更了解哪個類別的情況？
(A) 工作前景
(B) 管理
(C) 薪酬及福利
(D) 工作／生活的平衡

70. 相關細節——男子今日要做的事情

What will the man do today?
(A) Share a Web link with the woman
(B) Alert other supervisors about a discovery
(C) Create a summary of some content
(D) Post a review on the Web site

男子今天會做什麼？
(A) 將網頁連結分享給女子
(B) 提醒其他主管注意一項發現
(C) 撰寫特定內容的摘要
(D) 在網站上發表評論

- **alert (v.)** 提醒；通知 **supervisor (n.)** 主管 **discovery (n.)** 發現 **summary (n.)** 摘要 **content (n.)** 內容 **post (v.)** 發布

換句話說 **prepare an outline**（準備一份重點概要）→ **create a summary**（撰寫摘要）

71-73 Recorded message

You have reached the Menning Community College's Gardening Hotline. (71) **Our crew of Master Gardeners is happy to give you guidance on all types of problems related to gardening and plant care.** (72) **Please keep in mind, however, that this is a free service staffed by volunteers, so we may not always be right.** We take calls from nine a.m. to noon, Monday through Friday. (73) **Because our hours are short, we ask that callers take care to ask their question quickly and simply. Thank you.**

71-73 預錄訊息 加

您現在撥打的是門寧社區大學的園藝熱線。(71) **我們的園藝師團隊很樂意為您指點迷津，解答有關園藝及植物養護的各種疑難雜症。**(72) **不過請留意，本專線是由志工提供的免費服務，因此我們的建議未必總是正確無誤。**熱線接聽的時間為週一至週五上午九點至中午，(73) **由於服務時間短暫，故請來電者留意，發問時盡量快速且簡單扼要。謝謝您。**

- reach (v.) 與……取得聯繫 gardening (n.) 園藝 crew (n.) 工作人員 gardener (n.) 園丁 guidance (n.) 輔導；諮詢 related to 與……有關 staff (n.)（全體）職員；工作人員

71. 相關細節——該通電話的目的

What is the purpose of the hotline?
(A) To give updates
(B) To provide advice
(C) To accept donations
(D) To take reports on community problems

該支熱線電話的目的為何？
(A) 提供最新資訊
(B) 提供建議
(C) 接受捐贈
(D) 受理社區問題的通報

- advice (n.) 建議 accept (v.) 接受 donation (n.) 捐贈；捐款 community (n.) 社區

換句話說 give you guidance（為您指點迷津）→ provide advice（提供建議）

72. 相關細節——說話者針對潛在的電話接聽者提及的內容 難

What does the speaker mention about potential call recipients?
(A) They follow strict rules.
(B) They are currently busy.
(C) They are given regular training.
(D) They are not paid workers.

關於可能接聽電話的人，說話者提到了什麼？
(A) 他們遵守嚴格規定。
(B) 他們目前很忙碌。
(C) 他們定期接受訓練。
(D) 他們並非支薪員工。

- potential (adj.) 潛在的；可能的 recipient (n.) 接收者 strict (adj.) 嚴格的 currently (adv.) 目前 regular (adj.) 定期的 paid (adj.) 有償的；有支薪的

73. 相關細節——說話者要求聽者於通話時遵守的事情

What does the speaker ask listeners to do during their call?
(A) Be brief
(B) Take notes
(C) Speak clearly
(D) Remain polite

說話者要求聽者來電時做什麼？
(A) 簡短扼要
(B) 做好筆記
(C) 說話清楚
(D) 保持禮貌

- brief (adj.) 簡短的 take notes 做筆記 clearly (adv.) 清楚地 polite (adj.) 有禮貌的

換句話說 quickly and simply（快速且簡單扼要）→ brief（簡短扼要）

74-76 Excerpt from a meeting

74-76 會議摘錄 澳

Thanks for joining me, everyone. I'm excited to talk about my experiences at the Office Wellness Conference. There were lots of memorable presentations, but the one that impressed me the most was given by Edge Thinking. (74) **They're a consulting firm that specializes in helping companies make their offices healthier and happier places to work.** (75) **I contracted them to come in later this month to look around our office and determine how to improve it.** (76) **But there's one idea from their presentation that I want to try right away—standing desks. You can see some pictures of them up here on the screen.** They're supposed to have a variety of health benefits. What do you think?

感謝大家和我齊聚在此。我很高興能跟大家談談我參加「辦公室健康研討會」的所見所聞。這次研討會的很多場演講都值得回味，但是讓我印象最深刻的是「邊緣思維」主講的演講，(74) **他們是一家諮詢公司，專門幫企業打造更健康、更快樂的職場環境。**(75) **我已經跟他們簽約，請他們這個月過陣子到我們辦公室看看，判斷該如何改進。**(76) **但是他們的演講中提到了一個想法，我想現在就試試看，那就是「站立式辦公桌」，各位可以從螢幕上，看到這種桌子的幾張圖片，**據說對健康有多種益處。大家覺得怎麼樣？

- memorable (adj.) 難忘的　impress (v.) 給……深刻印象　specialize in 專攻；專營　contract (v.)（和……）簽訂合約　determine (v.) 決定　improve (v.) 改進　be supposed to 認為應該

74. 相關細節——「邊緣思維」公司的類型 難

What is Edge Thinking?

(A) A company that promotes healthy workplaces

(B) A government campaign targeting an industry

(C) An annual human resources conference

(D) A Web site operated by a research organization

「邊緣思維」是何種機構？

(A) 促進職場健康的公司

(B) 針對特定產業的政府活動

(C) 年度的人力資源相關會議

(D) 由研究機構營運的網站

- promote (v.) 推廣；提倡　target (v.) 針對　industry (n.) 行業　human resources 人力資源　operate (v.) 經營；營運　organization (n.) 機構；組織

換句話說 helping companies make their offices healthier（幫企業打造更健康的職場環境）
→ promotes healthy workplaces（促進職場健康）

75. 相關細節——說話者安排的事宜 難

What did the speaker arrange?

(A) A tour of a factory

(B) A team-building outing

(C) An assessment of an office

(D) A seminar on well-being

說話者安排了什麼？

(A) 工廠參訪

(B) 企業內訓之旅

(C) 對辦公室的評估

(D) 健康主題討論會

- outing (n.) 遠足；短途旅遊　assessment (n.) 評估

換句話說 look around our office and determine how to improve it（到我們辦公室看看，判斷該如何改進）→ an assessment of an office（對辦公室的評估）

76. 相關細節——說話者提供給聽者看的東西

What does the speaker show the listeners?
(A) Some revisions to a floor plan
(B) Images of furniture
(C) A list of job benefits
(D) A potential itinerary

說話者向聽者展示了什麼？
(A) 平面圖的幾項修改
(B) 家具的圖片
(C) 工作福利的清單
(D) 可能的行程

- revision (n.) 修改　floor plan 樓層平面圖　potential (adj.) 潛在的；可能的　itinerary (n.) 旅遊行程

換句話說 some pictures（幾張圖片）→ images（圖片）

77-79 Telephone message

77-79 電話留言　美

Hi, Dominick. It's Melody, calling from the event in Newark. It's going really well, I guess. (77) **A lot of potential distributors have stopped by our booth to pick up samples of our fruit juice.** (78) **Uh, the problem is that we've been much more popular than we expected. There are two more days in the show** and I have about twenty sample bottles left. I think if you shipped another few cases overnight, they would arrive by lunch tomorrow. (79) **I'll e-mail you all the details you'll need, so please check your inbox as soon as you get this.**

嗨，多明尼克，我是美樂蒂，目前人在紐瓦克的活動現場。我想一切進行得很順利，(77) **許多潛在經銷商來到我們的攤位，並索取我們的果汁樣品。**(78) **呃，問題是我們的人氣比原先預期的還要多上許多，活動還有兩天才結束，**而我只剩約 20 瓶樣品了，我想如果你連夜寄送幾箱過來，明天午餐前就會送到。(79) **我會把你會需要的詳情都用電子郵件寄給你，所以請在聽到這通留言後，馬上查看你的收件匣。**

- distributor (n.) 經銷商　stop by 造訪　ship (v.) 運送　overnight (adv.) 一夜間地
  detail (n.) 細節；詳情　inbox (n.) 收件匣

77. 相關細節——說話者參加的活動類型

What kind of event is the speaker most likely attending?
(A) A cosmetics convention
(B) An arts and crafts festival
(C) A food and beverage exposition
(D) A pharmaceutical trade show

說話者最有可能正在參加何種活動？
(A) 化妝品大會
(B) 藝術與手工藝品節
(C) 食品與飲料博覽會
(D) 製藥產業展

- craft (n.) 手工藝　beverage (n.) 飲料　exposition (n.) 博覽會；展覽　pharmaceutical (adj.) 製藥的

---

78. 掌握說話者的意圖——提及「我只剩約 20 瓶樣品了」的意圖

What does the speaker imply when she says, "I have about twenty sample bottles left"?
(A) More giveaway stock is urgently needed.
(B) Her return journey will not be difficult.
(C) A prediction about a product was correct.
(D) A display should be removed from a booth.

說話者說：「我只剩約 20 瓶樣品了」，其言下之意為何？
(A) 急需更多的贈品庫存。
(B) 她回程的行程沒有困難。
(C) 對產品的預測是正確的。
(D) 展品應從展位上撤下來。

- giveaway (n.) 贈品；免費樣品　stock (n.) 庫存；存貨　urgently (adv.) 急切地　journey (n.) 行程
  prediction (n.) 預測　display (n.) 展品

---

79. 相關細節——說話者提及她將做的事情

What does the speaker say she will do?
(A) Have lunch with a possible distributor
(B) Check the details of a contract
(C) Take an overnight flight
(D) Send the listener an e-mail

說話者說她會做何事？
(A) 與潛在經銷商共進午餐
(B) 確認合約的細節
(C) 搭乘夜間航班
(D) 發電子郵件給聽者

80-82 Advertisement

Cooking is a fun and rewarding hobby, and whether you're an experienced cook or a beginner in the kitchen, the Cessna Institute can help you to improve your skills. (80) **Thanks to a government grant, we are able to offer admission fees that are affordable to everyone, as they are income-based. You may be eligible to pay nothing at all!** Among the institute's instructors are several highly experienced local chefs, including Nelson Duncan. (81) **His restaurant just won the Armenta Prize!** (82) **Slots in all of our courses are going fast, so call us today at 555-0182 to sign up.** Don't miss your chance to become a more confident cook.

80-82 廣告 加

烹飪是有趣又令人獲益良多的愛好，無論您是老練的總舖師或是廚房菜鳥，「賽斯納學院」都能幫助您讓技巧更上層樓。(80) **多虧政府補助，本學院註冊費的定價可按照學員收入來調整，讓每個人都能負擔的起，您甚至可能無須支付任何費用！**本學院的講師陣容中，有好幾位都是本地的資深大廚，其中包括納爾森．鄧肯，(81) **他的餐廳才剛拿下阿曼塔獎！** (82) **本學院課程名額現正熱銷中，所以現在就來電 555-0182 報名吧。**想擁有更令人自豪的廚藝，就別錯過這次機會。

- rewarding (adj.) 有益處的　experienced (adj.) 經驗豐富的　institute (n.) 學院；教育機構　government (n.) 政府　grant (n.) 補助金　admission (n.) 入學　affordable (adj.) 負擔得起的　income (n.) 收入　-based (adj.) 以……為根據的　eligible (adj.) 有資格的　instructor (n.) 講師　prize (n.) 獎　slot (n.) 位置；區間　sign up 報名參加　confident (adj.) 有自信的

80. 相關細節——說話者強調賽斯納學院的相關事項

What does the speaker emphasize about the Cessna Institute?
(A) Its long history
(B) Its convenient location
(C) Its high admission requirements
(D) Its variable entrance costs

說話者強調「塞斯納學院」的那一點？
(A) 歷史悠久
(B) 地點交通便利
(C) 錄取要求高
(D) 入學費用可變動

- convenient (adj.) 便利的　location (n.) 地點；位置　requirement (n.) 要求；資格　variable (adj.) 可變的　entrance (n.) 入學

---

81. 相關細節——說話者針對鄧肯先生提及的內容

What does the speaker say about Mr. Duncan?
(A) He opened a new restaurant.
(B) His classroom is well-equipped.
(C) He studied at the Cessna Institute.
(D) His business received an award.

關於鄧肯先生，說話者說了什麼？
(A) 他開了一家新餐廳。
(B) 他的教室設備很齊全。
(C) 他曾在塞斯納學院就讀。
(D) 他的餐廳獲獎。

- equipped (adj.) 設備齊全的　institute (n.) 學院；教育機構　award (n.) 獎

換句話說 won the . . . prize（拿下……獎）→ received an award（獲獎）

---

82. 相關細節——建議聽者盡快報名的理由

Why are the listeners encouraged to register soon?

(A) Classes are filling up quickly.

(B) A special offer is about to end.

(C) The deadline is approaching.

(D) A new policy will be adopted shortly.

為什麼鼓勵聽者儘早報名？

(A) 課程很快就會額滿。

(B) 特別優惠即將結束。

(C) 截止日期快到了。

(D) 不久將採取一項新政策。

- fill up 充滿；填滿　be about to 即將　approach (v.) 接近　adopt (v.) 採取　shortly (adv.) 不久

換句話說 slots in all of our courses are going fast（名額現正熱銷中）
→ classes are filling up quickly（課程很快就會額滿）

83-85 Announcement

[83] **Attention, Dugan Fitness Center customers.** Please take a short break to listen to the following announcement. [84] **There is currently no hot water in the shower rooms.** We have called a repair service and they will arrive within the hour, but we don't know how long it will take to fix the problem. Also, while the repair work is taking place, the shower rooms may be entirely unavailable. We are deeply sorry for this inconvenience. [85] **To make it up to you, we would like to extend your membership by one week for free. The front desk staff will set that up when you leave today.**

83-85 宣布 英

[83] **杜根健身中心的貴賓，請注意。**請稍做休息，聆聽以下通知。[84] **淋浴間目前沒有供應熱水，**我們已經打電話給維修業者，他們預計一小時內會到達，但是我們不知道這個問題要費時多久才能解決。此外在維修進行期間，淋浴間可能會完全無法使用。造成大家本次不便，我們深表歉意。[85] **為了補償大家，我們會將各位的會籍免費延長一週，大家在離開時，我們櫃檯人員會幫大家處理好相關事宜。**

- attention (n.) 注意　break (n.) 暫停；休息　announcement (n.) 通知；公告　currently (adv.) 目前　repair (n.) 維修　fix (v.) 解決；處理　take place 發生；進行　entirely (adv.) 完全地　unavailable (adj.) 不可使用　inconvenience (n.) 不便；麻煩　extend (v.) 延長

83. 全文相關——聽者的身分

Who is the announcement most likely for?

(A) Theater patrons

(B) Shoppers

(C) Gym users

(D) Travelers

這項宣布最有可能的對象為何者？

(A) 劇院的顧客

(B) 購物者

(C) 健身房使用者

(D) 旅客

換句話說 fitness center customers（健身中心的貴賓）→ gym users（健身房使用者）

---

84. 相關細節——說話者宣布的內容

What does the speaker announce?

(A) A correction to an advertisement

(B) An issue with some plumbing

(C) A shortage of inventory

(D) A change in venue

說話者宣布了何事？

(A) 廣告更正

(B) 管線問題

(C) 庫存短缺

(D) 場地變更

- correction (n.) 更正　plumbing (n.) 水管；管道　shortage (n.) 不足；短缺　inventory (n.) 庫存　venue (n.) 場地；地點

---

85. 相關細節——說話者告知部分員工會做的事情

What does the speaker say some staff members will do?

(A) Arrange a form of compensation

(B) Oversee the sharing of a resource

(C) Make further announcements

(D) Help listeners leave the area

說話者說工作人員會做什麼？

(A) 安排補償措施

(B) 監督資源共享

(C) 做進一步通知

(D) 協助聽者離開

- **compensation (n.)** 補償　**oversee (v.)** 監督　**resource (n.)** 資源

換句話說 make it up to you（補償大家）→ compensation（補償）

86-88 Talk

86-88 談話　澳

(86) **As I said in my e-mail, I called you all here to talk about a serious problem at the laboratory.** When I returned from lunch yesterday, (87) **I found the doors of Chemical Storage Cabinet Two left wide open. It appears that nothing is missing, but this is still a major safety breach. You've all seen the sign saying "Cabinets Must Be Locked At All Times."** Please, please remember that there's a reason we put that sign up. All right. (88) **Uh, I know that this was one person's mistake, so I'm sorry to have to speak to all of you like this.** I hope you'll understand.

(86) **正如我在電子郵件所說，我叫大家來這裡，是要談談實驗室的一項嚴重問題。**昨天午餐後我回到實驗室時，(87) **發現二號化學品儲藏櫃的櫃門敞開著，似乎是沒有物品失蹤，但是依然是個重大安全疏失，你們都有看到標示牌寫著：「儲藏櫃必須隨時上鎖」。**拜託大家，請務必記住，我們貼這個標示是有原因的。好了，(88) **呃，我知道這是單一個人的失誤，所以我很抱歉得這樣跟所有人說話，**希望你們都能理解。

- **call (v.)** 召集；叫來　**serious (adj.)** 嚴重的　**laboratory (n.)** 實驗室　**chemical (n.)** 化學製品　**storage (n.)** 存放；儲藏　**appear (v.)** 看來；似乎　**missing (adj.)** 遺失的　**major (adj.)** 重大的　**breach (n.)** 缺口　**lock (v.)** 鎖住

86. 全文相關——說話者的工作地點

Where does the speaker work?

(A) At a research facility

(B) At a manufacturing plant

(C) At a city government agency

(D) At a shipping center

說話者在哪裡工作？

(A) 在研究機構

(B) 在製造工廠

(C) 在市府單位

(D) 在物流中心

換句話說 the laboratory（實驗室）→ a research facility（研究機構）

---

87. 掌握說話者的意圖——提及「我們貼這個標示是有原因的」的意圖　難

What does the speaker mean when he says, "there's a reason we put that sign up"?

(A) An activity can be dangerous.

(B) Storage spaces must be kept secure.

(C) Visitors need special assistance.

(D) Some old equipment is fragile.

說話者說：「我們貼這個標示是有原因的」，意思為何？

(A) 活動可能會有危險。

(B) 儲藏空間必須保持安全。

(C) 訪客需要特別協助。

(D) 陳舊設備容易損壞。

- **dangerous (adj.)** 危險的　**space (n.)** 空間　**secure (adj.)** 安全的　**assistance (n.)** 協助；幫助　**equipment (n.)** 設備　**fragile (adj.)** 脆弱的

---

88. 相關細節——說話者道歉的事情

What does the speaker apologize for?
(A) Not noticing a mistake earlier
(B) Not explaining a procedure
(C) Addressing all of the listeners
(D) Limiting access to an amenity

說話者為了何事道歉？
(A) 沒有及早發現錯誤
(B) 未解釋程序
(C) 對聽者全員講話
(D) 限制使用一項便利設施

- **notice (v.)** 注意到 **procedure (n.)** 程序 **address (v.)** 對……講話 **limit (v.)** 限制 **access (n.)** 使用權 **amenity (n.)** 便利設施

換句話說 speak to all of you（跟所有人說話）→ addressing all of the listeners（對聽者全員講話）

89-91 Introduction

Everyone, could I have your attention for a moment? (89) **Welcome to the launch of Ammett Gallery's show of Carlos Valdez's work.** We're so glad you could join us. We've collected more than forty of Mr. Valdez's paintings from various periods of his career. (90) **And as the highlight of tonight's event, I'd like to introduce Professor Mona Carlson of Flonning University. She's a leading expert on Mr. Valdez's work,** and she's agreed to say a few words about the contents and meaning of our show. (91) **We hope her speech will help you appreciate what you see as you continue circulating throughout the gallery this evening.** All right, please give a warm welcome to Professor Mona Carlson!

89-91 介紹 英

各位，可以請稍微注意到我這邊嗎？(89) **歡迎各位蒞臨「安美特畫廊」舉辦的卡洛斯・瓦爾德茲畫展開幕會**，很高興有您的參與。我們已收集了四十多幅瓦爾德茲先生的畫作，年代橫跨在他生涯的各個時期。(90) **而作為今晚活動的重頭戲，我要向各位介紹弗隆寧大學的莫娜・卡爾森教授。她是研究瓦爾德茲先生畫作的權威專家**，她同意就本次展覽的內容及意義說幾句話。(91) **我們希望她的演講，將有助於各位今晚接下來穿梭畫廊時，欣賞眼前的畫作。**好的，現在請熱烈歡迎莫娜・卡爾森教授！

- **attention (n.)** 注意 **launch (n.)** 開幕會 **collect (v.)** 蒐集 **period (n.)** 時期 **introduce (v.)** 介紹 **professor (n.)** 教授 **leading (adj.)** 主要的 **expert (n.)** 專家 **appreciate (v.)** 欣賞 **continue (v.)** 繼續 **circulate (v.)** 來回走動

89. 相關細節——聽者參加的活動

What event are the listeners attending?
(A) A guest lecture
(B) A welcome reception
(C) An exhibition opening
(D) A tour of an artist's workshop

聽者正在參加何種活動？
(A) 客座講座
(B) 歡迎接待會
(C) 展覽開幕會
(D) 藝術家工作室的參訪

換句話說 the launch of . . . Gallery's show（畫廊……畫展的開幕會）
→ an exhibition opening（展覽開幕會）

---

90. 相關細節——卡爾森女士的職業 難

Who most likely is Ms. Carlson?
(A) An art scholar
(B) A painter
(C) A gallery owner
(D) A museum donor

卡爾森女士最有可能是什麼人？
(A) 藝術學者
(B) 畫家
(C) 畫廊老闆
(D) 博物館捐贈者

換句話說 professor（教授）→ scholar（學者）

91. 相關細節——於卡爾森女士演講後發生的事情

According to the speaker, what will happen after Ms. Carlson speaks?

(A) Some refreshments will be served.

(B) Some photographs will be taken.

(C) The listeners will ask questions.

(D) The listeners will walk around.

根據說話者所言，卡爾森女士演講後會發生何事？

(A) 將會供應茶點。

(B) 將會拍照。

(C) 聽者將會提問。

(D) 聽者將會四處走動。

- refreshment (n.) 茶點　serve (v.) 供應；提供

換句話說 circulate（穿梭）→ walk around（四處走動）

92-94 Broadcast

You're listening to *Bondella Today*, the show about current affairs in our city. Up next today, (92) **there's the possible designation of the old Kirkland house on Third Street as a historic home.** Its newest owner, Albert Reynolds, submitted his application to the Bondella Cultural Heritage Board this week. (93) **Mr. Reynolds probably hopes to receive some of the city funding available for the restoration of historic homes**—the building is in bad condition. Personally, I hope he succeeds, because with a few improvements, the property could be quite striking. (94) **If you feel the same, why not speak up in support of Mr. Reynold's application at the board's next open meeting?** It will be held on Tuesday evening at City Hall.

92-94 電台廣播　美

您正在收聽的是《今日邦德拉》，本節目將帶您關心本市的最新時事。今天接下來的要聞是，(92) **位於第三街的柯克蘭舊宅可望被指定為歷史古宅。**本週，該棟舊宅的新屋主阿爾博特・雷諾茲向邦德拉文化資產委員會送交了申請書，(93) **雷諾茲先生大概是希望獲得一部分市政府用於修復各古厝的資金**——該棟建築屋況並不甚佳。就我個人，我希望他能成功，因為只要稍加整修，舊宅就能變得相當壯觀。(94) **若是您也有同感，何不在委員會下一場公開會議上，發言支持雷諾茲先生的申請案呢？**會議將於週二晚間在市政廳召開。

- current affairs 時事　up next 接下來；下一個　designation (n.) 指定　historic (adj.) 具歷史意義的　newest (adj.) 最新的　submit (v.) 提交　application (n.) 申請（書）　cultural heritage 文化遺產　board (n.) 委員會；董事會　funding (n.) 資助；資金　restoration (n.) 修復　condition (n.) 狀況　improvement (n.) 改進；改良　striking (adj.) 吸引人的　in support of 支持

92. 全文相關——廣播的主題　難

What is the main topic of the broadcast?

(A) A special status for a residence

(B) The activities of a citizens' organization

(C) The possible purchase of a structure

(D) A publication on a city's history

廣播的主題為何？

(A) 一棟住宅的特殊地位

(B) 民間團體的活動

(C) 可能的建物採購案

(D) 有關城市歷史的出版品

- status (n.) 狀態；資格身分　residence (n.) 住宅；住所　citizen (n.) 市民　organization (n.) 組織；團體　structure (n.) 建築物　publication (n.) 出版（品）

換句話說 the . . . house（宅）→ a residence（住宅）

93. 掌握說話者的意圖——提及「該棟建築屋況並不甚佳」的意圖 難

Why does the speaker say, "the building is in bad condition"?
(A) To express disapproval of a proposal
(B) To report the result of an official inspection
(C) To suggest that a project will be harder than expected
(D) To explain an assumption she has made

說話者為什麼會說：「該棟建築屋況並不甚佳」？
(A) 以表達對提案的反對
(B) 以報導官方的檢驗結果
(C) 以暗示工程會比預期困難
(D) 以解釋她做出的推斷

- express (v.) 表達　disapproval (n.) 不贊成；不同意　result (n.) 結果　official (adj.) 官方的　inspection (n.) 檢驗；檢查　assumption (n.) 推測；假設

94. 相關細節——說話者向聽者提出的建議 難

What does the speaker encourage some listeners to do?
(A) Apply for membership in a group
(B) Provide financial support for a cause
(C) Make a public comment on a matter
(D) See a property in person

說話者鼓勵部分聽者做什麼？
(A) 申請加入團體會員
(B) 為一項慈善事業提供資金
(C) 就某事公開發表意見
(D) 親自查看房產

- apply for 申請　financial (adj.) 財務的　cause (n.) 慈善事業　comment (n.) 評論　property (n.) 房產

換句話說 speak up（發言支持）→ make a public comment（公開發表意見）

95-97 Announcement + Chart

All right, everyone, I have an announcement to make. As you know, our survey to choose our new salad dressing flavor ended yesterday. (95) **First, thank you again for asking our customers to vote when you took their order at the counter.** We collected over two hundred votes in a week, which I think is quite good. So, here are the results. (96) **Look at how many votes the first-place dressing got!** It's the clear choice. Now, we want to make the launch of the new dressing a fun event. (97) **So I've decided that, for the first week, we're going to give diners two dollars off if they order the new dressing with their salad.** I think this will attract new customers.

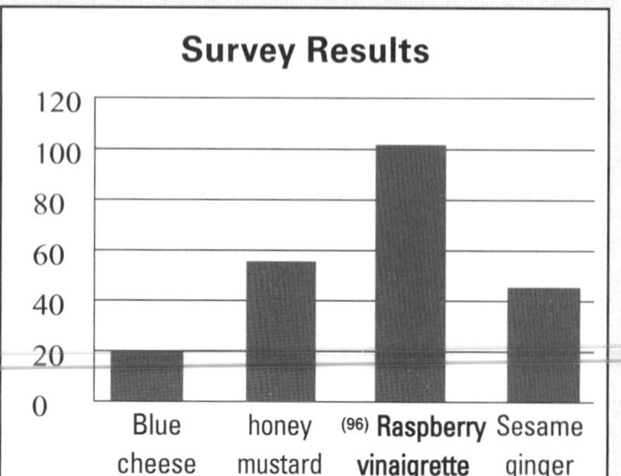

95-97 宣布＋圖表 加

好的，各位，我有一個消息要宣布。如大家所知，我們徵選新口味沙拉醬的調查昨天結束了。(95) **首先，再次感謝大家在櫃檯幫客人點餐的時候，請客人投票，**我們一週內就收集到兩百多票，我認為這相當不錯。那麼，票選結果出爐了。(96) **看看，第一名的沙拉醬得到這麼多票！**該如何選擇很清楚了。現在，我們想要舉辦趣味活動，來迎接新款沙拉醬的推出，(97) **所以我已經決定了，在推出的首週，如果客人點了新款沙拉醬配沙拉，就可獲得兩美元的優惠。**我認為這將吸引新顧客上門。

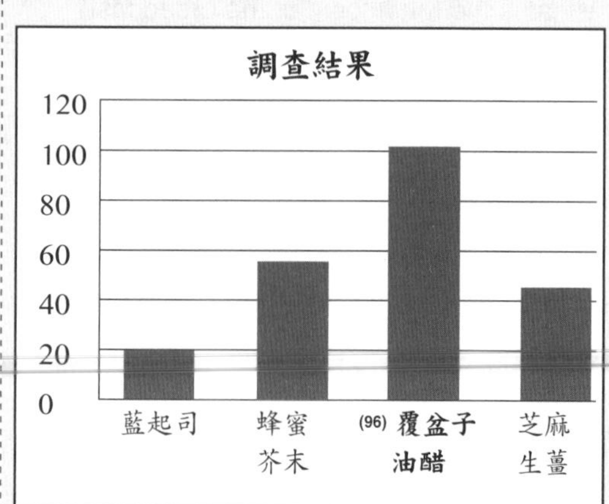

- announcement (n.) 宣布 survey (n.) 調查 flavor (n.) 口味 vote (v./n.) 投票；選票 collect (v.) 收集 quite (adv.) 很；非常 first-place (adj.) 第一名的 launch (n.) 推出；上市 diner (n.) 用餐者 attract (v.) 吸引

95. 全文相關——聽者的職業

Who most likely are the listeners?
(A) Restaurant staff
(B) Lunch customers
(C) Product developers
(D) Marketing specialists

聽者最有可能是何種身分？
(A) 餐廳員工
(B) 午餐顧客
(C) 產品開發人員
(D) 行銷專員

96. 圖表整合題——說話者提到的沙拉醬種類 難

Look at the graphic. Which type of salad dressing does the speaker point out?
(A) Blue cheese
(B) Honey mustard
(C) Raspberry vinaigrette
(D) Sesame ginger

請看圖表作答。說話者指出了哪種口味的沙拉醬？
(A) 藍起司
(B) 蜂蜜芥末
(C) 覆盆子油醋
(D) 芝麻生薑

97. 相關細節——說話者決定的事宜

What has the speaker decided to do?
(A) Contact an outside consultant
(B) Offer a promotional discount
(C) Discontinue two types of dressing
(D) Increase a regular supply order

說話者決定做什麼？
(A) 聯繫外部顧問
(B) 提供促銷折扣
(C) 停用兩種調味醬
(D) 增加定期供應的訂單

- promotional (adj.) 促銷的 discontinue (v.) 中斷；停止 increase (v.) 增加 regular (adj.) 定期的 supply (n.) 供應

換句話說 give . . . two dollars off（兩美元的優惠）→ offer a . . . discount（提供……折扣）

98-100 Telephone message + Price list

Hi. My name is Ichika Hironaka, and I'm calling with a question about tickets for the Boheim Horse Show. (98) **I'm planning to take my family to the show to celebrate my son's birthday.** (99) **There are four of us, so I'd like to take advantage of the group discount we're eligible for.** But I'm not yet sure that my daughter will be able to go. (100) **If I have to cancel her ticket, will I be able to get my money back? I'm worried that the rules on that kind of thing might be stricter for group tickets.** Please give me a call back at 555-0185.

98-100 電話留言＋票價表 英

你好，我的名字叫做廣中一香，我打來是想詢問波海姆馬秀的門票問題。(98) **我打算帶家人去看這次演出，來慶祝我兒子的生日，**(99) **我們有四個人，所以購票時，我想要使用符合資格的團體優惠，**但是我還不確定我女兒是不是也能去。(100) **如果我必須退掉她的門票，我能夠拿回退款嗎？我擔心團體票對這類情事的規定可能會更嚴格。**請打 555-0185 回電給我。

Boheim Horse Show	
Ticket pricing (per person)	
1–3 people	£30
(99) **4–10 people**	**£27**
11+ people	£24

波海姆馬秀	
票價（每人）	
1–3人	30 英鎊
(99) **4–10人**	**27 英鎊**
11人以上	24 英鎊

- celebrate (v.) 慶祝　take advantage of 利用　eligible (adj.) 符合條件的　strict (adj.) 嚴格的

98. 相關細節——預計與說話者一同看表演的人

Who will the speaker attend the show with?

(A) Work colleagues

(B) Relatives

(C) Potential clients

(D) Fellow members of a club

說話者會和誰一起前往馬秀？

(A) 同事

(B) 親人

(C) 潛在客戶

(D) 社團同好

換句話說 my family（家人）→ relatives（親人）

99. 圖表整合題——說話者需為每個人支付的金額

Look at the graphic. How much would the speaker like to pay per person?

(A) £33

(B) £30

(C) £27

(D) £24

請看圖表作答。說話者希望每人需支付的費用為何？

(A) 33 英鎊

(B) 30 英鎊

(C) 27 英鎊

(D) 24 英鎊

100. 相關細節——說話者擔憂的事情 難

What is the speaker concerned about?

(A) Rules may prohibit bringing certain items.

(B) The tickets may not be refundable.

(C) Part of the show may be canceled.

(D) A sale period may have ended.

說話者擔心什麼事？

(A) 某些物品可能依規定禁止攜帶。

(B) 門票可能不可退款。

(C) 部分節目可能會被取消。

(D) 促銷期可能已結束。

- rule (n.) 規定；規則　prohibit (v.) 禁止　bring (v.) 攜帶　refundable (adj.) 可退款的
  cancel (v.) 取消　period (n.) 期間

換句話說 be able to get my money back（夠拿回退款）→ be refundable（可退款）

ACTUAL TEST 6

PART 1 P. 68–71 21

1. 雙人照片——描寫人物的動作 美

(A) They're carrying a ladder.
(B) They're assembling some furniture.
(C) They're walking on a ramp.
(D) They're stacking boxes in a truck.

(A) 他們正在搬梯子。
(B) 他們正在組裝家具。
(C) 他們正走在坡道上。
(D) 他們正將箱子堆放在卡車裡。

- assemble (v.) 組裝　ramp (n.) 斜坡　stack (v.) 堆疊

2. 單人獨照——描寫人物的動作 加

(A) She's examining some merchandise.
(B) She's adjusting the handle of a shopping cart.
(C) She's trying a food sample in a store.
(D) She's reaching into her handbag.

(A) 她在查看商品。
(B) 她在調整購物推車的把手。
(C) 她在商店裡試吃食物。
(D) 她正伸手到包包裡拿東西。

- examine (v.) 查看　merchandise (n.) 商品　adjust (v.) 調整　reach into . . . 伸手進……拿東西

3. 綜合照片——描寫人物的動作 澳

(A) He's putting on a safety helmet.
(B) He's photographing a construction site.
(C) He's writing on a clipboard.
(D) He's leaning against a railing.

(A) 他正在戴上安全帽。
(B) 他正在拍攝工地。
(C) 他正在文件板夾上寫字。
(D) 他倚靠在欄杆上。

- photograph (v.) 拍照　construction site 工地　lean against . . . 靠在……　railing (n.) 欄杆

4. 事物與背景照——描寫戶外事物的狀態 英

(A) Some buildings overlook the water.
(B) Boats are sailing on a lake.
(C) A walkway stretches over a road.
(D) A field is surrounded by trees.

(A) 建築物俯瞰著水面。
(B) 船隻在湖上航行。
(C) 人行道順著道路延伸。
(D) 樹木圍繞著田野。

- overlook (v.) 俯瞰　sail (v.) 航行　lake (n.) 湖　walkway (n.) 人行道　stretch (v.) 延伸　field (n.) 田野　surround (v.) 圍繞

5. 綜合照片——描寫人物或事物 加

(A) The door of a car has been opened.
(B) Some repair work is taking place.
(C) A man is winding up a hose.
(D) Fuel is being put into a vehicle.

(A) 車門已經被打開。
(B) 正在進行維修工作。
(C) 男子正在捲收水管。
(D) 有人在幫汽車加油。

- repair (n.) 維修　take place 進行　wind up 捲收　hose (n.) 水管　fuel (n.) 燃油　vehicle (n.) 車輛

6. 綜合照片——描寫人物或事物 英 難

(A) Leaves are being raked into piles in a park.	(A) 公園裡的樹葉被耙成堆。
(B) Some passers-by are walking in the same direction.	**(B) 有些路人朝相同方向行走。**
(C) Seats have been set up in front of a stage.	(C) 舞台前已設置好座椅。
(D) Musical instruments are being laid out on a mat.	(D) 樂器正被擺放在墊子上。

- rake (v.)（用耙子）耙　pile (n.) 一堆　passer-by (n.) 路人，行人　direction (n.) 方向　musical instrument 樂器　lay (v.) 擺放

PART 2 P. 72

22

7. 以 When 開頭的問句，詢問業者聯絡的時間點 英⇄澳

When do you think we'll hear from the caterer?	你覺得我們何時會收到外燴業者的回覆？
(A) Yes, I think so.	(A) 對，我這麼覺得。
(B) Sometime this afternoon.	**(B) 今天下午吧。**
(C) A lower price quote.	(C) 較低的報價。

- caterer (n.) 外燴業者　quote (n.) 報價

8. 以助動詞 Have 開頭的問句，詢問對方是否找到不錯的研究所課程 加⇄英

Have you found a good graduate program yet?	你有找到不錯的研究所課程嗎？
(A) So that I can get a master's degree.	(A) 我這樣才能取得碩士學位。
(B) She graduated with honors.	(B) 她以優異成績畢業。
(C) Yes, and I've been accepted!	**(C) 有的，而且我已經錄取了！**

- graduate (adj./v) 研究所的；畢業　master (n.) 碩士　degree (n.) 學位　honors (n.)〔複〕優異成績　accept (v.) 錄取

9. 以 Where 開頭的問句，詢問張貼海報的位置 美⇄加 難

Where should I put up the posters?	我該在哪裡張貼海報？
(A) Start with the notice boards.	**(A) 先從布告欄開始。**
(B) I put them on your desk.	(B) 我把它們放在你桌上。
(C) By the end of the day.	(C) 今天下班前。

- notice board 布告欄

10. 以直述句傳達資訊 澳⇄美

I want to attend the training workshop this Thursday.	我這週四想參加培訓研習會。
(A) How long would you be gone?	**(A) 你會去多久？**
(B) Around one hundred employees.	(B) 大約一百名員工。
(C) In the meeting room.	(C) 在會議室。

- attend (v.) 參加　training (n.) 教育訓練　employee (n.) 員工

11. 表示建議的問句 澳⇄英

Would you like me to order you some lunch?	你要我幫你訂午餐嗎？
(A) The bakery downstairs.	(A) 樓下的麵包店。
(B) I brought a sandwich with me.	**(B) 我自己有帶三明治了。**
(C) I really liked it, too.	(C) 我也真的很喜歡它。

- order (v.) 訂購，點餐　bakery (n.) 麵包店　downstairs (adj./adv.) 樓下的（地）

12. 以 **How** 開頭的問句，詢問吸引客人上門的方法 美⇄英 難

How can we attract more customers to our bookshop?	我們如何吸引更多客人光臨我們書店？
(A) Yes, it's a busy place.	(A) 是的，這是個繁忙的地方。
(B) I'm not really a marketing expert.	**(B) 我不算是行銷專家。**
(C) Many people have already read it.	(C) 很多人已經讀過了。

- attract (v.) 吸引　expert (n.) 專家

13. 以選擇疑問句，詢問整修的時間點 加⇄美

Is the cafeteria renovation this week or next week?	自助式餐廳的整修時間是本週還是下週？
(A) It began this morning.	**(A) 今天早上就開始了。**
(B) That's a long time to wait.	(B) 還要等真久。
(C) Replacing the ovens.	(C) 替換爐具。

- cafeteria (n.)（自助）餐廳　renovation (n.) 翻修　replace (v.) 替換

14. 以 **What** 開頭的問句，詢問最想先練習的部分 英⇄加 難

What part of the sales presentation do you want to practice first?	你想先練習業務簡報的哪部分？
(A) For the clients from Lorman Associates.	(A) 給羅曼公司的客戶。
(B) It's a good way to increase your sales.	(B) 這是增加業績的好方法。
(C) Let's run through the introduction.	**(C) 我們來演練開場引言。**

- presentation (n.) 簡報　increase (v.) 增加　run through 排練

15. 以附加問句確認對方是否買票 英⇄澳

You bought a music festival ticket already, correct?	你已經買了音樂節的門票，對嗎？
(A) A three-day pass, please.	(A) 請給我三日票。
(B) I'm still deciding whether to go.	**(B) 我還在決定要不要去。**
(C) No, it's an annual event.	(C) 不是，這是年度活動。

- festival (n.) 節慶　pass (n.) 通行證　annual (adj.) 年度的

16. 以 **Where** 開頭的問句，詢問腳踏車的停放位置 加⇄美 難

Where did you park your bicycle?	你在哪裡停放腳踏車？
(A) Jackie has the same model in red.	(A) 賈姬有同樣的車型，是紅色的。
(B) Oh, I took the bus today.	**(B) 噢，我今天是搭公車。**
(C) From a shop on Barnhart Street.	(C) 從巴哈特街上的商店。

17. 以 **Be** 動詞開頭的問句，詢問今天 **IT** 人員是否會來安裝軟體 英⇄加

Is the IT crew going to install the new software today?
(A) As soon as we go out for lunch.
(B) Sure, I'll show you how to do it.
(C) They wear their uniforms every day.

資訊科技部門人員今天會來安裝新軟體嗎？
(A) 我們一出去吃午餐（，他們就會開始安裝）。
(B) 當然好，我教你怎麼做。
(C) 他們每天都穿制服。

- install (v.) 安裝　as soon as 一……就

18. 表示建議或提案的直述句 澳⇄美

I could also show you some smaller apartments downtown.
(A) Collect any small parts in this bag.
(B) Wasn't it difficult to relocate?
(C) I prefer to have more space.

我也可以讓您看看市區幾間較小的公寓。
(A) 請將小零件都收集好，放在這個袋子裡。
(B) 搬遷不是有點難嗎？
(C) 我偏好空間大一點的房子。

- downtown (adj./adv.) 市區的（地）　part (n.) 零件　relocate (v.) 搬遷

19. 以 **Which** 開頭的問句，詢問通往頂樓的電梯 加⇄澳 難

Which elevator goes to the top floor?
(A) Yes, the fifty-second floor.
(B) You'll need a special access code.
(C) The CEO's office.

哪一座電梯可抵達頂樓？
(A) 是的，52 樓。
(B) 你會需要特殊的通行碼。
(C) 執行長的辦公室。

- access code 通行碼；存取碼

20. 表示請託或要求的問句 英⇄加

Can you tell us about potential safety issues with the project?
(A) That information's on the next slide.
(B) I have some safety shoes right here, actually.
(C) Not that I am aware of.

你可以告訴我們此專案的潛在安全議題嗎？
(A) 該項資訊就在下一張投影片。
(B) 其實我這邊有一些安全鞋。
(C) 據我所知，沒有這種情況。

- potential (adj.) 潛在的　safety (n.) 安全性　issue (n.) 議題　aware (adj.) 意識到的

21. 以 **Who** 開頭的問句，詢問配送辦公用品的人 澳⇄英

Who's delivering the office supplies to our customer in the Trident Building?
(A) A few boxes of pens.
(B) Thanks, I appreciate that.
(C) Becky said she could do it.

誰會將辦公用品配送到我們在崔登特大樓的顧客？
(A) 幾盒筆。
(B) 謝謝，我很感激。
(C) 貝琪說她可以送去。

- deliver (v.) 配送　office supplies 辦公用品　appreciate (v.) 感激

22. 以 **When** 開頭的問句，詢問何時出發去看電影 美⇄澳

When are we leaving for the movie?
(A) That's fine with me.
(B) It depends—what's the traffic like?
(C) I moved it already.

我們什麼時候要出發去看電影？
(A) 我沒問題。
(B) 看情況——現在路況怎麼樣？
(C) 我已經移開它了。

- depend (v.) 看……而定　traffic (n.) 交通（量）

23. 以否定疑問句，確認廣告是否由馬丁負責 加⇄美

Didn't Martin direct the advertisement for our spring clothing range?
(A) It's on several cable TV channels.
(B) His clothing designs are excellent.
(C) No, he only offered suggestions.

馬丁不是執導我們春季服飾系列的廣告嗎？
(A) 已經在幾個有線電視頻道播出。
(B) 他的服裝設計很出色。
(C) 不是，他只有提供建議。

- direct (v.) 執導　advertisement (n.) 廣告　range (n.) 系列產品　excellent (adj.) 傑出的　offer (v.) 提供　suggestion (n.) 建議

24. 以選擇疑問句，詢問是否要使用公司手機 英⇄加 難

Do we have to use a company mobile phone, or is it optional?
(A) Well, there are major advantages to it.
(B) To handle business while traveling.
(C) Of course—just let your supervisor know.

我們一定要用公司手機，還是可選擇不用？
(A) 這個嘛，(用公司手機) 主要的好處有幾點。
(B) 為了在出差／旅行時處理公事。
(C) 當然——告知你的主管就好。

- optional (adj.) 非必需的　major (adj.) 主要的　advantage (n.) 好處，優點　handle (v.) 處理　supervisor (n.) 主管

25. 以 Who 開頭的問句詢問獲獎者 澳⇄英 難

Who received the award for Most Improved Employee?
(A) Right, she's doing much better now.
(B) I missed that part of the banquet.
(C) Great—you deserve it!

「最進步員工獎」的得獎者是誰？
(A) 對，她現在表現好很多。
(B) 我沒看到晚會的那個部分。
(C) 太好了——你當之無愧！

- receive (v.) 獲頒　award (n.) 獎項　improve (v.) 進步　banquet (n.) 晚會　deserve (v.) 應得

26. 以直述句傳達資訊 美⇄澳 難

We should assign the new interns to General Affairs.
(A) Please check the building directory.
(B) About ten vacant positions.
(C) I believe Human Resources needs some help, too.

我們應該指派新的實習生到總務部。
(A) 請查看大樓指南。
(B) 大約十個空缺職位。
(C) 我想人資部也需要一些協助。

- assign (v.) 指派　General Affairs 總務部　directory (n.) 指南　vacant (adj.) 空的　position (n.) 職位　Human Resources 人資部

27. 以 Why 開頭的問句詢問，為何傑瑞米沒有申請分公司經理的職位 加⇄美

Why didn't Jeremy apply for the branch manager role?
(A) He didn't meet the requirements.
(B) Only if there are no other applicants.
(C) I'd be happy to give you a reference.

傑瑞米為什麼不申請分公司經理的職位？
(A) 他不符合（職位的）要求。
(B) 只有在沒有其他應試者的情況下（，才能申請）。
(C) 我很樂意幫你寫推薦函。

- apply for . . . 申請；應徵⋯⋯　branch (n.) 分公司；分店；分部　role (n.) 職務　meet (v.) 符合　requirement (n.) 規定，要求　applicant (n.) 應試者；應徵者　reference 推薦（人／信）

28. 以附加問句，確認布蕾恩女士是否有去接機 澳⇄英

Ms. Blaine is picking up the investors from the airport, isn't she? **(A) I thought she had a schedule conflict.** (B) To the Regency Hotel. (C) Their flight departs at two.	布蕾恩女士去機場接投資人了，對嗎？ **(A) 我以為她行程撞期。** (B) 到瑞珍希飯店。 (C) 他們的班機兩點起飛。

- pick up 接送　investor (n.) 投資人　schedule conflict 行程撞期　flight (n.) 班機　depart (v.) 起飛；離開

29. 表示建議或提案的問句 加⇄英

Would you like these scented candles gift-wrapped? (A) I sent them to my sister. (B) They smell wonderful. **(C) Does that cost extra?**	您想將這些香氛蠟燭包裝成禮物嗎？ (A) 我已經寄給我姊妹。 (B) 聞起來很棒。 **(C) 需要多加費用嗎？**

- scented (adj.) 有香味的　gift-wrapped (adj.) 包裝成禮物的　cost (v.) 花費

30. 以 **How** 開頭的問句，詢問如何協助募款活動 美⇄加　難

How can I help out with the organization's fundraising event? (A) I'm just glad I could participate. (B) We raised more than expected. **(C) Wendy can give you some tasks.**	我可以如何幫忙機構的募款活動？ (A) 可以參與，我就很高興了。 (B) 我們籌得的金額超乎預期。 **(C) 溫蒂會給你一些工作。**

- organization (n.) 機構　fundraising (n.) 募款（活動）　participate (v.) 參與　raise (v.) 籌募　expect (v.) 預期　task (n.) 工作；任務

31. 以助動詞 **Did** 開頭的問句，詢問是否有請大翔清洗冷氣 美⇄澳

Did you remember to ask Hiroto to clean the air conditioner? (A) Don't forget the ceiling fans. **(B) I haven't seen him since yesterday.** (C) It is a bit cold in here.	你有記得叫大翔清洗空調嗎？ (A) 別忘了吊扇。 **(B) 我從昨天就沒看到他了。** (C) 這裡有點冷。

- air conditioner 冷氣；空調　ceiling (n.) 天花板　fan (n.) 電風扇

PART 3 P. 73–76

23

32-34 Conversation　　32-34 對話 英⇄澳

W: Hello. (32) **I made a reservation to hire a Montoya sedan from your company.** Here's the confirmation e-mail you sent me. **M:** Thank you. OK, I see that you'll have the vehicle for two days. Here are the keys. Do you have any questions?	女：哈囉，(32) **我有向你們公司預約租用一台「蒙特亞」的轎車**，這裡是你們傳給我的確認電郵。 男：謝謝您。好的，我這邊看到您會租車兩天，這是您的鑰匙，不知道您有任何問題嗎？

W: Yes. (33) **Is the satellite navigation system complicated? I've never used one before, so I'm a bit worried about whether I'll be able to figure it out.**	女：有的，(33) **這台車的衛星導航系統會很複雜嗎？我從來沒用過，所以有點擔心自己是否能夠搞懂用法。**
M: (34) **It's fairly simple, but also—there's a user manual in the glove compartment.**	男：(34) **用法很簡單的，而且手套箱裡有使用說明書。**
W: Oh, great. (34) **I'll take a look at that before I set off.**	女：噢，太好了，(34) **我出發前會看一下說明書。**

- reservation (n.) 預約　hire (v.) 租用　confirmation (n.) 確認　satellite (n.) 衛星　complicated (adj.) 複雜的　figure out 搞懂　user manual 使用說明書　glove compartment 手套箱　set off 出發

32. 全文相關——對話地點

Where are the speakers?
(A) At a restaurant
(B) At a vacation resort
(C) At a conference center
(D) At a car rental agency

說話者所在位置為何處？
(A) 在餐廳
(B) 在度假村
(C) 在會議中心
(D) 在租車公司

換句話說 hire a . . . sedan（租賃一台⋯⋯轎車）→ car rental（租車）

---

33. 相關細節——女子提出的問題

What problem does the woman mention?
(A) She has misplaced a set of keys.
(B) She does not know how long a trip will take.
(C) She did not receive an e-mail.
(D) She is unsure about operating a device.

女子提到什麼問題？
(A) 她忘記一組鑰匙放在哪裡。
(B) 她不知道路程有多久。
(C) 她沒有收到電子郵件。
(D) 她沒有把握操作一件裝置。

- misplace (v.) 誤放；忘了⋯⋯放在哪裡　receive (v.) 收到　unsure (adj.) 不確定的　operate (v.) 操作　device (n.) 裝置

---

34. 相關細節——女子提及她會做的事情

What does the woman say she will do?
(A) Check some instructions
(B) Use a storage compartment
(C) Make an initial payment
(D) Watch a video

女子說她會做何事？
(A) 查看說明書
(B) 使用置物箱
(C) 支付首付款
(D) 觀賞影片

- instruction (n.) 說明書　storage compartment 置物箱　initial (adj.) 首期；初次的　payment (n.) 款項

換句話說 a user manual（使用說明書）→ instructions（說明書）

35-37 Conversation

35-37 對話 英⇄加

W: Excuse me, Norman. (35) **I'd like to speak with you about something after you receive the delivery today.**

M: Oh, the delivery was this morning.

W: Ah, great! (36) **Well, the CEO wants to add a few more healthy dishes to our catering options.** What do you think about developing some soups?

M: Hmm . . . I don't know. We'd have to invest in special containers to transport them. That might be costly.

W: Good point. But I don't want to give up on this idea yet. (37) **I'm going to get on the Internet and see what kinds of containers are available.**

女： 不好意思，諾曼。(35) **你今天收到配送的貨品後，我想找你談一下事情。**

男： 噢，貨品今天早上送達了。

女： 哦，那就好！(36) **是這樣的，執行長想在我們的外燴餐單選擇裡，增加幾道比較健康的菜色**，你覺得來開發一些湯品怎麼樣？

男： 唔……我不知道，我們會需要採買特殊的容器來運送湯品，那樣成本可能會很高。

女： 這倒沒錯，但我還不想放棄這個點子。(37) **我來上網，看看有什麼類型的容器可以使用。**

- receive (v.) 收到　delivery (n.) 配送　add (v.) 增加　dish (n.) 菜色　catering (n.) 外燴　option (n.) 選項　develop (v.) 開發　invest (v.) 投資　container (n.) 容器　transport (v.) 運送　costly (adj.) 昂貴的　give up 放棄　available (adj.) 可用的

35. 掌握說話者的意圖——提及「貨品今天早上送達了」的意圖 難

What does the man mean when he says, "the delivery was this morning"?

(A) He needs to put away some stock.

(B) He is available to have a discussion.

(C) He does not require the woman's help.

(D) He is confused about a work schedule.

男子說：「貨品今天早上送達了」，意思為何？

(A) 他需要把存貨擺歸位。

(B) 他現在有空討論事情。

(C) 他不需要女子的協助。

(D) 他對於工作排程感到混亂。

- stock (n.) 存貨　confused (adj.) 不解的；困惑的

36. 相關細節——女子提及執行長想做的事情

According to the woman, what does the CEO want to do?

(A) Open a new branch

(B) Hire more servers

(C) Expand a menu

(D) Offer a discount

根據女子的說法，執行長想做何事？

(A) 開設新的分公司

(B) 僱用更多服務員

(C) 擴充菜單

(D) 提供折扣

- branch (n.) 分公司；分店　server (n.) 服務人員　expand (v.) 擴充

換句話說 add a few more . . . dishes（增加幾道……菜色）→ expand a menu（擴充菜單）

37. 相關細節——女子決定做的事情

What does the woman decide to do?

(A) Share an idea with an executive

(B) Visit a competitor

(C) Conduct online research

(D) Make an official announcement

女子決定做何事？

(A) 與主管分享想法

(B) 造訪競爭對手

(C) 上網搜尋

(D) 發出官方公告

- executive (n.) 主管　competitor (n.) 競爭對手　conduct (v.) 進行　official (adj.) 官方的　announcement (n.) 布告

換句話說 get on the Internet and see . . .（上網看看）→ conduct online research（上網搜尋）

38-40 Conversation

38-40 對話

美⇄加

W: (38) **Hi, this is Kathy in the IT department. How can I help you?**

M: Hi, Kathy. I just started working here in the marketing department, and I'm having trouble logging into my work computer.

W: I see. Are you using the user name and password you were assigned at the orientation?

M: Yes, and I double-checked those with HR, but (39) **whenever I enter them, the computer just freezes and then shuts down.**

W: That's strange. (40) **I'll send an employee up to take a look at it.** He'll be there in a few minutes.

女：(38) **嗨，我是資訊科技部門的凱西，我能幫你什麼忙呢？**

男：嗨，凱西，我剛到行銷部門這裡開始上班，在登入公司電腦的時候遇到了問題。

女：了解。你有使用新進人員說明會上，分配給你的使用者名稱和密碼嗎？

男：有的，我也有向人資部再次確認，但是 (39) **每當我輸入的時候，電腦就會當掉然後關機。**

女：這就怪了。(40) **我會派同仁上樓查看一下。**他等一下就會到了。

- department (n.) 部門　password (n.) 密碼　assign (v.) 分配　orientation (n.) 新進人員說明會　HR (=Human Resources) 人資部　freeze (v.)（電腦）當機　shut down 關機　employee (n.) 員工

38. 全文相關——女子的職業

Who most likely is the woman?

(A) An office receptionist

(B) A human resources manager

(C) An information technology technician

(D) A maintenance supervisor

女子最有可能是什麼身分？

(A) 辦公室接待員

(B) 人力資源部經理

(C) 資訊科技部的技術員

(D) 維修部的主管

39. 相關細節——男子碰到的問題

What problem does the man have?

(A) He forgot a password.

(B) He missed an orientation.

(C) He cannot get into his office.

(D) His computer is malfunctioning.

男子遇到什麼問題？

(A) 他忘記密碼。

(B) 他錯過了新人說明會。

(C) 他無法進入辦公室。

(D) 他的電腦運作異常。

- miss (v.) 錯過　malfunction (v.) 故障

換句話說 the computer freezes and shuts down（電腦就會當掉然後關機）
→ his computer is malfunctioning（他的電腦運作異常）

40. 相關細節——女子接下來要做的事

What will the woman probably do next?

(A) Go to pick up a machine

(B) Search for a publication

(C) Assign a task to a worker

(D) Approve a spending request

女子接下來很可能會怎麼做？

(A) 去收取機器

(B) 搜尋刊物

(C) 向員工指派任務

(D) 批准開銷請求

- publication (n.) 刊物　task (n.) 任務　approve (v.) 許可　spending (n.) 開銷

41-43 Conversation

41-43 對話

美⇄澳

W: Hi, Terry. (41) **I haven't seen you since you started fixing cars at Sheldon Auto.** Are you enjoying the job so far?

M: It could be better. I get along well with my coworkers, but (42) **I'm getting tired of the fifty-five-minute bus ride to work every day.**

W: That does sound frustrating. (43) **Well, I'm planning to go to a career fair at the community center this Saturday at two. Why don't you come with me?** You might find a job that suits you better.

M: That's not a bad idea at all. Would you like to get lunch first? I could pick you up at noon.

女： 嗨，泰瑞，(41) **自從你進到謝爾登汽車公司、從事修車工作後，我就沒再見到你了**，你目前還喜歡你的工作嗎？

男： 有待加強。我和同事相處得很融洽，但是 (42) **每天都要搭 55 分鐘的公車去上班，我開始感到厭煩了。**

女： 聽起來真的讓人不好受。(43) **這樣吧，我這週六兩點打算去社區中心的就業博覽會，你何不跟我一起去？**你也許會找到更適合的工作。

男： 這真是不錯的點子。妳會想先一起吃午餐嗎？我可以中午去接妳。

- fix (v.) 修理　so far 目前　get along with 相處　coworker (n.) 同事　ride (n.) 車程　frustrating (adj.) 令人氣惱的　career fair 就業展　community center 社區中心　suit (v.) 適合

41. 全文相關——男子的職業

What most likely is the man's job?

(A) Vehicle mechanic

(B) Parking attendant

(C) Car salesperson

(D) Delivery driver

該男子最有可能擔任什麼職務？

(A) 汽車技師

(B) 泊車服務員

(C) 汽車業務

(D) 配送司機

42. 相關細節——男子不喜歡這份工作的理由

難

What does the man say he dislikes about his job?

(A) The lack of promotion opportunities

(B) The competitive colleagues

(C) The irregular finish time

(D) The long commute

男子說他不喜歡自己工作的哪方面？

(A) 缺乏升遷機會

(B) 同事彼此競爭

(C) 下班時間不固定

(D) 長途通勤

- lack (n.) 缺乏　promotion (n.) 升遷　opportunity (n.) 機會　competitive (adj.) 競爭的　commute (n.) 通勤

換句話說 **the fifty-five-minute bus ride to work**（搭 55 分鐘的公車去上班）
→ **the long commute**（長途通勤）

43. 相關細節——女子建議男子做的事情

What does the woman suggest that the man do?

(A) Submit an application form

(B) Accompany her to an event

(C) Speak to their mutual friend

(D) Read a job advertisement

女子建議男子怎麼做？

(A) 提出申請表

(B) 陪她去參加活動

(C) 和共同朋友聊聊

(D) 看徵才廣告

- submit (v.) 提交　application form 申請表　accompany (v.) 陪伴　mutual (adj.) 共同的

換句話說 **come with me**（跟我一起去）→ **accompany her**（陪她）

44-46 Conversation with three speakers

44-46 三人對話 加⇄澳⇄英

M1: Hi, Olivia. Thanks for inviting us to your new home for this consultation. (44) **I'm James, and I'll be handling the decoration and arrangement of your living room and bedrooms.** This is my colleague, Joe.

M2: (44) **Hi, I'll be taking care of your bathrooms and kitchen.**

W: It's a pleasure to meet the two of you. (45) **Uh, as you can see, I don't even have any furniture, so you'll really have a lot to do.**

M2: Well, we love a challenge! (46) **Now, why don't you show us around?** That way, we can get some ideas for how to begin.

W: (46) **Sure.** Let's start with the upstairs rooms and work our way down.

M1: Sounds good.

男 1：嗨，奧莉維亞，謝謝妳邀請我們到妳的新家，進行此次諮詢。(44) **我是詹姆斯，我將負責處理您客廳和臥室的裝飾、布置事宜。**這是我的同事，喬。

男 2：(44) **嗨，我會負責您的浴室和廚房。**

女：很開心能和兩位見面。(45) **唔，如你們所見，我甚至連一件家具都沒有，所以你們真的有得忙了。**

男 2：喔，我們樂於接受挑戰！(46) **那麼，何不請您帶我們到處看看？**這樣我們比較能夠有想法，知道該如何開始著手。

女：(46) **沒問題。**我們就先從樓上的房間，接著再到樓下。

男 1：好主意。

- consultation (n.) 諮詢　handle (v.) 處理　decoration (n.) 裝飾　arrangement (n.) 布置　colleague (n.) 同事　take care of 處理　bathroom (n.) 浴室　pleasure (n.) 樂事　challenge (n.) 挑戰　upstairs (adj.) 樓上的

44. 全文相關——兩名男子的職業

Who most likely are the men?

(A) City officials

(B) Real estate agents

(C) Interior decorators

(D) Event planners

男子們最有可能是什麼身分？

(A) 市政府官員

(B) 房地產仲介

(C) 室內裝潢師

(D) 活動策劃人員

- agent (n.) 仲介　interior (n./adj.) 內部（的）　decorator (n.) 裝潢師

45. 相關細節——女子針對房子提及的事情

What does the woman mention about the property?

(A) It is currently unfurnished.

(B) It will also be used for business.

(C) It is located downtown.

(D) It is in need of repairs.

女子提到住宅的什麼情況？

(A) 目前未有家具。

(B) 也會做為商用。

(C) 位於市區。

(D) 需要維修。

- property (n.) 住宅　currently (adv.) 目前　unfurnished (adj.) 無家具擺設的　locate (v.) 位於　downtown (adv.) 在市區

換句話說 I don't even have any furniture（我甚至連一件家具都沒有）
→ It is currently unfurnished（目前未有家具）

46. 相關細節——男子接下來要做的事情

What will the men probably do next?
(A) Show the woman some paperwork
(B) Unload some equipment
(C) Interview the woman
(D) Tour the residence

男子們接下來很可能會做什麼？
(A) 給女子看一些文件。
(B) 卸載一些設備。
(C) 訪問女子。
(D) 參觀住宅內部。

- paperwork (n.) 文件　unload (v.) 卸載　equipment (n.) 設備　residence (n.) 住宅

47-49 Conversation

W: Peter, I just saw your e-mail. (47) **I'm sorry, but I won't be able to write that report by Friday. I have too many other tasks to take care of.**

M: Well, I really need that report this week. (48) **Could any of your other work be redistributed to your coworkers?**

W: Hmm . . . (48) **Angelina could add the new client details to the database.** She's done that before, when I've gone on vacation.

M: OK. (49) **Let me check her schedule for the week.** If she's not too busy, I'll ask her to handle that. Will that give you enough time to write the report?

W: Yes, I think it would.

47-49 對話　美⇄加

女： 彼得，我剛看了你的電子郵件。(47) **不好意思，我無法在週五前完成那份報告。我有太多其他事項要處理。**

男： 這個嘛，我這週真的需要那份報告，(48) **妳的其他工作，有沒有可以重新分派給同事的呢？**

女： 嗯…… (48) **可能可以請安潔莉娜，把新的客戶詳細資料新增到資料庫**，我之前請假時，她做過這項工作。

男： 好的，(49) **我會看一下她這週的行程**，如果她不會太忙，我會請她處理這部分，如此一來，妳會有足夠時間寫報告嗎？

女： 有的，我想我可以寫完。

- redistribute (v.) 重新分派　coworker (n.) 同事　detail (n.) 詳細資料

47. 相關細節——女子提到她沒辦法處理該工作的理由

Why does the woman say she is unable to accept an assignment?
(A) Her workload is too heavy.
(B) She does not have a necessary skill.
(C) It would violate a company policy.
(D) She is going out of town soon.

女子為何說她無法承接一份指派工作？
(A) 她的工作量太繁重。
(B) 她沒有必須的技能。
(C) 這會違反公司政策。
(D) 她很快就要外出遠行。

- accept (v.) 接受　assignment (n.) 指派工作　workload (n.) 工作量　violate (v.) 違反　policy (n.) 政策

換句話說 I have too many other tasks（我有太多其他事項）
→ Her workload is too heavy.（她的工作量太繁重。）

48. 相關細節——女子建議麻煩安潔莉娜做的事情

What does the woman suggest asking Angelina to do?
(A) Provide some training
(B) Contact new clients
(C) Update a database
(D) Postpone a vacation

女子建議要求安潔莉娜做什麼事？
(A) 提供培訓課程
(B) 聯絡新客戶
(C) 更新資料庫
(D) 延後休假

- training (n.) 培訓　postpone (v.) 延後

換句話說 add the new . . . details to the database（把新的……詳細資料新增到資料庫）
→ update a database（更新資料庫）

49. 相關細節——男子表示他會查看的事物

What does the man say he will check?
(A) A building directory
(B) A work calendar
(C) A staff handbook
(D) A survey report

男子表示會查看什麼？
(A) 樓層指南
(B) 工作行事曆
(C) 員工手冊
(D) 檢驗報告

換句話說 her schedule（她的行程）→ a work calendar（工作行事曆）

50-52 Conversation

M: Hi, this is Scott Rubin. I ordered some posters from your store earlier this week. (50) **Uh, I'm looking at the sample you sent me, and I don't think my company's logo is visible enough. Maybe dark blue wasn't a good choice for it.**

W: OK, we can make it a lighter shade of blue. (51) **I'll have my assistant do that this morning, and she'll e-mail you the revised sample this afternoon.** And since it's a minor change, there won't be any additional cost.

M: Great. Oh, and one other thing—regarding the scheduled pick-up time tomorrow, can we make it one p.m. instead of eleven a.m.? (52) **I have an early business lunch.**

50-52 對話

澳⇄美

男： 嗨，我是史考特・魯賓。我本週稍早有向貴店訂做一些海報，(50) **呃，我正在看妳寄給我的樣張，覺得我公司的標誌不夠明顯，也許標誌不太適合用深藍色。**

女： 好的，我們可調整為較淺色調的藍色。(51) **我今天早上會請助理處理，她今天下午會以電子郵件，將修改過的樣張傳給你**，因為這是小變動，我們不會收取額外費用。

男： 太好了。噢，還有一件事——關於原本排定明天取件的時間，我們可以從早上十一點，改到下午一點嗎？(52) **我近中午要參加商務午餐會議。**

- **visible (adj.)** 明顯的　**shade (n.)** 色調　**revise (v.)** 修訂　**minor (adj.)** 微小的　**regarding (prep.)** 關於……

50. 相關細節——男子擔憂的事情

難

What is the man concerned about?
(A) The price of a service
(B) The quality of an image
(C) The color of a logo
(D) The size of an order

男子擔心何事？
(A) 服務的價格
(B) 圖像的品質
(C) 標誌的顏色
(D) 訂單的大小

51. 相關細節——女子提及她助理將於今天下午做的事情

What does the woman say her assistant will do this afternoon?
(A) Prepare a revised invoice
(B) Print additional copies
(C) Send a design electronically
(D) Pack up some posters

女子表示她的助理下午會處理什麼事？
(A) 準備修改過的帳單
(B) 印出額外的副本
(C) 傳送設計圖的電子檔
(D) 打包部分海報

- **invoice (n.)** 請款帳單；發貨單　**electronically (adv.)** 以電子方式地　**pack up** 把……收拾好

換句話說 e-mail you . . .（以電子郵件傳給你）→ send . . . electronically（傳送……的電子檔）

---

52. 相關細節——男子欲更改取貨時間的理由

Why does the man want to change an appointment time?
(A) He has to attend a business gathering.
(B) His coworker is using a company car.
(C) He needs to pick up some clients.
(D) His office is scheduled to close early.

男子為什麼想要更改預約時間？
(A) 他要出席商務聚會。
(B) 他的同事在用公司配車。
(C) 他需要接送客戶。
(D) 他的辦公室預定提早關門。

- gathering (n.) 聚會

換句話說 have an . . . business lunch（要參加商務午餐會議）
→ attend a business gathering（出席商務聚會）

53-55 Conversation

M: [53]**Rachel, you know how our guests sometimes ask if we offer neighborhood tours? I'd like to try doing that. I think it would make their stay with us more memorable.**

W: That's a great idea. [54]**So many fascinating events have happened around here—there would be a lot to talk about.**

M: Exactly! [55]**So, do you think any of our workers could lead a tour, or should we try to find a professional tour guide?**

W: Hmm... Well, Michael knows the area pretty well. And he's very outgoing. Why don't you mention the idea to him when he comes in for his shift?

53-55 對話 澳⇄英

男： **(53) 瑞秋，妳知道客人有時會問，我們有沒有提供鄰近社區的導覽服務嗎？我想試試看，我覺得這會讓他們擁有更難忘的住宿回憶。**

女： 這是很好的點子。**(54) 這個地方發生過許多精彩事蹟，肯定會有不少話題可聊。**

男： 完全沒錯！**(55) 那麼，妳覺得我們有哪個員工可以來帶領導覽嗎？或者我們該找專業導遊？**

女： 嗯……這個嘛，麥可對社區熟門熟路，而且很活潑外向，你何不在他來值班的時候，把這個主意說給他聽？

- neighborhood (n.) 鄰近區域　memorable (adj.) 難忘的　fascinating (adj.) 精彩的
  professional (adj.) 專業的　outgoing (adj.) 外向的　shift (n.) 輪班（的時間）

53. 全文相關——說話者的職業

What type of business do the speakers most likely work for?
(A) A movie theater
(B) A hotel
(C) A museum
(D) A travel agency

說話者最有可能任職於何種業者？
(A) 電影院
(B) 飯店
(C) 博物館
(D) 旅行社

---

54. 相關細節——女子針對周邊環境提及的事情 

What does the woman mention about the surrounding neighborhood?
(A) It has a new leisure facility.
(B) It has an interesting history.
(C) It has a confusing layout.
(D) It lacks parking.

女子對於鄰近社區，提到了什麼事？
(A) 有新開幕的休閒設施。
(B) 擁有有趣的歷史。
(C) 格局配置令人困惑。
(D) 缺乏停車空間。

- facility (n.) 設施　confusing (adj.) 令人不解的　layout (n.) 配置　lack (v.) 缺乏……

55. 掌握說話者的意圖——提及「麥可對社區熟門熟路」的意圖 難

What does the woman imply when she says, "Michael knows the area pretty well"?
(A) It is surprising that Michael made a mistake.
(B) Michael might be able to answer a question.
(C) The man should not be concerned about a delay.
(D) She thinks Michael is suitable for a role.

女子說：「麥可對社區熟門熟路」，言下之意為何？
(A) 麥可犯錯一事令人驚訝。
(B) 麥可也許能回答某問題。
(C) 男子不應擔心延誤的事。
(D) 她認為麥可適合一項職務。

56-58 Conversation with three speakers

W1: **(56) Mr. Tarrant, many people are wondering what the best wireless earphones are these days. I'd like to review some of the most popular ones on our Web site.**
M: **(56) Great idea, Harumi!** That should increase our traffic. **(57) But, can you work out an agreement with manufacturers to get some free items to review?** Our budget wouldn't allow us to buy them ourselves.
W1: Oh, I'm not sure. I don't have many contacts in the electronics industry, actually.
M: Well, Janelle used to cover that field. Janelle?
W2: Yes, Mr. Tarrant?
M: **(58) Harumi needs some help with a new project. Could you sit down with her to talk it over?**
W2: Absolutely. Is now a good time, Harumi?

56-58 三人對話 英⇄加⇄美

女 1： **(56) 塔倫特先生，現在很多人都很好奇，時下最優質的無線耳機是哪幾款。我想要在我們的網站上，提供幾款最熱門機種的評點。**
男： **(56) 很棒的點子，晴美！**這樣應該能增加我們的流量。**(57) 不過，妳可以設法跟廠商談妥協議，以便獲得一些免費的品項來評測嗎？**我們預算有限，無法供應自購的開銷。
女 1： 噢，我不確定，其實我在電子產業沒有太多人脈。
男： 說起來，珍妮爾曾負責處理這個領域。珍妮爾？
女 2： 什麼事，塔倫特先生？
男： **(58) 晴美有項新專案需要協助，妳可以和她坐下來談一下嗎？**
女 2： 當然沒問題。晴美，現在方便嗎？

- wonder (v.) 想知道……　wireless (adj.) 無線的　traffic (n.) 流量　work out 設法處理……　agreement (n.) 協議　manufacturer (n.) 廠商，製造商　budget (n.) 預算　contact (n.) 人脈；熟人　electronics industry 電子產業　cover (v.) 處理；報導　field (n.) 領域

56. 相關細節——晴美欲評點的產品類別

What types of products does Harumi want to review?
(A) Security systems
(B) Digital cameras
(C) Game consoles
(D) Audio equipment

晴美想要評點哪類產品？
(A) 保全系統
(B) 數位相機
(C) 電玩主機
(D) 音訊設備

換句話說 earphones（耳機）→ audio equipment（音訊設備）

57. 相關細節——男子詢問晴美的事情 難

What does the man ask Harumi about?
(A) Determining some standards
(B) Encouraging readers to leave comments
(C) Clearing out a space for shipments
(D) Negotiating a deal with manufacturers

男子詢問晴美什麼事？
(A) 決定一些標準規範
(B) 鼓勵讀者留言
(C) 清出空間來擺放貨物
(D) 和廠商協商交易

- determine (v.) 決定　standard (n.) 標準規範　encourage (v.) 鼓勵　comment (n.) 留言；意見　shipment (n.) 貨物　negotiate (v.) 協商　deal (n.) 交易

換句話說 work out an agreement with manufacturers（跟廠商談妥協議）
→ negotiating a deal with manufacturers（和廠商協商交易）

---

58. 相關細節——男子要求珍妮爾做的事情

What does the man request that Janelle do?
(A) Monitor an online discussion
(B) Locate a project file
(C) Meet with a coworker
(D) Edit some articles

男子要求珍妮爾做什麼事？
(A) 監督看線上討論內容
(B) 找尋專案檔案
(C) 和同事開會
(D) 編輯文章

- monitor (v.) 監督　locate (v.) 找尋　coworker (n.) 同事　edit (v.) 編輯　article (n.) 文章

換句話說 sit down with her to talk it over（和她坐下來談一下）→ meet with a coworker（和同事開會）

59-61 Conversation

M: Veronica, I'd like your advice. Our gym's membership has been dropping over the last few months. (59) **How could we bring in some new members?**

W: (60) **Let me think... well, we could try to advertise more**. Instead of just putting ads in the newspaper, we could also hand out flyers, put up posters, and so on.

M: I like it, but (61) **I'm concerned about whether our funds can stretch that far**. The cost of regularly printing flyers and posters would add up pretty quickly.

W: Good point. Oh, then how about social media? I don't know if that would be as effective, but it would certainly be cheaper.

59-61 對話 加⇄美

男： 維若妮卡，我想聽聽妳的建議。我們健身房的會員人數，過去幾個月一直減少，(59) **我們該如何吸引新會員？**

女： (60) **我想想看……這樣吧，我們可以試著多打廣告**，不要只是在報紙登廣告，我們還可以發放傳單、張貼海報等。

男： 我覺得不錯，但是 (61) **我擔心我們的資金可能力有未逮**，定期印傳單和海報所累積的成本，很快就會水漲船高。

女： 你說得對。噢，那麼社群媒體怎麼樣？我不知道是否能達到相同效果，但價格絕對比較便宜。

- drop (v.) 下降　bring in 吸引　ad (n.) 廣告（= advertisement）　hand out 分發　flyer (n.) 傳單　concerned (adj.) 擔心的　fund (n.) 資金　stretch (v.) 支撐；延展　regularly (adv.) 定期地　effective (adj.) 有效的

59. 相關細節——男子向女子尋求的建議

What does the man ask for the woman's advice on?
(A) Evaluating suppliers
(B) Recruiting volunteers
(C) Participating in conferences
(D) Attracting customers

男子請女子提出哪方面的建議？
(A) 評估供應商
(B) 招募志工
(C) 參加會議
(D) 吸引顧客

- evaluate (v.) 評估　supplier (n.) 供應商　recruit (v.) 招募　volunteer (n.) 志工　attract (v.) 吸引

換句話說 bring in some new members（吸引新會員）→ attracting customers（吸引顧客）

60. 相關細節——女子提出的建議

What does the woman recommend?
(A) Relaxing some communication rules
(B) Analyzing posts on a Web platform
(C) Subscribing to a news source
(D) Increasing marketing methods

女子建議做何事？
(A) 放寬通訊規定
(B) 分析網路平台的貼文
(C) 訂閱新聞來源
(D) 增加行銷手段

- relax (v.) 放寬　communication (n.) 通訊；交流　analyze (v.) 分析　post (n.) 貼文　subscribe to . . . 訂閱……　source (n.) 來源　increase (v.) 增加

換句話說 advertise more（多打廣告）→ increasing marketing methods（增加行銷手段）

61. 相關細節——男子對於女子的建議有所猶豫的理由　難

Why is the man uncertain about the woman's suggestion?
(A) A venue may not be available.
(B) A budget may not be large enough.
(C) A timeline cannot be extended.
(D) A law may not allow a change.

男子為何對女子的建議感到遲疑？
(A) 場地可能無法取得。
(B) 預算可能不夠充沛。
(C) 無法延長時程。
(D) 法律可能不允許更動。

- venue (n.) 場地　available (adj.) 可用的　budget (n.) 預算　timeline (n.) 時程表　extend (v.) 延長

換句話說 funds（資金）→ a budget（預算）

62-64 Conversation + Map

M: Hello, Ms. Bailey? This is Tyler from Yenville Services. (62) **I'm supposed to mow the lawn and pull up some weeds at your house this morning,** but I can't seem to find it.

W: (63) **OK—well, it's the white house on the corner of Flint and Poole, across from the bank.**

M: Oh, really? That's the six hundred block. (64) **Aren't you located at five-sixty-one Flint Street?**

W: (64) **Ah, no, I'm at six-fifty-one Flint Street.**

M: Got it. Sorry for the confusion. I'll see you in a few minutes.

62-64 對話＋地圖　澳⇄英

男：哈囉，是貝莉女士嗎？我是「顏維爾服務」的泰勒。(62) **我今天早上排定要去貴府使用機器修剪草皮、並拔除野草**，但是我好像無法找到府上位置。

女：(63) **好的。我家就是弗林特街和玻里路轉角處的白色房子，位在銀行對面。**

男：噢，真的嗎？那邊是 600 號街區，(64) **貴府不是位於弗林特街 561 號嗎？**

女：(64) **啊，不是的，我是在弗林特街 651 號。**

男：了解，抱歉搞錯了。我很快就到。

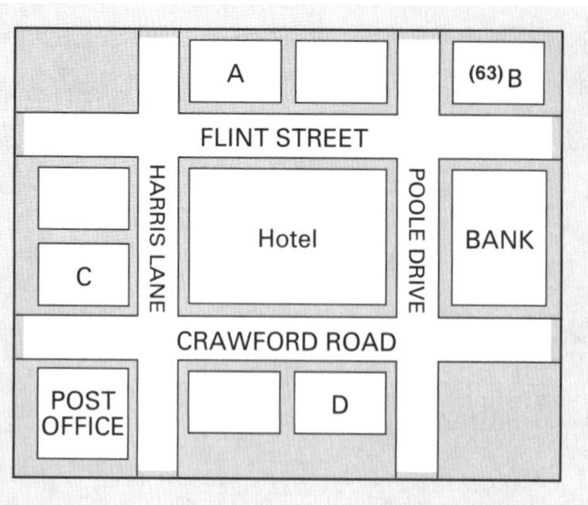

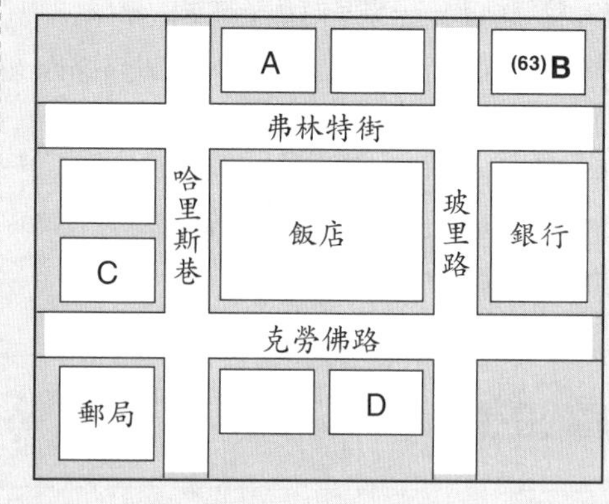

- be supposed to . . . 應該要……（執行某事） mow (v.)（用機器）修剪 lawn (n.) 草皮 weed (n.) 野草 corner (n.) 轉角；角落 across from . . . ……對面 confusion (n.) 困惑

62. 全文相關——男子的職業

Who most likely is the man?
(A) A painter
(B) A gardener
(C) A caterer
(D) A repair person

男子最有可能是什麼身分？
(A) 畫家
(B) 園丁
(C) 外燴業者
(D) 維修人員

63. 圖表整合題——女子住處的位置

Look at the graphic. Where does the woman live?
(A) At Location A
(B) At Location B
(C) At Location C
(D) At Location D

請看圖表回答。女子住在哪裡？
(A) A 位置
(B) B 位置
(C) C 位置
(D) D 位置

64. 相關細節——問題所在

What is the problem?
(A) A service has been canceled.
(B) The man had the wrong address.
(C) A road has been closed to traffic.
(D) The woman's house has been renovated.

發生的問題為何？
(A) 服務被取消。
(B) 男子掌握的地址有誤。
(C) 道路封閉，禁止通行。
(D) 女子的住宅已整修。

- cancel (v.) 取消 traffic (n.) 交通 renovate (v.) 翻修

65-67 Conversation + Advertisement

W: Are you finding everything you need today, sir?

M: I have a question about these beautiful Shanter dinnerware sets, actually. (65) **Can I use them to warm food up in the microwave?**

W: Yes, all of the pieces are made of microwave-safe ceramic. And, as you can see, they're on sale right now. How large of a set are you thinking of getting?

65-67 對話＋廣告 英⇄加

女： 先生您好，需要的商品目前都有找到嗎？

男： 其實，我對這些精美的「尚特」餐具組有個問題。(65) **我可以用來裝食物，放進微波爐裡加熱嗎？**

女： 可以的，套組所有用具使用的陶瓷材質，都可以安心以微波加熱。而且如您所見，餐具組現在折扣中，不知道您想購買多大的套組呢？

M: Well, that sale makes me want to buy a big one. (66) **But I really only need a four-person set.**

W: Sure. You can always come back and buy more later.

M: Oh, really? Won't they be gone in a few months?

W: (67) **No—Shanter tends to offer the same designs for years.** You'll have time.

男：這個嘛，優惠會讓我想買大一點的套組，(66) **但我真的只需要四人套組。**

女：沒問題。您可以隨時再次光臨添購。

男：噢，真的嗎？不會幾個月後就賣光吧？

女：(67) **不會的——尚特公司大多會長年銷售相同款式**，您還有時間考慮。

- **dinnerware (n.)** 餐具 **warm up** 加熱 **microwave (n.)** 微波爐 **on sale** 打折；優惠 **tend to . . .** 傾向；大多會……

65. 相關細節——男子針對餐具套組想了解的事情

What does the man want to know about the dinnerware sets?

(A) Why they are on sale

(B) How they should be washed

(C) How many pieces they include

(D) Whether they can be heated

有關餐具組，男子想知道何項資訊？

(A) 打折的原因

(B) 清洗的方式

(C) 內含幾件餐具

(D) 是否可以加熱

換句話說 warm food up in the microwave（食物放進微波爐裡加熱）→ they can be heated（可以加熱）

66. 圖表整合題——男子可省下的金額

Look at the graphic. How much money will the man save?

(A) $5

(B) $10

(C) $15

(D) $20

請看圖表作答。男子將可省下多少錢？

(A) 5 美元

(B) 10 美元

(C) 15 美元

(D) 20 美元

67. 相關細節——女子針對尚特品牌產品提及的事情 難

What does the woman say about Shanter's products?

(A) They are easy to return.

(B) They are designed to be long-lasting.

(C) They are not offered by many retailers.

(D) They are not discontinued often.

針對尚特品牌的產品，女子提出何項說明？

(A) 退貨方便。

(B) 以耐用為訴求設計而成。

(C) 許多零售商沒有販售該品牌。

(D) 商品不常停產。

- **return (v.)** 退貨 **long-lasting (adj.)** 耐用的；持久的 **offer (v.)** 供應 **retailer (n.)** 零售商 **discontinue (v.)** 停產

換句話說 offer the same designs for years（長年銷售相同的款式）
→ They are not discontinued often.（商品不常停產。）

68-70 Conversation + Departure board

68-70 對話＋發車時刻表 澳⇄美

M: Good morning, Nobuko. I got to the station a little early, so I bought you a coffee.

W: Oh, thank you, Jay!

M: No problem. Are you all ready to present to our clients?

W: Absolutely. (68) **I have the presentation file on a portable storage drive, and I also e-mailed it to myself, just in case.** So, what platform are we leaving from?

M: Let's check the departure board . . . (69) **Oh no, our train is delayed by a half an hour!**

W: How annoying! Well, the presentation isn't until after lunch, so we should still be on time. (70) **Why don't we go over our presentation strategy again while we wait?**

Destination	Scheduled Departure	Status
(69) Detroit	07:35	Delayed (30 minutes)
Indianapolis	07:55	On Time
Toledo	08:15	Delayed (45 minutes)
Milwaukee	08:25	Delayed (2 hours)

男：早安，信子。我比較早到車站，就幫妳買了杯咖啡。

女：噢，謝謝你，傑！

男：不客氣。妳準備好向我們的客戶發表簡報了嗎？

女：當然。(68) **我已經把簡報檔案存在攜帶式儲存硬碟，還將檔案寄到我自己的電子信箱，以備不時之需。** 那麼，我們要從哪個月台出發？

男：我看一下發車時刻表…… (69) **喔，不，我們要搭的列車誤點半小時！**

女：真氣人！這樣吧，簡報會要到午餐以後才開始，所以我們應該還是會準時到，(70) **我們何不在等車的時候，再檢視一次簡報策略？**

目的地	預計離站時間	狀態
(69) 底特律	07：35	誤點（30分鐘）
印第安納坡里斯	07：55	準點
托雷多	08：15	誤點（45分鐘）
密爾瓦基	08：25	誤點（2小時）

- present (v.) 做簡報　absolutely (adv.) 當然　portable (adj.) 攜帶式的　storage (n.) 儲存　departure (n.) 離站　board (n.) 看板　delay (v.) 誤點　annoying (adj.) 煩人的　strategy (n.) 策略

68. 相關細節——女子提到她帶來的東西

What does the woman say she has brought?

(A) A computer accessory

(B) Some refreshments

(C) Some gifts

(D) A printout

女子說她帶了什麼物品？

(A) 電腦配件

(B) 一些茶點

(C) 一些禮物

(D) 列印資料

換句話說 a portable storage drive（攜帶式儲存硬碟）→ a computer accessory（電腦配件）

69. 圖表整合題——說話者的目的地

Look at the graphic. What is the speakers' destination?

(A) Detroit

(B) Indianapolis

(C) Toledo

(D) Milwaukee

請看圖表作答。說話者的目的地為何？

(A) 底特律

(B) 印第安納坡里斯

(C) 托雷多

(D) 密爾瓦基

70. 相關細節——女子提出的建議

What does the woman suggest doing?
(A) Making a phone call
(B) Reviewing some plans
(C) Going to a departure platform
(D) Reserving some accommodations

女子提議做什麼事？
(A) 打電話
(B) 檢討計畫
(C) 前往離站月台
(D) 預約住宿處

- **review (v.)** 審視；檢討 **reserve (v.)** 預約 **accommodation(s) (n.)** 住宿處

換句話說 **go over**（檢視）→ **reviewing**（檢討）

PART 4 P. 77–79

24

71-73 Telephone message

Hello, Ms. Singh. This is Matt Miller calling from Wells Beaumont UK. (71) **Thank you for your interest in our senior laboratory researcher position. I'm happy to say that you are one of just a few candidates that we have chosen to move forward with.** (72) **We like that you've already been successfully managing teams of researchers and technicians for several years, as proven leadership ability is required for the role.** So, we would like you to come in for an interview next Tuesday at 9 a.m. (73) **Please call me back at your earliest convenience so that we can confirm this arrangement.** Thank you.

71-73 電話留言 澳

辛格小姐您好，我是英國威爾斯博蒙特公司的麥特．米勒。(71) **感謝您有意應徵本公司高階實驗室研究員的職位，很開心通知您，您是我們選中進入下一個階段的少數應徵者之一。**(72) **對於您已有成功管理研究人員與技師團隊的多年經驗，我們相當欣賞，因為此職位需要有實際成績證明的領導能力**，因此，我們希望請您於下週二早上 9 點前來面試。(73) **請於方便時盡早回電給我，以便確認時間安排。**謝謝您。

- **interest (n.)** 興趣 **senior (adj.)** 高階的；資深的 **laboratory (n.)** 實驗室 **researcher (n.)** 研究人員 **candidate (n.)** 人選 **forward (adv.)** 往前 **manage (v.)** 管理 **prove (v.)** 證明 **require (v.)** 必要；要求 **convenience (n.)** 方便 **confirm (v.)** 確認 **arrangement (n.)** 安排

71. 全文相關——聽者的身分

Who most likely is the listener?
(A) A job applicant
(B) A reference provider
(C) An external recruiter
(D) A career coach

聽者最有可能是什麼身分？
(A) 工作應試者
(B) 推薦人
(C) 外部招募人員
(D) 職涯指導人員

- **applicant (n.)** 求職應徵者 **reference (n.)** 推薦（信／人） **provider (n.)** 提供者；供應商 **external (adj.)** 外部的 **recruiter (n.)** 招募人員 **career (n.)** 職涯 **coach (n.)** 指導人員；教練

---

72. 相關細節——說話者提及聽者具備的條件 難

What does the speaker say the listener has?
(A) Relevant experience
(B) A large number of contacts
(C) A sample legal agreement
(D) Generous funding

說話者表示聽者具備什麼特點？
(A) 相關經驗
(B) 大量人脈
(C) 法律協議樣本
(D) 大量資金

- **relevant (adj.)** 相關的 **legal (adj.)** 法律的 **agreement (n.)** 協議 **generous (adj.)** 大量的；慷慨的 **funding (n.)** 資金

73. 相關細節——說話者提出的要求

What does the speaker ask the listener to do?
(A) Submit a document
(B) Return his call
(C) Visit a Web site
(D) Confirm some data

說話者請聽者做什麼事？
(A) 提交文件
(B) 回他電話
(C) 造訪網站
(D) 確認資料

- submit (v.) 提交　document (n.) 文件　confirm (v.) 確認

換句話說 call me back（回電）→ return his call（回他電話）

74-76 Excerpt from a meeting

Good morning, team. (74) **Today we begin development of our new range of office chairs.** (75) **Now, according to our market research data, office workers are looking for more comfortable chairs.** Because they sit at their desks for several hours a day, they prefer ergonomic seats that will reduce muscle and joint pain. So that will be the focus of this line. I know that some of you are familiar with this kind of design, but I want everyone to have an in-depth understanding as we begin this project. (76) **So, I've hired an expert in ergonomics to come in and speak to us today.** She'll be here in about an hour.

74-76 會議摘錄 美

團隊的伙伴們早安，(74) **我們今天會開始研發新系列的辦公椅。**(75) **現在，根據我們的市場研究資料，上班族都引頸企盼有更舒服的座椅**，因為上班族一天好幾個小時都坐在辦公桌前，因此偏好符合人體工學的椅子，以減輕肌肉和關節疼痛。因此，這次的系列會著重此特點。我知道你們有些人熟悉此類設計，但我希望這項專案開始之際，每個人都能深入了解。(76) **所以，我今天已經聘請人體工學專家，來公司和我們講解**，她再約一個小時就會到達。

- development (n.) 開發　ergonomic (adj.) 人體工學的　reduce (v.) 減少　muscle (n.) 肌肉
  joint (n.) 關節　pain (n.) 疼痛　in-depth (adj.) 深入的　expert (n.) 專家

74. 相關細節——說話者公司販售的產品

What product does the speaker's company sell?
(A) Automobiles
(B) Electronics
(C) Furniture
(D) Luggage

說話者的公司販售何種產品？
(A) 汽車
(B) 電子產品
(C) 家具
(D) 行李箱

換句話說 office chairs（辦公椅）→ furniture（家具）

75. 相關細節——公司目標客群的需求

What does the company's target market want?
(A) Better durability
(B) Increased comfort
(C) Improved safety
(D) Reduced cost

此公司的目標客群需求為何？
(A) 較佳的耐用度
(B) 舒適度增加
(C) 安全性提升
(D) 成本降低

- durability (n.) 耐用度　comfort (n.) 舒適度　safety (n.) 安全性

換句話說 more comfortable（更舒服的）→ increased comfort（增加舒適度）

76. 相關細節——說話者提及她完成的事情

What does the speaker say she has done?
(A) Employed a consultant
(B) Ordered some materials
(C) Talked to a facility manager
(D) Made a list of features

說話者表示她已經做了何事？
(A) 僱用諮詢人員
(B) 訂購材料
(C) 和設施經理談過話
(D) 製作特色清單

- **employ (v.)** 僱用 **consultant (n.)** 顧問 **material (n.)** 材料 **facility (n.)** 設施 **feature (n.)** 特色

換句話說 hired an expert（聘請專家）→ employed a consultant（僱用諮詢人員）

77-79 Telephone message

77-79 電話留言 (加)

Hi, Catherine, this is David. [(77)] **I'm calling about your trip to San Francisco this Thursday for the skills development workshop.** [(78)] **As you know, you were given special permission to turn in the travel request form on very short notice, several days after the usual deadline.** Luckily, we've still been able to accommodate most of your preferences—except one. [(79)] **You asked to take Coastal Airlines because of your rewards membership, but I've booked you on West Coast Air instead.** West Coast Air flies direct to San Francisco, and [(79)] **it's our policy to book direct flights when possible.** I hope you understand.

嗨，凱瑟琳，我是大衛。[(77)] **我這次來電，是關於妳這週四要前往舊金山，參加技能發展研習的事。** [(78)] **如妳所知，公司有給妳特殊許可，差旅需求表提交的預告期可以很短，比正常期限晚好幾天。** 幸好，我們仍能滿足妳大多數的偏好，只有一點例外，[(79)] **妳因為會員獎勵制度的關係，要求搭乘海岸航空班機，但是我已經幫妳改訂了西岸航空。** 西岸航空能直飛舊金山，而 [(79)] **本公司的政策是盡可能預訂直飛班機，** 希望妳能諒解。

- **permission (n.)** 許可 **turn in** 繳交 **on short notice** 緊急通知
  accommodate (v.) 顧及（需求、意見等） **preference (n.)** 偏好 **reward (n.)** 獎勵
  direct flight 直飛班機

77. 相關細節——聽者於週四要參加的活動

What event will the listener attend on Thursday?
(A) A trade exposition
(B) A recruitment fair
(C) A training workshop
(D) A grand opening

聽者將於週四參加什麼活動？
(A) 貿易展覽
(B) 徵才博覽會
(C) 培訓研習
(D) 盛大開幕活動

換句話說 the skills development workshop（技能發展研習）→ a training workshop（培訓研習）

---

78. 相關細節——說話者針對表格提及的事情 (難)

What does the speaker say about a form?
(A) It is incomplete.
(B) It was submitted relatively late.
(C) It includes an unusual request.
(D) It has been misplaced.

有關表單，說話者提到何項資訊？
(A) 內容不完整。
(B) 相對較晚繳交。
(C) 內有不常見的要求。
(D) 忘了表格放在哪裡。

- **incomplete (adj.)** 不完整的 **misplace (v.)** 誤放（某物）而找不到

換句話說 turn in（提交）→ submitted（繳交）

---

79. 掌握說話者的意圖——提及「西岸航空能直飛舊金山」的意圖 難

Why does the speaker say, "West Coast Air flies direct to San Francisco"?

(A) To point out a mistake that he discovered

(B) To answer a question about an itinerary

(C) To suggest an alternative travel option

(D) To explain why he made a decision

說話者為什麼說：「西岸航空能直飛舊金山」？

(A) 以指出他所發現的錯誤

(B) 以回答關於行程的問題

(C) 以建議另一個替代的旅行選項

(D) 以說明他做決定的原因

- itinerary (n.) 行程　alternative (adj.) 替代的

80-82 Advertisement

It's the middle of May, and that means it's time for Castleford's weeklong "Screenings Under the Stars" festival. [80] **Every evening from May eighteenth through twenty-fourth, the city will be showing a classic film on a large outdoor screen at Spruce Park**. No tickets are necessary. [81] **Simply come to the west side of the park with something comfortable to sit on**. Food trucks will be available each night from seven p.m., and the film will be introduced by an expert at eight. Don't miss this chance to enjoy classic cinema in a unique setting! [82] **To learn which films will be shown, visit our Web site, www.castleford-sus.com**. We hope to see you under the stars!

80-82 廣告 英

時至五月中，意味著克斯多弗市為期一週的「星光影」電影節開始了。[80] **從 5 月 18 日到 24 日的每天晚上，本市都將於雲杉公園的大型戶外螢幕播放一齣經典電影**。不需入場券，[81] **只要攜帶可以舒服坐靠的物品，前來公園西側即可**。餐車每晚七點開始營業，八點時將有專家介紹當晚影片。別錯過置身獨特場地中，欣賞經典電影的機會！[82] **想了解將會播放哪些電影，請至我們的網站 www.castleford-sus.com**。期待與您相會星空下！

- weeklong (adj.) 為期一週的　screening (n.) 電影放映　classic (adj.) 經典的　outdoor (adj.) 戶外的　available (adj.) 可使用的　introduce (v.) 介紹　expert (n.) 專家　unique (adj.) 獨特的　setting (n.) 環境設置；場景

80. 相關細節——說話者宣傳的活動

What type of event is the speaker advertising?

(A) An outdoor concert

(B) A movie festival

(C) A street parade

(D) A sports tournament

說話者在為何種活動打廣告？

(A) 戶外音樂會

(B) 電影節

(C) 街頭遊行

(D) 運動錦標賽

---

81. 相關細節——建議聽者做的事情

What are listeners encouraged to do?

(A) Try a special kind of food

(B) Wear warm clothing

(C) Bring their own seating

(D) Use public transportation

說話者鼓勵聽者做什麼事？

(A) 嘗試特殊食物

(B) 穿上保暖衣物

(C) 自行攜帶座椅

(D) 使用大眾運輸

- seating (n.) 座椅　public transportation 大眾運輸

換句話說 something . . . to sit on（可以……坐靠的物品）→ bring their own seating（自行攜帶座椅）

---

82. 相關細節——聽者應該造訪網站的理由

Why should listeners visit a Web site?
(A) To become a volunteer worker
(B) To download a map of a venue
(C) To see an entertainment lineup
(D) To purchase tickets in advance

聽者為什麼要造訪網站？
(A) 成為志工
(B) 下載場地地圖
(C) 瀏覽娛樂節目表
(D) 預購入場券

- **venue (n.)** 場地 **entertainment (n.)** 娛樂節目 **lineup (n.)** 節目表 **purchase (v.)** 購買 **in advance** 預先

換句話說 films（電影）→ entertainment（娛樂節目）

83-85 Excerpt from a meeting

83-85 會議摘錄 (美)

(83) I'd like to give you all an update on the project to add a new wing to the community center. As you know, we're currently collecting funding donations from local businesses. **(84) Well, I'm happy to say that we've already received more than sixty thousand dollars, and** we're still waiting for Joslyn Associates! **(84) It looks like we will easily meet our fund-raising goal.** This is great, because it means that construction can start on time and probably finish in early summer. **(85) I had been concerned about the August storms causing delays.**

(83) 針對要在社區中心新建側廳的專案，我想向大家更新一下狀況。如大家所知，我們目前正在向在地企業募集捐款。**(84) 那麼，我很開心的告訴大家，我們已經收到超過六萬美元的捐款，而且**我們還等著喬瑟琳公司的善款進來！**(84) 看來我們將輕易達到募資目標。**這是個好消息，表示建案能準時開工，而且大概可於初夏完工。**(85) 我之前一直擔心八月的暴風雨造成延宕。**

- **wing (n.)** 側廳 **community center** 社區中心 **collect (v.)** 募集 **funding (n.)** 資金 **donation (n.)** 捐款 **fund-raising (n.)** 募資 **construction (n.)** 工程 **concern (v.)** 使擔心 **delay (n.)** 延誤

83. 全文相關——獨白的主題 難

What is being discussed?
(A) A park restoration
(B) A building expansion
(C) An educational program
(D) An election campaign

說話者在討論何事？
(A) 公園整修
(B) 建物擴建工程
(C) 教育計畫
(D) 競選活動

換句話說 add a new wing to the community center（在社區中心新建側廳）
→ a building expansion（建物擴建）

---

84. 掌握說話者的意圖——提及「我們還等著喬瑟琳公司的善款進來」的意圖 難

What does the speaker imply when she says, "we're still waiting for Joslyn Associates"?
(A) She is worried that a deadline will not be met.
(B) She is unable to grant a request at this time.
(C) Joslyn Associates will contribute to an initiative.
(D) Joslyn Associates has a lot of influence in the city.

說話者說：「我們還等著喬瑟琳公司的善款進來」，言下之意為何？
(A) 她擔心無法趕上期限。
(B) 她此時無法准許一項請求。
(C) 喬瑟琳公司將捐獻支持企畫。
(D) 喬瑟琳公司在此城市舉足輕重。

- **deadline (n.)** 期限 **grant (v.)** 准許 **request (n.)** 請求 **contribute to** 貢獻；捐獻 **initiative (n.)** 企劃案 **influence (n.)** 影響力

---

85. 相關細節——說話者先前擔憂的事

What was the speaker concerned about before?
(A) Expensive permit fees
(B) A shortage of personnel
(C) Negative public opinion
(D) Poor seasonal weather

說話者先前擔心什麼事？
(A) 許可證費用昂貴
(B) 人手短缺
(C) 負面輿論
(D) 季節氣候惡劣

- permit (n.) 許可證 fee (n.) 費用 shortage (n.) 短缺 personnel (n.) 人員 negative (adj.) 負面的 seasonal (adj.) 季節性的

換句話說 August storms（八月暴風雨）→ poor seasonal weather（氣候惡劣）

86-88 Broadcast

[86] **Hi everyone, and welcome to another week of *Unwritten*, the podcast about the lives of great novelists.** Today, we're going to talk about Dorothy Pearson, the genius who wrote *Rose Branches* when she was just twenty years old. But first, I need to say something about last week's episode on Joong-Soo Ahn. [87] **Yes, you heard that right—it's "Joong-Soo", not "Juhng-Soo", which is what I called him throughout the episode. I'm sorry about that.** Some very kind listeners alerted me to the mistake through the show's social media accounts. [88] **I hope that all of you will let me know when I've gotten something wrong like that.** I always appreciate it.

86-88 廣播 英

[86] **嗨，大家好，歡迎收聽本週的《不成文》播客節目，一起探索各個偉大小說家的人生。**今天我們要討論的主角是天才作家桃樂絲・皮爾森，她年僅 20 歲時就寫下《玫瑰枝杈》。不過在開始前，有關上週介紹安俊洙的節目，我有事情向大家報告。[87] **是的，你沒聽錯，是「俊洙」，不是上一集全程都唸錯的「真洙」，對此我向大家道歉。**有些好心聽眾透過本節目的社群媒體，提醒我這個口誤。[88] **我希望我有講錯資訊的時候，大家都能提點我**，我一定感激不盡。

- novelist (n.) 小說家 genius (n.) 天才 alert (v.) 提醒；警示 account (n.) 帳號 appreciate (v.) 感激

86. 全文相關——獨白的主題

What is the topic of the podcast?
(A) Writing advice
(B) Book reviews
(C) Famous authors
(D) Publishing trends

此播客節目的主題為何？
(A) 撰寫建議
(B) 書評
(C) 知名作者
(D) 出版趨勢

換句話說 great novelists（偉大小說家）→ famous authors（知名作者）

87. 相關細節——說話者致歉的緣由

What does the speaker apologize for?
(A) Pronouncing a name incorrectly
(B) Misunderstanding a listener question
(C) Including a segment with bad sound quality
(D) Interrupting the show for an advertisement

說話者為了什麼事道歉？
(A) 名字發音錯誤
(B) 誤解聽眾的問題
(C) 播放音質差的片段
(D) 中斷節目插播廣告

- pronounce (v.) 發音 incorrectly (adv.) 錯誤地 misunderstand (v.) 誤解 segment (n.) 片段 interrupt (v.) 中斷

88. 相關細節——說話者鼓勵聽者做的事情

What does the speaker encourage listeners to do?
(A) Report any errors she makes
(B) Recommend ideas for future episodes
(C) Support the podcast's sponsor
(D) Follow her social media account

說話者鼓勵聽者做何事？
(A) 回報她犯下的各種失誤
(B) 建議未來節目構想
(C) 支持播客的贊助廠商
(D) 追蹤她的社群媒體帳號

- report (v.) 回報　error (n.) 失誤　recommend (v.) 建議　support (v.) 支持　sponsor (n.) 贊助商

換句話說 let me know when I've gotten something wrong（講錯資訊的時候提點我）
→ report any errors she makes（回報她犯下的各種失誤）

89-91 Excerpt from a meeting

Hi, everyone. I called you in for this meeting because I'd like your help. (89) **As you probably know, I'll be introducing the Axion mobile phone at the Sydney Technology Expo this weekend.** Though it won't be released until August, this will be the first time that the world hears about it. So the marketing team and I have been working hard on my presentation. (90) **Today, I'd like to practice it for you and hear your opinions and suggestions for revision.** All right? Good. (91) **Now, these printouts contain the latest version of the speech. Barbara, would you mind passing those out?** Everyone can make notes on them while I speak.

89-91 會議摘錄 澳

嗨，大家好。我召集大家來開會，是因為我需要大家的幫忙。(89) **大家大概都知道，我會在本週末的雪梨科技博覽會上，介紹「亞席恩」手機。**雖然手機要八月才會上市，但這將是全世界首次得知產品消息的時機。因此，行銷團隊和我一直緊鑼密鼓製作簡報發表內容。(90) **今天，我想在大家面前練習，並聽取各位的意見及改進的建議，**可以嗎？好的。(91) **現在，這些列印資料上有最新版本的講稿。芭芭拉，可以請妳發給大家嗎？**在我發表時，大家可以在資料上做筆記。

- call in 召集　introduce (v.) 介紹　release (v.) 上市；推出　suggestion (n.) 建議　revision (n.) 修改　printout (n.) 印出的資料　latest (adj.) 最新的　pass out 分發下去　make notes on 在……作筆記

89. 相關細節——說話者提及即將發生的事情

According to the speaker, what will happen soon?
(A) A project team will be formed.
(B) A leadership position will be filled.
(C) A product will be announced.
(D) A mobile app will be released.

根據說話者所說，何事即將發生？
(A) 將組成專案小組。
(B) 將有人填補領導職缺。
(C) 將發表產品。
(D) 將推出手機應用程式。

- form (v.) 組成　position (n.) 職位　fill (v.) 填補　announce (v.) 宣布

換句話說 introducing the . . . mobile phone（介紹……手機）
→ A product will be announced（將發表產品）

---

90. 相關細節——說話者希望聽者做的事情

What does the speaker want the listeners to do?
(A) Provide some feedback
(B) Create a recording
(C) Gather some supplies
(D) Revise some sales figures

說話者希望聽者做何事？
(A) 提供反饋
(B) 錄製影音
(C) 收集一些用品
(D) 修訂銷售數據

- recording (n.) 錄音／錄影檔　gather (v.) 收集　supplies (n.) 用品　revise (v.) 修訂　figure (n.) 數據

換句話說 your opinions and suggestions（各位的意見及建議）→ some feedback（反饋）

91. 相關細節——說話者要求芭芭拉發放的東西

What does the speaker ask Barbara to hand out?
(A) Entrance passes
(B) A set of prototypes
(C) A draft of a script
(D) Notepads

說話者要求芭芭拉分發何者？
(A) 入場通行證
(B) 一組產品原型
(C) 講稿草稿
(D) 筆記簿

92-94 Talk

Welcome, everyone, to your first day of work at Royston Industrial. (92) **My name is Manuel Gomez, and I'm going to give you a tour of this manufacturing plant.** By the end, you will be familiar with the facility and should have a good understanding of the process by which our products are made. Now, before we start, (93) **I need each of you to grab a helmet and goggles from the boxes here and put them on.** (94) **I know they're uncomfortable, but you can't be in the plant without them.** Just look around at the other workers. OK, are we ready to begin?

92-94 談話 加

歡迎大家，今天第一天來「羅伊斯頓工業」上班，(92) **我叫曼紐爾·戈梅茲，將會帶大家參觀一下這座製造工廠。**導覽結束時，大家可望熟悉這間設施，並且充分了解我們產品的製程。現在，我們開始之前，(93) **我想請每個人從這些箱子裡，取用安全帽、護目鏡並且戴好，**(94) **我知道戴起來不太舒服，但是沒有戴上這些裝備，就不能進入工廠，**看看周圍其他工人吧。好的，準備好開始了嗎？

- tour (n.) 參觀；導覽 manufacturing plant 製造工廠 facility (n.) 設施 process (n.) 程序 grab (v.) 拿取

92. 全文相關——獨白的地點

Where most likely is the talk taking place?
(A) At a fitness center
(B) At a construction site
(C) In a hospital
(D) In a factory

這段談話最有可能在哪裡進行？
(A) 健身中心
(B) 工地
(C) 醫院
(D) 工廠

換句話說 manufacturing plant（製造工廠）→ factory（工廠）

93. 相關細節——說話者要求聽者做的事情

What does the speaker ask the listeners to do?
(A) Wear safety gear
(B) Watch a demonstration
(C) Clean some machines
(D) Pack some boxes

說話者要求聽者做什麼事？
(A) 穿戴安全裝備
(B) 觀賞示範
(C) 清理機器
(D) 包裝箱子

- safety gear 安全裝備 demonstration (n.) 示範 pack (v.) 包裝

換句話說 a helmet and goggles（安全帽、護目鏡）→ safety gear（安全裝備）

94. 掌握說話者的意圖——提及「看看周圍其他工人吧」的意圖 難

What does the speaker mean when he says "Just look around at the other workers"?

(A) A requirement applies to everyone at a workplace.

(B) The listeners can learn a task by observing others.

(C) The listeners' negative feelings are common.

(D) There is serious competition for an opportunity.

說話者說：「看看周圍其他工人吧」，意思為何？

(A) 全員適用一項職場規定。

(B) 聽者可藉由觀察他人學會做工作任務。

(C) 聽者有負面感受是常見的。

(D) 針對機會的競爭很激烈。

- requirement (n.) 規定　apply to . . . 適用……　workplace (n.) 職場　task (n.) 任務　observe (v.) 觀察　competition (n.) 競爭　opportunity (n.) 機會

95-97 Telephone message + Form

95-97 電話留言＋表格 英

Hi Brian, it's Sophia Hines. (95) **I'm calling about the company's plan to supply wireless keyboards to all of our software helpline staff.** (96) **I just learned that some of the workers at our branch already have them. So instead of the forty that I originally requested, we're only going to need twenty-eight.** I sent you an e-mail about this too, but I wanted to call you directly so that you got the message as soon as possible. Am I too late? (97) **Has the order been processed already?** Let me know.

requested quantities of wireless keyboards

Branch	Quantity
Bristol	25
Manchester	35
(96) Norwich	40
Liverpool	45

嗨，布萊恩，我是蘇菲亞．海恩斯。(95) **我打來是想討論公司要為所有軟體客服專線人員，供應無線鍵盤的計畫。**(96) **我剛才得知，我們分公司的部分員工已經有無線鍵盤，所以我這邊需要的數量想從原先的 40，修改為僅 28 組。**我也有傳電子郵件通知你，但我想直接打給你，以便你盡早知道消息。我太晚通知了嗎？(97) **訂單已在處理當中了嗎？**再請跟我說。

無線鍵盤需求數量

分公司	數量
布里斯托	25
曼徹斯特	35
(96) 諾維奇	40
利物浦	45

- supply (v.) 供應　helpline (n.) 客服專線　branch (n.) 分公司　instead of . . . 取代

95. 相關細節——使用鍵盤的人

Who most likely will use the keyboards?

(A) Customer service representatives

(B) Data entry specialists

(C) Software designers

(D) Newspaper staff

何人最有可能使用此類鍵盤？

(A) 客服人員

(B) 資料登錄專員

(C) 軟體設計師

(D) 報社職員

換句話說 helpline staff（客服專線人員）→ customer service representatives（客服人員）

96. **圖表整合題——說話者任職的分公司**

Look at the graphic. Which branch does the speaker work for?

(A) Bristol

(B) Manchester

(C) Norwich

(D) Liverpool

請看圖表作答。說話者在哪家分公司工作？

(A) 布里斯托

(B) 曼徹斯特

(C) 諾維奇

(D) 利物浦

97. **相關細節——說話者提出的問題** 難

What does the speaker ask about?

(A) When a shipment will arrive

(B) How to start a return process

(C) Whom to notify about an issue

(D) Whether an order has been finalized

說話者詢問何事？

(A) 到貨時間

(B) 如何開始退貨流程

(C) 該向何人告知問題

(D) 訂單是否已最終確認

- shipment (n.) 貨物 return (n.) 退貨 notify (v.) 通知 issue (n.) 問題 finalize (v.) 最後確定

換句話說 the order been processed（訂單已在處理當中）
→ an order has been finalized（訂單已最終確認）

98-100 Talk + Schedule

All right, there's a change to today's demonstration schedule that I need to let you know about. Unfortunately, the materials we need to construct windmill sails didn't arrive in time, so the Miniature Windmill demonstration is cancelled. (98) **We've decided to run the eleven a.m. demonstration again in its place, as that one's sure to be popular.** (99) **I'll put up a notice at the museum entrance to alert visitors to the change.** And in addition to Family Fun Day, today is exciting because we're welcoming a new employee—John Dixon. Hi, John! (100) **He's going to observe some of your tours today so that he can learn how to give them.**

Exeter Science Museum

Family fun Day Demonstrations

9:00 A.M.	Invisible Ink
(98) **11:00 A.M.**	**Homemade Slime**
1:00 P.M.	Glitter Volcano
3:00 P.M.	Miniature Windmill
5:00 P.M.	Rocket Balloon Car

98-100 談話＋時間表 澳

好的，我想讓大家知道一下，今天的示範活動時程表將有變動。不幸的是，我們要用來製作風車葉片的材料未準時送達，因此微型風車的示範活動將會取消。(98) **在該時段，我們已決定再舉行一次早上 11 點的示範活動，因為該活動勢必大受歡迎。**(99) **我會在博物館入口處設置告示，來提醒訪客留意此項變動。**除了有家庭歡樂日，今天另一個讓人振奮的消息，就是我們迎來一名新進同仁——約翰．狄克森。嗨，約翰！(100) **他今天會觀摩你們今天帶領的部分導覽行程，以便學習導覽方法。**

艾克希特科學博物館

家庭歡樂日示範活動

上午 9：00	隱形墨水
(98) **上午 11：00**	**自製史萊姆**
下午 1：00	亮粉火山
下午 3：00	微型風車模型
下午 5：00	火箭氣球車

- demonstration (n.) 示範 material (n.) 材料 construct (v.) 建構 windmill sail 風車葉片 notice (n.) 公告；通知 entrance (n.) 入口處 alert (v.) 提醒；警示

98. 圖表整合題——說話者提及將會舉行兩次的示範活動

Look at the graphic. Which demonstration does the speaker say will take place twice?

(A) Invisible Ink

(B) Homemade Slime

(C) Glitter Volcano

(D) Rocket Balloon Car

請看圖表作答。說話者說何項示範活動會舉行兩次？

(A) 隱形墨水

(B) 自製史萊姆

(C) 亮粉火山

(D) 火箭氣球車

- **homemade (adj.)** 自製的

99. 相關細節——說話者表示他將做的事情

What does the speaker say he will do?

(A) Post an announcement

(B) Lead visitors on a tour

(C) Set up a temporary exhibit

(D) Hand out some badges

說話者表示他會做何事？

(A) 張貼公告

(B) 帶領訪客參觀

(C) 設置臨時展覽

(D) 分發一些徽章

- **post (v.)** 張貼 **announcement (n.)** 公告 **temporary (adj.)** 暫時的 **exhibit (n.)** 展覽 **hand out** 發送

換句話說 put up a notice（設置告示）→ post an announcement（張貼公告）

100. 相關細節——狄克森先生將會觀摩聽者的理由 難

Why will Mr. Dixon observe some of the listeners?

(A) To prepare to write an article

(B) To give performance evaluations

(C) To carry out scientific research

(D) To receive training for his job

狄克森先生為何要觀摩部分聽者？

(A) 以便準備寫文章

(B) 以便做績效評估

(C) 以便執行科學研究

(D) 以便接受工作培訓

- **prepare (v.)** 準備 **article (n.)** 文章 **performance (n.)** 表現 **evaluation (n.)** 評估 **carry out** 執行 **scientific (adj.)** 科學的 **research (n.)** 研究 **receive (v.)** 接受

換句話說 learn how to（學習……方法）→ receive training（接受培訓）

ACTUAL TEST 7

PART 1 P. 80–83

25

1. 單人獨照——描寫人物的動作 澳 

(A) A woman is framing a piece of art.
(B) A woman is removing a lid from a jar.
(C) A woman is kneeling by some decorative objects.
(D) A woman is positioning a vase on a stand.

(A) 女子正在為藝術品裱框。
(B) 女子正在取下罐子的蓋子。
(C) 女子跪在裝飾品旁邊。
(D) 女子正將花瓶放在檯子上。

- frame (v.) 裱框 remove (v.) 取下 lid (n.) 蓋子 jar (n.) 罐子 kneel (v.) 跪下 decorative (adj.) 裝飾的 object (n.) 物品 position (v.) 放置 vase (n.) 花瓶 stand (n.) 檯子

2. 雙人照片——描寫人物的動作 美

(A) They are putting on safety gloves.
(B) They are walking up some steps.
(C) They are using handheld measuring devices.
(D) They are standing close together.

(A) 他們正在戴上安全手套。
(B) 他們正走上階梯。
(C) 他們正在使用手持的測量裝置。
(D) 他們站得很近。

- put on . . . 戴上…… safety (n.) 安全 glove (n.) 手套 step (n.) 階梯 handheld (adj.) 手持的 measuring device 測量裝置

3. 多人照片——描寫人物的動作 加

(A) One of the men is using a pen to take notes.
(B) The woman is reaching for a calculator.
(C) The men are seated across from each other.
(D) One of the men is placing a cup to his mouth.

(A) 其中一名男子在用筆做筆記。
(B) 女子正伸手拿計算機。
(C) 男子坐在彼此對面。
(D) 其中一名男子正拿杯子喝東西。

- take notes 做筆記 reach for . . . 拿…… calculator (n.) 計算機 across from . . . 對面 place (v.) 擺放在

4. 事物與背景照——描寫戶外事物的狀態 英 

(A) Outdoor chairs are arranged in a row.
(B) Patio umbrellas have been closed.
(C) Seat cushions are leaning against a tree.
(D) Tables have been stacked upside down.

(A) 戶外的椅子排成一排。
(B) 露臺的傘已經闔上。
(C) 座墊靠著樹擺放。
(D) 桌子倒立疊放著。

- outdoor (adj.) 戶外 arrange (v.) 陳設 row (n.) 一排 patio (n.) 露臺 lean against . . . 倚靠著…… stack (v.) 疊放 upside down 顛倒

5. 綜合照片——描寫人物或事物 澳 

(A) Some flowers are being packed into a basket.
(B) Some bushes are being lifted out of the ground.
(C) Some potted plants are lined up on shelves.
(D) Some workers are planting a garden.

(A) 有人正將花朵包裝放進籃子。
(B) 有人正從地面上拔起灌木。
(C) 盆栽排列在架上。
(D) 有些工人正在栽植花園。

- pack (v.) 包裝 bush (n.) 灌木 lift (v.) 拔起 ground (n.) 地面 potted plant 盆栽 line up 排列整齊 shelf (n.) 架子（複數為 shelves） plant (v.) 栽植

6. 綜合照片——描寫人物或事物 (美) 難

(A) A display is being stocked with sandwiches.	(A) 有人在展示櫃裡放滿三明治。
(B) Prepared food is being weighed on a scale.	**(B)** 有人在用磅秤秤量調理食品。
(C) Some people are clearing trays from a work area.	(C) 有些人正在收走工作區域的托盤。
(D) Baking tools have been stored in cabinets.	(D) 烘焙用具已被存放在儲物櫃。

- stock (v.) 放滿 weigh (v.) 秤重 scale (n.) 磅秤 tray (n.) 托盤 baking tool 烘焙用具 store (v.) 存放

PART 2 P. 84

26

7. 以 **Who** 開頭的問句，詢問由誰負責櫥窗擺設 (加)⇄(美)

Who's going to organize our shop window this week?	本週是誰要安排本店的櫥窗擺設？
(A) For her organizational skills.	(A) 為了她的組織能力。
(B) They opened last week.	(B) 他們上週開張。
(C) Karen said she would.	**(C)** 凱倫說她會負責。

- organize (v.) 安排；組織 organizational (adj.) 籌備的

8. 以否定疑問句，確認影片是否有背景音樂 (英)⇄(澳)

Shouldn't there be music playing during this video?	這部影片不是應該有配樂嗎？
(A) Once the pop song ends.	(A) 這首流行歌曲結束時即可。
(B) Check if the speakers are turned on.	**(B)** 檢查一下喇叭有沒有開。
(C) There're a few in that drawer.	(C) 抽屜裡有一些。

- once…… (conj.) 一旦…… a few 一些 drawer (n.) 抽屜

9. 以 **How** 開頭的問句，詢問第一季的收益狀況 (加)⇄(美)

How were our revenues for the first quarter?	我們第一季的營收如何？
(A) By giving a brief summary.	(A) 藉由提出簡短摘要。
(B) Here's the report.	**(B)** 報告在這裡。
(C) On Third Avenue.	(C) 在第三大道。

- revenue (n.) 收益 quarter (n.) 季度 brief (adj.) 簡短的

10. 表示建議或提案的問句 (英)⇄(加)

Why don't we have our luncheon at a sushi restaurant?	我們何不在壽司餐廳舉行午餐會議？
(A) Do you know of one nearby?	**(A)** 你知道附近有哪家（壽司餐廳）可去嗎？
(B) The sales director plans to launch it online.	(B) 業務主任預計在線上推出。
(C) The rest of them arrived late.	(C) 其他人遲到。

- luncheon (n.) 午餐會 launch (v.) 推出；啟動 rest (n.) 其餘的人／物

11. 以直述句傳達資訊 (澳)⇄(英)

The copy machine on the second floor is out of order.	二樓的影印機故障了。
(A) You can cancel the order via their Web site.	(A) 你可以透過他們的網站取消訂單。
(B) Denby's Café has good coffee.	(B) 丹比咖啡廳的咖啡很好喝。
(C) I've already called a technician.	**(C)** 我已經聯絡了技術員。

- copy machine 影印機 out of order 故障 order (n.) 訂單 via (prep.) 透過 technician (n.) 技師

12. 以 **Why** 開頭的問句，詢問架上商品過少的理由 美⇄澳 難

Why is there so little merchandise on this shelf?	這個貨架上的商品怎麼那麼少？
(A) Haruki is about to restock it.	**(A) 春樹要來補貨了。**
(B) I think I sold one last year.	(B) 我想我去年賣出一個。
(C) A larger size may be available.	(C) 可能會有較大的尺寸。

13. 表示請託或要求的問句 加⇄英

Could you help me hang these party banners?	可以請你幫我吊掛這些派對布條嗎？
(A) I didn't know you went to that party.	(A) 我不曉得你有去那場派對。
(B) Sure, I can give you a hand.	**(B) 當然好，我可以幫你。**
(C) No, the band didn't play that song.	(C) 不，樂團沒有演奏那首歌

- hang (v.) 吊掛 banner (n.) 橫布條；橫幅 hand (n.) 幫忙

14. 以助動詞 **Does** 開頭的問句，詢問辦公室是否有回收桶 澳⇄美

Does this office have bins for recyclables?	這個辦公室有回收桶嗎？
(A) I've never been on a long cycling trip.	(A) 我從來沒有參加過長途單車旅行。
(B) Their products have improved over the years.	(B) 他們的產品這些年來已有所進步。
(C) Everything goes in the blue container over there.	**(C) 所有垃圾都是丟到那邊的藍色容器。**

- bin (n.) 垃圾桶 recyclable (n.) 資源回收物 improve (v.) 進步 container (n.) 容器

15. 以 **When** 開頭的問句，詢問舉辦免費演奏會的時間 英⇄美 難

When does the symphony orchestra hold its free concerts?	此交響樂團什麼時候會舉辦免費音樂會？
(A) Aren't those often crowded, though?	**(A) 但是那類音樂會，不是常人擠人嗎？**
(B) Yes, I'm a season ticket holder.	(B) 是的，我持有季票。
(C) At various venues throughout the city.	(C) 在市內的各個場地。

- symphony orchestra 交響樂團 crowded (adj.) 擁擠的 though (adv.) 不過；但是 holder (n.) 持有人 various (adj.) 各式各樣的 venue (n.) 場地；會場

16. 以 **Where** 開頭的問句，詢問用品儲藏室的鑰匙放在哪裡 英⇄加 難

Where do you keep the keys to the supply room?	你把用品儲藏室的鑰匙放在哪裡？
(A) On the first day of work.	(A) 第一天上班的時候。
(B) The door should be open.	**(B) 門應該是開的。**
(C) He asked for late check-in.	(C) 他要求延後入住。

- supply room 用品儲藏室

17. 以 **Be** 動詞開頭的問句，詢問交通是否總是處於壅塞狀態 美⇄澳 難

Is the traffic always this heavy here?	這裡的交通一直都這麼壅塞嗎？
(A) Yes, he can't lift them.	(A) 是的，他搬不動這些東西。
(B) It's rush hour.	**(B) 現在是尖峰時間。**
(C) The earlier shipment.	(C) 稍早到貨的貨物。

- traffic (n.) 交通 lift (v.) 拿起來 rush hour 尖峰時間 shipment (n.) 運送的貨物

18. 以 Who 開頭的問句，詢問由誰負責主導下一場研習會 加⇄美

Who's leading the next staff workshop? **(A) The board will decide.** (B) Thanks, I'll read over them. (C) When did you hire him?	誰負責帶領下一場員工研習？ **(A) 將由董事會決定。** (B) 謝謝，我會查閱內容。 (C) 你何時僱用他的？

- lead (v.) 帶領　board (n.) 董事會　read over 查看……的內容

19. 以 Where 開頭的問句，詢問最適合購買平板電腦的地方 英⇄澳

Where is the best place to buy a tablet? (A) They don't use gaming apps that often. **(B) The best deals are from online stores.** (C) You can plug it into this power outlet.	在哪裡買平板電腦會最合適？ (A) 他們不那麼常用遊戲應用程式。 **(B) 網路商店有最划算的交易。** (C) 你可以插到這個電源插座。

- tablet (n.) 平板電腦　that often 那麼常　deal (n.) 交易　power outlet 電源插座

20. 以直述句傳達資訊 美⇄加 難

These photos of the new product line look great. (A) At the main production facility. (B) Most of the phone lines were busy. **(C) We had a professional take them.**	這幾張新系列產品的照片真好看。 (A) 在主要生產設施。 (B) 多數的電話都忙線中。 **(C) 我們有請專業人員來拍照。**

- main (adj.) 主要的　facility (n.) 設施　professional (n.) 專業人員

21. 以否定疑問句確認下雨時是否改期 澳⇄英 難

Isn't there an alternative date for the art festival in case of rain? **(A) It would just be moved indoors.** (B) That isn't one of the exhibition themes. (C) I turned in my submission yesterday.	要是下雨了，藝術嘉年華不會改期舉辦嗎？ **(A) 只是會改到室內舉辦。** (B) 這並不在展覽主題當中。 (C) 我昨天交出資料了。

- alternative (adj.) 替代的　in case of . . . 假使　indoors (adv.) 室內　exhibition (n.) 展覽 theme (n.) 主題　turn in 交出　submission (n.) 提交（的資料）

22. 以 What 開頭的問句，詢問工廠視查的時間 美⇄澳 難

What time is the factory inspection scheduled for? (A) On a first-come, first-served basis. (B) Usually two to three hours. **(C) It may be postponed.**	工廠視察的時間安排在幾點？ (A) 採「先到先服務」的原則。 (B) 通常是二到三小時。 **(C)（時間）可能會延後。**

- inspection (n.) 視察　basis (n.) 基礎　postpone (v.) 延後

23. 以直述句傳達資訊 加⇄英 難

It looks like Conference Room B is double-booked for this afternoon. **(A) It's OK—it's two meetings for the same team.** (B) They don't sell many cooking supplies. (C) You can try requesting a single bedroom instead.	看起來會議室 B 今天下午被重複預訂了。 **(A) 沒關係——是同個團隊要開兩場會。** (B) 他們沒有販售太多烹飪用品。 (C) 你可以試著改要求單人房。

- conference room 會議室　double (adv.) 雙重地　supplies (n.) 用品　request (v.) 要求　instead (adv.) 作為替代

24. 以助動詞 **Have** 開頭的問句，詢問檔案是否已寄送 澳⇄英 難

Have you sent me the Gilliam account file yet?	你傳「吉利安」的帳戶檔案給我了嗎？
(A) That was a mistake—sorry.	(A) 弄錯了——抱歉。
(B) Isn't it on our internal Web site?	**(B) 不是放在我們的內部網站上嗎？**
(C) One hundred and twenty, by my count.	(C) 我算的是一百二十。

- account (n.) 帳戶　internal (adj.) 內部的　count (n.) 計算

25. 以附加問句，確認夾克可否放入洗衣機內清洗 美⇄加

I can put this jacket in the washing machine, right?	我可以把這件夾克放到洗衣機洗，對吧？
(A) Would you like help putting it on?	(A) 需要幫你穿上嗎？
(B) Our collection of winter apparel.	(B) 我們的冬裝系列。
(C) Just make sure it's set to cold water.	**(C) 只要確定水溫設為冷水即可。**

- apparel (n.) 服裝　make sure 確保　be set to . . . 設為……

26. 以選擇疑問句，詢問實習生前來的時間點 澳⇄加

Do the interns arrive Thursday or next Monday?	實習生是週四或下週一過來？
(A) The new application deadline.	(A) 新的申請截止日。
(B) I haven't gotten any updates about that.	**(B) 我還沒收到任何相關更新消息。**
(C) All right, we'll be finished shortly.	(C) 好的，我們很快會完成。

- application (n.) 申請　deadline (n.) 截止日　shortly (adv.) 很快地

27. 以 **Whose** 開頭的問句詢問耳機的主人 澳⇄英

Whose headset is this?	這是誰的頭戴式耳機？
(A) I'm heading the Planning Committee.	(A) 我正要前往規劃委員會。
(B) Mostly for its comfort.	(B) 主要是因為很舒適。
(C) Just set it on the side table.	**(C) 放在茶几上即可。**

- head (v.) 前往　mostly (adv.) 主要地

28. 以 **Why** 開頭的問句，詢問施工中斷的理由 美⇄加

Why was construction stopped on that shopping center project?	那個購物中心專案的工程為什麼停止了？
(A) We can stop somewhere else.	(A) 我們可以在其他地方停下來。
(B) Is there a sale going on now?	(B) 現在有特賣會嗎？
(C) The developer ran out of money.	**(C) 因為開發商資金用完了。**

- construction (n.) 工程　somewhere (n.) 某處　developer (n.) 開發商　run out of . . . 用完……

29. 以直述句傳達資訊 澳⇄美 難

These old documents are finally going to be shredded.	這些舊文件終於要被碎紙處理了。
(A) No, it doesn't need a title page.	(A) 不，不需要有標題頁。
(B) That should free up some space.	**(B) 這樣應該可以騰出一些空間。**
(C) For increasing the font size.	(C) 為了增加字級大小。

- shred (v.) 用碎紙機碎紙　free up 騰出；撥出　increase (v.) 增加

30. 以附加問句確認手冊的設計是否引人注意 (英)⇄(澳)

This brochure design is attractive, isn't it?
(A) I'd prefer a simpler layout, to be honest.
(B) Because the rooftop patio is closed.
(C) No, it's already been assigned to Derek.

這份手冊設計很吸睛，不是嗎？
(A) 老實說，我偏好簡單一點的版面。
(B) 因為頂樓露臺關閉了。
(C) 不，已經被指派給德瑞克了。

- brochure (n.) 手冊　attractive (adj.) 吸睛的　layout (n.) 版面　rooftop (n.) 屋頂　patio (n.) 露臺　assign (v.) 指派

31. 以助動詞 Do 開頭的問句，詢問兩小時是否足以完成所有發表 (加)⇄(美) (難)

Do you think two hours is enough time to fit in all the presentations?
(A) Well, smaller images will fit better on your slides.
(B) That projector is mounted closer to the screen.
(C) As long as none of the speakers run over time.

你覺得兩個小時夠讓所有簡報發表完嗎？
(A) 這個嘛，你的投影片比較適合放較小的圖片。
(B) 那部投影機架設在較靠近螢幕的位置。
(C) 只要講者都沒有超時就可以。

- fit in . . . 完成……　presentation (n.) 簡報　mount (v.) 架設

PART 3 P. 85–88

27

32-34 Conversation

W: Excuse me—do you know if bus number 7 goes to Bryson Rotary?

M: Yes, it does. (32) **Are you trying to get to Valmont Shopping Plaza?**

W: (32) **Actually, yes.** It's near the rotary, right?

M: That's right. This outbound bus will stop in front of the mall. (33) **But there's some paving work underway on the south side of Bryson Rotary.** Bus number 7 coming back this direction is being re-routed away from the rotary. It's confusing, so...

W: Oh, I see.

M: (34) **For your return trip, I'd recommend taking bus number 22 instead.** It stops about two blocks from here.

32-34 對話 (美)⇄(澳)

女： 不好意思——請問你知道 7 號公車是否會到布里森圓環嗎？

男： 會的，會到那裡。(32) **妳是想去佛蒙特購物廣場嗎？**

女： (32) **其實是的**，那裡就在圓環附近，對嗎？

男： 沒錯，去程公車會停靠在購物廣場前面。(33) **不過布里森圓環的南側，正在進行一些鋪路工程**，因此 7 號公車朝這個方向開回來時，會改道繞過圓環。這還蠻複雜的，所以說……。

女： 噢，我了解了。

男： (34) **妳回程的時候，我建議你改搭 22 號公車**，會停靠在離這裡約兩個街區的地方。

- rotary (n.) 環形交叉口　outbound (adj.) 向外的　pave (v.) 鋪（路）　underway (adj.) 進行中的　direction (n.) 方向　re-route (v.) 改變路線

32. 相關細節——女子準備要前往的地點

Where most likely is the woman going?
(A) To a shopping mall
(B) To a city park
(C) To a conference center
(D) To a railway terminal

女子最有可能要前往何處？
(A) 購物中心
(B) 市立公園
(C) 會議中心
(D) 火車總站

換句話說 Valmont Shopping Plaza（佛蒙特購物廣場）→ a shopping mall（購物中心）

33. 相關細節——針對布里森圓環提及的事情 難

What is mentioned about Bryson Rotary?
(A) It usually has heavy traffic.
(B) It is the site of a city festival.
(C) It has a subway stop.
(D) It is partially under construction.

對話裡提及了布里森圓環的何項資訊？
(A) 通常交通壅塞。
(B) 是城市節慶活動的舉辦地。
(C) 設有地鐵站。
(D) 有部分區域在施工。

- site (n.) 地點　partially (adv.) 部分地　construction (n.) 工程

換句話說 some paving work underway（進行一些鋪路工程）
→ partially under construction（部分區域在施工）

34. 相關細節——男子提出的建議

What does the man recommend doing?
(A) Parking in a garage
(B) Walking along a pedestrian street
(C) Returning via a different bus route
(D) Postponing a trip for a few hours

男子建議什麼做法？
(A) 在車庫停車。
(B) 沿著徒步區步行。
(C) 搭乘不同路線的公車回程。
(D) 將行程延後幾小時。

- garage (n.) 車庫　pedestrian (adj.) 步行的　via . . . (prep.) 藉由……　postpone (v.) 延後

換句話說 taking bus number 22 instead（改搭 22 號公車）
→ via a different bus route（搭乘不同路線的公車）

35-37 Conversation

M: Hi, Samantha. (35) **I just finished setting up all the displays for all the eco-friendly apparel we stock here in the store.**

W: I see. They look great. (36) **We'll put the collection boxes for Saturday's recycling initiative right in front of those windows.** That way, people will notice those brands when they're dropping off their old clothing.

M: Excellent. Oh, that reminds me . . . (37) **I have to print out the 10%-off coupons we're giving each customer who brings in used items. I'll do that right now.**

35-37 對話 澳⇄英

男： 嗨，莎曼珊，**(35) 我剛剛把店裡進貨的所有環保服飾，都擺到展示區就定位了。**

女： 了解，擺得很漂亮。**(36) 星期六我們舉辦回收活動時，就要把回收收集箱放在這些櫥窗的正前方，**這樣大家在投入舊衣的時候，就會注意到那些品牌。

男： 太棒了。噢，那倒是提醒了我……**(37) 我必須印出九折優惠券，來發給每名帶二手商品過來的顧客。我現在就去進行。**

- set up 設置　eco-friendly (adj.) 環保的　apparel (n.) 服飾　stock (v.) 進貨；存貨　collection (n.) 收集　recycle (v.) 回收　initiative (n.) 計劃　notice (v.) 注意　drop off 放入　used (adj.) 二手的

35. 全文相關——說話者的工作地點

Where most likely do the speakers work?
(A) At a fitness center
(B) At a home furnishings store
(C) At a coffee shop
(D) At a clothing store

說話者最有可能在哪裡工作？
(A) 健身中心
(B) 家具設備店
(C) 咖啡廳
(D) 服飾店

換句話說 apparel（服飾）→ clothing（服飾）

36. 相關細節——將於週六發生的事情

What is scheduled to take place Saturday?
(A) A grand opening celebration
(B) A safety inspection
(C) A closure for inventory
(D) A recycling collection event

星期六預計進行什麼活動？
(A) 隆重開幕會
(B) 安全檢查
(C) 關店盤點存貨
(D) 回收物收集活動

- inspection (n.) 視察　closure (n.) 關店　inventory (n.) 存貨

37. 相關細節——男子表示接下來要做的事情

What does the man say he will do next?
(A) Prepare some discount vouchers
(B) Place some boxes in storage
(C) Update a planning spreadsheet
(D) Process a customer refund

男子說他接下來要做什麼？
(A) 準備一些折價券
(B) 將一些箱子放到儲藏室
(C) 更新規劃試算表
(D) 處理顧客退款

- voucher (n.) 優惠券　storage (n.) 儲藏　spreadsheet (n.) 試算表　process (v.) 處理　refund (n.) 退款

換句話說 print out the 10%-off coupons（印出九折優惠券）
→ prepare some discount vouchers（準備一些折價券）

38-40 Conversation

W: Hi, welcome to the Electric Bike Superstore. How can I help you?

M: (38) **Well, I'm a do-it-yourself enthusiast and would like to buy an electric cargo bike to bring lumber and bricks home from the hardware store.** I'd want the model with the biggest carrying capacity.

W: Your best choice would be the Y10. It's durable and has a long-lasting battery. (39) **Its one drawback is that it's quite large and requires a lot of storage space.**

M: Can I see one?

W: Sure, follow me. (40) **Also . . . this week only, our store will attach any accessories, including cargo baskets, to your bike at no charge.**

38-40 對話

美⇄加

女： 您好，歡迎光臨電動單車超級商店。有什麼需要服務的嗎？

男： (38) **就是說呢，我很熱愛手作工藝，想買一台電動載貨單車，用來從五金行把木材、磚材載回家，**我想找提供最大載貨量的車款。

女： 最適合您需求的車款是 Y10，耐操耐用，又有強大的電池續航力，(39) **唯一缺點就是車身相當大，會佔蠻大空間。**

男： 我可以看一下嗎？

女： 沒問題，請跟我來。(40) **還有……本店這週有限定活動，會免費為您購買的單車加裝各類配件，包括載貨籃在內喔。**

- electric (adj.) 電動的　do-it-yourself (n.) 自己動手做　enthusiast (n.) 狂熱者　cargo (n.) 貨物　lumber (n.) 木材　brick (n.) 磚頭　hardware store 五金行　capacity (n.) 容量　durable (adj.) 耐用的　long-lasting (adj.) 持久的　drawback (n.) 缺點　storage (n.) 存放　attach (v.) 使隨附　accessory (n.) 配件

38. 相關細節——男子欲購買電動單車的理由 難

Why does the man want to purchase an electric bike?
(A) To add to a city's bike-share program
(B) To replace an older sport bike
(C) To transport building materials
(D) To shorten his daily commute

男子為何想購買電動單車？
(A) 想加入城市的單車共享計畫。
(B) 想替代較舊的運動單車。
(C) 想運送建材。
(D) 想縮短每日通勤時間。

- purchase (v.) 購買　share (v.) 共享　replace (v.) 替代　transport (v.) 運送　material (n.) 材料　shorten (v.) 縮短　commute (n.) 通勤

換句話說 bring lumber and bricks（把木材、磚材載回）→ transport building materials（運送建材）

39. 相關細節——女子提及 Y10 單車的缺點

According to the woman, what is a disadvantage of the Y10 bike?
(A) Its size
(B) Its appearance
(C) Its battery life
(D) Its cost

根據女子所說，Y10 單車的缺點是什麼？
(A) 尺寸
(B) 外觀
(C) 電池壽命
(D) 費用

40. 相關細節——女子提及本週店內提供的東西

What does the woman say the store is offering that week?
(A) Trial use of a charging station
(B) Extended warranties on bikes
(C) Reduced prices for repair services
(D) Free installation of accessories

女子表示商店當週提供什麼？
(A) 試用充電站
(B) 單車延長保固
(C) 維修服務費用調降
(D) 配件免費安裝

- trial (adj.) 試用的　charge (v.) 充電　extend (v.) 延長　warranty (n.) 保固期　reduce (v.) 降低　repair (n.) 維修　installation (n.) 裝設

41-43 Conversation

M: Hi, Myra. (41) **Some of the customer service representatives I oversee have pointed out an issue with our order entry software.** Uh . . .

W: What exactly is the problem?

M: Some promotional discounts aren't being applied properly. I tried to update the pricing feature of the program, but . . .

W: Oh, I've done that before. (42) **What happens with the program is that it has trouble processing promotional discounts without additional information.**

41-43 對話 澳⇄美

男： 嗨，米拉，(41) **有幾名我管理的客服員，都提出說我們的訂單輸入軟體有個問題**，這……

女： 具體來說，出了什麼問題呢？

男： 有些促銷折扣目前無法正確套用，我有試過更新程式的定價功能，但是……

女： 噢，那個問題我以前處理過，(42) **這種狀況是出在如果沒有額外資料，程式就無法處理促銷折扣。**

M: I see.	男： 原來如此。
W: On the screen, go to the window that says, "assign discount" and select the products that it applies to. (43) **You'll want to look at the instruction manual as you do it to ensure everything is accurate.**	女： 請點選螢幕上的「指定折扣」視窗，並選擇要套用折扣的產品。(43) **你也會需要在操作時查閱使用手冊，以便確保正確完成每個步驟。**

- representative (n.) 代表人　oversee (v.) 管理；帶領　entry (n.) 輸入　promotional (adj.) 促銷的　apply (v.) 套用　price (v.) 給……定價　feature (n.) 功能　process (v.) 處理　additional (adj.) 額外的　assign (v.) 指派　instruction manual 使用手冊　ensure (v.) 確保　accurate (adj.) 正確的；準確的

TEST 7

PART 3

41. 全文相關——男子的身分

Who most likely is the man?

(A) A customer service manager

(B) A software designer

(C) A shipping clerk

(D) An event planner

男子最有可能是什麼身分？

(A) 客服經理

(B) 軟體設計師

(C) 運務員

(D) 活動企劃

---

42. 掌握說話者的意圖——提及「那個問題我以前處理過」的意圖 難

Why most likely does the woman say, "I've done that before"?

(A) To argue that a task must be possible

(B) To acknowledge a mistake she made

(C) To explain why she is working alone

(D) To show understanding of a problem

女子會說：「那個問題我以前處理過」，最有可能的原因為何？

(A) 主張一項任務絕對可行

(B) 承認自己犯的錯誤

(C) 說明獨自工作的原因

(D) 對一項問題表示理解

- argue (v.) 主張　task (n.) 任務　acknowledge (v.) 承認

---

43. 相關細節——女子提出的建議

What does the woman suggest doing?

(A) Asking a team leader for additional help

(B) Referring to an instruction book during a process

(C) Sending a product back to its manufacturer

(D) Keeping a record of some actions

女子建議怎麼做？

(A) 要求團隊領導人額外協助

(B) 在進行程序時參考使用手冊

(C) 將產品寄回給製造商

(D) 保留一些動作的紀錄

- refer to . . . 參考　process (n.) 程序　manufacturer (n.) 製造商

換句話說 look at the instruction manual as you do it（在操作時查閱使用手冊）
→ referring to an instruction book during a process（在進行程序時參考使用手冊）

44-46 Conversation with three speakers

44-46 三人對話

英⇄澳⇄加

W: (44) **Thank you again, Mr. Taylor, for coming over today. Will you need to make another visit to finish the job?**	女： (44) **再次感謝你今天過來一趟，泰勒先生。你有需要再來一次，把工作完成嗎？**
M1: (44) **No, it's all done now. Your sink simply needed a new washer for the faucet. It was an easy fix.**	男 1： (44) **不需要的，目前都處理好了。您的水槽只是需要幫水龍頭換新的墊圈，很容易就修好了。**

W: Wow, that was fast. Your service is outstanding. **(45) I'll definitely tell my friends to call you when they have a plumbing problem.**	**女：** 哇，速度好快，你的服務真的太出色了。**(45) 我一定會跟朋友說，如果有水電問題，打電話找你就對了。**
M1: Oh, thank you.	**男 1：** 噢，謝謝妳。
W: Sure. And Tom, you had a question, right?	**女：** 不客氣。那麼湯姆，你有問題想問，是嗎？
M2: Yes. **(46) Mr. Taylor, I'm wondering roughly what you would charge to put in a new showerhead—you know, the kind that saves water.**	**男 2：** 是的，**(46) 泰勒先生，我想知道，若請你裝設新的蓮蓬頭，大概會收費多少？你知道，就是那種省水的蓮蓬頭。**
M1: Yes, that would be about sixty dollars for materials and installation.	**男 1：** 好的，材料費和安裝費用大約需要 60 美元。

- washer (n.) 墊圈　faucet (n.) 水龍頭　outstanding (adj.) 出色的　plumbing (n.) 水電　wonder (v.) 想知道　roughly (adv.) 大概　charge (v.) 收費　showerhead (n.) 蓮蓬頭　installation (n.) 安裝

44. 相關細節——泰勒先生剛完成的事情

What did Mr. Taylor just finish doing?
(A) Cleaning a power tool
(B) Unloading a truck
(C) Landscaping a yard
(D) Repairing a sink

泰勒先生剛完成何事？
(A) 清理電動工具
(B) 卸貨貨車
(C) 庭院造景工程
(D) 修理水槽

換句話說 fix（修）→ repairing（修理）

---

45. 相關細節——女子提及她將會做的事情

What does the woman say she will do?
(A) Organize a neighborhood event
(B) Refer others to Mr. Taylor's business
(C) Pay for services with a credit card
(D) Move a parked vehicle

女子說她會做何事？
(A) 籌備社區活動
(B) 向他人推薦泰勒先生的生意
(C) 以信用卡支付服務費
(D) 移動停靠的車輛

- organize (v.) 籌備　refer (v.) 推薦

換句話說 tell my friends to call . . .（跟朋友說打電話找……）→ refer others to（向他人推薦）

---

46. 相關細節——湯姆向泰勒先生要求的的東西

What does Tom ask Mr. Taylor for?
(A) A cost estimate
(B) A regular client discount
(C) A printed receipt
(D) A copy of a contract

湯姆向泰勒先生詢問什麼事？
(A) 費用估價
(B) 常客折扣
(C) 紙本收據
(D) 合約副本

- estimate (n.) 估算　regular client 常客　receipt (n.) 收據　contract (n.) 合約

換句話說 roughly what you would charge（大概會收費多少）→ a cost estimate（費用估價）

47-49 Conversation

47-49 對話 美⇄加

W: Hi, is there anything I can help you find here in the gift shop?

M: Yes, [(47)] **do you have any books with photos of your museum's permanent exhibits?**

W: Sure, there's this one here titled *Highlights of the City History Museum*. [(48)] **It has a whole chapter devoted to our collection of vintage memorabilia that trace the history of athletics in the region—no other area museum has exhibits like this.**

M: Interesting. I'd like to purchase it.

W: Great. [(49)] **I'll get a new, sealed copy for you from this cabinet. I have to ask the store manager for a key to open it**—just one moment.

女：您好，請問在我們禮品店有在找什麼嗎？我可以幫忙。

男：是的，[(47)] **你們有沒有什麼書籍，裡面收錄貴博物館常設展覽品的照片呢？**

女：當然有，這裡有本《市立歷史博物館的亮點》，[(48)] **裡面有一整個章節，專門介紹追溯本地區體育活動歷史的復古紀念品館藏——其他的地方博物館都看不到這類展品。**

男：很有意思，我想買這本。

女：太好了。[(49)] **我幫您從櫃子裡拿取一本全新、密封好的一冊。我得要請店長拿鑰匙來開櫃子**——請稍等一下。

- **permanent (adj.)** 固定的；永久的 **exhibit (n.)** 展覽品 **title (v.)** 給……取標題 **devote (v.)** 將……專用於 **collection (n.)** 收藏 **vintage (adj.)** 復古的 **memorabilia (n.)** 紀念品 **trace (v.)** 追溯 **athletics (n.)** 體育運動 **region (n.)** 區域

47. 相關細節——男子提及他正在找尋的東西

What does the man say he is looking for?

(A) A souvenir T-shirt

(B) A camera carrying bag

(C) An illustrated guidebook

(D) A set of drawing tools

男子說他正在找什麼東西？

(A) 紀念 T 恤

(B) 攝影機收納袋

(C) 圖解導覽書

(D) 一組畫具

- **souvenir (n.)** 紀念品 **illustrated (adj.)** 圖示的 **guidebook (n.)** 指南手冊 **drawing (n.)** 繪畫 **tool (n.)** 工具

換句話說 books with photos（收錄照片的書籍）→ an illustrated guidebook（圖解導覽書）

---

48. 相關細節——女子提及該博物館的特別之處 難

According to the woman, why is the museum special?

(A) It has free admission.

(B) It is the city's oldest museum.

(C) It has exhibits on sporting history.

(D) It allows visitors to take photographs.

根據女子說法，博物館為何特殊？

(A) 可以免費入場。

(B) 是該都市歷史最悠久的博物館。

(C) 有運動歷史的展覽品

(D) 允許遊客拍照。

- **admission (n.)** 入場 **allow (v.)** 允許

換句話說 athletics（體育活動）→ sporting（體育）

---

49. 相關細節——女子要向店長拿取的東西

What will the woman ask a manager for?

(A) A product code

(B) A key to a cabinet

(C) Some gift wrapping

(D) Some business cards

女子將向店長索取何物？

(A) 產品代碼

(B) 櫃子鑰匙

(C) 禮品包裝

(D) 名片

50-52 Conversation

50-52 對話 澳⇄英

M: Hi, Mona. (50) **We have a production problem with our line of spices that are packaged in the smallest sized jars**—our company label is being applied crookedly. It's strange because there are no issues with the labeling for our cans of pasta sauce.

W: Oh, that happens with Labeling Machine Number 2. (51) **You need to slow down its conveyor belt by changing the settings manually. I can help you with that.**

M: That would be great. It'll take time to resolve the issue, right? So we won't have much of that product to package this morning. (52) **I'll go to the packaging area and tell that team to take a break.**

男：嗨，夢娜，(50) **我們最小容量的罐裝系列香料，製造上發生了問題**：我們公司的標籤貼得歪七扭八。實在很奇怪，因為義大利麵醬的罐頭標籤，貼得並沒有問題。

女：噢，2 號標籤機會有這個狀況。(51) **你必須手動更改設定值，來放慢輸送帶的速度，我可以幫你處理。**

男：那就太好了。要解決這個問題，會需要點時間，對嗎？所以針對這項產品，我們今天早上就不會有太多貨量需要包裝，(52) **我會去到包裝區，跟團隊同仁說可稍作休息。**

- production (n.) 生產　spice (n.) 香料　package (v.) 包裝　jar (n.) 玻璃罐　label (n./v.)（貼）標籤　apply (v.) 貼上；塗上　crookedly (adv.) 歪斜地　manually (adv.) 手動地　resolve (v.) 解決　break (n.) 休息

50. 相關細節——說話者公司所生產的產品 難

What does the speakers' company most likely manufacture?

(A) Soft drinks

(B) Skincare products

(C) Eating utensils

(D) Food seasonings

說話者的公司最有可能製造什麼？

(A) 無酒精飲料

(B) 皮膚保養品

(C) 餐具

(D) 食物調味料

換句話說 spices（香料）→ food seasonings（食物調味料）

51. 相關細節——女子協助男子做的事情 難

What will the woman help the man do?

(A) Place products into shipping boxes

(B) Adjust a machine's operating speed

(C) Change the design of a logo

(D) Order additional equipment

女子會幫忙男子何事？

(A) 將產品放到出貨箱

(B) 調整機器運作速度

(C) 更改標誌的設計

(D) 訂購額外設備

- place (v.) 放置　adjust (v.) 調整　operate (v.) 運作　additional (adj.) 額外的　equipment (n.) 設備

換句話說 slow down its conveyor belt（放慢輸送帶的速度）
→ adjust a machine's operating speed（調整機器運作速度）

52. 相關細節——男子接下來會做的事

What will the man most likely do next?

(A) Phone a company technician

(B) Search for an instruction manual

(C) Inform a team of a work interruption

(D) Choose an alternative type of packaging

男子接下來最有可能做什麼事？

(A) 打電話給公司技師

(B) 尋找指導手冊

(C) 告知團隊作業中斷

(D) 選擇替代的包裝類型

- phone (v.) 打電話　technician (n.) 技術人員　search for 尋找　instruction manual 指導手冊
inform (v.) 告知　interruption (n.) 中斷　alternative (adj.) 替代的

換句話說 tell that team to take a break（跟團隊同仁說可稍作休息）
→ inform a team of a work interruption（告知團隊作業中斷）

53-55 Conversation with three speakers

M: Thank you, both, for stopping by my office. (53) **I recently did a walk-through of our largest property, Eastern Shopping Mall, and, well . . . the store directory and interior directional signs could be a lot better.**

W1: I noticed that recently too. Some are quite confusing. (54) **I'm actually running a focus group meeting next week with some of the owners of the shops in the mall.** Hopefully, they'll provide useful input. And Susan, you have an idea, right?

W2: Well, (55) **I used to work with Drew Hiller. He runs a firm that advises clients about design considerations for signs. I could get in touch with him.**

M: Yes, that's an excellent idea.

53-55 三人對話　加⇄美⇄英

男： 謝謝兩位過來我的辦公室。(53) **我最近實地訪查了我們規模最大的物業「東方購物中心」，然後，怎麼說……店櫃導覽和店內的方向引導標誌設計，都可以有很大改善空間。**

女 1： 這方面我最近也有注意到。有些設計十分讓人暈頭轉向。(54) **其實，我已準備在下週和購物中心的數名店櫃業主，舉辦焦點團體會議**，希望他們能提供實用的見解。還有，蘇珊，妳有個想法，對嗎？

女 2： 嗯，(55) **我曾和德魯．希勒合作過，他經營的公司，專門就標誌設計的考量提供建議給客戶，我可以和他接洽。**

男： 好的，這個主意很棒。

- walk-through (n.) 走訪視察　property (n.) 物業；房地產　directory (n.) 指南　interior (adj.) 室內的
directional (adj.) 指示方向的　notice (v.) 注意　focus group 焦點團體　hopefully (adv.) 但願……
input (n.) 見解　firm (n.) 公司　advise (v.) 建議　consideration (n.) 考量
get in touch with . . . 與……聯絡

53. 相關細節——男子提及需要改善的地方 難

According to the man, what needs improvement?
(A) A promotional flyer
(B) Some guidance signs
(C) Some outdoor gardens
(D) A restaurant in a food court

根據男子說法，何者需要改善？
(A) 促銷傳單
(B) 引導標誌
(C) 戶外花園
(D) 美食街的餐廳

- promotional (adj.) 促銷的　flyer (n.) 傳單　guidance (n.) 引導　outdoor (adj.) 戶外的

54. 相關細節——下週參加焦點團體的人

Who most likely will participate in next week's focus group?
(A) Maintenance workers
(B) Mall shoppers
(C) Store owners
(D) Real estate developers

何人最有可能參加下週的焦點團體？
(A) 維修工人
(B) 購物中心消費者
(C) 店家業主
(D) 房地產開發商

55. 相關細節——蘇珊提出的建議

What does Susan offer to do?
(A) Contact a consultant
(B) Post notices in a building
(C) Lead a training session
(D) Redesign a questionnaire

蘇珊提議做什麼事？
(A) 聯絡顧問
(B) 在大樓張貼公告
(C) 帶領培訓課程
(D) 重新設計問卷

- post (v.) 張貼 notice (n.) 公告 session (n.) 集會 questionnaire (n.) 問卷

換句話說 get in touch with（和……接洽）→ contact（聯絡）

56-58 Conversation

56-58 對話 美⇄加

W: **(56) Dan, we've gotten some employee feedback about the floor plan of our office.** And fortunately, it seems that most of the staff likes our setup.

M: That's encouraging. **(57) Any issues that stand out?**

W: **(57) Yes, our data analysts complained that it's difficult to locate previous research reports, because they're stored in the large filing cabinets in the research room. That's rather far from our work area.**

M: Oh, that is a problem.

W: **(58) Mr. Kim, the office manager, could buy a small bookshelf for this office. We could put the more recent reports there. I'll ask him to do that.**

女：**(56) 丹，我們已經收到部分員工針對我們辦公室的平面圖，所提出的意見反饋。**幸好大多數同仁似乎都喜歡我們的安排。

男：這話有如強心針。**(57) 有需要特別注意的問題嗎？**

女：**(57) 有的，我們的資料分析師抱怨說，要查找過往的研究報告會蠻困難的，因為這些報告存放在研究室的大型檔案櫃，那裡離我們的工作區域有點遠。**

男：噢，這倒是個問題。

女：**(58) 辦公室經理金先生，可以幫這間辦公室購買小型書架，我們可以把較近期的報告放在那裡，我會請他去進行。**

- floor plan 平面圖 seem (v.) 看似 setup (n.) 安排；設置 encouraging (adj.) 振奮人心的 stand out 特別突顯 analyst (n.) 分析師 locate (v.) 找尋 previous (adj.) 過往的 research (n.) 研究 store (v.) 存放 bookshelf (n.) 書架

56. 全文相關——對話主題

What are the speakers mainly discussing?
(A) A new work-from-home policy
(B) The layout of a workplace
(C) An upcoming video shoot
(D) New procedures for collecting data

說話者主要在討論什麼？
(A) 在家工作的新政策
(B) 工作場所的配置
(C) 即將進行的影片拍攝
(D) 用以收集資料的新程序

- policy (n.) 政策 workplace (n.) 工作場域 upcoming (adj.) 即將到來的 shoot (n.) 拍攝 procedure (n.) 程序

換句話說 he floor plan of our office（我們辦公室的平面圖）
→ the layout of a workplace（工作場所的配置）

57. 相關細節——女子回報的問題

What problem does the woman report?

(A) Some documents are hard to access.

(B) Some employees have long commutes to work.

(C) Some storage areas have no more space.

(D) Some hallways are often noisy.

女子回報了什麼問題？

(A) 有些文件難以取用。

(B) 有些員工的通勤時間長。

(C) 有些儲藏區的空間不夠。

(D) 有些走廊常有吵雜聲。

- **access (v.)** 接近；使用 **commute (n.)** 通勤 **hallway (n.)** 走廊

換句話說 **it's difficult to locate previous research reports**（要查找過往的研究報告會變困難的）
→ **Some documents are hard to access**（有些文件難以取用）

---

58. 相關細節——女子將要求金先生做的事情

What will the woman ask Mr. Kim to do?

(A) Move to a smaller office

(B) Purchase a piece of furniture

(C) Revise a research report

(D) Extend a submission deadline

女子會請金先生做什麼？

(A) 搬到較小的辦公室

(B) 購買一件家具

(C) 修改研究報告

(D) 延後繳交期限

- **purchase (v.)** 購買 **revise (v.)** 修改 **extend (v.)** 延長 **submission (n.)** 提交

換句話說 **buy a small bookshelf**（購買小型書架）→ **purchase a piece of furniture**（購買一件家具）

59-61 Conversation

M: Hi, Sarah. [59] **We've gotten a lot of compliments from customers in the three weeks since we added organic baked goods to our other health food selections.**

W: Good to hear. [60] **I'm wondering what else we can do to build interest in our business.**

M: I've been thinking about that too, and . . . other organic grocery stores have hands-on cooking classes.

W: Hmm. [60] **That's something worth exploring.** We had Isaiah, our herbal gardening expert, come in and answer customers' questions, but that's about it. OK, well . . .

M: Let's definitely consider it. [61] **Right now, I'll head over to the Kelley orchard down the road to pick up some blueberries for the store.**

59-61 對話

澳⇄英

男： 嗨，莎拉。[59] **自從我們在精選健康食品專區，新增有機烘焙產品後，這三週以來大獲顧客好評。**

女： 真是好消息。[60] **我正在思考我們還能怎麼做，來引發顧客對我們公司的興趣。**

男： 我也一直在想這件事，而說到這……其他有機生鮮食品店有舉辦手作料理課程。

女： 唔，[60] **還蠻值得深入探討。**我們以前請過香草園藝專家以賽亞，來現場回答顧客的問題，但也僅止於此。好吧，那麼……

男： 我們務必考慮看看。[61] **現在的話，我要去街口的凱利果園，幫店裡採買一些藍莓。**

- **compliment (n.)** 讚賞 **organic (adj.)** 有機的 **baked goods** 烘焙商品 **wonder (v.)** 想知道
hands-on (adj.) 親身實踐的 **worth (adj.)** 值得…… **explore (v.)** 探索；探究
herbal (adj.) 香草的；藥草的 **gardening (n.)** 園藝 **that's (about) it** 僅止於此 **head (v.)** 前往
orchard (n.) 果園

59. 相關細節——說話者的公司最近做的事情

What did the speakers' business do recently?
(A) Expanded its range of products
(B) Held an anniversary celebration
(C) Joined an industry association
(D) Renovated a shopping area

說話者的公司最近做了什麼？
(A) 拓展產品範圍
(B) 舉辦週年慶
(C) 加入產業協會
(D) 翻修了購物區

- expand (v.) 拓展　anniversary (n.) 週年紀念　celebration (n.) 慶祝　industry (n.) 產業　association (n.) 協會　renovate (v.) 整修

換句話說 added . . . goods to our . . . selections（在我們的專區新增產品）
→ expanded its range of products（拓展產品範圍）

60. 掌握說話者的意圖——提及「其他有機生鮮食品店有舉辦手作料理課程」的意圖 難

Why most likely does the man say, "other organic grocery stores have hands-on cooking classes"?
(A) To show surprise at a local trend
(B) To suggest offering in-store activities
(C) To highlight the health benefits of organic foods
(D) To express doubt about the effectiveness of a promotion

男子會說：「其他有機生鮮食品店有舉辦手作料理課程」，最有可能的原因為何？
(A) 對於當地趨勢表達驚訝
(B) 建議提供店內活動
(C) 強調有機食品的健康益處
(D) 表達對促銷效果的疑慮

- in-store (adj.) 店內的　highlight (v.) 強調　benefit (n.) 益處　effectiveness (n.) 效果　promotion (n.) 促銷

61. 相關細節——男子接下來要做的事情 難

What will the man probably do next?
(A) Water some plants
(B) Visit a nearby farm
(C) Clear off a display shelf
(D) Request a catalog

男子接下來很可能會做什麼？
(A) 幫植物澆水
(B) 造訪鄰近的農場
(C) 清理展示架
(D) 索取型錄

- water (v.) 澆水　nearby (adj.) 鄰近的　clear off 清理

換句話說 head over to the . . . orchard down the road（去街口的果園）
→ visit a nearby farm（造訪鄰近的農場）

62-64 Conversation + Map

M: Megan, I've updated our Web site. (62) **On the homepage, I added a quote from the article in *City-Life Review* that named us the best property management company in the area.**

W: Good. (63) **Next Tuesday I'll interview Anna Lopez, the owner of the flower shop nearby, for our neighborhood guide section of our site.**

M: Ah, I almost forgot . . . Here is a map I made—it shows four of the district's favorite restaurants. See?

62-64 對話＋地圖 加⇄英

男： 梅根，我已經更新我們的網站。(62) **在網站首頁，我新增了取自《都市生活評論》的文章引言，內容將我們選為本地區最佳的房地產管理公司。**

女： 做得好。(63) **我下週二會去訪問鄰近花店的老闆安娜・羅培茲，內容會用在網站上的「鄰里導覽」區塊。**

男： 啊，我差點忘了……這是我做的地圖，圖中標示出本地區最受歡迎的四家餐廳，看看覺得如何？

W: Oh, there's one problem. (64) **The Italian restaurant on Main Street just moved—it's next door to the Korean place on Fir Street now.**

M: OK. I'll change that part then.

女： 噢，有個問題。(64) **緬因街的義大利餐廳剛遷址——現在已經搬到佛爾街的韓式料理店隔壁。**

男： 好的，那我修改這個部分。

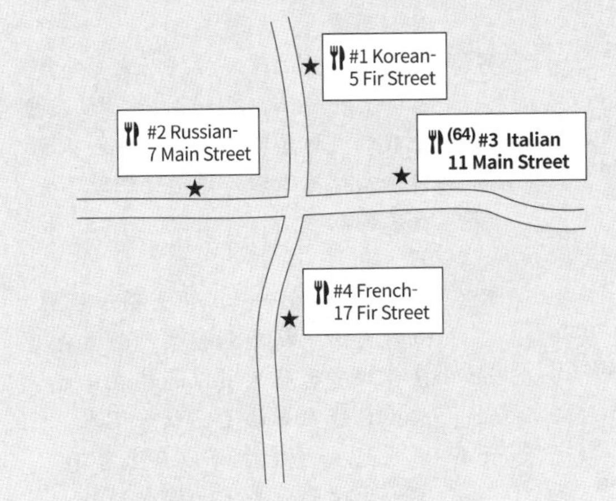

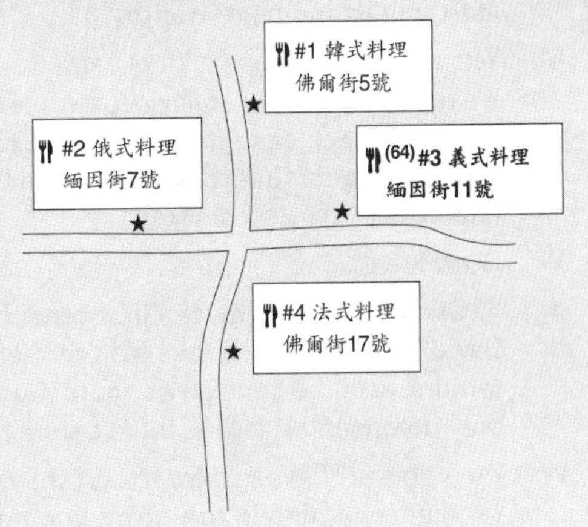

- **quote** (n.) 引言 **property** (n.) 房地產 **nearby** (adj./adv.) 鄰近的（地） **neighborhood** (n.) 鄰里 **guide** (n.) 導覽 **section** (n.) 分區 **district** (n.) 地區

62. 相關細節——男子放上公司網站的東西

難

What does the man say he put on the business's Web site?

(A) A link

(B) An apology

(C) Some praise

(D) Some prices

男子表示他在公司網站上放上了什麼？

(A) 連結

(B) 道歉訊息

(C) 讚譽

(D) 價目

---

63. 相關細節——女子表示她下週將會做的事情

What does the woman say she will do next week?

(A) Arrange a staff appreciation party

(B) Speak with a local business owner

(C) Purchase a navigation device

(D) View some vacant apartments

女子表示她下週要做什麼事？

(A) 安排職員感恩派對

(B) 和當地店家老闆對談

(C) 購買導航裝置

(D) 查看幾間公寓空房

- **arrange** (v.) 安排 **appreciation** (n.) 感恩 **device** (n.) 裝置 **vacant** (adj.) 空出的

換句話說 **interview the owner of the flower shop nearby**（訪問鄰近花店的老闆）
→ **speak with a local business owner**（和當地店家老闆對談）

---

64. 圖表整合題——不再正確的號碼

Look at the graphic. Which location number is no longer accurate?

(A) #1

(B) #2

(C) #3

(D) #4

請看圖表作答。哪一個地點的編號不再正確？

(A) 1 號

(B) 2 號

(C) 3 號

(D) 4 號

65-67 Conversation + Schedule

W: I'm all ready for tomorrow's interviews. (65) **We have to hire someone soon to help with the bimonthly special issues that we're going to start publishing next month.**

M: Yes, that's going to be a lot of extra work. We really need the interviews to go smoothly. (66) **I'll text each candidate a link to a map of our building so that they don't have trouble finding us.**

W: Good idea.

M: (67) **Oh, and by the way, the first candidate, David Meyer, will also take his proofreading test tomorrow in the conference room. So we can only do one interview in there before lunch.**

W: No problem. (67) **We can interview the other candidate coming in tomorrow morning in a small meeting room.**

Interview Schedule
Conference Room

David Meyer	10:00 A.M.
(67) **Erica Yang**	**11:00 A.M.**
LUNCH BREAK	12:00 P.M.-1:00 P.M.
Lance Dedham	1:30 P.M.
Joy Nelson	3:00 P.M.

65-67 對話＋日程表 美⇄澳

女：我已經準備好進行明天的面試了。(65) **我們需要快點僱用人手，來幫忙處理下個月要開始出版的特別號雙月刊事宜。**

男：是的，額外工作將接踵而來，我們真的要確保面試順利進行。(66) **我會把我們大樓地圖的連結，透過訊息傳給每位應徵者，這樣他們就不會找不到路。**

女：好主意。

男：(67) **噢，順帶一提，明天第一位應徵者大衛・梅爾的校稿測驗，也會在會議室進行，所以我們在午餐前，只能在會議室面試一個人。**

女：沒問題，(67) **我們可以在小會議室，面試明天早上會過來的另一名應徵者。**

面試時間表
會議室

大衛・梅爾	早上10點
(67) 艾瑞卡・楊	**早上11點**
午餐休息時間	中午12點至下午1點
蘭斯・戴德漢	下午1點30分
喬伊・尼爾森	下午3點

- hire (v.) 僱用　bimonthly (adj.) 雙月刊的　issue (n.)（刊物的）期；號　publish (v.) 出版　smoothly (adv.) 順利地　text (v.) 傳簡訊　candidate (n.) 人選　proofread (v.) 校對

65. 相關細節——女子提及雜誌將於下個月開始進行的事情

What does the woman say the magazine will start doing next month?

(A) Reducing rates for advertisements
(B) Publishing letters from subscribers
(C) Giving tours of its headquarters complex
(D) Releasing special issues regularly

女子說該份雜誌下個月會開始進行什麼事？

(A) 降低廣告費率
(B) 刊登訂閱者的來信
(C) 帶領參觀總公司大樓
(D) 定期推出特殊刊物

- rate (v.) 費率　subscriber (n.) 訂閱者　headquarters (n.) 總部　complex (n.) 綜合大樓　release (v.) 推出　regularly (adv.) 定期地

換句話說 bimonthly（雙月的）→ regularly（定期地）；
start publishing（開始出版）→ releasing（推出）

66. 相關細節——男子的計畫

What does the man plan to do?
(A) Take photos for a Web site
(B) Proofread some writing
(C) Set up audiovisual equipment
(D) Send out text messages

男子計劃做何事？
(A) 幫網站拍照
(B) 校對寫作內容
(C) 設置視聽設備
(D) 傳送簡訊

- audiovisual (adj.) 視聽的　equipment (n.) 設備

67. 圖表整合題——哪一位應徵者被安排在其他會議室面試　難

Look at the graphic. Which candidate will be interviewed in a different room?
(A) David Meyer
(B) Erica Yang
(C) Lance Dedham
(D) Joy Nelson

請看圖表作答。哪一位應徵者會在不同的會議室進行面試？
(A) 大衛・梅爾
(B) 艾瑞卡・楊
(C) 蘭斯・戴德漢
(D) 喬伊・尼爾森

68-70 Conversation + Store directory

W: Hi, Darnell. (68) **I heard we're having challenges with our store's level of staffing.**

M: (68) **Yes, it's been low, especially considering how busy it is.**

W: Well, it's lucky some of our cashiers can work overtime today, then.

M: True. All right, let's work on getting inventory onto the store floor. (69) **This afternoon, I'd like us to focus on one aisle only and restock all its shelves with printer paper, notebooks, and report covers.**

W: Sure. (70) **That part of the store does look a little empty, because of last week's fall clearance event.**

M: Exactly. And the clerks on the night shift can handle the other aisles, since they're less urgent.

General Goods Section

Aisle 1	Garden supplies
Aisle 2	Carpet and flooring
Aisle 3	Sports equipment
(69) Aisle 4	**Office stationery**

68-70 對話＋賣場分區圖　英⇄加

女：嗨，達尼爾，(68) **我聽說我們店裡的員工配置人數相當吃緊。**

男：(68) **是的，人力一直短少，尤其考量到目前繁忙的工作量。**

女：這樣啊，幸好今天我們有幾名收銀人員可以加班。

男：確實如此。好啦，我們來把存貨移動到店櫃樓層。(69) **今天下午，我希望大家只專注處理一個走道的貨架，將影印紙、筆記本和文件夾，全部都補貨上架。**

女：沒問題。(70) **由於上週舉行的秋季出清特賣，店裡那個區域確實看起來有點空。**

男：沒錯。其他走道的貨架可以由夜班店員處理，因為急迫性沒那麼高。

一般商品區

走道 1	園藝用品
走道 2	地毯與鋪地用品
走道 3	運動裝備
(69) 走道 4	**辦公文具**

- challenge (n.) 挑戰　staffing (n.) 員工配置　considering (prep.) 考慮到……　cashier (n.) 收銀員　overtime (adv.) 超時地　inventory (n.) 存貨　aisle (n.) 走道　restock (v.) 補貨　clearance (n.) 出清　shift (n.) 輪班　handle (v.) 處理　urgent (adj.) 緊急的

68. 相關細節——說話者提及的問題

What problem do the speakers mention?
(A) A missing form
(B) A delayed delivery
(C) A shortage of employees
(D) An out-of-date training manual

說話者提到什麼問題？
(A) 表格遺失
(B) 配送延誤
(C) 員工短缺
(D) 過時的培訓手冊

- missing (adj.) 下落不明的 shortage (n.) 短缺 out-of-date (adj.) 過時的 manual (n.) 手冊

換句話說 drop by（來訪）→ visit（造訪）

69. 圖表整合題——說話者於下午工作的走道

Look at the graphic. Which aisle will the speakers work in that afternoon?
(A) Aisle 1
(B) Aisle 2
(C) Aisle 3
(D) Aisle 4

請看圖表作答。說話者下午會處理哪一條走道？
(A) 走道 1
(B) 走道 2
(C) 走道 3
(D) 走道 4

70. 相關細節——女子提及上週發生的事情 難

According to the woman, what happened last week?
(A) A staff recruiting event
(B) A district managers' meeting
(C) A building renovation
(D) A seasonal sale

根據女子的說法，上週發生了什麼事？
(A) 徵才活動
(B) 地區經理的會議
(C) 大樓翻新
(D) 季節特賣會

- recruit (v.) 招募 district (n.) 地區 renovation (n.) 翻新 seasonal (adj.) 季節的

換句話說 fall clearance event（秋季出清特賣）→ a seasonal sale（季節特賣會）

PART 4 P. 89–91 28

71-73 Announcement

Attention riders. (71) **Once all the passengers from this arriving flight have boarded our shuttle, we will depart for Gate 2 of Delray Airport's main terminal.** From there you can proceed directly to the immigration inspection lanes. (72) **As a major gateway to overseas, Delray Airport handles a wide variety of aircraft.** (73) **During our ride, you are invited to look out the window and watch these planes being serviced in the runway parking area.** Please hold onto the safety rails while the vehicle is in motion, as it may make sudden stops. Thank you.

71-73 宣布 加

所有乘客請注意，(71) **待所有乘客從入境班機下機，都坐上我們的接駁車，我們將出發前往德瑞機場主航廈的第二登機門。**到航廈後，各位可直接前往查驗通關的通道。(72) **德瑞機場為接軌海外的主要樞紐，處理各種機型的起降作業，**(73) **歡迎您在搭車期間，看向窗外觀賞跑道停機區裡，正在養護的飛機，**也請在坐車期間抓好安全欄杆，以防車輛可能緊急煞車，謝謝大家。

- depart (v.) 出發 proceed (v.) 前往 immigration inspection 查驗通關處 lane (n.) 通道 overseas (n.) 海外地區 service (v.) 檢修 runway (n.) 跑道 safety rail 安全欄杆 in motion 行進中

71. 全文相關——做出宣布的地點

Where is the announcement being given?
(A) On a high-speed train
(B) On an airport shuttle bus
(C) In a baggage claim area
(D) At an airport departure lounge

這段宣布進行的地點為何處？
(A) 高速火車
(B) 機場接駁巴士
(C) 行李領取區
(D) 機場出境休息室

72. 相關細節——說話者針對德瑞機場提及的內容　難

What does the speaker mention about Delray Airport?
(A) It is one of two airports in the city.
(B) It mainly handles cargo planes.
(C) It offers international flights.
(D) It was recently expanded.

說話者提到德瑞機場的什麼事？
(A) 是此都市裡的兩座機場之一。
(B) 主要進出的是貨機。
(C) 提供國際班機。
(D) 近期剛擴建。

• mainly (adv.) 主要　cargo (n.) 貨物　international (adj.) 國際的　expand (v.) 擴大；發展

換句話說 overseas（海外）→ international（國際）

73. 相關細節——說話者建議聽者做的事情　難

What does the speaker encourage listeners to do?
(A) Observe airport operations
(B) Make use of luggage racks
(C) Request additional station stops
(D) Register for a notification service

說話者鼓勵聽者做什麼事？
(A) 觀察機場的運作
(B) 使用行李架
(C) 要求額外的停靠站
(D) 登記通知服務

• observe (v.) 觀察　operation (n.) 運作　luggage (n.) 行李　rack (n.) 架　register for 登記　notification (n.) 通知

換句話說 look out the window and watch these planes being serviced（往窗外觀賞正在養護的飛機）→ observe airport operations（觀察機場的運作）

74-76 Excerpt from a meeting

Welcome to today's meeting. (74) **Recently our technology advisor, Ms. Sharma, oversaw user testing for our new Language Learning Max mobile phone app. Her report on our app arrived yesterday, so I'd like to use this time to go over some of its key points.** Overall, users were positive about the app's design features. (75) **However, a number of people indicated that the digital images used to represent the vocabulary items were somewhat fuzzy and hard to see.** That's an important concern we need to address. (76) **So I made a short presentation on this issue. Let's turn our attention now to the first slide, which shows a sample image.**

74-76 會議摘錄　英

歡迎來到今天的會議。(74) **近期我們的技術顧問夏瑪小姐，就我們全新的「語言學習Max」手機應用程式，督導了使用者實測的進行，她對我們這款應用程式的報告昨天送達，因此我想藉由這個時間，來向大家說明幾項重點。**整體來說，使用者對於應用程式的設計要素均給予正面評價，(75) **不過有幾個人表示，用來呈現字彙項目的數位影像有點模糊難辨**，這是我們必須解決的重要問題。(76) **因此，我針對此問題做了簡短的簡報，請大家一起注意到第一張投影片，上面有一張範本影像。**

• advisor (n.) 顧問　oversee (v.) 監督　overall (adv.) 整體上　positive (adj.) 正面的　indicate (v.) 表示　represent (v.) 呈現　somewhat (adv.) 有一點　fuzzy (adj.) 模糊的　address (v.) 解決

74. 全文相關——會議的目的

What is the main purpose of the meeting?

(A) To address listeners' feedback on a plan

(B) To brainstorm names for a product

(C) To familiarize attendees with a software program

(D) To review a consultant's report

此會議的主要目的是什麼？

(A) 解決聽者對計畫提出的反饋

(B) 針對產品名稱進行腦力激盪

(C) 讓參加者熟悉某軟體程式

(D) 檢討顧問的報告

- **brainstorm (v.)** 腦力激盪 **familiarize (v.)** 使……熟悉 **attendee (n.)** 參加者

換句話說 **go over**（說明）→ **review**（檢討）

---

75. 相關細節——說話者提及手機應用程式的問題

難

According to the speaker, what is the problem with a mobile phone app?

(A) High user fees

(B) Slow loading speed

(C) Unclear illustrations

(D) Complex navigation

根據說話者說法，手機應用程式出了什麼問題？

(A) 使用費昂貴

(B) 載入速度慢

(C) 圖示不清楚

(D) 瀏覽方式繁複

- **fee (n.)** 費用 **load (v.)** 載入 **unclear (adj.)** 不清楚 **illustration (n.)** 圖示 **navigation** 瀏覽；訪問（網站等）

換句話說 **fuzzy and hard to see**（模糊難辨）→ **unclear**（不清楚）

---

76. 相關細節——說話者接下來要做的事情

What will the speaker probably do next?

(A) Evaluate design proposals

(B) Welcome a guest speaker

(C) Pass out sample items

(D) Discuss a presentation slide

說話者接下來大概會怎麼做？

(A) 評估設計提案

(B) 歡迎客座演講者

(C) 分發樣品

(D) 討論簡報投影片

- **evaluate (v.)** 評估 **proposal (n.)** 提議 **pass out** 傳遞 **discuss (v.)** 討論

77-79 Announcement

Thank you for shopping at Lorna's Market, the region's number-one full-service grocery store. (77) **We hope you are pleased with the recent upgrades we made to our layout and lighting.** To match the new interior, we are now looking for new members to join our team. (78) **Lorna's Market is currently hiring in the meat, grocery, and deli departments.** (79) **We are also seeking drivers for our new door-to-door delivery service, which we'll launch on June first.** Both full- and part-time hours are available. Apply online by visiting www.lornas-market.com.

77-79 宣布

澳

感謝您到羅娜超市購物，本店是服務全方位、在地第一名的生活雜貨超市。(77) **我們近期針對空間配置與照明有做更新調整，希望各位感到滿意。**為呼應煥然一新內部格局，我們現在正在招募新血，來加入本店團隊。(78) **羅娜超市的肉品、食品雜貨與熟食專區都在徵才，**(79) **另也正在誠徵司機，來協助執行六月一日我們將新推出的宅配到府服務。**全職、兼職人員皆歡迎加入。如有意願，請上網至 www.lornas-market.com 應徵。

- **region (n.)** 地區 **grocery (n.)** 食品雜貨 **pleased (adj.)** 滿意的 **lighting (n.)** 照明 **match (v.)** 因應；搭配 **deli (n.)** 熟食櫃檯 **launch (v.)** 推出

77. 相關細節——說話者針對羅娜超市提及的內容

What does the speaker mention about Lorna's Market?

(A) It was recently remodeled.

(B) It has a seafood department.

(C) It has a loyalty card program.

(D) Its management has changed.

針對羅娜超市，說話者提到了什麼？

(A) 近期剛整修。

(B) 設有海鮮專區。

(C) 設有集點卡計畫。

(D) 管理人員已更換。

- **recently (adv.)** 近期地 **remodel (v.)** 整修 **loyalty card (n.)** 集點卡；會員卡 **management (n.)** 管理人員

換句話說 **the recent upgrades we made to our layout and lighting**（我們近期針對空間配置與照明有做更新調整）→ **recently remodeled**（近期剛整修）

---

78. 全文相關——宣布的目的

What is the main purpose of the announcement?

(A) To remind shoppers about extended hours

(B) To publicize current job openings

(C) To encourage use of self-checkout machines

(D) To share the results of a survey

這段宣布的主要目的是什麼？

(A) 提醒消費者營業時間延長

(B) 宣傳目前的職缺

(C) 鼓勵使用自助結帳機器

(D) 分享調查的結果

- **remind (v.)** 提醒 **extend (v.)** 延長的 **publicize (v.)** 宣傳；公布 **job opening** 職缺 **encourage (v.)** 鼓勵 **survey (n.)** 調查

換句話說 **currently hiring**（現在正在招募）→ **current job openings**（目前的職缺）

---

79. 相關細節——將於六月一日開始的事情

According to the announcement, what will start on June 1？

(A) A series of cooking demonstrations

(B) The construction of a new location

(C) A home delivery service

(D) A prize giveaway contest

根據宣布內容，何事將於六月一日開始？

(A) 一系列烹飪展示活動

(B) 新據點的施工

(C) 宅配到府的服務

(D) 贈獎比賽

- **a series of** 一系列的 **demonstration (n.)** 示範 **prize (n.)** 獎品 **giveaway (n.)** 贈品

80-82 Tour information

Greetings, all. I'm Ellen Hoon. I'll be your volunteer guide for this tour of the city's historic district. (80) **I've studied this community for over twenty years in my role as professor of regional studies at South Central University,** and it's my favorite part of the city. Now . . . remember that people do live here. (81) **Please try not to look into windows or lean against gates as we explore the area.** Before we tour a replica of one of the historical homes, we'll now walk over to the Culture Center. (82) **It has detailed sketches created by the district's original architects that show some of the structures' floor plans.** Follow me this way.

80-82 觀光資訊 英

大家好，我是艾倫．胡恩，是大家這次參觀本市歷史街區的志工導遊。(80) **我擔任中南大學區域研究教授，已經對此社區進行超過二十年的研究**，而此區是我在本市最為情有獨鍾的地方。現在，請記得有居民實際居住在這裡。(81) **我們探訪此區時，請大家盡量不要往窗戶窺視，或倚靠大門口。**在參觀其中一間歷史住宅的仿製屋前，我們現在將先步行至文化中心，(82) **裡面有當初本區建築師所繪製的詳細素描稿，內容展示幾棟建築的平面圖。**請大家跟著我往這邊走。

- **volunteer (adj.)** 志工的 **district (n.)** 地區 **regional (adj.)** 地區的 **lean against . . .** 倚靠在…… **replica (n.)** 複製品 **original (adj.)** 原創的 **architect (n.)** 建築師 **floor plan** 平面圖

80. 全文相關——說話者的工作地點

Where most likely does the speaker work?
(A) At a transportation service
(B) At an architecture firm
(C) At an educational institution
(D) At a dining establishment

說話者最有可能在哪裡工作？
(A) 運輸業者
(B) 建築師事務所
(C) 教育機構
(D) 餐飲企業

換句話說 University（大學）→ an educational institution（教育機構）

81. 掌握說話者的意圖——提及「請記得有居民實際居住在這裡」的意圖

What does the speaker mean when she says, "remember that people do live here"?
(A) Listeners should be respectful toward residents.
(B) Older homes are more attractive to buyers.
(C) Residents depend on tourism revenue.
(D) It is unusual for a historic district to be occupied.

說話者提到：「請記得有居民實際居住在這裡」，用意為何？
(A) 聽者應尊重居民。
(B) 買主對較老舊的住宅更感興趣。
(C) 居民依賴觀光收入。
(D) 歷史街區難得會有居民居住。

- respectful (adj.) 尊重的　resident (n.) 居民　attractive (adj.) 吸引人的　depend on . . . 依賴……　tourism (n.) 觀光業　revenue (n.) 收益　unusual (adj.) 不尋常的　occupy (v.) 居住

82. 相關細節——說話者提及聽者接下來會看到的事物

What does the speaker say the listeners will see next?
(A) A live performance
(B) Some architectural drawings
(C) Some classic vehicles
(D) A body of water

據說話者所說，聽者接下來會看到什麼？
(A) 現場表演
(B) 建築繪圖
(C) 古董車
(D) 水域

換句話說 the structures' floor plans（建築的平面圖）→ architectural drawings（建築繪圖）

83-85 News report

This is a WRB News Radio update. (83) **This Sunday at one p.m., the city library kicks off its summer series of family movies with a screening of *Trek Across Peru*, an exciting adventure story.** All film showings are free and open to the public. For a complete schedule, visit www.wenville-library.org. (84) **The library also invites all residents to look through its entire collection of books and magazines by clicking on the "Browse" button on its homepage.** (85) **And to specially encourage our listeners to do that, WRB News Radio will be holding a call-in trivia contest about the library's offerings later today. This is how it will work.**

83-85 新聞報導 澳

您現在收聽的是 WRB 新聞電台的新聞快報。(83) **本週日下午一點，市立圖書館將展開一系列夏季家庭電影放映活動，首先放映的是熱血冒險故事《穿越秘魯》。**活動播放的所有電影均開放大眾免費觀賞，完整時刻表可至 www.wenville-library.org 查看。(84) **圖書館也邀請所有居民，在網站首頁點擊「瀏覽」按鈕，一覽全部的館藏書籍和雜誌。**(85) **為了特別鼓勵各位聽眾進行上述動作，WRB 新聞電台將針對圖書館提供的活動內容，於今天稍晚以聽眾現場來電的形式，舉辦小知識比賽。比賽辦法如下。**

- kick off 開始　screening (n.) 放映　(the) public (n.) 公眾　invite (v.) 邀請　resident (n.) 居民　entire (adj.) 全部的　browse (v.) 瀏覽　call-in (n.) 現場來電　trivia (n.) 小知識　contest (n.) 比賽

83. 全文相關——新聞報導的主題

What is the main topic of the news report?
(A) A profile of a local politician
(B) An upcoming community activity
(C) Driving conditions on area roadways
(D) Problems with an environmental project

此新聞報導的主題是什麼？
(A) 當地政治人物的簡介
(B) 即將進行的社區活動
(C) 區域道路的駕駛情況
(D) 環境專案的問題

- profile (n.) 簡介　politician (n.) 政客　upcoming (adj.) 即將到來的　community (n.) 社區　condition (n.) 情況　roadway (n.) 道路　environmental (adj.) 環境的

84. 相關細節——要求聽者做的事情

What are listeners invited to do?
(A) Participate in an opinion poll
(B) Attend an outdoor event
(C) Join a volunteer organization
(D) View an online catalog

活動邀請聽者做什麼事？
(A) 參與意見投票
(B) 參加戶外活動
(C) 加入志工組織
(D) 檢視線上書目

- participate (v.) 參與　poll (n.) 投票　attend (v.) 參加　volunteer (adj.) 志工的　organization (n.) 組織　view (v.) 檢視

換句話說 look through its entire collection of books and magazines . . . on its homepage（在網站首頁……一覽全部的館藏書籍和雜誌）→ view an online catalog（檢視線上書目）

85. 相關細節——將於接下來聽到的內容 難

What most likely will be heard next?
(A) A list of business closures
(B) A paid advertisement
(C) A call from a radio listener
(D) An explanation of a competition

接著最有可能聽到何項內容？
(A) 歇業公司的名單
(B) 付費廣告
(C) 電台聽眾的來電
(D) 比賽的說明

- list (n.) 清單　closure (n.) 關閉　paid (adj.) 付費的　advertisement (n.) 廣告　explanation (n.) 說明　competition (n.) 比賽

換句話說 how it will work（〔舉行的〕辦法）→ An explanation（說明）

86-88 Telephone message

Hi, Mr. Bowers. It's Nina Estrada, calling to follow up on our consultation yesterday. (86) **As senior designer at my firm, I'm confident I can guide you through every step of your hotel's renovation project.** Now, during my visit, you showed me some guest rooms, and . . . the wallpaper and lamps are quite old. (87) **So we'll want to focus on that element during the improvement process.** As we discussed, your hotel will be able to remain operational while the contractors do their work, so that will minimize revenue losses. (88) **Later today, I'll send you an e-mail with my recommendations, estimated costs, and so on in detail.** Take a look at it and let me know what you think.

86-88 電話留言 美

嗨，包爾斯先生，我是妮娜．艾斯特達，本次來電是針對我們昨天的諮詢，進行後續了解。(86) **身為公司資深設計師，我有信心能引導您逐步完成貴飯店翻新專案的各步驟。**說到這，在我拜訪的時候，您帶我參觀一些客房，而……壁紙和燈具都頗為老舊。(87) **因此，我們在整修過程中，會想著重在這項元素。**如我們所討論，貴飯店可在承包商施工時維持營運，以便將收益損失降到最低。(88) **我今天稍晚會將我的建議事項、費用估價等詳細資訊，用電子郵件寄給您，**請您看一下，並跟我說您的想法。

- follow up 後續了解 confident (adj.) 有信心的 wallpaper (n.) 壁紙 element (n.) 元素 contractor (n.) 承包商 minimize (v.) 降到最低 revenue (n.) 收益 loss (n.) 損失 estimate (v.) 預估 in detail 詳細的

86. 全文相關——說話者的職業

Who most likely is the speaker?

(A) An interior designer

(B) A convention organizer

(C) A hotel manager

(D) A real estate agent

說話者最有可能是什麼身分？

(A) 室內設計師

(B) 會議籌辦人員

(C) 飯店經理

(D) 房地產經紀人

87. 掌握說話者的意圖——提及「壁紙和燈具都頗為老舊」的意圖 難

Why most likely does the speaker say, "the wallpaper and lamps are quite old"?

(A) To indicate that she is impressed by some materials' durability

(B) To justify the decision to change a venue

(C) To emphasize the need to make updates

(D) To compliment a structure's vintage decorations

說話者會提到：「壁紙和燈具都頗為老舊」，最有可能是為什麼？

(A) 以表示她對部分建材的耐用度印象深刻

(B) 以解釋想改變場地的決定

(C) 以強調翻新的需求

(D) 以讚賞建築物的復古裝飾

- indicate (v.) 表示 impressed (adj.) 感到印象深刻的 durability (n.) 耐用度 justify (v.) 合理化 venue (n.) 場地 compliment (v.) 讚賞 structure (n.) 建築物 vintage (adj.) 復古的 decoration (n.) 裝飾

88. 相關細節——說話者提及她將於當天稍晚做的事情

What does the speaker say she will do later that day?

(A) Recruit additional workers

(B) Introduce the listener to a colleague

(C) Provide a written proposal

(D) Issue a partial refund

說話者表示她當天稍晚會做何事？

(A) 招募額外的工人

(B) 向同事介紹聽者

(C) 提供書面提案

(D) 發出部分退款

- recruit (v.) 招募 colleague (n.) 同事 proposal (n.) 計畫；提案 issue (v.) 分發 partial (adj.) 部分的

89-91 Introduction

(89) **Welcome, all, to the home of the city's most extensive collection of paintings and photographs from all different time periods.** All tours of our facility are self-guided—you don't need a tour guide or a special mobile phone app. (90) **Instead, you can hear explanations of all the exhibits through this pushbutton audio guide that I'll give you in a minute.** You simply push the button corresponding to the exhibit you are viewing, and then you'll hear a description of the work in the headphones. (91) **Finally, uh, I recommend beginning your tour in Gallery B, since our main gallery is already quite full at the moment.**

89-91 介紹 加

(89) **歡迎大家來參觀，這裡收藏橫跨不同時期的畫作和攝影作品，館藏為本市最豐。**我們設施的所有參觀行程均採自助導覽——各位不需要導遊或特殊的手機應用程式，(90) **而是可以透過我等一下將發給大家的按鈕式語音導覽，來聆聽所有展覽品的解說。**大家觀看展品時，只要按一下相對應的按鈕，就能在頭戴式耳機聽到該作品的說明。(91) **最後，呃，我建議大家先從 B 藝廊開始參觀，因為目前主藝廊的人潮已相當眾多。**

- extensive (adj.) 廣泛的；豐富的 collection (n.) 收藏 period (n.) 時期 explanation (n.) 解說 exhibit (n.) 展覽品 corresponding to . . . 對應 description (n.) 說明

89. 全文相關——該段介紹出現的地點 難

Where most likely is the introduction taking place?
(A) At a university student center
(B) At an art museum
(C) At a formal garden
(D) At a photo studio

這段介紹最有可能發生在何處？
(A) 在大學學生中心
(B) 在美術館
(C) 在正式花園
(D) 在攝影工作室

換句話說 the home of the city's most extensive collection of paintings and photographs（收藏橫跨不同時期的畫作和攝影作品，館藏為本市最豐）→ an art museum（美術館）

---

90. 相關細節——說話者提供給聽者的東西

What will the speaker give the listeners?
(A) An audio device
(B) A gift shop coupon
(C) A guide map to a facility
(D) A link to a mobile phone app

說話者會發給聽者什麼物品？
(A) 語音裝置
(B) 禮品店優惠券
(C) 設施的導覽地圖
(D) 手機應用程式的連結

換句話說 this pushbutton audio guide（按鈕式語音導覽）→ an audio device（語音裝置）

---

91. 相關細節——說話者提出的建議

What does the speaker suggest doing?
(A) Watching an introductory film
(B) Ordering a meal in advance
(C) Starting a tour in a less crowded area
(D) Filling out a feedback survey

說話者建議做什麼事？
(A) 觀賞介紹影片
(B) 事先訂餐
(C) 先從人較少的區域開始參觀
(D) 填寫意見回饋調查

- introductory (adj.) 介紹　meal (n.) 餐點　in advance 事先　crowded (adj.) 擁擠的　fill out 填妥　survey (n.) 調查

換句話說 full（人潮相當眾多）→ crowded（人多的）

92-94 Telephone message

Hi, Tony. [92] **I heard you got approval for your transfer to the company's overseas office in Hong Kong. Congratulations!** Related to that, you had asked me last week about having your belongings moved out of your apartment and put into storage. And, well . . . there are a lot of moving companies in this area. [93] **I wouldn't worry at all.** [94] **If you have time, go online and visit www.hongkong-sources.com. It has useful information about living in that area, and it'll help you out a lot I think.** Hope to talk again soon. Bye.

92-94 電話留言 美

嗨，東尼，[92] **我聽說你獲准調職了，會調到公司在香港的海外據點，恭喜你！**有關這件事，你上週問過我，要把你的個人物品從你的公寓搬出，並儲藏起來。這件事嘛……這一區有很多搬家公司，[93] **要是我就完全不會擔心。**[94] **如果你有空，可以上網到 www.hongkong-sources.com 這個網站。上面有關於居住在當地的實用資訊，我想會對你很有幫助。**希望很快有機會再聊，再見。

- approval (n.) 准許　transfer (n.) 調職　overseas (adj.) 海外的　related to . . . 相關　belongings (n.) 個人物品　storage (n.) 儲藏

92. 相關細節──說話者向聽者道賀的理由

Why most likely does the speaker congratulate the listener?

(A) He gave a successful presentation.

(B) He recently purchased a new house.

(C) His transfer request was granted.

(D) His sales team won an award.

說話者最有可能恭喜聽者的原因為何？

(A) 他的簡報很成功。

(B) 他近期買了新家。

(C) 他的調職申請獲准。

(D) 他的銷售團隊贏得獎項。

- presentation (n.) 簡報　grant (v.) 許可　award (n.) 獎項

換句話說 got approval for your transfer（申請調職獲准了）
→ **His transfer request was granted.**（他的調職申請獲准。）

93. 掌握說話者的意圖──提及「這一區有很多搬家公司」的意圖

What does the speaker imply when she says, "there are a lot of moving companies in this area"?

(A) She needs more details about a project.

(B) The region has many new residents.

(C) It will not be difficult to hire a mover.

(D) A new company might struggle at first.

說話者說：「這一區有很多搬家公司」，言下之意為何？

(A) 她需要了解更多此專案的細節。

(B) 該地區具有許多新居民。

(C) 不會太難僱用到搬家公司。

(D) 新公司剛開始可能很辛苦。

- resident (n.) 居民　hire (v.) 僱用　mover (n.) 搬家公司　struggle (v.) 掙扎；難處

94. 相關細節──說話者提及對聽者有幫助的東西

What does the speaker say will be helpful for the listener?

(A) Browsing a Web site

(B) Modifying a travel itinerary

(C) Completing an electronic form

(D) Holding a special staff meeting

據說話者說，何者對聽者有幫助？

(A) 瀏覽網站

(B) 修改旅遊行程

(C) 完成電子表格

(D) 舉行特殊員工會議

- browse (v.) 瀏覽　modify (v.) 修改　itinerary (n.) 行程　electronic (adj.) 電子的　hold (v.) 舉辦

換句話說 go online and visit www. hongkong-sources.com（上網到 www.hongkong-sources.com 這個網站）→ **browsing a Web site**（瀏覽網站）

95-97 Excerpt from a meeting + Chart

As you know, the interns will start next week. [95] **They'll first receive classroom instruction to become familiar with all the inventory management software products we've created for various industries.** Then we'll give them hands-on training in our newest program, Merchandise-Wiz, aimed at the shoe industry. [96] **This will help them to perform their duties related to monitoring our online customer service forum.** Now, we have one last-minute change for the practical module. [97] **The air conditioning is malfunctioning in the room Yuko was assigned, so we won't use that one.** Her trainee group is small, so we'll combine it with Jim's group and they'll meet in his assigned room.

95-97 會議摘錄＋表格 加

如各位所知，實習生下週會開始上班。[95] **他們首先會聽課，以便熟悉我們針對各種產業製作出來的各項存貨管理軟體產品。**接著，我們會提供他們實作教學，學習我們針對鞋業推出的最新程式「商品智慧王」，[96] **這將幫助他們執行監看我們線上客服論壇的相關職務。**現在，我們實務課程單元臨時有異動。[97] **結子分配到的會議室冷氣故障了，所以我們不會使用那一間，**她帶領的受訓小組人數較少，因此就和吉姆的小組合併，一起到他分配到的會議室去集合。

Name of Trainer	Room number
Gregor	305
Jim	307
Becky	309
(97) Yuko	**311**

訓練人員名稱	教室編號
葛瑞格	305
吉姆	307
貝琪	309
(97) 結子	**311**

- instruction (n.) 指導；教導　inventory (n.) 存貨　hands-on (adj.) 實作的　aim (v.) 以……為目標　perform (v.) 執行　duty (n.) 職務　monitor (v.) 監督　last-minute (adj.) 臨時的　practical (adj.) 實務的　module (n.) 單元　malfunction (v.) 故障　assign (v.) 指派　trainee (n.) 受訓學員　combine (v.) 結合

95. 全文相關——說話者的工作地點

What kind of business does the speaker most likely work for?

(A) At a merchandise display distributor

(B) At a software development firm

(C) At a footwear manufacturer

(D) At a package shipping company

說話者最有可能在何種行業工作？

(A) 商品展示架經銷商

(B) 軟體開發公司

(C) 鞋類製造商

(D) 包裹貨運公司

- merchandise (n.) 商品　display (n.) 展示架　distributor (n.) 經銷商　development (n.) 開發　footwear (n.) 鞋類　manufacturer (n.) 製造商　package (n.) 包裹　shipping (n.) 貨運

96. 相關細節——說話者提及實習生要做的事 難

According to the speaker, what will interns be required to do?

(A) Oversee an online messaging board

(B) Create posts for a social media account

(C) Test a feature of a computer program

(D) Compile statistics about clients

根據說話者的說法，實習生將需要做什麼事？

(A) 監看線上留言板

(B) 為社群媒體帳戶建立貼文

(C) 測試電腦程式的功能

(D) 彙整客戶相關統計資料

- board (n.)（留言）板　account (n.) 帳戶　compile (v.) 彙整　statistics (n.) 統計資料

換句話說 monitoring our online customer service forum（監看我們線上客服論壇）
→ oversee an online messaging board（監看線上留言板）

97. 圖表整合題——無法用於受訓的會議室

Look at the graphic. Which room will most likely NOT be used for training?

(A) 305　(C) 309

(B) 307　**(D) 311**

請看圖表作答。哪間會議室最不可能用來進行教育訓練？

(A) 305　(C) 309

(B) 307　**(D) 311**

98-100 Announcement + Sign

OK, big announcement . . . (98) **In June, we're going to move all warehouse staff to a "four-ten workweek". You'll have four days of ten-hour shifts and then three days off.**

98-100 宣布＋指示牌 美

好的，這裡有重大消息要宣布…… (98) **六月時，我們所有倉庫員工，將為改為實施「4/10工作週」模式，也就是每週四天要輪班 10 小時，另外三天休息。**

(99) **This will make it easier for our temporary staff to help out as we approach the summer season, when we experience peak demand for our services.** There will be a full meeting on this change next Monday. (100) **Also, yesterday I put up a new sign in the loading dock area. It informs visitors that they need to wear identification badges.** There's now a lot of information on that wall. But we do need to ensure procedures are being followed correctly.

(99) **如此一來，我們的臨時員工可以更容易協助我們，迎接夏季這個我們服務需求旺季的到來。**針對此異動，我們下週一會開完整的會議。(100) **此外，我昨天在卸貨平台區設置了新標示，以便告知訪客必須佩戴識別證。**牆面上已經有許多資訊，但我們務必確保程序要確實遵循。

Sign

1	Delivery Drivers Must Sign in at Office
2	(100) Visitors Must Wear ID Badges
3	Area Monitored by Security Camera
4	Parking for Delivery Vehicles Only

標示

1	宅配司機必須在辦公室簽到
2	(100) 訪客務必配戴識別證掛牌
3	全區設有保全監視器
4	停車場僅供貨運車輛使用

- announcement (n.) 宣布　warehouse (n.) 倉庫　workweek (n.) 工作週　shift (n.) 輪班　temporary (adj.) 暫時的；臨時的　approach (v.) 即將；接近　peak (n.) 尖峰　demand (n.) 需求　loading dock 卸貨平台　identification (n.) 識別證　badge (n.) 識別證；名牌　procedure (n.) 程序

98. 相關細節——說話者最先提到的更動事項

What does the speaker first announce a change to?

(A) A work schedule

(B) The staff dress code

(C) A stocking system

(D) A floor plan

說話者一開始宣布何者有異動？

(A) 工作時間表

(B) 職員服裝規定

(C) 存貨系統

(D) 樓層平面圖

99. 相關細節——說話者提及將於夏季發生的事情 

According to the speaker, what will happen in the summer?

(A) A new product will be launched.

(B) A busy period will begin.

(C) A facility will close temporarily.

(D) A sales contest will take place.

根據說話者說法，夏季會發生什麼事？

(A) 即將推出新產品。

(B) 即將進入旺季。

(C) 一座設施會暫時關閉。

(D) 將舉行業績競賽。

- launch (v.) 推出　period (n.) 時期　facility (n.) 設施　temporarily (adv.) 暫時的　contest (n.) 競賽

換句話說 when we experience peak demand for our services（我們服務需求旺季）
→ a busy period（旺季）

100. 圖表整合題——說話者於昨天設置的標示

Look at the graphic. Which sign did the speaker install yesterday?

(A) Sign #1

(B) Sign #2

(C) Sign #3

(D) Sign #4

請看圖表作答。說話者昨天裝設了何項標示？

(A) 1 號標示

(B) 2 號標示

(C) 3 號標示

(D) 4 號標示

ACTUAL TEST 8

PART 1 P. 92–95

29

1. 單人獨照——描寫人物的動作 美

(A) He is carrying a bucket.
(B) He is adjusting his hat.
(C) He is leaning against a ladder.
(D) He is painting the side of a house.

(A) 他提著水桶。
(B) 他正在調整帽子。
(C) 他倚靠著梯子。
(D) 他正在油漆房子的側面。

- bucket (n.) 水桶 adjust (v.) 調整 lean against . . . 靠在…… ladder (n.) 梯子

2. 雙人照片——描寫人物的動作 澳

(A) They are clapping their hands.
(B) They are running side by side.
(C) They are drinking from bottles.
(D) They are facing one another.

(A) 他們正在鼓掌。
(B) 他們正在並肩跑步。
(C) 他們正在喝著水瓶的水。
(D) 他們彼此面對面。

- clap (v.) 拍手 side by side 肩並肩；一起 bottle (n.) 瓶子 face (v.) 面向；正對 one another 彼此；互相

3. 綜合照片——描寫人物或事物 加

(A) A man is working with a hand tool.
(B) Bricks are being stacked in piles.
(C) An outdoor garden is being planted.
(D) A man is sweeping a walking path.

(A) 男子手持工具工作中。
(B) 有人正在堆疊磚頭。
(C) 有人正在栽種戶外花園。
(D) 男子正在清掃步道。

- hand tool 手動工具 brick (n.) 磚（狀物） stack (v.) 把……堆疊 in piles 成堆 outdoor (adj.) 戶外的；露天的 plant (v.) 栽種 sweep (v.) 清掃；打掃 path (n.) 小徑

4. 事物與背景照——描寫室內事物的狀態 英 難

(A) The door of a laundry machine is being opened.
(B) There is a seating area in the center of the room.
(C) A bin has been set up near some appliances.
(D) Some laundry is being folded beside a basket.

(A) 有人正打開洗衣機的門。
(B) 房間中央有個座位區。
(C) 幾台家電旁邊放了一個容器。
(D) 有人在籃子旁邊摺洗好的衣服。

- laundry (n.) 待洗或洗好的衣物 seating (n.) 座位 bin (n.) 容器；箱 appliance (n.) 家電；裝置 fold (v.) 摺疊

5. 綜合照片——描寫人物或事物 澳 

(A) People are stepping onto an escalator.
(B) Baggage is being pulled off a cart.
(C) A walkway is lined with columns.
(D) The woman is inspecting the man's luggage.

(A) 人們正踏上手扶梯。
(B) 行李正從推車中行李提起。
(C) 走道兩旁排列著圓柱。
(D) 女子正在檢查男子的行李。

- step (v.) 踏（進） baggage (n.) 行李 walkway (n.) 走道 line (v.) 沿……排列 column (n.) 圓柱 inspect (v.) 檢查 luggage (n.) 行李箱

6. 綜合照片——描寫人物或事物 美

(A) Cars are parked along a parade route.	(A) 汽車沿著遊行路線停放。
(B) Performers are climbing onto a raised stage.	(B) 表演者正登上架高的舞台。
(C) There are spectators watching from windows.	(C) 觀眾透過窗戶觀看。
(D) Musical instruments are being played on a street.	**(D) 有人正在街頭吹奏樂器。**

- parade (n.) 遊行　route (n.) 路；路線　performer (n.) 表演者　climb (v.) 爬；攀登　spectator (n.) 觀眾；旁觀者　musical instrument 樂器

PART 2 P. 96

30

7. 以 What 開頭的問句，詢問幾點關門 美⇄加

What time do you close this evening?	你們今天晚上幾點打烊？
(A) We're open until ten o'clock.	**(A) 我們開到十點。**
(B) This tie matches with those clothes.	(B) 這條領帶和那些衣服很搭。
(C) On Friday the twelfth.	(C) 12 日星期五。

- tie (n.) 領帶　match (v.) 和……相配

8. 以 Who 開頭的問句，詢問手冊是誰製作的 澳⇄英

Who made this brochure for the trade show?	商展的宣傳手冊是誰製作的？
(A) Yes, with a special printer.	(A) 是的，用特殊的印表機。
(B) Sorry—this copy is for Valerie.	(B) 抱歉，這份是要給薇樂莉的。
(C) Someone on the design team.	**(C) 設計部門的人。**

- brochure (n.)（宣傳用）小冊子　trade (n.) 貿易　copy (n.)（印刷品等）一份

9. 以助動詞 Do 開頭的問句，詢問是否還有多的紙張 加⇄美

Do you have any extra paper?	你還有額外的紙張嗎？
(A) A one-year subscription.	(A) 訂閱一年。
(B) I'll look in the storage closet.	**(B) 我去儲藏櫃看看。**
(C) That dish is already pretty spicy.	(C) 那道菜已經很辣了。

- extra (adj.) 額外的　subscription (n.) 訂閱　storage closet 儲藏櫃　spicy (adj.) 辛辣的；加香料的

10. 以 When 開頭的問句，詢問整修完成的時間 英⇄澳

When will the renovation project be finished?	整修工程何時會完工？
(A) Probably by early spring.	**(A) 很可能是初春。**
(B) For the new staff lounge.	(B) 提供給新的員工休息室。
(C) Due to some budget concerns.	(C) 由於預算考量。

- renovation (n.) 整修；翻新　lounge (n.) 休息室　budget (n.) 預算　concern (n.) 關係；利害關係

11. 以 **Where** 開頭的問句，詢問可以製作海報的地方 美⇄加

Where should we go to have the posters made?
(A) No, it isn't that difficult.
(B) Because I need to frame them.
(C) Elm Street Printing does good work.

我們要去哪裡印海報？
(A) 不，沒那麼難。
(B) 因為，我需要把它們裱框。
(C) 榆樹街印刷廠印得很漂亮。

- frame (v.) 給（圖畫等）裝框

12. 以 **How** 開頭的問句，詢問用軟體加入視訊會議的方法 英⇄加

How can I join a video conference with this software?
(A) Yes, I enjoyed listening to her presentation.
(B) Click the camera button on the screen.
(C) The cashier will check their membership cards.

我如何用這個軟體加入視訊會議？
(A) 是的，我很喜歡她的簡報。
(B) 按下螢幕上的攝影機按鈕。
(C) 收銀員會檢查他們的會員卡。

- video conference 視訊會議　presentation (n.) 演講；簡報　cashier (n) 收銀員

13. 以選擇疑問句，詢問對方正在尋找的工作類型 澳⇄英 難

Are you looking for a part-time or a full-time position?
(A) I'm hoping to work twenty hours per week.
(B) Not anymore—Kazuki let me borrow his.
(C) The dental clinic might be hiring.

你正在找兼職還是正職工作？
(A) 我希望每週工作 20 小時。
(B) 不需要了，一樹把他的借給我了。
(C) 牙科診所也許在徵人。

- per (prep.) 每；每一　borrow (v.) 借；借入　dental clinic 牙科診所　hire (v.) 僱用

14. 以 **Who** 開頭的問句，詢問誰負責訂購清潔用品 加⇄美 難

Who is in charge of ordering cleaning supplies?
(A) Are we running low already?
(B) A charger for mobile devices.
(C) That surprised me too.

誰負責訂購清潔用品？
(A) 我們已經快用完了嗎？
(B) 行動裝置的充電器。
(C) 我也很吃驚。

- in charge of . . . 負責　supply (n.) 用品　run low 快用完；不足　charger (n.) 充電器　mobile (adj.) 行動的　device (n.) 裝置；設備

15. 以否定疑問句，確認是否由法蘭克主導研討會 澳⇄美 難

Wasn't Frank supposed to lead tomorrow's workshop?
(A) I've read only the first one.
(B) I doubt he did it.
(C) Haven't you seen the updated schedule?

法蘭克不是應該帶領明天的研習嗎？
(A) 我只讀了第一個。
(B) 我不相信是他做的。
(C) 你沒有看更新的時程表嗎？

- be supposed to . . . 應該要……　lead (v.) 帶領　doubt (v.) 懷疑；不相信

16. 表示建議或提案的問句 英⇄加 難

Why don't we take the subway to get to the airport?
(A) He has to change planes in Madrid.
(B) We have too many heavy bags.
(C) To register for flight update texts.

我們何不搭地鐵去機場？
(A) 他必須在馬德里轉機。
(B) 我們有太多袋重物。
(C) 登記接收航班更新簡訊。

- subway (n.) 地下鐵　plane (n.) 飛機　register for 登記……　flight (n.) 航班　text (n.)（手機等的）文字訊息

17. 以助動詞 **Have** 開頭的問句，詢問是否在地方雜誌上登過廣告 澳⇄英

Have we ever advertised in local magazines?	我們曾在地方雜誌上登過廣告嗎？
(A) She used to work as a television reporter.	(A) 她以前是電視台記者。
(B) No, but we could consider it.	**(B) 沒有，但我們可以考慮。**
(C) When did you send it?	(C) 你何時寄出的？

• advertise (v.) 登廣告；宣傳　local (adj.) 本地的；地方性的　consider (v.) 考慮

18. 以附加問句確認這裡是否很冷 加⇄美

It's chilly in here, isn't it?	這裡真冷，不是嗎？
(A) We couldn't hear the sound.	(A) 我們聽不到聲音。
(B) He's on another line now.	(B) 他正在接聽另一線電話。
(C) I just turned the heat up.	**(C) 我剛把暖氣調暖了。**

• chilly (adj.)（天氣、房間等）寒冷的　turn up 調高（溫度、聲音等）　heat (n.) 暖氣設備

19. 以 **When** 開頭的問句，詢問禮品卡何時到期 英⇄澳

When does this gift card expire?	這張禮品卡何時到期？
(A) It's good for five years.	**(A) 有效期限五年。**
(B) They retired from their positions last month.	(B) 他們上個月退休了。
(C) Thank you for thinking of me.	(C) 謝謝你想到我。

• expire (v.) 到期；結束　good (adj.) 有用的　retire (v.) 退休；退役

20. 以直述句傳達資訊 美⇄美 難

I heard a Mexican restaurant opened up nearby.	我聽說附近開了一家墨西哥餐廳。
(A) Oh, where did you find the key?	(A) 噢，你在哪裡找到鑰匙？
(B) We went there for lunch on Monday.	**(B) 我們週一中午去了那間吃飯。**
(C) The maximum weight for packages.	(C) 包裹的重量上限。

• nearby (adv.) 在附近　maximum (adj.) 最大的　weight (n.) 重量　package (n.) 包裹

21. 以否定疑問句確認今天是否會到貨 澳⇄美

Isn't the shipment of office furniture going to arrive here today?	那批辦公家具不是預定今天到貨嗎？
(A) Check the assembly instructions.	(A) 查看組裝說明書。
(B) By using a mobile phone app.	(B) 透過使用手機應用程式。
(C) Yes, it's out for delivery now.	**(C) 是的，現在已在配送途中。**

• shipment (n.) 運輸（的貨物）　assembly (n.) 組裝　instruction (n.)（常用複數）說明

22. 表示建議或提案的問句 英⇄澳

Should we add a video to our next presentation?	我們下次簡報應該加上影片嗎？
(A) I haven't watched that one yet.	(A) 我還沒看過那一個。
(B) The previous marketing director.	(B) 前任行銷總監。
(C) Only if it's really necessary.	**(C) 只有在真的有需要的情況下。**

• add (v.) 增加　previous (adj.) 先前的　director (n.) 主管；首長　necessary (adj.) 必需的

23. 以 **How** 開頭的問句，詢問飲料的銷售狀況 加⇄英 難

How have sales been for our newest energy drink?
(A) The figures are being compiled now.
(B) Solar is a good option for clean energy.
(C) I went to a discount supermarket.

我們的最新能量飲料的銷量如何？
(A) 銷售數字正在彙整。
(B) 太陽能是清潔能源的優質選項。
(C) 我去了一家折扣超市。

- newest (adj.) 最新的 figure (n.) 數字 compile (v.) 彙編；收集 option (n.) 選項 discount (adj.) 折扣的

24. 以直述句傳達資訊 加⇄澳

The vending machine in the break room is out of order.
(A) All the guest rooms were booked.
(B) I already called the technician.
(C) Bending exercises to stay healthy.

休息室的販賣機故障了。
(A) 所有客房均已訂滿。
(B) 我已經打電話給技師了。
(C) 維持健康的屈體運動。

- vending machine 自動販賣機 break room 休息室 out of order 故障 book (v.) 預訂 technician (n.) 技師；技術員 bend (v.) 彎曲

25. 以 **Where** 開頭的問句，詢問售票處位置 英⇄澳 難

Where is the ticket office located?
(A) Sure, I'll ask a parking attendant.
(B) Before the performance begins.
(C) Mark picked up our tickets yesterday.

售票處在哪裡？
(A) 當然，我會問停車場服務員。
(B) 在表演開始之前。
(C) 馬克昨天幫我們取票了。

- attendant (n.) 服務員；隨從 performance (n.) 表演

26. 以附加問句，確認筆電是否不該放在外面 美⇄加 難

This notebook shouldn't be sitting out, should it?
(A) At the employee performance review.
(B) He prefers electronic books.
(C) An intern may have left it there.

這台筆記型電腦不應該擱在外面，不是嗎？
(A) 在員工績校考核期間。
(B) 他偏好電子書。
(C) 可能是實習生留在那裡的。

- sit (v.) 擱置 performance review 績效考核 electronic (adj.) 電子的

27. 以 **Why** 開頭的問句，詢問會議時間較短的理由 澳⇄英

Why was this week's meeting so short?
(A) There wasn't much new agenda.
(B) Usually twice a week.
(C) No, our team is actually overstaffed.

本週會議為什麼這麼短？
(A) 新的討論事項不多。
(B) 通常一週兩次。
(C) 不，我們團隊其實人手太多。

- agenda (n.) 議程；待議事項 actually (adv.) 實際上 overstaffed (adj.) 人員過多的

28. 以選擇疑問句詢問，造景工程人員前來的日子 加⇄英

Is the landscaping crew coming today or tomorrow?
(A) Probably some fences and gardens.
(B) They should be here this afternoon.
(C) The candidate's recent résumé.

造景工程人員是今天還是明天會來？
(A) 也許一些籬笆和花園。
(B) 他們應該今天下午過來。
(C) 應徵者最近的履歷表。

- landscaping (n.) 景觀美化 crew (n.)（一組）工作人員 fence (n.) 籬笆 candidate (n.) 應徵者 recent (adj.) 最近的；最新的 résumé/resume (n.) 履歷表

29. 表示請託或要求的直述句 澳⇄英

Someone will have to let me into the warehouse.	必須有人讓我進入倉庫。
(A) I have an access card.	**(A) 我有門禁卡。**
(B) Most of our workers live in apartments, not houses.	(B) 我們大部分的員工住公寓，而不是平房。
(C) They're trying to save money on shipping.	(C) 他們正設法節省運費。

- warehouse (n.) 倉庫　access (n.) 進入（的權利）

30. 以附加問句確認新地毯的外觀 美⇄加

The new carpeting looks great, doesn't it?	新的地毯看起來很漂亮，不是嗎？
(A) A few of them arrived late.	(A) 他們有幾位遲到了。
(B) The color is quite attractive.	**(B) 顏色很吸引人。**
(C) From an online clothing store.	(C) 從一家網路服飾店。

- quite (adv.) 相當；很　attractive (adj.) 有吸引力的

31. 表示請託或要求的問句 美⇄英

Could you help me set up this display case?	你可以幫我設置這個展示櫃嗎？
(A) She was able to log on successfully.	(A) 她可以順利登入。
(B) Why did they raise prices?	(B) 他們為什麼漲價？
(C) Let's do that after our break.	**(C) 我們休息時間結束後來做。**

- set up 安裝；擺放　display case 展示櫃　raise (v.) 提高　break (n.) 休息；暫停

PART 3 P. 97–100

31

32-34 Conversation

M: Hi, Karen. While you were away, the maintenance crew took away all the old file cabinets. (32) **So now we have more space to set up desks for the part-time staff. See?**

W: (32) **Oh, I'm really happy to see that.** Everything looks terrific. (33) **But . . . the carpets still have some stains. Shouldn't we get them cleaned professionally?**

M: I was thinking the same thing. (33) **I heard B & R Services does good work.** Plus, they use eco-friendly cleaning equipment. (34) **Their Web site is B-and-R.com.**

W: (34) **Great. Let's take a look now—we can go over all their service options.**

32-34 對話 加⇄英

男： 嗨，凱倫，妳不在的時候，維修人員把所有的舊檔案櫃都搬走了，(32) **所以我們現在有更多空間，可以擺放兼職人員用的辦公桌，妳看如何？**

女： (32) **噢，我真的相當滿意**，一切配置看起來無可挑剔，(33) **但是……地毯還是有些汙漬，我們是否應該找專業人員，把汙漬清理掉？**

男： 我正有此意。(33) **我聽說 B&R 服務公司能力很好**，而且他們使用環保的清潔用具，(34) **他們的網址是 B-and-R.com。**

女： (34) **太棒了，我們現在就來看看，我們可以查看他們所有服務選項。**

- maintenance (n.) 維修；保養　crew (n.)（一組）工作人員　terrific (adj.) 非常好的　stain (n.) 汙漬　professionally (adv.) 專業地　eco-friendly (adj.) 環保的　equipment (n.) 設備；用具　go over 仔細查看

32. 相關細節——女子感到滿意的地方

What does the woman say she is pleased with?
(A) A larger work area
(B) An extended vacation
(C) Some budget decisions
(D) Some recent sales results

女子說她對什麼很滿意？
(A) 辦公空間擴增
(B) 假期延長
(C) 預算決策
(D) 近期銷售結果

- extend (v.) 延長　vacation (n.) 假期　budget (n.) 預算　result (n.) 結果

換句話說 more space to set up desks for the part-time staff（有更多空間可以擺放兼職人員用的辦公桌）→ a larger work area（辦公空間擴增）

33. 相關細節——B&R 服務公司的種類

What kind of business most likely is B & R Services?
(A) An event planning firm
(B) A temporary staffing agency
(C) An interior decorating provider
(D) A carpet cleaning company

B&R 服務公司最可能是何種業者？
(A) 活動規劃公司
(B) 派遣人員仲介公司
(C) 室內裝潢供應商
(D) 地毯清潔公司

- planning (n.) 規劃　temporary (adj.) 臨時的；暫時的　staff (v.) 為……提供人員
agency (n.) 仲介；代理機構　decorate (v.) 裝飾；布置　provider (n.) 供應商；供應者

34. 相關細節——說話者接下來要做的事情

What will the speakers probably do next?
(A) Review information on a Web site
(B) Prepare a presentation
(C) Rearrange some devices
(D) Ask for approval from a manager

說話者接下來很可能做什麼？
(A) 查看網站上的資訊
(B) 準備簡報
(C) 重新排列一些裝置
(D) 請求經理的批准

- review (v.) 查看　rearrange (v.) 重新排列／布置　device (n.) 裝置　approval (n.) 批准；同意

換句話說 go over all their service options（查看他們所有服務選項）→ review information（查看資訊）

35-37 Conversation

W: Hi, Mr. Jones? This is a courtesy call from Southern Asian Airways. (35) **There's been a change in the itinerary for your flight to Mumbai on November nineteenth. That flight will leave from New York, not Washington, D.C.**

M: (36) **Right. I got an update e-mail on Friday explaining that.**

W: Oh good, you're all confirmed then. Is there anything else I can help you with?

M: Yes, actually. (37) **How can I ask for all vegetarian options for the in-flight meals?**

35-37 對話 美⇄澳

女： 嗨，瓊斯先生嗎？這裡是南亞航空，本次來電想知會您：(35) **您於 11 月 19 日飛往孟買的航班路線有變動，班機將會從紐約起飛，而不是華盛頓特區。**

男： (36) **好的，我週五有收到電子郵件，說明了這項最新變動。**

女： 噢，好的，那麼您都確認完畢了。還有其他需要我服務的地方嗎？

男： 其實有的，(37) **我要如何選擇全素的飛機餐？**

W: On our Web site, go to "My Flight" and then follow the instructions for "tailoring food options."

M: Terrific. Thank you for the call.

女：請上我們的網站，點選「我的航班」，然後依照「客製餐飲選項」的指示進行。

男：太好了，謝謝妳的來電。

- courtesy call 禮貌性致電／問候等 itinerary (n.) 路線；行程 flight (n.) 航班 confirm (v.) 確認 vegetarian (adj.) 素食的 option (n.) 選項 in-flight meal 飛機餐 instruction (n.) 操作說明 tailor (v.) 定製；專門製作 terrific (adj.)（口語）非常好

35. 相關細節——女子告知的行程變更事宜

According to the woman, what has changed about a trip itinerary?

(A) The operator of a flight

(B) The departure point

(C) The duration

(D) The number of connecting flights

根據女子說法，行程有何變動？

(A) 航班操作員

(B) 起飛地點

(C) 飛航時間

(D) 轉機航班的數量

- operator (n.) 操作員 departure (n.) 出發；離開 duration (n.) 持續期間 connecting (adj.) 連接的

換句話說 leave（起飛）→ departure（起飛）

---

36. 相關細節——男子提及週五發生的事情

What does the man say happened on Friday?

(A) He received a notification message.

(B) He canceled a previous booking.

(C) He changed the date of a trip.

(D) He was given a ticket discount.

男子說週五發生了什麼事？

(A) 他收到通知訊息。

(B) 他取消之前的預訂。

(C) 他更改了旅程日期。

(D) 他的機票得到折扣。

- receive (v.) 收到 notification (n.) 通知 cancel (v.) 取消 previous (adj.) 之前的 booking (n.) 預訂

換句話說 got an update e-mail（收到更新資訊的電子郵件）
→ received a notification message（收到通知訊息）

---

37. 相關細節——男子想知道的事情

What does the man want to know about?

(A) Choosing a seating option

(B) Checking in large baggage

(C) Requesting special meals

(D) Using an airport lounge

男子想知道何事的相關資訊？

(A) 選擇座位選項

(B) 托運大件行李

(C) 要求特殊餐點

(D) 使用機場休息室

- seating (n.) 座位 baggage (n.) 行李 request (v.) 要求

換句話說 ask for all vegetarian options for the . . . meals（選擇全素的餐點）
→ requesting special meals（要求特殊餐點）

38-40 Conversation

38-40 對話

加⇄英

M: Hi, I'm Fred Mason. I have a two o'clock dental appointment to see Dr. Evans. [38] **I was told to be here fifteen minutes ahead of time.** It's my first visit to the clinic.

W: Oh yes, normally you can download and print out our patient information forms. But we're updating our Web site. [39] **So . . . please fill out these forms here—only the parts that are circled or highlighted.**

M: No problem.

W: Just bring them back to me when you're done. [40] **Plus, here are notepads and a calendar with dental care tips printed on them—it's a gift packet for new patients.**

M: Great, thank you.

男：嗨，我是佛瑞德．馬森。我有和艾文斯醫師約在二點看診。[38] **我聽你們說，要提前 15 分鐘到**。這是我第一次看診。

女：噢，好的。通常您可以下載然後印出我們的病人資料表，但我們的網站正在更新當中，[39] **所以……請填寫這邊的幾張表格，只需填寫圈起來或特別標示的地方即可。**

男：沒問題。

女：填完之後，拿回來給我就好。[40] **另外，這邊有一些便條冊和一份行事曆，上面印有牙齒保健要點；這是我們送給新病患的贈品組。**

男：太好了，謝謝妳。

- **dental (adj.)** 牙齒的；牙科的　**appointment (n.)**（事務性）約會；預約　**ahead of . . .** 在……之前　**clinic (n.)** 診所　**fill out** 填寫　**circle (v.)** 圈出；畫圓圈　**highlight (v.)** 強調；使凸顯　**calendar (n.)** 日曆　**packet (n.)** 小包；小袋

38. 相關細節——男子先前收到的指示

What was the man previously instructed to do?

(A) Bring his old dental records

(B) Enter through a side door

(C) Arrive early for an appointment

(D) Refer acquaintances to a clinic

男子先前受要求做何事？

(A) 攜帶舊的牙科病歷表

(B) 透過側門進入

(C) 提早到達約診

(D) 介紹熟人到診所看診

- **enter (v.)** 進入　**refer (v.)** 使求助於　**acquaintance (n.)** 認識的人

---

39. 相關細節——女子針對文件提及的事項

難

What does the woman say about some paperwork?

(A) It had already been filled out electronically.

(B) It has marked sections for completion.

(C) It contains some printing errors.

(D) It was recently revised.

關於一些文件，女子說了什麼？

(A) 已經透過電子方式填完。

(B) 有標示出需要填寫的部分。

(C) 內有一些印刷錯誤。

(D) 最近修訂過。

- **electronically (adv.)** 用電子方式　**mark (v.)** 標明　**section (n.)**（事物的）部分　**completion (n.)** 完成　**error (n.)** 錯誤　**revise (v.)** 修訂

換句話說 the parts that are circled or highlighted（圈起來或特別標示的地方）
→ marked sections（標示的部分）

40. 相關細節——女子給男子的東西

What does the woman give the man?
(A) Some tooth care tools
(B) Some customized stationery
(C) Some coupons for future visits
(D) Some bottled water

女子送給男子什麼？
(A) 牙齒保健工具
(B) 訂製的文具
(C) 未來可使用的優待券
(D) 瓶裝水

- tool (n.) 工具　customized (adj.) 客製化的；訂製的　stationery (n.) 文具　bottled (adj.) 瓶裝的

41-43 Conversation

M: Good news, Ah-Reum. (41) **Our latest mobile phone app for language learning got a positive review from Nancy Batra—you know, the technology columnist for *The Watmon Times*.**

W: Yes, I just read it. That'll help boost its sales, for sure. (42) **I'm wondering if we should proceed with developing a mobile phone app for self-study in mathematics. There could be strong demand . . .**

M: (42) **It's worth considering**, and, well . . . many students are learning from home.

W: OK. (43) **I'll go ahead and e-mail Greg, our expert advisor on mobile apps, and set up a time to discuss our plans.**

41-43 對話　澳⇄美

男：雅瀷，有個好消息：(41) **我們最新的語言學習手機 APP 受到南西．貝特拉給出正面評論；妳知道，就是那位《華曼時報》的科技專欄作家。**

女：是啊，我剛看到文章了，這勢必有助提高銷量。(42) **我正在想，我們是不是該接著開發自學數學的手機 APP，可能不少人會有相關需求……**

男：(42) **這很值得考慮**，而且說起來……很多學生目前都在家上課。

女：好的，(43) **我會著手寄電子郵件，給我們的手機 APP 專家顧問葛瑞格，安排時間討論我們的計畫。**

- latest (adj.) 最新的　positive (adj.) 正面的　columnist (n.) 專欄作家　boost (v.) 提高
  wonder (v.) 想知道　proceed with . . . 繼續做……　demand (n.) 需求　worth (adj.) 值得（做……）
  expert (adj.) 專家的　advisor (n.) 顧問

41. 相關細節——南西．貝特拉的身分

Who most likely is Nancy Batra?
(A) A visiting professor
(B) An in-house translator
(C) A departmental intern
(D) A newspaper journalist

南西．貝特拉最可能的身分為何？
(A) 客座教授
(B) 公司的翻譯員
(C) 部門的實習生
(D) 報社新聞工作者

換句話說 columnist（專欄作家）→ journalist（新聞工作者）

42. 掌握說話者的意圖——提及「很多學生目前都在家上課」的意圖　難

Why does the man say, "many students are learning from home"?
(A) To decline an assignment
(B) To suggest delaying a product release
(C) To express agreement with the woman
(D) To admit that he is concerned about market competition

男子為什麼說：「很多學生目前都在家上課」？
(A) 以推辭一項工作
(B) 以建議延後產品推出
(C) 以表達同意女子
(D) 以承認他擔心市場競爭

- decline (v.) 婉拒　assignment (n.) 工作；任務　delay (v.) 延後　release (n.) 發行
  agreement (n.) 同意　admit (v.) 承認　concerned (adj.) 擔心的　competition (n.) 競爭

43. 相關細節——女子接下來要做的事情

What will the woman probably do next?
(A) Contact a consultant
(B) Make a delivery
(C) Proofread a report
(D) Set up some equipment

女子接下來很可能會做什麼？
(A) 聯絡顧問
(B) 送出貨物
(C) 校對報告
(D) 設置設備

- contact (v.) 聯絡　consultant (n.) 顧問　proofread (v.) 校對　equipment (n.) 設備

換句話說 e-mail our expert advisor（寄電郵給我們的專家顧問）→ contact a consultant（聯絡顧問）

44-46 Conversation with three speakers

M1: Ms. Jacobs? The desktop computer in the side office is working again.

W: That was fast. Was it a problem with the electrical outlet in the wall?

M1: No, (44) **actually one monitor cable wasn't secured tightly enough, so I just needed to plug it in again.** It was an easy fix.

W: Ah, I see. Oh, (45) **hi, Stan. The computer's been fixed.**

M2: (45) **Great. I'll have the intern I'm overseeing get back to her digital art project.**

W: Excellent, we're all set.

M1: (46) **And Ms. Jacobs . . . if you have time, please leave a client review on the Web site for my repair business.** I would really appreciate it.

44-46 三人對話　加⇄英⇄澳

男 1：雅各布女士？側邊辦公室的桌上型電腦又可以用了。

女：動作真快。是牆壁插座的問題嗎？

男 1：不是，(44) **其實是螢幕有一條電線沒有插緊，所以我只需要重新把線插進去，**很簡單就修好了。

女：啊，了解。噢，(45) **嗨，史丹，電腦已經修好了。**

男 2：(45) **太好了，我會叫我管理的實習生，回去繼續進行她的數位藝術專案。**

女：好極了，一切搞定。

男 1：(46) **另外，雅各布女士，如果您有時間的話，請針對我的維修業務，到網站上留下客戶評價，**對此我會非常感謝。

- electrical outlet 插座　secure (v.) 把……弄牢　tightly (adv.) 牢固地　plug in 插上…的插頭　fix (n./v.) 修理　oversee (v.) 監督　set (adj.) 準備好的　review (n.) 評論　repair (n.) 修理　appreciate (v.) 感謝

44. 相關細節——導致問題的原因

What has caused a problem?
(A) An outdated software program
(B) A malfunctioning monitor
(C) A loose cable connection
(D) A faulty electrical outlet

問題的起因是什麼？
(A) 軟體程式過時
(B) 螢幕故障
(C) 電線連接鬆脫
(D) 插座異常

- outdated (adj.) 過時的　malfunction (v.) 故障；失靈　loose (adj.) 鬆開的　connection (n.) 連接　faulty (adj.) 有錯誤的；有缺陷的

換句話說 wasn't secured tightly enough（沒有插緊）→ loose（鬆脫）

45. 相關細節——史丹提及與自身有關的事情

What does Stan mention about himself?
(A) He supervises an intern.
(B) He has a project due soon.
(C) He previously tried to fix a computer.
(D) He referred Ms. Jacobs to a service.

史丹提到他自己的什麼事？
(A) 他有管理一名實習生。
(B) 他有個專案期限快到了。
(C) 他先前嘗試修理電腦。
(D) 他把服務轉介給雅各布女士。

• **supervise (v.)** 管理　**due (adj.)** 到期的　**previously (adv.)** 先前地

換句話說 **overseeing**（管理）→ **supervise**（管理）

---

46. 相關細節——要求女子做的事情

What is the woman asked to do?
(A) Distribute his business card
(B) Provide online feedback
(C) Present a warranty document
(D) Review an installation procedure

女子受要求做何事？
(A) 發送他的名片
(B) 提供線上意見回饋
(C) 出示保固文件
(D) 檢查安裝程序

• **distribute (v.)** 分發　**business card** 名片　**present (v.)** 出示　**warranty (n.)** 保證書
installation (n.) 安裝　**procedure (n.)** 程序

換句話說 **leave a client review on the Web site**（到網站上留下客戶評價）
→ **provide online feedback**（提供線上意見回饋）

47-49 Conversation

M: Hi, I'm Kevin. I'm here for my training to be a historical tour guide.
W: Yes, I'm your trainer. (47) **I heard you got a high score on your written exam on the city's historical facts.** Congratulations!
M: Oh, thank you! I studied hard for it.
W: OK. Well, today (48) **I'll show you around the city's history museum. It's important because every walking tour of the city originates from its lobby.** It's a great introduction to our past.
M: I see. (49) **Should I be taking notes on what we talk about?**
W: That would be a great idea, if it will help you remember.

47-49 對話 加⇄美

男： 嗨，我是凱文，我來這裡參加歷史導覽員的培訓。
女： 好的，我是你的培訓導師。(47) **我聽說，你在本市歷史知識的筆試成績拿到高分，恭喜你！**
男： 噢，謝謝妳！我很用功準備。
女： 很好，那麼今天 (48) **我會帶你走一遍本市的歷史博物館，這裡相當重要，因為本市每場徒步導覽都是從這裡的大廳出發**，博物館可以讓我們好好地初步認識過去歷史。
男： 了解。(49) **我應該把我們討論的內容記下來嗎？**
女： 如果這能幫助你記憶，倒是個好辦法。

• **written exam** 筆試　**show somebody around** 帶某人到處參觀　**originate (v.)** 起源；創始
introduction (n.) 介紹　**take notes** 記筆記

47. 相關細節——女子提及男子最近完成的事情

According to the woman, what did the man do recently?
(A) Took a knowledge test
(B) Opened a souvenir shop
(C) Published a guidebook
(D) Trained a tour leader

根據女子所說，男子最近做了何事？
(A) 參加知識測驗
(B) 開了紀念品店
(C) 出版了導覽書
(D) 訓練了一名領隊

- souvenir (n.) 紀念品　publish (v.) 出版

換句話說 exam（考試）→ test（測驗）

48. 相關細節——女子強調城市的歷史博物館很重要的理由 難

Why does the woman say the city's history museum is important?
(A) It is the city's oldest tourist attraction.
(B) It is larger than other museums.
(C) It has new interactive exhibits.
(D) It is the starting point for walking tours.

女子為何說城市的歷史博物館很重要？
(A) 是市區最古老的旅遊景點。
(B) 比其他博物館還大。
(C) 有新的互動式展覽品。
(D) 是徒步導覽的起點。

- tourist attraction 旅遊景點　interactive (adj.) 互動的　exhibit (n.) 展覽（品）

換句話說 originates from（從……開始）→ starting（起始）

49. 相關細節——男子向女子詢問的事情

What does the man ask the woman about?
(A) Taking special transportation to a venue
(B) Introducing himself to a group of people
(C) Earning a professional qualification
(D) Keeping a record of a conversation

男子詢問女子何項相關事項？
(A) 搭乘特殊交通工具去會場
(B) 把自己介紹給一群人
(C) 取得專業資格
(D) 把對話記錄下來

- transportation (n.) 交通工具；運輸　venue (n.) 會場　introduce (v.) 介紹　earn (v.) 取得　professional (adj.) 專業的　qualification (n.) 資格

換句話說 taking notes on what we talk about（把我們討論的內容記下來）
→ keeping a record of a conversation（把對話記錄下來）

50-52 Conversation

W: Hi, I read about the rain garden at Cailson City Park—you know, (50) **that sunken garden that collects rainwater so plants can absorb it. I'm a homeowner and would like to build one.**

M: (50) **Well, we have all the soil and plants you would need here at this store.** (51) **For a rain garden project, I would recommend selecting plants that are native to this area.** They're best adapted to our local weather patterns.

W: I see.

M: (52) **To help you choose, here on this tablet is a Web site called www.rain-resources.com. It tells all about rain gardens.** You can look at it as you browse around.

50-52 對話 英⇄澳

女：嗨，我之前讀到凱爾森市立公園裡，有座「雨水花園」，你知道，(50) **就是那種會收集雨水、提供給植物吸收的下凹式花園。我自己有棟房子，想要蓋一座這種花園。**

男：(50) **這樣的話，您會需要的所有土壤和植物，我們店裡都一應俱全。(51) 以雨水花園工程來說，我會建議選擇種植本地的原生植物，**因為會最能夠適應本地的天氣型態。

女：了解。

男：(52) **為了幫助您選擇，這邊的平板電腦上有個網站：www.rain-resources.com，上面有雨水花園的各類資訊。**您一邊逛本店商品時，可以一邊查看網站。

- sunken (adj.) 下陷的　absorb (v.) 吸收　homeowner (n.) 屋主　soil (n.) 土壤　native (adj.) 原生種的　adapt (v.) 適應　browse (v.) 隨意觀看（店內商品）

50. 全文相關——對話的地點 難

Where most likely is the conversation taking place?
(A) At a city park
(B) At a garden supply shop
(C) At an organic farm
(D) At a natural history museum

這段對話最可能發生在何處？
(A) 在市立公園
(B) 在園藝用品店
(C) 在有機農場
(D) 在自然歷史博物館

51. 相關細節——男子針對工程提出的建議 難

What does the man suggest doing for a project?
(A) Placing some plants in an indoor area
(B) Checking a local weather forecast daily
(C) Choosing plants that normally grow in a region
(D) Starting it during a warmer season

男子對工程有何建議？
(A) 將部分植物擺在室內區域
(B) 每天查看當地天氣預報
(C) 選擇通常生長在地方的植物
(D) 在較溫暖的季節動工

- place (v.) 放置　indoor (adj.) 室內的　weather forecast 天氣預報

換句話說 selecting plants that are native to this area（選擇種植本地的原生植物）
→ choosing plants that normally grow in a region（選擇通常生長在地方的植物）

52. 相關細節——男子展示給女子看的事物

What does the man show the woman?
(A) A directional sign
(B) An informational Web site
(C) An artificial body of water
(D) A price list for services

男子展示什麼給女子看？
(A) 方向指示標誌
(B) 提供資訊的網站
(C) 人工水域
(D) 服務價目表

- directional (adj.) 方向的　artificial (adj.) 人工的

53-55 Conversation with three speakers

M: Thank you for giving me the chance to tell you about my company's products. (53) **At Carelli Graphics, our sole focus is producing high-quality posters to inspire and encourage workers.** This one, called "Success," is our top seller.

W1: Very nice!

M: (54) **What's more, our company only uses recycled or sustainably-sourced wood and paper in our products.**

W1: (54) **I like that.** (55) **Sandra?**

W2: (54) **Yes, I like that too.** (55) **Uh, and I wanted to say that my department is having a day of activities to improve our teamwork soon.** This one, with the title "Collaboration", would be great for us.

M: I'll set it aside.

53-55 三人對話　加⇄美⇄英

男：謝謝給予機會，讓我向妳們說明本公司的產品。(53) **我們凱爾里平面設計專心致力在製作高品質海報，用來啟發員工並提振士氣**，這張名為「成功」的海報，是我們最暢銷的產品。

女 1：很不錯！

男：(54) **此外，我們公司只會使用再生或取自永續來源的木材和紙張，來製作產品。**

女 1：(54) **這點我很喜歡，**(55) **珊卓拉妳呢？**

女 2：(54) **是啊，我也喜歡。**(55) **噢，我還想說的是，我的部門即將舉行一日活動，以便促進團隊合作精神**，這張標題為「合作」的海報，會很適合我們使用。

男：我就把那張放在這邊。

- sole (adj.) 唯一的 produce (v.) 生產 inspire (v.) 啟發 recycle (v.) 回收再利用 sustainably (adv.)（環境）永續地 source (v.) 從（某地）獲取…… collaboration (n.) 合作 set aside 把……擱在一邊；撥出

53. 相關細節——男子的公司販售的產品類型

What kind of products does the man's company sell?
(A) Adjustable desks
(B) Instructional books
(C) Business software
(D) Motivational posters

男子的公司販賣何種產品？
(A) 可調整式書桌
(B) 學習用書
(C) 商用軟體
(D) 勵志海報

- adjustable (adj.) 可調整的 instructional (adj.) 教學的 motivational (adj.) 鼓動人心的

換句話說 posters to inspire and encourage workers（啟發員工並提振士氣的海報）
→ motivational posters（勵志海報）

54. 相關細節——女子們中意喜歡男子公司的特點 難

What do the women say they like about the man's company?
(A) It provides a fast delivery service.
(B) It uses environmentally-friendly materials.
(C) It participates in community fundraisers.
(D) It has a wide selection of products.

女子們說，她們中意男子公司的何項特質？
(A) 提供快速送貨服務。
(B) 使用環保原料。
(C) 參與社區募款活動。
(D) 產品種類多樣。

- delivery (n.) 送貨；投遞 environmentally-friendly (adj.) 環保的 participate (v.) 參加 community (n.) 社區 fundraiser (n.) 募款活動 a (wide) selection of . . . 各式……可供挑選

換句話說 recycled or sustainably-sourced wood and paper（再生或取自永續來源的木材和紙張）
→ environmentally-friendly materials（環保原料）

55. 相關細節——珊卓拉針對自己部門談到的事情

What does Sandra say about her department?
(A) It will sponsor a running race.
(B) It will be given a different name.
(C) It will have team-building day.
(D) It will merge with another department.

關於她的部門，珊卓拉說了什麼？
(A) 會贊助一場賽跑。
(B) 會有不同的名稱。
(C) 會舉行一日內訓活動。
(D) 會和另一個部門合併。

- sponsor (v.) 贊助 race (n.) 比賽 merge (v.) 合併

換句話說 a day of activities to improve our teamwork（一日活動以便促進團隊合作精神）
→ team-building day（一日內訓）

56-58 Conversation

M: Hi, thanks for calling Darvi's Restaurant. How may I help you?

W: Hi. (56) **I'm making plans to have an outdoor meal to celebrate our company's tenth year**

56-58 對話 澳⇄美

男：嗨，這裡是達維餐廳，感謝您的來電，請問需要什麼服務嗎？

女：嗨，(56) **我正在規劃舉辦戶外聚餐宴會，用來慶祝我們公司開業十週年。**我們想

in business. We'd like to have it on Sunday evening, but—would you be able to cater it in that case? I know that you're closed then . . .

要辦在週日晚上，但是——這樣你們方便幫我們供餐嗎？我知道那個時段你們沒有營業……

M: **(57) Don't worry—we can schedule catering for any time, even before we open and after we close our dining room to customers.**

男：**(57) 別擔心，我們的外燴服務可以安排在任何時段，即使是我們餐廳開始營業前或對外打烊後，還是可以的。**

W: Oh, that's good news. And could we substitute some ingredients in the meals?

女：噢，那真是太好了。另外，我們可以更換餐點中的部分食材嗎？

M: Absolutely. **(58) For that, I'd recommend calling the owner, Mr. Darvi, on his mobile and speaking with him. His number is on our Web site.**

男：當然可以。**(58) 要做更換的話，我建議撥打手機給老闆達維先生，和他討論一下，他的手機號碼可從我們網站上查到。**

- outdoor (adj.) 戶外的　celebrate (v.) 慶祝　cater (v.) 提供外燴　schedule (v.) 安排時間　dining room 餐廳　substitute (v.) 用……代替　ingredient (n.) 食料　absolutely (adv.)（表示贊同）沒錯

56. 相關細節——女子正在計劃的活動

What kind of event is the woman planning?

(A) An awards banquet
(B) A birthday party
(C) An anniversary celebration
(D) A cooking contest

女子正在規劃何種活動？

(A) 頒獎晚宴
(B) 生日派對
(C) 週年慶祝會
(D) 烹飪比賽

57. 相關細節——男子針對餐飲服務提及讓女子安心的事情 

What does the man say to reassure the woman about a catering service?

(A) It has won recognition from publications.
(B) It is used by the area's biggest companies.
(C) It can be provided in a range of venues.
(D) It is available outside of regular business hours.

關於供餐服務，男子對女子做出何項保證？

(A) 有獲得到報章媒體的好評。
(B) 當地的大型企業都選用他們。
(C) 可在不同場地提供服務。
(D) 可在一般營業時間外供應。

- reassure (v.) 使安心　recognition (n.) 讚賞　publication (n.) 出版物　a range of . . . 一系列……　venue (n.) 會場　available (adj.) 可用的　regular (adj.) 一般的

換句話說 before we open and after we close our dining room to customers（我們餐廳開始營業前或對外打烊後）→ outside of regular business hours（一般營業時間外）

58. 相關細節——男子提出的建議

What does the man suggest doing?

(A) Requesting a discount for a large group
(B) Reserving a particular banquet room
(C) Phoning a business proprietor directly
(D) Ordering meals from an online menu

男子建議做什麼？

(A) 要求大型團體的折扣。
(B) 預訂特定的宴會廳。
(C) 直接打電話給餐廳老闆。
(D) 從線上菜單訂餐。

- request (v.) 要求　reserve (v.) 預訂　particular (adj.) 特定的　banquet (n.) 宴會　phone (v.) 打電話給……　proprietor (n.) 經營者　order (v.) 點餐

換句話說 calling the owner（打給老闆）→ Phoning a . . . proprietor（打電話給……老闆）

59-61 Conversation

59-61 對話

英⇄澳

W: Welcome to Marino's Farmer's Market. Oh, hi, Mr. Blakely.

M: Hi. I placed an order online for two pounds of yellow corn, for pick-up.

W: Yes, my assistant will be right out with your order.

M: Great. (59) **Hey, I like your new Web site—it's really easy to order from.**

W: Thank you. (59) **I designed it myself, and supplied all the photos.**

M: Wow! (60) **And I have to say that your corn is the best I've ever tasted**—and I grew up on a farm.

W: So glad to hear that! (61) **Now, while you're waiting, why don't you explore our new floral section? We have some beautiful bouquets of fresh-cut tulips and roses.**

女：歡迎光臨馬利諾農夫市集。噢，布萊克利先生您好。

男：嗨，我在網路上訂了兩磅黃玉米，現在來取貨。

女：好的，我的助理會馬上把您訂的貨品拿過來。

男：太好了。(59) **話說，我很喜歡你們的新網站——在上面下單非常簡單。**

女：謝謝你。(59) **網站是我自己設計的，而且所有的照片都是我提供的。**

男：哇！(60) **還有我要說你們的玉米是我吃過最好吃的**，而我可是在農場上長大的。

女：聽到你這麼說，我很開心！(61) **在你現在等待的期間，何不參考一下我們新設的花卉專區？我們有些使用現採的鬱金香、玫瑰做成的美麗花束。**

- place an order 下訂單　assistant (n.) 助理　supply (v.) 供給　taste (v.) 嚐　explore (v.) 探索　section (n.) 區域

59. 相關細節——女子提及她做過的事情

難

What does the woman say she did?

(A) Uploaded some images to the Internet

(B) Repaired some harvesting equipment

(C) Packed a box of produce for pick-up

(D) Submitted an order form to a manufacturer

女子說她做了何事？

(A) 上傳影像到網路上

(B) 修理採收用具

(C) 把農產品裝箱供人取貨

(D) 把訂單交給製造商

- upload (v.) 上傳　repair (v.) 修理　harvest (v.) 收成　equipment (n.) 用具　pack (v.) 裝（箱）　produce (n.) 農產品　submit (v.) 交出　manufacturer (n.) 製造商

換句話說 supplied all the photos（提供所有照片）→ uploaded some images（上傳影像）

60. 掌握說話者的意圖——提及「我可是在農場長大的」的意圖

難

Why most likely does the man say, "I grew up on a farm"?

(A) To support an opinion

(B) To explain a misunderstanding

(C) To offer assistance

(D) To show curiosity

男子說：「我可是在農場上長大的」，最可能的原因為何？

(A) 印證一個看法

(B) 解釋誤會

(C) 提供協助

(D) 顯示好奇心

- support (v.) 證實　opinion (n.) 看法　misunderstanding (n.) 誤會　assistance (n.) 協助　curiosity (n.) 好奇心

61. 相關細節——女子建議男子做的事情

What does the woman suggest the man do?

(A) Feed some farm animals

(B) Park closer to an entrance

(C) Read over a promotional flyer

(D) Look at some flower arrangements

女子建議男子做什麼？

(A) 餵食農場動物

(B) 把車停得更靠近入口

(C) 查閱廣告傳單

(D) 查看一些花束

- feed (v.) 飼養　park (v.) 停放（車輛等）　entrance (n.) 入口　promotional (adj.) 宣傳的　flyer (n.)（廣告）傳單　flower arrangement 插花

62-64 Conversation + Graph

M: Hi, Leilani. Well, (62) **our initiative to move into new markets has succeeded. Our drinks are being sold in more places than ever before, and sales are strong overall.**

W: Excellent! How are sales for our Tropical Sun drink?

M: They're up. (63) **Surveyed consumers say they like its blend of mango and strawberry flavors.** Here's a sales chart broken down by size of container.

W: I see . . . It seems our most popular container size historically is still our best seller.

M: Yes. (64) **But I was surprised to see that this one is our second-best seller. So let's look at its sales figures in more depth**. I'll bring up more charts.

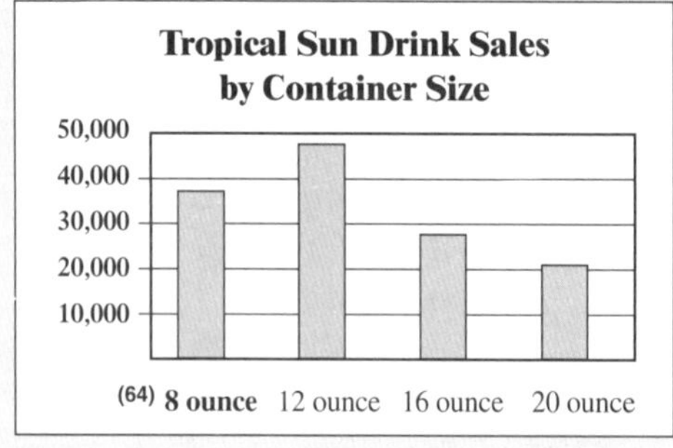

62-64 對話＋圖表 加⇄英

男： 嗨，蕾拉妮，(62) **我們打入新市場的計畫很成功，我們飲料的銷售地點比以前大有斬獲，而且整體銷售額也非常強勁。**

女： 太好了！我們「熱帶豔陽」這款飲料的銷量如何？

男： 銷量有所成長，(63) **顧客受訪時說到，他們很喜歡融合芒果和草莓的風味。**這邊是根據容量大小細分的銷售量圖表。

女： 了解⋯⋯看起來我們歷來銷量最佳的一款包裝容量，仍然是賣得最好。

男： 是的，(64) **但讓我驚訝的是，銷量居次的會這一款，所以我們不妨來更深入看看這一款的銷售數字**，我會拿更多圖表過來。

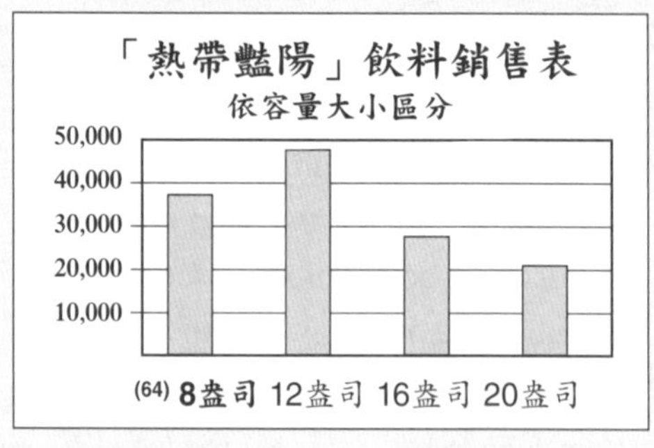

- initiative (n.) 計畫；行動　overall (adj.) 全面的　excellent (adj.) 極好的　flavor (n.) 風味　blend (n.) 混合　break down 把⋯⋯細分　container (n.) 容器　figure (n.) 數字　in depth 詳盡地

62. 相關細節——公司完成的事情 難

According to the speakers, what has the company done?

(A) Relocated its head office

(B) Expanded its sales territory

(C) Created a new corporate logo

(D) Replaced a celebrity spokesperson

根據說話者，公司完成了何事？

(A) 遷移總部

(B) 擴展銷售區域

(C) 製作新的公司標誌

(D) 更換明星代言人

- relocate (v.) 搬遷　head office 總公司；總部　expand (v.) 擴展　territory (n.) 領域　corporate (adj.) 公司的　replace (v.) 取代；更換　celebrity (n.) 名人　spokesperson (n.) 代言人；發言人

換句話說 move into new markets（打入新市場）→ expanded its sales territory（擴展銷售區域）

63. 相關細節——針對熱帶豔陽飲料提及的內容 難

What is mentioned about the Tropical Sun drink?
(A) It is stocked mostly in restaurants.
(B) It has a combination of flavors.
(C) It will soon be sold at discounts.
(D) It comes in glass bottles.

關於「熱帶豔陽」飲料，對話中提到什麼？
(A) 大部分供貨給餐廳。
(B) 混合不同風味。
(C) 即將折價銷售。
(D) 以玻璃瓶裝。

- **stock (v.)** 進貨　**mostly (adv.)** 大部分地　**combination (n.)** 結合　**come in** 以（某形式）販售

換句話說 its blend of . . . flavors（融合……的風味）→ a combination of flavors（混合不同風味）

64. 圖表整合題——說話者關注的飲料容量

Look at the graphic. Which size of drink's sales data will the speakers focus on?
(A) 8 ounce
(B) 12 ounce
(C) 16 ounce
(D) 20 ounce

請見圖表作答。說話者們將會關注哪一款容量的飲料銷售資料？
(A) 8 盎司
(B) 12 盎司
(C) 16 盎司
(D) 20 盎司

65-67 Conversation + Menu

W: Well, it sure has been quiet here.

M: I'll say. (65) **Some of our hardware engineers don't have much to do these days.** But we'll be busier when we start working on product updates.

W: True. Oh, that reminds me—(66) **you know Enzio's Café? They've just streamlined the way you order for delivery—now it's only two steps.** You click the menu item on the Web site and then click "order." I'll show you.

M: Oh, that's nice. So, (67) **do you want to order today's special?**

W: (67) **Well, it is the cheapest one. But it's on the light side. Why don't we order the special tomorrow?** It'll be more filling.

M: Good plan.

Enzio's Cafe—Daily Specials

Monday	Chicken curry $13
Tuesday	Vegetable pasta $10
(67) **Wednesday**	**Cheese pizza $12**
Thursday	Grilled salmon $14

65-67 對話＋菜單 美⇄澳

女：嗯，這裡真的很安靜。

男：對啊，(65) **我們一些硬體工程師這幾天沒有太多事情可做**，但是等我們開始進行產品更新時，就會比較忙了。

女：那倒是真的，噢，這讓我想到：(66) **你知道恩齊歐咖啡館嗎？他們才剛簡化外送點餐的方式，現在只要兩個步驟就好了。**你在網站上點選菜單上的品項後，再點「下單」就好，我展示給你看。

男：噢，真的不錯。那麼，(67) **妳想點今天的特餐嗎？**

女：(67) **嗯，特餐是最便宜的餐點，但分量不多，我們何不明天再點特餐？**明天的特餐比較吃得飽。

男：好主意。

恩齊歐咖啡館——每日特餐

星期一	咖哩雞	$13
星期二	蔬菜義大利麵	$10
(67) **星期三**	**起司披薩**	**$12**
星期四	烤鮭魚	$14

- I'll say（表贊同）的確 remind (v.) 提醒 streamline (v.) 使簡化；使提升效率 step (n.) 步驟 light (adj.) 少量的；輕淡的 filling (adj.) 有飽足感的

65. 相關細節——男子針對部分員工提及的事情

What does the man say about some employees?
(A) They have been telecommuting.
(B) They will transfer to overseas offices.
(C) Their workloads have been reduced.
(D) They are attending a product launch.

關於部分員工，男子說了什麼？
(A) 他們一直遠距工作。
(B) 他們將調往海外據點。
(C) 他們的工作量減少了。
(D) 他們正在參加產品發表會。

- telecommute (v.) 遠距辦公 transfer (v.) 調任 overseas (adj.) 國外的 workload (n.) 工作量 reduce (v.) 減少 attend (v.) 參加 launch (n.) 發布會

換句話說 don't have much to do（沒有太多事情可做）→ workloads have been reduced（工作量減少）

66. 相關細節——女子提及恩齊歐咖啡館最近完成的事 難

According to the woman, what has Enzio's Café recently done?
(A) Raised its food prices
(B) Renovated its dining room
(C) Opened an additional location
(D) Simplified an ordering process

根據女子，恩齊歐咖啡館最近完成何事？
(A) 調漲餐飲價格
(B) 整修餐廳
(C) 開新分店
(D) 簡化點餐程序

- raise (v.) 增加 renovate (v.) 整修；翻新 dining room 餐廳 additional (adj.) 額外的 location (n.) 地點 simplify (v.) 簡化 process (n.) 程序

換句話說 streamlined the way you order（簡化點餐方式）
→ simplified an ordering process（簡化點餐程序）

67. 圖表整合題——說話者可能會訂購的特餐 難

Look at the graphic. What special will the speakers probably order for delivery?
(A) Chicken curry
(B) Vegetable pasta
(C) Cheese pizza
(D) Grilled salmon

請見圖表作答。說話者很可能會點哪一道特餐外送？
(A) 咖哩雞
(B) 蔬菜義大利麵
(C) 起司披薩
(D) 烤鮭魚

68-70 Conversation + List

M: Hi, Judy. (68) **Well, it's only your first week here on the job, but it looks like you're learning quickly.** Is there anything I can help you with?

W: Actually, yes. (69) **I'm processing a returned headset, and the purchaser said he returned it because it's a faulty product. There's sound only on one side. Uh, no return code appears on the computer.**

68-70 對話＋清單 加⇄美

男： 嗨，茱蒂。(68) **嗯，妳才來上班一個星期，但看起來已經駕輕就熟了**，有什麼我可以幫忙的嗎？

女： 老實說，有的。(69) **我正在處理一個退貨的耳機，買家說退貨的原因是為耳機有瑕疵，只有一邊有聲音。呃，電腦上沒有顯示退貨代碼。**

M: Oh, you have to enter it manually. (69) **Here's a list of the codes.**

W: Ah, thank you.

M: No problem. If you have any questions later, just ask another associate. (70) **I'm headed to the back of the warehouse now to see if the picking crew needs help.**

Return code	Reason for return
01	Damaged in shipping
(69) **02**	**Defective—does not work properly**
03	Wrong item shipped
04	Changed mind—do not want

男：噢，妳必須手動輸入代碼。(69) **這邊是代碼清單。**

女：噢，謝謝你。

男：不客氣。如果妳晚點遇到任何問題，只要詢問另一名同事即可。(70) **我現在要去倉庫後面，看看揀貨員是否需要協助。**

退貨代碼	退貨原因
01	運送途中受損
(69) **02**	**瑕疵品：無法正常運作**
03	貨品送錯
04	改變心意：不想要貨

- process (v.) 處理　return (v.) 退回　purchaser (n.) 買主　faulty (adj.) 有缺陷的　appear (v.) 出現　enter (v.) 輸入　manually (adv.) 手動地　associate (n.) 同事　head (v.) 前往　warehouse (n.) 倉庫　picking (n.) 揀貨；撿料

68. 相關細節——男子提及有關女子的事情

What does the man mention about the woman?

(A) She is working overtime.

(B) She is a new employee.

(C) She will soon go on vacation.

(D) She is handling a colleague's responsibilities.

男子提到關於女子的什麼事？

(A) 她加班工作。

(B) 她是新進員工。

(C) 她即將休假。

(D) 她正在處理同事的工作。

- handle (v.) 處理　colleague (n.) 同事

69. 圖表整合題——應輸入的退貨代碼

Look at the graphic. Which return code will most likely be entered?

(A) Code 01

(B) Code 02

(C) Code 03

(D) Code 04

請見圖表作答。最有可能會輸入的退貨代碼為何？

(A) 代碼 01

(B) 代碼 02

(C) 代碼 03

(D) 代碼 04

70. 相關細節——男子接下來要做的事情

What will the man probably do next?

(A) Go to a different part of a building

(B) Use a loudspeaker to ask for assistance

(C) Write down some questions

(D) Restart a handheld device

男子接下來很可能會做什麼？

(A) 前往大樓的另一個地方

(B) 使用擴音器要求協助

(C) 寫下一些問題

(D) 重啟一個手持裝置

- loudspeaker (n.) 擴音器　assistance (n.) 協助　handheld (adj.) 手持的　device (n.) 裝置

71-73 Advertisement

For everything you need to live and work smartly at home, (71) **visit Caldarr Center. We guarantee the lowest everyday prices on all the TVs, laptops, and mobile phones that we sell.** (72) **And, for your convenience, we've just started a new curbside pickup option.** Simply select the items you want from our Web site, then schedule a pick-up time, and a store associate will bring your goods to your car. (73) **And for help in choosing the right product, we invite all our shoppers to look over our customer reviews Web page—read their honest opinions about the products they bought here at Caldarr Center.**

71-73 廣告 加

想要在家聰明生活、工作，(71) **就請光臨卡爾達中心**，這裡有你所需的一切。(71) **我們保證，本店販售的所有電視、筆記型電腦和手機，每天都是最低價。**(72) **而且為了讓您更便利，本店剛推出了新的路邊取貨服務選項**，只要從我們的網站上，選擇想要的貨品後，排定取貨時間，門市人員就會將您訂的貨品送到您的愛車旁邊。(73) **若在挑選合適產品時需要協助，在此邀請各位消費者來查看我們的顧客評論網頁，看看顧客對於從卡爾達中心購買的商品，給予的真心意見。**

- guarantee (v.) 保證 convenience (n.) 方便 curbside (n.) 路邊 associate (n.) 同事 goods (n.)〔複〕商品；貨物

71. 相關細節——卡爾達中心所屬的產業

What kind of business most likely is Caldarr Center?
(A) A home furnishings retailer
(B) An electronics store
(C) A telecommunications service
(D) A maker of office supplies

卡爾達中心最可能是何種業者？
(A) 家飾用品零售商
(B) 電子用品店
(C) 電信服務商
(D) 辦公用品製造商

- furnishing (n.) 家具；室內陳設 telecommunications (n.) 電信

換句話說 the TVs, laptops, mobile phones（電視、筆記型電腦和手機）→ electronics（電子用品）

72. 相關細節——卡爾達中心最近完成的事情

According to the advertisement, what has Caldarr Center done recently?
(A) Added a new way to shop
(B) Launched a loyalty program
(C) Expanded its range of products
(D) Hired new staff members

根據廣告，卡爾達中心最近做了什麼？
(A) 新增購物方式
(B) 推出熟客回饋方案
(C) 擴大產品範圍
(D) 僱用新員工

- add (v.) 增加 launch (v.) 推出 loyalty program 熟客回饋方案 expand (v.) 擴大 range (n.) 範圍 hire (v.) 僱用

73. 相關細節——說話者建議聽者做的事情

What does the speaker encourage listeners to do?
(A) Browse a customer feedback page
(B) Upgrade some warranty coverage
(C) Purchase special gift cards
(D) Vote on a potential improvement

說話者鼓勵聽者做何事？

(A) 瀏覽顧客回饋意見網頁。
(B) 升級保固範圍。
(C) 購買特別禮品卡。
(D) 票選可能需要改善的地方。

- browse (v.) 瀏覽 warranty (n.) 保證書 coverage (n.) 保險範圍 purchase (v.) 購買 vote (v.) 投票 potential (adj.) 可能的 improvement (n.) 改善

換句話說 look over our customer reviews Web page（查看我們的顧客評論網頁）
→ browse a customer feedback page（瀏覽顧客回饋意見網頁）

74-76 Announcement

74-76 宣布 澳

(74) Welcome aboard the Northern Express train, offering service to Portland Station with intermediate stops in Dover and Cumberland. The first car of this train is for passengers seated in Business Class, and the remaining cars are for passengers seated in Coach Class. (75) Car Four is the train's Quiet Car, where passengers are asked to maintain a library-like atmosphere. Please refrain from making any mobile phone calls while riding in this car. (76) In just a few moments, we will open our café car, where passengers may purchase a variety of light snacks. Please watch your step as you pass between the cars of the moving train. Thank you, and enjoy your trip.

(74) 歡迎搭乘北方特快車，本車終點站為波特蘭站，中途停靠多佛和坎伯蘭站。本列車第一節供商務車廂旅客乘坐，其餘為普通車廂，供一般乘客搭乘。(75) 第四節車廂是本車的安靜車廂，車廂內旅客須保持宛如圖書館的安靜氛圍；搭乘該節車廂時，請不要透過手機通話。(76) 再過不久，本列車咖啡餐車將會開放，乘客可前往購買各類輕食。列車行進期間，穿越車廂行走時，請留意您的腳步。謝謝各位，祝您旅途愉快。

- aboard (adv.) 在（交通工具）上　intermediate (adj.) 中間的　passenger (n.) 乘客　seated (adj.) 就坐的　remaining (adj.) 其餘的　coach class（列車）普通車廂　maintain (v.) 維持　atmosphere (n.) 氣氛　refrain (v.) 避免　a variety of . . . 各式各樣的……　pass (v.) 經過；穿過

74. 相關細節——說話者針對北方特快列車提及的內容 難

What is mentioned about the Northern Express Train?
(A) It costs more than ordinary trains.
(B) It operates several times each day.
(C) It makes no stops en route to its destination.
(D) It is divided into two seating classes.

關於北方特快車，獨白中提及什麼？
(A) 票價比一般列車高。
(B) 每天營運數班車次。
(C) 終點站前無停靠站。
(D) 車廂等級分為兩種。

- cost (v.) 花費　operate (v.) 營運　en route 在途中　destination (n.) 目的地　divide (v.) 劃分

75. 相關細節——向第四節車廂乘客要求的事情

What are passengers in Car Four of the train asked to do?
(A) Present photo identification
(B) Store luggage between cars
(C) Avoid mobile phone conversations
(D) Move forward to the next car

列車第四節車廂的旅客被要求做什麼？
(A) 出示有照片的身分證件
(B) 將行李存放在車廂間
(C) 避免手機交談
(D) 往前移到下一節車廂

- present (v.) 出示　identification (n.) 身分證件　store (v.) 儲存　luggage (n.) 行李　avoid (v.) 避免　conversation (n.) 交談；談話　forward (adv.) 向前

換句話說 refrain from taking any mobile phone calls（不要透過手機通話）
→ avoid mobile phone conversations（避免手機交談）

TEST 8 PART 4

76. 相關細節——即將發生的事情

According to the announcement, what will happen shortly?
(A) Tickets will be inspected.
(B) A video will be shown.
(C) Boarding will be completed.
(D) Refreshments will be available.

根據宣布內容，何事即將發生？
(A) 驗票。
(B) 播放影片。
(C) 登車完畢。
(D) 可購買點心。

- inspect (v.) 檢查　board (v.) 登上（交通工具）　refreshment (n.) 茶點

換句話說 snacks（點心）→ refreshments（點心）

77-79 Recorded message

Thank you for calling Worldways Health. [77] **We are the area's best-known clinic offering health care services and advice for people who travel internationally.** [78] **Due to the high volume of calls in anticipation of the holiday period, our wait times are longer than usual. We apologize and ask that you please stay on the line.** The next available representative will be with you as soon as possible. [79] **Please take this time to ensure that you have any relevant travel and health insurance paperwork at hand.** This will enable your call to proceed smoothly.

77-79 預錄訊息 英

這裡是「世界通健康中心」，感謝您的來電。[77] **在為出國旅客提供醫療照顧服務和建議的方面，我們是本地最知名的診所。** [78] **由於預期到假日即將到來，民眾來電眾多，等候時間會比平常還久，對此我們深表歉意，並請您不要掛斷電話。**下個客服專員一有空，將會盡快為您服務。[79] **請利用這段時間，確認手邊已備妥各項相關的旅行與健康保險文件，**以利後續通話順利進行。

- clinic (n.) 診所　internationally (adv.) 國際地　volume (n.) 總量；總數
in anticipation of . . . 預料……　holiday (n.) 假日　period (n.) 期間　apologize (v.) 道歉
available (adj.) 有空的　representative (n.) 代表　ensure (v.) 確保　relevant (adj.) 相關的
insurance (n.) 保險　paperwork (n.) 書面資料　at hand 在手邊　enable (v.) 使能夠
proceed (v.)（繼續）進行　smoothly (adv.) 順利地

77. 全文相關——錄製語音訊息的業者

What kind of business recorded the message?
(A) A real estate firm
(B) A travel agency
(C) A medical clinic
(D) A mobile app developer

錄製這段訊息的為何種業者？
(A) 不動產仲介公司
(B) 旅行社
(C) 醫療診所
(D) 手機應用程式開發商

---

78. 相關細節——說話者道歉的原因

What does the speaker apologize for?
(A) A recent price increase
(B) An upcoming holiday closure
(C) Extended holding times
(D) Possible audio problems

說話者為何道歉？
(A) 近期的漲價
(B) 即將在假日公休
(C) 等候時間拉長
(D) 音訊可能有問題

- increase (n.) 增加　upcoming (adj.) 即將到來的　closure (n.) 關閉；打烊
holding time（電話）等候時間

換句話說 our wait times are longer than usual（等候時間會比平常還久）
→ extended holding times（等候時間拉長）

79. 相關細節——建議聽者做的事情

What is the listener encouraged to do?
(A) Meet a representative in person
(B) Prepare some documentation
(C) Use a business's other locations
(D) Try calling on another day

說話者鼓勵聽者做何事？
(A) 親自和專員見面
(B) 準備一些文件
(C) 利用公司的其他分部
(D) 改天再試著來電

- **in person** 親自 **prepare (v.)** 準備 **documentation (n.)**（總稱）文件 **location (n.)** 地點

換句話說 have any . . . paperwork at hand（備妥各項……文件）
→ prepare some documentation（準備一些文件）

80-82 Telephone message

80-82 電話留言

Hi, Mr. Martino? It's Sheila calling from 10 Westmont Street. (80) **You're probably on your way to my home to install new water pipes in the basement.** I had scheduled the two p.m. service visit on your Web site. (81) **In the section for driving directions, I typed "white house on the right," and . . .** there are a lot of white houses in the area. (81) **So I wanted to let you know my house has a large number "10" on the mailbox.** You'll see it. (82) **I'll move my car out of the driveway now so you can park your truck close to the house.** OK, see you soon.

嗨，馬提諾先生？我是衛斯特蒙街十號的席拉。(80) **你很可能正在前來我家的路上，要來幫地下室安裝新水管**，我在你們的網站上，和你約好下午兩點時過來。(81) **在行車指南的部分，我有輸入：「右手邊的白色房子」，而……**這一區有很多白色房子，(81) **所以我想告訴你，我家的信箱上有標示大大的「10」號**，你到時會看到的。(82) **我將會把我的車從車道移開，這樣你就能靠著房子來停放你的卡車。**好的，待會見。

- **install (v.)** 安裝 **basement (n.)** 地下室 **schedule (v.)** 預約 **section (n.)** 區塊 **type (v.)** 打字 **mailbox (n.)** 信箱 **driveway (n.)** 私人車道

80. 全文相關——聽者的職業

Who most likely is the listener?
(A) A neighbor
(B) A plumber
(C) A house painter
(D) A delivery person

聽者最可能的身分為何？
(A) 鄰居
(B) 水電工
(C) 房屋油漆工
(D) 送貨員

---

81. 掌握說話者的意圖——提及「這一區有很多白色房子」的意圖 難

What most likely does the speaker mean when she says, "there are a lot of white houses in the area"?
(A) A maintenance service could become popular.
(B) A neighborhood has few nearby businesses.
(C) Some renovations will make a home stand out.
(D) Some instructions may have been unclear.

說話者說：「這一區有很多白色房子」，意思最可能為何？
(A) 有項維修服務可能變得很流行。
(B) 某個街區附近很少有商家。
(C) 整修一下會讓房子較為顯眼。
(D) 有些指示可能不甚明確。

- **maintenance (n.)** 維修；保養 **neighborhood (n.)** 社區 **renovation (n.)** 整修 **stand out** 突出 **instruction (n.)** 指示 **unclear (adj.)** 不清楚的

---

82. 相關細節——說話者接下來要做的事情

What does the speaker say she will do next?
(A) Add her signature to an agreement
(B) Make a space available for parking
(C) Take some letters to a post office
(D) Put up some signs outside a structure

說話者說，她接下來會做什麼？
(A) 在協議上簽名
(B) 挪出停車空間
(C) 把信件拿去郵局
(D) 在建築物外放置標誌

- signature (n.) 簽名　agreement (n.) 協議　space (n.) 空間　available (adj.) 可得到的　post office 郵局　put up 懸掛；張貼　sign (n.) 標誌　structure (n.) 建築物

換句話說 move my car out of . . . so that you can park your truck（把我的車移開……以便你停放卡車）→ make a space available for parking（挪出停車空間）

83-85 News report

In local news, the long-awaited Shorepoint Shopping Mall will open to the public this Friday, after nearly three years of construction. (83) **Work on the mall fell behind schedule after adjustments were made to the layout of the indoor food court section to allow for more space separating its fifteen restaurants.** (84) **The mall, located alongside Highway 4, can be reached by City Bus Number 62, which stops in front of its main entrance.** (85) **The mall's management will broadcast its Grand Opening Day ceremony online via social media platforms. Members of the public who won't be able to attend in person are invited to watch the live video from nine-thirty to ten a.m. on Friday.** Those who do will be rewarded with access to many of the same special discounts as in-person visitors.

83-85 新聞報導 澳

接著關注在地新聞：經過將近三年的施工後，眾所期盼的岸點購物中心將於本週五對外開幕。(83) **工程進度落後的原因，在於室內美食廣場格局設計經過多項調整，以便讓廣場內 15 家餐廳之間的區隔空間擴大。**(84) **購物中心坐落四號公路沿線，可搭乘市立公車 62 路到達，停靠點就在購物中心大門口。**(85) **購物中心管理單位將透過社群媒體平台，播送隆重的開幕儀式，無法親臨現場參加的民眾，歡迎在週五上午九點半到十點觀看直播影片，**觀賞影片者也和現場參加者一樣，能取得多項特別折扣。

- long-awaited (adj.) 期待已久的　construction (n.) 建設　adjustment (n.) 調整　layout (n.) 平面圖　indoor (adj) 室內的　separate (v.) 分隔　locate (v.) 使……坐落於　alongside (prep.) 在……旁邊　entrance (n.) 入口　management (n.) 管理階層　broadcast (v.) 播送　ceremony (n.) 典禮　via (prep.) 透過　in person 親自　reward (v.) 獎賞　access (n.) 使用權

83. 相關細節——報導中提及購物中心延後完工的理由 難

According to the report, what delayed the mall's completion?
(A) Changes to its floor plan
(B) Difficulty receiving some permits
(C) A shortage of construction workers
(D) The hiring of a new contractor

根據報導，何事造成購物中心延後完工？
(A) 變更樓層平面圖
(B) 難以取得部分許可證
(C) 建築工人短缺
(D) 僱用新的承包商

- completion (n.) 完工　floor plan (n.)（建築物的）平面圖　permit (n.) 許可證　shortage (n.) 短缺　contractor (n.) 承包商

換句話說 adjustments were made to the layout（格局設計經過多項調整）→ changes to its floor plan（變更樓層平面圖）

84. 相關細節——說話者提及購物中心的特色

What does the speaker say is a feature of the mall?
(A) A performance space
(B) An indoor garden
(C) A large entrance hall
(D) A public transportation stop

說話者提到購物中心的何項特色？
(A) 表演空間
(B) 室內花園
(C) 寬敞的入口大廳
(D) 大眾運輸停靠站

換句話說 City Bus（市立公車）→ public transportation（大眾運輸）

85. 相關細節——邀請聽者參與的事情 難

What are listeners invited to do?
(A) Stream footage of an opening-day event
(B) Submit feedback surveys to mall management
(C) Register for an e-mail update program
(D) Participate in a phone-in talk show

說話者邀請聽者做何事？
(A) 在線上串流觀賞開幕日活動
(B) 提供意見調查給購物中心管理部門
(C) 註冊電子郵件更新方案
(D) 打電話參與脫口秀

- stream (v.) 線上串流收看　footage (n.)（影片）片段　submit (v.) 提交　survey (n.) 調查　register (v.) 登記；註冊

86-88 Excerpt from a meeting

(86) **Finally, I'd like to review the brochure we're creating for Revdecc Plus. As a high-end health club, they focus on providing a comfortable workout environment for their members.** The brochure's front page shows people running near a tall building, and . . . it doesn't capture their brand image. We'll need to revise it. Now, we've had design challenges before. (87) **The changes shouldn't be hard to make, and I'm confident we can give it more impact**. Let's work on that now. (88) **Then, at four this afternoon, let's get together again as a team, and discuss what we've done.**

86-88 會議摘錄 英

(86) **最後，我想檢討我們為「瑞夫戴克＋」製作的宣傳冊，他們作為高檔健身會館，致力於提供會員舒適的健身環境**，目前手冊的封面，是人們在一棟大樓附近跑步，而……這並未掌握到他們的品牌形象，我們需要對此修改。我們過去也碰過設計上的挑戰，(87) **修改應該不難，而且我有信心我們可以讓封面更衝擊人心**。我們現在著手修改吧，(88) **然後今天下午四時，團隊再集合起來，討論大家的進展**。

- brochure（宣傳用）小冊子　workout (n.) 健身　environment (n.) 環境　capture (v.)（用圖文）描繪　revise (v.) 修改　confident (adj.) 有信心的　impact (n.) 衝擊（力）

86. 相關細節——「瑞夫戴克＋」的產業類別

What kind of business most likely is Revdecc Plus?
(A) A publishing company
(B) A real estate developer
(C) A fitness center
(D) An advertising agency

「瑞夫戴克＋」最可能是何種業者？
(A) 出版社
(B) 不動產開發商
(C) 健身中心
(D) 廣告代理商

換句話說 a health club（健身會館）→ a fitness center（健身中心）

87. 掌握說話者的意圖——提及「我們過去也碰過設計上的挑戰」的意圖 

Why most likely does the speaker say, "we've had design challenges before"?

(A) To suggest buying new design software

(B) To emphasize the need to recruit more staff

(C) To reassure the listeners about a task

(D) To praise the listeners for an accomplishment

說話者會說：「我們過去也碰過設計上的挑戰」，最可能的原因為何？

(A) 以建議購買新的設計軟體

(B) 以強調招聘更多員工的需求

(C) 以使聽者對任務放寬心

(D) 以表揚聽者的成就

- emphasize (v.) 強調　recruit (v.) 招聘　reassure (v.) 使安心　task (n.) 任務；工作　praise (v.) 表揚　accomplishment (n.) 成就

88. 相關細節——說話者建議下午要做的事情

What does the speaker recommend doing in the afternoon?

(A) Distributing some brochures

(B) Holding a team meeting

(C) Working past the end of a shift

(D) Visiting a client together

說話者建議下午做何事？

(A) 分發一些手冊

(B) 舉行團隊會議

(C) 輪班時間後繼續工作

(D) 一同拜訪客戶

- distribute (v.) 分發　shift (n.) 輪班　client (n.) 客戶

換句話說 let's get together again as a team, and discuss . . .（團隊再集合起來討論……）
→ holding a team meeting（舉行團隊會議）

89-91 Excerpt from a workshop

Hello, everyone. I'm Ed Tanaka, your instructor for this three-day workshop. (89) **As we put our brushes to the canvas and try to create beautiful works of art, I will teach you various techniques for coloring and shading your works.** (90) **What makes this workshop unique is that it takes place entirely in an open-air setting, surrounded by the beautiful nature we're aiming to capture in our creations.** (91) **Now, as we move to this park's rose garden, please mind your footing, as there is some uneven ground and loose gravel.** Follow me this way.

89-91 研習摘錄 加

大家好，我是田中艾德，在這場三天的研習中，擔任各位的講師。(89) **我們於帆布揮灑畫筆、嘗試創作美麗的藝術作品時，我會教導大家多種為作品上色和營造明暗的技巧。** (90) **這次研習的獨特之處，在於全程都是在戶外環境進行，周圍環繞著美麗的自然風景，也就是我們希望在創作中捕捉的事物。** (91) **現在，當我們前往公園的玫瑰花園的途中，請留意腳步，因為地面有些不平整和礫石鬆動的地方。** 請跟著我往這邊走。

- instructor (n.) 講師　brush (n.) 畫筆　technique (n.) 技巧　color (v.) 著色　shade (v.) 畫陰影於……　entirely (adv.) 完全地　setting (n.) 環境　surround (v.) 圍繞　aim (v.) 打算要……　capture (v.)（用圖文）描繪　creation (n.) 作品　uneven (adj.) 不平的　loose (adj.) 鬆動的　gravel (n.) 礫石

89. 相關細節——研習教導的事物

What most likely is being taught in the workshop?
(A) Hiking for fitness
(B) Growing plants
(C) Writing journals
(D) Painting pictures

研習中最可能教導什麼？
(A) 健行
(B) 栽種植物
(C) 寫日記
(D) 畫圖

90. 相關細節——說話者提及研習的特別之處

According to the speaker, what is special about the workshop?
(A) It has a high enrollment.
(B) It is being held outdoors.
(C) It is taught by two instructors.
(D) It takes place over multiple days.

根據說話者，研習有何特殊之處？
(A) 報名人數很多。
(B) 在戶外進行。
(C) 由二名講師授課。
(D) 為期數日。

- enrollment (n.) 報名人數　outdoors (adv.) 在戶外　multiple (adj.) 多個的

換句話說 takes place . . . in an open-air setting（在戶外環境進行）
→ is being held outdoors（在戶外進行）

91. 相關細節——向聽者提出的建議 難

What are listeners advised to do?
(A) Obtain parking permits
(B) Carry minimal belongings
(C) Avoid picking flowers
(D) Walk carefully

聽者被建議做何事？
(A) 取得停車證
(B) 盡量減少攜帶個人物品
(C) 不要摘花
(D) 小心行走

- obtain (v.) 獲得　permit (n.) 許可證　carry (v.) 攜帶　belongings (n.) 擁有物；行李

換句話說 mind your footing（留意腳步）→ walk carefully（小心行走）

92-94 Announcement 澳

OK, important announcement. (92) **The new office on Taylor Street passed its safety inspection and is now ready for us to move into.** Isn't that exciting? We'll finally have space to grow. Now, we're going to try to finish the moving process over the first three days of next week. (93) **This means that we need to have all office supplies packed and ready to move by Monday morning.** So, there's work to do, and . . . it's Thursday afternoon. (94) **For now, I'll get a plastic bin for you to throw away unwanted items and place it right here by the entrance.** Please use it freely. We don't want to pack and move things that you won't actually need.

92-94 宣布

好的，在此有項重要宣布：(92) **泰勒街的新辦公室通過了安全檢查，我們現在可以準備遷入了**，是不是令人雀躍不已呢？我們總算有擴大發展的空間了。現在，我們要設法在下週的前三天完成搬遷程序，(93) **這意味我們必須在週一早上前，把辦公室所有用品打包好、準備搬遷**，因此我們有得忙的，而……現在是週四下午了，(94) **我馬上會準備一個塑膠箱，放在門口處，讓各位把不要的物品丟進去**。請盡情使用，畢竟沒有人會想把實際上用不到的東西打包、搬走。

- pass (v.) 通過　safety (n.) 安全　inspection (n.) 檢查　process (n.) 過程　office supply 辦公用品
pack (v.) 打包（行李等）　bin (n.) 箱子；容器　throw away 扔掉

92. 相關細節——說話者的公司即將要做的事情

What will the speaker's company do soon?

(A) Relocate to a different office

(B) Host a visit from potential clients

(C) Rearrange its current workspace

(D) Undergo a safety inspection

說話者的公司即將進行何事？

(A) 搬到不同的辦公室

(B) 接待潛在客戶來訪

(C) 重新配置目前的辦公空間

(D) 接受安全檢查

- relocate (v.) 搬遷 host (v.) 接待 potential (adj.) 潛在的 rearrange (v.) 重新布置 undergo (v.) 接受

換句話說 move（搬遷）→ relocate（搬遷）

93. 掌握說話者的意圖——提及「現在是週四下午了」的意圖 難

What does the speaker imply when he says, "it's Thursday afternoon"?

(A) An executive is probably busy.

(B) A deadline is approaching.

(C) A previously stated date is incorrect.

(D) A meeting will be postponed.

說話者說：「現在是週四下午了」，言下之意為何？

(A) 主管很可能在忙。

(B) 期限正在逼近。

(C) 先前說的日期有誤。

(D) 有個會議將延後。

- executive (n.)（公司等）主管 deadline (n.) 截止日期 approach (v.) 接近 previously (adv.) 先前地 state (v.) 說明 incorrect (adj.) 錯誤的 postpone (v.) 延期

94. 相關細節——說話者提及接下來要做的事情

What does the speaker say he will do next?

(A) Clean a workstation

(B) Wait next to an external door

(C) Organize a supply closet

(D) Set up a waste container

說話者說他接下來將做什麼？

(A) 打掃工作區

(B) 在外門旁邊等

(C) 整理用品櫃

(D) 放一個垃圾箱

- workstation (n.) 工作區 external (adj.) 外部的 organize (v.) 整理 supply closet 用品櫃 container (n.) 容器

換句話說 a . . . bin for you to throw away（供丟棄的箱子）→ a waste container（垃圾箱）

95-97 Excerpt from a meeting + Diagram

OK, now I'd like to mention our display counter at the front of the supermarket, by the café. [95] **This is exclusively for products that the manufacturer has stopped making, and all the featured items are priced thirty percent off.** Now, your shelf diagram for our imported items is no longer accurate. [96] **Trevoli Foods announced it will stop producing its sauces in bottles, so I took those items off the shelf and moved them to the promotional display.** I also posted a sign directing shoppers to that area. [97] **Please do stress to our customers there's no need to present any coupons—they simply pay the marked prices.**

95-97 會議摘要＋圖表 美

好了，現在我想提一下我們放在超級市場前面、咖啡店旁邊的展示櫃。[95] **那一櫃是專門陳列廠商已經停產的商品，而且所有架上商品都以七折販售。**目前，你們幫本店的進口食品製作的貨架圖表已經需要勘誤：[96] **「崔佛利食品」宣布將停產瓶裝醬料，因此我已把該項產品從架上拿下來，改放到促銷展示區，**我也張貼了告示牌，引導顧客前往該區，[97] **請務必向我們的顧客強調，只要照標價結帳即可，不需出示任何折價券。**

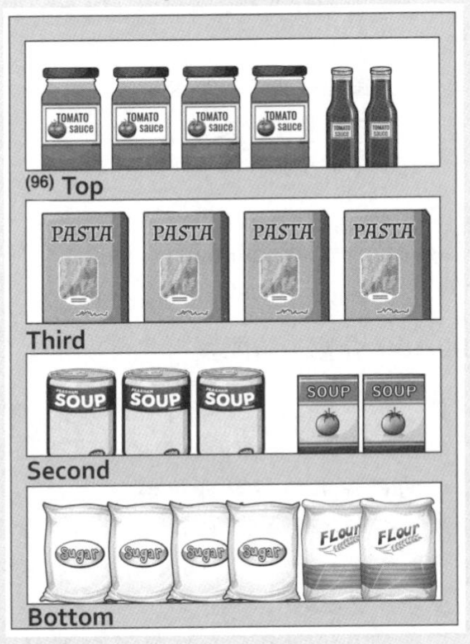

- mention (v.) 談到　exclusively (adv.) 專門地　manufacturer (n.) 製造商　feature (v.) 以……作為主打　diagram (n.) 圖解　import (v.) 進口　accurate (adj.) 正確的　announce (v.) 宣布　promotional (adj.) 促銷的　direct (v.) 給……指路　stress (v.) 強調

95. 相關細節——說話者提及折價出售的商品 難

According to the speaker, what is being sold at reduced prices?

(A) Health foods

(B) Cooking tools

(C) Products sold in bulk

(D) Discontinued merchandise

根據說話者，何者正在折價出售？

(A) 健康食品

(B) 烹飪用具

(C) 大批出售的商品

(D) 停產的商品

- in bulk 大量　discontinue (v.) 停止；中斷

換句話說 products that the manufacturer has stopped making（廠商已經停產的商品）
→ discontinued merchandise（停產的商品）

96. 圖表整合題——說話者下架哪一層的產品

Look at the graphic. Which shelf did the speaker remove items from?

(A) The top shelf

(B) The third shelf

(C) The second shelf

(D) The bottom shelf

請見圖表作答。說話者已把哪一層的商品取下？

(A) 頂層

(B) 第三層

(C) 第二層

(D) 底層

97. 相關細節——針對促銷活動，說話者向聽者提出的要求

What are listeners asked to emphasize about a sale?
(A) It applies mostly to high priced items.
(B) It involves a mobile app.
(C) It will last for only one day.
(D) It does not require coupons.

針對促銷活動，聽者被要求強調何事？
(A) 大部分適用於高價商品。
(B) 需要使用手機應用程式。
(C) 只會持續一天。
(D) 不需要折價券。

- apply (v.) 適用　mostly (adv.) 主要地　involve (v.) 需要　last (v.) 持續　require (v.) 需求

98-100 Introduction + Schedule

Hi, I'm Jessica, and I'll be your trainer today. (98) **You've already been introduced to the high-quality travel bags and rolling suitcases that we produce here at Bocavian, Incorporated.** Now, each of our afternoon training modules will last one hour, with just one adjustment. I'll spend more time focusing on presentations, as you will present quite often in your career here. (99) **That means we'll spend less time on software training, but it's OK because you learned its main functions yesterday.** All right, let's begin. (100) **First, the policy guide runs to fourteen pages, so please take a moment to make sure your copy has every page.**

Day 2 training
1:00 P.M. to 5:00 P.M.

Module 1	Company policies
Module 2	Making presentations
(99) Module 3	**Software training**
Module 4	Customer relations

98-100 介紹＋時間表 英

嗨，我是各位今天的指導員潔西卡。(98) **先前已經向大家介紹過我們波卡維亞公司製造的高品質旅行袋和附輪行李箱**，接下來，下午我們每個培訓單元時間都會是一小時，只有一個地方需要調整：我會花較多時間聚焦在簡報製作，因為各位在這裡工作期間，常會需要做簡報，(99) **這也表示我們軟體訓練的時間會減少，但是沒關係，因為大家昨天已學過主要功能了**。好的，我們開始吧。(100) **首先，公司規章指南共有 14 頁，所以請花點時間確認講義有沒有缺頁。**

第二天培訓
下午 1：00 至 5：00

單元一	公司規章
單元二	簡報製作
(99) **單元三**	**軟體訓練**
單元四	客戶關係

- introduce (v.) 介紹　rolling suitcase 附輪行李箱　module (n.) 單元　adjustment (n.) 調整　present (v.) 做簡報

98. 全文相關——獨白出現的地點

Where most likely is the introduction taking place?
(A) At a luggage manufacturer
(B) At a graphic design firm
(C) At a jewelry seller
(D) At a software developer

做出這段介紹的最可能地點為何？
(A) 行李箱製造商
(B) 平面設計公司
(C) 珠寶銷售商
(D) 軟體開發公司

換句話說 the . . . travel bags and rolling suitcases（旅行袋和附輪行李箱）→ luggage（行李箱）

99. 圖表整合題——縮短時間的課程

Look at the graphic. Which module most likely will be shortened?
(A) Module 1
(B) Module 2
(C) Module 3
(D) Module 4

請見圖表作答。哪個單元時間最可能縮短？
(A) 單元一
(B) 單元二
(C) 單元三
(D) 單元四

100. 相關細節——要求聽者做的事情

What does the speaker tell the listeners to do?
(A) Look at some product samples
(B) Share materials with a partner
(C) Ensure that a booklet is complete
(D) Turn off any personal electronics

說話者要求聽者做何事？
(A) 查看幾個產品樣本
(B) 和夥伴共用資料
(C) 確認手冊內容完整
(D) 關閉個人電子用品

- **share (v.)** 共用 **ensure (v.)** 確保 **booklet (n.)** 小冊子 **complete (adj.)** 完整的 **electronics (n.)**〔複〕電子用品

ACTUAL TEST 9

PART 1 P. 104–107

33

1. 單人獨照——描寫人物的動作 澳

(A) She's opening a storage container.
(B) She's repairing some office equipment.
(C) She's cleaning a whiteboard.
(D) She's making a copy of a document.

(A) 她正打開儲藏容器。
(B) 她正在維修辦公設備。
(C) 她正在清理白板。
(D) 她正在影印文件。

- storage (n.) 貯存　container (n.) 容器　repair (v.) 修理　equipment (n.) 設備　whiteboard (n.) 白板

2. 雙人照片——描寫人物的動作 英

(A) They're carrying safety helmets.
(B) They're parking next to some trees.
(C) They're pushing some bicycles.
(D) They're riding side by side.

(A) 他們正拿著安全帽。
(B) 他們正把車停在樹旁邊。
(C) 他們正在推腳踏車。
(D) 他們正在並肩騎車。

- safety helmet 安全帽　bicycle (n.) 腳踏車　ride (v.) 騎乘　side by side 並肩地

3. 綜合照片——描寫人物或事物 加

(A) Garden waste is being put into a bag.
(B) A man is holding the handle of a wooden gate.
(C) The lids of some bins have been raised.
(D) A man is organizing bottles on a shelf.

(A) 有人正將花園的垃圾裝袋。
(B) 男子握著木門的把手。
(C) 垃圾箱的蓋子正被掀起。
(D) 男子正在整理架上的瓶子。

- lid (n.) 蓋子　bin (n.) 垃圾箱；容器　raise (v.) 舉起　organize (v.) 整理　shelf (n.) 架子

4. 事物與背景照——描寫室內事物的狀態 美

(A) Newspapers have been folded to fit in a display.
(B) Racks have been positioned in front of a window.
(C) Merchandise is being removed from boxes.
(D) A magazine has been left on a store counter.

(A) 報紙已折疊就緒、擺出架上。
(B) 窗戶前放置了置物架。
(C) 商品正從箱中取出。
(D) 雜誌遺留在商店的櫃檯上。

- fold (v.) 折疊　fit (v.) 適合；相合　rack (n.) 置物架　position (v.) 放置　merchandise (n.) 商品
  remove (v.) 移開；拿開

5. 綜合照片——描寫人物或事物 澳 難

(A) Some people are boarding a public bus.
(B) There is a basket in the corner of a shelter.
(C) A woman has set her backpack down on a bench.
(D) A map has been attached to a standing sign.

(A) 有些人正在搭上公車。
(B) 在遮雨亭的角落有個籃子。
(C) 女子把背包放在長椅上。
(D) 告示立牌上貼著地圖。

- board (v.) 登上（交通工具）　basket (n.) 籃；簍　shelter (n.) 遮蔽（處）　attach (v.) 使附著

6. 綜合照片——描寫人物或事物 英 難

(A) A large group of people is waiting in a line.	(A) 一大群人正在排隊等候。
(B) A podium has been placed on a raised stage.	(B) 架高的舞台上放著講台。
(C) A speaker is gesturing toward the back of a room.	(C) 演講者正向會議室後方比手勢。
(D) A graph is being projected onto a screen.	**(D) 圖表投射在螢幕上。**

- podium (n.) 講台　place (v.) 放置　raised (adj.) 升高的；凸起的　gesture (v.) 做手勢　project (v.) 投射（光線等）

PART 2 P. 108

34

7. 以助動詞 Did 開頭的問句，詢問是否有看籃球賽 英⇄加

Did you see the basketball game last night?	你看了昨晚的籃球賽嗎？
(A) A big group of fans.	(A) 一大群粉絲。
(B) The company sponsors a basketball team.	(B) 公司贊助一支籃球隊。
(C) Yes, I watched it on television.	**(C) 有，我用電視收看。**

- sponsor (v.) 贊助

8. 以 How 開頭的問句，詢問鑰匙歸還的方式 澳⇄美

How would you like me to return the key?	你希望我如何歸還鑰匙？
(A) Use your key card.	(A) 用你的鑰匙卡。
(B) You can give it to the receptionist.	**(B) 你可以交給接待員。**
(C) That would be great.	(C) 那就太好了。

- return (v.) 歸還　receptionist (n.) 接待員

9. 以 Where 開頭的問句，詢問會議紀錄所在地點 加⇄英

Where can I find the notes from the departmental meeting?	我可以到哪裡查找部門會議的紀錄？
(A) In the shared folder on the network.	**(A) 網路上的共享資料夾。**
(B) To the director of marketing.	(B) 給行銷主管。
(C) Make sure they're less than two pages long.	(C) 確保不要超過兩頁。

- note (n.) 紀錄　departmental (adj.) 部門的　shared (adj.) 共用的　director (n.) 主管

10. 以直述句傳達資訊 澳⇄英

The computer won't accept my password.	電腦不接受我的密碼。
(A) Our newest desktop model.	(A) 我們最新款的桌上型機型。
(B) Ah, I know what the problem is.	**(B) 哦，我知道問題出在哪裡。**
(C) No, they're mine.	(C) 不，是我的。

- accept (v.) 接受　newest (adj.) 最新的

11. 以間接問句詢問是誰把蛋糕放在桌上 美⇄澳 難

Do you know who left this cake on the table?
(A) I thought you did.
(B) It used to be Sophie's.
(C) For our tenth anniversary.

你知道桌上的蛋糕是誰留下的嗎？
(A) 我以為是你。
(B) 以前是蘇菲的。
(C) 為了我們的十週年慶。

- anniversary (n.) 週年紀念日

12. 以 **When** 開頭的問句，詢問電影節的舉辦時間 英⇄加

When is the Wexler Film Festival held?
(A) At the city's convention center.
(B) I don't think it's a regular event.
(C) Holova makes high-quality film, too.

魏斯勒電影節何時舉行？
(A) 在市立會議中心。
(B) 我想那不是定期活動。
(C) 賀勒瓦也會拍優質電影。

- regular (adj.) 定期的　high-quality (adj.) 高品質的

13. 以 **Why** 開頭的問句，詢問為何要把食物從冰箱取出 英⇄美

Why do we have to take our food out of the break room fridge?
(A) The cleaning crew is coming by.
(B) Anything without a label on it.
(C) We can also buy snacks on-site.

我們為何要把食物從休息室的冰箱取走？
(A) 清潔人員要來了。
(B) 沒貼標籤的都是。
(C) 我們也可以現場購買點心。

- break room 休息室　fridge (n.) 冰箱　crew (n.)（一組）工作人員　label (n.) 標籤
  on-site (adv.) 在現場；就地

14. 以否定疑問句確認是否在奧斯汀站下車 澳⇄美

Isn't Austin Station your stop?
(A) As soon as the bus comes.
(B) There's no stop sign here.
(C) No, I get off at Cook Street.

你不是要在奧斯汀站下車嗎？
(A) 等巴士來的時候。
(B) 這裡沒有「停車讓行」標誌。
(C) 不是，我要在庫克街站下車。

15. 以選擇疑問句詢問處理文件的方式 加⇄英

Should we staple these documents or just attach them with paperclips?
(A) They're attached to my most recent e-mail.
(B) Let's just use paperclips for now.
(C) So that we can hand them out at the workshop.

我們該把這些文件訂起來，還是用迴紋針別起來就好？
(A) 附在我最新收到的電子郵件裡。
(B) 目前用迴紋針就好。
(C) 以便我們能在研習會上分發。

- staple (v.) 用訂書機訂　attach (v.) 固定　hand out 分發

16. 以直述句傳達資訊 美⇄澳 難

I'm working the Saturday morning shift this week.
(A) Could you send it to my apartment?
(B) That's my day to relax.
(C) No, mine starts this evening.

在這個星期，我週六上早班。
(A) 你可以寄到我的公寓嗎？
(B) 我那天休假。
(C) 不是，我的（輪班）從今晚開始。

- shift (n.) 輪班　relax (v.)（使）放鬆

17. 以助動詞 **Will** 開頭的問句，詢問是否要設置投影機 英⇄加

Will I have to set up the projector for the presentation?
(A) A conference table and some chairs.
(B) I found it quite informative.
(C) We have an IT specialist for that.

我需要設置投影機供做簡報使用嗎？
(A) 一張會議桌和幾把椅子。
(B) 我覺得資訊很豐富。
(C) 我們有名資訊工程專員會處理。

• conference (n.) 會議　informative (adj.) 資訊豐富的　specialist (n.) 專業人員

18. 以附加問句確認是否可帶高階主管參觀辦公室 澳⇄英 難

We're going to take the executives on a tour of our office, aren't we?
(A) Will there be enough time for that?
(B) The new chief financial officer.
(C) Oh, I already have one.

我們要帶主管們參觀我們的辦公室，不是嗎？
(A) 有足夠時間參觀嗎？
(B) 新任財務長。
(C) 噢，我已經有一個了。

• executive (n.) 主管　chief (adj.) 主要的　financial (adj.) 財務的

19. 以 **How far** 開頭的問句，詢問可提前多久準備醬料 美⇄加

How far in advance can we make the pasta sauce?
(A) No more than a day.
(B) First, wash the tomatoes.
(C) There's one a few miles from here.

我們可以提前多久做義大利麵醬？
(A) 最多提早一天。
(B) 首先，把番茄洗乾淨。
(C) 離這裡數英里遠的地方有一個。

20. 以 **Why** 開頭的問句，詢問移動糖果展示架的理由 美⇄加

Why has the Henderson's Candy display been moved?
(A) Do you have a location in mind?
(B) Thanks, but I don't really like candy.
(C) The aisle was becoming too crowded.

為何「韓德森糖果」的展示架移走了？
(A) 你有想要去哪裡嗎？
(B) 謝謝，但我不是很喜歡吃糖果。
(C) 走道變得太擠了。

• in mind 想到；心裡　aisle (n.) 走道　crowded (adj.) 擁擠的

21. 以 **Where** 開頭的問句，詢問會議舉行的地點 英⇄澳 難

Where's the session on contract negotiation being held?
(A) Here's the conference program.
(B) Mr. Nakano has finally agreed to sign.
(C) It was shipped from London on Thursday.

合約談判的講習會在哪裡舉行？
(A) 研討會的議程表在這邊。
(B) 中野先生終於同意簽約。
(C) 週四從倫敦送來的。

• session (n.) 講習會　contract (n.) 合約　negotiation (n.) 協商　agree (v.) 同意　ship (v.) 運輸

22. 以 **What** 開頭的問句，詢問如何慶祝羅佩茲女士退休 加⇄美 難

What are we doing to celebrate Ms. Lopez's retirement next month?
(A) Coffee can help when you're feeling tired.
(B) The events committee is meeting this week.
(C) Yeah, she's a local celebrity.

我們要如何慶祝羅佩茲女士下個月退休？
(A) 覺得疲倦時，咖啡可有助你提神。
(B) 活動委員會本週要開會。
(C) 是啊，她是在地名人。

• celebrate (v.) 慶祝　retirement (n.) 退休　committee (n.) 委員會　celebrity (n.) 名人

23. 表示請託或要求的問句 澳⇄英

Would you mind writing a post for the company blog?
(A) Yes, it got many comments from readers.
(B) A pencil and some paper.
(C) What would you like it to be about?

你介意幫公司的部落格寫篇貼文嗎？
(A) 是的，收到很多讀者的留言。
(B) 一枝鉛筆和幾張紙。
(C) 你想要什麼主題的文章？

- post (n.)（網路）貼文　comment (n.) 評論

---

24. 以否定疑問句確認行政人員的業務量是否過於繁重 加⇄英

Don't you think the administrators' workload is too heavy?
(A) It's under twenty kilograms.
(B) My computer uploads quickly.
(C) Only during our busy season.

你不覺得行政人員的工作量太重了嗎？
(A) 不到 20 公斤。
(B) 我的電腦上傳速度很快。
(C) 只在我們旺季的時候。

- administrator (n.) 行政人員　workload (n.) 工作量　heavy (adj.) 沉重的

---

25. 以 **Be** 動詞開頭的問句，詢問工作時可否戴耳機 美⇄澳 

Are we allowed to wear headphones while we work?
(A) I mostly wear casual clothing.
(B) You'll need a phone for client calls.
(C) It's not a very noisy office.

我們工作時可以戴耳機嗎？
(A) 我通常穿輕便服裝。
(B) 你需要一支與客戶通話的電話。
(C) 辦公室不會太吵。

- allow (v.) 允許　mostly (adv.) 通常　noisy (adj.) 嘈雜的

---

26. 表示建議或提案的直述句 加⇄澳 難

We should print out the booking confirmation.
(A) To my work e-mail address, please.
(B) They usually just ask for identification.
(C) I packed some books to read on the train.

我們應該印出預約確認信。
(A) 請寄到我工作用的電郵信箱。
(B) 他們通常只要求查看身分證件。
(C) 我帶了幾本書要在列車上讀。

- booking (n.) 預訂　confirmation (n.) 確認　address (n.) 地址　identification (n.) 身分證明
  pack (v.) 將……裝入行李

---

27. 以 **Which** 開頭的問句，詢問對方想要修剪哪一棵樹 美⇄加 難

Which one of these trees did you want us to trim?
(A) We made an appointment for lawn care, actually.
(B) Because their leaves are falling in the swimming pool.
(C) Is that the longest term you have available?

你想要我們修剪的是哪一棵樹？
(A) 其實我們是預約草坪維護。
(B) 因為葉子一直掉到游泳池裡。
(C) 那是你們最長的期限了嗎？

- trim (v.) 修剪　appointment (n.) 預約　lawn (n.) 草坪　care (n.) 照護　actually (adv.) 實際上
  term (n.) 期限

---

28. 以選擇疑問句，詢問擺節日裝飾品的時間點 澳⇄英

Shall we put up the holiday decorations today or tomorrow?
(A) I made a banner for the reception desk.
(B) Plus the first two days of next week.
(C) My schedule is completely open.

我們要今天擺設假期的裝飾品，還是明天？
(A) 我幫接待處製作了橫幅布條。
(B) 加上下週的前二天。
(C) 我的行程完全沒有安排。

• decoration (n.) 裝飾物　banner (n.) 橫幅　reception (n.) 接待

29. 以附加問句，確認該份試算表是否為最新版本 美⇄澳 難

This is the most up-to-date version of the spreadsheet, isn't it? (A) The number in the bottom right corner. **(B) I haven't made any changes lately.** (C) There are a few dates that would work for me.	這是最新版的試算表，對嗎？ (A) 右下角的數字。 **(B) 我最近沒有做任何更動。** (C) 有幾個我方便的日期。

• up-to-date (adj.) 最新的　spreadsheet (n.) 試算表　bottom (n.) 底部

30. 表示請託或要求的問句 加⇄美

Can I get a copy of my medical records from this clinic? **(A) You'll have to fill out some forms first.** (B) Well, that's not what our records show. (C) We keep medications in the back room.	我可以拿一份我在診所的就醫紀錄嗎？ **(A) 你必須先填一些表格。** (B) 這個嘛，我們紀錄上不是這樣。 (C) 我們把藥品存放在後面房間。

• medical (adj.) 醫療的　clinic (n.) 診所　fill out 填寫　medication (n.) 藥物

31. 以 Who 開頭的問句詢問尼克不在時，由誰負責批准採購要求 英⇄美 難

Who's responsible for approving purchasing requests when Nick is away? (A) That's an excellent idea. **(B) Just leave it; he'll be back this afternoon.** (C) It's for a filing cabinet for the sales department.	尼克不在公司時，是誰負責核准採購要求？ (A) 那個點子很棒。 **(B) 擱著就好，他今天下午就會回來。** (C) 為了業務部要用的檔案櫃

• responsible (adj.) 負責的　approve (v.) 批准　purchasing (n.) 採購　request (n.) 要求

PART 3 P. 109–112

35

32-34 Conversation

M: Lynette, while you were at your meeting, I took a call from Carla Burns at Snadler Associates. (32) **She has that law conference in Sydney next month.** She said she asked you to plan her trip by today, and she's worried that she hasn't heard back from you.

W: (33) **Oh, I took care of all of her flight and hotel bookings this morning.** I just didn't have time to tell her before my meeting.

M: OK. (34) **Well, please send her a confirmation e-mail right now.** I want her to know that everything has been arranged.

32-34 對話 澳⇄美

男： 麗奈特，妳開會的時候，我接到史奈德勒公司的卡拉．伯恩斯打來的電話，(32) **她下個月要到雪梨參加法律研討會**，她說已經請妳在今天之前，規劃好她的行程，但還沒接到妳的回覆，因此很擔心。

女： (33) **噢，我今早已經打點好她一切的航班和飯店預定事宜**，只是開會前沒有時間告知她。

男： 好的。(34) **這樣的話，請現在寄電子郵件給她進行確認**，我希望讓她了解，一切都安排好了

• conference (n.) 會議；研討會　take care of . . . 處理……　booking (n.) 預訂　confirmation (n.) 確認　arrange (v.) 安排

32. 相關細節——男子提及下個月將會發生的事情

What does the man say will happen next month?
(A) A conference will take place.
(B) A new law will go into effect.
(C) A tour will be given.
(D) A staff member will retire.

男子說，下個月會有何事舉行？
(A) 將舉行研討會
(B) 新法律將生效
(C) 將舉辦導覽
(D) 有名員工要退休

- take place 舉行　go into effect 生效　retire (v.) 退休

---

33. 相關細節——女子提及她完成的事情

What does the woman say she did?
(A) Picked up some materials
(B) Made some reservations
(C) Had lunch with a client
(D) Posted a job listing

女子說她完成了何事？
(A) 領取材料
(B) 做好預約
(C) 和客戶吃午餐
(D) 貼出職缺列表

- material (n.) 材料　reservation (n.) 預訂　post (v.) 張貼　listing (n.) 列表

換句話說 took care of all of her flight and hotel bookings（打點好她一切的航班和飯店預定事宜）
→ made some reservations（做好預約）

---

34. 相關細節——男子要求女子馬上完成的事情

What does the man ask the woman to do immediately?
(A) Listen to a telephone message
(B) Make copies of a file
(C) Correct a mistake
(D) Send a notification

男子要求女子立刻做什麼事？
(A) 聽電話留言
(B) 影印檔案
(C) 修正錯誤
(D) 寄出通知

- correct (v.) 改正　notification (n.) 通知

換句話說 a confirmation e-mail（電子郵件確認）→ a notification（通知）

35-37 Conversation with three speakers

M1: Welcome to Riverside Coffee. What can I get for you?
W: [35] **I'd like a latte, but do you have almond milk? I'd like that instead of regular milk, please.**
M1: Oh, I'm sorry, but we don't have that.
M2: Excuse me, [36] **Carl. We actually started carrying almond milk last week because customers kept asking for it.**
M1: Oh, I had no idea. [36] **Thanks for the correction, Bill.** OK ma'am, it looks like we'll be able to accommodate you. There's a fifty-cent additional charge for substitutions, though. Is that OK?

35-37 三人對話

加⇄英⇄澳

男 1： 歡迎光臨河濱咖啡館，請問要點什麼呢？
女： [35] **我要一杯拿鐵，但你們有提供杏仁奶嗎？我想要用杏仁奶代替一般用的牛奶，謝謝。**
男 1： 噢，很抱歉，但我們沒有供應杏仁奶。
男 2： 抱歉打岔一下，[36] **卡爾，我們其實從上週起就有開始供應杏仁奶，因為顧客持續反映有這項需求。**
男 1： 噢，我不知道，[36] **謝謝你糾正我，比爾。**好的，女士，看來我們可以為您做調整，不過更換別的乳品須多付 50 美分，這樣方便嗎？

W: That's no problem. (37) **Oh, I have this coupon for a free drink for frequent customers, too.** Can I use it to pay for this drink?	女： 沒問題。(37) **噢，我還有這張常客優惠券，可以免費兌換飲品**，我能用來抵付這杯飲料嗎？
M2: Sure.	男 2: 當然可以。

- carry (v.) 出售…… correction (n.) 更正 accommodate (v.) 提供……方便 charge (n.) 收費 substitution (n.) 替換；代替 frequent (adj.) 頻繁的

35. 相關細節——女子提出的要求

What does the woman ask for?
(A) A take-away cup
(B) A sales receipt
(C) A gift certificate
(D) An ingredient replacement

女子提出何項要求？
(A) 外帶杯
(B) 銷貨收據
(C) 禮券
(D) 更換成分

- take-away (n.) 外帶

換句話說 would like that instead of regular milk（想要用來代替一般用的牛奶）
→ an ingredient replacement（更換成分）

36. 相關細節——比爾指正卡爾的事情 難

What does Bill correct Carl about?
(A) The name of a drink
(B) The operating hours of a café
(C) The availability of an item
(D) The cost of a change

比爾糾正卡爾什麼事？
(A) 飲料品名
(B) 咖啡館營業時間
(C) 品項是否可供應
(D) 變更的費用

- operation hours 營業時間 availability (n.) 可得性

37. 相關細節——女子使用的支付方式

How does the woman want to pay for her order?
(A) With cash
(B) With a voucher
(C) With a credit card
(D) With a mobile app

女子想要如何支付她點的飲料？
(A) 用現金
(B) 用兌換券
(C) 用信用卡
(D) 用手機應用程式

- voucher (n.) 兌換券

換句話說 coupon（優惠券）→ voucher（兌換券）

38-40 Conversation **38-40 對話** 英⇄加

W: All right, now let's talk about who to cast in the side parts. First up is the character of "the uncle." (38) **Uh, I liked Simon Witherspoon—I think he'd give the play a lively energy.**	女： 好的，現在讓我們來討論次要角色的人選。首先是「叔叔」這個角色，(38) **嗯，我覺得西蒙・魏斯朋還不錯，我想他會為這齣戲劇注入活力。**
M: It's true that he's quite a dynamic performer. (39) **But the character really needs to be able to sing, and the music part of Simon's audition was not impressive.**	男： 他確實是名充滿活力的演員，(39) **但是這個角色真的需要唱功堅強的演員，而西蒙試鏡時，音樂方面的表現並不亮眼。**

W: Well, then let's get him a singing coach! I think it's worth the investment.

M: I'm not convinced. [40] **Let's move on to another character for now, and talk about casting the uncle again later.**

女： 那麼，我們就幫他聘請歌唱教練！我覺得這值得投資。

男： 我並不認同。**[40] 我們現在先接著選另一個角色，晚點再討論「叔叔」的人選。**

- cast (v.) 為……選演員　play (n.) 戲劇　lively (adj.) 生氣勃勃的　dynamic (adj.) 充滿活力的　performer (n.) 表演者　impressive (adj.) 令人印象深刻的　worth (adj.) 值得（做……）　investment (n.) 投資　convinced (adj.) 確信的

38. 相關細節——說話者徵選演員的目的　難

What are the speakers most likely choosing cast members for?

(A) A television program

(B) A feature film

(C) A stage show

(D) An online advertisement

說話者最可能正在為何事選角？

(A) 電視節目

(B) 劇情長片

(C) 舞台劇

(D) 網路廣告

換句話說 the play（戲劇）→ a stage show（舞台劇）

39. 相關細節——男子針對魏斯朋先生的敘述

What does the man say about Mr. Witherspoon?

(A) He does not have a necessary skill.

(B) He should play another character.

(C) He will have to audition again.

(D) He has a scheduling conflict.

關於魏斯朋先生，男子說了什麼？

(A) 他沒有所需的技能。

(B) 他應該演另一個角色。

(C) 他需要再次試鏡。

(D) 他的行程撞期。

- scheduling conflict 行程衝突

40. 相關細節——男子決定做的事情

What does the man decide to do?

(A) Speak with an investor

(B) Rewatch a performance

(C) Postpone a discussion

(D) Move a location

男子決定怎麼做？

(A) 和投資者討論

(B) 重看表演

(C) 延後討論

(D) 遷移地點

- investor (n.) 投資者　performance (n.) 表演　postpone (v.) 延後

換句話說 talk about . . . again later（晚點再討論）→ postpone a discussion（延後討論）

41-43 Conversation

W: Good morning. [41] **I'd like to check out. Here's my room key.**

M: Thank you. Just a moment . . . OK, Ms. Suzuki, here's the bill for your stay.

W: [42] **Oh, this is charging me for two nights, but I arrived yesterday morning.** I'm attending the engineering convention.

41-43 對話　美⇄澳

女： 早安，**[41] 我想要退房，這是我的房間鑰匙。**

男： 謝謝您，請稍等……好的，鈴木女士，這是您的住宿帳單。

女： **[42] 噢，帳單上向我收取兩個晚上的住宿費，但我是昨天早上才到達的，**來參加一場工程大會。

M: Hmm . . . I'm not sure why, but our system has you listed for July first and second in Room 407.	男：唔……我不清楚原因，但我們系統列的資料顯示，您是於 7 月 1 日和 2 日住在 407 號房。
W: Well, I did originally book two nights, but I changed my reservation about a week ago. Oh! (43) **Would you like to see my confirmation e-mail? I think I have the printout here in my purse.**	女：這個嘛，我起初確實訂了兩個晚上，但大約一週前，我已經更改了訂房內容。對了！(43) **你要看我的電子郵件確認信嗎？我想我的包包裡有印出的紙本。**
M: That would be very helpful.	男：那會非常有幫助。

- bill (n.) 帳單　stay (n.) 停留　charge (v.) 收費　convention (n.) 會議　list (v.) 把……列入　originally (adv.) 起初地　reservation (n.) 預訂　confirmation (n.) 確認　purse (n.)（女用）提包

41. 全文相關——對話的地點

Where most likely is the conversation taking place?
(A) In a parking garage
(B) In a banquet hall
(C) In a seminar room
(D) In a hotel lobby

這段對話最可能發生在哪裡？
(A) 立體停車場
(B) 宴會廳
(C) 研討室
(D) 飯店大廳

42. 掌握說話者的意圖——提及「我是昨天早上才到達的」的意圖

What does the woman imply when she says, "I arrived yesterday morning"?
(A) She was not present for a talk.
(B) There is an error on an invoice.
(C) She did not have time for a social activity.
(D) There was strong competition for an opportunity.

女子說：「我是昨天早上才到達的」，言下之意為何？
(A) 她沒有出席演說。
(B) 帳單上有錯誤。
(C) 她沒有時間進行社交活動。
(D) 某個機會的競爭很激烈。

- present (adj.) 在場的　invoice (n.) 請款帳單；發貨單　competition (n.) 競爭　opportunity (n.) 機會

43. 相關細節——女子接下來會做的事情 難

What will the woman most likely do next?
(A) Look over a timetable
(B) Make a call to a colleague
(C) Search through her handbag
(D) E-mail the man from a device

女子接下來最有可能做何事？
(A) 查看時間表
(B) 打電話給同事
(C) 在手提包裡找東西
(D) 透過裝置發電郵給男子

- colleague (n.) 同事　device (n.) 裝置

換句話說 purse（包包）→ handbag（手提包）

44-46 Conversation　　44-46 對話　英⇄澳

W: **(44) Delmer, I've finished loading the products onto the truck for the eleven o'clock shipment. It just left. I'm going to take my break now.**

M: Sure, Megan. But can I talk to you for a minute first? **(45) I noticed you rubbing your back earlier. Are you having back pain?**

W: A little bit, actually. But I'm sure that it will go away once I get the chance to relax this weekend.

M: I hope so. If it doesn't, come and see me. **(46) I can recommend a massage therapist who specializes in treating lower back pain.** Several other workers have gone to see her, and they say she's great.

女： **(44) 戴爾瑪，我已經把貨品搬上卡車，以備妥 11 點出貨，而剛才貨車出發了，現在我要去休息一下。**

男： 當然好的，梅根，但我方便先跟妳聊一下嗎？**(45) 我稍早注意到妳在揉妳的背，妳的背在痛嗎？**

女： 其實是有一點，不過我確定只要這個週末有機會休息，背痛就會消退。

男： 希望如此，如果還是會痛，就來找我，**(46) 我可以介紹一名專門治療下背疼痛的按摩治療師**，好幾個其他同事都去給她服務過，個個都讚不絕口。

- load (v.) 裝載　shipment (n.) 運輸（的貨物）　notice (v.) 注意到　rub (v.) 揉搓　back pain 背痛　massage therapist 按摩治療師　specialize in . . . 專門從事……　treat (v.) 治療；處理

44. 全文相關——女子的職業

Who most likely is the woman?

(A) An assembly line manager

(B) A truck driver

(C) A warehouse worker

(D) A sales clerk

女子最可能的身分為何？

(A) 生產線經理

(B) 卡車司機

(C) 倉庫工人

(D) 銷售人員

---

45. 相關細節——男子擔憂的事情

What is the man concerned about?

(A) The status of a shipment

(B) The woman's health

(C) The opinion of an executive

(D) The woman's job satisfaction

男子擔心何事？

(A) 出貨的狀況

(B) 女子的健康

(C) 主管的意見

(D) 女子的工作滿意度

- status (n.) 狀態　executive (n.) 主管　satisfaction (n.) 滿意

---

46. 相關細節——男子提供給女子的東西　難

What does the man offer the woman?

(A) Help from another staff member

(B) Use of a special piece of equipment

(C) A career development opportunity

(D) A referral to a service provider

男子提議給女子何者？

(A) 另一名員工的協助

(B) 使用特殊設備

(C) 生涯發展機會

(D) 介紹服務業者

- equipment (n.) 設備　referral (n.) 介紹　provider (n.) 提供者

換句話說 recommend a massage therapist（介紹按摩治療師）
→ a referral to a service provider（介紹服務業者）

47-49 Conversation

47-49 對話

加⇄美

M: Hi, Jody. It's Randall Fisher. Did you get the draft lease I sent you for legal review? (47) **If everything looks good, I'd like to move my music shop into the space as soon as possible.**

W: I was planning to e-mail you about that. (48) **As your business lawyer, I'm concerned that the agreement doesn't allow you to transfer the lease or sublet the space. You'd be stuck there for the entire lease period. That's not very advantageous to you.**

M: Oh, I see.

W: (49) **Of course, you could ask the landlord to revise that part of the lease, but you might have to give him something in return—higher rental fees, for example. Would you consider that?**

男：嗨，朱蒂，我是藍道·費雪。妳收到我寄過去給妳進行法律審查的租約草稿了嗎？(47) **如果內容看起來都沒問題，我想盡快把我的樂器行遷到那個地點。**

女：我正打算針對此事寄電子郵件給您，(48) **作為您的商務律師，我擔心的是，該份合約不允許您轉讓租約、或是將空間轉租，您必須在那裡待到租約期滿，此點對您不太有利。**

男：噢，我懂了。

女：(49) **當然，你可以要求房東針對這部分修改租約，但你可能必須提供對方一些好處作為交換，例如支付較高的租金。這部分你會考慮嗎？**

- draft (n.) 草稿　lease (n.) 租約　legal (adj.) 法律的　agreement (n.) 協議　transfer (v.) 轉讓　sublet (v.) 分／轉租　stuck (adj.) 動不了的　entire (adj.) 全部的　advantageous (adj.) 有利的　landlord (n.) 房東　revise (v.) 修改　in return 作為交換　rental fee 租金

47. 相關細節——男子希望做的事情

What does the man hope to do?

(A) Release some music

(B) Rent some machinery

(C) Sell a piece of property

(D) Relocate a retail store

男子希望做什麼？

(A) 發表音樂作品

(B) 租用機器

(C) 出售房地產

(D) 搬遷零售商店

- release (v.) 發表　property (n.) 房地產　relocate (v.) 搬遷　retail store 零售商店

換句話說 move my music shop（搬遷我的樂器行）→ relocate a retail store（搬遷零售商店）

48. 相關細節——女子提出的問題

難

What problem does the woman mention?

(A) A contract's terms are unfavorable.

(B) A space has some security issues.

(C) A local regulation is complicated.

(D) A certification has expired.

女子提到什麼問題？

(A) 合約的條款不甚有利。

(B) 場地有安全問題。

(C) 有項當地規範很複雜。

(D) 有份證書過期了。

- term (n.) 條款　unfavorable (adj.) 不利的　security (n.) 安全　regulation (n.) 規定　complicated (adj.) 複雜的　certification (n.) 證書　expire (v.) 到期

換句話說 not very advantageous（不太有利）→ unfavorable（不甚有利）

49. 相關細節——女子向男子提出的問題 難

What does the woman ask the man about?
(A) His familiarity with a process
(B) His willingness to negotiate
(C) His ability to prove a claim
(D) His access to a resource

女子詢問男子何事？
(A) 對程序的熟悉度
(B) 協商的意願
(C) 證明主張的能力
(D) 資源的使用權限

• familiarity (n.) 熟悉　process (n.) 程序　willingness (n.) 願意　negotiate (v.) 協商　prove (v.) 證明　claim (n.) 聲稱　access (n.) 使用權　resource (n.) 資源

50-52 Conversation with three speakers

50-52 三人對話

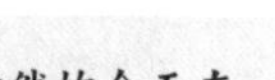

M: Hi, Heather. (50) **I'm glad you could join us for this meeting even though you're working from home today.** Can you see and hear us alright?

W1: Hi, Simon and Donna. Yes, the video and audio seem to be working just fine.

M: Great. Let's get started, then. Donna?

W2: All right. (51) **As you both know, we'll be talking today about our proposed revisions to the employee handbook.** Heather, do you have your materials at hand?

W1: Yep.

W2: Great. (52) **Then let's begin by discussing how each of our assigned sections is coming along.**

男：　嗨，海瑟。(50) **很高興雖然妳今天在家工作，仍然可以和我們一起開會。**妳可以清楚看到我們、聽見我們說話嗎？

女 1：嗨，賽門和唐娜。可以的，影像和聲音功能似乎都沒問題。

男：　太好了，那麼我們開始吧。唐娜？

女 2：好的，(51) **如兩位所知，我們今天要討論員工手冊的提議修改事宜。**海瑟，妳手邊有資料嗎？

女 1：有的。

女 2：非常好。(52) **那麼，我們首先開始討論各自分配到的部分進展如何。**

• propose (v.) 提議　revision (n.) 修訂　at hand 在手邊　assign (v.) 分配　section (n.) 部分　come along 進展

50. 相關細節——男子針對會議提及的內容 

What does the man mention about the meeting?
(A) It was not originally scheduled for today.
(B) It includes a remote participant.
(C) It is being recorded.
(D) It might last past closing time.

關於會議，男子提到什麼？
(A) 原本預定時間不是今天。
(B) 與會者當中有人遠距參與。
(C) 會議過程正被錄下。
(D) 可能會超過下班時間。

• originally (adv.) 起初地　schedule (v.) 預定的　include (v.) 包含　remote (adj.) 遙遠的　last (v.) 持續　past (prep.) 晚於

---

51. 相關細節——說話者正在進行的專案 難

What kind of project are the speakers working on?
(A) Recruiting for staff openings
(B) Developing a questionnaire
(C) Organizing a training program
(D) Rewriting a set of policies

說話者正在進行何種專案？
(A) 招聘員工職缺
(B) 開發問卷
(C) 規劃培訓課程
(D) 修訂一套方針

• recruit (v.) 招聘　opening (n.) 職缺　questionnaire (n.) 問卷　organize (v.) 籌劃　policy (n.) 方針；政策

換句話說 revisions to the employee handbook（員工手冊的提議修改）
→ rewriting a set of policies（修訂一套方針）

52. 相關細節——說話者接下來要做的事情 難

What will the speakers do next?

(A) Give individual progress updates

(B) Read the minutes of a previous meeting

(C) Choose their preferred assignments

(D) Wait for an additional attendee

說話者接下來會做什麼？

(A) 回報各自的最新進度

(B) 查閱先前會議紀錄

(C) 選擇各自偏好的任務

(D) 等待另一名與會者

- individual (adj.) 個別的　progress (n.) 進展　minutes (n.)〔複〕會議紀錄　previous (adj.) 先前的　prefer (v.) 偏好　assignment (n.) 工作；任務

換句話說 how each of our assigned sections is coming along（各自分配到的部分目前進展如何）
→ individual progress（各自的進度）

53-55 Conversation

W: Good evening, sir. Is Ireland your final destination?

M: (53) **Yes, I'm visiting Dublin for a few days on business.**

W: All right. Then you'll need to fill out this landing card and submit it to Immigration when the plane lands.

M: Oh, OK. (54) **Do you have a pen I can borrow?**

W: (54) **Sure.** Here you are.

M: Thanks. Oh, this card is asking for my passport number, but I don't have it memorized. And my passport is in my bag in the overhead compartment.

W: (55) **Well, the "Fasten Seatbelts" sign is off, so you can open up the compartment now if you'd like.** Just make sure to close it when you're finished.

53-55 對話 英⇄澳

女： 晚安，先生，您的最終目的地是愛爾蘭嗎？

男： (53) **是的，我要去都柏林出差幾天。**

女： 好的，那麼您必須填寫這張入境卡，並在飛機降落後送交入境查驗。

男： 噢，沒問題。(54) **可以跟妳借支筆嗎？**

女： (54) **當然可以**，請用。

男： 謝謝。噢，入境卡上要填我的護照號碼，但我沒有背下來，而我把護照收在袋子裡了，現在放在座位上方的行李置物櫃。

女： (55) **這部分的話，「請繫好安全帶」的燈號未亮起，所以如果您有需要，現在可以打開置物櫃**，只要務必在拿完物品後，將置物櫃關上即可。

- destination (n.) 目的地　fill out 填寫　landing (n.) 著陸　submit (v.) 交出　immigration (n.) 移民　land (v.) 降落　passport (n.) 護照　memorize (v.) 背熟　overhead (adj.) 在頭頂上的　compartment (n.) 隔間

53. 相關細節——男子提及與本此旅程有關的事情

What does the man say about his trip?

(A) He plans to visit a friend.

(B) It will be one week long.

(C) It has been enjoyable.

(D) He is traveling for work.

關於他的旅程，男子說了什麼？

(A) 他計劃去拜訪朋友。

(B) 會長達一週。

(C) 旅程目前很愉快。

(D) 當前行程為差旅。

換句話說 visiting . . . on business（出差）→ traveling for work（差旅）

54. 相關細節——女子協助男子的方式

How does the woman assist the man?
(A) By giving him an extra cushion
(B) By agreeing to talk to another passenger
(C) By accepting a container for disposal
(D) By lending him a writing tool

女子如何協助男子？
(A) 多給他一個靠墊
(B) 同意和另一位乘客談談
(C) 接受供丟棄的容器
(D) 出借書寫工具

- container (n.) 容器 disposal (n.) 清除；拋棄

換句話說 a pen（筆）→ a writing tool（書寫工具）

55. 相關細節——女子表示男子可以做的事情 難

According to the woman, what can the man do?
(A) Lean his seat back
(B) Access a storage area
(C) Leave part of a form blank
(D) Turn off an overhead light

根據女子所說，男子可以做何事？
(A) 把他的座椅往後傾
(B) 使用儲物空間
(C) 將部分表格留白
(D) 關掉座位上方的燈

- lead back 向後靠 access (v.) 使用 storage (n.) 儲存

換句話說 open up the compartment（打開置物櫃）→ access a storage area（使用儲物空間）

56-58 Conversation

M: Hey, Krista. (56) **How's your design for the concert hall coming along?**
W: It's going well, Curtis. How are you doing?
M: I'm busy! (57) **I don't know if you've heard, but we're going to choose three students from the local university to do internships here this summer.** I'm in charge of the program.
W: No, I hadn't heard that! Is there anything I can do to help?
M: Definitely! (58) **As a senior employee, it'd be great if you could give a talk to the students about your work and the skills it requires.** Would you be willing to do that sometime in July?
W: (58) **Sure.** I'd be happy to.

56-58 對話 加⇄美

男： 嗨，克莉絲塔，(56) **妳的音樂廳設計案進行得如何？**
女： 一切順利，柯提斯，你最近還好嗎？
男： 忙到不行！(57) **不知道妳有沒有聽說，我們要從在地的大學裡選出三名學生，讓他們今年夏天來實習**，我就負責這個專案。
女： 沒有，我沒有聽說這個消息！我可以幫上什麼忙嗎？
男： 當然！(58) **身為資深員工，如果妳可以跟學生講解妳的工作和所需的技巧，那就太好了**。妳願意七月時，找個時間幫這個忙嗎？
女： (58) **當然好**，我很樂意。

- in charge of . . . 負責…… senior (adj.) 資深的 willing (adj.) 樂意的 sometime (adv.) 在某個時候

56. 全文相關——說話者的工作地點

Where do the speakers most likely work?
(A) At a public relations agency
(B) At an architectural firm
(C) At a recording studio
(D) At an art museum

說話者最可能在哪裡工作？
(A) 公關公司
(B) 建築公司
(C) 錄音室
(D) 美術館

換句話說 design（設計）→ architectural（建築的）

57. 相關細節——男子提及即將發生的事情

What does the man say will happen soon?
(A) A computer program will be upgraded.
(B) A building will be remodeled.
(C) Some interns will be selected.
(D) Business hours will change temporarily.

據男子說，何事即將發生？
(A) 電腦程式將要升級。
(B) 大樓將要改建。
(C) 將選出實習生。
(D) 營業時間將暫時變動。

- remodel (v.) 改建　temporarily (adv.) 暫時地

換句話說 choose three students from the local university to do internships（從在地的大學裡選出三名學生來實習）→ Some interns will be selected.（將選出實習生。）

58. 相關細節—女子同意做的事情

What does the woman agree to do?
(A) Calculate a budgetary requirement
(B) Telecommute for a short period
(C) Deliver a speech to a group
(D) Conduct some phone interviews

女子同意做何事？
(A) 計算預算需求
(B) 短期內遠距工作
(C) 對團體發表演說
(D) 執行電話訪問

- calculate (v.) 計算　budgetary (adj.) 預算的　requirement (n.) 需求　telecommute (v.) 遠距工作　deliver a speech 發表演說　conduct (v.) 執行

換句話說 give a talk（講解）→ deliver a speech（發表演說）

59-61 Conversation

W: Hi, Marcus. Where are you right now?
M: (59) **I'm on the fourth floor, putting up a wall fan for the accountants.**
W: Oh, OK. I'm back from my trip to the hardware store, and I was wondering where you'd gone.
M: Yeah, the fan was delivered after you left, and they asked me to put it up right away. (60) **It's getting warm up here because of the sunlight bouncing off the new skyscraper across the street.**
W: Really? That's too bad. (61) **Well, let me know if you need anything.**
M: Oh, actually—I left my blue screwdriver on my desk.
W: Uh . . . yes, I see it. I'll be there in a minute.

59-61 對話　英⇄加

女：嗨，馬可斯，你現在人在哪裡？
男：(59) **我在四樓，幫會計部安裝壁扇。**
女：噢，好的。我從五金行回來，想確認一下你去哪裡了。
男：是啊，妳離開之後，電扇送到了，而且他們要求我立刻安裝。(60) **因為對面新蓋了摩天大樓，將陽光反射過來，所以這裡越來越熱了。**
女：真的嗎？那可太糟了。(61) **好啦，如果有需要什麼，就告訴我。**
男：噢，其實我把我的藍色螺絲起子忘在我桌上了。
女：嗯……有的，我看到了，我稍後就拿過去。

- fan (n.) 風扇　accountant (n.) 會計人員　hardware store 五金行　wonder (v.) 想知道　right away 立刻　bounce (v.)（使）反彈　skyscraper (n.) 摩天大樓　screwdriver (n.) 螺絲起子

59. 相關細節——男子表示他現在正在做的事情

What does the man say he is currently doing?
(A) Repairing some electronics
(B) Assembling some furniture
(C) Packing a moving crate
(D) Installing an appliance

男子說他現在正在做什麼？
(A) 修理電子產品
(B) 組裝家具
(C) 裝箱準備搬遷
(D) 安裝電器

- repair (v.) 修理　electronics (n.) 電子產品　assemble (v.) 組裝　crate (n.) 板條箱　install (v.) 安裝　appliance (n.)（家用）電器

換句話說 putting up a wall fan（安裝壁扇）→ installing an appliance（安裝電器）

---

60. 相關細節——鄰近大樓的問題 難

What is the problem with a nearby building?
(A) It is blocking some light.
(B) It is increasing noise levels.
(C) It is reflecting some heat.
(D) It is causing higher winds.

附近的大樓有何問題？
(A) 把光線擋住。
(B) 使噪音增加。
(C) 將熱氣反射。
(D) 造成較強的風勢。

- block (v.) 阻擋　increase (v.) 增加　reflect (v.) 反射　cause (v.) 導致

換句話說 the sunlight bouncing off . . .（陽光反射過來）→ It is reflecting some heat.（將熱氣反射。）

---

61. 掌握說話者的意圖——提及「我把我的藍色螺絲起子忘在桌上了」的意圖 難

What does the man mean when he says, "I left my blue screwdriver on my desk"?
(A) He is willing to lend his belongings to the woman.
(B) He will not be able to complete his task right away.
(C) He does not mind returning to his workstation.
(D) He would like the woman to bring a tool to him.

男子說：「我把我的藍色螺絲起子忘在我桌上了」，其意思為何？
(A) 他願意把個人物品借給女子。
(B) 他無法立刻完成他的工作。
(C) 他不介意回到他的工作區。
(D) 他想要女子把工具帶過去給他。

- belongings (n.) 擁有物　task (n.) 任務　mind (v.) 介意　workstation (n.) 工作區　tool (n.) 工具

62-64 Conversation + Wheater forecast

W: Kendrick, I'm concerned about the weather this week. (62) **We should probably schedule a few extra employees to repair potential damage to the power lines.**

M: Why? What's going on?

W: (63) **Well, as you can see on this forecast I printed out, there's going to be one day of high winds. We'll want at least one extra crew per district on standby that day, I think.**

M: Hmm. This forecast is from the Clancy Weather Service, though, isn't it? They're not always reliable, in my experience. (64) **Why don't you see what a few other meteorological services are predicting?** If it's similar, then I'll approve your suggestion.

18°C / 24°C	15°C / 21°C	16°C / 21°C	17°C / 26°C
Tuesday	Wednesday	(63) **Thursday**	Friday

62-64 對話＋天氣預報 美⇄澳

女： 肯卓里，本週的天氣讓我很擔心，(62) **到時電線可能會毀損，我們可能應該多安排一些額外的維修人力。**

男： 為什麼？狀況是如何呢？

女： (63) **這個嘛，我把天氣預報印出來了，你可以從上面看到，其中一天會颳起強風，我認為當天，每一區我們至少要多派一組人員待命。**

男： 唔，但是這份預報是「坎西天氣服務」製作的，不是嗎？依我的經驗，他們的預報未必準確。(64) **妳何不看看其他幾家氣象業者的預報內容？**如果其他家的結果也類似，那麼我就批准妳的建議。

18°C / 24°C	15°C / 21°C	16°C / 21°C	17°C / 26°C
星期二	星期三	(63) **星期四**	星期五

- concerned (adj.) 擔心的 schedule (v.) 安排 potential (adj.) 可能的 power line 電源線 forecast (n.) 預報 crew (n.)（一組）工作人員 per (prep.) 每；每一 district (n.) 區 on standby 待命；備用 reliable (adj.) 可靠的 meteorological (adj.) 氣象的 predict (v.) 預報 approve (v.) 批准 suggestion (n.) 提議

62. 全文相關——說話者的職業

What industry do the speakers most likely work in?
(A) Energy utilities
(B) Rail transportation
(C) Road construction
(D) Groundskeeping

說話者最可能在何種產業工作？
(A) 公用能源事業
(B) 鐵路運輸
(C) 道路工程
(D) 場地管理

- utilities (n.)（水電等）公用事業 transportation (n.) 運輸 construction (n.) 建造

換句話說 the power lines（電線）→ energy utilities（公用能源事業）

63. 圖表整合題——女子建議增派人力的日子

Look at the graphic. Which day does the woman suggest scheduling extra workers for?
(A) Tuesday
(B) Wednesday
(C) Thursday
(D) Friday

請見圖表作答。女子建議哪一天要安排額外的人手？
(A) 週二
(B) 週三
(C) 週四
(D) 週五

64. 相關細節——男子建議先做的事情 難

What does the man recommend doing first?
(A) Asking a supervisor for approval
(B) Giving workers a chance to volunteer
(C) Determining some crews' responsibilities
(D) Checking some different forecasts

男子建議先做何事？
(A) 請求主管批准
(B) 給工人志願服務的機會
(C) 決定部分工作人員的職責
(D) 查看別家預報結果

- supervisor (n.) 主管 approval (n.) 批准 volunteer (v.) 志願 determine (v.) 決定 responsibility (n.) 職責

換句話說 see what a few other meteorological services are predicting（看看其他幾家氣象業者的預報內容）→ checking some different forecasts（查看別家預報結果）

65-67 Conversation + Gate design

M: Hi Sonya, it's Kwang-Min Cho. I've picked the new gate for my yard.

W: Great! Let me just get your file out. OK, which one do you want?

M: (65) **I like the one you showed me that is curved at the top and closed at the bottom.**

W: Good choice! It has an appealing mix of style and functionality.

65-67 對話＋門的設計圖 加⇄英

男： 嗨，桑雅，我是趙光明。我已經選好我的院子要裝設的新大門款式了。

女： 太好了！我來把您的檔案叫出來。好了，您想要哪一款呢？

男： (65) **我喜歡妳上次給我看過，上面是弧形、下面是封閉式的那一款。**

女： 真有眼光！那一款兼具時尚和實用性，很吸引人。

M: That's what I thought. [(66)] **I want a gate that will make the yard look nice, but that will also keep animals out of the vegetable garden I'm planning.**

W: Absolutely. [(67)] **Now, I'll call to make sure the wholesaler has it in stock.** If it is, the landscaping crew will be able to finish the fencing as scheduled.

男：我正是這麼覺得。(66) **我想要能讓院子外觀變好看的大門，但也要能擋住動物，不讓牠們跑進我計劃種植的菜園。**

女：這是當然。(67) **我會馬上打電話給批發商，確認有庫存**，如果有貨，景觀工程人員就能按照預定時間，把圍籬裝好。

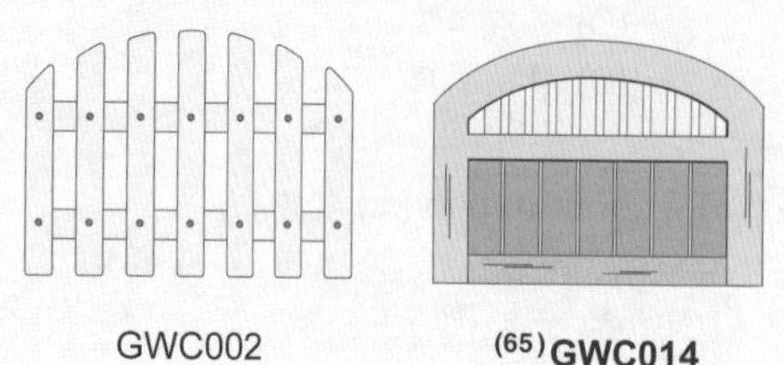

GWC002　　(65) **GWC014**

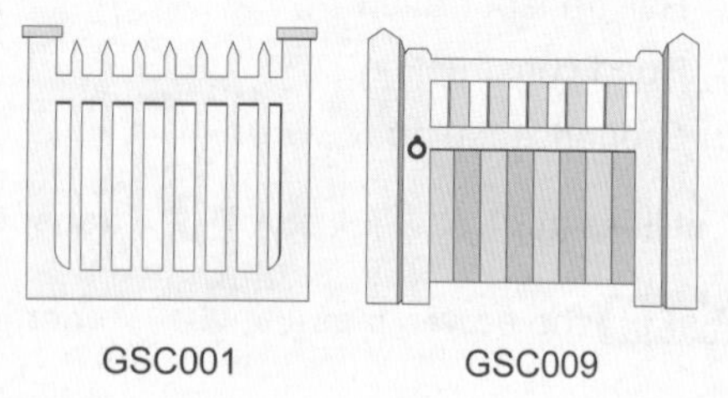

GSC001　　GSC009

- pick (v.) 挑選　gate (n.) 大門　yard (n.) 院子　curved (adj.) 弧形的　bottom (n.) 底部　appealing (adj.) 有吸引力的　functionality (n.) 實用性　wholesaler (n.) 批發商　in stock 有現貨的　landscaping (n.) 景觀美化　crew (n.)（一組）工作人員　fencing (n.) 柵欄；籬笆

65. 圖表整合題——男子選擇的大門

Look at the graphic. Which gate does the man choose?

(A) GWC002

(B) GWC014

(C) GSC001

(D) GSC009

請見圖表作答。男子選了哪一款大門？

(A) GWC002

(B) GWC014

(C) GSC001

(D) GSC009

66. 相關細節——男子針對院子的敘述 難

What does the man say about his yard?

(A) He will keep a pet there.

(B) He will grow produce there.

(C) He plans to have parties there.

(D) He will put in a swimming pool there.

關於他的院子，男子說了什麼？

(A) 他會在院子養寵物。

(B) 他會在院子種植農作。

(C) 他計劃在院子開派對。

(D) 他會在院子建造游泳池。

- pet (n.) 寵物　produce (n.) 農產品

換句話說 vegetable（菜）→ produce（農作）

67. 相關細節——女子接下來將致電的對象

Who will the woman most likely call next?

(A) A supplier

(B) An employee

(C) Another client

(D) An inspector

女子接下來最可能打電話給誰？

(A) 供應商

(B) 員工

(C) 另一名客戶

(D) 檢查員

換句話說 wholesaler（批發商）→ supplier（供應商）

68-70 Conversation + Episode list

68-70 對話＋集數列表

加⇄美

M: [(68)] **All right, we now have a full tank of gas.** We shouldn't have to stop again unless we want some snacks.

W: Great! Well, since there're a few more hours of highway ahead of us, why don't you find something for us to listen to?

M: Sure. [(69)] **I just subscribed to a new podcast for this trip, actually. It's a series of interviews with successful entrepreneurs.**

W: That sounds good. Maybe we'll get some ideas that we can apply at the trade show tomorrow.

M: Exactly. OK, let's see, I'm most interested in the third episode here . . . [(70)] **but since we have enough time to listen to all of them, I'll just start with the oldest one.**

	Showing: Newest first
"Amita Mittal" June 23	40 minutes
"Mateo Lozano" June 16	39 minutes
"Josh Dennis" June 9	42 minutes
(70) **"Verna Armstrong"** **June 2**	**44 minutes**

男：(68) **好了，我們現在油箱加滿了，**除非我們要買零食，否則應該不用再停下來了。

女：太好了！說到這個，既然我們接下來還要在公路上開好幾個小時，你何不找點東西，讓我們可以邊聽呢？

男：當然沒問題。(69) **其實我才剛為了這次遠行，訂閱了一個新的播客節目，那是一系列成功企業家的訪談節目。**

女：聽起來不錯，也許我們可以聽到一些可以在明天的商展上，派上用場的點子。

男：正是如此。好啦，我看一下，我最感興趣的是這裡的第三集⋯⋯ (70) **但既然我們有時間可以聽完所有集數，我就從頭開始播放。**

	排序：日期最新者在前
〈阿米塔・密托〉 6月23日	40 分鐘
〈馬提歐・羅札諾〉 6月16日	39 分鐘
〈喬許・丹尼斯〉 6月9日	42 分鐘
(70) **〈維納・阿姆斯壯〉** **6月2日**	**44** 分鐘

- full (adj.) 滿的　highway (n.) 公路　ahead of . . . 在⋯⋯前面　subscribe (v.) 訂閱　actually (adv.) 實際上　a series of . . . 一系列⋯⋯　entrepreneur (n.) 企業家　apply (v.) 應用

68. 相關細節——男子剛完成的事情

What most likely has the man just finished doing?

(A) Buying food at a roadside store

(B) Putting fuel in a vehicle

(C) Arranging some baggage

(D) Receiving advice about a route

男子最可能剛做完什麼事？

(A) 在路邊商店購買食物

(B) 為車輛加油

(C) 整理行李

(D) 聽取對路線的建議

- roadside (adj.) 路邊的　fuel (n.) 燃料　vehicle (n.) 車輛　arrange (v.) 整理　baggage (n.) 行李　route (n.) 路線

換句話說 now have a full tank of gas（現在油箱加滿了）→ putting fuel in a vehicle（為車輛加油）

69. 相關細節——針對節目中人物的敘述

難

What is mentioned about the people featured on the podcast?

(A) They founded their own businesses.

(B) They have spoken at a famous event.

(C) They are in the same industry.

(D) They conducted interesting research.

關於播客節目的焦點人物，對話中提及什麼？

(A) 他們自行創業。

(B) 他們在有名的活動中演講。

(C) 他們從事相同產業。

(D) 他們執行有趣的研究。

- feature (v.) 以……為主要角色　found (v.) 創立　conduct (v.) 執行

換句話說 entrepreneurs（企業家）→ founded their own businesses（自行創業）

70. 圖表整合題——男子最先播放的節目

Look at the graphic. Which episode will the man play first?
(A) "Amita Mittal"
(B) "Mateo Lozano"
(C) "Josh Dennis"
(D) "Verna Armstrong"

請見圖表作答。男子會先播放哪一集？
(A)〈阿米塔・密托〉
(B)〈馬提歐・羅札諾〉
(C)〈喬許・丹尼斯〉
(D)〈維納・阿姆斯壯〉

PART 4 P. 113–115

71-73 Telephone message

Hi. (71) **My name is Sally Fuller, and I'd like to use your overnight delivery service to send a package.** But I'm having a problem—I can't seem to find your storefront. (72) **My map app says that it's at 650 Jackson Avenue—is that right?** Because I'm parked in front of that building now, and I don't see your sign anywhere. (73) **Um, I know that I need to drop this package off by eleven in order for it to ship overnight, so please call me back at this number as soon as you get this message.** Thanks.

71-73 電話留言 英

嗨，(71) **我叫做莎莉・富勒，我想要使用你們的隔日配送服務，來寄一個包裹**，但我現在有個問題：我好像找不到你們的店面。(72) **我的地圖應用程式顯示，店面是在傑克森大道650號，那個地址對嗎？**因為我現在就停在那一棟的前面，但四處都看不到你們的招牌。(73) **唔，我知道必須在11點前把包裹送到，才能夠在隔日送達，所以請你們聽到留言後，立刻回撥這個號碼給我**，謝謝。

- overnight (adj.) 一夜間的　package (n.) 包裹　sign (n.) 招牌　drop off 把……放下　ship (v.) 運送

71. 全文相關——說話者致電的公司類型

What kind of business is the speaker calling?
(A) A fitness center
(B) A hardware store
(C) An employment agency
(D) A shipping company

說話者正打電話給何種業者？
(A) 健身中心
(B) 五金行
(C) 人力仲介
(D) 貨運公司

換句話說 delivery（配送）→ shipping（貨運）

72. 全文相關——來電的目的

What is the purpose of the call?
(A) To confirm an address
(B) To make an appointment
(C) To ask about parking options
(D) To learn about a pricing system

這通電話的目的是什麼？
(A) 確認地址
(B) 預約會面
(C) 詢問停車選項
(D) 了解定價系統

- confirm (v.) 確認　pricing (n.) 定價

73. 相關細節—說話者擔憂的事情

難

What is the speaker concerned about?

(A) An additional fee

(B) A limited amount of time

(C) An identification requirement

(D) A large number of customers

說話者擔心什麼事情？

(A) 額外的費用

(B) 時間有限

(C) 需要身分證明

(D) 顧客人數眾多

74-76 News report

74-76 新聞報導

加

This is Terrence Barnes from KTQN News with an announcement regarding traffic in Thornlin. (74) **The substantial number of citizens and visitors driving to the Wilvard Center for tonight's sold-out charity concert is causing serious congestion downtown.** Traffic has slowed to a standstill on some streets. (75) **In response, officials from the Thornlin Department of Transportation have issued a statement on its Web site.** (76) **It asks those without urgent business downtown to keep away from the area in order to prevent the situation from growing worse. KTQN urges our listeners to do the same.**

這裡是 KTQN 新聞的泰倫斯．巴尼斯，現在為您播報松林市路況的相關消息。(74) **今晚有場慈善音樂會在維爾佛德中心舉行，門票已熱賣一空，目前有大量居民與來賓開車前往參加，造成市區嚴重塞車，**部分街道車流幾乎寸步難行。(75) **對此，松林市交通局官員已在網站發布聲明，**(76) **要求未有要事前往市區的民眾，就不要進到該區域，以防止情況惡化。KTQN 呼籲各位聽眾遵守指示。**

- announcement (n.) 宣布　regarding (prep.) 關於　traffic (n.) 交通（量）　substantial (adj.) 大量的　citizen (n.) 市民　charity (n.) 慈善事業　congestion (n.) 壅塞　standstill (n.) 停滯　in response 回應　official (n.) 官員　transportation (n.) 運輸　issue (v.) 發布　statement (n.) 聲明　urgent (adj.) 緊急的　situation (n.) 情況　grow worse 惡化　urge (v.) 力勸

74. 相關細節——交通問題的起因

What has caused traffic problems?

(A) Bad weather

(B) A street closure

(C) Holiday travel

(D) A major event

造成交通問題的成因為何？

(A) 天候不佳

(B) 道路封閉

(C) 假期旅遊潮

(D) 大型活動

換句話說 charity concert（慈善音樂會）→ a major event（大型活動）

---

75. 相關細節——說話者提及政府部門的作為

According to the speaker, what has a government department done?

(A) Issued a mass text message

(B) Sent personnel to an area

(C) Posted a statement online

(D) Suspended a transportation service

根據說話者，政府部門有何動作？

(A) 廣發簡訊

(B) 派遣人員到某地區

(C) 在網路上張貼聲明

(D) 暫停一項運輸服務

- mass (adj.) 大批的　personnel (n.)（總稱）人員　post (v.) 張貼　suspend (v.) 暫停

換句話說 issued a statement on its Web site（在網站發布聲明）
→ posted a statement online（在網路上張貼聲明）

---

76. 相關細節——要求聽者做的事情

What are the listeners asked to do?
(A) Visit a city Web site
(B) Avoid a neighborhood
(C) Drive more slowly than usual
(D) Await a second radio announcement

聽者被要求怎麼做？
(A) 造訪市政府網站
(B) 避開一個街區
(C) 放慢行車速度
(D) 等待第二則廣播通知

• avoid (v.) 避免 neighborhood (n.) 街區 await (v.) 等待

換句話說 keep away from the area（不要進到該區域）→ avoid a neighborhood（避開一個區域）

77-79 Excerpt from a meeting

77-79 會議摘要 美

All right, we're here to discuss the results of last week's focus group testing our new hand lotion. [77] **Jeremy has kindly organized the data into these charts—thanks, Jeremy.** [78] **Now, this lotion was developed to provide long-lasting moisturizing, so we had assumed that the advertising would focus on that. But really, we need to reflect consumers' actual experience with the product**—and as you can see, the "scent" category received the highest approval rating, at 74%. I know that this change would mean that marketing team might not have its materials ready by September twenty-fifth as planned. [79] **But I don't see a problem with moving that due date back a few weeks. What do you all think?**

好的，我們在此要來討論上週焦點團體試用我們新款護手霜的結果，[77] **傑瑞米很用心的把資料整理成這幾張圖表，謝謝你，傑瑞米。**[78] **這款護手霜的開發宗旨，在於提供長效保濕，因此我們預設產品廣告會要主打這一點。但實際上，我們必須反映出消費者對產品的真實體驗**——而就像各位所見，「香味」這一項滿意度最高，達到 74%，我知道要做這個變動，代表行銷團隊可能無法按照計畫，在 9 月 25 日前把素材準備好，[79] **但我不覺得把期限延後幾週會有任何問題，大家覺得如何？**

• focus group 焦點團體 organize (v.) 整理 long-lasting (adj.) 持久的 moisturize (v.) 使濕潤 assume (v.) 假定 advertising (n.)（總稱）廣告 reflect (v.) 反映 scent (n.) 香味 approval (n.) 認可 rating (n.) 評價 material (n.) 素材 due date 期限

77. 相關細節——說話者感謝傑瑞米的事情 難

What does the speaker thank Jeremy for?
(A) Creating some visual aids
(B) Leading a discussion group
(C) Organizing the current meeting
(D) Preparing some lotion samples

說話者為什麼感謝傑瑞米？
(A) 製作視覺輔助資料
(B) 帶領討論小組
(C) 安排這次會議
(D) 準備護手霜樣品

• visual aid 視覺輔助資料

換句話說 organized the data into these charts（把資料整理成這幾張圖表）
→ creating some visual aids（製作視覺輔助資料）

---

78. 掌握說話者的意圖——提及「『香味』這一項滿意度最高，達到 74%」的意圖 難

Why does the speaker say, "the 'scent' category received the highest approval rating, at 74%"?
(A) To show disappointment with all of the results
(B) To indicate a new direction for a marketing campaign
(C) To congratulate some of the listeners on an achievement
(D) To request that the listeners ignore some design flaws

說話者為什麼說：「『香味』這一項滿意度最高，達到 74%」？
(A) 以對各項結果表示失望
(B) 以指出行銷活動的新方向
(C) 以恭喜部分聽者的成就
(D) 以要求聽者忽視設計瑕疵

- disappointment (n.) 失望　indicate (v.) 指出　direction (n.) 方向　achievement (n.) 成就
  ignore (v.) 忽視　flaw (n.) 瑕疵

79. 相關細節——說話者就何事詢問聽者的意見

What does the speaker ask for the listeners' opinions on?
(A) Performing more market research
(B) Contacting a manufacturer
(C) Forming a special team
(D) Extending a deadline

說話者針對何事詢問聽者的意見？
(A) 執行更多市場研究
(B) 聯絡製造廠商
(C) 成立特別團隊
(D) 延後截止期限

- manufacturer (n.) 製造商　form (v.) 成立　extend (v.) 延展

換句話說 moving that due date back a few weeks（把期限延後幾週）
→ extending a deadline（延後截止期限）

80-82 Advertisement

As the summer heat rises, you may find that your shirts, dresses, and suits become dirty and wrinkled more quickly. (80) **If you don't have hours to spend in the laundry room, try Zantrey Cleaners.** We'll wash or dry clean your apparel carefully to ensure that colors stay bright and fabrics stay strong. (81) **And for even more convenience, you can now have your items picked up and dropped off right at your door! Customers can try this great new service once for free as part of a special offer.** (82) **Simply download ZantryGo, our convenient app for smartphones, and the offer will be automatically applied to your first order.** Do it today to stay fresh throughout the summer!

80-82 廣告 澳

隨著夏季高溫上升，您可能發覺您的襯衫、洋裝和西裝更快變髒、變皺，(80) **如果您沒空在洗衣房裡耗上好幾小時，就來「任崔洗衣店」吧**，本店會小心仔細地將您的衣物做清洗或乾洗，確保衣物顏色保持鮮豔、質地堅韌如常。(81) **更方便的是，現在您可以在家門口直接取送衣物！目前特殊優惠活動實施中，消費者有機會免費試用一次這項新的優質服務**，(82) **只要以智慧型手機下載本店的便利應用程式「任崔Go」，首筆訂單就能自動享有上述優惠。** 現在就下載，讓您整個夏天清爽無比！

- heat (n.) 高溫　wrinkle (v.) 起皺　laundry room 洗衣間　apparel (n.) 服裝　ensure (v.) 保證
  fabric (n.) 布料　convenience (n.) 方便　drop off 把……放下　convenient (adj.) 方便的
  automatically (adv.) 自動地　apply (v.) 適用

80. 全文相關——廣告的服務

What type of service is being advertised?
(A) Sign printing
(B) Clothes cleaning
(C) Automobile repair
(D) Air conditioner maintenance

廣告主打何種服務？
(A) 招牌印刷
(B) 衣物清洗
(C) 汽車修理
(D) 空調維修

81. 相關細節——說話者提及免費提供的服務

What does the speaker say is available for free?
(A) A care product
(B) Delivery service
(C) An initial inspection
(D) An extended warranty

根據說話者，何者可以免費取得？
(A) 保養品
(B) 運送服務
(C) 初步檢查
(D) 延長保固

換句話說 have your items picked up and dropped off right at your door（在家門口直接取送衣物）
→ delivery service（運送服務）

---

82. 相關細節——聽者獲得優惠的方式

How can listeners receive the offer?
(A) By installing a mobile app
(B) By mentioning the advertisement to a clerk
(C) By spending a certain amount of money
(D) By joining a mailing list

聽者要如何得到優惠？
(A) 安裝手機應用程式
(B) 對店員提及這則廣告
(C) 消費特定金額
(D) 加入郵寄名單

- install (v.) 安裝　certain (adj.) 特定的　mail (v.) 郵寄

換句話說 download our convenient app for smartphones（以智慧型手機下載本店的便利應用程式）
→ installing a mobile app（安裝手機應用程式）

83-85 Broadcast

Welcome back to "Everyday Parenting" on WTUY Radio. [83] **Before the break, I was talking to Byron Young about his popular blog, "While We're Young", which is full of humorous and heartfelt writings about his children.** Now, it's your turn to talk to Mr. Young. [84] [85] **Call us now at 555-0139 with your burning questions about parenting.** Remember, he's a full-time parent to three kids, [85] **so you can ask him about anything.** Sleep issues, fights between siblings, problems adjusting to school—he's dealt with it all.

83-85 電台廣播 英

歡迎回到 WTUY 電台的《每日育兒經》節目。[83] **剛才進廣告前，我正和拜倫・楊聊到他的當紅部落格「青春飛揚」，內容全是關於自家小孩的創作，真情流露之餘又令人莞爾。**現在，換各位聽眾和楊先生聊天了。[84] [85] **請即時撥打 555-0139，把關於育兒的棘手問題告訴我們**，別忘了，他可是三個孩子的全職奶爸，[85] **所以任何問題都難不倒他**：睡眠問題、手足爭吵、學校適應的問題，他全都處理過。

- parenting (n.) 育兒　humorous (adj.) 幽默的　heartfelt (adj.) 真誠的　burning (adj.) 迫切的
  sibling (n.) 手足　adjust (v.) 適應

83. 相關細節——說話者採訪楊先生的內容

What did the speaker interview Mr. Young about?
(A) An award he won
(B) A structure he built
(C) His personal Web site
(D) His new book

說話者針對何事訪問楊先生？
(A) 他得到的獎項
(B) 他建造的建築
(C) 他的個人網站
(D) 他的新書

換句話說 blog（部落格）→ personal Web site（個人網站）

---

84. 相關細節——說話者建議聽者做的事情

What does the speaker encourage listeners to do?
(A) Attend a celebration
(B) Phone the radio station
(C) Make an online purchase
(D) Write down some information

說話者鼓勵聽者做何事？
(A) 參加慶祝活動
(B) 打電話到電台
(C) 線上購物
(D) 寫下資訊

- attend (v.) 參加　celebration (n.) 慶祝活動　phone (v.) 打電話給……　purchase (n.) 購買

換句話說 call（撥打）→ phone（打電話）

85. 掌握說話者的意圖——提及「他可是三個孩子的全職奶爸」的意圖 難

What does the speaker imply when she says, "he's a full-time parent to three kids"?
(A) Mr. Young does not have much time to talk.
(B) Mr. Young's productivity is impressive.
(C) Mr. Young is an expert on a topic.
(D) Mr. Young often engages in an activity.

說話者說：「他可是三個孩子的全職奶爸」，言下之意為何？
(A) 楊先生沒什麼時間聊天。
(B) 楊先生的生產力亮眼。
(C) 楊先生是某個主題的專家。
(D) 楊先生常參與一項活動。

- productivity (n.) 生產力 impressive (adj.) 令人印象深刻的 engage in . . . 參加……

86-88 Instructions

(86) **Thank you for watching this tutorial on Londa, the mobile app that helps you track your spending and balance your personal budget.** Let's start with the basics. When you open up Londa for the first time, you'll need to create a user account by linking accounts, cards, and so on from any banks you choose. (87) **This may sound complicated, but—Londa is designed to be simple.** Just enter the requested information like this, and you can complete set-up pretty quickly. One clear advantage of Londa that you can see at this stage is that it supports a long list of banks. (88) **Londa can collect and organize details about funds and transactions from all of these institutions.**

86-88 解說 加

(86) **感謝觀看手機應用程式「隆達」的教學影片，這款程式可幫助追蹤您的開銷並平衡個人收支。**讓我們從基本項目開始：您首次開啟隆達時，會需要連結您所選擇的各個銀行帳號、卡片等資料，以便建立使用者帳戶。(87) **聽起來可能很複雜，但是隆達的設計讓一切化繁為簡**，只要依此方式輸入所需資料，很快就能完成帳號設定。如您所見，隆達在這個階段有個顯而易見的優點，即支援的銀行名單相當完備，(88) **隆達可以收集、彙整所列各家機構的資金和交易細節資訊。**

- tutorial (n.) 指導 track (v.) 追蹤 spending (n.) 開銷 balance (v.) 使……平衡 budget (n.) 預算 account (n.) 帳戶 complicated (adj.) 複雜的 enter (v.) 輸入 set-up (n.) 設定 advantage (n.) 優點 stage (n.) 階段 collect (v.) 收集 transaction (n.) 交易 institution (n.) 機構

86. 相關細節——隆達協助用戶的事情

What does Londa help users do?
(A) Learn a foreign language
(B) Improve their physical fitness
(C) Manage their finances
(D) Follow current affairs

隆達幫助使用者做何事？
(A) 學習外語
(B) 促進身體健康
(C) 管理財務
(D) 追蹤時事

- improve (v.) 改善 physical (adj.) 身體的 manage (v.) 管理 finance (n.) 財務 current affairs 時事

換句話說 track your spending and balance your personal budget（追蹤您的開銷並平衡個人收支）
→ manage their finances（管理財務）

87. 掌握說話者的意圖——提及「隆達的設計讓一切化繁為簡」的意圖

Why does the speaker say, "Londa is designed to be simple"?
(A) To provide reassurance about user-friendliness
(B) To justify a lack of sophisticated features
(C) To explain why an optional service is not necessary
(D) To express confusion about some advertising claims

說話者為何要說：「隆達的設計讓一切化繁為簡」？
(A) 以保證容易操作
(B) 以說明為何未有複雜功能
(C) 以解釋為何不需要非必須服務
(D) 以表達對廣告說詞的疑惑

- reassurance (n.) 釋疑；寬慰 user-friendliness (n.) 易使用性 justify (v.) 證明……正當 lack (n.) 缺少 sophisticated (adj.) 複雜的 feature (n.) 功能 confusion (n.) 困惑 claim (n.) 宣稱

88. 相關細節——說話者提及隆達的優點 難

According to the speaker, what is an advantage of Londa?
(A) It can be downloaded for free.
(B) It offers excellent customer support.
(C) It can retrieve data from many sources.
(D) It does not require much storage space.

根據說話者，何者為隆達的優點之一？
(A) 可以免費下載。
(B) 提供優質的客服協助。
(C) 可以從多項來源取得資料。
(D) 儲存空間需求不大。

- retrieve (v.) 擷取（資訊） source (n.) 來源 storage (n.) 儲存

換句話說 collect and organize details . . . from all of these institutions（收集、彙整各家機構的細節資訊）→ retrieve data from many sources（從多項來源取得資料）

89-91 Telephone message

Hi, Ms. Stephens? My name is Valerie Fleming. I saw your Internet ad for your used car. I just moved into town, and (89) **I'm having trouble getting around just by bus. It's like the times on the bus schedules are just suggestions!** Anyway, so I'm interested in buying your car. (90) **But I have a question about it—can the seats be adjusted electronically?** I've found that that tends to allow a much more comfortable ride. Uh, so please call me back and let me know. (91) **I'm going to be trying out another car around seven this evening,** but otherwise I should be able to answer the phone immediately. Thanks.

89-91 電話留言 美

嗨，史蒂芬斯女士？我叫做薇樂莉．佛萊明，在網路上看到妳的二手車廣告。我剛搬到鎮上，而 (89) **我覺得這裡出門很難只靠公車代步，公車時刻表上的時間好像只是僅供參考！**總之，我因此有興趣向妳買車，(90) **但我對那台車有個問題：座椅能夠電動調整嗎？**我覺得這往往能讓駕車時感覺更舒適。唔，所以再請回電告訴我。(91) **我今晚七點左右會去試試另一輛車，**但其他時間我應該都能立刻接電話，謝謝。

- ad (n.) 廣告 used (adj.) 二手的 adjust (v.) 調整 electronically (adv.) 以電子方式 tend (v.) 往往會 comfortable (adj.) 舒服的 otherwise (adv.) 除此之外 immediately (adv.) 立即地

89. 相關細節——說話者有興趣買車的理由 難

Why is the speaker interested in buying a car?
(A) She often has to move large items.
(B) She wants to go on unplanned trips out of town.
(C) She lives in an area with unreliable public transportation.
(D) She likes to have privacy when going on journeys.

說話者為何有興趣買車？
(A) 她常必須搬運大型物品。
(B) 她想要到外地隨意旅行。
(C) 她住的地區不能仰賴公共運輸。
(D) 她喜歡旅行時保有隱私。

- unreliable (adj.) 不可靠的 public transportation 公共運輸

90. 相關細節——說話者詢問的特色

What feature does the speaker ask about?
(A) Electronic door locks
(B) Power seats
(C) Darkened windows
(D) Temperature control systems

說話者詢問什麼特色？
(A) 電子門鎖
(B) 電動座椅
(C) 深色窗戶
(D) 溫度控制系統

- darken (v.)（使）變暗 temperature (n.) 溫度

91. 相關細節——說話者晚上要做的事情

What does the speaker say she will do in the evening?

(A) Go for a test drive

(B) Attend a job interview

(C) Have dinner with friends

(D) Suggest a sale price

說話者說她晚上要做什麼？

(A) 試駕車輛

(B) 參加面試

(C) 和朋友吃晚餐

(D) 提議售價

換句話說 trying out another car（試試另一輛車）→ go for a test drive（試駕車輛）

92-94 Speech

Thank you for the warm welcome. [(92)] **I am honored to be taking over as interim CEO until a permanent replacement for Ms. Riley can be found.** Now, given the circumstances of my appointment, I want to assure you that I will not be making any major changes to our overall direction and practices. [(93)] **However, I will make an effort to facilitate the exchange of information and ideas between staff in different areas of the company.** This will give us a solid basis of trust as we enter the next era of Shorman Industries. All right. Now it's time to hear from you. [(94)] **Please ask me anything you'd like to know about my or the company's plans.**

92-94 演講 澳

謝謝大家的熱烈歡迎。[(92)] **在找到雷利女士固定的繼任人選前，我很榮幸能暫代執行長一職。** 目前，考量到我的職務性質，我想跟各位保證，我不會對本公司整體方向與常規做出重大改變。[(93)] **然而，我會致力促進公司各不同部門員工之間，多多交流資訊與想法，** 這會讓我們薛爾曼工業在邁進下一個時代之際，有堅實的互信基礎。好的，現在該聽聽各位的想法了，[(94)] **大家對我或公司的計畫如有任何想知道的事情，都請提出。**

- honored (adj.) 榮幸的　take over 繼任　interim (adj.) 臨時的　CEO (chief executive officer) (n.) 執行長　permanent (adj.) 固定的　replacement (n.) 接替者　circumstance (n.) 情況　appointment (n.) 職位　assure (v.) 向⋯⋯保證　major (adj.) 重大的　overall (adj.) 總體的　practice (n.) 慣常做法　facilitate (v.) 促進　exchange (n.) 交換　solid (adj.) 穩固的　era (n.) 時代

92. 相關細節——說話者針對執行長任命一事提及的內容

What does the speaker mention about his appointment to CEO?

(A) It has not been officially announced.

(B) It has caused controversy.

(C) It will be temporary.

(D) It was unexpected.

關於就任執行長，說話者提到了何事？

(A) 尚未正式宣布

(B) 已經引起爭議

(C) 為暫時性質

(D) 來得出乎意料

- officially (adv.) 正式地　announce (v.) 宣布　cause (v.) 導致　controversy (n.) 爭議　temporary (adj.) 臨時的　unexpected (adj.) 出乎意料的

換句話說 interim（臨時的）→ temporary（暫時的）

93. 相關細節——說話者提及他欲做的事情 難

What does the speaker say he will try to do?

(A) Expand a training initiative

(B) Improve internal communication

(C) Upgrade the safety of a facility

(D) Increase employee benefits

說話者說他會努力進行何事？

(A) 擴大培訓計畫

(B) 改善內部溝通

(C) 升級設施安全

(D) 增加員工福利

- expand (v.) 擴大　initiative (n.) 計畫　internal (adj.) 內部的　facility (n.) 設施　benefit (n.) 福利

換句話說 facilitate the exchange of information and ideas between staff in different areas of the company（促進公司各不同部門員工之間，多多交流資訊與想法）
→ improve internal communication（改善內部溝通）

94. 相關細節——接下來要發生的事情

What most likely will take place next?
(A) A question-and-answer session
(B) A welcome reception
(C) A slide presentation
(D) A photo shoot

接下來最可能進行何者？
(A) 問答時間
(B) 歡迎會
(C) 投影片簡報
(D) 照片拍攝

95-97 Talk + Table

I appreciate your letting me speak to you about the advantages of choosing Vallond for your video hosting needs. (95) **I know that you have been making videos on how to care for the trees, bushes, and flowers that you sell.** Well, you won't find a better way to make those videos available on the Web than Vallond. Our platform is straightforward, fast, and reliable, and (96) **all of our service packages allow you to include links to other pages in your videos.** That's a great way to engage viewers. (97) **Now, since you've already made over a hundred videos, I want to recommend our package that has a five-hundred-video limit.** It even gives you special access to viewing statistics!

Vallond Video Hosting Packages

Package	Features	Monthly Cost
Package A	20 videos	Free
Package B	100 videos	$25
(97) **Package C**	**500 videos + viewing statistics**	**$100**
Package D	Unlimited videos + viewing statistics	$300

95-97 談話＋表格 英

感謝容我為各位解說，在選用影音代管平台方面，選擇「佛隆德」將帶來哪些優點。(95) **我知道你們正持續製作影片，介紹如何照顧貴店販賣的樹木、灌木和花卉**，若要上架那些影片到網路上以供收看，「佛隆德」是你們的最佳選擇。我們的平台操作簡單又快速可靠，而且 (96) **我們所有方案都開放在影片中添加連結，可連接到其他網頁**，有利促進觀眾參與度。(97) **目前，因為你們已經製作超過一百支影片，我想要推薦我們影片上限 500 支的方案**，方案還特別開放各位查閱觀看數據！

佛隆德影片代管套裝方案

方案	特色功能	月費
方案 A	20 支影片	免費
方案 B	100 支影片	$25
(97) **方案 C**	**500 支影片＋查看統計資料**	**$100**
方案 D	無限量影片＋查看統計資料	$300

- **appreciate (v.)** 感謝 **advantage (n.)** 優勢 **care for . . .** 照料…… **bush (n.)** 灌木 **available (adj.)** 可得到的 **straightforward (adj.)** 直接明確的 **reliable (adj.)** 可靠的 **allow (v.)** 允許 **engage (v.)** 吸引 **access (v.)** 存取（資料） **view (v.)** 觀看 **statistics (n.)** 統計資料

95. 全文相關——聽者的工作地點 難

Where most likely do the listeners work?
(A) At a commercial farm
(B) At a plant shop
(C) At a public park
(D) At a landscaping firm

聽者最可能任職於何種業者？
(A) 商業農場
(B) 花木商店
(C) 公立公園
(D) 造景公司

換句話說 trees, bushes, and flowers（樹木、灌木和花卉）→ plant（花木）

96. 相關細節——說話者提及所有方案都有提供顧客的項目 難

What does the speaker say all packages allow customers to do?

(A) Customize the video player's appearance
(B) Place regional restrictions on videos
(C) Enable viewers to share videos
(D) Display a Web link in a video

說話者說，所有方案都開放顧客做何事？

(A) 客製影片播放器外觀
(B) 為影片添加區域限制
(C) 讓觀眾可以分享影片
(D) 在影片顯示網路連結

- **customize (v.)** 客製 **appearance (n.)** 外觀 **place (v.)** 放置 **regional (adj.)** 地區的 **restriction (n.)** 限制 **enable (v.)** 使能夠

換句話說 include links to other pages（添加連接到其他網頁的連結）
→ display a Web link（顯示網路連結）

97. 圖表整合題——說話者推薦的方案

Look at the graphic. Which package does the speaker recommend?

(A) Package A
(B) Package B
(C) Package C
(D) Package D

請見圖表作答。說話者推薦何項套裝方案？

(A) 方案 A
(B) 方案 B
(C) 方案 C
(D) 方案 D

98-100 Telephone message + Text message

Hi, this is Jake Coleman. You sent me a text message today about my appointment on October seventeenth. (98) **I'm sorry I didn't call earlier—I was in the middle of a tennis match when the text arrived, and I didn't see it until after your closing time.** (99) **Anyway, I'll need to move my appointment to a little later that day.** Does Greg have any openings around four p.m.? (100) **Also, I was wondering—do you sell the shampoo that you use?** I really liked the way it made my hair feel last time. Call me back and let me know.

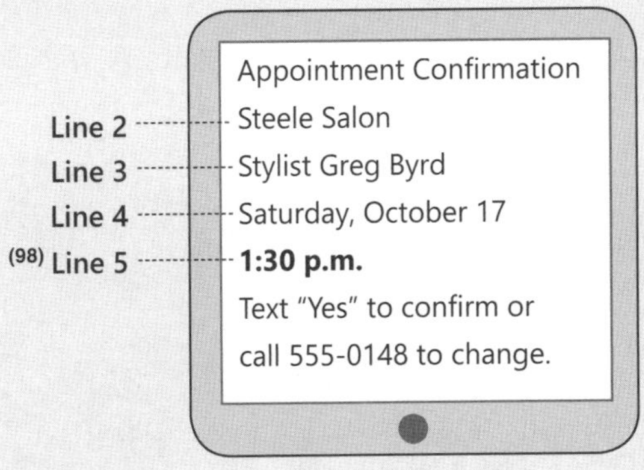

98-100 電話留言＋文字簡訊 加

嗨，我是傑克．柯曼。你們今天發了簡訊給我，內容關於我在 10 月 17 日的預約。(98) **很抱歉我未能早點致電——簡訊傳來時，我正在參加網球比賽，而直到過了你們關店時間，我才看到簡訊。**(99) **總之，我當天的預約需要稍微延後，**葛瑞格下午四點左右有空檔嗎？(100) **還有，我也想問一下：你們有在販賣店裡用的洗髮精嗎？**上次使用過後，頭髮的感覺真的讓我很滿意。再請回電告知我。

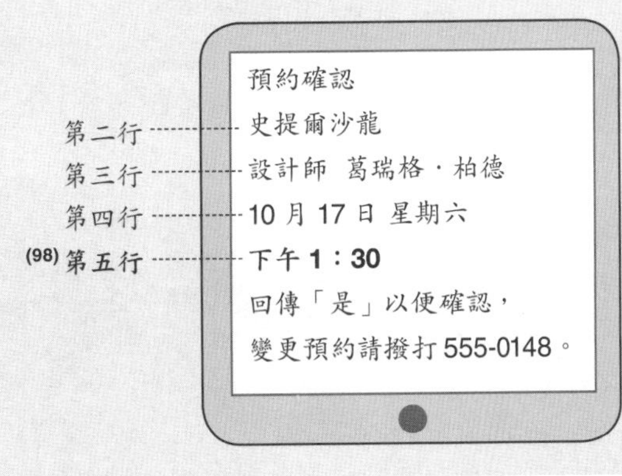

- appointment (n.) 預約　in the middle of . . . 正忙於……　text (n./v.) 簡訊／傳簡訊
  opening (n.) 空檔　wonder (v.) 想知道

98. 相關細節——說話者提及簡訊傳來時，他正在做的事情

What does the speaker say he was doing when the text message arrived?

(A) Playing a sport

(B) Making a call

(C) Seeing a movie

(D) Boarding a flight

說話者說簡訊傳來時，他正在做什麼？

(A) 從事運動

(B) 撥打電話

(C) 觀看電影

(D) 航班登機

換句話說 **in the middle of a tennis match**（正在參加網球比賽）→ **playing a sport**（從事運動）

---

99. 圖表整合題——說話者欲更改簡訊的哪一行資訊

Look at the graphic. Which line includes information that the speaker would like to change?

(A) Line 2

(B) Line 3

(C) Line 4

(D) Line 5

請見圖表作答。說話者想要更改的資訊位在哪一行？

(A) 第二行

(B) 第三行

(C) 第四行

(D) 第五行

---

100. 相關細節——說話者提及他想知道的事情

What does the speaker want to know about the salon?

(A) Whether its shampoos contain certain chemicals

(B) Whether it offers a product for purchase

(C) How much it charges for a hair treatment

(D) How long the effects of one of its services will last

有關髮型沙龍，說話者想知道何事？

(A) 店內洗髮精是否含有特定化學物質

(B) 是否販售一項產品

(C) 護髮的費用

(D) 其中一種服務的效果會持續多久

- contain (v.) 包含　chemical (n.) 化學製品　charge (v.) 收費　effect (n.) 效果
  last (v.) 持續

換句話說 **sell the shampoo**（販賣那款洗髮精）→ **offers a product for purchase**（販售一項產品）

ACTUAL TEST 10

PART 1 P. 116–119 37

1. 單人獨照——描寫人物的動作 美

(A) He's pulling a bottle from a bag.
(B) He's tying one of his shoes.
(C) He's jogging on a paved path.
(D) He's relaxing on a park bench.

(A) 他正從袋子裡取出瓶子。
(B) 他正在繫一隻鞋的鞋帶。
(C) 他正在鋪面道路上慢跑。
(D) 他正坐在公園長椅上休息。

- pull (v.) 拉；抽出 tie (v.) 繫 pave (v.) 鋪設 path (n.) 小徑

2. 單人獨照——描寫人物的動作 澳

(A) She's standing in front of a bookcase.
(B) She's climbing a staircase in a library.
(C) She's carrying a stack of books.
(D) She's resting one arm on a counter.

(A) 她站在書架前面。
(B) 她正爬上圖書館裡的階梯。
(C) 她正在搬一疊書。
(D) 她的一隻手臂靠在櫃檯上。

- bookcase (n.) 書架 climb (v.) 爬；攀登 staircase (n.) 樓梯間 stack (n.) 一疊 rest (v.) 靠；倚

3. 雙人照片——描寫人物的動作 英

(A) They are having coffee inside a café.
(B) They are looking at the screen of a mobile device.
(C) One of the men is reaching for something on the table.
(D) One of the men is adjusting some sliding windows.

(A) 他們正在咖啡館裡喝咖啡。
(B) 他們正觀看行動裝置的螢幕。
(C) 一名男子正伸手拿取桌上物品。
(D) 一名男子正在調整拉窗。

- device (n.) 裝置 reach for . . . 伸手拿…… adjust (v.) 調整 sliding (adj.) 滑動的

4. 綜合照片——描寫人物或事物 加

(A) Some people are posing for a photograph.
(B) A walking tour is taking place in a forest.
(C) A boat is being rowed down a river.
(D) Leaves are being removed from the water.

(A) 一些人正在擺拍照姿勢。
(B) 森林中正在舉辦健行。
(C) 有人正在河中划船。
(D) 有人正在移除水裡的樹葉。

- pose (v.) 擺姿勢 take place 發生 forest (n.) 森林 row (v.) 划（船） remove (v.) 移除

5. 事物與背景照——描寫室內事物的狀態 澳

(A) Papers have been attached to a bulletin board.
(B) Chairs have been left in a conference room.
(C) A small trash bin is being emptied.
(D) Cords have been connected to a computer.

(A) 紙張固定在布告欄上。
(B) 椅子留在會議室裡。
(C) 有人正把小垃圾桶清空。
(D) 電線連接到電腦上。

- attach (v.) 固定 bulletin board 布告欄 trash bin 垃圾桶 empty (v.) 倒空 connect (v.) 連接

6. 綜合照片——描寫人物或事物 美 難

(A) A plastic container holds a set of tools.	(A) 塑膠容器裝著工具。
(B) A piece of pottery is being shaped.	**(B)** 有人正為陶器塑形。
(C) Some artwork is being displayed on walls.	(C) 牆上展示著藝術品。
(D) A woman is picking up an apron.	(D) 女子正拾起圍裙。

- container (n.) 容器　hold (v.) 容納　pottery (n.) 陶器　shape (v.) 使成形　artwork (n.) 藝術品　display (v.) 陳列　apron (n.) 圍裙

PART 2 P. 120

38

7. 以 **Who** 開頭的問句，詢問是誰發現漏水 加⇄英

Who discovered the water leak?	是誰發現漏水狀況？
(A) Our insurance covered most of it.	(A) 大部分都在我們保險理賠範圍。
(B) No, I heard about it this morning.	(B) 不，我今天早上聽說的。
(C) The tenant in Apartment 3A.	**(C) 3A** 室的房客。

- discover (v.) 發現　leak (n.) 漏出；滲漏　insurance (n.) 保險　cover (v.) 給……保險　tenant (n.) 房客

8. 以 **When** 開頭的問句，詢問可以開始上班的時間點 美⇄加 

If we decide to hire you, when will you be able to start?	如果我們決定錄用你，你何時能開始上班？
(A) Excellent—I look forward to it.	(A) 太好了，我很期待。
(B) My current employer requires two weeks' notice.	**(B)** 我目前的雇主要求提前兩週通知。
(C) As long as we can agree on the contract terms.	(C) 只要我們都同意合約條款。

- look forward to . . . 期待……　current (adj.) 現在的　require (v.) 要求　notice (n.) 通知　contract (n.) 合約　term (n.) 條款

9. 以 **How much** 開頭的問句，詢問新沙發所需的空間大小 澳⇄美 

How much space will we need for the new sofa?	新沙發會需要多大的空間？
(A) All employees will be allowed to use it.	(A) 所有員工都可以使用。
(B) Its measurements are in the catalog.	**(B)** 型錄裡有寫尺寸。
(C) Wherever there's empty space.	(C) 只要有空著的地方。

- measurement (n.) 尺寸

10. 表示請託或要求的問句 澳⇄英

Can you show me how to use the library's scanner?	你可以示範如何使用圖書館的掃描器嗎？
(A) Yes, just a few minutes ago.	(A) 是的，就在幾分鐘前。
(B) It creates digital images of documents.	(B) 會產生文件的電子檔。
(C) Did you try reading the posted instructions?	**(C)** 你試過查看張貼的操作說明嗎？

- post (v.) 張貼　instruction (n.) 用法說明

11. 以 **Why** 開頭的問句，詢問為何必須提供醫師證明 ⓐ加⇄英

Why do I have to provide a note from my doctor? **(A) It's company policy.** (B) Once you return to work. (C) Oh, are you feeling unwell?	為什麼我必須提供醫師證明？ **(A) 這是公司政策。** (B) 你一回來上班的時候。 (C) 噢，你不舒服嗎？

- note (n.) 短箋　policy (n.) 政策　unwell (adj.) 身體不適的

12. 以直述句傳達資訊 美⇄澳 難

There's a package for you at Reception. (A) I'm sorry, but I won't have time to attend. **(B) That must be my new business cards.** (C) Melissa is going to the post office later.	接待處有你的包裹。 (A) 抱歉，但我沒有時間參加。 **(B) 那一定是我的新名片。** (C) 梅莉莎晚點要去郵局。

- package (n.) 包裹　reception (n.) 接待處　business card 名片

13. 以 **What** 開頭的問句，詢問方向盤上按鈕的用途 加⇄美

What are these buttons on the steering wheel for? (A) The premium model is two thousand dollars more. (B) I often drive on mountain roads. **(C) Controlling the car's audio system.**	方向盤上的這些按鈕作用為何？ (A) 頂級款式要價超過二千元。 (B) 我常開山路。 **(C) 操控車內音響系統。**

- steering wheel 方向盤　premium (adj.) 頂級的；優質的

14. 以 **Be** 動詞開頭的問句，詢問路易斯五金行是否為連鎖店 英⇄澳 難

Is Lewis Hardware a chain store? **(A) I'm only aware of the Greenley location.** (B) Most hardware stores sell chains. (C) Monday through Saturday.	路易斯五金行是連鎖店嗎？ **(A) 我只知道在葛林利的那一家。** (B) 大部分五金行都有賣鏈條。 (C) 週一到週六。

- chain store 連鎖店　aware (adj.) 知道的　location (n.) 地點；位置　hardware store 五金行　chain (n.) 鏈條

15. 以 **Where** 開頭的問句，詢問這盒甜甜圈的來源 英⇄加 難

Where did this box of donuts come from? (A) Brumfield Bakery makes great donuts. **(B) There was a meeting in here earlier.** (C) I like the plain ones best.	這盒甜甜圈是從哪裡來的？ (A) 柏菲德烘焙坊做的甜甜圈很好吃。 **(B) 稍早這裡有場會議。** (C) 我最喜歡原味的。

- plain (adj.) 未修飾的

16. 以選擇疑問句詢問夾克的顏色 澳⇄加

Is your jacket the black one or the tan one? **(A) I didn't bring a jacket.** (B) On the coat rack is fine. (C) Do you have the same style in red?	你的外套是黑色的，還是棕褐色的？ **(A) 我沒有穿外套來。** (B) 掛在衣帽架上就好。 (C) 你們有同款紅色的嗎？

- tan (adj.) 棕褐色的　coat rack 衣帽架

17. 以附加問句確認是否有收到電子郵件 美⇄美

You got my e-mail about the project delay, right? (A) Yes, let's call the projector technician. (B) Sure—here's my e-mail address. **(C) Yes—such a frustrating situation.**	你收到我關於專案延期的電子郵件了，對嗎？ (A) 對的，讓我們打電話給投影機技師。 (B) 當然好，這是我的電郵信箱。 **(C) 對的，真是令人失望的狀況。**

- delay (n.) 延期 technician (n.) 技師 frustrating (adj.) 令人沮喪的

18. 以 **When** 開頭的問句，詢問最後一次確認社群媒體頁面的時間點 英⇄美 難

When did you last check our social media page? (A) Online businesses don't usually take checks. (B) A few inquiries from customers. **(C) Nick has taken over that responsibility.**	你上次查看我們的社群媒體頁面，是什麼時候？ (A) 網路商家通常不收支票。 (B) 顧客的一些詢問。 **(C) 尼克接手了那個職務。**

- last (adv.) 上一次地 check (v./n.) 檢查／支票 inquiry (n.) 詢問 take over 接管 responsibility (n.) 職責；工作

19. 以助動詞 **Has** 開頭的問句，詢問下午的管理講習是否已經開始 加⇄英

Has the afternoon session on management started? **(A) It's not even one-fifteen yet.** (B) Thanks for letting me know! (C) Industry trends, I think.	下午的管理講習開始了嗎？ **(A) 現在還不到一點十五分。** (B) 謝謝你告訴我！ (C) 我想是產業趨勢。

- session (n.) 講習會 management (n.) 管理；經營 industry (n.) 產業；工業

20. 表示建議或提案的直述句 美⇄加 難

Let's send everyone home while the labeling machine is being repaired. (A) OK—I'll buy some additional envelopes. **(B) We'll need them to work overtime tomorrow.** (C) It's not attaching the labels correctly.	在標籤機修理期間，我們讓大家先回家去吧。 (A) 好的，我要額外買一些信封。 **(B) 我們明天要請他們加班。** (C) 標籤沒有貼對。

- label (v./n.) 貼標籤／標籤 repair (v.) 修理 additional (adj.) 額外的 envelope (n.) 信封 overtime (adv.) 加班地 attach (v.) 貼上；使附著

21. 以 **Which** 開頭的問句，詢問列車出發的月台 澳⇄美

Which platform is our train leaving from? (A) He's a personal trainer. **(B) Just follow me this way.** (C) That's why we'd better hurry.	我們的列車是從哪個月台發車？ (A) 他是個私人健身教練。 **(B) 跟著我往這邊走就好。** (C) 所以我們最好趕快。

- had better . . . 最好做……

22. 以 Who 開頭的問句詢問給伊莎貝爾花束的人是誰 英⇄澳 難

Who gave Isabelle that bouquet of flowers?	是誰送給伊莎貝爾那束花？
(A) Her team loves to celebrate work anniversaries.	**(A) 她的團隊喜歡慶祝就職週年紀念日。**
(B) You can set them on the table for now.	(B) 你現在可以暫時放在桌上。
(C) There was some extra flour in the kitchen.	(C) 廚房有些額外的麵粉。

- bouquet (n.) 花束　celebrate (v.) 慶祝　anniversary (n.) 週年紀念　for now 暫時　flour (n.) 麵粉

23. 以 Where 開頭的問句，詢問放置圖表的位置 英⇄加 難

Where should I put the chart comparing our sales with competitors'?	我該把我們和同業的銷量對照圖放在哪裡？
(A) Only for the northeastern market.	(A) 只有東北區市場。
(B) They're serious competition, actually.	(B) 其實，競爭很激烈。
(C) Make a separate slide.	**(C) 做成另一張投影片。**

- competitor (n.) 競爭對手　northeastern (adj.) 東北的　competition (n.) 競爭　separate (adj.) 個別的

24. 表示建議或提案的直述句 美⇄澳 難

It may be time for us to get a staff accountant.	也許我們是時候聘請一名會計員了。
(A) Tuesday at nine a.m.	(A) 週二早上九點。
(B) Can we afford one?	**(B) 我們負擔得起嗎？**
(C) We can place orders without an account.	(C) 我們沒有帳號也能下訂單。

- accountant (n.) 會計人員　afford (v.) 負擔得起　account (n.) 帳戶

25. 以否定疑問句確認是否想一起吃披薩 加⇄美 難

Didn't you want to share a pizza?	你不想一起吃披薩嗎？
(A) This restaurant is famous online.	(A) 這家餐廳在網路上很有名。
(B) Because it's too big for one person.	(B) 因為很大塊，一個人吃不下。
(C) That was before I saw they have lasagna.	**(C) 我看到有千層麵之前還想。**

26. 以 Why 開頭的問句，詢問請求遭拒的原因 英⇄美 

Why was my expense reimbursement request denied?	為何我的請款單遭到退回？
(A) No idea. Mine have always been approved.	**(A) 不知道，我的一直都會獲准。**
(B) After the finance director reviewed it.	(B) 等財務主管看過。
(C) No, it wasn't that expensive.	(C) 不，沒那麼貴。

- expense (n.) 費用；開支　reimbursement (n.) 報銷；退款　deny (v.) 拒絕給予
  approve (v.) 批准；同意　finance (n.) 財務　director (n.) 主管；首長

27. 以附加問句確認書架是否會被搬到新辦公室 英⇄美 難

Those bookshelves aren't being moved to the new office, are they?	那些書架不會要搬去新辦公室吧，是嗎？
(A) No, a second-hand furniture store is coming to pick them up.	**(A) 不會，會有二手家具店來載走。**
(B) A replacement set of shelves made of dark wood.	(B) 深色木頭製成的架子，用來替換。
(C) Dave and John are, but they'll take the subway there.	(C) 是戴夫和約翰，但他們會搭地鐵前往。

- bookshelves (n.) 書架　second-hand (adj.) 二手的　replacement (n.) 代替物

28. 以選擇疑問句詢問內訓活動的項目 澳⇄美 難

Should the next team-building event be a day hike or a bike ride?	下次的內訓活動該是一日健行，還是單車行？
(A) To improve relationships among team members.	(A) 為了改善團隊成員的關係。
(B) A weekend afternoon would be better.	(B) 週末下午比較好。
(C) Not everyone likes outdoor activities.	**(C) 不是大家都喜歡戶外活動。**

- team-building (n.) 企業團隊培訓　hike (n.) 健行

29. 以助動詞 Do 開頭的問句，詢問是否在該大樓內的公司上班 加⇄英

Do you work at one of the businesses in this building?	你是在這棟大樓的公司上班嗎？
(A) The travel agency is closing soon.	(A) 旅行社很快要關門了。
(B) Here's my identification badge.	**(B) 這是我的識別證。**
(C) Some discounts at the first-floor café.	(C) 一樓咖啡館的一些折扣。

- identification (n.) 識別；身分證明

30. 以否定疑問句，確認參加焦點團體是否會獲得酬勞 美⇄加 難

Aren't we supposed to be paid for participating in this focus group?	我們參加這個焦點團體，不是應該獲得酬勞嗎？
(A) The money will be sent electronically.	**(A) 費用將會用以電子轉帳。**
(B) Testing a video game for Hanjoon Entertainment.	(B) 為「漢俊娛樂」測試電玩遊戲。
(C) Well, the participants meet all the qualifications.	(C) 嗯，參加者符合所有資格。

- be supposed to . . . 應當……　electronically (adv.) 以電子方式　meet (v.) 符合
qualification (n.) 資格

31. 以直述句傳達資訊 澳⇄英 難

We offer reduced-price admission for university students.	我們對大學生有提供門票折扣。
(A) But your Web site says you do.	(A) 但你們的網站上說你們有。
(B) Some of the museums downtown.	(B) 市中心的一些博物館。
(C) I graduated last year, unfortunately.	**(C) 不巧，我去年畢業了。**

- reduce (v.) 降低　admission (n.) 入場費；門票錢

PART 3　P. 121–124　39

32-34 Conversation　32-34 對話 美⇄加

W: Oh, hello, Mr. Quinn. It's good to see you again. How are your new glasses working out?	女：噢，哈囉，昆恩先生，很高興再見到您。您的新眼鏡合用嗎？
M: The prescription lenses are great, but it turns out that the frames are a little tight. That's why I'm here. (32) **Could you widen these parts that go over my ears?**	男：鏡片度數配得很好，但後來覺得鏡框有點緊，所以我又過來一趟。(32) **妳可以把耳朵上面的這幾個部分調鬆一點嗎？**

W: Absolutely. It will take just a few minutes. (33) **Why don't you have a seat in our waiting area?** (33) (34) **We just got some new magazines.**	女： 當然可以，只要幾分鐘就可以完成了。(33) **您何不到等候區坐一下？** (33) (34) **我們剛放上了幾本新雜誌。**
M: (34) **Well, I can't read comfortably without my glasses.** I'll just listen to music on my phone.	男： (34) **這個嘛，沒戴眼鏡，我會看書會很吃力**，我聽聽手機裡的音樂就好了。

- work out 發展；結果　prescription (n.) 處方　turn out 結果是……（尤指意外結果）　frame (n.) 框；支架　tight (adj.) 緊的　widen (v.) 使變寬

32. 相關細節——男子來店的目的

What is the purpose of the man's visit?

(A) To inquire about a bill

(B) To pick up an order

(C) To renew a prescription

(D) To request a fit adjustment

男子到店的目的是什麼？

(A) 洽詢帳單

(B) 取貨

(C) 更新處方

(D) 要求調整合適大小

- inquire (v.) 詢問　bill (n.) 帳單　renew (v.) 更新　prescription (n.) 處方　adjustment (n.) 調整

---

33. 相關細節——女子告知可以使用的東西

What does the woman say is available?

(A) Some publications

(B) Some beverages

(C) Internet access

(D) Charging stations

女子說可以取用何物？

(A) 出版品

(B) 飲料

(C) 網路連線

(D) 充電站

換句話說 magazines（雜誌）→ publications（出版品）

---

34. 相關細節——男子提及的問題

What problem does the man mention?

(A) He did not bring a required item.

(B) He is unable to use an amenity.

(C) He can only wait a short duration.

(D) His contact information has changed.

男子提到何項問題？

(A) 他沒有攜帶需要的東西。

(B) 他無法使用休閒設施。

(C) 他只能等一小段時間。

(D) 他的聯絡資料有變動。

- amenity (n.) 便利設施；娛樂設施　duration (n.) 持續時間

換句話說 magazines（雜誌）→ an amenity（休閒設施）

35-37 Conversation　　35-37 對話　英⇄加

W: Good afternoon, Mr. Morgan. (35) **This is Chelsea Vasquez calling from Habernathy Credit Union. I've got some good news about your request for a business loan. You've been approved.**	女： 午安，摩根先生，(35) **這裡是賀伯納西信用合作社的崔兒喜·維斯奎茲，這邊要向您告知關於您申請企業貸款的好消息：貸款已經通過了。**
M: That's fantastic! (36) **Our community will really benefit from the bicycle shop I'm going to open.** I know there are a lot of people who will be happy to buy their bikes locally.	男： 好極了！(36) **我要開的自行車行，真的會對我們社區貢獻良多**，我知道很多人會很高興能從在地店家購買腳踏車。

TEST 10

PART 3

W: We agree, Mr. Morgan. (37) **Now, there are a few documents we need to go over together before we can release the money. When can you come into the office?**

M: I'm free tomorrow morning.

女： 我們也認同，摩根先生。(37) **現在，在我們撥款之前，有幾份文件需要一起仔細核對，您什麼時候方便前來辦公室？**

男： 我明天早上有空。

- loan (n.) 貸款 approve (v.) 批准 benefit (v.) 受惠 go over 仔細核對 release (v.) 釋放

35. 全文相關——女子的工作地點

Where does the woman work?

(A) At a city department

(B) At a financial institution

(C) At a news outlet

(D) At a law office

女子工作的地點為何？

(A) 市政府的部門

(B) 金融機構

(C) 新聞媒體

(D) 法律事務所

---

36. 相關細節——男子計劃要做的事情

What does the man plan to do?

(A) Donate money to a charity

(B) Bid for a government contract

(C) Organize a community activity

(D) Launch a retail business

男子計劃做何事？

(A) 捐款給慈善機構

(B) 投標政府合約

(C) 籌備社區活動

(D) 開設零售店家

- donate (v.) 捐獻；捐贈 charity (n.) 慈善事業 bid (v.) 投標 organize (v.) 組織；安排 launch (v.) 開始；發起 retail (n.) 零售

換句話說 open the bicycle shop（開自行車行）→ launch a retail business（開設零售店家）

---

37. 相關細節——女子要求男子前往辦公室的理由

Why does the woman ask the man to visit her office?

(A) To discuss an idea

(B) To submit a payment

(C) To review some paperwork

(D) To meet a manager

女子為何要求男子去她的辦公室？

(A) 討論想法

(B) 繳交款項

(C) 檢閱文件

(D) 會見經理

- discuss (v.) 討論 submit (v.) 提交 payment (n.) 支付的款項 review (v.) 仔細審核

換句話說 go over（仔細核對）→ review（檢閱）

38-40 Conversation

W: Hi, Lorenzo. It's good to see you. Are you enjoying the conference so far?

M: Yes, very much. (38) **Before lunch, I attended a session on using the advanced functions of the Medina Laboratory Automation System.** That's the system my lab has.

W: (39) **Oh, that must have been very useful, then.**

38-40 對話

英⇄澳

女： 嗨，羅倫佐，很高興看到你。研討會進行到目前，你還喜歡嗎？

男： 是的，很喜歡。(38) **午餐之前，我參加了介紹「麥地納實驗室自動系統」進階功能操作的講習**，我的實驗室就是使用那款系統。

女： (39) **噢，那麼一定很有幫助囉。**

M: [39] **Yes,** I took detailed notes. I can't wait to go back and tell my lab manager about it. Anyway, how has the conference been for you?	男： [39] **是啊**，我很仔細記了筆記。我等不及要回去和我的實驗室經理講述內容了。不提這個了，那妳覺得研討會如何？
W: [40] **Fine, but—I'm a bit nervous for this afternoon. I'm going to present on my current research.**	女： [40] **不錯，但是我對這個下午有點緊張，因為我要發表目前的研究內容。**
M: Right, I saw that in the program. Good luck! I'm sure you'll do fine.	男： 對啊，我在時程表上有看到。祝妳好運！我確信妳會表現得很好。

- **session (n.)**（活動的）一場；一節　**advanced (adj.)** 先進的　**function (n.)** 功能　**automation (n.)** 自動化　**lab (=laboratory) (n.)** 實驗室　**detailed (adj.)** 詳細的　**nervous (adj.)** 緊張的　**present (v.)** 發表；呈現　**current (adj.)** 目前的

38. 相關細節——男子提到今天上午發生的事情

According to the man, what took place in the morning?
(A) A training workshop
(B) A laboratory meeting
(C) A university class
(D) An inventory check

根據男子所說，早上有何事舉行？
(A) 培訓研習會
(B) 實驗室會議
(C) 大學課程
(D) 存貨盤點

TEST 10 PART 3

39. 掌握說話者的意圖——提及「我很仔細記了筆記」的意圖 難

Why does the man say, "I took detailed notes"?
(A) To explain why he could not be contacted
(B) To emphasize the value of some information
(C) To show willingness to share a resource with the woman
(D) To decline the woman's offer of assistance

男子為什麼說：「我很仔細記了筆記」？
(A) 解釋為何聯絡不到他
(B) 強調資訊的價值
(C) 表示樂意和女子分享資源
(D) 婉拒女子想協助的提議

- **emphasize (v.)** 強調　**value (n.)** 重要性；價值　**willingness (n.)** 樂意　**resource (n.)** 資源　**decline (v.)** 婉拒　**assistance (n.)** 協助

40. 相關細節——使女子感到緊張的事情

What is the woman nervous about?
(A) Leading a research project
(B) Interviewing for a job opening
(C) Learning the result of an application
(D) Giving a conference presentation

女子為了何事感到緊張？
(A) 帶領研究計畫
(B) 工作職缺面試
(C) 得知申請結果
(D) 在研討會發表簡報

- **application (n.)** 申請　**presentation (n.)** 簡報

換句話說 present（發表）→ giving a . . . presentation（做簡報）

41-43 Conversation with three speakers

41-43 三人對話 美⇄澳⇄加

W: Hi. You're the site supervisor, right? (41) **We're the crew from Soto Contractors, and we're here to put in the countertops.**

M1: Uh, hi . . . I think there's been a mistake. You're not scheduled to work today.

W: Really? This is when the project manager told us to come.

M1: Well, luckily he's on site today. (42) **Eric,** could you come over here? This woman is from Soto Contractors.

M2: Uh-oh—didn't you get my voice mail? (42) **The kitchen blueprints were changed suddenly last week.**

W: Oh, no, I missed that. (43) **Does that mean you're canceling our contract?**

M2: (43) **No, the material is still granite, so we'll need your specialized skills.** But now we're behind schedule. Could you come in next Monday?

W: I'll check and let you know.

女：嗨，你就是工地主任，對嗎？(41) **我們是索托承包公司的工作人員，要來安裝廚房檯面。**

男 1：呃，嗨……我想是弄錯了，你們不是排在今天施工。

女：真的嗎？專案經理告訴我們在這個時間過來。

男 1：這樣啊，剛好今天他人在現場。(42) **艾瑞克**，你可以過來一下嗎？這位小姐是索托承包公司的人。

男 2：唉呀，妳沒有收到我的語音訊息嗎？(42) **廚房的設計藍圖上週突然更改了。**

女：噢，不，我沒收到。(43) **那表示你們要取消我們的合約嗎？**

男 2：(43) **不會的，建材還是花崗岩，所以我們會需要你們的專門技術**，但現在我們進度延後了，你們可以下週一過來嗎？

女：我確認後再告訴你。

- **site** (n.) 工地 **supervisor** (n.) 管理人 **crew** (n.)（一組）工作人員 **countertop** (n.) 廚房檯面 **blueprint** (n.) 藍圖 **miss** (v.) 未看／聽到 **material** (n.) 材料 **granite** (n.) 花崗岩 **specialized** (adj.) 專門的；專業的

41. 相關細節——女子帶工作人員來做的事情

What has the woman's crew come to do?

(A) Connect power wiring

(B) Modify an outdoor space

(C) Install some interior surfaces

(D) Set up temperature control systems

女子的工作人員前來進行何事？

(A) 連接電線

(B) 改造戶外空間

(C) 安裝室內檯面

(D) 設置溫度控制系統

- **wiring** (n.) 線路 **modify** (v.) 改造 **install** (v.) 安裝 **surface** (n.)（桌子、櫥櫃等）檯面 **temperature** (n.) 溫度

換句話說 **put in the countertops**（安裝廚房檯面）→ **install some interior surfaces**（安裝室內檯面）

---

42. 相關細節——艾瑞克指出的問題

What problem does Eric report?

(A) A budget limit has been reached.

(B) Some design plans have been revised.

(C) Some construction materials have flaws.

(D) The weather has been unfavorable.

艾瑞克告知何項問題？

(A) 預算已達上限。

(B) 有些設計圖修改了。

(C) 有些建材有瑕疵。

(D) 天氣不盡理想。

- **budget** (n.) 預算 **limit** (n.) 限制 **revise** (v.) 修訂 **construction** (n.) 建造 **flaw** (n.) 瑕疵 **unfavorable** (adj.) 不適宜的

換句話說 **blueprints were changed**（設計藍圖更改了）→ **Some design plans have been revised.**（有些設計圖修改了。）

43. 相關細節——艾瑞克提及讓女子安心的事項

難

What does Eric say to reassure the woman?

(A) Her company's expertise will still be necessary.

(B) Her company can probably complete a job swiftly.

(C) Her company will not be blamed for an issue.

(D) Her company will receive a cancelation fee.

艾瑞克說了什麼來讓女子放心？

(A) 仍然需要她公司的專門技術。

(B) 她的公司很可能可以快速完成工作。

(C) 有個問題不會歸咎於她的公司。

(D) 她的公司會收到合約取消費用。

- expertise (n.) 專門技術 swiftly (adv.) 快速地 blame (v.) 把……歸咎於 cancelation fee 取消費

換句話說 specialized skills（專門技術）→ expertise（專門技術）

44-46 Conversation

44-46 對話

加⇄英

M: [(44)] **Thanks for coming to this exit interview,** Ichika. So, let's start with the most important question—[(44)] **why did you decide to leave?**

W: It's for the usual reason—I got a better job at another company.

M: Could you tell me more about that? What makes that job more attractive?

W: Well, to be honest, I'll be doing the same work for more pay. [(45)] **Our pay here is below market rate, you know.**

M: [(46)] **Yes, we've heard this comment from other departing employees. I'll be sure to pass it on to management again, though.** Now, tell me your impression of your supervisor.

男：[(44)] **一佳，謝謝妳過來接受離職訪談。**那麼，我們從最重要的問題開始吧：[(44)] **妳為什麼決定離職？**

女：是由於很常見的理由：我在另一家公司找到更好的工作。

男：可以請妳說得更詳細一點嗎？那份更吸引妳的地方是什麼？

女：這麼嘛，老實說就是：工作內容相同，但薪水較高。[(45)] **你知道，我們這裡的薪資比市場行情低。**

男：[(46)] **是的，我們已經從其他離職員工那裡，聽過這項批評了，不過我一定再次將把這個意見轉達給管理階層。**那麼現在，說說妳對妳主管的印象吧。

- exit interview 離職訪談 leave (v.) 離職 attractive (adj.) 有吸引力的 market rate 市場行情 comment (n.) 批評；意見 depart (v.) 離開 pass (v.) 傳達 management (n.) 管理階層 impression (n.) 印象 supervisor (n.) 管理者

44. 相關細節——女子決定的事情

What has the woman decided to do?

(A) Ask for a pay raise

(B) Suspend a subscription

(C) Obtain an academic degree

(D) Resign from her position

女子決定做什麼？

(A) 要求加薪

(B) 中止訂閱

(C) 取得學位

(D) 辭去職位

- raise (n.) 提高 suspend (v.) 使中止 subscription (n.) 訂閱 obtain (v.) 得到 academic degree 學位 resign (v.) 辭職

換句話說 leave（離職）→ resign（辭職）

---

45. 相關細節——女子提及的問題

What problem does the woman mention?
(A) Her compensation is unusually small.
(B) The market for a service is shrinking.
(C) A required task is unpleasant.
(D) Her workload has increased.

女子提及何項問題？
(A) 她的薪酬較正常低。
(B) 一項服務的市場正在萎縮。
(C) 職務內容令人不舒服。
(D) 她的工作量增加了。

- **compensation (n.)** 報酬；薪水 **unusually (adv.)** 異於尋常地 **shrink (v.)** 縮小 **unpleasant (adj.)** 令人不快的 **workload (n.)** 工作量

換句話說 pay（薪水）→ compensation（薪酬）

---

46. 相關細節——男子承諾的事情

What does the man promise to do?
(A) Consider a request
(B) Supervise a transition
(C) Deliver some feedback
(D) Make an introduction

男子承諾會做何事？
(A) 考慮要求
(B) 監督過渡期
(C) 傳達回饋意見
(D) 進行介紹

- **consider (v.)** 考慮 **request (n.)** 要求；請求 **supervise (v.)** 監督 **transition (n.)** 過渡期；轉變 **deliver (v.)** 傳送 **introduction (n.)** 介紹

47-49 Conversation with three speakers

W1: Hi, Mr. Semwal. My name's Andrea, and this is my friend Tracy. (47) **We really enjoyed your talk on the process of launching your startup.**
M: Oh, thank you. Are you two students here?
W2: Yes, we're business majors. Uh, Mr. Semwal, I have a question that I didn't get to ask during the Q&A. Could I ask it now?
M: Sure, Tracy, go ahead.
W2: So, (48) **you're an inspiration to us, but—when you were young, who inspired you?**
M: Well, I wouldn't be here without Deborah Gold, who was my professor during my senior year in university. She was a mentor to me.
W1: (49) **She wrote *A History of Innovation*, right?**
M: (49) **Yes, and I'd recommend that to both of you.** It's a bestseller for a reason.

47-49 三人對話 英⇄澳⇄美

女 1： 嗨，山沃爾先生，我名叫安卓雅，而這位是我朋友崔西。(47) **我們真的很喜歡您關於自行創業過程的演講。**
男： 噢，謝謝妳們。兩位是這裡的學生嗎？
女 2： 是的，我們主修商科。那個，山沃爾先生，我有個問題，問答時間沒有機會問，方便現在問您嗎？
男： 當然，崔西，請說。
女 2： 就是，(48) **您是啟發我們的榜樣，但是當您年輕時，是受到誰的啟發呢？**
男： 哦，我能有今日成就，都是多虧了黛博拉．高德，她是我大學四年級時的教授，是我的導師。
女 1： (49) **她寫了《創新的歷史》一書，對嗎？**
男： (49) **是的，我也推薦妳們兩位去讀。**那本書會暢銷不是沒有原因的。

- **process (n.)** 過程 **launch (v.)** 發起 **startup (n.)** 新創公司 **major (n.)**（大學科系）主修學生 **inspiration (n.)** 鼓舞人心的人／物 **inspire (v.)** 啟發；鼓舞 **professor (n.)** 教授 **senior (adj.)**（大學）四年級生的 **innovation (n.)** 創新

47. 全文相關——男子的身分 難

Who is the man?
(A) An author
(B) A musician
(C) An entrepreneur
(D) A politician

男子的身分為何？
(A) 作家
(B) 音樂家
(C) 企業家
(D) 政治人物

48. 相關細節——崔西向男子提出的問題

What does Tracy ask the man about?
(A) Challenges he faced
(B) His advice for youth
(C) His hopes for the future
(D) People who influenced him

崔西詢問男子何事？
(A) 他面對的挑戰
(B) 他給年輕人的建議
(C) 他對未來的希望
(D) 影響他的人

- **challenge (n.)** 挑戰　**face (v.)** 面對　**youth (n.)** 年輕人　**influence (v.)** 影響

換句話說 inspired（啟發）→ influenced（影響）

49. 相關細節——男子建議的事情

What does the man recommend doing?
(A) Seeking a mentor relationship
(B) Reading a certain book
(C) Traveling to other countries
(D) Choosing a small university

男子有何建議？
(A) 尋找導師關係
(B) 閱讀特定書籍
(C) 去其他國家旅行
(D) 選擇小型大學

- **seek (v.)** 尋找　**relationship (n.)** 關係　**certain (adj.)** 特定的；某個的

53-55 Conversation

W: Noah, I was just checking our page on City-Consumers.com, and I noticed that (50) **we got a two-star rating for Ashley's work on the Loper Incorporated photos. The review said she was too hurried and made the subjects feel nervous.**

M: That's not good. (51) **I'll talk to her about how to make customers comfortable.** She has such a great eye for composition. If she can learn how to handle people better, she'll be a real asset.

W: I hope so, because right now she's costing us money. (52) **We'll have to give Loper Incorporated some of their fee back in order to save our relationship with them.**

50-52 對話 美⇄澳

女：諾亞，我剛才查看了我們在 City-Consumers.com 網站上的頁面，發現 (50) **艾希莉為羅普公司做的攝影服務讓我們得到兩顆星的評價。評論寫道，她做事太趕，讓拍攝的對象感到緊張。**

男：那樣不行，(51) **我會和她解說如何讓顧客覺得自在**，她在構圖方面很有眼光，如果她可以提升人際互動的能力，就真的大有可為了。

女：我希望如此，因為她現在正造成我們損失，(52) **我們得退還一些費用給羅普公司，以維護和他們的關係。**

- **notice (v.)** 注意到　**rating (n.)** 評價；評分　**hurried (adj.)** 匆忙的　**subject (n.)** 對象
composition (n.)（繪畫或照片的）構圖　**handle (v.)** 對待　**asset (n.)** 人才；資產

50. 相關細節——女子告訴男子的事情

What does the woman tell the man about?
(A) A negative review
(B) A broken Web link
(C) A scheduling error
(D) A security risk

女子告訴男子何項相關事情？
(A) 負面評論
(B) 網頁連結失效
(C) 排程錯誤
(D) 安全風險

51. 相關細節——男子打算和艾希莉的談談原因

Why will the man speak to Ashley?
(A) To ask for her help
(B) To give her some news
(C) To express his gratitude
(D) To provide some guidance

男子為何要和艾希莉談談？
(A) 請她幫忙
(B) 告知消息
(C) 表達感謝
(D) 提供指導

- express (v.) 表達 gratitude (n.) 感謝 provide (v.) 提供 guidance (n.) 指引；指導

52. 相關細節——女子提及說話者的公司必須做的事情

According to the woman, what must the speakers' company do?
(A) Issue a partial refund
(B) Save copies of some images
(C) Replace a software program
(D) Make an official announcement

根據女子所說，說話者的公司必須做什麼？
(A) 退回部分費用
(B) 儲存影像複本
(C) 更換軟體程式
(D) 發出正式聲明

- issue (v.) 發給 partial (adj.) 部分的 refund (n.) 退款；退還 replace (v.) 替換 official (adj.) 正式的

換句話說 give . . . some of their fee back（退還一些費用給他們）
→ issue a partial refund（退回部分費用）

53-55 Conversation

M: I can ring up your purchase over here, ma'am. So, did you find everything you were looking for today?

W: Yes, and more! (53) **I just came to get some holiday greeting cards, but then I saw that you have these Cantling journals.**

M: Oh, yes, we just got them last month. Have you seen them before?

W: I bought one when I visited London, and I really like it. (54) **Since Cantling is a British company, it was a surprise to see its journals here.**

M: I'm glad you like them. (55) **We try to stock a variety of interesting products.**

W: Well, I'll be back soon, then!

M: Excellent. OK, your total is twenty-four dollars and thirty-eight cents. How would you like to pay?

53-55 對話 加⇄英

男： 我這邊可以幫您結帳，女士。好的，今天在找的商品都買齊了嗎？

女： 都齊了，還多買了不少！(53) **我原本只是來買些節日用的賀卡，但我看到你們有在賣這種「肯特林」牌的日記簿。**

男： 噢，是的，我們上個月才剛進貨。您以前有看過嗎？

女： 我之前去倫敦時，有買過一本，真的是很喜歡，(54) **因為肯特林是英國廠牌，所以很意外在這裡看到他們出的日記簿。**

男： 很高興您喜歡。(55) **本店會致力供應各式各樣新奇的商品。**

女： 哦，那麼我很快會再來店！

男： 太好了。好的，您的消費總金額是 24 元 38 分錢，請問要如何付款呢？

- ring up 結帳 purchase (n.) 購買的物品 holiday greeting 節日問候 journal (n.) 日誌 stock (v.) 進貨 a variety of . . . 各式各樣的……

53. 相關細節——男子店內主要販售的產品

What does the man's store mainly sell?
(A) Cosmetics
(B) Health food
(C) Housewares
(D) Stationery

男子的店裡主要販售何物？
(A) 化妝品
(B) 健康食品
(C) 家用器具
(D) 文具

換句話說 greeting cards, journals（賀卡，日記簿）→ stationery（文具）

54. 相關細節——女子提及有關肯特林產品的內容 難

What do we know about the journal the woman buys?
(A) It was recently released.
(B) It is imported from abroad.
(C) It is not often sold at a discount.
(D) It has been discontinued.

有關女子買的日記簿，可推知何者正確？
(A) 最近才剛推出
(B) 從國外進口而來
(C) 不常打折出售
(D) 已經停產了

- release (v.) 發行 import (v.) 進口 abroad (n.) 國外 discontinue (v.) 停止；中止

55. 掌握說話者的意圖——提及「我很快會再來店」的意圖 難

What does the woman most likely mean when she says, "I'll be back soon"?
(A) She expects to use up a purchase quickly.
(B) She hopes that the man will do a favor for her.
(C) She parked close to the store's entrance.
(D) She intends to become a regular customer.

女子說：「我很快會再來店」，最可能的意思為何？
(A) 她預期買的東西很快會用完。
(B) 她希望男子可以幫她一個忙。
(C) 她把車停在靠近店門口。
(D) 她有意成為常客。

- expect (v.) 預期 use up 用完 favor (n.) 幫助 entrance (n.) 入口；門口 intend (v.) 想要；打算 regular (adj.) 經常的

56-58 Conversation

M: Noland Airport customer service. How can I help you?

W: Hi, I'm calling from Clementas Company. [56] **One of our executives is flying into your airport next month, and he'll be on a tight schedule, so his arrival has to go smoothly.** Do you have any services you can offer?

M: Yes—I'd recommend "Airport Concierge". An attendant would greet your executive at the disembarking gate and assist him through the arrival process. [57] **They could even have a private car service take him wherever he needs to go from the airport.**

56-58 對話 加⇄美

男： 這裡是諾蘭機場顧客服務中心，請問需要什麼服務？

女： 嗨，我這裡是喀門塔斯公司。[56] **我們有一位高階主管下個月會飛抵你們機場，而他的行程很緊湊，因此要確保他的入境過程順暢無阻，**你們可以提供什麼服務嗎？

男： 有的，我會推薦「機場禮賓」服務，屆時下機時將有專人在機門迎接貴公司主管，並協助他通過入境程序，[57] **甚至還能享有專車服務，從機場載他前往任何需要去的地點。**

W: [57] **Oh, a local contact is going to pick him up.** But otherwise, that sounds great.[58] **How do I reserve it?**	**女：** (57) **噢，到時會由當地的聯絡人員去接他，**不過其他部分聽起來不錯，(58) **我要怎麼預約此服務？**
M: It's operated by a separate company. [58] **I'll give you its number.**	**男：** 那是別的公司負責營運的，(58) **我來給你他們的電話號碼。**

- executive (n.) 主管　tight (adj.)（時間）緊湊的　smoothly (adv.) 順利地　recommend (v.) 推薦　concierge (n.)（飯店）櫃台人員；禮賓部　attendant (n.) 服務員　greet (v.) 迎接；問候　disembark (v.) 下（交通工具）　process (n.) 過程　private (adj.) 私人的　contact (n.) 聯絡人　otherwise (adv.) 除此之外　reserve (v.) 預訂　separate (adj.) 不同的

56. 相關細節——女子針對公司主管提及的內容

What does the woman say about a company executive?
(A) He does not speak a local language.
(B) He will bring a lot of luggage.
(C) He has a minor injury.
(D) He will not have much time.

關於公司的高階主管，女子說了什麼？
(A) 他不會說當地語言。
(B) 他會攜帶大量行李。
(C) 他受了輕傷。
(D) 他的時間不多。

- luggage (n.) 行李　minor (adj.) 輕微的；不嚴重的　injury (n.) 受傷

換句話說 be on a tight schedule（行程很緊湊）→ not have much time（時間不多）

57. 相關細節——女子提及不必要的安排 難

According to the woman, what will not be necessary?
(A) Arranging ground transportation
(B) Giving a special greeting
(C) Reserving a private rest space
(D) Sending electronic flight updates

根據女子說法，何者是不必要的？
(A) 安排陸上交通
(B) 提供特殊迎接服務
(C) 預訂私人休息場所
(D) 寄送航班更新的電子訊息

- arrange (v.) 安排　transportation (n.) 運輸；交通工具　rest (n.) 休息　space (n.) 空間　electronic (adj.) 電子的

58. 相關細節——女子可能會於對話結束後做的事情

What will the woman most likely do after the conversation?
(A) Forward a confirmation e-mail
(B) Make another phone call
(C) Begin a car journey
(D) Visit a travel Web site

在此對話後，女子最可能做何事？
(A) 轉寄確認電子郵件
(B) 撥打另一通電話
(C) 開始行車上路
(D) 瀏覽旅遊網站

- forward (v.) 轉寄；轉交　confirmation (n.) 確認　journey (n.) 旅行

59-61 Conversation

59-61 對話

澳⇄美

M: **(59) Mona, remember how you said the building's windows were getting dirty, but you were concerned about the cost of having them washed? Well, I found a company that does it for much cheaper than others, so I went ahead and scheduled a service visit.**

W: That's great, but . . . why are they so much cheaper than other companies?

M: It's interesting, actually. **(60) They use robots to do the work.** They say the quality is the same and there's less of a safety hazard.

W: Wow! That sounds like it's worth a try. **(61) OK, I'll let the rest of our team know about the service visit.** Oh, wait—when are they coming?

M: Next Thursday morning.

男： **(59) 莫娜，還記得妳說過大樓的窗戶越變越髒，但妳擔心請人清洗窗戶的費用嗎？跟妳說，我找到一家清洗窗戶的業者，費用比其他家便宜很多，所以我就直接預約前來服務的時間了。**

女： 太好了，但是……他們為什麼比其他公司便宜這麼多？

男： 其實蠻有趣的：**(60) 他們使用機器人來工作**，他們說服務品質都一樣，但安全風險較少。

女： 哇！聽起來值得一試。**(61) 好的，我會向團隊的其他成員告知有人會來做這次服務。**噢，等等，他們什麼時候過來？

男： 下週四早上。

- **concerned (adj.)** 擔心的 **go ahead** 著手做 **schedule (v.)** 預約 **quality (n.)** 品質 **hazard (n.)** 危險；危害 **worth . . .** 值得做… **rest (n.)** 剩餘部分

59. 相關細節——男子預約的服務

What service does the man say he has scheduled?

(A) Plant care

(B) Appliance repair

(C) Window cleaning

(D) Furniture removal

男子說他已預約了何種服務？

(A) 照顧植物

(B) 家電維修

(C) 清洗窗戶

(D) 搬運家具

---

60. 相關細節——男子提及服務的特別之處

According to the man, what is special about the service?

(A) It is done outside of business hours.

(B) It does not involve hazardous chemicals.

(C) It is not available in all seasons.

(D) It is performed by machines.

根據男子所說，這項服務有何特別之處？

(A) 是在非上班時段進行。

(B) 不會使用有害的化學物質。

(C) 並非一年四季都提供。

(D) 是由機器執行。

- **involve (v.)** 包含；需要 **hazardous (adj.)** 危險的 **chemical (n.)** 化學製品 **available (adj.)** 可得到的 **perform (v.)** 執行

換句話說 use robots to do the work（使用機器人來工作）→ performed by machines（是由機器執行）

---

61. 相關細節——女子提及她將會做的事情

What does the woman say she will do?

(A) Watch a demonstration

(B) Inform some colleagues

(C) Permit an inconvenience

(D) Take the rest of the day off

女子說她將會做何事？

(A) 觀看示範

(B) 通知同事

(C) 容許不便

(D) 提前下班

- **demonstration (n.)** 實地示範 **inform (v.)** 通知 **colleague (n.)** 同事 **permit (v.)** 容許；允許 **inconvenience (n.)** 不便 **take . . . off** 在……期間休假

換句話說 let the rest of our team know（向團隊的其他成員告知）→ inform some colleagues（通知同事）

62-64 Conversation + Ticket

M: Caroline, where are you? The concert's about to start!

W: Yes, (62) **sorry that I'm running late! I didn't know that the stadium doesn't allow backpacks. I had to run back to the parking area to put mine in my car.**

M: That's too bad. Well, are you almost here now?

W: Yeah. Our area is near Flash Burgers, right?

M: No, I don't think so. I didn't see that on my way in.

W: Hmm. Oh, I made a mistake! (63) **I confused the "section" and "row" numbers on my ticket.** I'll be there in a minute.

M: Great. (64) **But wait—since you're right by Flash Burgers, could you pick me up a Flash Meal?** I'm really hungry.

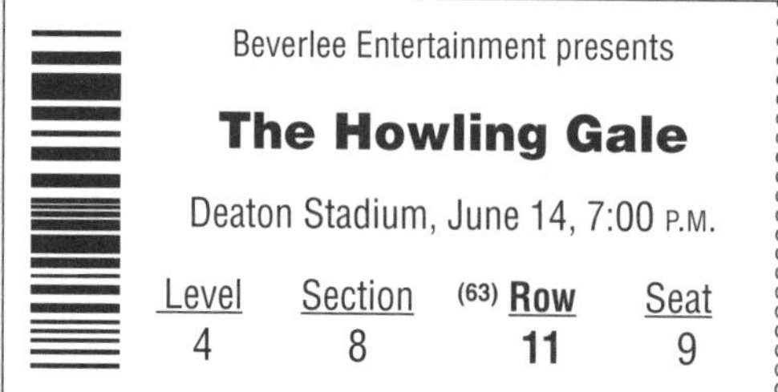

62-64 對話＋門票 澳⇄英

男：卡洛琳，妳人在哪裡？音樂會快要開始了！

女：我知道，(62) **抱歉，我會晚點到！我不知道不能把背包帶進體育場，所以必須跑回停車場，把我的背包放進車裡。**

男：太糟糕了，那妳現在差不多要到了嗎？

女：快了，我們的座位區就在「閃光漢堡」附近，對嗎？

男：不，我想不是，我進來的一路上沒有看到漢堡店。

女：唔，噢，我搞錯了！(63) **我把門票上「區」和「排」的號碼搞混了**，我馬上就到。

男：太好了。(64) **不過等等，既然妳人在閃光漢堡旁邊，可以幫我買一份閃光餐嗎？**我真的很餓。

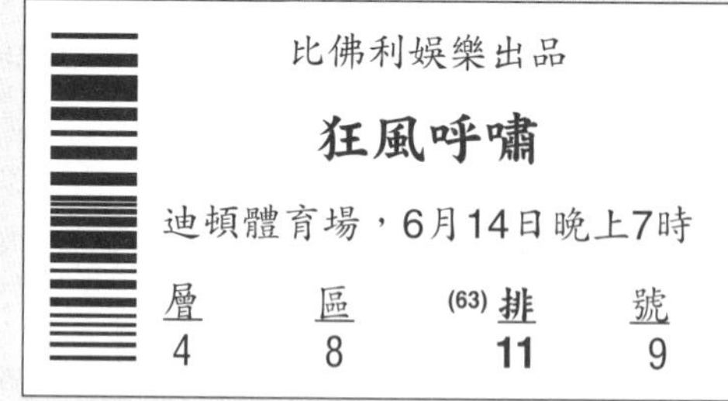

- be about to 即將　stadium (n.) 體育場　confuse (v.) 混淆　section (n.) 區域　row (n.) 一排；一列

62. 相關細節——女子遲到的原因

Why is the woman late?

(A) It took her a long time to find parking.
(B) She was unaware of an admission policy.
(C) She misunderstood a spoken invitation.
(D) There was traffic around the stadium.

女子為什麼遲到？

(A) 她找停車位找了很久。
(B) 她未注意到一項入場規定。
(C) 她誤解了口頭邀約。
(D) 體育場周圍交通壅塞。

- unaware (adj.) 不知道的　admission (n.) 准許進入　policy (n.) 政策；方針　misunderstand (v.) 誤解　invitation (n.) 邀請　traffic (n.) 交通（量）

換句話說 didn't know（不知道）→ was unaware of（未注意到）

63. 圖表整合題——女子走錯的區域 難

Look at the graphic. What section did the woman go to by mistake?

(A) 4　(B) 8
(C) 11　(D) 9

請見圖表作答。女子誤走到哪一區？

(A) 4　(B) 8
(C) 11　(D) 9

64. 相關細節——男子向女子提出的要求

What does the man ask the woman to do?
(A) Bring him some refreshments
(B) Send him a photograph
(C) Look for concert staff
(D) Wait by a landmark

男子要求女子做何事？
(A) 帶些點心給他
(B) 寄照片給他
(C) 尋找音樂會工作人員
(D) 在地標旁等候

- refreshment (n.) 點心；飲料　landmark (n.) 地標

換句話說 pick me up a . . . Meal（幫我買一份餐點）→ bring him some refreshments（帶些點心給他）

65-67 Conversation + Announcement

W: Otto, do you have a moment? (65) **I'd like to pitch an article series for our Saturday edition.**

M: Sure, Bridget. What is it?

W: (66) **I want to interview each of the winners of the Jasper Environmental Awards. It's a great program, and it should get more attention.** We only ran a short news piece on it after they were announced.

M: Tell me about the winners.

W: (67) **Well, I would start with the winner of the "Waste Management" category.** She leads a group that collects the healthy but unattractive produce that local supermarkets throw away, and then distributes it to people who need it.

M: OK. That does sound like a good fit for the weekend. (67) **Ask her if she's interested.**

2nd Annual Jasper Environmental Awards Winners

Conservation Jamie Wright	(67) ***Waste Management*** **Taylor Bowers**
Technology Hyun-Jin Wi	*Communications* Cameron Kennedy

65-67 對話＋公告　英⇄加

女：奧圖，你有空嗎？(65) **我想要提案做一個系列報導，刊載週六專刊上。**

男：當然可以，布莉姬，是什麼報導？

女：(66) **我想要訪問賈士伯環境獎的各項得主，那個獎是很棒的計畫，應該得到更多關注。**之前我們只在得獎者宣布後，登了一則很短的新聞。

男：跟我說明一下這些得獎者。

女：(67) **那麼，我會從「廢棄物管理」項目的得獎者開始。**她帶領一群團隊夥伴收集因為賣相不好、而在當地市場遭到丟棄的健康農產品，然後把農產品分送給需要的人。

男：好的，那聽起來確實很適合週末刊出。(67) **去詢問她是否有興趣吧。**

第二屆年度賈士伯環境獎得主

保育類 傑米・萊特	(67) **廢棄物管理** **泰勒・鮑爾斯**
科技類 魏玄振	通訊傳播類 卡麥隆・甘迺迪

- pitch (v.) 提案；極力勸說　edition (n.) 版本　winner (n.) 得獎者　environmental (adj.) 環境的　award (n.) 獎；獎金　attention (n.) 注意　announce (v.) 宣布　waste (n.) 廢棄物　management (n.) 管理　category (n.) 類別　lead (v.) 帶領　unattractive (adj.) 不具吸引力的　produce (n.) 農產品　throw away 拋棄　distribute (v.) 分配；分發　fit (n.) 適合

65. 全文相關——女子的身分

Who most likely is the woman?
(A) A city official
(B) A reporter
(C) A nonprofit executive
(D) A marketing consultant

女子最可能的身分為何？
(A) 市政府官員
(B) 記者
(C) 非營利組織的主管
(D) 行銷顧問

66. 相關細節——女子針對獎項談及的內容 難

What does the woman say about the awards program?
(A) It deserves more publicity.
(B) It selects surprising winners.
(C) It added a new category this year.
(D) Its ceremony can be viewed online.

關於該獎項計畫，女子說了何事？
(A) 應該更受大眾關注。
(B) 選出令人意外的得獎者。
(C) 今年新增一項類別。
(D) 頒獎典禮可以在網路上觀看。

- **deserve (v.)** 值得；應得 **publicity (n.)**（公眾）注意 **select (v.)** 選擇 **surprising (adj.)** 令人吃驚的 **ceremony (n.)** 典禮；儀式 **view (v.)** 觀看

換句話說 more attention（更多關注）→ more publicity（更受大眾關注）

67. 圖表整合題——女子可能聯絡的對象

Look at the graphic. Whom will the woman most likely contact?
(A) Jamie Wright
(B) Taylor Bowers
(C) Hyun-Jin Wi
(D) Cameron Kennedy

請見圖表作答。女子最可能將聯絡誰？
(A) 傑米・萊特
(B) 泰勒・鮑爾斯
(C) 魏玄振
(D) 卡麥隆・甘迺迪

68-70 Conversation + Expense code list

M: Hi, Ms. Diaz, it's your bookkeeper. (68) **I'm entering your salon's operating expenses now, and—there's an invoice from a company called "Baxell" for a few dozen manicure kits.** Can you confirm that you placed that order?

W: Yes, I did. Why? Is there a problem with the invoice?

M: (69) **Well, I hadn't heard of Baxell, and your invoices for this kind of expense usually come from Reidmont.** So I thought I should check.

W: I see. (70) **Yes, I learned about Baxell at a trade show last month and decided to try them out.** You might see more invoices from them in the future.

68-70 對話＋費用代碼表 加⇄美

男：嗨，迪亞茲女士，我是您的記帳員。(68) **我正在輸入您的美容沙龍的營業費用，然後——有一張列有好幾十套美甲套組的費用帳單，來自一家叫「百克索」的公司**，可以請您確認是否訂了這批貨嗎？

女：是的，我有訂。怎麼了嗎？那張費用帳單有問題嗎？

男：(69) **這個嘛，我沒聽說過「百克索」，而且貴店這類開銷的帳單通常是從「瑞得蒙」公司收到**，因此我想應該確認一下。

女：了解。(70) **對的，我上個月在一場商展上知道百克索這家公司，決定試用他們的產品**，你以後可能會看到更多他們開立的帳單。

Operating Expenses	
(68) 520	**Business Supplies**
530	Utilities
540	Telecommunications
550	Repair and Maintenance

營業費用	
(68) 520	**營業用品費**
530	公用事業費
540	電信費
550	維修費

- bookkeeper (n.) 記帳員　enter (v.) 輸入　operating expense 營業費用　invoice (n.) 發貨單；請款帳單　a few dozen 幾十個　confirm (v.) 確認　expense (n.) 費用　trade (n.) 貿易；行業

68. 圖表整合題——輸入費用的代碼 難

Look at the graphic. Which code will the expense most likely be entered under?

(A) 520

(B) 530

(C) 540

(D) 550

請見圖表作答。該筆費用最可能輸入在何項代碼之下？

(A) 520

(B) 530

(C) 540

(D) 550

69. 相關細節——男子擔心該張帳單的理由 難

Why is the man concerned about the invoice?

(A) Its due date has already passed.

(B) It does not include some details.

(C) It is from an unfamiliar company.

(D) It requests an unusual amount of money.

男子對該費用帳單有何顧慮？

(A) 到期日已經過去。

(B) 未有詳細資料。

(C) 來自陌生的公司。

(D) 要求異於尋常的金額。

- due date 到期日　include (v.) 包含　detail (n.) 細節；詳述　unfamiliar (adj.) 不熟悉的　unusual (adj.) 不尋常的　amount (n.) 總額

換句話說 hadn't heard of（沒聽說過）→ unfamiliar（陌生的）

70. 相關細節——女子最近做過的事情

What did the woman most likely do recently?

(A) Watched a television news show

(B) Cleared out a storage area

(C) Attended an industry event

(D) Delegated a task to an employee

女子最近最可能做過什麼事？

(A) 觀看電視新聞節目

(B) 清出儲藏空間

(C) 參加產業活動

(D) 委派工作給員工

- storage (n.) 儲存　clear out 清除　industry (n.) 行業　delegate (v.) 把……委派給……　task (n.) 工作；任務

換句話說 a trade show（商展）→ an industry event（產業活動）

71-73 Excerpt from a meeting

All right, everyone, it's 11:01, so we'd better get started. (71) **Remember, it's now company policy that meetings can't go over thirty minutes.** I'm sure that will help our productivity overall, but it does mean that we need to really focus right now. (72) **I've made a list of everything we're going to talk about today. Please take a look at it now.** (73) **As you can see, we've got to decide on the venue, program, and food for our yearly holiday party.** I have a few suggestions for the first of these.

71–73 會議摘錄 澳

好了，各位，現在是 11 點 01 分，所以我們最好開始吧。(71) **記住，公司現在規定會議不能超過 30 分鐘，**我相信那對我們整體的產能有幫助，但的確也意味我們現在真的必須聚精會神。(72) **我把今天要討論的所有事項列成了一張清單，現在請先看一下。**(73) **如各位所見，我們必須決定我們年度佳節派對的場地、節目和餐飲。**對於第一個事項，我有一些建議。

- policy (n.) 規定；政策 productivity (n.) 生產力 overall (adv.) 總體上 focus (v.) 聚焦；集中 venue (n.) 舉行地點 yearly (adj.) 一年一次的 suggestion (n.) 建議

71. 相關細節——公司近期採取的政策

What did the company recently adopt a policy on?
(A) How meeting notifications are sent out
(B) How many people must attend a meeting
(C) How meeting spaces can be used
(D) How long meetings can last

公司最近採行了何事的相關政策？
(A) 會議通知如何發送
(B) 會議必須有多少人參加
(C) 會議空間可以如何利用
(D) 會議可以持續多久

- adopt (v.) 採取 notification (n.) 通知 last (v.) 持續

72. 相關細節——說話者要求聽者先做的事情

What does the speaker ask the listeners to do first?
(A) Put away some snacks
(B) Examine an agenda
(C) Prepare to take notes
(D) Write their names on a form

說話者要求聽者先做什麼？
(A) 把零食收起來
(B) 查看議程
(C) 準備記筆記
(D) 在表格上寫下名字

- put away 把……收起來 examine (v.) 仔細檢查 agenda (n.) 議程 take notes 記筆記 form (n.) 表格

換句話說 a list of everything we're going to talk about（要討論的所有事項清單）→ an agenda（議程）

73. 相關細節——會議的目的

What is the purpose of the meeting?
(A) To discuss a safety issue
(B) To choose a new employee
(C) To evaluate a training program
(D) To plan an annual gathering

會議的目的是什麼？
(A) 討論安全問題
(B) 選擇新進員工
(C) 評估培訓計畫
(D) 規劃年度聚會

- evaluate (v.) 評估 annual (adj.) 年度的 gathering (n.) 集會

換句話說 our yearly . . . party（我們的年度派對）→ an annual gathering（年度聚會）

74-76 Telephone message

74-76 電話留言

英

Hi, Mr. Price. This is Julie at Stonebend Furniture. (74) **I received the delivery of the Muldock chair prototype this morning. Your craftmanship is excellent, but . . . the wood has water damage.** (75) **So I looked at the packaging, and it's the wrong choice for that type of wood. Hickory is quite sensitive to moisture, and I assumed you knew that . . . but** I guess it's not native to your area. Anyway, I'll need to know that you can ship the product safely before I make a larger production order. (76) **Could you look into the matter until you find a more suitable packaging method?** Thanks.

嗨，普萊斯先生，我是彎石家具的茱莉。(74) **我今天早上收到「莫爾達克」座椅的原型樣品，你的做工非常出色，但是……木頭上有水漬汙損，**(75) **因此我仔細檢查了包裝，發現你選錯了包裝材料來裝這種木料。山胡桃木對濕氣很敏感，我以為你會知道……但**我猜山胡桃木不是你們當地的原生種。總之，我必須確信你可以把產品安全送達，才能訂下較大量的生產訂單。(76) **你可以研究一下這件事，找出更合適的包裝方法嗎？**謝謝。

- prototype (n.) 原型　craftmanship (n.) 技藝　damage (n.) 損害　packaging (n.) 包裝　hickory (n.) 山胡桃木　sensitive (adj.) 敏感的；易受傷害的　moisture (n.) 濕氣　assume (v.) 以為；假定　native (adj.) 原生的　ship (v.) 運送；裝運　production (n.) 生產　suitable (adj.) 合適的　method (n.) 方法

TEST 10

PART 4

74. 相關細節——說話者於上午做的事情

難

What did the speaker do in the morning?

(A) Finalized a digital drawing

(B) Browsed a furniture catalog

(C) Checked a sample item

(D) Received a sales proposal

說話者早上做了什麼？

(A) 完成數位畫作

(B) 瀏覽家具型錄

(C) 檢查樣本

(D) 收到銷售提案

- finalize (v.) 完成　browse (v.) 瀏覽；隨意翻閱　proposal (n.) 提案

換句話說 prototype（原型樣品）→ a sample item（樣品）

75. 掌握說話者的意圖——提及「我猜山胡桃木不是你們當地的原生種」的意圖

難

What does the speaker imply when she says, "I guess it's not native to your area"?

(A) She knows why a cost might be high.

(B) She understands how a mistake happened.

(C) She is suggesting entering a new market.

(D) She is doubtful about a product's authenticity.

說話者說：「我猜山胡桃木不是你們當地的原生種」，言下之意為何？

(A) 她知道費用可能很高的原因。

(B) 她了解錯誤何以發生。

(C) 她建議進入新市場。

(D) 她懷疑產品的真實性。

- doubtful (adj.) 懷疑的　authenticity (n.) 真實性

76. 相關細節——說話者要求聽者做的事情

What does the speaker ask the listener to do?

(A) Give his opinion

(B) Expedite an order

(C) Update some machinery

(D) Search for an alternative

說話者要求聽者做何事？

(A) 說出他的意見

(B) 迅速完成訂單

(C) 更新機具設備

(D) 尋找替代方案

- opinion (n.) 意見　expedite (v.) 迅速完成　machinery (n.) 機器　search (v.) 尋找　alternative (n.) 替代方案

換句話說 find a more suitable . . . method（找出更合適的包裝方法）
→ search for an alternative（尋找替代方案）

77-79 Tour information

Attention, passengers. [77] **Thank you for joining us for this cruise around the coast of Mapsalak National Park.** [78] **In case you haven't noticed already, there are two whales passing by on our left.** We can tell from the large bumps on their backs that they are humpback whales. Oh, one of them just jumped out of the water! It seems like they're putting on a show for us. I hope you all saw that. [79] **If not, or if you'd like to see more, I recommend buying a "Whales of Mapsalak" DVD from our gift shop when we return to land.** It's full of really amazing footage.

77-79 觀光資訊 美

各位旅客請注意，[77] **感謝大家參加這次的遊航，一同漫遊環繞馬薩拉克國家公園沿海地區，**[78] **還沒注意到的朋友，請看我們的左手邊，正有兩隻鯨魚游過**，從牠們背上的大塊凸起，我們可以分辨出牠們是座頭鯨。噢，其中一隻剛才躍出了水面！看起來就像正在為我們表演，希望大家都看到了。[79] **如果沒有，或者大家還看不過癮，我建議等我們返航靠岸後，可以到我們的禮品店買一片《馬薩拉克的鯨魚》DVD**，裡面收錄了相當令人嘆為觀止的片段。

- cruise (n.) 乘船遊覽　coast (n.) 海岸　national park 國家公園　in case 假如　notice (v.) 注意　whale (n.) 鯨魚　bump (n.) 凸起；腫塊　humpback whale 座頭鯨　amazing (adj.) 驚人的　footage (n.) 影片片段

77. 全文相關——聽者所在的地點

Where most likely are the listeners?
(A) On a bus
(B) On a boat
(C) On a footpath
(D) On an aircraft

聽者最可能在哪裡？
(A) 在巴士上
(B) 在船上
(C) 在步道上
(D) 在飛機上

換句話說 cruise（遊航）→ boat（船）

78. 相關細節——說話者告知聽者的事情

What does the speaker point out to the listeners?
(A) Some wild animals
(B) Some rare plants
(C) A famous building
(D) A large body of water

說話者指引聽者觀看何者？
(A) 野生動物
(B) 罕見植物
(C) 著名建築物
(D) 一大片水域

79. 相關細節——說話者建議聽者做的事情

What does the speaker encourage listeners to do later?
(A) Return some rental gear
(B) Purchase a video souvenir
(C) Post their photographs online
(D) Recommend the tour to others

說話者鼓勵聽者稍後做何事？
(A) 歸還租用的設備
(B) 購買影像紀念品
(C) 將照片張貼到網路上
(D) 向其他人推薦該行程

- return (v.) 歸還　rental (adj.) 租借的　gear (n.) 裝備；用具　purchase (v.) 購買　souvenir (n.) 紀念品　post (v.) 張貼；發布　photograph (n.) 照片

80-82 Announcement

80-82 宣布

加

Managers, thank you for joining me today. [80] **I wanted to let you know that Arvina Software is going to restructure.** Instead of employees being grouped by function, such as sales or finance, we're going to be divided into business units that each focus on customers in a particular industry, such as transportation or retail. I believe this will improve our service and lead to higher revenues. Obviously, this will be a major change. [81] **But don't worry—from now on, you'll be involved in every step of the process.** Your input will be crucial. [82] **I only ask that you keep this information to yourselves until the plans are finalized.** Telling employees now would only cause unnecessary worries about the transition.

感謝各位經理今天來和我開會。[80] **在此想要告訴大家，「艾爾維納軟體」將要重整，**我們劃分員工部門的方式，會從原來依業務、財務等職務區分，改成分為數個營業單位，分別關注如運輸業、零售業等特定產業客戶，我相信這會改善我們的服務，並造就更高的收益。顯然，這會是個很大的改變，[81] **但別擔心：從現在起，各位將參與這個過程的每個步驟。**大家的參與至關重要，[82] **我只要求各位在計畫確定之前，對消息要守口如瓶，**現在就告訴員工，只會讓他們對此轉變產生無謂的擔憂。

- restructure (v.) 改組；重建　instead of . . . 而不是　function (n.) 職務；功能　divide (v.) 劃分　unit (n.) 單位　focus (v.) 集中　particular (adj.) 特定的　industry (n.) 行業　transportation (n.) 運輸（業）　retail (n.) 零售　improve (v.) 增進　lead (v.) 導致　revenue (n.) 收益　obviously (adv.) 明顯地　involve (v.) 使參與　process (n.) 過程　input (n.) 投入；參與　crucial (adj.) 重要的　finalize (v.) 敲定　cause (v.) 導致；引起　unnecessary (adj.) 不必要的　transition (n.) 轉變；過渡期

80. 全文相關——獨白的主題

What is the speaker announcing?
(A) The revision of a document
(B) The relocation of a workplace
(C) The reorganization of a company
(D) The retirement of an executive

說話者正在宣布何事？
(A) 文件的修訂
(B) 工作場所的搬遷
(C) 公司組織重整
(D) 主管的退休

- revision (n.) 修正；修訂　relocation (n.) 搬遷　workplace (n.) 工作場所　reorganization (n.) 組織重組　retirement (n.) 退休　executive (n.) 主管

換句話說 restructure（重整結構）→ reorganization（組織重整）

81. 掌握說話者的意圖——提及「這會是個很大的改變」的意圖

難

What does the speaker imply when he says, "this will be a major change"?
(A) The listeners might be feeling concerned.
(B) A process will take place over a long period.
(C) He is optimistic about an outcome.
(D) A previous project had a limited impact.

說話者說：「這會是個很大的改變」，言下之意為何？
(A) 聽者可能會感到擔憂。
(B) 過程會持續很長時間。
(C) 他對結果很樂觀。
(D) 先前的計畫影響有限。

- concerned (adj.) 擔心的　period (n.) 期間；時期　optimistic (adj.) 樂觀的　outcome (n.) 結果　previous (adj.) 先前的　impact (n.) 衝擊

82. 相關細節——向聽者提出的要求 難

What are the listeners asked to do?
(A) Schedule regular planning sessions
(B) Conserve some office supplies
(C) Monitor the results of a transition
(D) Avoid disclosing some information

聽者被要求做何事？
(A) 安排定期規劃會議
(B) 節約使用辦公用品
(C) 密切注意轉變的結果
(D) 避免透露消息

- schedule (v.) 排定 regular (adj.) 定期的 planning (n.) 規劃 session (n.) 會議 conserve (v.) 節約 office supplies 辦公用品 monitor (v.) 監控 result (n.) 結果 avoid (v.) 避免 disclose (v.) 揭露

換句話說 keep this information to yourselves（對消息要守口如瓶）
→ avoid disclosing some information（避免透露消息）

83-85 Telephone message

(83) Hello, this is Joo-Hee from Regency Comfort Suites calling for Desmond Smith regarding your reservation for March fourth. It turns out that on that day, we're washing all the hallway carpets on the fourth floor, where your room is located. (84) But rest assured that, as a member of our loyalty program, your comfort and convenience are extremely important to us. (85) We'd like to offer you one of our executive suites on the fifth floor at no extra charge. Uh, if you'd like to take advantage of this offer, call me back at (513) 555-0106. Have a nice day.

83-85 電話留言 英

(83) 哈囉，這裡是瑞珍舒適套房飯店的珠熙，來電找戴斯蒙德．史密斯，討論有關 3 月 4 日訂房的事宜。我們後來發現，飯店當天要清洗所有四樓走廊的地毯，即您預訂房間所在的樓層。(84) 但請放心，由於您有加入我們的忠實顧客方案，您的舒適與便利就是我們的要務，(85) 我們想要提供您免費改住五樓的一間行政套房。噢，如果您有意接受這項提議，請回撥（513）555-0106 告知我。祝您有愉快的一天。

- regarding (prep.) 關於…… reservation (n.) 預訂 turn out . . . 最終發現…… hallway (n.) 走廊 rest assured （用於安慰）請別擔心 loyalty program 常客回饋方案 comfort (n.) 舒適 convenience (n.) 便利 extremely (adv.) 極其地 executive suite 行政套房 charge (n.) 收費 take advantage of . . . 利用……

83. 全文相關——說話者的工作地點

Where does the speaker work?
(A) At a hotel
(B) At a travel agency
(C) At an architectural firm
(D) At a cleaning company

說話者在哪裡工作？
(A) 飯店
(B) 旅行社
(C) 建築師事務所
(D) 清潔公司

---

84. 相關細節——說話者針對聽者提及的內容 難

What does the speaker indicate about the listener?
(A) He has recently been hired.
(B) He has won a competition.
(C) He is a member of a rewards club.
(D) He is a professional public speaker.

有關聽者，說話者提到何事？
(A) 他最近受僱。
(B) 他贏得比賽。
(C) 他是回饋專案的會員。
(D) 他是專業演說家。

- competition (n.) 比賽 reward (n.) 獎勵；獎賞 professional (adj.) 專業的

換句話說 our loyalty program（我們的忠實顧客方案）→ a rewards club（回饋專案）

---

85. 相關細節——說話者提及聽者可以做的事情 難

What does the speaker say the listener can do?
(A) Try out a new offering
(B) Submit a form electronically
(C) Enjoy upgraded accommodations
(D) Participate in a celebration remotely

說話者表示聽者可以做何事？
(A) 試用新的贈品
(B) 以電子方式提交表單
(C) 享受住宿升級
(D) 遠距參加慶祝會

- offering (n.) 禮物　submit (v.) 提交　form (n.) 表格　electronically (adv.) 用電子方式 accommodation (n.) 住宿　participate in . . . 參加……　celebration (n.) 慶祝活動 remotely (adv.) 遠距地

換句話說 suites（套房飯店）→ accommodation（住宿）

86-88 Talk

Thank you all for coming to the McAllister Convention Center's open house. (86) **I hope you've enjoyed the tour of our facilities, and that you might decide to host your next conference or employee retreat here.** We are completely booked up for the next six months, so remember to contact us well in advance. (87) **Let me also remind you that our largest conference room is fully equipped with the latest audio-visual equipment, so we're the ideal venue for any events that rely on the use of advanced technology.** (88) **We also contract with the full-service event-planning agency, A Perfect Night, so we can help your occasion be a huge success.**

86-88 談話 澳

謝謝大家前來參加「麥克艾利瑟」會議中心的開放參觀日，(86) **希望各位喜歡本次設施導覽，也盼望大家未來決定把下場會議或員工休憩之旅辦在這裡。**本中心接下來的六個月，設施都已全部訂滿，因此請記得要早早聯絡我們。(87) **容我向大家重申，本中心最大的會議室備有最新型的全套視聽設備，因此若要舉辦各類要用到先進科技的活動，這裡就是理想地點。** (88) **我們也和提供全方位服務的活動規劃公司「完美夜晚」簽約合作，可以幫助各位的盛會圓滿成功。**

- facility (n.) 設施　host (v.) 主辦　conference (n.) 會議　retreat (n.) 避靜；靜修 in advance 事先；提前　remind (v.) 提醒　equip (v.) 配備　latest (adj.) 最新的　equipment (n.) 設備 venue (n.) 會場　rely on 依賴　advanced (adj.) 先進的　contract (v.) 與……訂合約 agency (n.) 代理商　occasion (n.) 盛會；場合　huge (adj.) 巨大的

86. 全文相關——聽者的身分 難

Who most likely are the listeners?
(A) Company shareholders
(B) Potential clients
(C) Volunteer workers
(D) Safety inspectors

聽者最可能的身分為何？
(A) 公司股東
(B) 潛在客戶
(C) 志工
(D) 安檢人員

---

87. 相關細節——說話者針對會議中心提及的內容

What does the speaker mention about the convention center?

(A) It is the largest venue in the region.

(B) It will be renovated soon.

(C) It is affordable to rent.

(D) It uses modern technology.

關於會議中心，說話者提到何事？

(A) 是當地最大的會場。

(B) 即將進行整修。

(C) 租金實惠。

(D) 使用現代科技。

- region (n.) 地區　renovate (v.) 整修　affordable (adj.) 負擔得起的　rent (v.) 租用　modern (adj.) 現代的

換句話說 latest（最新型的）→ modern（現代的）

88. 相關細節——「完美夜晚」該公司的類型

What type of company is A Perfect Night?

(A) A prepared-meal delivery provider

(B) A chauffeur service

(C) An event organizer

(D) An employment agency

「完美夜晚」屬於何種業者？

(A) 調理食品外送公司

(B) 私人駕駛服務

(C) 活動籌辦公司

(D) 人力仲介

- meal (n.) 一餐　provider (n.) 供應商　chauffeur (n.) 私人司機　organizer (n.)（活動等）籌辦者　employment (n.) 職業

換句話說 event-planning agency（活動規劃公司）→ event organizer（活動籌辦公司）

89-91 Excerpt from a workshop

All right, let's move on to a particularly difficult area—handling customer complaints. (89) **On the screen, you can see the four-step process you should follow when you get a complaint.** First, stay calm, even if the customer is upset. Second, listen well and make sure you understand the problem. Ask questions if needed, but not in a challenging way. Third, acknowledge the problem. (90) **Don't say, "That doesn't sound so bad."** Would you like to hear that? Finally, provide a resolution, such as an apology or refund. (91) **Now, these are skills that are best learned by doing, so let's partner up and act out sample situations.** Take one of these papers with scenario suggestions.

89-91 研習會摘錄 (美)

好的，接著讓我們來討論一個特別棘手的部分：處理客訴。(89) **在螢幕上，各位可以看到在接獲投訴時，應該遵循的四階段程序。**第一，保持冷靜，不要受顧客的脾氣影響。第二，要仔細聆聽、確定你了解問題。如果有需要可以提問，但不要咄咄逼人。第三，要承認問題，(90) **不要說：「聽起來沒那麼嚴重。」**這種話你會想聽嗎？最後，要提供解決方法，例如道歉或退款。(91) **現在，這些技巧最好是要從做中學，所以請大家找好搭檔，練習扮演實境案例。**這裡有些情境提示，來各拿一張吧。

- particularly (adv.) 尤其地　handle (v.) 處理　complaint (n.) 投訴　process (n.) 步驟　challenging (adj.) 挑撥的　acknowledge (v.) 承認　resolution (n.) 解決　apology (n.) 道歉　partner up 成為搭檔　act out 演出……　situation (n.) 情況　scenario (n.) 情節；場景　suggestion (n.) 建議；示意

89. 相關細節——說話者在螢幕上展示的東西

What does the speaker show on a screen?

(A) A list of actions

(B) A customer profile

(C) A set of statistics

(D) A Web page

說話者在螢幕上展示何物？

(A) 一連串行動

(B) 顧客檔案

(C) 統計數字

(D) 網頁

90. 掌握說話者的意圖——提及「這種話你會想聽嗎？」的意圖 難

Why does the speaker say, "Would you like to hear that"?

(A) To confirm that she should set up some audio equipment

(B) To express surprise at the listeners' interest in a story

(C) To make the listeners consider another person's perspective

(D) To indicate that a certain part of the workshop is unpopular

說話者為什麼會說：「這種話你會想聽嗎？」

(A) 以確定她應該準備音響設備

(B) 以表達對於聽者對故事感興趣的驚訝

(C) 以讓聽者考量對方的觀點

(D) 以指出研習的特定部分不受歡迎

- confirm (v.) 確認 set up 設置 equipment (n.) 設備 express (v.) 表達 surprise (n.) 驚訝 perspective (n.) 觀點；角度 indicate (v.) 表明 certain (adj.) 特定的 unpopular (adj.) 不受歡迎的

91. 相關細節——聽者接下來要做的事情

What will the listeners most likely do next?

(A) Take a short break

(B) Vote on a suggestion

(C) Open some packages

(D) Engage in role plays

聽者接下來最可能做什麼？

(A) 休息一下

(B) 表決提議

(C) 拆開包裹

(D) 做角色扮演

- break (n.) 休息 vote (v.) 投票 engage in 參與；參加 role (n.) 角色 play (n.) 演出

換句話說 partner up and act out sample situations（搭檔練習扮演實境案例）
→ engage in role plays（做角色扮演）

92-94 News report

Now, on to our top story in local news. (92) **This is the first day that vehicles will not be allowed to use Fourth Street between Scott Street and Sutter Avenue.** Brilson city council decided to turn that section of the roadway into a pedestrian zone in order to create a pleasant shopping and leisure destination. (93) **If the zone is a success, its northern boundary may eventually be extended up to Bailey Street.** (94) **To prepare citizens for the zone's implementation, the city government erected signs on neighboring streets and hung notices in the affected public buses last month.** For the next few days, however, drivers and bus passengers in the area should expect some difficulties and delays.

92-94 新聞報導 加

現在接著要播報當地新聞頭條：(92) **從即日起，車輛將禁止開進位在史考特街和蘇特大道之間的第四街路段。**布里森市議會已決定將該路段改設為行人徒步區，以期打造舒適的購物與休閒空間。(93) **如果徒步區成效甚佳，後續可能會將範圍往北延伸至貝利街。**(94) **為了讓市民預備徒步區的實施，市政府上個月就已在鄰近街道設立告示，並在受到影響的公車上掛出公告，**然而在接下來幾天，那區域的用路人和公車乘客應該可以想見仍會遇到一些困難和延誤。

- city council 市議會　section (n.) 區域；地段　roadway (n.) 道路；車道　pedestrian (adj.) 步行的　zone (n.) 區域；分區　pleasant (adj.) 宜人的　leisure (adj.) 休閒的　destination (n.) 目的地；終點　northern (adj.) 北方的　boundary (n.) 範圍　eventually (adv.) 最後　extend (v.) 延伸；擴大　citizen (n.) 市民；居民　implementation (n.) 實施　erect (v.) 豎立　neighboring (adj.) 鄰近的　notice (n.) 告示　affect (v.) 影響　passenger (n.) 乘客　expect (v.) 預期

92. 全文相關——新聞報導的主題 難

What is the news report mainly about?
(A) A forthcoming mode of transportation
(B) The banning of automobiles from a street
(C) Some work to improve the quality of a road
(D) The creation of additional parking facilities

這則新聞的主題為何？
(A) 即將啟用的運輸方式
(B) 街道禁止汽車通行
(C) 改善道路品質的工程
(D) 創設更多停車設施

- forthcoming (adj.) 即將發生的　mode (n.) 方法；種類　ban (v.) 禁止　automobile (n.) 汽車　improve (v.) 改善　quality (n.) 品質　creation (n.) 創造　facility (n.) 設施；設備

換句話說 vehicles will not be allowed（車輛將禁止開進）→ the banning of automobiles（禁止汽車通行）

93. 相關細節——說話者針對徒步區提及的內容 難

What does the speaker indicate about a project?
(A) It is intended to reduce environmental damage.
(B) It is opposed by a merchants' association.
(C) Its scope might expand in the future.
(D) It was carried out successfully in other cities.

關於計畫，說話者指出何事？
(A) 意在降低對環境的傷害。
(B) 受到商會的反對。
(C) 範圍未來可能延伸。
(D) 在其他城市實施成功。

- intend (v.) 想要　reduce (v.) 減少　environmental (adj.) 環境的　oppose (v.) 反對　merchant (n.) 商人　association (n.) 協會　scope (n.) 範圍　expand (v.) 擴大　carry out 執行；實行

換句話說 its . . . boundary may . . . be extended（可能會將範圍……延伸）
→ its scope might expand（範圍可能延伸）

94. 相關細節——上個月政府為市民做的事情 難

What did the city government do for citizens in the past month?
(A) Notified them of an upcoming change
(B) Surveyed them about a proposal
(C) Relaxed a local regulation
(D) Held a special public event

市政府上個月為市民做了什麼？
(A) 通知他們即將進行的變動
(B) 調查他們對提案的看法
(C) 放寬當地規定
(D) 舉行特別公開活動

- notify (v.) 通知　upcoming (adj.) 即將來臨的　survey (v.) 調查　proposal (n.) 提案　relax (v.) 放寬　regulation (n.) 規定

95-97 Telephone message + Café layout

95-97 電話留言＋咖啡館平面圖 澳

Hi, my name is Silvio Esposito. (95) **I was at your café this afternoon to network with a professional contact, and I think I left my umbrella behind.** I didn't notice until later because the rain had stopped by the time we left. Did you happen to find it? It's a black umbrella with white trim around the edges, and (96) **I was sitting in the booth closest to the window,** in case that helps. If you do find it, please set it aside behind your counter and let me know. (97) **It was a present from my daughter, so I'd really like to get it back.** My number is 555-0196. Thank you.

嗨，我叫做西維奧・艾波西托，(95) **今天下午有到你們的咖啡館，和一名工作上的友人碰面交流，而現在我發現忘記把傘帶走了**，因為我們離開時雨已經停了，所以我等到後來才發現。你們有看到嗎？雨傘是黑色的，邊緣有白色裝飾，另外，(96) **我當時坐在最靠窗戶的座位隔間**，不知這是否有助尋找。如果你們真的找到了，請收存在櫃檯並通知我，(97) **那把傘是女兒送我的禮物，所以我真的希望能夠取回**。我的電話是 555-0196，感謝你。

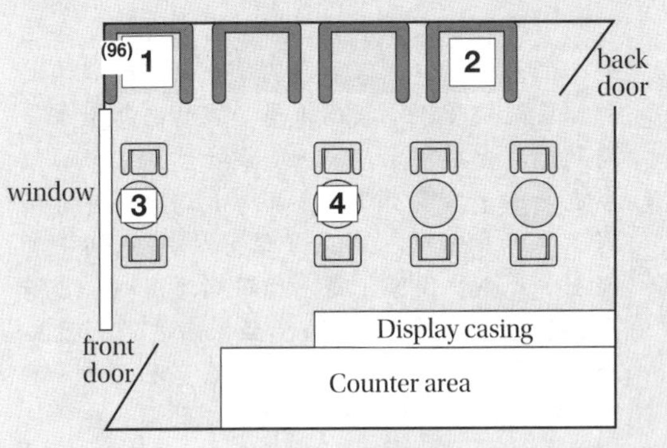

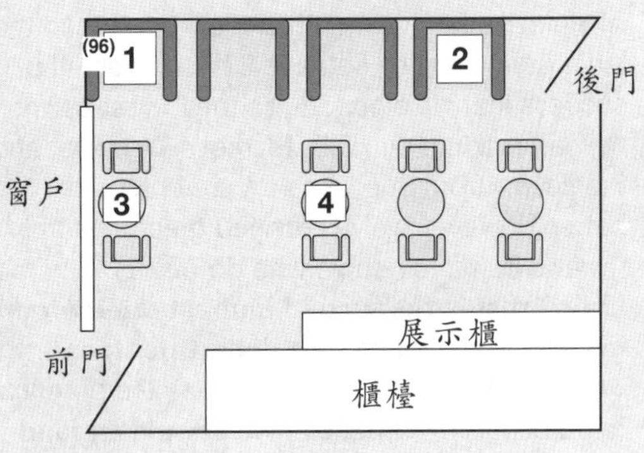

- **network (v.)** 建立人脈　**professional (adj.)** 專業的　**contact (n.)** 聯絡人　**notice (v.)** 注意到
  trim (n.) 裝飾；鑲邊飾　**edge (n.)** 邊緣　**booth (n.)**（隔開的）坐席　**set aside** 把……放在一邊

95. 相關細節——說話者在咖啡館內主要從事的活動 難

What was the speaker mainly doing at the café?

(A) Engaging in a leisure activity

(B) Completing some freelance work

(C) Speaking with a business associate

(D) Studying for a professional exam

說話者在咖啡館主要在做何事？

(A) 參與休閒活動

(B) 完成接案工作

(C) 和生意夥伴談話

(D) 準備專業考試

- **engage in . . .** 參加……　**leisure (adj.)** 休閒的　**associate (n.)** 生意夥伴；同事
  exam (=examination) (n.) 考試

換句話說 **network with a professional contact**（和一名工作上的友人碰面交流）
→ **speaking with a business associate**（和生意夥伴談話）

96. 圖表整合題——說話者坐過的位置

Look at the graphic. At which location was the speaker sitting?

(A) 1

(B) 2

(C) 3

(D) 4

請見圖表作答。說話者先前坐在哪個位置？

(A) 1

(B) 2

(C) 3

(D) 4

97. 相關細節——說話者提到與雨傘有關的敘述

What does the speaker say about the umbrella?
(A) It was expensive.
(B) It was a gift.
(C) Its design is unique.
(D) It belongs to a relative.

關於雨傘，說話者提及何事？
(A) 價格昂貴。
(B) 是件禮物。
(C) 設計很獨特。
(D) 物主為親戚。

- expensive (adj.) 昂貴的　unique (adj.) 獨特的　belong to . . . 屬於……

換句話說 a present（禮物）→ a gift（禮物）

98-100 Excerpt from a meeting + Chart

All right, it's been a month since we released the Little Artist painting set, and it hasn't been the success that we'd hoped. It's the lowest-selling new art product on Hall's Market's Web site, and the figures from Success Arts are only a little better. However, we've received great customer reviews from the people who do buy it. (98) **In fact, Little Artist is the second highest rated product in Delta Mall Online's art department, and third on Creative Ideas.** So clearly it has the potential to be popular. (99) **I believe we should expand our advertising campaign for it.** (100) **Jenny, how much money do we have available to put towards that?** You know our budget the best.

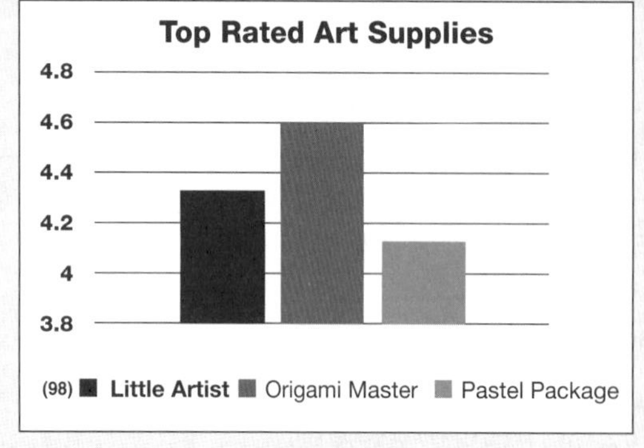

98-100 會議摘錄＋圖表 英

好的，我們推出「小藝術家」繪畫套組至今已經一個月了，但並未如我們原先希望的那樣大賣，反而銷量在「霍爾市集」網站的新上市藝術類產品中敬陪末座，而「成功美術」上的數字也是五十步笑百步。然而，我們從確實有購買產品的顧客中，得到了很好的評價。(98) **實際上，「小藝術家」是「德塔網路商城」藝術商品區中評價第二高的產品，而在「創意點子」則是評價第三名，**所以顯然有潛力熱賣。(99) **我相信，我們應該擴大該套組的廣告宣傳。**(100) **珍妮，我們現在有多少資金可以用來投入廣告呢？**妳最了解我們的預算。

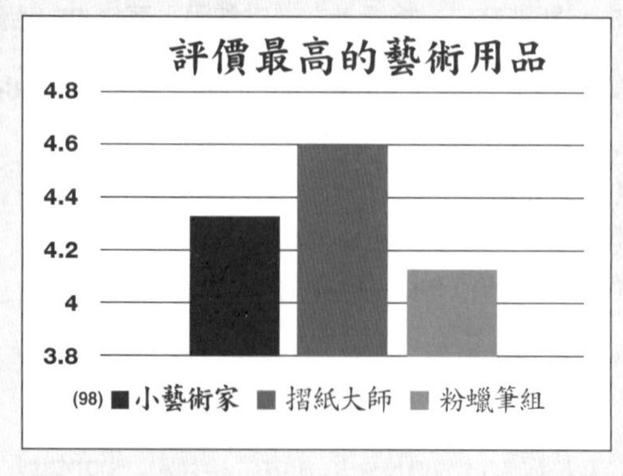

- release (v.) 推出　figure (n.) 數字　in fact 事實上　rate (v.) 評價　department (n.) 部門　clearly (adv.) 顯然地　potential (n.) 潛力　expand (v.) 擴大　advertising campaign 廣告活動　available (adj.) 可用的　budget (n.) 預算

98. 圖表整合題——該圖表所屬的網站 難

Look at the graphic. What Web site is the chart for?
(A) Hall's Market
(B) Success Arts
(C) Delta Mall Online
(D) Creative Ideas

請見圖表作答。此圖表用於哪個網站？
(A) 霍爾市集
(B) 成功美術
(C) 德塔網路商城
(D) 創意點子

99. 相關細節——說話者提出的建議 難

What does the speaker propose doing?
(A) Hiring a consulting firm
(B) Expanding a product line
(C) Renegotiating a contract
(D) Increasing a promotional effort

說話者提議做何事？
(A) 聘請顧問公司
(B) 擴大產品線
(C) 重新協商合約
(D) 加強促銷

- **consult (v.)** 諮詢　**firm (n.)** 公司　**renegotiate (v.)** 重新談判　**increase (v.)** 增加　**promotional (adj.)** 促銷的　**effort (n.)** 努力

換句話說 expand our advertising campaign（擴大廣告宣傳）
→ increasing a promotional effort（加強促銷）

---

100. 相關細節——說話者詢問珍妮的事情

What does the speaker ask Jenny about?
(A) Some financial resources
(B) Some employees' availability
(C) A manufacturing process
(D) A competitor's practices

說話者詢問珍妮何事？
(A) 財務資源
(B) 員工是否有空
(C) 製造流程
(D) 競爭同業的業務

- **financial (adj.)** 財務的　**resource (n.)** 資源　**availability (n.)** 可得性　**manufacture (v.)** 製造　**process (n.)** 過程　**competitor (n.)** 競爭對手　**practice (n.)** 工作；業務

換句話說 money（資金）→ some financial resources（財務資源）

分數對照表

聽力測驗

答對題數	分數
96-100	480-495
91-95	435-490
86-90	395-450
81-85	355-415
76-80	325-375
71-75	295-340
66-70	265-315
61-65	240-285
56-60	215-260
51-55	190-235
46-50	160-210
41-45	135-180
36-40	110-155
31-35	85-130
26-30	70-105
21-25	50-90
16-20	35-70
11-15	20-55
6-10	15-40
1-5	5-20
0	5

閱讀測驗

答對題數	分數
96-100	460-495
91-95	410-475
86-90	380-430
81-85	355-400
76-80	325-375
71-75	295-345
66-70	265-315
61-65	235-285
56-60	205-255
51-55	175-225
46-50	150-195
41-45	120-170
36-40	100-140
31-35	75-120
26-30	55-100
21-25	40-80
16-20	30-65
11-15	20-50
6-10	15-35
1-5	5-20
0	5

◆ 以上換算表是依據本書收錄的試題訂定，建議使用該表格，推算自己取得的分數。舉例來說，若聽力部分答對 61 至 65 題，對應分數會落在 240 至 285 區間。計分方式並非答對題數為 61 題，對應分數就是 240 分、或是答對題數為 65 題，對應分數就是 285 分。**請注意，本換算表僅用於幫助考生判斷自己的英語實力大致落在哪個區間，並不適用於實際多益測驗成績換算。**

答案紙

ACTUAL TEST 01

LISTENING SECTION																				
	1	Ⓐ Ⓑ Ⓒ Ⓓ	11	Ⓐ Ⓑ Ⓒ Ⓓ	21	Ⓐ Ⓑ Ⓒ Ⓓ	31	Ⓐ Ⓑ Ⓒ Ⓓ	41	Ⓐ Ⓑ Ⓒ Ⓓ	51	Ⓐ Ⓑ Ⓒ Ⓓ	61	Ⓐ Ⓑ Ⓒ Ⓓ	71	Ⓐ Ⓑ Ⓒ Ⓓ	81	Ⓐ Ⓑ Ⓒ Ⓓ	91	Ⓐ Ⓑ Ⓒ Ⓓ
	2	Ⓐ Ⓑ Ⓒ Ⓓ	12	Ⓐ Ⓑ Ⓒ Ⓓ	22	Ⓐ Ⓑ Ⓒ Ⓓ	32	Ⓐ Ⓑ Ⓒ Ⓓ	42	Ⓐ Ⓑ Ⓒ Ⓓ	52	Ⓐ Ⓑ Ⓒ Ⓓ	62	Ⓐ Ⓑ Ⓒ Ⓓ	72	Ⓐ Ⓑ Ⓒ Ⓓ	82	Ⓐ Ⓑ Ⓒ Ⓓ	92	Ⓐ Ⓑ Ⓒ Ⓓ
	3	Ⓐ Ⓑ Ⓒ Ⓓ	13	Ⓐ Ⓑ Ⓒ Ⓓ	23	Ⓐ Ⓑ Ⓒ Ⓓ	33	Ⓐ Ⓑ Ⓒ Ⓓ	43	Ⓐ Ⓑ Ⓒ Ⓓ	53	Ⓐ Ⓑ Ⓒ Ⓓ	63	Ⓐ Ⓑ Ⓒ Ⓓ	73	Ⓐ Ⓑ Ⓒ Ⓓ	83	Ⓐ Ⓑ Ⓒ Ⓓ	93	Ⓐ Ⓑ Ⓒ Ⓓ
	4	Ⓐ Ⓑ Ⓒ Ⓓ	14	Ⓐ Ⓑ Ⓒ Ⓓ	24	Ⓐ Ⓑ Ⓒ Ⓓ	34	Ⓐ Ⓑ Ⓒ Ⓓ	44	Ⓐ Ⓑ Ⓒ Ⓓ	54	Ⓐ Ⓑ Ⓒ Ⓓ	64	Ⓐ Ⓑ Ⓒ Ⓓ	74	Ⓐ Ⓑ Ⓒ Ⓓ	84	Ⓐ Ⓑ Ⓒ Ⓓ	94	Ⓐ Ⓑ Ⓒ Ⓓ
	5	Ⓐ Ⓑ Ⓒ Ⓓ	15	Ⓐ Ⓑ Ⓒ Ⓓ	25	Ⓐ Ⓑ Ⓒ Ⓓ	35	Ⓐ Ⓑ Ⓒ Ⓓ	45	Ⓐ Ⓑ Ⓒ Ⓓ	55	Ⓐ Ⓑ Ⓒ Ⓓ	65	Ⓐ Ⓑ Ⓒ Ⓓ	75	Ⓐ Ⓑ Ⓒ Ⓓ	85	Ⓐ Ⓑ Ⓒ Ⓓ	95	Ⓐ Ⓑ Ⓒ Ⓓ
	6	Ⓐ Ⓑ Ⓒ Ⓓ	16	Ⓐ Ⓑ Ⓒ Ⓓ	26	Ⓐ Ⓑ Ⓒ Ⓓ	36	Ⓐ Ⓑ Ⓒ Ⓓ	46	Ⓐ Ⓑ Ⓒ Ⓓ	56	Ⓐ Ⓑ Ⓒ Ⓓ	66	Ⓐ Ⓑ Ⓒ Ⓓ	76	Ⓐ Ⓑ Ⓒ Ⓓ	86	Ⓐ Ⓑ Ⓒ Ⓓ	96	Ⓐ Ⓑ Ⓒ Ⓓ
	7	Ⓐ Ⓑ Ⓒ Ⓓ	17	Ⓐ Ⓑ Ⓒ Ⓓ	27	Ⓐ Ⓑ Ⓒ Ⓓ	37	Ⓐ Ⓑ Ⓒ Ⓓ	47	Ⓐ Ⓑ Ⓒ Ⓓ	57	Ⓐ Ⓑ Ⓒ Ⓓ	67	Ⓐ Ⓑ Ⓒ Ⓓ	77	Ⓐ Ⓑ Ⓒ Ⓓ	87	Ⓐ Ⓑ Ⓒ Ⓓ	97	Ⓐ Ⓑ Ⓒ Ⓓ
	8	Ⓐ Ⓑ Ⓒ Ⓓ	18	Ⓐ Ⓑ Ⓒ Ⓓ	28	Ⓐ Ⓑ Ⓒ Ⓓ	38	Ⓐ Ⓑ Ⓒ Ⓓ	48	Ⓐ Ⓑ Ⓒ Ⓓ	58	Ⓐ Ⓑ Ⓒ Ⓓ	68	Ⓐ Ⓑ Ⓒ Ⓓ	78	Ⓐ Ⓑ Ⓒ Ⓓ	88	Ⓐ Ⓑ Ⓒ Ⓓ	98	Ⓐ Ⓑ Ⓒ Ⓓ
	9	Ⓐ Ⓑ Ⓒ Ⓓ	19	Ⓐ Ⓑ Ⓒ Ⓓ	29	Ⓐ Ⓑ Ⓒ Ⓓ	39	Ⓐ Ⓑ Ⓒ Ⓓ	49	Ⓐ Ⓑ Ⓒ Ⓓ	59	Ⓐ Ⓑ Ⓒ Ⓓ	69	Ⓐ Ⓑ Ⓒ Ⓓ	79	Ⓐ Ⓑ Ⓒ Ⓓ	89	Ⓐ Ⓑ Ⓒ Ⓓ	99	Ⓐ Ⓑ Ⓒ Ⓓ
	10	Ⓐ Ⓑ Ⓒ Ⓓ	20	Ⓐ Ⓑ Ⓒ Ⓓ	30	Ⓐ Ⓑ Ⓒ Ⓓ	40	Ⓐ Ⓑ Ⓒ Ⓓ	50	Ⓐ Ⓑ Ⓒ Ⓓ	60	Ⓐ Ⓑ Ⓒ Ⓓ	70	Ⓐ Ⓑ Ⓒ Ⓓ	80	Ⓐ Ⓑ Ⓒ Ⓓ	90	Ⓐ Ⓑ Ⓒ Ⓓ	100	Ⓐ Ⓑ Ⓒ Ⓓ

ACTUAL TEST 02

LISTENING SECTION																				
	1	Ⓐ Ⓑ Ⓒ Ⓓ	11	Ⓐ Ⓑ Ⓒ Ⓓ	21	Ⓐ Ⓑ Ⓒ Ⓓ	31	Ⓐ Ⓑ Ⓒ Ⓓ	41	Ⓐ Ⓑ Ⓒ Ⓓ	51	Ⓐ Ⓑ Ⓒ Ⓓ	61	Ⓐ Ⓑ Ⓒ Ⓓ	71	Ⓐ Ⓑ Ⓒ Ⓓ	81	Ⓐ Ⓑ Ⓒ Ⓓ	91	Ⓐ Ⓑ Ⓒ Ⓓ
	2	Ⓐ Ⓑ Ⓒ Ⓓ	12	Ⓐ Ⓑ Ⓒ Ⓓ	22	Ⓐ Ⓑ Ⓒ Ⓓ	32	Ⓐ Ⓑ Ⓒ Ⓓ	42	Ⓐ Ⓑ Ⓒ Ⓓ	52	Ⓐ Ⓑ Ⓒ Ⓓ	62	Ⓐ Ⓑ Ⓒ Ⓓ	72	Ⓐ Ⓑ Ⓒ Ⓓ	82	Ⓐ Ⓑ Ⓒ Ⓓ	92	Ⓐ Ⓑ Ⓒ Ⓓ
	3	Ⓐ Ⓑ Ⓒ Ⓓ	13	Ⓐ Ⓑ Ⓒ Ⓓ	23	Ⓐ Ⓑ Ⓒ Ⓓ	33	Ⓐ Ⓑ Ⓒ Ⓓ	43	Ⓐ Ⓑ Ⓒ Ⓓ	53	Ⓐ Ⓑ Ⓒ Ⓓ	63	Ⓐ Ⓑ Ⓒ Ⓓ	73	Ⓐ Ⓑ Ⓒ Ⓓ	83	Ⓐ Ⓑ Ⓒ Ⓓ	93	Ⓐ Ⓑ Ⓒ Ⓓ
	4	Ⓐ Ⓑ Ⓒ Ⓓ	14	Ⓐ Ⓑ Ⓒ Ⓓ	24	Ⓐ Ⓑ Ⓒ Ⓓ	34	Ⓐ Ⓑ Ⓒ Ⓓ	44	Ⓐ Ⓑ Ⓒ Ⓓ	54	Ⓐ Ⓑ Ⓒ Ⓓ	64	Ⓐ Ⓑ Ⓒ Ⓓ	74	Ⓐ Ⓑ Ⓒ Ⓓ	84	Ⓐ Ⓑ Ⓒ Ⓓ	94	Ⓐ Ⓑ Ⓒ Ⓓ
	5	Ⓐ Ⓑ Ⓒ Ⓓ	15	Ⓐ Ⓑ Ⓒ Ⓓ	25	Ⓐ Ⓑ Ⓒ Ⓓ	35	Ⓐ Ⓑ Ⓒ Ⓓ	45	Ⓐ Ⓑ Ⓒ Ⓓ	55	Ⓐ Ⓑ Ⓒ Ⓓ	65	Ⓐ Ⓑ Ⓒ Ⓓ	75	Ⓐ Ⓑ Ⓒ Ⓓ	85	Ⓐ Ⓑ Ⓒ Ⓓ	95	Ⓐ Ⓑ Ⓒ Ⓓ
	6	Ⓐ Ⓑ Ⓒ Ⓓ	16	Ⓐ Ⓑ Ⓒ Ⓓ	26	Ⓐ Ⓑ Ⓒ Ⓓ	36	Ⓐ Ⓑ Ⓒ Ⓓ	46	Ⓐ Ⓑ Ⓒ Ⓓ	56	Ⓐ Ⓑ Ⓒ Ⓓ	66	Ⓐ Ⓑ Ⓒ Ⓓ	76	Ⓐ Ⓑ Ⓒ Ⓓ	86	Ⓐ Ⓑ Ⓒ Ⓓ	96	Ⓐ Ⓑ Ⓒ Ⓓ
	7	Ⓐ Ⓑ Ⓒ Ⓓ	17	Ⓐ Ⓑ Ⓒ Ⓓ	27	Ⓐ Ⓑ Ⓒ Ⓓ	37	Ⓐ Ⓑ Ⓒ Ⓓ	47	Ⓐ Ⓑ Ⓒ Ⓓ	57	Ⓐ Ⓑ Ⓒ Ⓓ	67	Ⓐ Ⓑ Ⓒ Ⓓ	77	Ⓐ Ⓑ Ⓒ Ⓓ	87	Ⓐ Ⓑ Ⓒ Ⓓ	97	Ⓐ Ⓑ Ⓒ Ⓓ
	8	Ⓐ Ⓑ Ⓒ Ⓓ	18	Ⓐ Ⓑ Ⓒ Ⓓ	28	Ⓐ Ⓑ Ⓒ Ⓓ	38	Ⓐ Ⓑ Ⓒ Ⓓ	48	Ⓐ Ⓑ Ⓒ Ⓓ	58	Ⓐ Ⓑ Ⓒ Ⓓ	68	Ⓐ Ⓑ Ⓒ Ⓓ	78	Ⓐ Ⓑ Ⓒ Ⓓ	88	Ⓐ Ⓑ Ⓒ Ⓓ	98	Ⓐ Ⓑ Ⓒ Ⓓ
	9	Ⓐ Ⓑ Ⓒ Ⓓ	19	Ⓐ Ⓑ Ⓒ Ⓓ	29	Ⓐ Ⓑ Ⓒ Ⓓ	39	Ⓐ Ⓑ Ⓒ Ⓓ	49	Ⓐ Ⓑ Ⓒ Ⓓ	59	Ⓐ Ⓑ Ⓒ Ⓓ	69	Ⓐ Ⓑ Ⓒ Ⓓ	79	Ⓐ Ⓑ Ⓒ Ⓓ	89	Ⓐ Ⓑ Ⓒ Ⓓ	99	Ⓐ Ⓑ Ⓒ Ⓓ
	10	Ⓐ Ⓑ Ⓒ Ⓓ	20	Ⓐ Ⓑ Ⓒ Ⓓ	30	Ⓐ Ⓑ Ⓒ Ⓓ	40	Ⓐ Ⓑ Ⓒ Ⓓ	50	Ⓐ Ⓑ Ⓒ Ⓓ	60	Ⓐ Ⓑ Ⓒ Ⓓ	70	Ⓐ Ⓑ Ⓒ Ⓓ	80	Ⓐ Ⓑ Ⓒ Ⓓ	90	Ⓐ Ⓑ Ⓒ Ⓓ	100	Ⓐ Ⓑ Ⓒ Ⓓ

答案紙

ACTUAL TEST 03

LISTENING SECTION																			
1	Ⓐ Ⓑ Ⓒ Ⓓ	11	Ⓐ Ⓑ Ⓒ Ⓓ	21	Ⓐ Ⓑ Ⓒ Ⓓ	31	Ⓐ Ⓑ Ⓒ Ⓓ	41	Ⓐ Ⓑ Ⓒ Ⓓ	51	Ⓐ Ⓑ Ⓒ Ⓓ	61	Ⓐ Ⓑ Ⓒ Ⓓ	71	Ⓐ Ⓑ Ⓒ Ⓓ	81	Ⓐ Ⓑ Ⓒ Ⓓ	91	Ⓐ Ⓑ Ⓒ Ⓓ
2	Ⓐ Ⓑ Ⓒ Ⓓ	12	Ⓐ Ⓑ Ⓒ Ⓓ	22	Ⓐ Ⓑ Ⓒ Ⓓ	32	Ⓐ Ⓑ Ⓒ Ⓓ	42	Ⓐ Ⓑ Ⓒ Ⓓ	52	Ⓐ Ⓑ Ⓒ Ⓓ	62	Ⓐ Ⓑ Ⓒ Ⓓ	72	Ⓐ Ⓑ Ⓒ Ⓓ	82	Ⓐ Ⓑ Ⓒ Ⓓ	92	Ⓐ Ⓑ Ⓒ Ⓓ
3	Ⓐ Ⓑ Ⓒ Ⓓ	13	Ⓐ Ⓑ Ⓒ Ⓓ	23	Ⓐ Ⓑ Ⓒ Ⓓ	33	Ⓐ Ⓑ Ⓒ Ⓓ	43	Ⓐ Ⓑ Ⓒ Ⓓ	53	Ⓐ Ⓑ Ⓒ Ⓓ	63	Ⓐ Ⓑ Ⓒ Ⓓ	73	Ⓐ Ⓑ Ⓒ Ⓓ	83	Ⓐ Ⓑ Ⓒ Ⓓ	93	Ⓐ Ⓑ Ⓒ Ⓓ
4	Ⓐ Ⓑ Ⓒ Ⓓ	14	Ⓐ Ⓑ Ⓒ Ⓓ	24	Ⓐ Ⓑ Ⓒ Ⓓ	34	Ⓐ Ⓑ Ⓒ Ⓓ	44	Ⓐ Ⓑ Ⓒ Ⓓ	54	Ⓐ Ⓑ Ⓒ Ⓓ	64	Ⓐ Ⓑ Ⓒ Ⓓ	74	Ⓐ Ⓑ Ⓒ Ⓓ	84	Ⓐ Ⓑ Ⓒ Ⓓ	94	Ⓐ Ⓑ Ⓒ Ⓓ
5	Ⓐ Ⓑ Ⓒ Ⓓ	15	Ⓐ Ⓑ Ⓒ Ⓓ	25	Ⓐ Ⓑ Ⓒ Ⓓ	35	Ⓐ Ⓑ Ⓒ Ⓓ	45	Ⓐ Ⓑ Ⓒ Ⓓ	55	Ⓐ Ⓑ Ⓒ Ⓓ	65	Ⓐ Ⓑ Ⓒ Ⓓ	75	Ⓐ Ⓑ Ⓒ Ⓓ	85	Ⓐ Ⓑ Ⓒ Ⓓ	95	Ⓐ Ⓑ Ⓒ Ⓓ
6	Ⓐ Ⓑ Ⓒ Ⓓ	16	Ⓐ Ⓑ Ⓒ Ⓓ	26	Ⓐ Ⓑ Ⓒ Ⓓ	36	Ⓐ Ⓑ Ⓒ Ⓓ	46	Ⓐ Ⓑ Ⓒ Ⓓ	56	Ⓐ Ⓑ Ⓒ Ⓓ	66	Ⓐ Ⓑ Ⓒ Ⓓ	76	Ⓐ Ⓑ Ⓒ Ⓓ	86	Ⓐ Ⓑ Ⓒ Ⓓ	96	Ⓐ Ⓑ Ⓒ Ⓓ
7	Ⓐ Ⓑ Ⓒ Ⓓ	17	Ⓐ Ⓑ Ⓒ Ⓓ	27	Ⓐ Ⓑ Ⓒ Ⓓ	37	Ⓐ Ⓑ Ⓒ Ⓓ	47	Ⓐ Ⓑ Ⓒ Ⓓ	57	Ⓐ Ⓑ Ⓒ Ⓓ	67	Ⓐ Ⓑ Ⓒ Ⓓ	77	Ⓐ Ⓑ Ⓒ Ⓓ	87	Ⓐ Ⓑ Ⓒ Ⓓ	97	Ⓐ Ⓑ Ⓒ Ⓓ
8	Ⓐ Ⓑ Ⓒ Ⓓ	18	Ⓐ Ⓑ Ⓒ Ⓓ	28	Ⓐ Ⓑ Ⓒ Ⓓ	38	Ⓐ Ⓑ Ⓒ Ⓓ	48	Ⓐ Ⓑ Ⓒ Ⓓ	58	Ⓐ Ⓑ Ⓒ Ⓓ	68	Ⓐ Ⓑ Ⓒ Ⓓ	78	Ⓐ Ⓑ Ⓒ Ⓓ	88	Ⓐ Ⓑ Ⓒ Ⓓ	98	Ⓐ Ⓑ Ⓒ Ⓓ
9	Ⓐ Ⓑ Ⓒ Ⓓ	19	Ⓐ Ⓑ Ⓒ Ⓓ	29	Ⓐ Ⓑ Ⓒ Ⓓ	39	Ⓐ Ⓑ Ⓒ Ⓓ	49	Ⓐ Ⓑ Ⓒ Ⓓ	59	Ⓐ Ⓑ Ⓒ Ⓓ	69	Ⓐ Ⓑ Ⓒ Ⓓ	79	Ⓐ Ⓑ Ⓒ Ⓓ	89	Ⓐ Ⓑ Ⓒ Ⓓ	99	Ⓐ Ⓑ Ⓒ Ⓓ
10	Ⓐ Ⓑ Ⓒ Ⓓ	20	Ⓐ Ⓑ Ⓒ Ⓓ	30	Ⓐ Ⓑ Ⓒ Ⓓ	40	Ⓐ Ⓑ Ⓒ Ⓓ	50	Ⓐ Ⓑ Ⓒ Ⓓ	60	Ⓐ Ⓑ Ⓒ Ⓓ	70	Ⓐ Ⓑ Ⓒ Ⓓ	80	Ⓐ Ⓑ Ⓒ Ⓓ	90	Ⓐ Ⓑ Ⓒ Ⓓ	100	Ⓐ Ⓑ Ⓒ Ⓓ

ACTUAL TEST 04

LISTENING SECTION																			
1	Ⓐ Ⓑ Ⓒ Ⓓ	11	Ⓐ Ⓑ Ⓒ Ⓓ	21	Ⓐ Ⓑ Ⓒ Ⓓ	31	Ⓐ Ⓑ Ⓒ Ⓓ	41	Ⓐ Ⓑ Ⓒ Ⓓ	51	Ⓐ Ⓑ Ⓒ Ⓓ	61	Ⓐ Ⓑ Ⓒ Ⓓ	71	Ⓐ Ⓑ Ⓒ Ⓓ	81	Ⓐ Ⓑ Ⓒ Ⓓ	91	Ⓐ Ⓑ Ⓒ Ⓓ
2	Ⓐ Ⓑ Ⓒ Ⓓ	12	Ⓐ Ⓑ Ⓒ Ⓓ	22	Ⓐ Ⓑ Ⓒ Ⓓ	32	Ⓐ Ⓑ Ⓒ Ⓓ	42	Ⓐ Ⓑ Ⓒ Ⓓ	52	Ⓐ Ⓑ Ⓒ Ⓓ	62	Ⓐ Ⓑ Ⓒ Ⓓ	72	Ⓐ Ⓑ Ⓒ Ⓓ	82	Ⓐ Ⓑ Ⓒ Ⓓ	92	Ⓐ Ⓑ Ⓒ Ⓓ
3	Ⓐ Ⓑ Ⓒ Ⓓ	13	Ⓐ Ⓑ Ⓒ Ⓓ	23	Ⓐ Ⓑ Ⓒ Ⓓ	33	Ⓐ Ⓑ Ⓒ Ⓓ	43	Ⓐ Ⓑ Ⓒ Ⓓ	53	Ⓐ Ⓑ Ⓒ Ⓓ	63	Ⓐ Ⓑ Ⓒ Ⓓ	73	Ⓐ Ⓑ Ⓒ Ⓓ	83	Ⓐ Ⓑ Ⓒ Ⓓ	93	Ⓐ Ⓑ Ⓒ Ⓓ
4	Ⓐ Ⓑ Ⓒ Ⓓ	14	Ⓐ Ⓑ Ⓒ Ⓓ	24	Ⓐ Ⓑ Ⓒ Ⓓ	34	Ⓐ Ⓑ Ⓒ Ⓓ	44	Ⓐ Ⓑ Ⓒ Ⓓ	54	Ⓐ Ⓑ Ⓒ Ⓓ	64	Ⓐ Ⓑ Ⓒ Ⓓ	74	Ⓐ Ⓑ Ⓒ Ⓓ	84	Ⓐ Ⓑ Ⓒ Ⓓ	94	Ⓐ Ⓑ Ⓒ Ⓓ
5	Ⓐ Ⓑ Ⓒ Ⓓ	15	Ⓐ Ⓑ Ⓒ Ⓓ	25	Ⓐ Ⓑ Ⓒ Ⓓ	35	Ⓐ Ⓑ Ⓒ Ⓓ	45	Ⓐ Ⓑ Ⓒ Ⓓ	55	Ⓐ Ⓑ Ⓒ Ⓓ	65	Ⓐ Ⓑ Ⓒ Ⓓ	75	Ⓐ Ⓑ Ⓒ Ⓓ	85	Ⓐ Ⓑ Ⓒ Ⓓ	95	Ⓐ Ⓑ Ⓒ Ⓓ
6	Ⓐ Ⓑ Ⓒ Ⓓ	16	Ⓐ Ⓑ Ⓒ Ⓓ	26	Ⓐ Ⓑ Ⓒ Ⓓ	36	Ⓐ Ⓑ Ⓒ Ⓓ	46	Ⓐ Ⓑ Ⓒ Ⓓ	56	Ⓐ Ⓑ Ⓒ Ⓓ	66	Ⓐ Ⓑ Ⓒ Ⓓ	76	Ⓐ Ⓑ Ⓒ Ⓓ	86	Ⓐ Ⓑ Ⓒ Ⓓ	96	Ⓐ Ⓑ Ⓒ Ⓓ
7	Ⓐ Ⓑ Ⓒ Ⓓ	17	Ⓐ Ⓑ Ⓒ Ⓓ	27	Ⓐ Ⓑ Ⓒ Ⓓ	37	Ⓐ Ⓑ Ⓒ Ⓓ	47	Ⓐ Ⓑ Ⓒ Ⓓ	57	Ⓐ Ⓑ Ⓒ Ⓓ	67	Ⓐ Ⓑ Ⓒ Ⓓ	77	Ⓐ Ⓑ Ⓒ Ⓓ	87	Ⓐ Ⓑ Ⓒ Ⓓ	97	Ⓐ Ⓑ Ⓒ Ⓓ
8	Ⓐ Ⓑ Ⓒ Ⓓ	18	Ⓐ Ⓑ Ⓒ Ⓓ	28	Ⓐ Ⓑ Ⓒ Ⓓ	38	Ⓐ Ⓑ Ⓒ Ⓓ	48	Ⓐ Ⓑ Ⓒ Ⓓ	58	Ⓐ Ⓑ Ⓒ Ⓓ	68	Ⓐ Ⓑ Ⓒ Ⓓ	78	Ⓐ Ⓑ Ⓒ Ⓓ	88	Ⓐ Ⓑ Ⓒ Ⓓ	98	Ⓐ Ⓑ Ⓒ Ⓓ
9	Ⓐ Ⓑ Ⓒ Ⓓ	19	Ⓐ Ⓑ Ⓒ Ⓓ	29	Ⓐ Ⓑ Ⓒ Ⓓ	39	Ⓐ Ⓑ Ⓒ Ⓓ	49	Ⓐ Ⓑ Ⓒ Ⓓ	59	Ⓐ Ⓑ Ⓒ Ⓓ	69	Ⓐ Ⓑ Ⓒ Ⓓ	79	Ⓐ Ⓑ Ⓒ Ⓓ	89	Ⓐ Ⓑ Ⓒ Ⓓ	99	Ⓐ Ⓑ Ⓒ Ⓓ
10	Ⓐ Ⓑ Ⓒ Ⓓ	20	Ⓐ Ⓑ Ⓒ Ⓓ	30	Ⓐ Ⓑ Ⓒ Ⓓ	40	Ⓐ Ⓑ Ⓒ Ⓓ	50	Ⓐ Ⓑ Ⓒ Ⓓ	60	Ⓐ Ⓑ Ⓒ Ⓓ	70	Ⓐ Ⓑ Ⓒ Ⓓ	80	Ⓐ Ⓑ Ⓒ Ⓓ	90	Ⓐ Ⓑ Ⓒ Ⓓ	100	Ⓐ Ⓑ Ⓒ Ⓓ

答案紙

ACTUAL TEST 05

LISTENING SECTION																				
	1	Ⓐ Ⓑ Ⓒ Ⓓ	11	Ⓐ Ⓑ Ⓒ Ⓓ	21	Ⓐ Ⓑ Ⓒ Ⓓ	31	Ⓐ Ⓑ Ⓒ Ⓓ	41	Ⓐ Ⓑ Ⓒ Ⓓ	51	Ⓐ Ⓑ Ⓒ Ⓓ	61	Ⓐ Ⓑ Ⓒ Ⓓ	71	Ⓐ Ⓑ Ⓒ Ⓓ	81	Ⓐ Ⓑ Ⓒ Ⓓ	91	Ⓐ Ⓑ Ⓒ Ⓓ
	2	Ⓐ Ⓑ Ⓒ Ⓓ	12	Ⓐ Ⓑ Ⓒ Ⓓ	22	Ⓐ Ⓑ Ⓒ Ⓓ	32	Ⓐ Ⓑ Ⓒ Ⓓ	42	Ⓐ Ⓑ Ⓒ Ⓓ	52	Ⓐ Ⓑ Ⓒ Ⓓ	62	Ⓐ Ⓑ Ⓒ Ⓓ	72	Ⓐ Ⓑ Ⓒ Ⓓ	82	Ⓐ Ⓑ Ⓒ Ⓓ	92	Ⓐ Ⓑ Ⓒ Ⓓ
	3	Ⓐ Ⓑ Ⓒ Ⓓ	13	Ⓐ Ⓑ Ⓒ Ⓓ	23	Ⓐ Ⓑ Ⓒ Ⓓ	33	Ⓐ Ⓑ Ⓒ Ⓓ	43	Ⓐ Ⓑ Ⓒ Ⓓ	53	Ⓐ Ⓑ Ⓒ Ⓓ	63	Ⓐ Ⓑ Ⓒ Ⓓ	73	Ⓐ Ⓑ Ⓒ Ⓓ	83	Ⓐ Ⓑ Ⓒ Ⓓ	93	Ⓐ Ⓑ Ⓒ Ⓓ
	4	Ⓐ Ⓑ Ⓒ Ⓓ	14	Ⓐ Ⓑ Ⓒ Ⓓ	24	Ⓐ Ⓑ Ⓒ Ⓓ	34	Ⓐ Ⓑ Ⓒ Ⓓ	44	Ⓐ Ⓑ Ⓒ Ⓓ	54	Ⓐ Ⓑ Ⓒ Ⓓ	64	Ⓐ Ⓑ Ⓒ Ⓓ	74	Ⓐ Ⓑ Ⓒ Ⓓ	84	Ⓐ Ⓑ Ⓒ Ⓓ	94	Ⓐ Ⓑ Ⓒ Ⓓ
	5	Ⓐ Ⓑ Ⓒ Ⓓ	15	Ⓐ Ⓑ Ⓒ Ⓓ	25	Ⓐ Ⓑ Ⓒ Ⓓ	35	Ⓐ Ⓑ Ⓒ Ⓓ	45	Ⓐ Ⓑ Ⓒ Ⓓ	55	Ⓐ Ⓑ Ⓒ Ⓓ	65	Ⓐ Ⓑ Ⓒ Ⓓ	75	Ⓐ Ⓑ Ⓒ Ⓓ	85	Ⓐ Ⓑ Ⓒ Ⓓ	95	Ⓐ Ⓑ Ⓒ Ⓓ
	6	Ⓐ Ⓑ Ⓒ Ⓓ	16	Ⓐ Ⓑ Ⓒ Ⓓ	26	Ⓐ Ⓑ Ⓒ Ⓓ	36	Ⓐ Ⓑ Ⓒ Ⓓ	46	Ⓐ Ⓑ Ⓒ Ⓓ	56	Ⓐ Ⓑ Ⓒ Ⓓ	66	Ⓐ Ⓑ Ⓒ Ⓓ	76	Ⓐ Ⓑ Ⓒ Ⓓ	86	Ⓐ Ⓑ Ⓒ Ⓓ	96	Ⓐ Ⓑ Ⓒ Ⓓ
	7	Ⓐ Ⓑ Ⓒ Ⓓ	17	Ⓐ Ⓑ Ⓒ Ⓓ	27	Ⓐ Ⓑ Ⓒ Ⓓ	37	Ⓐ Ⓑ Ⓒ Ⓓ	47	Ⓐ Ⓑ Ⓒ Ⓓ	57	Ⓐ Ⓑ Ⓒ Ⓓ	67	Ⓐ Ⓑ Ⓒ Ⓓ	77	Ⓐ Ⓑ Ⓒ Ⓓ	87	Ⓐ Ⓑ Ⓒ Ⓓ	97	Ⓐ Ⓑ Ⓒ Ⓓ
	8	Ⓐ Ⓑ Ⓒ Ⓓ	18	Ⓐ Ⓑ Ⓒ Ⓓ	28	Ⓐ Ⓑ Ⓒ Ⓓ	38	Ⓐ Ⓑ Ⓒ Ⓓ	48	Ⓐ Ⓑ Ⓒ Ⓓ	58	Ⓐ Ⓑ Ⓒ Ⓓ	68	Ⓐ Ⓑ Ⓒ Ⓓ	78	Ⓐ Ⓑ Ⓒ Ⓓ	88	Ⓐ Ⓑ Ⓒ Ⓓ	98	Ⓐ Ⓑ Ⓒ Ⓓ
	9	Ⓐ Ⓑ Ⓒ Ⓓ	19	Ⓐ Ⓑ Ⓒ Ⓓ	29	Ⓐ Ⓑ Ⓒ Ⓓ	39	Ⓐ Ⓑ Ⓒ Ⓓ	49	Ⓐ Ⓑ Ⓒ Ⓓ	59	Ⓐ Ⓑ Ⓒ Ⓓ	69	Ⓐ Ⓑ Ⓒ Ⓓ	79	Ⓐ Ⓑ Ⓒ Ⓓ	89	Ⓐ Ⓑ Ⓒ Ⓓ	99	Ⓐ Ⓑ Ⓒ Ⓓ
	10	Ⓐ Ⓑ Ⓒ Ⓓ	20	Ⓐ Ⓑ Ⓒ Ⓓ	30	Ⓐ Ⓑ Ⓒ Ⓓ	40	Ⓐ Ⓑ Ⓒ Ⓓ	50	Ⓐ Ⓑ Ⓒ Ⓓ	60	Ⓐ Ⓑ Ⓒ Ⓓ	70	Ⓐ Ⓑ Ⓒ Ⓓ	80	Ⓐ Ⓑ Ⓒ Ⓓ	90	Ⓐ Ⓑ Ⓒ Ⓓ	100	Ⓐ Ⓑ Ⓒ Ⓓ

ACTUAL TEST 06

LISTENING SECTION																				
	1	Ⓐ Ⓑ Ⓒ Ⓓ	11	Ⓐ Ⓑ Ⓒ Ⓓ	21	Ⓐ Ⓑ Ⓒ Ⓓ	31	Ⓐ Ⓑ Ⓒ Ⓓ	41	Ⓐ Ⓑ Ⓒ Ⓓ	51	Ⓐ Ⓑ Ⓒ Ⓓ	61	Ⓐ Ⓑ Ⓒ Ⓓ	71	Ⓐ Ⓑ Ⓒ Ⓓ	81	Ⓐ Ⓑ Ⓒ Ⓓ	91	Ⓐ Ⓑ Ⓒ Ⓓ
	2	Ⓐ Ⓑ Ⓒ Ⓓ	12	Ⓐ Ⓑ Ⓒ Ⓓ	22	Ⓐ Ⓑ Ⓒ Ⓓ	32	Ⓐ Ⓑ Ⓒ Ⓓ	42	Ⓐ Ⓑ Ⓒ Ⓓ	52	Ⓐ Ⓑ Ⓒ Ⓓ	62	Ⓐ Ⓑ Ⓒ Ⓓ	72	Ⓐ Ⓑ Ⓒ Ⓓ	82	Ⓐ Ⓑ Ⓒ Ⓓ	92	Ⓐ Ⓑ Ⓒ Ⓓ
	3	Ⓐ Ⓑ Ⓒ Ⓓ	13	Ⓐ Ⓑ Ⓒ Ⓓ	23	Ⓐ Ⓑ Ⓒ Ⓓ	33	Ⓐ Ⓑ Ⓒ Ⓓ	43	Ⓐ Ⓑ Ⓒ Ⓓ	53	Ⓐ Ⓑ Ⓒ Ⓓ	63	Ⓐ Ⓑ Ⓒ Ⓓ	73	Ⓐ Ⓑ Ⓒ Ⓓ	83	Ⓐ Ⓑ Ⓒ Ⓓ	93	Ⓐ Ⓑ Ⓒ Ⓓ
	4	Ⓐ Ⓑ Ⓒ Ⓓ	14	Ⓐ Ⓑ Ⓒ Ⓓ	24	Ⓐ Ⓑ Ⓒ Ⓓ	34	Ⓐ Ⓑ Ⓒ Ⓓ	44	Ⓐ Ⓑ Ⓒ Ⓓ	54	Ⓐ Ⓑ Ⓒ Ⓓ	64	Ⓐ Ⓑ Ⓒ Ⓓ	74	Ⓐ Ⓑ Ⓒ Ⓓ	84	Ⓐ Ⓑ Ⓒ Ⓓ	94	Ⓐ Ⓑ Ⓒ Ⓓ
	5	Ⓐ Ⓑ Ⓒ Ⓓ	15	Ⓐ Ⓑ Ⓒ Ⓓ	25	Ⓐ Ⓑ Ⓒ Ⓓ	35	Ⓐ Ⓑ Ⓒ Ⓓ	45	Ⓐ Ⓑ Ⓒ Ⓓ	55	Ⓐ Ⓑ Ⓒ Ⓓ	65	Ⓐ Ⓑ Ⓒ Ⓓ	75	Ⓐ Ⓑ Ⓒ Ⓓ	85	Ⓐ Ⓑ Ⓒ Ⓓ	95	Ⓐ Ⓑ Ⓒ Ⓓ
	6	Ⓐ Ⓑ Ⓒ Ⓓ	16	Ⓐ Ⓑ Ⓒ Ⓓ	26	Ⓐ Ⓑ Ⓒ Ⓓ	36	Ⓐ Ⓑ Ⓒ Ⓓ	46	Ⓐ Ⓑ Ⓒ Ⓓ	56	Ⓐ Ⓑ Ⓒ Ⓓ	66	Ⓐ Ⓑ Ⓒ Ⓓ	76	Ⓐ Ⓑ Ⓒ Ⓓ	86	Ⓐ Ⓑ Ⓒ Ⓓ	96	Ⓐ Ⓑ Ⓒ Ⓓ
	7	Ⓐ Ⓑ Ⓒ Ⓓ	17	Ⓐ Ⓑ Ⓒ Ⓓ	27	Ⓐ Ⓑ Ⓒ Ⓓ	37	Ⓐ Ⓑ Ⓒ Ⓓ	47	Ⓐ Ⓑ Ⓒ Ⓓ	57	Ⓐ Ⓑ Ⓒ Ⓓ	67	Ⓐ Ⓑ Ⓒ Ⓓ	77	Ⓐ Ⓑ Ⓒ Ⓓ	87	Ⓐ Ⓑ Ⓒ Ⓓ	97	Ⓐ Ⓑ Ⓒ Ⓓ
	8	Ⓐ Ⓑ Ⓒ Ⓓ	18	Ⓐ Ⓑ Ⓒ Ⓓ	28	Ⓐ Ⓑ Ⓒ Ⓓ	38	Ⓐ Ⓑ Ⓒ Ⓓ	48	Ⓐ Ⓑ Ⓒ Ⓓ	58	Ⓐ Ⓑ Ⓒ Ⓓ	68	Ⓐ Ⓑ Ⓒ Ⓓ	78	Ⓐ Ⓑ Ⓒ Ⓓ	88	Ⓐ Ⓑ Ⓒ Ⓓ	98	Ⓐ Ⓑ Ⓒ Ⓓ
	9	Ⓐ Ⓑ Ⓒ Ⓓ	19	Ⓐ Ⓑ Ⓒ Ⓓ	29	Ⓐ Ⓑ Ⓒ Ⓓ	39	Ⓐ Ⓑ Ⓒ Ⓓ	49	Ⓐ Ⓑ Ⓒ Ⓓ	59	Ⓐ Ⓑ Ⓒ Ⓓ	69	Ⓐ Ⓑ Ⓒ Ⓓ	79	Ⓐ Ⓑ Ⓒ Ⓓ	89	Ⓐ Ⓑ Ⓒ Ⓓ	99	Ⓐ Ⓑ Ⓒ Ⓓ
	10	Ⓐ Ⓑ Ⓒ Ⓓ	20	Ⓐ Ⓑ Ⓒ Ⓓ	30	Ⓐ Ⓑ Ⓒ Ⓓ	40	Ⓐ Ⓑ Ⓒ Ⓓ	50	Ⓐ Ⓑ Ⓒ Ⓓ	60	Ⓐ Ⓑ Ⓒ Ⓓ	70	Ⓐ Ⓑ Ⓒ Ⓓ	80	Ⓐ Ⓑ Ⓒ Ⓓ	90	Ⓐ Ⓑ Ⓒ Ⓓ	100	Ⓐ Ⓑ Ⓒ Ⓓ

答案紙

ACTUAL TEST 07

LISTENING SECTION																			
1	Ⓐ Ⓑ Ⓒ Ⓓ	11	Ⓐ Ⓑ Ⓒ Ⓓ	21	Ⓐ Ⓑ Ⓒ Ⓓ	31	Ⓐ Ⓑ Ⓒ Ⓓ	41	Ⓐ Ⓑ Ⓒ Ⓓ	51	Ⓐ Ⓑ Ⓒ Ⓓ	61	Ⓐ Ⓑ Ⓒ Ⓓ	71	Ⓐ Ⓑ Ⓒ Ⓓ	81	Ⓐ Ⓑ Ⓒ Ⓓ	91	Ⓐ Ⓑ Ⓒ Ⓓ
2	Ⓐ Ⓑ Ⓒ Ⓓ	12	Ⓐ Ⓑ Ⓒ Ⓓ	22	Ⓐ Ⓑ Ⓒ Ⓓ	32	Ⓐ Ⓑ Ⓒ Ⓓ	42	Ⓐ Ⓑ Ⓒ Ⓓ	52	Ⓐ Ⓑ Ⓒ Ⓓ	62	Ⓐ Ⓑ Ⓒ Ⓓ	72	Ⓐ Ⓑ Ⓒ Ⓓ	82	Ⓐ Ⓑ Ⓒ Ⓓ	92	Ⓐ Ⓑ Ⓒ Ⓓ
3	Ⓐ Ⓑ Ⓒ Ⓓ	13	Ⓐ Ⓑ Ⓒ Ⓓ	23	Ⓐ Ⓑ Ⓒ Ⓓ	33	Ⓐ Ⓑ Ⓒ Ⓓ	43	Ⓐ Ⓑ Ⓒ Ⓓ	53	Ⓐ Ⓑ Ⓒ Ⓓ	63	Ⓐ Ⓑ Ⓒ Ⓓ	73	Ⓐ Ⓑ Ⓒ Ⓓ	83	Ⓐ Ⓑ Ⓒ Ⓓ	93	Ⓐ Ⓑ Ⓒ Ⓓ
4	Ⓐ Ⓑ Ⓒ Ⓓ	14	Ⓐ Ⓑ Ⓒ Ⓓ	24	Ⓐ Ⓑ Ⓒ Ⓓ	34	Ⓐ Ⓑ Ⓒ Ⓓ	44	Ⓐ Ⓑ Ⓒ Ⓓ	54	Ⓐ Ⓑ Ⓒ Ⓓ	64	Ⓐ Ⓑ Ⓒ Ⓓ	74	Ⓐ Ⓑ Ⓒ Ⓓ	84	Ⓐ Ⓑ Ⓒ Ⓓ	94	Ⓐ Ⓑ Ⓒ Ⓓ
5	Ⓐ Ⓑ Ⓒ Ⓓ	15	Ⓐ Ⓑ Ⓒ Ⓓ	25	Ⓐ Ⓑ Ⓒ Ⓓ	35	Ⓐ Ⓑ Ⓒ Ⓓ	45	Ⓐ Ⓑ Ⓒ Ⓓ	55	Ⓐ Ⓑ Ⓒ Ⓓ	65	Ⓐ Ⓑ Ⓒ Ⓓ	75	Ⓐ Ⓑ Ⓒ Ⓓ	85	Ⓐ Ⓑ Ⓒ Ⓓ	95	Ⓐ Ⓑ Ⓒ Ⓓ
6	Ⓐ Ⓑ Ⓒ Ⓓ	16	Ⓐ Ⓑ Ⓒ Ⓓ	26	Ⓐ Ⓑ Ⓒ Ⓓ	36	Ⓐ Ⓑ Ⓒ Ⓓ	46	Ⓐ Ⓑ Ⓒ Ⓓ	56	Ⓐ Ⓑ Ⓒ Ⓓ	66	Ⓐ Ⓑ Ⓒ Ⓓ	76	Ⓐ Ⓑ Ⓒ Ⓓ	86	Ⓐ Ⓑ Ⓒ Ⓓ	96	Ⓐ Ⓑ Ⓒ Ⓓ
7	Ⓐ Ⓑ Ⓒ Ⓓ	17	Ⓐ Ⓑ Ⓒ Ⓓ	27	Ⓐ Ⓑ Ⓒ Ⓓ	37	Ⓐ Ⓑ Ⓒ Ⓓ	47	Ⓐ Ⓑ Ⓒ Ⓓ	57	Ⓐ Ⓑ Ⓒ Ⓓ	67	Ⓐ Ⓑ Ⓒ Ⓓ	77	Ⓐ Ⓑ Ⓒ Ⓓ	87	Ⓐ Ⓑ Ⓒ Ⓓ	97	Ⓐ Ⓑ Ⓒ Ⓓ
8	Ⓐ Ⓑ Ⓒ Ⓓ	18	Ⓐ Ⓑ Ⓒ Ⓓ	28	Ⓐ Ⓑ Ⓒ Ⓓ	38	Ⓐ Ⓑ Ⓒ Ⓓ	48	Ⓐ Ⓑ Ⓒ Ⓓ	58	Ⓐ Ⓑ Ⓒ Ⓓ	68	Ⓐ Ⓑ Ⓒ Ⓓ	78	Ⓐ Ⓑ Ⓒ Ⓓ	88	Ⓐ Ⓑ Ⓒ Ⓓ	98	Ⓐ Ⓑ Ⓒ Ⓓ
9	Ⓐ Ⓑ Ⓒ Ⓓ	19	Ⓐ Ⓑ Ⓒ Ⓓ	29	Ⓐ Ⓑ Ⓒ Ⓓ	39	Ⓐ Ⓑ Ⓒ Ⓓ	49	Ⓐ Ⓑ Ⓒ Ⓓ	59	Ⓐ Ⓑ Ⓒ Ⓓ	69	Ⓐ Ⓑ Ⓒ Ⓓ	79	Ⓐ Ⓑ Ⓒ Ⓓ	89	Ⓐ Ⓑ Ⓒ Ⓓ	99	Ⓐ Ⓑ Ⓒ Ⓓ
10	Ⓐ Ⓑ Ⓒ Ⓓ	20	Ⓐ Ⓑ Ⓒ Ⓓ	30	Ⓐ Ⓑ Ⓒ Ⓓ	40	Ⓐ Ⓑ Ⓒ Ⓓ	50	Ⓐ Ⓑ Ⓒ Ⓓ	60	Ⓐ Ⓑ Ⓒ Ⓓ	70	Ⓐ Ⓑ Ⓒ Ⓓ	80	Ⓐ Ⓑ Ⓒ Ⓓ	90	Ⓐ Ⓑ Ⓒ Ⓓ	100	Ⓐ Ⓑ Ⓒ Ⓓ

ACTUAL TEST 08

LISTENING SECTION																			
1	Ⓐ Ⓑ Ⓒ Ⓓ	11	Ⓐ Ⓑ Ⓒ Ⓓ	21	Ⓐ Ⓑ Ⓒ Ⓓ	31	Ⓐ Ⓑ Ⓒ Ⓓ	41	Ⓐ Ⓑ Ⓒ Ⓓ	51	Ⓐ Ⓑ Ⓒ Ⓓ	61	Ⓐ Ⓑ Ⓒ Ⓓ	71	Ⓐ Ⓑ Ⓒ Ⓓ	81	Ⓐ Ⓑ Ⓒ Ⓓ	91	Ⓐ Ⓑ Ⓒ Ⓓ
2	Ⓐ Ⓑ Ⓒ Ⓓ	12	Ⓐ Ⓑ Ⓒ Ⓓ	22	Ⓐ Ⓑ Ⓒ Ⓓ	32	Ⓐ Ⓑ Ⓒ Ⓓ	42	Ⓐ Ⓑ Ⓒ Ⓓ	52	Ⓐ Ⓑ Ⓒ Ⓓ	62	Ⓐ Ⓑ Ⓒ Ⓓ	72	Ⓐ Ⓑ Ⓒ Ⓓ	82	Ⓐ Ⓑ Ⓒ Ⓓ	92	Ⓐ Ⓑ Ⓒ Ⓓ
3	Ⓐ Ⓑ Ⓒ Ⓓ	13	Ⓐ Ⓑ Ⓒ Ⓓ	23	Ⓐ Ⓑ Ⓒ Ⓓ	33	Ⓐ Ⓑ Ⓒ Ⓓ	43	Ⓐ Ⓑ Ⓒ Ⓓ	53	Ⓐ Ⓑ Ⓒ Ⓓ	63	Ⓐ Ⓑ Ⓒ Ⓓ	73	Ⓐ Ⓑ Ⓒ Ⓓ	83	Ⓐ Ⓑ Ⓒ Ⓓ	93	Ⓐ Ⓑ Ⓒ Ⓓ
4	Ⓐ Ⓑ Ⓒ Ⓓ	14	Ⓐ Ⓑ Ⓒ Ⓓ	24	Ⓐ Ⓑ Ⓒ Ⓓ	34	Ⓐ Ⓑ Ⓒ Ⓓ	44	Ⓐ Ⓑ Ⓒ Ⓓ	54	Ⓐ Ⓑ Ⓒ Ⓓ	64	Ⓐ Ⓑ Ⓒ Ⓓ	74	Ⓐ Ⓑ Ⓒ Ⓓ	84	Ⓐ Ⓑ Ⓒ Ⓓ	94	Ⓐ Ⓑ Ⓒ Ⓓ
5	Ⓐ Ⓑ Ⓒ Ⓓ	15	Ⓐ Ⓑ Ⓒ Ⓓ	25	Ⓐ Ⓑ Ⓒ Ⓓ	35	Ⓐ Ⓑ Ⓒ Ⓓ	45	Ⓐ Ⓑ Ⓒ Ⓓ	55	Ⓐ Ⓑ Ⓒ Ⓓ	65	Ⓐ Ⓑ Ⓒ Ⓓ	75	Ⓐ Ⓑ Ⓒ Ⓓ	85	Ⓐ Ⓑ Ⓒ Ⓓ	95	Ⓐ Ⓑ Ⓒ Ⓓ
6	Ⓐ Ⓑ Ⓒ Ⓓ	16	Ⓐ Ⓑ Ⓒ Ⓓ	26	Ⓐ Ⓑ Ⓒ Ⓓ	36	Ⓐ Ⓑ Ⓒ Ⓓ	46	Ⓐ Ⓑ Ⓒ Ⓓ	56	Ⓐ Ⓑ Ⓒ Ⓓ	66	Ⓐ Ⓑ Ⓒ Ⓓ	76	Ⓐ Ⓑ Ⓒ Ⓓ	86	Ⓐ Ⓑ Ⓒ Ⓓ	96	Ⓐ Ⓑ Ⓒ Ⓓ
7	Ⓐ Ⓑ Ⓒ Ⓓ	17	Ⓐ Ⓑ Ⓒ Ⓓ	27	Ⓐ Ⓑ Ⓒ Ⓓ	37	Ⓐ Ⓑ Ⓒ Ⓓ	47	Ⓐ Ⓑ Ⓒ Ⓓ	57	Ⓐ Ⓑ Ⓒ Ⓓ	67	Ⓐ Ⓑ Ⓒ Ⓓ	77	Ⓐ Ⓑ Ⓒ Ⓓ	87	Ⓐ Ⓑ Ⓒ Ⓓ	97	Ⓐ Ⓑ Ⓒ Ⓓ
8	Ⓐ Ⓑ Ⓒ Ⓓ	18	Ⓐ Ⓑ Ⓒ Ⓓ	28	Ⓐ Ⓑ Ⓒ Ⓓ	38	Ⓐ Ⓑ Ⓒ Ⓓ	48	Ⓐ Ⓑ Ⓒ Ⓓ	58	Ⓐ Ⓑ Ⓒ Ⓓ	68	Ⓐ Ⓑ Ⓒ Ⓓ	78	Ⓐ Ⓑ Ⓒ Ⓓ	88	Ⓐ Ⓑ Ⓒ Ⓓ	98	Ⓐ Ⓑ Ⓒ Ⓓ
9	Ⓐ Ⓑ Ⓒ Ⓓ	19	Ⓐ Ⓑ Ⓒ Ⓓ	29	Ⓐ Ⓑ Ⓒ Ⓓ	39	Ⓐ Ⓑ Ⓒ Ⓓ	49	Ⓐ Ⓑ Ⓒ Ⓓ	59	Ⓐ Ⓑ Ⓒ Ⓓ	69	Ⓐ Ⓑ Ⓒ Ⓓ	79	Ⓐ Ⓑ Ⓒ Ⓓ	89	Ⓐ Ⓑ Ⓒ Ⓓ	99	Ⓐ Ⓑ Ⓒ Ⓓ
10	Ⓐ Ⓑ Ⓒ Ⓓ	20	Ⓐ Ⓑ Ⓒ Ⓓ	30	Ⓐ Ⓑ Ⓒ Ⓓ	40	Ⓐ Ⓑ Ⓒ Ⓓ	50	Ⓐ Ⓑ Ⓒ Ⓓ	60	Ⓐ Ⓑ Ⓒ Ⓓ	70	Ⓐ Ⓑ Ⓒ Ⓓ	80	Ⓐ Ⓑ Ⓒ Ⓓ	90	Ⓐ Ⓑ Ⓒ Ⓓ	100	Ⓐ Ⓑ Ⓒ Ⓓ

答案紙

ACTUAL TEST 09

LISTENING SECTION																			
1	Ⓐ Ⓑ Ⓒ Ⓓ	11	Ⓐ Ⓑ Ⓒ Ⓓ	21	Ⓐ Ⓑ Ⓒ Ⓓ	31	Ⓐ Ⓑ Ⓒ Ⓓ	41	Ⓐ Ⓑ Ⓒ Ⓓ	51	Ⓐ Ⓑ Ⓒ Ⓓ	61	Ⓐ Ⓑ Ⓒ Ⓓ	71	Ⓐ Ⓑ Ⓒ Ⓓ	81	Ⓐ Ⓑ Ⓒ Ⓓ	91	Ⓐ Ⓑ Ⓒ Ⓓ
2	Ⓐ Ⓑ Ⓒ Ⓓ	12	Ⓐ Ⓑ Ⓒ Ⓓ	22	Ⓐ Ⓑ Ⓒ Ⓓ	32	Ⓐ Ⓑ Ⓒ Ⓓ	42	Ⓐ Ⓑ Ⓒ Ⓓ	52	Ⓐ Ⓑ Ⓒ Ⓓ	62	Ⓐ Ⓑ Ⓒ Ⓓ	72	Ⓐ Ⓑ Ⓒ Ⓓ	82	Ⓐ Ⓑ Ⓒ Ⓓ	92	Ⓐ Ⓑ Ⓒ Ⓓ
3	Ⓐ Ⓑ Ⓒ Ⓓ	13	Ⓐ Ⓑ Ⓒ Ⓓ	23	Ⓐ Ⓑ Ⓒ Ⓓ	33	Ⓐ Ⓑ Ⓒ Ⓓ	43	Ⓐ Ⓑ Ⓒ Ⓓ	53	Ⓐ Ⓑ Ⓒ Ⓓ	63	Ⓐ Ⓑ Ⓒ Ⓓ	73	Ⓐ Ⓑ Ⓒ Ⓓ	83	Ⓐ Ⓑ Ⓒ Ⓓ	93	Ⓐ Ⓑ Ⓒ Ⓓ
4	Ⓐ Ⓑ Ⓒ Ⓓ	14	Ⓐ Ⓑ Ⓒ Ⓓ	24	Ⓐ Ⓑ Ⓒ Ⓓ	34	Ⓐ Ⓑ Ⓒ Ⓓ	44	Ⓐ Ⓑ Ⓒ Ⓓ	54	Ⓐ Ⓑ Ⓒ Ⓓ	64	Ⓐ Ⓑ Ⓒ Ⓓ	74	Ⓐ Ⓑ Ⓒ Ⓓ	84	Ⓐ Ⓑ Ⓒ Ⓓ	94	Ⓐ Ⓑ Ⓒ Ⓓ
5	Ⓐ Ⓑ Ⓒ Ⓓ	15	Ⓐ Ⓑ Ⓒ Ⓓ	25	Ⓐ Ⓑ Ⓒ Ⓓ	35	Ⓐ Ⓑ Ⓒ Ⓓ	45	Ⓐ Ⓑ Ⓒ Ⓓ	55	Ⓐ Ⓑ Ⓒ Ⓓ	65	Ⓐ Ⓑ Ⓒ Ⓓ	75	Ⓐ Ⓑ Ⓒ Ⓓ	85	Ⓐ Ⓑ Ⓒ Ⓓ	95	Ⓐ Ⓑ Ⓒ Ⓓ
6	Ⓐ Ⓑ Ⓒ Ⓓ	16	Ⓐ Ⓑ Ⓒ Ⓓ	26	Ⓐ Ⓑ Ⓒ Ⓓ	36	Ⓐ Ⓑ Ⓒ Ⓓ	46	Ⓐ Ⓑ Ⓒ Ⓓ	56	Ⓐ Ⓑ Ⓒ Ⓓ	66	Ⓐ Ⓑ Ⓒ Ⓓ	76	Ⓐ Ⓑ Ⓒ Ⓓ	86	Ⓐ Ⓑ Ⓒ Ⓓ	96	Ⓐ Ⓑ Ⓒ Ⓓ
7	Ⓐ Ⓑ Ⓒ Ⓓ	17	Ⓐ Ⓑ Ⓒ Ⓓ	27	Ⓐ Ⓑ Ⓒ Ⓓ	37	Ⓐ Ⓑ Ⓒ Ⓓ	47	Ⓐ Ⓑ Ⓒ Ⓓ	57	Ⓐ Ⓑ Ⓒ Ⓓ	67	Ⓐ Ⓑ Ⓒ Ⓓ	77	Ⓐ Ⓑ Ⓒ Ⓓ	87	Ⓐ Ⓑ Ⓒ Ⓓ	97	Ⓐ Ⓑ Ⓒ Ⓓ
8	Ⓐ Ⓑ Ⓒ Ⓓ	18	Ⓐ Ⓑ Ⓒ Ⓓ	28	Ⓐ Ⓑ Ⓒ Ⓓ	38	Ⓐ Ⓑ Ⓒ Ⓓ	48	Ⓐ Ⓑ Ⓒ Ⓓ	58	Ⓐ Ⓑ Ⓒ Ⓓ	68	Ⓐ Ⓑ Ⓒ Ⓓ	78	Ⓐ Ⓑ Ⓒ Ⓓ	88	Ⓐ Ⓑ Ⓒ Ⓓ	98	Ⓐ Ⓑ Ⓒ Ⓓ
9	Ⓐ Ⓑ Ⓒ Ⓓ	19	Ⓐ Ⓑ Ⓒ Ⓓ	29	Ⓐ Ⓑ Ⓒ Ⓓ	39	Ⓐ Ⓑ Ⓒ Ⓓ	49	Ⓐ Ⓑ Ⓒ Ⓓ	59	Ⓐ Ⓑ Ⓒ Ⓓ	69	Ⓐ Ⓑ Ⓒ Ⓓ	79	Ⓐ Ⓑ Ⓒ Ⓓ	89	Ⓐ Ⓑ Ⓒ Ⓓ	99	Ⓐ Ⓑ Ⓒ Ⓓ
10	Ⓐ Ⓑ Ⓒ Ⓓ	20	Ⓐ Ⓑ Ⓒ Ⓓ	30	Ⓐ Ⓑ Ⓒ Ⓓ	40	Ⓐ Ⓑ Ⓒ Ⓓ	50	Ⓐ Ⓑ Ⓒ Ⓓ	60	Ⓐ Ⓑ Ⓒ Ⓓ	70	Ⓐ Ⓑ Ⓒ Ⓓ	80	Ⓐ Ⓑ Ⓒ Ⓓ	90	Ⓐ Ⓑ Ⓒ Ⓓ	100	Ⓐ Ⓑ Ⓒ Ⓓ

ACTUAL TEST 10

LISTENING SECTION																			
1	Ⓐ Ⓑ Ⓒ Ⓓ	11	Ⓐ Ⓑ Ⓒ Ⓓ	21	Ⓐ Ⓑ Ⓒ Ⓓ	31	Ⓐ Ⓑ Ⓒ Ⓓ	41	Ⓐ Ⓑ Ⓒ Ⓓ	51	Ⓐ Ⓑ Ⓒ Ⓓ	61	Ⓐ Ⓑ Ⓒ Ⓓ	71	Ⓐ Ⓑ Ⓒ Ⓓ	81	Ⓐ Ⓑ Ⓒ Ⓓ	91	Ⓐ Ⓑ Ⓒ Ⓓ
2	Ⓐ Ⓑ Ⓒ Ⓓ	12	Ⓐ Ⓑ Ⓒ Ⓓ	22	Ⓐ Ⓑ Ⓒ Ⓓ	32	Ⓐ Ⓑ Ⓒ Ⓓ	42	Ⓐ Ⓑ Ⓒ Ⓓ	52	Ⓐ Ⓑ Ⓒ Ⓓ	62	Ⓐ Ⓑ Ⓒ Ⓓ	72	Ⓐ Ⓑ Ⓒ Ⓓ	82	Ⓐ Ⓑ Ⓒ Ⓓ	92	Ⓐ Ⓑ Ⓒ Ⓓ
3	Ⓐ Ⓑ Ⓒ Ⓓ	13	Ⓐ Ⓑ Ⓒ Ⓓ	23	Ⓐ Ⓑ Ⓒ Ⓓ	33	Ⓐ Ⓑ Ⓒ Ⓓ	43	Ⓐ Ⓑ Ⓒ Ⓓ	53	Ⓐ Ⓑ Ⓒ Ⓓ	63	Ⓐ Ⓑ Ⓒ Ⓓ	73	Ⓐ Ⓑ Ⓒ Ⓓ	83	Ⓐ Ⓑ Ⓒ Ⓓ	93	Ⓐ Ⓑ Ⓒ Ⓓ
4	Ⓐ Ⓑ Ⓒ Ⓓ	14	Ⓐ Ⓑ Ⓒ Ⓓ	24	Ⓐ Ⓑ Ⓒ Ⓓ	34	Ⓐ Ⓑ Ⓒ Ⓓ	44	Ⓐ Ⓑ Ⓒ Ⓓ	54	Ⓐ Ⓑ Ⓒ Ⓓ	64	Ⓐ Ⓑ Ⓒ Ⓓ	74	Ⓐ Ⓑ Ⓒ Ⓓ	84	Ⓐ Ⓑ Ⓒ Ⓓ	94	Ⓐ Ⓑ Ⓒ Ⓓ
5	Ⓐ Ⓑ Ⓒ Ⓓ	15	Ⓐ Ⓑ Ⓒ Ⓓ	25	Ⓐ Ⓑ Ⓒ Ⓓ	35	Ⓐ Ⓑ Ⓒ Ⓓ	45	Ⓐ Ⓑ Ⓒ Ⓓ	55	Ⓐ Ⓑ Ⓒ Ⓓ	65	Ⓐ Ⓑ Ⓒ Ⓓ	75	Ⓐ Ⓑ Ⓒ Ⓓ	85	Ⓐ Ⓑ Ⓒ Ⓓ	95	Ⓐ Ⓑ Ⓒ Ⓓ
6	Ⓐ Ⓑ Ⓒ Ⓓ	16	Ⓐ Ⓑ Ⓒ Ⓓ	26	Ⓐ Ⓑ Ⓒ Ⓓ	36	Ⓐ Ⓑ Ⓒ Ⓓ	46	Ⓐ Ⓑ Ⓒ Ⓓ	56	Ⓐ Ⓑ Ⓒ Ⓓ	66	Ⓐ Ⓑ Ⓒ Ⓓ	76	Ⓐ Ⓑ Ⓒ Ⓓ	86	Ⓐ Ⓑ Ⓒ Ⓓ	96	Ⓐ Ⓑ Ⓒ Ⓓ
7	Ⓐ Ⓑ Ⓒ Ⓓ	17	Ⓐ Ⓑ Ⓒ Ⓓ	27	Ⓐ Ⓑ Ⓒ Ⓓ	37	Ⓐ Ⓑ Ⓒ Ⓓ	47	Ⓐ Ⓑ Ⓒ Ⓓ	57	Ⓐ Ⓑ Ⓒ Ⓓ	67	Ⓐ Ⓑ Ⓒ Ⓓ	77	Ⓐ Ⓑ Ⓒ Ⓓ	87	Ⓐ Ⓑ Ⓒ Ⓓ	97	Ⓐ Ⓑ Ⓒ Ⓓ
8	Ⓐ Ⓑ Ⓒ Ⓓ	18	Ⓐ Ⓑ Ⓒ Ⓓ	28	Ⓐ Ⓑ Ⓒ Ⓓ	38	Ⓐ Ⓑ Ⓒ Ⓓ	48	Ⓐ Ⓑ Ⓒ Ⓓ	58	Ⓐ Ⓑ Ⓒ Ⓓ	68	Ⓐ Ⓑ Ⓒ Ⓓ	78	Ⓐ Ⓑ Ⓒ Ⓓ	88	Ⓐ Ⓑ Ⓒ Ⓓ	98	Ⓐ Ⓑ Ⓒ Ⓓ
9	Ⓐ Ⓑ Ⓒ Ⓓ	19	Ⓐ Ⓑ Ⓒ Ⓓ	29	Ⓐ Ⓑ Ⓒ Ⓓ	39	Ⓐ Ⓑ Ⓒ Ⓓ	49	Ⓐ Ⓑ Ⓒ Ⓓ	59	Ⓐ Ⓑ Ⓒ Ⓓ	69	Ⓐ Ⓑ Ⓒ Ⓓ	79	Ⓐ Ⓑ Ⓒ Ⓓ	89	Ⓐ Ⓑ Ⓒ Ⓓ	99	Ⓐ Ⓑ Ⓒ Ⓓ
10	Ⓐ Ⓑ Ⓒ Ⓓ	20	Ⓐ Ⓑ Ⓒ Ⓓ	30	Ⓐ Ⓑ Ⓒ Ⓓ	40	Ⓐ Ⓑ Ⓒ Ⓓ	50	Ⓐ Ⓑ Ⓒ Ⓓ	60	Ⓐ Ⓑ Ⓒ Ⓓ	70	Ⓐ Ⓑ Ⓒ Ⓓ	80	Ⓐ Ⓑ Ⓒ Ⓓ	90	Ⓐ Ⓑ Ⓒ Ⓓ	100	Ⓐ Ⓑ Ⓒ Ⓓ

Answer Key

Actual Test 01

1 (D)	21 (B)	41 (C)	61 (C)	81 (C)
2 (C)	22 (C)	42 (D)	62 (C)	82 (B)
3 (A)	23 (A)	43 (B)	63 (D)	83 (B)
4 (C)	24 (B)	44 (A)	64 (D)	84 (A)
5 (B)	25 (B)	45 (B)	65 (B)	85 (C)
6 (C)	26 (A)	46 (D)	66 (B)	86 (D)
7 (C)	27 (A)	47 (C)	67 (D)	87 (C)
8 (B)	28 (C)	48 (B)	68 (A)	88 (A)
9 (B)	29 (B)	49 (A)	69 (D)	89 (A)
10 (C)	30 (B)	50 (B)	70 (A)	90 (B)
11 (A)	31 (A)	51 (C)	71 (A)	91 (C)
12 (B)	32 (A)	52 (D)	72 (B)	92 (C)
13 (C)	33 (B)	53 (A)	73 (C)	93 (A)
14 (A)	34 (C)	54 (C)	74 (D)	94 (D)
15 (A)	35 (D)	55 (D)	75 (C)	95 (B)
16 (B)	36 (D)	56 (B)	76 (A)	96 (D)
17 (C)	37 (B)	57 (A)	77 (C)	97 (C)
18 (A)	38 (D)	58 (A)	78 (A)	98 (D)
19 (C)	39 (A)	59 (D)	79 (D)	99 (B)
20 (B)	40 (B)	60 (A)	80 (B)	100 (C)

Actual Test 02

1 (D)	21 (C)	41 (C)	61 (B)	81 (C)
2 (C)	22 (B)	42 (B)	62 (A)	82 (D)
3 (C)	23 (C)	43 (A)	63 (D)	83 (C)
4 (A)	24 (A)	44 (B)	64 (C)	84 (A)
5 (B)	25 (A)	45 (A)	65 (C)	85 (A)
6 (A)	26 (B)	46 (C)	66 (D)	86 (B)
7 (C)	27 (B)	47 (A)	67 (D)	87 (B)
8 (B)	28 (B)	48 (C)	68 (B)	88 (C)
9 (A)	29 (C)	49 (B)	69 (B)	89 (D)
10 (C)	30 (A)	50 (D)	70 (C)	90 (B)
11 (A)	31 (C)	51 (B)	71 (B)	91 (A)
12 (B)	32 (D)	52 (A)	72 (D)	92 (A)
13 (A)	33 (D)	53 (B)	73 (C)	93 (B)
14 (B)	34 (B)	54 (A)	74 (D)	94 (D)
15 (C)	35 (A)	55 (C)	75 (A)	95 (D)
16 (A)	36 (D)	56 (D)	76 (B)	96 (A)
17 (C)	37 (C)	57 (A)	77 (C)	97 (A)
18 (A)	38 (A)	58 (D)	78 (D)	98 (C)
19 (B)	39 (D)	59 (A)	79 (A)	99 (C)
20 (B)	40 (B)	60 (C)	80 (C)	100 (B)

Actual Test 03

1 (C)	21 (C)	41 (B)	61 (C)	81 (A)
2 (C)	22 (B)	42 (D)	62 (D)	82 (A)
3 (A)	23 (A)	43 (A)	63 (B)	83 (B)
4 (D)	24 (A)	44 (D)	64 (A)	84 (D)
5 (B)	25 (C)	45 (D)	65 (B)	85 (B)
6 (C)	26 (C)	46 (B)	66 (C)	86 (D)
7 (A)	27 (B)	47 (D)	67 (D)	87 (B)
8 (C)	28 (B)	48 (C)	68 (A)	88 (B)
9 (A)	29 (A)	49 (A)	69 (B)	89 (D)
10 (A)	30 (B)	50 (A)	70 (B)	90 (A)
11 (C)	31 (A)	51 (D)	71 (D)	91 (D)
12 (B)	32 (C)	52 (B)	72 (A)	92 (C)
13 (B)	33 (A)	53 (A)	73 (D)	93 (C)
14 (B)	34 (C)	54 (B)	74 (C)	94 (D)
15 (A)	35 (A)	55 (C)	75 (B)	95 (A)
16 (B)	36 (C)	56 (C)	76 (A)	96 (D)
17 (C)	37 (C)	57 (B)	77 (B)	97 (A)
18 (C)	38 (D)	58 (C)	78 (C)	98 (C)
19 (C)	39 (C)	59 (B)	79 (D)	99 (A)
20 (A)	40 (B)	60 (A)	80 (B)	100 (C)

Actual Test 04

1 (D)	21 (B)	41 (A)	61 (D)	81 (A)
2 (A)	22 (B)	42 (C)	62 (C)	82 (B)
3 (D)	23 (C)	43 (D)	63 (A)	83 (A)
4 (B)	24 (A)	44 (C)	64 (C)	84 (C)
5 (C)	25 (C)	45 (D)	65 (A)	85 (A)
6 (A)	26 (A)	46 (B)	66 (A)	86 (B)
7 (B)	27 (A)	47 (B)	67 (B)	87 (D)
8 (C)	28 (A)	48 (A)	68 (B)	88 (A)
9 (C)	29 (B)	49 (D)	69 (D)	89 (C)
10 (A)	30 (C)	50 (D)	70 (C)	90 (D)
11 (B)	31 (B)	51 (B)	71 (C)	91 (B)
12 (A)	32 (C)	52 (A)	72 (D)	92 (D)
13 (A)	33 (B)	53 (A)	73 (A)	93 (C)
14 (C)	34 (A)	54 (C)	74 (A)	94 (B)
15 (B)	35 (A)	55 (B)	75 (B)	95 (D)
16 (C)	36 (D)	56 (D)	76 (D)	96 (A)
17 (A)	37 (C)	57 (B)	77 (D)	97 (C)
18 (B)	38 (D)	58 (B)	78 (A)	98 (B)
19 (A)	39 (A)	59 (B)	79 (C)	99 (C)
20 (C)	40 (C)	60 (C)	80 (B)	100 (D)

Actual Test 05

1 (D)	21 (B)	41 (B)	61 (D)	81 (D)
2 (A)	22 (A)	42 (A)	62 (C)	82 (A)
3 (B)	23 (A)	43 (C)	63 (B)	83 (C)
4 (C)	24 (B)	44 (D)	64 (B)	84 (B)
5 (A)	25 (B)	45 (C)	65 (B)	85 (A)
6 (C)	26 (B)	46 (A)	66 (B)	86 (A)
7 (A)	27 (C)	47 (C)	67 (A)	87 (B)
8 (B)	28 (C)	48 (C)	68 (B)	88 (C)
9 (C)	29 (A)	49 (B)	69 (D)	89 (C)
10 (B)	30 (C)	50 (D)	70 (C)	90 (A)
11 (A)	31 (B)	51 (A)	71 (B)	91 (D)
12 (C)	32 (B)	52 (C)	72 (D)	92 (A)
13 (C)	33 (D)	53 (D)	73 (A)	93 (D)
14 (A)	34 (C)	54 (B)	74 (A)	94 (C)
15 (C)	35 (A)	55 (D)	75 (C)	95 (A)
16 (A)	36 (C)	56 (D)	76 (B)	96 (C)
17 (B)	37 (B)	57 (A)	77 (C)	97 (B)
18 (A)	38 (A)	58 (A)	78 (A)	98 (B)
19 (B)	39 (D)	59 (A)	79 (D)	99 (C)
20 (C)	40 (D)	60 (D)	80 (D)	100 (B)

Actual Test 06

1 (C)	21 (C)	41 (A)	61 (B)	81 (C)
2 (A)	22 (B)	42 (D)	62 (B)	82 (C)
3 (C)	23 (C)	43 (B)	63 (B)	83 (B)
4 (A)	24 (A)	44 (C)	64 (B)	84 (C)
5 (D)	25 (B)	45 (A)	65 (D)	85 (D)
6 (B)	26 (C)	46 (D)	66 (B)	86 (C)
7 (B)	27 (A)	47 (A)	67 (D)	87 (A)
8 (C)	28 (A)	48 (C)	68 (A)	88 (A)
9 (A)	29 (C)	49 (B)	69 (A)	89 (C)
10 (A)	30 (C)	50 (C)	70 (B)	90 (A)
11 (B)	31 (B)	51 (C)	71 (A)	91 (C)
12 (B)	32 (D)	52 (A)	72 (A)	92 (D)
13 (A)	33 (D)	53 (B)	73 (B)	93 (A)
14 (C)	34 (A)	54 (B)	74 (C)	94 (A)
15 (B)	35 (B)	55 (D)	75 (B)	95 (A)
16 (B)	36 (C)	56 (D)	76 (A)	96 (C)
17 (A)	37 (C)	57 (D)	77 (C)	97 (D)
18 (C)	38 (C)	58 (C)	78 (B)	98 (B)
19 (B)	39 (D)	59 (D)	79 (D)	99 (A)
20 (A)	40 (C)	60 (D)	80 (B)	100 (D)

Actual Test 07

1 (C)	21 (A)	41 (A)	61 (B)	81 (A)
2 (D)	22 (C)	42 (D)	62 (C)	82 (B)
3 (D)	23 (A)	43 (B)	63 (B)	83 (B)
4 (A)	24 (B)	44 (D)	64 (C)	84 (D)
5 (C)	25 (C)	45 (B)	65 (D)	85 (D)
6 (B)	26 (B)	46 (A)	66 (D)	86 (A)
7 (C)	27 (C)	47 (C)	67 (B)	87 (C)
8 (B)	28 (C)	48 (C)	68 (C)	88 (C)
9 (B)	29 (B)	49 (B)	69 (D)	89 (B)
10 (A)	30 (A)	50 (D)	70 (D)	90 (A)
11 (C)	31 (C)	51 (B)	71 (B)	91 (C)
12 (A)	32 (A)	52 (C)	72 (C)	92 (C)
13 (B)	33 (D)	53 (B)	73 (A)	93 (C)
14 (C)	34 (C)	54 (C)	74 (D)	94 (A)
15 (A)	35 (D)	55 (A)	75 (C)	95 (B)
16 (B)	36 (D)	56 (B)	76 (D)	96 (A)
17 (B)	37 (A)	57 (A)	77 (A)	97 (D)
18 (A)	38 (C)	58 (B)	78 (B)	98 (A)
19 (B)	39 (A)	59 (A)	79 (C)	99 (B)
20 (C)	40 (D)	60 (B)	80 (C)	100 (B)

Actual Test 08

1 (C)	21 (C)	41 (D)	61 (D)	81 (D)
2 (D)	22 (C)	42 (C)	62 (B)	82 (B)
3 (A)	23 (A)	43 (A)	63 (B)	83 (A)
4 (C)	24 (B)	44 (C)	64 (A)	84 (D)
5 (C)	25 (C)	45 (A)	65 (C)	85 (A)
6 (D)	26 (C)	46 (B)	66 (D)	86 (C)
7 (A)	27 (A)	47 (A)	67 (C)	87 (C)
8 (C)	28 (B)	48 (D)	68 (B)	88 (B)
9 (B)	29 (A)	49 (D)	69 (B)	89 (D)
10 (A)	30 (B)	50 (B)	70 (A)	90 (B)
11 (C)	31 (C)	51 (C)	71 (B)	91 (D)
12 (B)	32 (A)	52 (B)	72 (A)	92 (A)
13 (A)	33 (D)	53 (D)	73 (A)	93 (B)
14 (A)	34 (A)	54 (B)	74 (D)	94 (D)
15 (C)	35 (B)	55 (C)	75 (C)	95 (D)
16 (B)	36 (A)	56 (C)	76 (D)	96 (A)
17 (B)	37 (C)	57 (D)	77 (C)	97 (D)
18 (C)	38 (C)	58 (C)	78 (C)	98 (A)
19 (A)	39 (B)	59 (A)	79 (B)	99 (C)
20 (B)	40 (B)	60 (A)	80 (B)	100 (C)

Actual Test 09

1 (D)	21 (A)	41 (D)	61 (D)	81 (B)
2 (D)	22 (B)	42 (B)	62 (A)	82 (A)
3 (C)	23 (C)	43 (C)	63 (C)	83 (C)
4 (A)	24 (C)	44 (C)	64 (D)	84 (B)
5 (B)	25 (C)	45 (B)	65 (B)	85 (C)
6 (D)	26 (B)	46 (D)	66 (B)	86 (C)
7 (C)	27 (A)	47 (D)	67 (A)	87 (A)
8 (B)	28 (C)	48 (A)	68 (B)	88 (C)
9 (A)	29 (B)	49 (B)	69 (A)	89 (C)
10 (B)	30 (A)	50 (B)	70 (D)	90 (B)
11 (A)	31 (B)	51 (D)	71 (D)	91 (A)
12 (B)	32 (A)	52 (A)	72 (A)	92 (C)
13 (A)	33 (B)	53 (D)	73 (B)	93 (B)
14 (C)	34 (D)	54 (D)	74 (D)	94 (A)
15 (B)	35 (D)	55 (B)	75 (C)	95 (B)
16 (B)	36 (C)	56 (B)	76 (B)	96 (D)
17 (C)	37 (B)	57 (C)	77 (A)	97 (C)
18 (A)	38 (C)	58 (C)	78 (B)	98 (A)
19 (A)	39 (A)	59 (D)	79 (D)	99 (D)
20 (C)	40 (C)	60 (C)	80 (B)	100 (B)

Actual Test 10

1 (B)	21 (B)	41 (C)	61 (B)	81 (A)
2 (A)	22 (A)	42 (B)	62 (B)	82 (D)
3 (C)	23 (C)	43 (A)	63 (C)	83 (A)
4 (C)	24 (B)	44 (D)	64 (A)	84 (C)
5 (D)	25 (C)	45 (A)	65 (B)	85 (C)
6 (B)	26 (A)	46 (C)	66 (A)	86 (B)
7 (C)	27 (A)	47 (C)	67 (B)	87 (D)
8 (B)	28 (C)	48 (D)	68 (A)	88 (C)
9 (B)	29 (B)	49 (B)	69 (C)	89 (A)
10 (C)	30 (A)	50 (A)	70 (C)	90 (C)
11 (A)	31 (C)	51 (D)	71 (D)	91 (D)
12 (B)	32 (D)	52 (A)	72 (B)	92 (B)
13 (C)	33 (A)	53 (D)	73 (D)	93 (C)
14 (A)	34 (B)	54 (B)	74 (C)	94 (A)
15 (B)	35 (B)	55 (D)	75 (B)	95 (C)
16 (A)	36 (D)	56 (D)	76 (D)	96 (A)
17 (C)	37 (C)	57 (A)	77 (B)	97 (B)
18 (C)	38 (A)	58 (B)	78 (A)	98 (C)
19 (A)	39 (B)	59 (C)	79 (B)	99 (D)
20 (B)	40 (D)	60 (D)	80 (C)	100 (A)

新制多益 聽力高分金榜演練

關鍵10回滿分模擬1000題

作　　者	YBM TOEIC R&D
譯　　者	黃詩韻／蔡裴驊／劉嘉珮 關亭薇（前言及各題考點）
編　　輯	高詣軒
校　　對	申文怡
主　　編	丁宥暄
內文排版	林書玉／劉秋筑
封面設計	林書玉
製程管理	洪巧玲
出 版 者	寂天文化事業股份有限公司
發 行 人	黃朝萍
電　　話	+886-(0)2-2365-9739
傳　　真	+886-(0)2-2365-9835
網　　址	www.icosmos.com.tw
讀者服務	onlineservice@icosmos.com.tw
出版日期	2022 年 10 月 初版一刷 （寂天雲隨身聽 APP 版）

郵撥帳號 1998620-0 寂天文化事業股份有限公司

訂書金額未滿 1000 元，請外加運費 100 元。

〔若有破損，請寄回更換，謝謝。〕

國家圖書館出版品預行編目 (CIP) 資料

新制多益聽力高分金榜演練 : 關鍵 10 回滿分模擬 1000 題 (寂天雲隨身聽 APP 版)/YBM TOEIC R&D 著 ; 黃詩韻 , 蔡裴驊 , 劉嘉珮 , 關亭薇譯 . -- 初版 . -- [臺北市] : 寂天文化事業股份有限公司 , 2022.10

面；　公分

ISBN 978-626-300-156-5(16K 平裝)

1.CST: 多益測驗

805.1895　　111014466

YBM 실전토익 LC 1000 3